To

BURNING SOULS

Burn brightly, live lightly!

D

DAVID CHERNUSHENKO

For Anna, Gaia and Eric.

I work to leave you a world of beauty,
equity and mutual respect.

There are two ways to be fooled.

One is to believe what isn't true;

the other is to refuse to believe what is true.

Soren Kierkegaard

The End of History

Bearing Truth

American Science Academy Awards Gala
Washington, DC, November 2018

"Ladies and gentlemen,
He is an educator, climate scientist, writer, TV sensation and the most generous man I know. Please welcome our Science Communicator Award recipient, Dr. Sagan Cleveland!"

Sagan took a deep breath, then pulled himself out of his chair and mounted the stairs to the stage, hoping he looked steadier than he felt. The applause was reassuring. They hadn't given up on him. But would they be with him an hour from now? Would *he* be with them?

He'd tapered his dosage, but he wasn't as sharp as he'd like. Or once was.

Placing his notes carefully upon the lectern, he scanned the cavernous banquet hall as the applause continued. His secret was safe. Just him and Simone. He smiled.

"Thank you, Madam President," he began, nodding to where she was now seated. "Thanks for inviting me to shock the bow ties off this esteemed group." A gentle laughter rippled across the hall.

"Academy members and patrons, I am truly honoured to accept this award. If my auto-assembling parents from Detroit could be here they would be so—"

He paused, making an act of reflecting on his words. "Come to think of it, my mama would have said, 'Sagan, you going as a *penguin*?'"

He caressed the satin lapel of his tuxedo, absorbing the warm laughter. "That just may be where I got my sharp tongue and devilish wit. Well, if I'm a penguin then I'm at a convention of them." He looked left, then right, grinning.

"OK, you're not here for stand up. Though you may wish you were." He could see people nodding. Others cleared their throats or smiled tightly.

"Does everybody have a seat? Not that it's going to be long," he clarified, his tone shifting. "It will, though, be true. Which is what makes it hard to swallow. And what makes it science. In this age of slippery truth, there's nothing I will say that hasn't been, that cannot be corroborated: with verifiable observation, witnesses, un-doctored video and more. But I want to go light on stats tonight, and visuals."

He could see people near the front nodding. *Powerpoint ties your hands*, Simone had said. Right, as usual. He'd be working from a loose script.

"Truth! Ah yes, I made my reputation by telling the truth. Some lame jokes, yeah, but never overstating what is known. Or sugar-coating facts."

Sagan placed both palms on the lectern and relaxed his shoulders.

"The Earthly biosphere that gave birth to the human species, and all those from which we evolved—the web of life upon which we rely—is in a death spiral. Human intervention has set us on a course from which it's not likely we can pull out. Bets have been placed and the wheel has been spun. The house will win, and we have precious little to say about it.

"We could have, but too few of us did. Too few, too faintly... too *late*!" He raised his voice on the last word. Now he lowered it again.

"Life as we know it," he said, just above a whisper, "is about to get *really* bad."

He paused, and held it for several seconds.

"Nervous laughter!" he noted, smiling himself. "I made you uncomfortable."

"*Is he serious? Was that a joke?* No, friends. Though plenty have treated me as if I were a joke. Me and anyone who dared confront them with truths. Uncomfortable truths. You might even say, *inconvenient* ones..."

Chuckling and nodding, the audience exhaled.

"*That* dude became a punchline too. Where is he now? On a stage, somewhere, just like me. Still telling the truth; *selling* the truth while there may be a microscopic window of opportunity to save our species, and the civilization we cling to so dearly."

Sagan shook his head in dismay.

"He, like me, and many of you, will die knowing he gave everything. To a lot of grateful and appreciative people. To a lot of confused people. And to plenty who didn't *want* to know. Who shouted him down. Folks who call us names, troll us online, probe into our personal affairs, get our work de-funded, and even threaten us with death, in the most imaginative ways. Every...damn...day!" He pounded the lectern with his left fist, his right hand holding him steady.

A shiver ran across his shoulders. Had they turned on the air conditioning? Or should he wrap this up quickly?

"But you know what? The deniers and skeptics are going to go down in the same spiral of destruction as we who drank Al Gore's Kool-Aid while it was still cool.

"My friends, I can't soften the blow. I do not have a list of fix-it tips. *Change your light bulbs. Wear a sweater. Ride a bike!* That list would have been great in 1992. It was 'the turn-around decade'. Trouble is, we didn't turn around."

He looked up, making an effort to include the tables furthest away, as he'd once been coached, hundreds of lectures ago.

"What I have on offer tonight is a science talk with a little politics and religion. Quite a mix, huh? I'll 'vulgarize' the complicated parts. '*Voolgareezay!*' That's what the French say, did you know? Simplifying so everybody can get it."

He thought again of Simone, far away, yet always on call.

"Tonight, when I have once more delivered the *voolgar* facts, I'm going to leave it to you to decide what you'll do with it."

Sagan's dark eyes, devoid now of mischief, fixed on the nearest table.

"So, let's roll, 'cause delay is what got us into this mess."

Wolves at the Gate

Dateline: September 10, 2025, Southern France
Weather: Hot, dry, silent

Simone's mind was spinning like the hard drive on her first laptop. Writing columns for papers that no longer published, for readers who no longer cared. No longer dared.

Another scorching night in the Drome. Which farm was burning now? Which wood lot? Which walled estate? Were there even any left to burn?

Chateau d'Inferno. Lovely little French wine. A hint of scorched earth, with atomic after-taste. Sniff. Swirl. Sip. Spit. *That would be Chateau Cruas-Meysse; or maybe Cote-du-Fessenheim!* If nuclear reactors grew grapes.

Dry mouth, addled brain. Simone flipped over in her narrow bed and groped for her water. Balm for the lips.

Lips. *Loose lips lose lives*, the wartime British posters had said. *Loose lips might sink ships*, read the American version. A stickler for accuracy, that Simone Cohen. Accuracy and truth. Twenty-five years of speaking truth. Until it became too dangerous. Not just for her, but the people she cared about most.

Fake news. She flinched at the memory.

Some thought it was Trump who'd led the assault. During the 2016 campaign, and then in office. Wrong! It started much earlier and went far wider. Deeper too. Propaganda campaigns, surging in tandem with attacks on journalism, and journalists; on science, and scientists. The return of populism.

Truth is the first casualty. Truth-tellers come next. Her words.

Once truth is whatever you want it to be, we are on the road to social collapse, with empathy and humanity the first to die. Her again.

Dezinformatsiya, the Russians called it. Disinformation. They would know.

Simone felt the disk speeding up. The hard drive in her head.

Things fall apart. The centre cannot hold. Yeats.

It was underway before 2016, but that election unclipped the leashes; all around the world. Authoritarians, populists, supremacists, xenophobes, ideologues, profiteers...Putin, Bannon, Erdogan, Duterte, Orban, Salvini, Bolsonaro...

The best lack all conviction, while the worst are full of passionate intensity. More Yeats. The Second Coming, of course.

Lacking conviction are the institutions that hold society's most deplorable in check. Her words, again. *Democratic governance, the rule of law, and a century of international cooperation—crumbling, faster than anyone could predict.*

Almost anyone. Punching a gaping hole in this over-crowded lifeboat. Taking down a lot of good people. Bad ones too. With nobody even trying to bail now.

Simone stirred. A light breeze had brought the sound of distant barking. The curtains flapped, and for a moment she felt her bare skin cooling.

Hobbes saw it coming. *No arts; no letters; no society...*

She gave her head a shake, but the spinning continued.

Not with a bang but a whimper. Eliot saw it too.

These quotations she had collected since high school formed an anthology in her head. She had clung to them as tightly as memories. After this long, they felt like part of her own history. They witnessed it all, answered her, soothed her when she found herself staring down the big, unanswerable questions. *Why are we here? What's the point? Is there a point?*

Serving quotations on a silver platter; turning them, playing with them. She'd always loved that. Most people loved when she did it. Some hated it. Especially when it was their words—their claims and promises played back at them.

Nasty journalist!

A journalist's job isn't to make friends. That's what she believed. Still did. It's what drove her: truth, honesty, justice. Simone's jaw clenched.

That which does not kill me makes me stronger. Nietzsche.

That one got her through some gut-puking training sessions, tough races and their real life equivalents. She became stronger and stronger, until strong wasn't enough, and telling the truth was far too dangerous. *Ride for your life, little woman!*

Simone felt her thighs, her forearms, her shoulders, her pecs. A shrivelled version of the athlete she'd once been. Imagined herself to be.

Cast out at 52. Alone and silenced. No way to communicate, to persuade, to use even the drop of influence she might still have on anybody still out there. Her many followers. Once.

No way to bait her haters, either. If they were still out there, still gunning for her. Not without revealing herself, and the bulls eye on her back. So far from those she loved, dead and alive—and not entirely sure who was which.

The drive kept spinning. Replaying, reliving, hallucinating… it was hard to tell.

Dogs barked in the distance. Searching for food, or fighting over it. Another reason to fix the gap in the fence alongside the field.

He who has a why to live for can bear almost any how. Nietzsche again. That's what she'd believed. She still might, if she hadn't run out of whys—beyond fixing fences or finding water and food to get Ibrahim and her through the coming winter.

That was it for clever quotes from her 1990 Ontario high school curriculum.

Happy days!

It occurred to her, not for the first time, that the most interesting people from that period were not the cool kids. More the cyclists, the closet poets and the kids who quoted existentialists. The late bloomers. A fleeting smile crossed her lips. They were the ones who forced the world to take notice. The ones with whom she'd landed big interviews.

The biggest ones, though, the people who helped propel her rising star, weren't from high school. They came from a tighter group. At grad school. In England.

They had been full of conviction, Jenny, Jiro and Sagan. Her group of four. The intensity shifted, but it took them as far as they could go on their trajectories. Before it undid them.

Simone took a deep breath, trembling as she exhaled. Then, to her surprise, she felt tears, cool as they rolled down her cheeks, salty as they reached her tongue.

Then came a drowsiness, long overdue.

With a jolt, Simone awoke. Her whole body was tense. That cracking sound? Had she dreamt it? For a full minute she lay perfectly still, listening. Nothing. Just another of her strange dreams.

Breathing deeply, she tried to settle again. Now there were voices! She was sure of it. Sitting up, she listened intently. More silence. The mighty mouse, reduced to hearing voices!

She lowered her bare feet gently to the floor and felt her way to the bathroom. At the open window, she nudged the curtain and peered cautiously into the courtyard below. Pitch black. She'd been here once before, she recalled, frowning. A night of murder.

Breathe, hold and relax. The biathlete's mantra, settling on a target before squeezing the trigger. The last time she'd been at this window, she'd had a rifle and a half dozen men on her side. Now they were just two, with Ibrahim on watch duty, carrying their only gun. Two against how many? And what?

Tonight there was nothing to see. Or hear—beyond the pounding of her heart. She stared again into the blackness. Then she felt the spider. That tingle in her scalp. Could it be him?

And if it was? A surge of adrenaline hit her. *Avenge her friend!* But with what?

The crunch of gravel! Barely distinguishable, but getting louder. Tires on the driveway. What happened to Ibrahim? Asleep? Fled? Or worse! She shuddered.

And the intruder lights? But now there *was* a light. A single one; faint, advancing in pace with the sound.

Simone went rigid. Then relaxed, as it came to her—she had just enough time to grab the hatchet from outside the door.

The Turn Around Decade

High Tea

Cambridge, England, September 1997

The door to Aunty's Tea House opened and shut for the dozenth time since Sagan had claimed his table. Sitting alone at a table for four, the only one he'd been able to snag, he apologized to another hopeful group.

"I'm expecting friends." A friend. An acquaintance, really.

All of this was new to him. The bustling tea house. Scones. Clotted cream. Cups with saucers. "You're in for a culture shock," his professor at Cornell had warned him. So had several Churchill Scholar alumni he'd spoken with at the Manhattan send-off party. He hadn't really believed it. Same language. Similar food. Beer.

It's not like I'm going to Japan, he'd thought. Or even France.

Yet here he was a week after arriving, baffled by the accents, unsure of the food and pining for an ice-cold beer. He'd expected making friends to be easier too.

Rather than the jovial global village they'd described, the Cambridge University he was discovering was mostly white, upper-class and straight. None of which fit Sagan Cleveland.

He'd spent much of his life struggling to escape labels. Admission to Cornell had been his first chance.

Everyone's an equal in the science lab! More like tolerated. *Great to have you here Sagan.* Learn your place! Implied, not spoken.

He craved so much more, even if he couldn't define what he was missing.

But Cambridge: bright young minds from every continent; a hothouse of ideas, music and art. A dream-come-true year with the Scott Polar Research Institute, on full scholarship. A quick train ride to London, with all its marvels and temptations. A mere hop to Amsterdam, Paris and a whack of other places his parents had never been.

Only now, this feeling was creeping over him again. The fog. He'd thought he was free of it. Though you never really are, he knew.

You're barely into your second week, he reminded himself. *When was making friends a problem for you?*

Sagan Cleveland was the bright-eyed kid with the big smile. The joker. Trim, fit and always dapper. Sharpest dresser in any class. *Sagan does not go unnoticed!* Under-appreciated, sure. That came with the territory. But he'd learned how to lift people up, warm people up, and by doing so, pick himself up. Then, when things were back on track, man could he fly.

Sensing the need to defend the table once more, he pulled himself out. He hoped the young woman from his staircase in residence would show up.

"High tea?" he'd proposed. One British culinary experience he could embrace.

But if she didn't show soon, he'd have to share his table. Yes, that's what he'd do. *The next person who asks gets the pleasure of my company. Or me, theirs.* Maybe that's how you made friends here.

"Sorry. Excuse me!" A gangly Asian student was standing in front of him juggling a loaded tray.

"Is it ok for me to have a seat at your table? It is very busy," the fellow continued in accented English.

"Sure," Sagan replied, indicating the seat across from him. "Finders keepers."

"Pardon me?"

Sagan laughed. "Since my date hasn't shown up, it's her loss, and your gain."

"Oh, I see. But I do not want to take another person's seat."

"Go ahead," Sagan said, with a casual wave. "I'm not sure she'll come. And it's not really a date."

The fellow began removing items from his tray, arranging them carefully on the table. Watching casually at first, Sagan soon found himself staring. The long, slender hands placed the teacup just so. Then adeptly, as if the motion had been rehearsed, poured the amber liquid from a greater height than Sagan would have dared. Not a splash. Not a dribble from the spout or the lid of the pot. Sagan smiled. They make teapots better here than back home.

Raising the cup to his lips for a first sip verging on reverence, the newcomer became aware of Sagan's interest, and paused. Sagan quickly apologized.

"I shouldn't have been staring, but I found your movements so... precise. Like a dance." He winced. "Sorry if that's weird!"

"Oh no. I am flattered," the tea pourer said with a slow nod, his face and voice showing no emotion.

"Tea is an important part of Japanese life. We even have a ceremony for it. But not for everyday tea. Only a special kind, performed for a guest. And *never* with scones and cream!" he proclaimed in horror, pronouncing scones the British way—*scawns*.

"Mmm," he sighed, closing his eyes. "Warm scones are *so* delicious!"

Sagan sensed mischief, hiding behind the manners.

"Damn right!" he declared. "Strawberry jam, and a nice Darjeeling. You don't get them where I'm from. Maybe in some fancy Boston hotel."

"Are you from Boston?"

"Hardly," said Sagan. "Inner city Detroit. And you?"

"Tokyo. My education was in Tokyo. But my hometown is called Namie, in Fukushima Prefecture."

"Japanese!" Sagan exclaimed. "That explains the tea ceremony! And your politeness. I guess Detroit explains my... impoliteness."

"Oh, I did not find you impolite. I think, perhaps, I found you a bit... lonely?"

Sagan chuckled. "It showed, did it? I moved into college early, but haven't had much luck connecting with people."

"Yes, I also came early. But I have been fortunate to make some friends quickly at my college, Clare Hall."

"Clare!" said Sagan. "I love the bridge."

"No, no," his table mate corrected. "Clare *Hall*. Very small. Just graduate students. Not so traditional."

Sagan nodded. "I'm at Churchill. It's also modern, but it's pretty big. And mostly undergrads. I feel a bit of an outsider."

"Imagine being Japanese?" A grin followed.

Sagan threw back his head and laughed.

"As we're sharing our souls, maybe we should swap names! I'm Sagan."

"Sorry. Sei-gin?"

"Close. Sei-*gan*. As in Carl Sagan, the scientist. And educator. He's best known for his TV series in the '80s —Cosmos."

"So, you are... his son?"

"No, not related," said Sagan. "We have a different, um, complexion."

"Skin colour," he added, as the fellow's eyes indicated confusion. "My parents were big fans," he explained. "Papa was crazy about science, cosmology especially. Building cars by day, exploring the universe in his free time. He was such a fan of Carl Sagan that I got stuck with the name. It started as a nickname, when I showed an interest as a kid. Then it stuck. I made it official when I turned 18."

"*Very* interesting!" said the fellow, with a slow nod. Was he being genuine or sarcastic, Sagan wondered. He'd go with genuine.

"Listen to me, I haven't even asked *your* name. See if you can match my story."

"Ohhh," came the reply, followed by an intake of air through the teeth. "I think I can. Do you want my family name, or, how did you say—nickname?"

"Save the best for last," Sagan proposed.

"Well... my real name is Ebitsubo Jiro'"

"OK, which is your first name?"

"Jiro. Very common in Japan. Not so original as Sagan."

"And your nickname?"

"My nickname," Jiro said slowly, his eyes shimmering, "is John!"

"John?" Sagan said loudly, his pitch rising. "How's that supposed to rival mine?"

Jiro grinned. "Because," he said, "I also am named after a TV star. And I also have a father who lives a different life at home. You see, my father is a highly respected engineer. But secretly, he wants to be British. Secretly," he said, leaning forward and in a hushed voice, "my father likes British comedy. Most unusually in Japan, he likes Monty Python. So he named me after—"

"Sagan!"

A woman's voice had cut in before Jiro could finish.

"I'm so sorry," said a petite, dark-haired woman as she rushed toward their table.

"My supervisor went on forever and—"

"No need to apologize," Sagan said with a smile and a nod to his table mate. "This tea samurai took pity on me. Jenny, allow me to introduce my new friend Jiro-John."

"It is a pleasure to meet you," Jiro said, rising and offering a slight bow. Fully upright, he towered over Jenny.

"Jiro-John?" Jenny was not sure she had heard correctly.

"Ah," said Sagan, as she took a seat and began to wipe the steam off her wire-rimmed glasses. "You missed the back story. Jiro was explaining why his eccentric father named him John. Something about Monty Python."

"*Cleese!*" Jenny exclaimed. "Your dad named you after *John Cleese?*"

Jiro's sheepish smile confirmed her guess.

"That *is* unusual," Jenny said. "Can we call you Bruce just to be clear!"

Jiro exploded with laughter. Sagan furrowed his brow and looked at Jenny.

"Sorry," she said, "I guess Python didn't make it to America."

"Oh, it did. I liked their film about the reluctant messiah…"

"*Life of Brian!*" chimed Jenny and Jiro. Glancing at one another, they laughed.

"Yeah," said Sagan, wrinkling his face, "I'm more of a Robin Williams guy."

"That's all right," said Jenny. "Python wasn't so big in Malaysia either, despite our colonial history."

"Now hang on!" said Sagan, holding up a hand. "Before we get into history lessons, we need to do two things. First, Jenny needs tea."

"And scones," suggested Jiro.

"Naturally," said Sagan. "Second, we need to settle on what to call Jiro-John."

"I have an idea," Jenny said tentatively. "How about JJ?"

"JJ?" said Jiro. "OK," he agreed, with a straight face. "Just to keep things clear!"

Chuckling with the others, Sagan could feel the fog dissipating.

When they rose to leave an hour later, Sagan felt certain that Cambridge had been the right choice after all. They agreed to meet again the following week. And they consented to JJ inviting a fourth person.

"A Canadian," he indicated. "I believe you will like her."

Three Plus One

Jiro walked faster than usual, which was saying something. He could cover distance quickly with his long stride and light gait.

In Japan, he was always the tallest man in the subway car or the crowd. He had literally stood out from the time he'd turned thirteen, shooting up quickly over the heads of his peers, and then his father. Then his older brother too; which Katsuo deeply resented.

In Japanese culture women often ranked men according to the three takais: tall nose, high salary, tall stature. As a young man, Jiro was embarrassed by the attention. During adolescence his height had been a curse, turning him into some sea creature in his mind: a studious kid overtaken by gangly limbs he could barely control. That his brother used it against him didn't help matters.

On a damp October afternoon in Cambridge, though, he received no special notice as he kept his pace brisk to stay with the person cycling alongside him. She was a markedly shorter, muscular woman with blond hair that protruded from her helmet.

They arrived at Aunty's at almost the exact time as the others: Sagan coming from his lab on a classic student bike—old, battered and black with a wicker basket—and Jenny by foot from a meeting with her thesis supervisor.

They watched JJ's invitee dismount adeptly and secure her lightweight bike with a solid U-lock. Like most students, Sagan had casually leaned his ancient machine against the first available wall.

"Hey," the original trio greeted one another as they converged at the door.

JJ gestured to the others to enter ahead of him, delaying a proper introduction. Sagan delayed it further with a cat-like pounce toward the one available table.

This gave the helmeted woman a chance to peel off and hang her gear, unaware she was being stared at. She looked up just as Jenny's expression turned from disbelief to glee.

"Simone?!"

"Jenny?" the woman exclaimed. "No way!"

JJ and Sagan exchanged baffled looks as the two embraced, then pulled back to stare at one another, both beaming.

"You have met already?" JJ said tentatively.

"Only once," Jenny replied, her eyes alight. "And it was five years ago, but Simone is someone you do not forget."

Her face pink, Simone shrugged.

"Hi," said Sagan, from across the table. "I'm Sagan. You know JJ, of course."

Simone was puzzled. "You mean John?"

"Jiro!" corrected Jenny.

"We call him JJ," Sagan interjected, "to keep things clear."

"Monty Python!" declared Simone. "I love it. You three must be fans."

"Two out of three," clarified Sagan. "But that ain't bad!"

"Meatloaf!" Simone declared. "Nice."

Sagan was impressed. Jenny and JJ, on the other hand, seemed to have missed the musical reference.

Once all four were seated with a steaming pot of tea and basket of warm scones, JJ stood and, over the buzz of the room, gave "Simone Cohen" a formal welcome.

Fighting the smile that was tugging at his lips, Sagan responded in an imitation of JJ. "Thank you, esteemed JJ-san. And welcome, Simone, to our little club. There was a fourth chair calling to be filled by someone with the right credentials."

"Which are…?" Simone asked.

"As yet to be confirmed," Sagan replied with a straight face. "But a love of high tea is essential." He gestured to JJ, who stood and raised the teapot.

Sagan smiled at Simone's look of amazement as JJ poured four cups. When they had all taken a sip, Sagan asked what he had been itching to learn. He figured JJ would have been too.

"Just how exactly do you girls know each other?"

Simone was the first to reply. "Remember Rio? 1992?"

"Of course," said Sagan. "The Earth Summit."

"Well," said Simone, "Jenny and I were there. As youth members of our national delegations."

"We met on a bus," added Jenny.

"A long ride?" Sagan guessed.

"A memorable ride," said Jenny. "Right after, I was accepted into engineering at the University of Singapore. I only passed because of Simone."

"What?!" said Simone.

"Wah!" exclaimed JJ. "A woman in engineering?" Six eyes turned to stare at him.

"That was, I think, sexist?" he said sheepishly.

Sagan confirmed this with an emphatic nod.

"So sorry," JJ said. "In Japan, it is almost unheard of."

"To be fair to JJ," said Jenny, "I was the only one in my class. And nobody, apart from my parents, thought I would get into Cambridge."

"Busting down barriers!" Sagan said. JJ and Simone nodded in support.

"Though it is a bit embarrassing," Jenny said quietly, "I must tell Simone how she saved me from expulsion." She paused and looked at her hands. Simone glanced at the men and shrugged, while JJ moved to refill the cups.

"I failed a final exam," Jenny explained. "In first year. A very hard course. I had frozen completely. This meant I was going to fail that class, and there was nothing I could do about it."

"Oh no," JJ whispered.

Jenny lifted her head and locked eyes with Simone. "Then I thought of you. That confident journalism student from Canada. So determined. The way you pressured your government to support NGO participation in Rio—*the Global Forum!* I said to myself that Simone would not simply give up. I steeled my nerve, and went to the dean. I told him, 'Sir, the best inventors and entrepreneurs say we must not be afraid of failing. We can learn from it. I have now learned what it is like to freeze when under pressure, and I am certain I can learn from this.' Since he seemed receptive, I said what I had rehearsed. I asked for a make-up exam under what I thought would be 'fair' conditions. If I did not achieve 100 percent, I would drop out."

Sagan shook his head. "Gutsy!"

"And he agreed?" said Simone.

"He said it was an excellent suggestion, but he needed to make the same offer to the entire class. So nobody could accuse him of lowering standards—for a woman. Anyone who asked for such a retest could have one."

"And..." Simone prompted. JJ and Sagan leaned in closer.

"One hundred percent," Jenny exclaimed, "or I wouldn't be drinking tea with you!" She looked around the table beaming, her cheeks flushed.

"Bravo!" said Sagan, clapping.

Jenny was not yet done. "Most important is how he created a new policy. He had long felt that there was too much pressure on students, with serious effects on mental health."

Sagan felt a slight shiver as he leaned in again to listen.

"The emphasis has always been on rote learning," Jenny said. "But the world needs innovators. So the dean used my case to question a lot of practices, and try new, collaborative approaches. More team projects."

"*Sugoi*" said JJ, prompting all heads to turn his way. "Terrific," he translated.

"Thanks," said Jenny. "But it was Simone. My memory of her at least. She would never have just given up!"

Simone wanted none of it. "You defended your own dream. And triggered even bigger changes." Jenny was shifting in her seat, picking at the scone on her plate.

"Are you also a scientist?" asked Simone, turning to Sagan.

"Yep," he said. "Atmospheric chemistry."

Suddenly JJ pushed back his chair and stood. "So sorry," he said with an awkward bow, "Evening lecture." He patted his pockets in search of a wallet.

"Go!" said Jenny, waving him away. "We'll cover your tea."

"And finish your scones!" Sagan volunteered.

With a quick nod, JJ turned and hand-sliced his way between tables.

"It's the *Silly Walk* for polite people!" Sagan remarked. "Don't you just love that guy?"

Vulgar Talk

It was a Friday evening in November and the Churchill College bar was hot and noisy. The four were squeezed around a table up against a brick wall, just inside the entrance. Sagan had claimed the spot early, but competition for space and the barkeeper's attention was fierce and was likely to stay that way for another few hours.

They had been discussing the quirky side of Cambridge culture.

"You know how men are expected to wear *dinner jacket?*" Sagan shouted. "*DJ* — to even some of the most ordinary gatherings?" Mostly, Simone realized, it was Sagan doing the speaking. With the occasional prompt.

"I figured that was a myth," Simone piped in, breaking her silence.

"Oh no, it's true," JJ confirmed. "At social events for my law class the men often wear DJ!"

"Well," said Sagan, "at Churchill even undergrads dress up. Some rowers hosted a female crew for dinner. There they were, splashing sherry on their suits as they overcooked the pasta."

His mimed juggling of implements earned laughs from JJ and Jenny, and a smile from Simone.

"Right?" He said, looking around. "So, I figured I'd better get my own."

"I'll bet that's not cheap," said Jenny.

"Ah, but here's the secret. You can find them at the market. Used."

"DJ? At the outdoor market?" Jenny sounded doubtful.

"Yep," continued Sagan, "got mine for 20 pounds. They're 300 in a store. I got the shirt and tie new for another 30. That's full DJ for 50 quid! Under a hundred bucks."

Proud as a peacock, Simone noted.

"Anybody for another pint?" proposed a smiling JJ. With their orders, he headed to the crowded bar.

"Have you chosen a thesis topic?" Jenny asked Sagan, out of the blue.

"I have indeed. The impact of methane release on the atmosphere. From livestock rearing and thawing permafrost."

"That's a big scope for a master's thesis," Jenny commented.

Sagan nodded. "That's the first thing my supervisor said: 'Pick cow farts or sinking igloos, not both.'"

Jenny and Simone laughed. *Such a clown.*

"Which appeals more to you personally?" Simone poked.

"I'm tempted by the permafrost," he replied with a grin. "The field work won't be as risky."

"Don't be too sure," said Simone. "Though melting tundra won't smell as ripe."

"Methane is methane!" said Jenny with scientific precision.

"But if I go with the frozen stuff, I won't get the thrill of making 5 billion people hate me. When I conclude beef and dairy production must be outlawed."

"It is true," said JJ, piping in as he arrived with their drinks. "People do not like their eating habits or business practices questioned."

Jenny reached out to help JJ distribute the glasses.

"Run with the arctic methane," Simone advised. "Veganism is a tough sell."

"But that's what I find exciting! Using science to help people lead informed lives." Sagan's eyes were shining. "Science isn't just for scientists."

"*Vulgarisation!*" Simone said, to the bewilderment of the others. "It's a French way of saying dumbing down," she explained. "But not in a negative light."

"Vool-ga-ree-za-see-onn," tried Sagan.

"Good try," she said with a smile. "*Popularize* is a better term. It's what David Suzuki does—the Canadian scientist and TV host. And Carl Sagan." *Of course! Why didn't I make that connection earlier?!*

"Exactly!" said Sagan. "That's how he drew in people like my parents. Urban black folks who only just made it through high school."

"But can you make a living this way?" said JJ, sounding skeptical. "Popularizing."

"If you're good at it," answered Simone.

"Which I intend to be," declared Sagan, pushing out his chest.

Simone had noticed his joking on day one. His love of attention. But not his ego.

"So JJ, what brought you to Cambridge to study law?"

It was Jenny, shouting over the din. Keen to hear from the quiet guy. Not that she was any more talkative. *Two introverts, two extroverts. An interesting quartet.*

"It's not so interesting," JJ said waving one arm, palm forward. At their insistence, he recounted how he had earned a domestic law degree several years earlier, in Tokyo.

"In Japan, it is not so common to pursue a career as a lawyer. It is quite rare to hire a lawyer to resolve a dispute, or even to seek reparations using the courts." He paused to sip his beer, then resumed with another prompt from Jenny.

"Then why choose law in the first place?"

JJ looked at his hands. "I did not," he said. "My father and older brother, they... twisted my elbow."

"Arm," offered Simone.

"Parental persuasion," Sagan noted, chuckling.

"It was mostly my brother. It is he who wanted to be a lawyer, but he pursued engineering, like my father. He believes Japan needs people trained in trade agreements, intellectual property and financial law. So, it was the will of my family that I study law. Now international business law."

"That's what you're taking here?" asked Simone.

"Not directly. I am doing the one-year LLM. But I want to work with a law firm in London when I have completed the degree. To get practical experience."

"And keep some distance from your brother," Sagan poked.

"Family obligations are very important," said JJ, his tone sharp, and his voice rising. Jenny peered at JJ thoughtfully. Simone felt her discomfort at the way the conversation had turned.

Ease off Sagan.

"But wouldn't you like to make your own decisions?"

JJ looked down at his hands. "I must do what is best for the family, not just me."

Never cause someone to lose face. Time for a lifeline.

"Does your programme require you to write a thesis?" Simone asked.

JJ looked up at her, taking a moment to process the question. "No," he said. "Thank goodness. My writing in English is not so good. I have several major papers, but no thesis."

"Phew!" he added, wiping his brow with an exaggerated gesture that brought smiles back to their faces.

"Well," Simone announced, looking at her unfinished pint, "the camaraderie is *ichiban*, but my Saturday cycling buddies wait for nobody, least of all a hung-over Canadian."

"Cycling in this cold!" Jenny exclaimed.

Simone scoffed. "Cold? Come to Ottawa in February." Jenny shivered.

"Are you walking back to Clare Hall, or riding?" JJ asked Simone.

"Riding," she replied, "but I'd be glad roll slowly alongside you."

"I once tried to cycle drunk," Sagan volunteered as the other three stood to leave. "Didn't make it ten feet before I keeled over." Swaying in his chair, legs flailing, he plunked his head on the table.

Chuckling to herself at Sagan's antics, Simone noticed JJ smile.

"*Oyasumi nasai!*" JJ said. "Good night, my provocative friend."

"What do you make of Sagan?" Simone asked JJ as he strode briskly down Wilberforce Road. The orange street lamps illuminated their route, but offered no heat to counter the piercing autumn wind. "I'm thinking there's a lot more to him than we're seeing."

JJ was slow to answer, choosing his words with care. He glanced up as the moon made a brief appearance between scudding clouds.

"It takes a lifetime just to understand ourselves. It is no wonder we must put on an act sometimes, to hide how confused we are."

Digging Deeper

Simone hated rowing machine workouts. But the December weather and reduced daylight hours had driven many college crews indoors.

Everybody hated the ergometer. The "erg." It felt as bad as it sounded. Just stare at your screen and pull. At least in a boat you were travelling. Even if your view was the back of a crew member—straining as you pulled together in rhythm, then sliding smoothly forward, blades feathered, until the micro-second when all eight oars dropped into the water and you exploded into another stroke.

There was poetry to rowing. Like the perfect diagonal stride on cross-country skis. But it carried a risk that only a severe wipe-out on skis could rival: 'catching a crab.' Failing to get your blade out of the water at the critical moment brought the entire boat to a shuddering halt. And worse. Rowers had been injured by loose handles surging at them at chest height. Neck height, in her case.

Dancing on the edge of danger. It was part of the thrill. Thrill and risk are twins, Simone understood—on skis, on a bicycle, in a rowing shell—and she'd choose risk any day over the *erg*.

"Ten minutes down, ten more to go for the stroke side," called their coxswain as she paced behind the four ergometers arranged side by side in the boathouse. "Then you can hand your sweaty seats over to the bow four." 'Lizzie the coxy' was petite, but her voice commanded attention.

"Unh!" The four of them groaned.

"If I don't spew first," Simone heard Gerda say in her Austrian accent.

Ten more minutes, Simone told herself. *Think of something pleasant.*

It wouldn't be sex. She could barely remember the last time… Actually, she could. A year ago, in Japan. Liam. Australian. Wrote for the *Sydney Herald*. But she'd gone without since. Looking for Mr. Good Enough. Mr. Perfect didn't exist.

She could hear Sagan's laugh. Picture his smile.

Sagan was a charmer. Single too, it seemed. But could they…? The issue wasn't skin colour, though she'd only ever dated white guys. Nor his provocative remarks and clothing choices. She wasn't even put off by his exploits. It was more basic. Was he attracted to women? Partly at least. Sexual orientation was a continuum. The science showed it. And if he was somewhere in the middle, could it work? Was he open to it? Was she?

"Five minutes. Keep the rate up."

"Thanks Lizzy, but I can't see!" Gerda's eyes would be as full of sweat as Simone's. The waiting four chuckled.

Nobody could make her laugh like Sagan. Sometimes it was goofy, playing for laughs. Usually, though, it was clever. Word play. Her father had raised her on it.

She could never tell which of Sagan's tales was true and which invented, or at least embellished. But he left her in stitches on numerous occasions. When the 'gang of four' met up for tea or beer, or went to a concert or party together. Less so, with Jenny recently. She had declined several invitations, or simply failed to show.

Sagan, though, always showed. With the four, or Simone's classmates, or Jiro's law colleagues or—apparently—all sorts of others. He seemed ready to try anything, from today's counter-culture to ancient customs: slam poetry; 'Real Tennis,' with its bizarre rules; an afternoon at Ladbroke's quizzing locals on how to pick a horse; or even a weekend of 'beagling.'

"It's like fox-hunting," he'd explained, "but without horses or a fox." He'd laughed at their puzzled looks. "Mostly it's a way for aristocratic boys to have a jolly day out among peers. Me being the *obvious* exception." Not much of an explanation, but he refused to expand. "Sworn to secrecy!" he'd said with a wink.

There was the very public Sagan, and another she was left to guess at.

"Ten last pulls," Lizzy shouted. "Make them count!"

Back to the Land

Simone had great expectations for Christmas in Strasbourg—reconnecting with her mother's family, speaking French for the first time in months, and finally meeting François, the husband of her cousin Nicole, who had been away when she and her parents had visited eight years earlier.

As a child, she had become close to Nicole, despite their age gap. Seven years her senior, Nicole had spent a summer in Ottawa, mostly at the family's cottage northwest of Montréal, as an *au pair* to Simone. They'd exchanged cards and letters regularly over the years. Whenever photos were included, someone would remark on how similar they looked. "Identical twins," she'd heard more than once, as she approached adulthood.

It was only natural to visit while just across the Channel. Natural too that she would want to meet François, about whom she had heard so much: passionate, devoted to environmental protection and animal welfare and, most of all, to questioning France's 'nuclear energy obsession'.

Waiting for Simone at the Strasbourg central station were Nicole and her two children—Marc, 14 and Sylvie, 12. Simone sensed in their stiff smiles that something was amiss.

"Is François at work?" she asked innocently as they drove back to the family apartment. The uncomfortable silence which followed was unexpected.

"No," Nicole responded after a long pause. "François is away." Marc and Sylvie, seated behind Simone, were silent for the entire drive.

"François no longer lives with us," Nicole announced without emotion as she hung Simone's coat in the front hall wardrobe of the spacious family apartment. She had waited until the children were out of earshot. "He moved out in October."

Simone's dismay must have shown. Nicole apologized for not warning her, explaining that only close friends and family knew. Was it temporary or permanent, she wondered? His coats and shoes were still in the wardrobe.

Two days later, with Christmas nearly upon them, Simone had yet to learn more. She wanted to ask, but there were always others around, namely the children. Neither had mentioned their father. Reminders of him were everywhere, though. Photos of the family, mostly on outdoor expeditions, lined the front hallway. His desk in the office where Simone was sleeping had not been touched.

She found her inquisitive self battling with respect for family. Though it went against her nature, she forced her mouth to remain shut, recalling a piece of wisdom she had heard from a great documentary filmmaker—that you could learn as much from staying silent as from pressing hard.

In a quiet moment on the morning of December 24th, Nicole chose to open up after sending Marc and Sylvie out to do errands. Simone had been seated in the living room, flipping through a photo album labelled *Summer Vacation 1993*. It seemed to be the last in a series. She was lingering over a photo of François pointing to what Simone knew to be deer tracks, with a younger Marc and Sylvie looking entranced beside him.

"*Saint François d'Assise*. Patron saint of animals and nature," declared Nicole, coming up behind her and placing her hands on Simone's shoulders. "That's him in a nutshell." Simone detected a hint of nostalgia.

"He got side-tracked by that whole nuclear campaign. Which pulled him into politics. It never seemed right for him. He gave it everything, mind you, for longer than he should have. Then he walked away. *Assez!*"

"Not that François didn't love people," she clarified, peering in for a closer look at the photos. "But he didn't connect with people in the same profound way as he did with animals. No games. An animal is what it appears to be, and respect is the key." She paused, turning to the next page.

"Remarkable," she added wistfully.

"So what happened?" Simone said gently. "If I'm not prying."

"I'll tell you when you are," Nicole answered with a tight smile. "Technically, we're still a couple. Just not together. Physically or emotionally. After these last crazy years."

"He was involved with the Green Party, wasn't he?" Simone knew this much.

"Yes, he was once *the* François Dirringer, accidental leader of *Les Verts*."

"Accidental?"

"You'll have to ask him some day. I'll give you my version. Then we'd better start wrapping, before the invasion." Nicole glanced toward the presents on the dining room table.

"You talk, while I wrap," Simone offered, pulling herself up.

"Helpful as always, Simone. Even when you were little."

"I'll do anything to get a story," Simone joked, strolling toward the dining room.

Nicole followed and took a seat across from where Simone would be working.

"François grew to distrust any group that places human needs above those of the natural order we inherit from our creator. People who *say* the right things yet always put their own interests above ecological and spiritual ones."

"*When a bird, or a tree or a river or a whole ecosystem can always be sacrificed to human needs,*" she mimicked, "*where does that leave humanity? What are we left to pursue? To worship? Power. Money. Members. Voters.*"

She had been staring blankly across the table as she spoke. Looking into Simone's eyes, she continued.

"Odd that he found himself leading a political party, you are thinking? Indeed! François saw an opportunity to further his goals through politics, as a result of his anti-nuclear campaigns here in Alsace, and the community-building with like-minded Germans. He had a chance to do something bigger. More profound.

"He was reluctant at first. One morning he told me, 'I'm not the right person for this,' and that afternoon I found him folding pamphlets with a trio of volunteers." Nicole chuckled and shook her head.

Simone smiled at the image. She had wrapped two gifts, and silently moved on to a third.

"The start of some crazy years. Five, almost. First as local councillor, then as head of *Les Verts* here in the Bas-Rhin region. He was good at it. A natural communicator. Gentle, but persuasive— though he could be fiery when needed. He spoke honestly and candidly. Suicide in politics, some say."

"That one next," Nicole pointed, seeing Simone had paused. "For Marc."

"Nice!" Simone sized up the skateboard, still in its box.

"Did François ever enjoy politics?"

"Interaction with the public, sure. Policy debate, the opportunity to say publicly what he truly believed. But the internal fighting got to him. *If this is how like-minded people treat each other, how can we expect better from our opponents?* He reached a point where one day he cracked: *I've done what I can. I'll be of service some other way, where I can keep my soul!*"

Simone shook her head. "That's pretty strong!"

"Strong," Nicole agreed, her voice louder, "but honest. He didn't like what he had become. Neither did I. He was... no longer his best self. Irritable, after having to justify his actions all day in public. He became like a turtle, pulling into its shell."

Nicole wrapped her arms across her chest.

"For the last year, or more, he was coming home so worn down he didn't want to engage with anyone. For the first time in our lives I would find him watching TV. Anything that was on, while turning down dinners with friends. This was a guy who used to love discussing big ideas." Nicole sat still, lost in thought.

Sensing she might not have another chance, Simone prepared to ask the crucial question. Nicole beat her to it.

"I told him one evening, out in the park where we'd still walk some nights, that he had a choice: get out of politics, or get out of the house. But I'd much prefer he get out of politics."

"And?"

"He chose both. After we had strolled for a while in silence, he said: 'Nicole. It may not look like it, but I love you as much as ever. And that's why I have to leave.'"

"Sounds like a line from a movie," Simone said with a hint of sarcasm.

Nicole turned to Simone, her eyes narrowing. "He needed time for silence. A retreat. And when he'd had enough time alone, being of service to the land, maybe he would once again have the passion to serve people."

Nicole gestured toward the front hall. "He took his old climbing backpack, a few books, and headed south to our land in the Drome."

"Do you have a house there?"

Nicole snorted. "A shed is more like it. A run-down farmhouse. We'd dreamt of fixing it up. But we didn't get there often. When we did, we'd end up sleeping in a tent. Just using the old wood stove, after we'd repaired the chimney. It was such an expedition to get there, we mostly ended up resting and walking in the mountains. I'm not much good with my hands. That's François' thing. He'll dive right in without me."

"So, he's been gone for a few months. When do you think he'll be back?"

"You mean, *do* I think he'll be back?"

"Oh!" exclaimed Simone, meeting Nicole's eyes. Pausing, Nicole shrugged.

"He'll lose himself in his projects. Rebuilding. Establishing gardens. Then getting involved in the community, when he's ready. I doubt he'll return."

"And you?" said Simone, watching her cousin closely. "Will you visit?"

Nicole's eyes flashed. "It's his escape, not mine! I have my career, my friends... I'm not the one who had to get away. The kids can visit if they wish."

"Marc and Sylvie—how are they?" Simone had noted how quiet they were.

"Oh," Nicole replied with a shrug. "Kids sense a lot more than parents imagine. He was unhappy. We were unhappy. It couldn't go on."

Simone nodded. "Have you heard from François since?"

"Funny you should ask. There was a card in the mail yesterday." Nicole glanced toward the living room. "An...unusual one. A nativity scene. Baby Jesus, in a manger, but with the animals all wild, come to see the Christ child. Something only François could send. It's on the mantelpiece."

Simone put down the scissors and ribbon, and strolled toward the fireplace. "It *is* strange," she called out. "Mind you, no more than Three Wise Men and a virgin mother surrounded by admiring sheep and cows!" She laughed, a deep generous laugh.

Nicole joined her briefly, though there was pain behind the laugh. "He'd like you," she said abruptly. "You'd like him. Maybe when you're done at Cambridge he'll be ready for a visit. You can be my spy. Let me know if he's OK."

"I'd like that. I've never been to the Drome. Let's not call it spying, though."

"I was kidding, of course."

"Of course."

The rest of the holiday passed without mention of François. *How sad*, thought Simone. She could visit him in the fall, after graduation. If he was still there. If he would have her.

Intervention

he bathtub in Simone's residence was rarely used. Enveloped in steam, she had all the time in the world—to soak, and to think. She sighed as the heat penetrated her aching muscles.

What should she do about Jenny? Or should she do anything at all? Jenny was a perfectly capable adult who might not take kindly to meddling.

She worried about JJ also; and Sagan—especially Sagan, come to think of it—who seemed determined to outdo himself. Or do himself in. Whichever came first.

But in Jenny's case, there was urgency. The tingle in her scalp told her so. The spider was rarely wrong.

Jenny's PhD would take four years minimum. She was barely halfway through, far from home, with a scholarship that didn't cover trips home; working too hard and eating too little. Simone could see her headed for a dark place.

What if the spider was right, and she did nothing? A young woman like Jenny, with no family around. Sure, the four of them had become a kind of family, but Jenny needed a mother, and the real one was far away, unaware of what her daughter was doing to herself.

Jenny was proving hard to entice out of her lab. Simone had yet to see her in the new year. And only once or twice in December. Sagan remarked on it too, in his own way, when Jenny failed to join them for a pub supper at the start of term.

"The ghost of Churchill College," he had joked, acting out the part, "floating through the dining hall."

"She's lost a lot of weight," he added, no longer laughing, "and there was never much to lose." JJ had winced at the description.

Minus Jenny, the three of them had traded holiday stories. JJ's week in London sounded dismal. Seven meetings with a series of Japanese investment banks, arranged and attended by his brother Katsuo. His *overbearing* brother, it seemed, even if he wouldn't come out and say it.

Sagan had also spent a week in London, but his was full of "earthly delights"—as he told it. And he'd clearly kept a lot to himself. He'd mentioned paying homage to Freddie Mercury— something about a wall in Kensington. Then he'd flown to Amsterdam "for the night life."

"Never made it to Paris," he said with a devious smile. "I was *distracted*."

As for Jenny, all Simone knew was what she'd told them in early December: she'd be working through the holiday to prepare for a meeting with her supervisor.

What to do? Play the mother? Yes, the guys had encouraged her. But it was risky. Then again, she'd kick herself if she didn't. She'd lost a friend to an eating disorder in high school and had seen several suffering from anxiety at university. Like everyone else, she had done nothing. Just distanced herself, not having any idea what to do. Never again.

Simone shivered. Her bath was getting cold. Time to act.

She would send a note. Something gentle. An offer to help, or find Jenny help if she wanted it. Perhaps she needed little more than mentoring—a regular 'check in' date with a female friend. She'd also invite Jenny to the Burns supper at Clare Hall. Sagan was coming. He could tie her up and drag her over from Churchill if it came to that. And JJ would be there. Simone had seen the spark between them, though both were too timid to act on it. She might have to play a role there too.

But first things first.

* * *

Jenny seethed for two days after getting Simone's note.

What gives her the right to meddle?! I worked my tail off to get here, and I'm not throwing it all away just because other people think I should have 'work-life balance.' What does that even mean? My parents didn't have 'work-life balance.'

Most of the world would laugh at the idea. Or cry. Such a privileged western conceit. *Look at Simone with her rowing and cycling, and formal hall meals with her classmates. Reeking of privilege. And Sagan. Especially Sagan, with his generous scholarship. Shouldn't he be in the lab instead of chasing beagles? Even JJ, drunk three nights a week. Who pays for that?*

Jenny wrote a scathing reply to Simone. She carried it with her for a week. Each time she planned to stop by Clare Hall and drop it off, it was after midnight—too late to ring the bell at her residence, too late to walk into the entrance hall and leave it in her mail slot. Always too late.

Sitting alone at breakfast one morning she read the note from Simone one more time; picturing her not as a finger-wagging aunt but a concerned friend.

As passionate as she was about her work, Jenny sometimes missed the company of friends. Once, pedalling furiously down Barnet Walk towards her lab, she thought she saw JJ ahead. She slowed to say hello, only to find it was someone else. The sting took her aback.

Simone could be right. I enjoy their company. It takes my mind off of school. They make me laugh. Especially Sagan. The silly clown. Simone makes me laugh too, and think. Shows how you can be good at many things; driven even, but not let it consume you. Maybe the sports and the meals with friends is how she stays so healthy. Maybe Sagan's constant joking and wild weekends is how he deals with his own... issues. He's obviously done well in school, despite his background and the challenge of being... different. He's having the adventures he wouldn't dare to back home. And JJ. Goofy JJ. Sweet, but so very shy. Maybe the beer is how he handles his stress:

studying and writing in a foreign language; family expectations; a
brother who dictates his life.

Dear Simone,

Thank you for caring enough to reach out.
To be honest, I do not like the food here, I never
had an exercise routine, and I am so focused on
my work that I have no spare time. Is your offer
still open? And may I still come to the dinner
with you guys?

Jenny

The skirl of bagpipes resounded off the low ceiling and
large windows of Clare Hall's main lounge. Simone couldn't
help wondering if Ralph Erskine had imagined bagpipes when
he designed the college. Once a year, a piper would lead guests
into the dining hall at the Robert Burns Night Supper.

Sagan marched beside Jenny, five rows behind the piper and
haggis and just in front of her and JJ. Smiling JJ towered over
the three of them.

Simone laughed at the sight of Sagan. His grin was the
biggest in the room, as were his eyes—kid-in-a-candy-store eyes.
"My first Robbie Burns night!" they announced. "First bagpipes,
first haggis!"

He was paying close attention to Jenny, she noticed. What a
treat it was to have her join them. What a relief. And here she
was, laughing at Sagan's jokes about haggis. Wasn't it nice that
Sagan was so attentive. She felt the heat in her face. *Jealous? I'm
not jealous. We've all missed her.*

Sagan could sense JJ's energy. The friendly giant. Mostly, though,
he felt Simone. Her gaze, if not burning into his back, was
sending sparks. He'd never met a woman like her. So... fun

wasn't the right word, it was something more intense than mere fun. Feisty! That was it. Simone was feisty, and he liked it. He liked her. He'd wondered if he could... but no. He just wasn't wired that way. Maybe if he tried hard enough he could force himself. But it would be just that: forced. He'd forced himself once. It left the girl in tears, and then him too, later, at home.

There'd been nothing forced about Jeroen. From the moment they made eye contact in the Amsterdam club. The throbbing beat drowned out their words, but who needed words. They'd danced. They'd touched. Then Jeroen had guided him out the door and home to his funky little apartment. Up the stairs in that narrow little house.

When it feels right, it feels right. Simple as that. And Simone, as much as he loved her feistiness, would never feel right. He had to speak to her soon. It wasn't right playing games, and that's what he'd been doing.

Sagan looked to his left and nudged Jenny. "Haggis, mmm!" he shouted, in competition with the bagpipes. "Sheep's stomach stuffed with lungs and heart." Jenny was giggling. "Simmered in boiling water for two hours." She tried to stifle her laughter with her hand.

Lovely girl Jenny. A bit intense, though. Needs a little TLC, and I know just the man to offer it. It was so obvious. If the two of them weren't so damn shy...

Suddenly, he had an idea. Simone would help, he was sure.

* * *

What a joy to be with his friends. This fourth week of January was turning out much better than the first.

Katsuo! Deciding everything for him. Spouting his nonsense. "Do your people proud Jiro. Remember where you come from... Learn from the *gaijin*, but never, ever believe you will be one of them... Our father has spared no expense for your studies... I have tapped into my network... These meetings—don't embarrass me!"

"Yes, big brother," he'd replied. "You are right big brother. I will do my best." All the while, his teeth grinding, his insides churning.

Still smiling, JJ took a deep breath. Tonight would be fun. It was great to see Jenny, even in a big group. She was so serious and hardworking.

He had tried to make her laugh, with his stories. Like Sagan did. She would laugh a bit, but always looked sad when he was done. Maybe alone, just the two of them… he wouldn't have to compete for attention, struggling to be heard and seen. Even by a little Chinese-Malaysian girl. He imagined enveloping her; her tiny figure, protected by him. Not that she needed protection, he scolded himself. But he liked the idea. Tiny, like so many Japanese women. Only not Japanese, he remembered.

What would his parents think? He knew what Katsuo would say. But Katsuo wouldn't need to know.

No Ordinary Picnic

imone's 11-month International Relations course had two requirements: exams in March, and a thesis due in mid-August, followed by an oral defence. She'd proposed an unusual topic: "Motivating broad support for a sustainable model of global development depends less on delivering facts or persuasive cases for change than on emotional and values-based triggers." In lay terms: you can't get people to be 'green' by telling them to change, or that it's good for them; you must get them to adopt new behaviour by choice.

Research in this area was in its infancy, notably in the fields of environmental stewardship and resource management, but she could draw on work from other social change theory and practice. Some had looked at the effective yet horrific propaganda machines of Nazi Germany, socialist USSR and Maoist China. Some tapped recent work in health promotion, international development and, most recently, the prevention of smoking and drunk driving. Simone was pulling together data from a wide variety of fields, and her supervisor had helped her craft a solid outline.

Life was mostly going to plan. School—tick. Sport—tick. Social and cultural life—tick. Love life—gong!.

When in doubt, go cycling. That was her motto. Some days, she chose to ride alone. It gave her time to contemplate. Other days, she enjoyed a group ride. For the camaraderie and the extra push. But today's ride would be different. Very different.

She had borrowed a road bike for Sagan, knowing his classic Flying Pigeon with wicker basket was not going to cut it, even on the modest ride she had planned. She was waiting with it and her own bike at the entrance to her residence. As he pulled up, she began to giggle.

Like the dorky friends of the main character in the 1970s film *Breaking Away*, Sagan was dressed in what he had: baggy shorts, full-fingered gloves and striped knee socks. She should not have laughed, but she couldn't help it.

"Where did you get those socks? The Village People!?"

"I'm having my DJ pressed for the YMCA ball," he replied, with a straight face. "You are hereby un-invited!"

If she hadn't known better, Simone would have worried she'd offended him.

"Come closer my dear," she camped, "we need the seat at the right height for your fashionable legs!"

"Touché!" said Sagan, as he mounted the borrowed bike to give it a test.

"Have you ever ridden one like this?" she asked, tightening the seat post.

"Yes, my elitist little racer."

"Just checking," she said defensively. "Though my friend Peter has several others, he'd prefer you return this one intact."

As they rolled out onto Grange Road, Simone leading the way, Sagan belted out a modified line from his Queen repertoire. "Fat bottomed lassies are riding today…!"

"No fat there, skinny lad," she called back, then promptly accelerated, pulling steadily away as they headed towards Madingley Road and the countryside. Sagan discovered how hard it is to sing, or taunt, when gasping for air.

Simone had plenty of time to think as she allowed the distance between them to close gradually. She liked him. She liked him a lot. But it seemed clear this would never be more than friendship. Maybe a very good one, but no more. Still, she had reached the point where she needed to be sure.

There was a scenic lay-by along the route where they would stop and eat the light lunch she had packed. That's where she would ask. She shouldn't. *It's his business, not mine.* Did she have the right? No more, and no less than he did to play games.

"Whew," declared a winded Sagan, as they came to a halt. "I retract the fat part." They leaned their bikes on a stone wall bordering the rest area.

"It's all muscle, and I earned every ounce," Simone said, striking a bodybuilder pose. He laughed. "You, on the other hand, may be a slender one, but you've got potential. You just need endurance work."

"Was that flattery?" said Sagan.

"As close to it as this girl knows. At least when talking to boys."

"Gets all nervous with the opposite sex," Sagan chuckled. "You can relax. We don't bite. At least I don't."

Simone handed him a substantial sandwich. "Enjoy!" she said. They could talk after. When she felt more settled.

Sagan's eyes lit up. "Another Clare Hall feast!"

"Haggis left-overs," she said in a serious voice.

"From January?" Sagan eyed the contents with sudden suspicion. When he spotted the bacon, lettuce and tomato, his face lit up. "It's a BLT. A *real* BLT. You're the best!"

"Alas," said Simone, "no Canadian bacon at Sainsbury."

Sagan shrugged as he took a large bite, the mayonnaise dribbling down his chin.

Seated on the wall, they ate in silence, looking out over the fields below them, brown and dormant. It was mild for mid-February, but spring was still a month away. Simone breathed in, detecting a faint scent of smoke in the air. Someone in the distance was burning off a field. A harmful practice, she thought, but old habits were hard to break.

Soon, thought Simone. *Relax and say what you need to.*

Holding out a hand, she took Sagan's sandwich wrappings. After stowing them in her bike pannier, she walked slowly back. There would not be a better time.

"Sagan?" she began, looking him in the eye. He had been watching her closely.

"Mmm hmm."

"This is as personal a question as anyone could ask, but that's what I'm trained to do. Not beat around the bush. Get right to the point…" She glanced away.

"Yes," said Sagan after waiting for her to re-establish eye contact.

"I need to—"

"Yes!" he said. This time more forcefully.

"Sorry?" This was not going as planned.

He slid off the wall and stepped towards her, placing a hand on each of her shoulders. "The answer is *yes*."

"I didn't even ask the question!" she said.

"You didn't have to," he said to her gently. "It's what everyone wants to know. Or seems to need to," he added with an edge.

"I'm sorry," Simone said. "It's just that…"

"In your case, you *do* need to know." He looked down as he spoke. "I owe it to you," he added softly, looking into her eyes again.

"That's OK, Sagan, I understand." She had known, but hadn't wanted to.

"Well Simone, you may understand, I mean, I'm sure you do. But most people say they *understand*." He used his fingers to emphasize the word with air quotes. "But they don't really. They might *tolerate* me, but they do not respect me the same way once they know. They *sympathize*. Then judge anyway."

"I don't!" she protested.

He smiled. "I know Simone. I tested you, for longer than I should have. Told you outrageous things. Sometimes exaggerated them, to see if you'd walk away."

"Never!," she said, feeling her face flush.

"But you didn't. You wouldn't. So, I do owe it to you. To be totally open."

Sagan paused and took a deep breath. "For the first time, I'm telling someone close to me that I'm gay. I'm gay, and at ease with that fact. And I'm honoured to have you as my friend."

He had taken her hands in his. Her heart too, it seemed. More than she'd realized.

They looked away from each other. Then in one bold move, Simone stepped toward him and wrapped her arms around his chest. He responded with a gentle embrace of her shoulders, and leaned his head onto hers.

They stayed locked this way for a long time, tears streaming down all four cheeks. A group of cyclists passed by, glancing their way.

"Awww-kward! Looks like a break-up," the rider at the front called back to his buddies, unaware how far his voice would travel. At this, Simone and Sagan ended the hug. Making blurry eye contact, they started to giggle, which turned into full-on laughter, and then more tears.

"Simone. I hope you won't take this the wrong way, but... I love you."

"Sentiment accepted Sagan. I love you too."

"Now help me find a boyfriend," she blurted, stomping a foot. "I haven't had sex in ages!"

"What! A hot cycling chick like you?" He looked her over admiringly.

"Precisely," she scowled. "So what's my problem?"

"Well, if I've just been designated your 'harmless gay confidante,' I'll tell you. You're a bit intimidating. Smart, funny, don't take fools gladly. Buns of steel. Not many guys are comfortable with that, but they're out there. Don't rush it."

"Rush it?" she squealed. "It's been a year!"

Sagan raised his eyebrows. "I know how *that* feels. Try fishing in a pool a fraction the size. With everyone afraid to make the first move for fear of getting a punch in the face. Maybe kicked in the ribs for sport!"

"Ouch," she winced.

"Yes, it can be that bad. But it can also be good. Really good," he added, beaming. "So, be patient and keep being who you are."

"Thanks Sagan, my harmless confidante," Simone said with a smile. "Let's get back on our horses. I'm not done making a cyclist out of you."

"Is it my socks?"

"Actually," she laughed, "the socks are growing on me."

On the ride back, Simone set a comfortable pace, then instructed Sagan in the art of drafting to reduce wind resistance. "Not too close. A touch of the tires could send us both into the ditch. Or oncoming traffic."

He caught on quickly, even taking the lead for a part of the ride.

"Fast learner," said Simone.

"Always have been," he called back, then promptly veered into the gravel.

"With a tendency to be cocky," Simone added.

"That's pretty much what it said on my report cards."

While Simone reset the seat at its original height, she picked up where their conversation had ended. "Just one more thing."

"Fire away."

"Do your parents know?"

"I've never *told* anyone," Sagan confided. "I've only just fully admitted it to myself. Being far away from home is liberating."

"So, you've never spoken about it with your family?"

"Forbidden territory. They would never say anything, but *they know*. How could they not?" Sagan pointed at his socks. "Papa's in total denial. Mama's just sad. They hope it'll go away if they ignore it." He paused, looking down at the ground.

"*You are SAVED!*" he exclaimed, tapping his palm on Simone's forehead. She chuckled at the cliché.

"My younger brother Demar despises me for it. Young black men, there's only one role you can play: tough, and straight. I can't blame him, but it's torn us apart. He won't look me in the eye. Michelle's the only one who accepts me. No questions, just love. She's only ten."

"Does this explain not going home for Christmas?"

"Who's the clever girl?"

"I thought so," Simone nodded. "One more thing. Final question, I promise!"

Sagan rolled his eyes. "Shoot, oh relentless one."

"Will you tell JJ and Jenny?"

"I don't know," he said, pausing to think. "That's not true," he answered at last. "I will. But I want you there."

* * *

He invited them to the Churchill Bar for 5 p.m. on a Monday. It would be nearly empty. Once seated, with two pairs of expectant eyes on him, and another urging him along, he found his tongue turned to dried leather. The pint he had drained before they got there was of little help. It was only when he felt Simone's hand settle on his shoulder that he found the courage to begin.

"May I tell you the *real* story of my Christmas vacation?," he said, looking down at the table.

Feeling a gentle squeeze, he looked directly at Jenny, then JJ. She dipped her head slightly, while JJ nodded more deeply. He was safe here, they were saying.

So—unplanned, uncensored, uninhibited—he let it all spill out. His self-doubt, his awakening and now, finally, the freedom to be himself; as risky as that could sometimes still be. Finally, realizing he had been talking non-stop for what seemed like hours, he paused and again made eye contact. Would they or wouldn't they?

Jenny was first to speak. "True friends embrace you as you are."

JJ nodded, his eyes echoing her words. Then he rose and spoke for the first time since they had settled in around the table.

"I think Sagan needs another beer."

"I think we all do," said Jenny.

Simone leaned over and kissed him on the cheek. "One less barrier," she said.

What's New in Renewables

"*R enewable energy: climate solution, or pie in the sky?*" Jenny had read from a brochure a week earlier. "It's next Thursday night. Who wants to go?"

"I'm up for anything," Sagan said. So true, thought Simone.

"OK," JJ shrugged, "sounds interesting." Simone smiled. Anywhere Jenny would be was interesting to JJ.

"I'm game," Simone said. "There might be something useful for my thesis."

When neither Jenny nor Sagan appeared at the agreed upon time, Simone assumed the worst: Jenny would be in the lab, and Sagan distracted by something new. With the lecture hall rapidly filling, she and JJ decided to go in and hold two places.

On each of their seats they found a handout with the speaker's biography and list of publications. "Robert McIlraith, engineering professor from Edinburgh University," JJ read, stumbling over the last name.

"I believe it's *Mack-ill-raith*," said Simone. "Tricky—even for English speakers."

"I hope there will be time for questions," said JJ.

Simone was intrigued. "About anything in particular?"

JJ was about to respond when a breathless Sagan dropped into the seat on her left.

"Jenny twisted an ankle—at aerobics class," he panted. "She's in her room—with an ice pack." He looked across to JJ, who Simone heard sigh.

For close to an hour, the professor laid out the case for replacing fossil fuels with 'renewables,' and elaborated on the merits of various promising technologies. The three listened with interest. Simone noticed JJ taking notes.

The professor closed by inviting questions from the audience. Surprised that JJ was not raising his hand, Simone nudged him with her elbow. When he did not respond, she decided to ask a question of her own. Maybe he needed her to get the ball rolling.

"How much of Great Britain's needs could be met by renewable energy if all available resources were fully exploited?" Simone asked.

"That's quite a question," the professor began. "You say, *needs,* plus *available*, plus *fully exploited*. I would need a date, of course, so let's use 2025—not too soon, yet not so far—if that's OK?"

Feeling the many eyes on her, Simone nodded. Sagan gave her a light bump with his shoulder. JJ readied his pen.

"The short answer is simple," the professor began. "Renewable energy can meet all our *needs* by 2025. Note my emphasis. If we can cut our energy demand in half—through efficient buildings and appliances; and if we can improve the efficiency of our transportation fleet; and if we can use public transit or walk or bicycle most of the time and drive or fly only when we *must*; and if we plan our cities and towns more intelligently, with greater density and less need to hop around willy-nilly—then we'll have accomplished half the goal!

"If you don't start with *conservation*, you're throwing away half your money, whether it's at fossil or nuclear or renewable power. As for *which* renewables should be part of the mix, here in the UK solar is not a great option. But as prices come down, and efficiency improves, it will make sense to ensure any suitable roof is covered with PV panels. Hydro-electric turbines are viable on some rivers in Scotland, but you don't want to go blocking every blasted river now do you? Where will I do my fly-fishing?"

He paused, smiling, as a ripple ran through the audience. Simone heard Sagan chuckle.

"So, what else? Have you tried to ride a bike along the coast of East Anglia?" Simone saw a number of heads nodding along with hers. "Or taken a UK beach holiday?" Many were chuckling or shaking their heads.

"I don't have to tell *you* there's a wee bit of wind around these isles! You won't even have to put all your turbines on land. If the Danes can stick them in the ocean, then with a bit of Scottish ingenuity we could generate enough power to shut down the nuclear plants which so many of you young folk are out protesting. Your grannies too! And don't get me started on the cost of decommissioning and waste handling."

Sagan was entranced. As much by the speaker's delivery, Simone sensed, as his grasp of the subject. JJ, though, seemed tense.

"*Decommissioning*?" The speaker snorted. "Bollocks! We don't have a clue how to dispose of the waste, or even the irradiated concrete from the buildings. And nobody's setting aside money for *that* rainy day. Yet we're making economic comparisons between '*expensive*' renewables, and '*cheap*' nuclear power. 'Too cheap to meter,' they used to say. Have you heard of anyone having to 'decommission' a PV panel or a turbine and store *them* in a salt mine for 100,000 years? That's what you have to ask when you start making cost comparisons with nuclear. But nobody does, do they!"

Prof. McIlraith was turning red in the face. JJ, to Simone's surprise, was also.

"When you calculate how many panels and turbines are needed, you'd better ask why British homes have no insulation, or double-glazed windows or decent caulking. If we're not prepared to take those steps, we'd be foolish to spend money by the bloody bagful. And office towers have their lights on all night. And we don't bother to turn off the telly when we stroll down to the pub!"

"I hope I answered your question," the breathless professor laughed, looking again at Simone. When she tilted her head, a number of people sighed.

"You want your money's worth!" he teased. "If we can do just half of what I've been ranting about, we can meet *all* the UK's energy *needs*, economically—as prices will come way down with manufacturing at scale. But we'll need to build an *integrated* system. Complimentary technologies, not one magic bullet.

"Indeed we must!" he declared earnestly. "This is the turn-around decade, as I once heard it put. We must be on our way to turning this Titanic by the year 2000 or I'm afraid catastrophic climate change is certain; and the cost to everyone enormous."

Frowning, he looked at Simone and nodded.

"Thank you," she mouthed, as the moderator jumped in.

"I noted a lot of interest at the mention of pubs," he said. "Let's have two last questions."

JJ's hand shot up, startling Simone.

"Thank you professor *Mack-ill-raissu,*" he began cautiously. He was sweating heavily. "You mentioned the costs associated with nuclear plants. But after Three Mile Island and the Chernobyl crisis, how vulnerable are modern plants?"

"Interesting," said the professor. "You are perhaps Japanese?" JJ nodded.

"So, like France, in Japan the government and private companies have worked together to generate much of the country's electrical needs. In countries with few domestic energy sources, this is a policy decision, not a financial one. Hardly surprising after the Second World War, and the energy crisis in the seventies. Denmark went a different route, mind you. As for vulnerability, there's terrorism, of course; hard to foresee and prevent. Next is mechanical failure, though newer systems have a lot of redundancy and safety measures built in. Then, related to this, is human error. In fact, Three Mile Island was a combination of human error and instrument hiccup.

"*Hiccup!*" he repeated, oozing sarcasm. "*Terribly sorry for the meltdown, folks, we had a bit of a hiccup.*"

Sagan gave Simone a jab as he chuckled. JJ scowled and shook his head.

"But the two *big* threats are from natural factors. Nuclear plants are dependent on water to cool them. When the supply is interrupted, it takes mere minutes to reach a critical stage. The temperature of water is also crucial. Imagine a drought year, where the supply from a river is unusually low, and warm. Then, my friend, you have a problem. Finally, there is the risk of major disasters. Earthquakes, flooding, maybe a tsunami in coastal locations. Those are the ones I worry about. Short, sharp shocks taking out power supplies, water to and from the reactor, and maybe road access for emergency crews. The Japanese have done a lot to avoid such risks, but nothing's perfect. Plan for the worst. Sorry for the bad news, son."

Simone turned to see JJ nodding slowly. His face was blank, his mind seemingly elsewhere. He had taken no notes.

"One last question. You in the bright jumper." The moderator was pointing to Sagan. "Did you three come together?"

Sagan nodded. "We were four, but one came up lame. I'm asking this for her."

Simone felt JJ stir and noticed his pen was again at the ready.

"Our friend Jenny Fung's research is on battery storage," Sagan explained. "Using affordable materials so storage devices will be available to communities with no central energy supply. For example rural Asia, where solar might be combined with batteries to power a village. How important is storage in this renewable future?"

"Indeed!" said the professor. "Storage is essential. Many renewables—wind and solar especially—are 'intermittent.' When they're on, they're on; when they're not, they're not. So how to design a grid around sources that drop out when it's cloudy, or in winter, or when there's no wind? Storage, of course! But what kind, and at what cost?

"We've come a long way from the lead-acid days. There's nickel metal hydride, nickel cadmium, and work now happening with lithium ion. Great progress will be made, but these are high-tech solutions. They won't be cheap, and they require mining and processing. But there are low-tech solutions, getting back to Jenny's objective. A 'battery' is simply a way to hold energy until needed.

"The simplest and oldest of all? Raise water up, then run it down as needed. As small as a water tower, as big as a mountain lake. A second approach is compression. Think of a giant balloon, or hobby rockets."

Simone could hear JJ's pen scribbling furiously.

"I will end by going back to some technology. How about hydrogen? Use your wind turbine to create hydrogen through electrolysis, then run it through a fuel cell to power a building, or a bus or even a car. Speaking of cars, when we reach the point where electric vehicles have sufficiently good batteries, I can see a day where any car at rest—which is most of the time—could be called on for emergency power. Sell back to the utility at a peak price. Nifty way to pay off your car loan, eh?"

The moderator stepped in, chuckling. "A big thank you to Robert McIlraith!" he said, prompting vigorous applause. "So, we have homework. We heard about the turn-around decade. There's 20 months left. Go home, go to work and turn things around."

Simone and Sagan smiled at one another. When they turned to JJ, though, he was gone.

"There he is," said Sagan, pointing to where JJ was working his way toward the stage. They watched as he introduced himself to Prof. McIlraith, exchanged a few words, then offered a piece of paper. In response, the professor gave JJ one of his own. When JJ bowed, the professor responded, a little less deeply.

"What was that?" Sagan said to Simone.

"Meishi!" she replied.

"What?"

"Ritual exchange of business cards."

"Oh!" said Sagan. "JJ has business cards?"

"Hey guys." JJ was back. "We are invited to join the professor at the pub."

Sagan beamed. "I'm in!" Simone was too.

"Enjoy yourselves," said JJ as they headed to the door. "But I want to take the professor's *meishi* to Jenny. And share his offer."

"Offer?" chanted Simone and Sagan.

"I'll tell you later," he called as he disappeared into the crowd.

* * *

JJ mopped the beads of sweat from his brow and listened to his heart pounding. On his brisk walk to Jenny's residence he had rehearsed what he would say, but waiting now for her to answer his knock, the clever words slipped away.

"Here Jenny," he blurted, thrusting his hand out to her as she opened the door in a nightgown and ankle bandage.

"I brought you the business card of a professor who says he would be pleased to offer you any guidance you might need with your experiments since Sagan asked a question related to your work on energy storage during the discussion period."

"Why thank you," she said with a smile, after listening patiently. "That's so thoughtful. Please, come in. Would you like some tea?"

"Oh no," he protested. "I shouldn't. It is late, and you are injured."

"Well maybe you can help me make the tea," she suggested, waving him inside. "I'll need water from the small kitchen," she said, pointing toward an electric kettle.

"Of course," he said. "I can make the tea myself. I am quite familiar with—"

"I know you are," she said, placing a hand on his arm. "Very adept at pouring too."

He hurried out with the kettle. When he returned, she had prepared a plate of biscuits and shortbread. "Sorry, no scones," she said with a shrug.

"Oh no matter," he said, waving his hand. "Just being with you is—" They both turned crimson.

After a period of awkward small talk, he took a deep breath, raised his eyes to meet hers and mumbled the words he feared most. "I like you Jenny!"

She looked away briefly, then, blushing again, smiled warmly.

"I thought so," she said. "But I've never before had a boyfriend, so I'm not so good at judging."

"And you," he said tentatively, "do you—"

"I like you too JJ. I have from the first day."

"Oh my," he said exhaling. "I am also very new to this. To having a… girlfriend."

"Then we can learn together. Neither of us will know if we're doing it wrong."

"Yes. We can go slowly, and learn from one another."

* * *

Simone and Sagan were past the point where cycling was possible. Just walking their bikes was a challenge. The professor proved to be not only a lover of beer, but generous. And deaf to "no thanks, I've had enough."

"English ale is fine," he had declared when they took their seats in the alcove closest to the bar. "But this pub can do better. That's why I come whenever I'm in Cambridge. Am I rright Ferrgus?" he called towards the bar.

"Yerr always rright professor," answered the publican, playfully exaggerating the Scottish brogue to match his customer. "Five pints of the best, I assume?"

'Yeh assume rright Ferrgus!"

"That would be the Caledonian Deuchars IPA," he announced to Simone, Sagan, the panelists and the moderator, all of whom had accepted his offer of "a wee pint to cap off a fine evening." There would be nothing "wee" about it.

"Whoa!" Sagan said, blinking as they emerged into the well-lit square. He had done most of the drinking, while Simone asked most of the questions. Their course set, after considerable debate, they made their way loudly towards Garret Hostel Lane, which would take them down a dark Barnet Walk.

Sagan began to chuckle. "I was just remembering JJ. His mad dash, and the card thing. *Meeshu*. For Jenny. What was that about?" He paused to look at Simone, then snickered loudly. "He's twice her height!"

Simone glared. "What's so funny? I think they'd be great together."

"Maybe it's a business arrangement!"

"What are you implying, you drunken lout?"

"Well, his law degree and... financial connections." Sagan spoke slowly, working to complete an idea. "Imagine Jenny's inventions funded by Japanese banks."

"*She's* still a student," said Simone, "and his brother has plans for *him*."

They had navigated their way past University Library and were now faced with a decision.

"Sagan, you're in no shape to walk home!"

"That's why I have a bike!"

"No way. I've got a camping mat in my room. If you promise not to take advantage of me, since I'm a little drunk, you can sleep with me. In my room, that is."

"Thought you'd never ask, you sexy creature. Got spare pyjamas?"

"Nope."

"A pillow?"

"A rolled-up sweater."

"Good enough!"

* * *

Jenny awoke to find herself pinned between JJ and the wall, the two of them sharing her single bed. He was lying on top of the covers, an arm draped over her, fully dressed except for the coat and shoes he had removed at the door. For a moment she lay still, recalling how she'd ended up in this position. Then, as it became painfully clear she needed to use the toilet, she attempted to shift her guest. Pushing with all her might, she could barely budge him. Trapped, she had a moment of panic. Then, as the absurdity of the situation hit her, she started to giggle. The giggle turned to a full-on cackle. With the bed shaking now, JJ's eyes sprang open.

"Where am—"

She gasped as her shy almost-lover dropped over the edge of the bed, flailing helplessly.

"Ow!" he cried.

"Oh!" she called.

Then she heard him laugh. Relieved and released, she jumped up, pecked him on the cheek, and excused herself, grabbing a towel on her way to the bathroom.

Yawning, JJ pushed himself up and returned to the bed. He lay there for awhile, recalling how they had talked late into the night.

He looked up when she returned to the room several minutes later. Wrapped in just her towel, she had a look he had never seen.

"Your turn," she announced, handing him a spare towel.

"OK!" he exclaimed, feeling a rush of blood. When he returned from what must have been his fastest shower ever, he found Jenny sitting in bed, again with that look.

"JJ," she said, "I have two requests." He nodded instantly.

"First, I would like you to make us tea." Again, he nodded.

"Then I would like us to begin our lessons. I'm taking a day off."

"Work-life balance is important," he said supportively.

A Day at the Races

Her exams over, Simone joined a class visit to key international institutions based in Belgium, including the North Atlantic Treaty Organization, where they participated in a discussion with a panel of NATO generals on the future of the institution.

"Why are we still spending money on troops and weapons when the Cold War is over?" a classmate from Liverpool had asked. "Can't we shift to addressing poverty and economic development?"

Seeing many students nodding, a Canadian general put up his best defence.

"History has a way of surprising you, son. Conflicts spring up out of the most innocuous things. Water. Unresolved borders. Ethnic tension, triggered by economic uncertainty. Firebrand leaders getting people worked up. Politicians looking to distract from their scandals. People fleeing civil war and drought, seeking refuge in countries that cannot or will not accept them. There are many reasons to maintain robust military capability and coordination."

Many students did not buy it. Of those who did, most were from countries that had seen this sort of tension recently. Or were living it still.

Simone recounted some of this several weeks later as the gang strolled in the sunlight along the banks of the River Thames at Henley. They were making their way towards the finish line for the Oxford-Cambridge boat races they had come to see—the best place for viewing, she informed them.

"How was *your* trip?" Jenny asked Sagan. "Switzerland, was it?"

"*Ja! Oui!* A conference in Geneva. My lab director had his paper accepted. *Our* paper really, so he made sure I got to go. *The potential for permafrost thawing to contribute sequestered methane to the earth's atmosphere,*" he recited.

"I wanted a less sexy title," he added with a straight face, "but got outvoted."

"Ah, the dumbing down of learning," Simone said indignantly, playing along. Jenny rolled her eyes. JJ simply nodded, missing the joke.

"Good talks?" wondered Jenny. "Useful contacts?"

"Both," Sagan replied. "And the discussion was stimulating—at the session, and well into the night. You know climate scientists! Big partiers."

They smiled, assuming it was another joke.

"Seriously!" he said. Many a theory has been tested at a hotel bar."

"Our work on methane struck a chord," he elaborated. "People have been fixated on CO_2. It's the most prevalent gas, and human activity plays such a prominent role in its release. But methane is the hidden danger."

"And this has been ignored until now?" Jenny asked, looking directly at him.

"Not ignored, just downplayed. But several journals were interested in our work. And a couple of IPCC members—the Intergovernmental Panel on Climate Change. They're going to look at this more closely in an upcoming report."

"That's exciting," said Jenny, halting abruptly. The others stopped as well.

"I've pretty much locked up my PhD position at Penn State," Sagan continued.

"Congrats Sagan," said Simone.

"Thank you dahling," he replied with affection.

"How was your Queen pilgrimage?" she asked, waving to herd the group along. The races would be starting soon.

"Great. I took a train to Montreux. Wanted to see the town and lake. Experience the calm. That's what drew them there, you know. That, and the music scene. I especially wanted to see the new statue." His eyes were shining.

JJ smiled. Sagan had shared his plans the last time the four of them were together.

Only Jenny was unmoved.

"Sagan," she said cautiously, "why is Freddie Mercury so important to you? It must be more than just his... orientation."

Sagan nodded, considering her question.

"I was thinking about that as I sat there, watching the sunset cast some amazing colours on the statue. It's a giant thing. I was thinking, what's the big deal, he was a rock singer? Charismatic, showy, supremely talented musically, but so what?" He glanced at the three of them in turn. "I don't think the 'gay idol' thing has much to do with it. You have to remember, he wasn't truly 'out' until late in his career." He paused.

"Short career," he added wistfully. "And he was no role model. Never tried to be."

"There was something about him that made a lot of us think, 'that guy isn't letting life go half-lived.' Art, production, charitable work... I bet we don't know the half of it either."

Simone was watching Sagan intently. He had taken on a new energy. Something she hadn't seen before. The others must have felt it too. They were giving him the space he seemed to need.

"Did I answer your question, Jenny?" he said, returning to the present.

"Mostly," she said. "Yes, you did," she corrected. "Even if not in words."

"I'm not sure I have the words," he said, smiling. "Why do people fall in love?"

A perfect segue to the great unspoken subject, thought Simone, but Sagan spoke first.

"So, you two, how was romantic Scotland?"

Jenny and JJ glanced at each other, then away, both blushing. Then back again.

Carpe Diem

T all and handsome—with a hockey player's broken nose for a touch of ruggedness—and most obviously brilliant. Sometimes a bit too brilliant in his own mind. Paul Racine was as Jenny had described. Intense, to be sure, and serious, but he was showing flashes of humour during their dinner at a quiet Indian restaurant.

"I sometimes feel I'm in a Masterpiece Theatre drama," he said about the hierarchy at his college. "Then there's that absurdly polite way of never actually saying what they think about things, about you, while they make it *bloody* clear in other ways."

Simone laughed. She knew it well. "I bet they don't let you wear that *Habs* cap in the dining hall," she poked. Paul removed his Montreal Canadiens hat promptly, scowling briefly before smiling and combing his hair with his fingers.

They shared a love for the outdoors and a "real winter," she learned. Paul described working in the New Brunswick woods, where his uncle tapped maple syrup and ran a small logging operation, complete with horses to pull logs over the snow. They laughed at the way that so many here whined about the cold: "the wind's coming straight down from Siberia," he moaned, placing the hat back on his head and pulling the brim down over his face.

The hat. She wondered if he slept in it, and if she was about to find out. She quivered slightly at the thought, while trying to focus on another of his stories.

Paul liked to talk, she noted. His work *was* fascinating, and she liked the way his passion for ocean protection spilled out of him, though a little more interest in *her* would be nice. But hey, it was a first date.

When he wrapped an arm around her on the walk to his residence, she put her own around his waist. It was nice to feel desired. And it was clear how this evening would end. "I've got a queen size mattress," he'd volunteered at dinner. "When you're six-four, you need the extra leg room." *What other smooth moves did he know?*

Her eyes traced the edges of his muscular body as he unlocked his room, pausing to admire the contours of his jeans. Definitely good enough.

First to Leave

They had only just come together, it seemed to JJ now, as they basked in the late-June sun on the sloping 'Backs' of the River Cam. He was leaving much too soon. The closest friends he had ever known.

On the previous afternoon, he had been awarded his degree, with Jenny and Sagan attending as 'family'. Since graduates were allowed two guests only, he had agonized over who to pick. Simone had spared him in the end, offering to skip the ceremony but join them for dinner. To everyone's surprise, she arrived late and left early.

"Hot date," Jenny whispered, as they watched Simone leave the restaurant. Though she had been the matchmaker, when prodded for details she offered the minimum: "Paul. Engineer. Handsome. French Canadian. For more, ask Simone."

Sagan was doing so now, he saw, in his unique fashion.

"Alert, alert!," Sagan called loudly, startling a number of tourists who were fighting to control their errant punts. "Reward for anyone who finds the real Simone Cohen!" Wincing and covering his ears, JJ saw Jenny and Simone smile and shake their heads.

"Last seen with a hunky Quebec hockey player!" Sagan bellowed.

"New Brunswick," Simone corrected, in a much quieter voice.

"New Brunswick," he mimicked. "'I have a commitment with Paul Slapshot from New Brunswick.'"

"Commitment?" JJ asked, puzzled.

"Slapshot?" Jenny said.

"No commitment," Simone said patiently. "Though I find him... compelling."

"He's not just a hockey player," said Jenny in defence of her colleague. "Paul is modelling ways to replace diesel marine engines with cleaner, more efficient propulsion."

"Pro-pul-sion!" exclaimed Sagan, with a thrust of the hips. Simone rolled her eyes, as JJ joined Sagan in laughter.

"OK little boys," Jenny scolded. "Simone is getting the... *attention* she deserves. But I am sensing one of us is not!" She glared at Sagan.

JJ felt his face redden. As nobody wanted to follow this line further, they went quiet. For several minutes they watched as students and tourists drifted by.

"So..." Sagan broke into their thoughts. "In honour of JJ's graduation and his departure tomorrow, perhaps we might offer a proper farewell."

JJ waved his hand vigorously. "Not necessary!"

"Yes. It is," said Sagan, turning serious. "I may be a joker, but I want to say a few serious things before we split up for... maybe forever."

"No!" objected the others.

"You never know. Who can tell where life's going to take us. And if we'll be together again, all in one place."

JJ felt a twinge of sadness. Sagan was right.

"So JJ, it has been an honour and a pleasure. I don't regret for one moment sharing my table. Seems like years ago, that tea ceremony."

He felt the warmth of Sagan's familiar smile, but it did not last.

"Promise me one thing JJ: every now and then, ask yourself, does this feel right for me? Can I honour my family by using my talents in a way that fulfills *me*, that recharges *me*. OK?" Sagan's eyes communicated a deep affection.

He nodded, looking down. Thinking.

"Here endeth the sermon!" Sagan declared with a laugh.

They all smiled, then leaned their heads back, the warm sun on their faces.

"Well JJ," Simone broke in, "tell us about the next chapter. High finance is it?"

"*Hai! So desu.* I accepted a one-year trial with the Tokyo Industrial Investment Bank. London office. Tokyo Industrial is a close partner with the company my father and brother work for—TEPCO—a major energy company. I will be developing contacts with British universities. Some European ones too. Sort of a 'talent scout' for joint ventures in the energy industry."

"And close by," Sagan said, glancing at Jenny. "I can hear you now, JJ! 'Excuse me boss, I must head up to Cambridge for some talent scouting, what what!'"

He felt himself blush. Jenny, he saw, hid her face behind her hand.

"You'll have to be a devoted company man and all that," Sagan said, "but I'm glad you and Jenny will be close while she finishes her PhD."

Jenny was beaming now.

"Not that either of you will have a lot of free time," Simone noted, breaking the spell. "But... work isn't everything."

"We should check in on each other," suggested Sagan. "Every few months; a *work-isn't-everything* check-up."

"Deal!" said Simone. "If we're going to change the world, we'll need to live past 40. So, JJ, go easy on the drinking! I know *salaryman* culture."

"Not me!" He waved his hand in protest. "Asleep by nine, I promise."

Simone—his first friend at Cambridge—was not to be put off. "Don't let them drag you in," she warned. Then suddenly she was standing, opening her arms to him. "Take care, *tomodachi*."

"Offer me a good story tip, and I'll be there," she added, stepping back.

He watched her stride away in silence. And kept watching, as a strapping man in a peaked cap who had been waiting at a distance stepped forward. He gave the three of them a sheepish grin and a wave, before pivoting to receive Simone's shoulder in the crook of a muscular arm.

JJ turned to Jenny and spoke quietly. "Will he treat her well?"

She shrugged. "Paul's a nice guy. Polite, generous…"

"But?"

"Yes, but?" echoed Sagan.

"Well…" Jenny said, "he likes to be in control."

He and Sagan nodded, but neither smiled.

"Let her have some fun," said Jenny. "What's the worst that can happen?"

Seaside Rendezvous

August 1998

The day after JJ's departure, Simone had a troubling meeting with her thesis supervisor. The 'absent-minded professor' had provided minimal feedback until then, leading her to believe she was on firm ground.

"You must remember," he said, his face pinched. "This is an *academic* paper. It's not the style that counts. It's the quality of the evidence."

"OK," Simone acknowledged, "but I have multiple sources for my arguments."

"That may be," he said, shifting papers from one pile to the next on his overcrowded desk. "But not a lot of published material."

"It's a very young field, and rapidly evolving. That's why it's so important! Understanding human motivations—"

"Quite interesting. No question. In an activist kind of way." He pronounced activist with disdain. Fear even, Simone sensed.

"I remain neutral, and offer evidence from all sides."

"I'm not saying it crosses over into opinion, just that your bias shows."

"What bias is that?"

"The reader cannot help feeling he needs to be changed."

"That's true," she admitted. She stated her assumptions in the opening chapter. Environmental degradation and the associated human and economic impacts were already severe, and certain to get worse. "But I don't pre-judge what changes are required. I'm looking at how you would get people to agree, and then, more importantly to act or support policies that encourage action. I leave open what those might be. Whether it's government intervention or market solutions. Or some combination."

"Most convincing," he said, "but more academic language would serve you well."

Weeks later, Simone shook her head as she finished recounting the story to Jenny and Sagan. They had spent the day cycling lazily along the coastline of The Wash, ending at a pub in Kings Lynn, with a view over the River Great Ouse. The air was warm and still, with seagulls providing a background chorus. Their train to Cambridge wouldn't leave for an hour.

"Academic language: how the world was saved!" Sagan oozed sarcasm. "You'll be fine," he added reassuringly.

"You will," Jenny agreed.

"Wanna hear *my* story?" Sagan asked as baskets of fish and chips were placed in front of them.

They ate while he described how he, like Simone, was taken to task for presentation. Quite radically, he had included sections that resembled a graphic novel. A graphic artist he met in college welcomed the chance to try presenting scientific content with her drawings. She'd taken a stab at using a computer to generate animation, but gave up. The software was still too rudimentary. Probably for the better, Sagan concluded. His masters thesis was pushing enough boundaries.

"Maybe I'll do my PhD as an interactive video game," he had joked to her. They'd laughed, just as Simone and Jenny did now.

"I kept the cool colour graphics and some illustrations," he told them, "but not without courting disapproval. Black and white photos and bar charts are *avant-garde* to many of the fellows, it seems. Thankfully my supervisor backed me. *One must take risks in science*," Sagan quoted, affecting a German accent.

"Here's to your oral defences," Jenny proposed, leading a toast.

Obstacles aside, Simone and Sagan submitted their theses on time. Jenny, they knew, had at least two more years of research to do before submitting hers.

"Now for my dilemma," she announced, looking from one to the other. "I was hoping you might have some advice."

"We'd be glad to," said Simone, glancing at Sagan. He nodded.

"You guys know I'm on a scholarship," Jenny began. "From MalayGas. I was chosen on my academic record. Nobody cared what research I was going to do."

"But now they do?" Simone guessed.

"A change of leadership."

"Which means..." said Sagan.

"To qualify for my third and fourth year of funding, MalayGas needs to know how my work contributes to oil and gas development."

"Will it?" Asked Sagan. "Or *could* it?"

Jenny pursed her lips. "Not without major changes."

"And selling your soul?" suggested Simone.

Jenny laughed. "Not *selling* it. But leasing it for awhile, perhaps."

"Is there some way you could meet their needs while staying true to your own objectives?" asked Simone. "Bringing clean power to those who have none." She recalled her conversation with Jenny on a bus six years earlier.

"Maybe," said Jenny. "If I try hard enough."

"Or pitched your current research creatively enough," suggested Simone.

Sagan jumped to his feet. "Ladies, we have work to do!" he announced as he headed into the pub. Jenny looked as puzzled as Simone felt. Several minutes later Sagan returned carrying three cold lemonades, a pen and a notepad.

When they boarded their train, Jenny was clutching a folded sheet of paper on which she had written two paragraphs.

Hockey Fight

Staring at her screen, alone in the lab, Jenny felt her stomach growl. Supper hour was long past, but she needed to understand the results of this experiment. Paul was long gone, working shorter hours these days. She smiled.

When the piercing sound of the phone finally broke her focus, she opted to ignore it. Many rings later, she sighed and reached for the handset.

"Jenny here," she said icily.

The warm, bemused chuckle melted her in an instant.

"JJ!" she squealed, "how did you know I'd be in the lab?"

"Oh," he said gently, "it's only 10 p.m. Quite predictable. Did you get dinner?"

"What!" she scolded in jest, "Are you taking over for Simone?"

"I am equally interested in your welfare. Besides, I think she has been rather, how should we say, preoccupied."

"Agreed," Jenny laughed. "I hope she's finding time to prepare her defence."

"I expect she'll have everything under control," JJ said.

"And you," Jenny said warmly. "How's the job?"

"Oh, too early to tell. For now, I am mostly doing a lot of reading. Corporate policy. Government policy. Energy policy. Policy policy."

"Hmm," said Jenny, "I expect it will get more interesting." A long silence followed.

"JJ?" she said, "I have a question for you. Perhaps an offer."

"Go ahead my sweet Malaysian girlfriend."

"JJ was a cute nickname, but may I use Jiro now? It seems more… dignified. More… you."

After a moment of reflection, he answered. "Sure. Call me Jiro. And you? Is there a proper Chinese name I can use?"

"That's very considerate, JJ, I mean Jiro!" They both laughed. "But I've always been called Jenny. When speaking English, which is most of the time now."

"Good night Jiro," she said at the end of the call. She liked how it sounded.

"Good night, girlfriend Jenny! Take good care of yourself."

Jenny sat for a moment in the quiet of the deserted lab. Girlfriend. She liked how that sounded too. How Jiro said it. And how thoughtful he was to check in on her. She should get something to eat.

* * *

"Aw, c'mon Simone! Just try it." Paul was holding a Montreal Canadiens cap he had offered her as a surprise. They had just finished dressing in anticipation of a Sunday brunch.

"That's generous of you Paul, but *A*, I don't wear baseball caps, even with hockey team logos, and *B*, I'm not about to dress in matching his-and-hers hats, like I'm some kind of trophy girlfriend." Simone was bristling now.

"That's so insulting!" Paul shouted, his voice filling the bedroom. "My friend in Moncton goes to all the trouble to find this hat for you, and sends it all the way here, and you won't even try it on." His hands were clenched.

"Don't go playing passive-aggressive with me Paul. If you'd taken the time to notice if I ever wore hats, to ask me if I liked the Habs even, maybe you could have come up with a gift that was for me, not for you."

Paul banged a fist down on his desk. "You can be so self-centred!" He stomped out of the room, slamming the door behind him.

"Look who's talking!" she called after him.

Sister Pledge

"**S**orry about the time," Jenny whispered, when Simone responded to her timid knocks on the bedroom door. "I wanted to catch you before you leave. Sagan told me you were doing a last high tea tomorrow, but I can't make it.

"I was going to try and reach you too," said Simone, waving Jenny inside. "Have a seat on the bed. I'll climb back in."

"I was worried you may not want to stop by the lab," said Jenny, watching Simone's face closely. "You know, bump into Paul."

"Ah yes," Simone said cautiously. "What did he tell you?"

"Not much," said Jenny. "Just that it's over."

Simone shrugged. "Short but intense. Full on and then, I guess, full off. He was what I needed."

"Was?"

"Still could be, I guess. But no..." said Simone. Jenny waited.

"I'm heading out in two days, and he's here for another couple of years, like you. We agreed the long distance thing wouldn't work." Jenny nodded, biting her tongue.

"We'll cross paths again. Canada's a small place." Simone laughed.

Jenny looked around the bare room, where once there had been posters, a computer, and sports gear hanging to dry. Simone's beloved bicycle was packed in a special bag, she noticed.

"Simone?" she said. "Do you remember David Suzuki's warning in Rio?"

Simone nodded. "Turn this supertanker around by the year 2000, or kiss our chances goodbye."

"Yes," said Jenny quietly. She paused. "How do you think we're doing?"

"There's lots of promising signs," Simone said tentatively. "Technologies, laws, treaties. But the myth hasn't changed. It's still economy vs. environment. 'Of course we want to save the Earth,' she mimicked, 'but not by killing jobs.' They say it when things are going badly, and again when they're going well."

"Too few people get it enough to act," Jenny added, letting her dejection show. "Or they get it, but are paralyzed by fear."

"Or hope," said Simone.

Jenny cocked her head. "How do you mean?"

"Well, just like fear can freeze you, so can hope. It's as if somebody else will take care of things. The government, God, the free market... When I hear people talk about hope, I don't hear them say, 'but I'll do everything I can to make sure my hope isn't in vain'. Hope has to be tied to action."

"I'd never thought about it that way."

"You're talking to the newly-minted Master of global behavioural change and communication," said Simone, playfully lifting her nose.

"Right," said Jenny, catching on. "The thesis wasn't 'too well-written' after all?"

"Nah," Simone said. "They praised me for my first-hand interviews."

"It was thorough," said Jenny. "I enjoyed reading it."

Simone chuckled. "How often are 'enjoyed' and 'thesis' used together?"

Jenny smiled. "That's what it's going to take, though, isn't it? You don't bore people into making big changes. Or bombard them with facts."

"That's what I like about Sagan's approach," Simone said. "Have you seen him?"

"How could I miss him," Jenny laughed. "Floating around Churchill. His examiners suggested he publish a graphic book on climate change, not just polar regions and methane."

"That would be cool!"

"He doesn't really belong in university," said Jenny.

Simone shook her head. "You need the credentials to back up your claims."

"I guess," said Jenny. "People trust scientists. More than politicians or the media."

"People doubt the media?!" Simone's voice was laden with irony.

"Not you," Jenny clarified. "And not when stories are supported by evidence."

"You mean research, like yours. Now your funding's confirmed."

"Thanks to you and Sagan," Jenny was quick to acknowledge.

Simone reached out and took her hands. "You'd do the same for us."

Jenny nodded as her thoughts drifted. It had been so simple, recasting her original research plan as something beneficial to oil and gas exploration sites, just as they discussed on that golden August evening. Portable, stable power storage to run critical computer and communications equipment; simpler and less dangerous. She hadn't sold her soul. It was just a short-term rental. She looked into Simone's eyes and smiled. How close they'd become in one short year.

"So here we are," Simone said, breaking the silence. "September 1998. That window of opportunity is closing. But you, me, Sagan... we'll jam it open while the supertanker changes direction. Mixed metaphor. It's nearly midnight."

"Very nearly," Jenny noted.

The Last Tea

"It's just the two of us," said Sagan, offering Simone a pained smile.

"High noon at Aunty's tea shop," she said. "The last ones standing."

"Sconing!" he suggested.

"Is that a verb?"

"English is remarkably flexible."

"More so than *the* English," Simone said glancing around at the mix of local and foreign customers. "Though our examiners were flexible, weren't they—after all?"

"They were. Plus, you and I know how to sweet talk." Sagan winked.

"Here's to sweet talking," said Simone, raising her tea cup, pinky finger extended.

"To sweet talking!" he toasted, imitating her gesture.

Smiling, they tapped together Aunty's china. Sagan caught the admonishing look from an older gentleman at the table to their right.

"Sagan, I'll see my parents in a few months in Canberra—my father was just posted there. Will you be with yours, or is that beyond sweet talking?" Simone's concern touched him.

"One thing at a time," he said. "They'll drive to Penn State and bring my stuff."

"Your sister?"

He smiled. "She'll visit. Even if I'm not welcome in Detroit."

"But not your brother."

"Not likely." He furrowed his brow. "Mom's worried about Demar," he added softly. "Running with a bad crowd. Trying to fit in."

"Almost inevitable," said Simone, nodding.

"No!" Sagan said, shaking his head. "Not inevitable. But it's damn hard to break away. Chart your own path."

"*You* have!" Simone was staring at him, her eyes shining.

"Sure," he laughed, "but I'll tell you how hard it was—if you've got a week!"

She nodded slowly. "I can only imagine,"

"I'm not looking for pity," he said, looking away.

"And I," said Simone softly but firmly, "am not offering any. Just trying to understand. Maybe even empathize."

"Thanks." Relaxing, his smile returned. "Maybe it will make sense some day."

"*Life can only be understood backwards, but it must be lived forward!*"

"Whoa!" he said. "Did you just make that up?"

"Nope," said Simone. "Kierkegaard."

"Who?"

"Soooren Kierkegaard. Danish existentialist. With Monty Python pronunciation."

"Of course," he said sarcastically. "Must have missed him in school."

She laughed. "I have this brain that pops out quotes, as you know. Nietzsche, Python, Queen—"

"Queen is mine!" he growled. Simone raised her hands in mock surrender.

"*Life can only be understood forwards…?*" he tried.

"*Backwards,*" she corrected, "*but it must be lived forward!*"

They strolled along a bustling Trinity Lane in silence, taking in the excitement of a school year about to start. Full circle, he thought.

As they passed the large display windows of Heffer's Bookstore, Simone stopped abruptly. "Don't move!" Ten minutes later, she emerged holding a tiny package.

"Read it when it feels right," she instructed him, offering the mystery book.

Gaining altitude, the plane was passing just south of Cambridge, Sagan realized with a thrill. *Wow! Churchill, Clare Hall, Trinity, King's Parade…* Tiny now, yet so large.

One year ago. He recalled himself sitting at Aunty's, alone.

Simone's gift! Carefully he removed the wrapping paper. *Man's Search for Meaning.* Viktor Frankl.

He opened the book to find an inscription.

> He who has a why to live for
> can bear almost any how.
>
> Love always,
> Simone

St. François

Drome, France, October 1998

S imone's pitch to the *Ottawa Herald* to report on the ambitious environmental plans of the Sydney 2000 Olympic Games had been accepted. Now, in addition to Christmas with family in Canberra, she would spend the first two weeks of December in Sydney. *Aussie Aussie Aussie, oi oi oi!*

But first, autumn in France—by bicycle. Picking grapes for two weeks near Colmar would replenish her bank account. Then she'd head southwest to Chambéry where she had done an exchange when she was 14. She'd visit with her host family. Last and best, she'd ride through the Alps to the Drome, to finally meet François.

Everyone said she should do it someday. That someday was now.

Ma chère Simone, he had written in response to her self-invitation. *It would be lovely to see you, though I cannot offer much. Just pure water, a roof and all the physical labour you desire.*

Now, after three weeks on the road, here she was coasting down a narrow lane towards an uncertain welcome.

To her great surprise, François was waiting at the gate. He swung it open with an ear-splitting screech. Like the high wall into which it was anchored, the gate was a remnant of another era. He waved her through with a bow and a wry smile, his crinkled eyes and ruddy cheeks showing the 42 years of age his muscled upper body did not.

"Go, go," he encouraged, "no point losing momentum. I'll meet you at the end of the drive, where it turns to gravel.

"Be careful as you dismount," he called after her. "The loose stone devours bicycle tires."

He was right. After a thousand kilometres without mishap, Simone found herself suddenly on her side, her feet still clipped to the pedals.

"So much for my dignity," she muttered as François arrived to help her up.

"Ah, dignity," he said, helping unclip her pedals and lifting the bike off her. "We are usually harder on ourselves than others. Don't you find?"

"But still—" she said, massaging her left hip.

"But still, this is not how Simone the adventurer wished to begin her visit. So, let's try again. I see a dusty, sweaty young woman, who has traversed the Alps like few French ever will, and arrived within an hour of her prediction. And she wishes to say..."

"François Dirringer I presume?" She smiled and shook his hand. "What a pleasure to meet you at last."

"Then I say, Simone Cohen, welcome to my very humble abode."

She'd expected a hermit, going through the motions of allowing her to visit. He proved anything but. Not that he was chatty. Certainly not when working, as they often were. But he was charming. Witty too. And curious.

"Have you done any farming?" he asked, as they walked the perimeter of the property the morning after she arrived, accompanied by Belle, François' energetic young border collie.

"Just a little gardening with my parents," she admitted.

François' five acres lay a kilometre or so down the hill from Le Tilleret, a village of 100 inhabitants, along a narrow paved road. More or less square, the property was bounded along the road by a deteriorating wall and gate, and on the other sides by a combination of hedges, dilapidated fences and a field belonging to Chloe and Pascal Martin. "Friends and co-conspirators" was how he described the organic farming couple. A dozen or so small farms were within a ten-minute walk.

"How about construction?" he asked. "A fit, strong woman like you!"

"I helped build an extension on the family home," she said. "I put in the insulation batts and vapour barrier. I even nailed on some shingles. Until I got sent down." She scowled at the memory. "I wasn't keeping the rows straight."

"Yes, that could cause problems," François laughed.

"We don't use asphalt shingles much in Europe," he said. He paused and pointed toward the Martin's barn in the distance. "We usually follow our traditional styles and materials. They look nice, but aren't too energy efficient. Not that your shingles are."

"So what *is* efficient?" Simone asked as they continued strolling.

"Ah," said François, "that's a question with no simple answer. People tend to reduce everything to specific, separate materials and choices—what's the best insulation or roof type? But we need to take a systems approach. What matters is that the individual parts work together. Complementing each other."

"Is that what you mean by permaculture? What you were telling me last night about the layout of the land, the trees and plants, for best use of sun and shade?" Simone had noticed how few tall trees there were. How harsh the sun was in the summer, with so little shade.

"Yes." His face lit up. "Smart girl! Woman, I should say." He smacked himself on the wrist, then smiled.

He had already shared with her his vision for the land and his thoughts on permaculture and its relationship to building techniques. So far, he had used permaculture design in establishing shady and sunny zones in the gardens, placing drought-tolerant varieties and thirsty ones in the appropriate places. Also in selecting plants that worked symbiotically with one another "to stave off pests, without need for harmful—and expensive—chemicals."

"Companion planting," Simone offered. She was familiar with the North American indigenous idea of planting corn, climbing beans and squash with one another, in a specific arrangement.

"Sort of," said François. "That is permaculture on a small scale. But it's the same principle. Take lessons from nature. But don't romanticize it," he added.

This day he was showing her how the overall farm would work. And how he had established his priorities for what to work on first, since he was only one person. She thought for a moment that she heard a hint of longing. One man, working alone, without colleagues—or family. Striving to create a place they would want to visit. Maybe even settle.

"Well I'm here to help," she offered quickly. Maybe a bit too loudly. "I have two more weeks until I need to leave for Marseille, to catch my flight to Sydney, and I can't think of what else I'd rather be doing."

"Young and full of energy," he said admiringly. "The sky is the limit!"

"You're hardly old yourself," she mocked in a shaky voice.

He threw his head back and laughed.

"I spend a lot of time building up the depleted soil," he continued as they arrived at a plot where some squash, broccoli and peppers had not yet been harvested. He pointed to some places where a rich, dark, aromatic soil contrasted with the surrounding lighter and dustier soil. "With leaves, kitchen scraps, straw and manure from neighbours' farms…" He waved to the west. "And 'humanure', as you know."

Simone had been tutored in the art of adding a ladle of sawdust into the outhouse pit, after each 'visit'. She was not the least bit fazed by the idea, after years of using an outhouse at the cottage, and learning to 'shit in the woods' on canoe trips.

"Sufficiently composted," he emphasized, "so heat kills any pathogens."

On another day, Francois outlined his plans for the house, and the 'energy positive' philosophy that guided him. The house occupied a central location on the land, at the end of the drive coming up from the road. Vehicles would park in the gravel courtyard bounded by the house on the right, a large but rickety older barn on the left and a new, partially-walled but fully-roofed structure which provided shelter for the tractor, a work bench and the chopping and stacking firewood.

With winter approaching, François was focused on making the house airtight and insulating the floor and roof, now that the walls had been rebuilt and high-efficiency windows and doors had been fitted. Simone helped install a solar hot water device on the roof—a system evidently of his own making. She identified old radiators, painted black to absorb the sun, connected by recycled copper pipes to a substantial water tank built into the centre of the main room. It would supplement the wood stove and furnish hot water. Even heat a bath someday—once he had built a bathroom, as intended.

"I'm not planning on tromping to the outhouse in my old age," he joked.

"You'll need something more comfortable if you want visits…" Simone said, trailing off as she realized where she was going. François suggested they return to work.

Simone found his low-tech approach intriguing, noting how much he did with used materials, clever design and a lot of elbow grease.

When not working, or cooking, or canning, François took her onto some overgrown paths accessed from a back gate, long rusted away. These eventually connected to some well-maintained trails in the mountains that ringed the Saou Forest further up the valley.

"A great place to hide," he commented cryptically.

Later, he elaborated. With northern France under Nazi occupation, and mandatory labour recently introduced in the Vichy south, many local men, and some women, had headed into the hills. Some became *maquisards* resistance fighters. Many others in the region harboured Jews and political escapees, and provided safe passage for downed Allied airmen. The *Maquis du Vercors* was one of the most active resistance movements. They were feared by their occupiers and the collaborator Vichy government, as they seemed to strike from out of nowhere, and vanish just as quickly.

Simone was intrigued. "I knew about "the resistance" but had no idea it was this widespread. And in rural areas too. I pictured young men sneaking through the sewers of Paris. Blowing up railway bridges, that sort of thing."

"Like in the movies," François acknowledged. "But "la résistance" grew to be very broad and diverse. It spanned social class, age and religion. Initially under the occupation, most people were too scared to speak up. As long as they were not personally affected too badly, they saw little reason to take risks."

"I guess that's the problem with resisting." said Simone.

"It's easier to keep your head down," François continued, "and hope you won't be targeted. But then, when you become a target, when first they come for others and finally they come for you, how does that saying go?"

Simone recited it verbatim in English, as François nodded.

One day, at François' suggestion, Simone got back on her bike to do a loop of the area surrounding the farm. The lavender harvest was over, but the distinct scent of the local flower was everywhere.

At a high point in the ride, while looking west toward the Rhone from the ruins of a medieval seigneury—a place that once offered protection not just to the owners, but to local peasants in times of war and lawlessness—Simone was struck by what she saw. The conical tower of a nuclear reactor, its plume of steam clearly visible.

All around her, modern society was juxtaposed against a slower, less mechanical past. Patches of forest and natural spaces interspersing with cultivated fields, criss-crossed by roads, rail tracks and a superhighway. In one direction, dozens of wind turbines turned majestically on the ridge of the low mountains, and in the other a nuclear station loomed. Both systems fed into intrusive power lines.

How had François escaped from fighting the Fessenheim plant on the Rhine, Simone wondered, to end up in the shadow of the Cruas-Meysse plant on the Rhone?

"There is no escaping big power structures," he said, when she mentioned it later. "Nuclear plants, coal mines, oil wells, pipelines. You can resist them locally, you know, piecemeal. But ultimately, all you win is a skirmish. The only real victory will be to replace the whole power structure with something better. I am now trying to do that. First on my own and then, I hope, with others who think like me."

"Everywhere is downstream or downwind from something that can kill. But I'm here to nurture. I've had my fill of fighting." This was the François that Nicole described.

François inspired her. He'd done what he could in activism, then politics, and now in a more practical way, rooted to his land. She could imagine herself settling here. But not yet. Staying in the safe and comfortable south of France wasn't going to change the big world beyond, as the nuclear plant showed. Permaculture, energy positive buildings, soil restoration... she had to get out there and tell these stories. She had to find more of these stories. She needed to make her own mark.

Throughout her visit Simone was tight-lipped about what Nicole had shared, and what she knew of the children. For his part, François never mentioned them. Perhaps he felt it unfair to use her as a go-between. Indeed it would have been.

Simone did, though, when she wrote to Nicole some months later, to reassure her that François was well; and that the gardens were fertile and the main house nearly complete.

Life Gets in
the Way

Staying in Touch

Pennsylvania State University, April 1999

The envelope from Simone, delivered to the office he shared with two other doctoral students, took him by surprise. There had been no communication since September. Six months! The stamp depicted a scene of outdoor skating, with a backdrop he assumed was an Ottawa skyline.

Sagan had thought often of Simone, JJ and Jenny, but done nothing.

Now, this envelope. This big honking envelope. He slit it open. Clippings. So many clippings! *By Simone Cohen. Simone Cohen on assignment. Special feature by Simone Cohen.* He glanced quickly at the headlines, but was looking for a letter. I want *your* news, Simone, not news about others. Even if you wrote it.

* * *

Dear Sagan,

Every day I've wanted to write. OK, every week. But I spend all day writing, and I've been trying to settle into a new life. Now I have a real address where you can write me. A phone number too.

97

My clippings will give you a pretty good idea of what I'm up to.

After an amazing couple of months in France, I joined my parents in Canberra. You may recall I planned to write about the Sydney 2000 'Green Olympics.' I spent several weeks digging around. The organizing committee was quite open. They felt they were doing a good job but not getting credit, so they were keen to show everything. Which is rare.

They won't be perfect, but they're far ahead of what anyone has tried: innovative building design, less toxic materials, a 'model' athletes village that showcases all kinds of energy- and water-efficient features. It's denser than recent sprawling suburbs, plus it's linked to both rail and a fast ferry into central Sydney. To top it off, the main venue at Homebush Bay is on remediated land. You can credit the Olympics with prodding several levels of government to clean up the soil and riverbank.

With the stench coming out of the IOC, it's nice to see something positive. Truth be told, though, what's happening in Sydney isn't about the Olympics. It's forward-thinking people—in government, business and civil society—who seized the Olympic platform to push a positive legacy for the games. Their bigger goal is to profile sustainable practices. Companies now have products and expertise that can be sold around the world. Developers, architects, engineers...

I should have just let you read the articles! They ran as a series over three weekend editions. HeraldMedia, the national chain, picked them up. For me that was a coup. The features editor has hinted at a possible job.

That was a long way of getting to my big news: I'm a reporter and feature writer for a major Canadian daily!!! Rap my knuckles for excessive punctuation!!!!!

I've found a cosy apartment in an old building in Centretown. Lots of light, with funky restaurants around the corner. No guest room, but the futon sofa folds down.

I'd better wrap this up and get out for my ski before the snow is gone. This season was great, though a little milder than I remember. But who am I to judge, you're the expert. "You can't judge climate by one year of weather." I can hear you now.

All this could be yours! You can skate, right? Next winter, it's onto the Rideau Canal for you. I'll treat you to a Beavertail. It's yummier than it sounds!

Oh, you'll see my piece about your upcoming election. I did a scan of each party's policies. If Gore wins the nomination, that should bring real attention to the climate issue. Are there ever some dinosaurs down there! Not just Republicans, but mostly so. Good luck with that! Go Gore (black that out, journalists are neutral!)

Send me your phone number and I'll give you a call. You can be my issue expert.

Hugs and high teas,
Simone

P.S. I called Jenny at her lab one night. She's making good progress. You'll love this bit: Prrrofessorrr McIlraith has offered to be a research advisor. They connected when he was in town in

January. (Score one for JJ's meishi.) I suspect a pub was involved. He told her: "I was so charmed by your friends, I figured you had to be worth going the extra mile to help." (insert accent)

* * *

Pennsylvania State University
April 11, 1999

Dear Simone,

This is the first letter I've written in ages. Hasn't electronic mail reached Canada?

I'm settling in fine. Got a decent room in an older house near campus. Most important is the garage. For my bike, which makes me an oddity. Everything here is so car-centric. Most grad students have cars. Lots of undergrads too. The parking lots on American campuses are huge. I miss Cambridge's streets. They had life. You ran into friends. You popped into shops on a whim.

I had a thought about cars. Why do we all own one? What if there was one per residence. Or block, in a student ghetto. What if you could sign it out like a book? A car club, pay an annual fee. Then when you use it you pay per mile (oops, 1.6 kilometres). Think how much everyone would save in repairs and insurance!

What do you think of Gore's chances? I was thinking of volunteering. Never was much into politics. Couldn't see the point. Whoever got elected just kept on doing what corporations and privileged folks wanted anyhow and the small guy got the shaft.

Forgive my cynicism, but you know where I come from. Every time African Americans imagined a breakthrough, after the race riots and when the unions had real power, nothing much changed. Look how Detroit keeps getting worse. Carter, Reagan, Bush, Clinton... why should Gore be different? That's why I'm holding back. Even if he wins, will he get support from Congress? The only real success I've seen was the Montreal Protocol on ozone. It was so bad, people could see and feel it. Not so for climate or biodiversity. It's a slow death, so why rush? Don't want to scare voters.

Here I am preaching to the converted. Sort of like within my field. But are the people who need to hear it listening? What does it take? More evidence? Scarier predictions? I'm not sure. They shut us off. "The sky is falling, the sky is falling," we say. And then it doesn't, 'cause it won't for decades. So the deniers say, "Ha, wrong again! It's just a hoax." I often hear that. "It's a way to get research funding." That one pisses me off! Like we get kicks from predicting disaster.

Maybe that's why we're so cautious. Scientists avoid definitive statements. "Trends indicate... Evidence suggests... More research is needed to establish causal connections..." But it's <u>science</u>. Nothing is ever 100%. Still, if we don't get more bold and find ways to connect, we'll be muttering "I told you so." in our old age.

Sorry, I needed to get that off my chest. My skinny chest. I should get to the gym. Maybe I'll meet someone. Then again, I could get my teeth knocked out. Progressive campus or not.

I'm heading north this summer. Way north. We're teaming up with a group of Carleton University researchers. That's in Ottawa, I learned, so what a great excuse to see you. Find me a bike and show me around.

Thinking of you,
Sagan

The Great White North

Ottawa, July 1999

Sagan had heard good things about Ottawa from Simone, whenever she tried to tempt him to visit. More than a government town, she insisted. Music and comedy clubs, great restaurants, a thriving summer festival scene and dozens of picturesque paths and rural roads for riding. He'd only just stepped out of the airport into the hot, humid air and already he was wishing for more than two free days before his trip began.

Simone! Damn he missed the girl! They had exchanged some letters and emails, they had phoned a few times, but he should have tried harder. And now there she was, waiting as promised, the trunk of the car popped open.

"Simone Cohen drives a car!" he exclaimed with a shake of the head. "Who'd have thunk it?"

"You wanted me to collect you by bike? With all your gear?" She gave him a friendly punch in the arm, then opened her arms.

Ooh he'd missed those hugs.

"You Canadians like your cars small!"

"Doing our part to off-set emissions from south of the border," she said with a straight face as she heaved the first of his two large duffel bags into the trunk.

"Ooh, you always take the bait."

"Shut up and get in," she said. "We've got riding to do."

103

As they drove, Sagan commented on the forested land. "Is all Ottawa this green?"

Seventy years earlier, Simone explained, Ottawa's planners had established a greenbelt around the original city. The Airport Parkway they were on passed through it. Suburban growth had long ago leapt this greenbelt into surrounding rural land, but residents considered it sacred.

As they approached what seemed to be the city proper, she pointed out some key landmarks. "We're passing over the Rideau River now. On the left is Carleton University."

"Nice setting!" Sagan said, noting the trees, and the large park to his right.

"We're about to pass over the Rideau Canal—sorry, no skating in July. On our right is an area called the Glebe. Nice place to stroll. Maybe tomorrow afternoon, if you can still walk!"

He grimaced. She had promised hills.

"You hungry Sagan? Airplanepretzels won't get you through tonight's warm-up ride." She gestured at the string of eateries that had appeared. "If you like Lebanese, you've landed in the capital of shawarma. Second only to Beirut!"

"Can't say I know it," he said, looking out as he rolled down his window. "But I'll try anything. Just be gentle with the hills tomorrow. I've been slacking."

"No longer a skinny lad?" said Simone, reaching to pinch his spare tire.

Partway into their Gatineau Hills ride, Simone adjusted her ambition. Sagan would never manage the full loop she'd planned.

"So out of shape!" he gasped as he coasted to a stop next to her. She had dismounted at Champlain Lookout, enjoying the view for the umpteenth time as she waited. She handed Sagan an energy bar, which he gratefully accepted.

Looking out over the fields and the Ottawa River in the distance while he refueled, he remarked on how amazing it was to have such natural beauty within easy reach of the city.

"Growing up, I only got into nature when church camp took us on a day trip. But I payed for that with some serious preaching the rest of the time!"

Simone smiled. "I was so lucky. Still am. I get into the woods, or out riding on rural roads as often as I can. But I have to go further and further afield now. You don't see it from here, but Ottawa just keeps on eating up green space and farmland."

Sagan nodded. "Like every other city."

"Pretty much," she agreed. "The planet's going to be one big city unless we take serious steps to curtail the sprawl. And limit population growth."

Sagan shook his head. "Obvious, yet so controversial."

"Like limiting resource consumption and waste production," said Simone. "Obvious, yet nobody wants to go there. Or even have an adult conversation."

Sagan disagreed. "The conversations happen. At conferences and in journals, just not at the political level. All the politicians ever do is posture."

"It's about getting elected," Simone reminded him. "And re-elected. Never get out ahead of talk radio or the tabloids."

"Newspapers!" Sagan exclaimed. "They still have those?" He leaned away to avoid the punch from Simone.

"For now," she said, pursing her lips. "But they're getting slimmer, and we're all worrying about the possible impact of the internet."

"And here I was hoping you could help me get the word out," said Sagan.

"How so?" asked Simone.

He paused before answering, taking a gulp of water to wash down the rest of his snack. "Simone," he began. "We're in deep doo-doo. I don't know what our field work is going to show this year, but I'm expecting it to surpass all our worst-case projections. Again! Temperature increases at the poles. Soil subsidence. Permafrost melting. And the methane releases that come with them. It's one big positive feedback loop. Only here, positive means bad!"

"But nobody's listening?" Simone guessed where he was going.

"Worse than that," Sagan scoffed. "Nobody's talking. The science community is so cautious. They don't want to overstate what's known. They don't want to be found to have cried wolf. Only the opposite is likely to be the case."

"But it will be too late by the time people figure it out," she said, completing his thought.

Sagan nodded deeply and slowly. She had never seen him so pained.

"You got it, girl." He fixed his eyes on hers. "So why do non-experts like you get it, while so many supposedly smart people don't?"

She thought for a moment. "Because I have no vested interest. Journalists, reporters like me at least, are about figuring out what's true and telling it as straight as we can. We don't have to live with the consequences, in a direct sense. We can report unpleasant things, then move on to the next big story. No election cycles. No next quarterly statements."

"Simone," Sagan began, an idea forming. "If I fed you some of the stuff I'm getting, and material from others who want to tell the story as it should be, can you find a way to get it out there?"

"Well," Simone laughed lightly, "I'm still only one step above the bottom rung. But I'll do my best. You know I share your passion; your commitment to telling truth."

"Maybe I can help you climb a few rungs!" Sagan proposed, a grin forming.

She laughed. "Or get me yanked off the ladder!"

* * *

The heavily-loaded plane roared as it fought to gain altitude. The weekly First Air flight to Iqaluit was bursting with cargo and passengers. For regular passengers, it was an odd feeling, this ponderous lift off, but they knew it would get there. Rookies like Sagan glanced around nervously while the veterans chuckled. One of many rites of initiation.

The land of the midnight sun, thought Sagan, thrilled to be on his way to conduct real field research. Part of a top-notch team. *The Show, at last. How did I get so lucky?*

On landing in Iqaluit, the team had several hours to kill. Jill Klassen, a young researcher from Carleton, suggested a walk into town before squeezing into a smaller plane for an even hairier flight to their research site on the western side of Baffin Island.

Descending the sloping road, Sagan squinted as he caught site of Kuujuusi Inlet, sparkling in the sun of the summer afternoon. Though ice-free for several weeks now, the water would be barely above freezing, connected as it was to Frobisher Bay, which was cooled by the Baffin Island Current. This climatic influence accounted for the lack of trees. Permafrost lay just below.

He inhaled deeply. So pure. Could there be anywhere less polluted than this? Could it stay that way? He inhaled again, picking up a faint salty scent.

They headed along the shore, picking their way among the rocks and beached vessels. Jill stopped to watch a group of men performing repairs on an outboard motor. As Sagan strolled over to join her, one of the men turned to utter a greeting.

"Hey, where you from?"

Sagan and Jill exchanged glances. "Ottawa," offered Jill. "He's from the States."

Sagan nodded. "Detroit, sort of. Studying in Pennsylvania."

"Oh," came the man's reply. "Way more interesting than Ottawa."

"Anything's more interesting than Ottawa," the youngest of the group quipped. They all laughed. Jill too, Sagan noticed.

Noting Sagan's expression, the young man explained: "Every third person we see is from Ottawa. Government. Some scientists."

"You've nailed us," said Jill. "We're studying changes to the climate."

"You want to know about climate changes!" said the first man. In his fifties, Sagan guessed. "We can tell you about that for free.

Then you can take the summer off and go fishing!" He smiled broadly. "Until mid-August, when it starts freezing up again."

"Whoa!" shivered Sagan. "We're here 'til the *end* of August."

"Why do you think we packed parkas?" said Jill, punching his shoulder lightly.

"I thought it was a precaution." Sagan's voice betrayed his worry.

"Parkas? T-shirts? Nowadays, who can tell!" It was a new voice. An older man than the others. He was seated on a long flat rock, with a view of the repairs. From under a frayed Ski-Doo ball cap, his face spoke of a lifetime exposed to the elements.

"Weather's changing. Hard to predict. Old knowledge not much good."

"Mmm," echoed several, nodding. Not the younger ones, Sagan noted.

"For generations, Inuit have learned to read signals." The man pointed to the clear blue sky, then out to the water. "Clouds, ice, moss. Whether to expect a long winter. When the ice will start to break up."

"We don't do it for fun." His eyes bored into Sagan's. "It's survival."

"How do you mean?" asked Sagan.

"When you're heading out, making a long crossing," he explained patiently, "you need to know the ice. Same for weather. Even if you're not crossing ice. We have ways to read signs of a storm. Get stranded in a blizzard, you can be lost in minutes."

"My older brother," It was the young man again. "died two years ago making a crossing by Ski-Doo. Ice must have opened up. In early May! Too soon." He shook his head and looked away.

"Never found him," he continued shakily. "Not even a call for help on the radio."

"I'm so sorry to hear that," Jill said. Sagan nodded, imagining the family's pain.

"Yah, it happens." The young man looked down and prodded the gravel with the toe of his boot.

"It always has," said the elder of the group. "But more now. We have to adapt. Hunting and fishing. Storing food outside where it should stay frozen, then suddenly you find it half-thawed, full of maggots. In February!"

"Mm hmm," nodded the others, grimacing at the memory.

"What about animal behaviour?" asked Jill.

"Plenty of changes," said a man wearing an Edmonton Oilers cap. His left hand was missing two fingers. "With the thinning of the ice, earlier springs, many animals act different. Seal. Walrus. Polar bears. Whales even. Not so much here, but talk to people on the mainland. Further west: Northwest Territories, Yukon, Alaska. You're going to be flying soon, eh? Ask your pilot."

Sagan exchanged glances with Jill.

"They talk to people across the North. See lots of changes. Especially on the mainland. Runways like a roller coaster. Buildings sinking. They'll have stories."

"Well boys," he said loudly, looking around. "Better put this motor together and be ready for high tide."

"For sure," said the Oilers fan. "Fish while the fishing's good. Global warming or not, ice will be back in the bay. Wanna have our fish caught and dried. Can't afford store prices." The others muttered agreement. "Besides, we don't like southern food."

All but one nodded. "Maybe we'd better learn," the youngest man said with a grin. "Big Mac with fries—to go!" They all laughed, Jill and Sagan joining in.

Walking slowly back to the airport, Sagan reflected on what he'd heard.

"All the climate models have the two poles warming much faster than the rest of the planet," he said to Jill. "If those guys are seeing changes now, at under one degree warming—global average—just think what will happen by the middle of the century!"

"Best case scenario: 3-5 degrees," Jill said gravely. "Worst case: 6-8."

They walked in silence most of the way back. As they approached the terminal, Sagan paused and looked at Jill. "Do you feel like me, about our work?"

"How so?"

"Stories from elders are compelling to *us*, but the world needs proof. Fast!"

Sagan had his work cut out for him, and work he would. But never alone. Everyone doing research in the Arctic was seeing these changes. Perhaps not everyone felt it as deeply as he did now, but their collective work was essential to constructing the story, as accurately as possible. As for telling it, he had an ace up his sleeve. Or at least sitting in Ottawa. He'd tell her everything.

Ottawa Herald, November 10, 1999

Disappearing sea ice may be canary in climate coal mine

By Simone Cohen

Arctic sea ice is disappearing at a faster rate than previously forecasted, according to a recent study in the journal *Nature*. The international team which authored the paper has been tracking sea ice cover since 1979. According to recent measurements, multi-year ice has thinned by more than 10 percent since the first measurements were taken at locations close to the North Pole.

As the extent of ice cover is dictated by both the temperature and duration of the winter season, this multi-year ice provides the most reliable indicator of overall shifts in global temperature, as it takes many years to form and to melt.

Team leader and co-author Roger Smithson of the Scott Polar Institute, based at Cambridge University, described the team's surprise at the extent of the shrinkage.

"Scientists are not prone to hyperbole, so we are cautious when it comes to making predictions," he stated at a recent press conference, "but the extent of ice loss over the past decade has surprised most experts and is causing us to reevaluate our forecasts."

Forecasts are likely to be significantly altered in two areas: the date by which sea ice will have shrunk to where summer shipping traffic will become possible without the expense and logistical requirements of ice-breaker accompaniment; and the date by which multi-year ice will have vanished entirely and only seasonal ice will be found, with none in the warmest months.

Smithson was blunt about the implications of the team's findings. "We can expect feedback loops from the loss of sea ice to accelerate and intensify the warming of the Arctic, and by extension, the planet as a whole. Whereas sea ice reflects the sun's rays, the much darker open water absorbs those rays and creates heat, leading to even warmer oceans."

While forecasts published in the recent reports of the Intergovernmental Panel on Climate Change estimate a 1-3 degrees Celsius warming for the planet as a whole by 2050, the polar regions are expected to warm by as much as 4-7 degrees by 2050.

Family Pride

To: MightyNorthernPen@magma.ca
From: Jenny.Fung@Cambridge.ac.uk
Subject: News from Olde England
Date: January 15, 2000

Dear Simone,

I guess Y2K was a lot of panic for nothing. Still, saving files was not a wasted effort. I shudder to think what I'd do if three years of research were wiped out.

It was great to hear that you'll be traveling in the U.S. and dropping in on Sagan. If his family isn't keeping an eye on him, you can do it for us, OK?

Speaking of families, they can certainly cause grief. Not mine, but Jiro's! My parents have supported my choices. Even my engagement to a Japanese man. This is significant, not just for reasons of race and culture. Older people have not forgotten how brutal the Japanese occupation was. My parents have not yet met Jiro. We could not afford to both fly to KL over the holidays. I went alone. My first visit in three years! But his parents came to London in January. I returned in time to overlap with their visit. Of course, there is the language challenge between me and Mrs. Ebitsubo. Mr. Ebitsubo speaks excellent English, remember?

Jiro taught me a few Japanese phrases. We were getting along well until Katsuo arrived. You could see an immediate change in the parents. Mrs. Ebitsubo went quiet, which did not surprise me. But the deference Mr. Ebitsubo showed did. They seemed to be warming up to us, until Katsuo lectured on about Japanese pride and all this outdated bullshit! Pardon me, but I am still quite shaken. Sadly, my Jiro also turns into a different person around his brother. Though he is taller (and better looking), he shrinks in the presence of Katsuo. He just nods and says things like, "You must be right." and "You know best."

Oh my, I have gone on. I wanted to say how I enjoy your articles. I loved your story about the 'Living Machine' for treating sewage and toxic effluent. I was also intrigued by The Natural Step methodology. You are saving me and your readers time by summarizing these inspiring advances. Those who wish can dig deeper. I think the World Wide Web is going to be really useful, for research, and especially discussion forums. We need upbeat stories of solutions and innovators, to offset the negative. How about a mandatory ratio: 3 parts good to 1 bad?

I am getting good lab results and have identified applications that will keep MalayGas happy. I'll tell more later.

Your Asian sister,
Jenny

What Bleeds Leads

T wo days and 170 kilometres. The Canadian Ski Marathon
was not most people's idea of fun, but it was Simone's. Until
the final 30 kilometres.

She'd wanted to do it for years, but knew it was foolish to
try without logging the training distances. That meant having
time, good snow and a job that didn't keep sending you out of
town. This year it had all come together. She'd only had a few
short work trips since December. Snow had been plentiful, and
she'd linked up with some old skiing friends from school, which
made training a lot more fun, and wimping out on a frigid day
unthinkable.

One last checkpoint, and then it would be downhill—
gradually, and with a cross-breeze—for the final leg. Double-
pole, double-pole, double-pole. Like an automaton. Plant poles,
bend and push, swing up, repeat.

Why did she like this so much? You could get frostbite. You
would get blisters. For the next two days, you'd hardly be able
to lift your arms. She smiled. Blame it on her parents. Edward
and Nadine Cohen had introduced their tiny daughter to skiing
during their posting to Norway in the Seventies. Back in Ottawa
they kept it up. Every weekend, out they went. Like church.
Often straight from church. Occasionally, instead of church.

"The outdoors is my church," her father had said. Though
she stopped attending church in her teens, Simone embraced

the outdoors as a kind of religion too. Nature, sport and healthy living. With an occasional visit to church.

She and her parents were Unitarian Universalists—"UUs", for short. A church with centuries of tradition, diverse roots and a relatively forgiving dogma. Not really a dogma at all, Simone thought. More the encouragement of spiritual exploration and right living. The Seven Principles were sufficiently loose as to allow her to find something of value and a home of sorts.

The inherent worth and dignity of every person; justice, equity and compassion in human relations; acceptance of one another... Simone could recall the principles from memory. Even at the end of a ski marathon. She smiled. Then coughed.

These were noble goals, not rules. She preferred that to commandments. Coming back to Ottawa after Japan and Cambridge, she had begun to seek clarity, in her life and profession. What was she was trying to do? Encourage the world to aim just a little bit higher, and remember just how noble a person and a society could be when they put their minds to it. Minds and spirit.

The seventh principle was the one that really grabbed her— *respect for the interdependent web of existence of which we are a part.* She'd always loved the outdoors and respected nature, in a romantic kind of way. But now, she had words to define a goal—to promote respect for the interdependent web of all existence. It may not be what drove her outside at minus twenty degrees Celsius, grunting along on skinny skis with drool frozen on her chin, but it sure as hell explained the passion she felt for her vocation.

More and more, Simone found herself attending service. Her free-floating life was packed with adventure, but it needed grounding in something, somewhere. Something bigger than herself. A community devoted to lifting people up, not tearing them down.

Her parents had not grown up in a UU community. Her father, Edward Cohen was 'Jewish, with too many questions'. He admired many aspects of his parents' faith—they had immigrated to Montreal from Southeastern France in the 1920s—but was neither pressured nor inclined to practice Judaism. Though he remained proud and very aware of his ethnic and religious roots.

Simone's mother had similarly wandered from her Ukrainian Orthodox upbringing. Her grandparents had left Ukraine in the early days of the Russian Revolution, when, as intellectuals with property and anti-Russian leanings, it became clear they could not stay. They settled in Strasbourg. Two generations later, granddaughter Nadine came to Canada looking for adventure in the summer of 1967. She found it, in the name and arms of one Edward Cohen.

Simone loved the way her parents told this story. Free-spirited Sixties youth charting their own course, respectful of their families, religious upbringing and cultures, but wary of the baggage. They kept what they liked and adopted or adapted to new things which they had come to admire and respect. Hence their eventual home as UUs. Hence, Simone believed, her own faith in humanity—even when it didn't seem to deserve it—and her commitment to fighting ecological destruction and climate disruption, even when that put her at odds with powerful people, and occasionally her own friends and neighbours. And editors!

Simone coughed as a breath of icy air hit her lungs. The temperature had begun to be drop. Like her own energy level. You can only gut it out for so long. Pushing, until you get pushback.

Marsha Delorean, the Features editor, had called her into the *Herald*'s meeting room two days earlier under instruction from the editor-in-chief. Apparently her writing 'lacked balance.' It was 'overly rosy, too uncritical.' What this meant, Simone responded sarcastically, was you could never just tell an uplifting and inspiring story. You always had to find a naysayer, to crap on what some inspired individual or group or company or government was doing to address a challenge. That was 'balance'.

"Since when does a feature need alternate points of view?" Simone had argued. "Aren't we looking for unique stories? Where somebody is pioneering something, or taking a stand against something, or showing what's possible? What's the value in equal treatment for sourpusses? Didn't we agree I was to offer readers something fresh? Signs of hope, to balance all the gloom: poverty, deforestation, mill closures, fishery collapse..."

"Yes," Marsha said, her eyes narrowing, "and that's still what we want from you. But remember, there is a fine line between raising hope and creating false hope. That's where you may be lacking still in critical judgement."

"I accept your feedback as intended," Simone said. "But—"

Marsha chuckled, shaking her head. "Simone is bound to have a 'but'. It's why I hired you, and it's why I went to bat for you with the boss. Say what you need to."

"People are constantly being pelted by bad news. The world's going to hell in a handbasket, they're told, and there's nothing they can do about it. But there is. Plenty can be done; plenty's being done already. Solutions that make clear environmental and social sense. Good economic sense too, in the medium or long term. But we're always told that they'll hurt the economy or take away jobs. That's the closing note of most pieces. *Look at this excellent idea. Forget about it, though.*"

"You do have to tell all sides," Marsha countered.

"Do we, really? Isn't there a double standard? When the business section—heck, the front page some days—heaps praise on the latest gadget or hot company, do you ever learn who was hurt in the process? Who the latest boy wonder stepped on to amass his fortune? When the big banks report billion dollar profits, has anyone been assigned to find out who paid for that? Maybe it's sweatshop labour in Vietnam, or murdered activists in Bolivia, who tried to protect their water from the mining company. Or Canadians on low incomes being encouraged to run up credit balances on cards they shouldn't have been offered. No, good day on the stock market is just good news! But someone creates a cleaner, more efficient process and we have to mention the lost jobs in the legacy industry. Can't we just report something like sustainable forestry as good news for its own sake?"

Marsha let her rant a long time before stepping in. "For as long as I've been in this business, it's been accepted that good news won't sell. There's no drama. *If it bleeds, it leads.* People want their adrenaline. Why do people listen to talk radio?"

"Yes," Simone said, more quietly. "But has anyone ever tested that assumption? Has anyone run a week of good news stories to see what happens? Upbeat banners above stories that don't promptly negate the headline."

"Not that I know," Marsha admitted.

"So," Simone challenged, "how about the *Herald* be the one to test whether people stop reading; or write in to complain; or cancel subscriptions if we run too much good news. Do you think anyone would have the balls?"

Marsha chuckled. Men held all the top positions.

"What if you pitched it as an experiment? One we could track. Sales figures. Letters for and against. Then compare the data against the same time in other years."

"We'd have to do it in secret," Marsha said. She had identified a crucial hitch. "Semi-secret at least. Say, just the front page editor and editor-in-chief being in on it. Or else the results could be skewed. And we definitely couldn't tip off the readers."

Simone agreed. "Business as usual. Once the trial's over, we'd get a great story out of it. Whatever the result." She was getting more and more excited.

"If you get the OK from the top," she prompted Marsha, "I'll suggest a list of stories to pitch. They may not all be breaking news; good news doesn't work that way. It builds. It grows. Not like a crisis or a scandal. That stuff just happens. Maybe that's what people love about bad news: the pure randomness. 'It could happen to you!' But could it? Are many of our scary leads truly relevant? Or do we run them for shock value?"

"The world is a dangerous place," said Marsha, completing Simone's thought. "Stay home and close the curtains," she added with melodrama. "Boowahahaha!"

"Pretty much," laughed Simone. "Or just, 'What the heck, I'm not in charge of my fate anyway. It must be God's will.' Fatalism gets reinforced."

Marsha couldn't let Simone go entirely unchallenged. "Don't upbeat stories lead people to a kind of false optimism? Apathy even? 'Hey, it'll all work out. The government is on top of things. May as well get out of the way and hope for the best?'"

"If all they do is hope," Simone agreed.

"So how is good news better in the end?" Marsha prodded.

"It's fundamentally different. Stories of people, or institutions, acting to solve problems are. Accomplishing goals beyond just profit. You know, the 'triple bottom line' of sustainability: economic, social and environmental. Those are stories of a different cloth. They plant a seed. They inspire and, perhaps, lead a reader to act. Goodness doesn't appear out of nowhere. Just like evil. The soil is prepared. Or poisoned."

"And we're doing too much poisoning," Marsha suggested. "Of minds. And spirit?"

"Exactly, Marsha. Exactly."

"Well, thanks Simone. You've taken me back a few decades, when I was full of conviction and intensity like you. I want to find it again."

"I'll be your tag-team partner," said Simone, pausing to size up her editor. "So, we're on? The good news caper is afoot?"

"I can't promise anything," said Marsha. "I just run the features section. Some days not even that, it would appear." She gave Simone an accusing glare, then laughed. "I haven't pitched a big idea for awhile. This is going to be fun. However it turns out."

"Merde!" Simone said. "That's French for *break a leg.*"

"Oh right. I thought you were saying I'll be in deep shit."

"Nah, just stirring some up. But if it hits the fan put me on cleanup."

"For a year!" Marsha threatened as Simone left the meeting room.

A shit disturber, Simone thought as she recalled the encounter now. It beat some of the things people were calling her. She smiled as the finish line came into sight. And at what was to come in the week ahead. Once she could lift her arms again.

Election Shock

To: MightyNorthernPen
From: SayItAgain@hotmail.com
Subject: Noooooooooo!
Date: December 2, 2000

How exactly does one immigrate to Canada? Or cross over in the dark and claim refugee status? It's like Bush brought together a bunch of Texas oil barons and had them draw up a manifesto for raising the temperature of the planet. Kyoto bye bye!

Sagan

To: SayItAgain@hotmail.com
From: MightyNorthernPen@magma.ca
Subject: Re: Noooooooooo!
Date: December 3, 2000

Hey Sagan, I hear you. People are odd when it comes to choosing leaders. Bush looks like he's going to be captive to the people he surrounds himself with. He won't be the first puppet president, though. Or the last. Stick it out and finish that PhD. You'll be a hot commodity. That would be the time to flee.

Get plenty of exercise—it clears the head.

By the way, I loved that sound clip. Was that campus radio? I like the way you wove together the science, humour and music. You have a real flair. Do more of this stuff. I forwarded it to Jenny and Jiro. I'm sure they'll love it.

Simone

Care Packages

To: MightyNorthernPen@magma.ca
From: Jenny.Fung@CambridgeUni.ac.uk
Subject: News from Olde England
Date: April 21, 2001

Dear Simone,

It was a treat to get your package. *Natural Capitalism* looks great. I glanced through it before Jiro snatched it away. I must not resent him. His work is not so rewarding. His bank wants him to focus on making 'conventional' energy more efficient. Strange word, isn't it: 'conventional'. As if extracting a finite resource and using convoluted processes to make it usable and somewhat safe is conventional. But the sun, wind, water, biological matter and ground heat sources are 'alternative'. What might we say instead? Maybe 'natural' energy vs. 'risky'. We must find words that resonate.

Paul and I are developing a kit for remote and mobile energy supply. My research has identified the most efficient and economic battery types for a variety of applications (off-grid villages, mining and forestry camps, boats). His work on charge controllers and inverters that run sensitive electronics matches well with my batteries. Our Prof. McIlraith has assigned students to identify appropriate sources to power our system for various conditions and climates: Engineers saving the world!

Sister Jenny

Hot Stuff

Montreal, June 2001

"If you'd told me there'd be all these fit guys in lycra, I'd have come last year!" Sagan declared.

Simone watched him scan the crowd of cyclists surrounding them as they waited for the signal to set them on their way. Montreal's Tour de L'Île was an annual mass participation ride; more festival than sporting event. There would be few sore muscles at the end of this brilliant day. Plenty of sunburns, though.

"Now I have to compete with you for the buffest ones!" she said, laughing.

Sagan rolled his eyes. "Celibate Simone. Haven't we had this conversation?"

"Indeed," she said, looking fondly at her friend. "You said something about me being a hot babe, but a little intense."

"I've got it!" he said, as if formulating an idea. "I could announce I'm riding with *the* Simone Cohen—award winning journalist. They'll all come flocking."

"Don't you dare," she growled. "And if *you're* going to announce *my* credentials, I'll do it right back. *Woo hoo!*" she called out. "Meet DJ Sagan, budding media star. Before it goes to his head." A number of people turned briefly to look. Not seeing anyone they recognized, they looked away.

"Please!" Sagan said calmly, adjusting his sunglasses. "I wish to remain anonymous."

"Not much problem there," Simone assured him. "This crowd watches Quebec television. Not PBS from central Pennsylvania."

Just then, a starter pistol was fired in the distance. Slowly the riders around them began to move.

For awhile they rolled along in silence, taking in the sights, sounds and smells of Montreal's various neighbourhoods; a cosmopolitan blend of incomes, languages and ethnicities in constant evolution. Passing through La Petite Italie, they stopped to enjoy pastry and espresso seated at a sidewalk table.

"This is great!" Sagan marvelled. "The costumes, the riders. Just ordinary folks."

"I knew you'd like it." said Simone.

"You knew! Okay, you who know everything, tell me about your award." Simone shrugged. "Come on," Sagan urged. "False modesty can't fool me."

She began by recounting the conversation which prompted the experiment. How she hadn't expected the guys at the top to go for it. But Marsha, her features editor and mentor, must have made a convincing pitch. Once the concept received support from two senior editors and the publisher, she and Marsha developed a plan for tracking their results, all the while keeping from colleagues and readers the fact that good news stories would be given top placement over the course of an entire week.

"Early feedback from readers was almost entirely positive," Simone told Sagan. "Letters praising the shift away from doom and gloom came flooding in. We decided to extend into a second week, and finally a third. By that time, it was obviously an experiment. The contrast with our normal headlines was too stark."

Sagan nodded. "I can see that."

"When it became clear that it was a deliberate campaign, we started to be accused of manipulation. Mostly by competitors and media commentators. That was enough to halt the trial, and prompt an explanation. But no apology."

Simone quoted from the publisher's statement. "*Journalistic integrity was never compromised. The stories were real, and essential news was still printed. The prominence given to good news over bad was the only substantive difference.*"

Sagan gave her a high five. "Leading the peloton once again!"

"Aw shucks," she said with a shrug. "I had a hunch, but never, ever thought it would play out so well. National coverage. International too."

"I know," said Sagan. "Even the U.S. of A. The heart of corporate mind control. The *Good News Experiment.*"

"We've been calling it the *Newsworthy Experiment,*" she said, "since it questioned what's considered newsworthy. Even if people are likely to fall back into their old ways, and the myth that bad news sells."

"Old habits die hard," said Sagan.

"Marsha and I co-authored a series about the experiment. We pointed out how strange it is that we can run inflammatory headlines for months on end and nobody bats an eye. But two weeks of upbeat stories above the fold, and it's manipulation. 'Spoon feeding us pablum', one competitor called it. A journalism prof accused us of 'dumbing down' the news."

"But who got the last laugh," said Sagan, "and the award."

"That wasn't just me—and Marsha. Four of us received a Canadian Journalism Award, and the *Herald* was singled out for courage in journalism."

"But it was *your* idea."

"It was, but you know most big ideas require a team to make happen."

Sagan stared at Simone and shook his head. "You know what I like about you?"

"My awesome glutes?" she ventured, turning to model her shorts.

"In addition to those," he laughed. "You have guts and a serious ego, and yet you still don't let it go to your head."

"Well," Simone said in a serious tone, "if any of that's true, I have a role model."

Salaryman

London, July 2001

Oh no, do not vomit. He took a slow breath and closed his eyes. The Northern Line train squealed as it made one of a series of curves on its way up to Highgate. *Do not vomit. Do not miss your station.*

He was no better than the salarymen he'd pitied riding the Tozai line out to Gyotoku. Heads lolling back and forth as they fell asleep, then woke, panic-stricken, searching to see if they'd overshot their station. He'd never be one of them. But he was. Different city, different subway, but a drunken *sarariman* nonetheless.

Simone had warned him. Had she seen the signs? His drinking. The 'energy analyst' job which he'd embellished for the sake of his friends, but was really just a junior position, where he might slowly make his way up, toeing the company line, hoping for something more interesting.

Katsuo! Always making me do what he wants. And me, always agreeing. "Spineless Jiro," he called me. Good thing Jenny didn't understand. Putting me down in front of my fiancée, and our parents! "Let's see if our father stands up for you: your career ambitions and your engagement to this Chinese girl."

He really was going to vomit. Breathe. It's Tufnell Park. Two more stops.

128

Simone and Sagan, why did I think I was like them? Choosing their own paths. Even Jenny. But me? Just tell Jiro what to do. He will let you wipe your shoes on him.

Simone and Sagan. He smiled. He so much looked forward to seeing them again. He really should write. Look at Simone, sending packages with articles and even books. That last one was so interesting. Inspiring things done by bold people. People with a spine.

Archway. One more stop. Maybe he wouldn't vomit after all. Not tonight. And tomorrow, he would go home right after work. Make excuses. 'Wedding preparations'. His co-workers would laugh. 'Doesn't the woman take care of those things?' Maybe some women, in some relationships.

Emerging onto the street at Highgate, Jiro took in a lungful of surprisingly fresh air. Tomorrow, he would take a walk through Highgate Wood. Then he would write an email to Simone and Sagan, telling them how happy he was that they would be at the wedding.

Jiro smiled. *Soon I will be married to the brilliant and beautiful Jenny Fung and we will begin a new life together.*

Kindness of Strangers

Newark Airport, September 11, 2001

T he images on the departure area TV screens made no sense.
Planes flying into the Twin Towers, over and over. Just
across the water from where they stood, dumbfounded, like
thousands of others. Millions of others. No flights would be leaving
American airspace any time soon. Certainly not today. There
was little chance of reaching England in time for the wedding.

"Poor Jenny and Jiro," whispered Simone, turning to look
through misted eyes into Sagan's.

He nodded silently, but she could see he had gone elsewhere.

"Canada!" he suddenly blurted.

"What about Canada?" said Simone. "There were no attacks
there."

"Exactly," he said, with a surge of excitement. "What if we
could get to Montreal and fly out of there!"

Simone looked doubtful. "Let's think this through. If we can
get a rental car, that's about 8-10 hours, depending on traffic
and the border. Perhaps a late night flight could get us to the
UK. Maybe Amsterdam or Paris."

"We'd have to buy new tickets," Sagan noted. "Plus, there's
the drop-off fee, assuming we can even take the car over the
border." His enthusiasm was ebbing.

"That's... two grand each," he concluded, shaking his head.

Simone turned to face him squarely, her hands on his shoulders. "I got you."

"No way!" he protested. "You can't"

"I can. And I will." she said firmly. "Pay me back when you're rich and famous."

Sagan found himself speechless.

"The big question is whether Canadian airspace is open. Let's find a phone and... no, we won't accomplish anything here." Simone tugged his arm, jolting him into action.

"I'll call my parents in Ottawa," she said as they strode towards the exit from the secure area. "No, the *Herald* news desk." She was thinking and talking on the move. "You go straight to rentals. Take anything they've got."

"Even a Cadillac?"

"Grab a limo if you have to. We'll find others to share it."

"I walked most of the airport looking for a phone," reported a sweating Simone, when she found Sagan in the car rental area. "Then all I got was busy signals."

"And everything's rented," he said with a weak shrug.

"At least we tried for whatever that's worth." Then it came to her. "We'll hitchhike!"

"This is America—nobody hitchhikes!"

"Not normally. But the world has just changed."

Perhaps it was Sagan's sign. "Must reach Montreal," it read. "Best friends to marry and we're the gift."

Ahmed, a limo driver heading back to Albany, got them halfway there. He called ahead to his uncle Mohammed, owner of the company. His son Youssef could get them to the border. Crossing might be difficult, but they'd be on the home stretch by then.

Youssef took down their names, passport numbers and Simone's credit card details. His brother Daoud had a travel agency in Syracuse. If planes were leaving Canada, Daoud would meet them with the tickets at a freeway layby. Simone and Sagan watched from their rear seat as this support network sprung into action.

They did not make it to the wedding—no flights were leaving Canada for at least 48 hours. All they managed was a phone call to England. But the heroic effort of strangers to get a "mixed race couple" to a wedding, was something they would never forget.

Ahmed, Mohammed and Youssef—refugees from persecution in Syria—would be targeted by hateful remarks in the aftermath of 9/11, they later learned. The mosque in Albany was covered in graffiti. Daoud lost longstanding clients. "We can't do business with your kind!"

The world had indeed changed.

Family Secrets

J enny sat at the table in her small Cambridge kitchen. She had risen at dawn so she could be alone. Wrapped in a housecoat, a cup of tea in her hands, she stared at the writing on the envelope in front of her. "To be read on the morning of your wedding."

Dearest Jenny,

This may come as a surprise, the complete story at least.

During the Vietnam "boat people" crisis, thousands fled the country to avoid reprisals from the Viet Cong regime. Especially Hoa Chinese, who were being harshly persecuted. So great was their desperation to escape that some handed children to family members or strangers on board a boat when it became clear there was not room for everyone. Others began the journey as a family, but one or more parents perished, or were kidnapped or murdered during the voyage. On the perilous trip, it was not uncommon for a child to reach the shores of Malaysia with no adult taking responsibility for them, or even knowing their name or place of origin.

Jenny knew much of this. Her parents had actively assisted *boat people*. Her mother was a nurse, while her father ran a family restaurant in an oceanside town. Why they were retelling the story on the morning of her wedding was not clear.

One such child—emaciated and badly sunburned—was brought to the intensive care ward in which I worked. At this time—1977— the numbers of boat people were still small, and the attitude of the Malaysian government and people still generous. Within two years, that would change, as the country became the first landing point for tens of thousands of refugees. In these early days, the quality of medical care was quite high, and a difficult case was not yet being triaged as unlikely to survive. So fortunate. Within several weeks, it was clear that this tiny girl had great tenacity. We estimated her age at 3, but it was hard to say.

Your father and I first met when I came to his restaurant on my evenings off. He tells me he struck up a conversation to learn how he could help out. Of course, he also says I'm the prettiest girl he ever met, so I'm still not sure which is the truth.

On one visit, I told him of this remarkable child, and her will to survive. He asked if he might come to see her. This was not allowed, but since he was liked by the doctors and nurses in my unit, who knew of his donations of food, I was able to bring him in.

What came next was remarkable. Both because of how quickly it happened, and how little doubt either of us had. Your father turned to me and said, with a seriousness I had not yet seen: "You and I must marry quickly. Then we can adopt *her. We will bless her with the gift of a family, and she will bless us in many ways."*

Your father has always had a special intuition. You see, we would try for many years to have more children, but without success. Somehow, he knew this was a special opportunity, for us and this child. The child of course, is you.

We have indeed been blessed and we love you beyond words. It is a lucky man who will have your hand in marriage, but we know you will have taken great care in making your choice. We look forward to welcoming Jiro into our family.

Jenny dabbed her eyes quickly as Jiro entered the kitchen. She looked up to see him smiling, his arms spread for his usual morning embrace. Noting her face, he hesitated. Then, his expression darkening, he froze. Eyes closed, he inhaled slowly.

She knew these signs. He was preparing to deal with difficult emotions. A feeling familiar to her.

When he opened his eyes, she held out the letter. As he read, Jenny followed the various changes of expression on his face. When done, he shook his head and uttered one of the Japanese-isms she had come to love, if not always fully understand.

"Wah!" *Wow. Amazing. Holy smokes. Terrific. You have to be kidding.* On this day, he did not leave her to guess. "What an incredible act!"

She rose and buried her nose in his chest; as high as she would ever get without assistance. Kissing the top of her head, Jiro whispered that he also had a story to share.

"Is it good news?" Jenny asked, stepping back and looking him in the eyes.

"Very much," he replied, holding her gaze. "It is also a story of love and generosity." She nodded for him to start.

"I will go straight to the point, then give the background, OK?" She nodded again.

"My father, speaking also for my mother, has given our marriage his blessing. He has instructed Katsuo to never again speak of racial purity. Not in their presence."

"Wah!" Jenny grinned, stepping back. "That is indeed a blessing."

"But that's not all."

"Stop." Jenny held up her hand.

"But..."

"No," she said, forcefully. "This is important, correct?"

Jiro nodded.

"So it deserves my full attention. We will make time, I promise."

"But there's one more short thing," said Jiro, with insistence.

"OK, really short." Jenny was visibly agitated.

"This will seem strange coming from my father. But I think it is the true Ebitsubo-san. The one who calls me John, in private."

"Go on."

"*Marry for love*, he told me. *It has worked for your mother and me.*"

Jenny took Jiro's hands in hers and stepped back to look in his eyes. "That is exceptional advice," she agreed, before continuing with a frown. "But he left out another *very* important lesson."

He frowned in return. "And what is that?"

"Don't be late for your own wedding!" she cried, pushing him toward the bedroom.

Deadlines

Gulf of Mexico, March 2002

Simone was trying to work, but this kid wouldn't leave her alone. Marsha was holding a prominent place in the weekend paper, if she could file that night. It would be tight, but she might just pull it off, if the annoying first mate would just get the hint.

She'd flown to Mississippi to interview local fishermen on the impact of pollution from offshore drilling accidents. Was the oil economy wiping out the traditional one, for want of stringent safety standards, or could they co-exist? After several days of speaking to affected men and women, she chartered a fishing excursion boat to take her out to one of the massive new drilling platforms. She was greeted there by the company's 'community outreach' officer who stayed close at hand as the rig's chief engineer gave her a tour. Now, on the ride back, she needed to write.

Who do you work for? How do you become a journalist? Do you have to go to college first? Does it pay well?

"Look!" she barked at last. "Can't you see I'm writing? I've got a deadline."

"What are you writing about? You sticking it to the oil companies. I know some crab fishermen who'd love that!"

Simone sighed loudly and looked up. "OK, here's the deal," she said. "If you leave me alone for the next hour, maybe find me a cold drink, you can send me all your questions by email. I'll answer when I'm not under such stress."

"Deal," said the lanky, dark-haired young man, his intense eyes locked on hers. He brought her a 7Up, then sat and watched her type. She felt relief when eventually he drifted away.

"Hey look," Simone said in a more friendly voice when he returned later to tell her that they would be docking, "sorry I was sharp. I need to finish this article, and these oil spill stories make me cranky." The young man nodded.

"I could interview *you*," she said with a smile. "What did you say your name was?"

"I didn't," he replied sullenly, "and I don't want to be interviewed."

"Just thought you might like a taste of what a journalist does."

"Nah," he said. "It's probably not my thing."

Simone shrugged. "Still," she said taking a business card from her backpack, "if you change your mind, here's how to reach me."

"See-moan," he read, nodding as he scanned the card. "Sounds French. Mine's Elmore," he volunteered, looking her in the eye. "*Elmore Lambert.*"

He used a Louisiana French pronunciation, Simone noticed.

"Dad was a proud Cajun. *Zachary Lambert.* For all the good it did him," he added with a shrug.

"Indeed," Simone said, registering the boy's emotional wobble.

"Don't be too quick to rule out journalism," she called back to him as she made to leave the boat. "Send me an email."

"Send me an email," Elmore muttered to himself as he watched Simone step ashore, her laptop case hanging from one shoulder and a camera bag from the other. "Thanks," he added sarcastically. "You send me a computer and an email account and maybe I will."

"Not!" he said more loudly, knowing she was out of earshot.

Later, he blushed as he remembered the encounter. Sure, she'd been arrogant, but hadn't he been a bit of a prick? And she did apologize. She even offered to give him advice. But he'd turned her down. He could hear his father calling him out for his rudeness. *Is that how you were raised?* Or maybe not. Zachary Lambert didn't seek advice, or help, from anybody. It was like a religion. But how had that panned out for him? A shiver ran up Elmore's spine at the memory of his father's final days.

Compared to his father, Elmore told himself often, his life had not been *that* hard. But whatever the physical pain Zachary had endured, at least he had been, and continued to be, admired. In their small bayou town, people pronounced the name Zachary Lambert with admiration.

Elmore Lambert, though, was always said with disdain. He couldn't remember a time before the taunting; at school and at home.

"Elmore Lambert, you throw like a girl! Stop using your wrist." How many times had he heard that—from his uncle, his cousins, the gym teacher?

Fag, queer, homo and other words he didn't understand, but they were always said with that tone. That curl of the lip. He knew one thing, though. You didn't want to be one. He wasn't going to be one. Even if it took work. Hard work. And constant vigilance. Don't get caught singing a Disney princess song. Or skipping instead of running. Or lacking enthusiasm for sports or guns or motorbikes. Or girls.

But there was fishing. Fishing was Elmore's escape. The quiet, and the time with his father on a Sunday. Out in a boat. On a jetty. In the bayou.

Best never be caught on his own though. He'd learned that. A group of boys coming across a solitary one was bad news. Never be the weakest.

The life of Elmore's father may have been tougher, seen from the outside: a grade ten education, physical work, dangerous work. Accidents. Raising two kids, mostly alone. Wandering wife. Just enough money. But Zachary Lambert had never needed to fit in.

Zachary was the guy a parent would point to and say, "Son, you wanna be like him! Never complains, first to lend a hand, doesn't want hand-outs." Among adults, other things were said: "Shame about his wandering wife. And that son."

Some suspected he was too soft on the boy. Nobody could recall seeing him raise a hand in anger, or his voice. Not that the boy was one to make trouble. It seemed to follow him though. By junior high, there was a steady stream of missing homework assignments, lunches taken, lunch money taken. Finally, the schoolyard fights. "Quite a scrapper, that Elmore. You'd never know it from looking at the kid. Learned a few tricks from his Uncle Clem, I reckon. Clem could fight!"

Everything changed in the fall of grade 10, when Elmore had to be rushed from school in an ambulance. Surrounded and jumped, it was said.

When Zachary brought Elmore home from an extended recovery period in Baton Rouge, a lot changed. No more taunting. Collective guilt. Everyone had been complicit. To students, he no longer existed. A pale, scrawny, black-haired ghost. Elmore was fine with that. He had checked out.

From the start of grade 11, he was putting in time. His locker, once a magnet for hate, got a wide berth. Still, he earned solid grades and was on his way to the only thing that mattered: graduating, then getting the hell out.

"There's more than one way to get ahead," his father often reminded him. "You don't wanna do this back-breakin' work like me. Wadin' in chemicals and god knows what. Keep yer head down. Get yer diploma. Then move to some place where they can see further than the end of their fishing rod. Any rod."

Elmore's hospital stay changed Zachary too. Whether it was his decades as a pipe-fitter in the chemical soup of a string of processing plants, or the crushing debt from his son's medical bills, Zachary's health went into decline. He faced it with a stoicism perfected over generations; since his Acadian ancestors were forcibly deported from Nova Scotia. 'Faut le tougher!' You tough it out.

It took Elmore and his uncle Clement to cart him into a public hospital for a diagnosis, when he no longer had the strength to refuse.

"I hardly know where to start," the emergency doctor emerged to tell them, a pained expression on his face. "Respiratory problems. Stomach tumour. Lesions..."

Home Zachary had come, with nothing but ointment and painkillers. Prescription renewable. You could get drugs cheaper on the black market, Elmore learned. And food from the food bank. Useful, when there was no money. Elmore learned to lie, so his father wouldn't know where things came from. Something he had never done. Zachary raised him to tell the truth. No exceptions.

The final months of Zachary's illness—in the winter of Elmore's grade 12 year—were particularly tough. Oddly though, Elmore's devotion to his father during this time earned him grudging admiration. From neighbours, who saw him rolling Zachary out onto the porch for air and some late afternoon sun; from Clement, who came by when he could; and from the principal, who exempted him from final exams and personally delivered his diploma.

When his father died, Elmore lost the only person he truly cared for. The only one who showed concern for him, in his spartan way.

Elmore had admired many things about his father, but his inability to accept help was never one of them. Zachary may have preferred to suffer, but that didn't give him the right to make others suffer. Elmore suffered. Now he was owed.

A week after the funeral, he headed to Gulfport, where Claude Richard, a buddy of his uncle, offered him work on a chartered fishing boat, using the only employable skills he had.

Those skills proved to be his ticket into the world of respectable work. With connections, and information. Oh, what a party of businessmen let loose on a boat for a day with an open bar would say out loud! He heard it all, but never let on. *Listen. Learn. Be invisible, unless they ask for advice.* On fishing, or tourism. Sometimes, ahem, where to find a lady for the evening. That's how—a month after his brief encounter with Simone—Elmore came into contact with one of the country's more charismatic oil patch investors.

Citizen Science

Clearfield, Pennsylvania, April 2002

"And that's our show for this week. Join me and the crew next Sunday afternoon for *Un-Blinding Me with Science*. Remember to keep supporting your local public television affiliate. I'm Sagan Cleveland. Keep your eyes on the skies, your brain on the whys, and beware of the lies. Later!"

Sagan sat still, smiling, waiting for the director's cue. "Switch to camera two. Pull back...and go to theme. That's a wrap, Sagan. We're off the air."

"Nice job everyone!" It was Paula Jones, the station producer.

Sagan waited while his microphone was removed, then headed back to the control room to thank the rest of the crew. Television was a team effort. The on-screen talent is all the viewer sees, but they are only as good as the production crew.

"Thank you Celine, Rob, Manuel," he said, looking in turn to each of the three in the control room. "Have a great week!"

"You too Sagan. Take care. Nice job," they replied. Celine the sound technician gave Sagan the thumbs up.

"Oh Sagan, before you go," He turned to see Paula striding toward him.

"Yes sir, madam producer. At your service." He snapped her a salute.

She rolled her eyes in response. Paula was dedicated to making a great show, as their ratings proved. And she was fun to work with.

"In two weeks we start our travelling shows, Sagan. Four in total."

"And you were worried I'd forget?"

"I've not known you to forget much of anything. But I wanted to see if you had thoughts on how to involve students and teachers from the high schools we're visiting. Here's a list of my initial ideas."

"Give me a minute," he said, taking the hand-written sheet. "I'll take a look."

"No hurry," she said, waving a hand. "You can get back to me during the week. Send an email, or call."

"If it's just the same, I like to deal with things when they're fresh. When I get back home, or on campus, I tend to get buried in my work."

"Right," said Paula, with a nod of recognition. "Doctoral thesis deadline."

Sagan tilted his head toward the door. "Want to grab a bite down the road, and talk while we eat?"

"You never heard of Sunday dinner with family?" she admonished.

"Right, sorry. Sunday dinners haven't been on my radar for a while."

"Well then," said Paula, scrutinizing him, "we'll have you over some time and reintroduce you. But right now, let's grab a few minutes in the green room."

Seated on a worn sofa, with a magazine to support Paula's notes, Sagan worked quickly, jotting ideas in the margin and occasionally commenting or asking questions.

"These are urban schools, right? Concrete jungles?"

"Mostly," nodded Paula. "That's my understanding."

"Let's film people outside in that sterile environment, then again in the nearest spot that approaches being natural—a park, or the banks of a stream. I'd like to show how hard it is to expect people to understand nature when they're never in it."

"And to respect a world they never see or touch," Paula added. She was an avid hiker and Girl Guide leader.

"Do you think we can work that in—showing the schools in their urban context? I was going to propose it for next year's theme."

"*Next* year?" Paula sounded surprised. "Aren't you moving on up with that PhD?"

"What!" Sagan said in mock offence. "Forget my people?"

Paula laughed. "All right, all right. I like the idea for these initial high school shows. We can chat about the future later. I assume you'll know by late spring where you're headed, if it's no longer Penn State? You know we've had network interest."

"Netverks," Sagan said in a vampire voice, rubbing his hands together. "Very scary!"

"Seriously Sagan! I speak for the team when I say we want the best for you, but we'd also like to keep you here on the farm." She smiled with affection.

"I am touched, and honoured," he said gently.

"You're a hoot, Sagan. And you have a knack for explaining science in a way that's neither boring nor *edutainment*, if you know what I mean."

"Far too well."

"So, let's nail these next shows, and see where life takes us."

"But I want it all," Sagan sang, "and I want it now!"

She shook her head. "I still don't get it. Try some Springsteen."

"G'night Paula," Sagan said, grimacing. "Get on home for Sunday dinner."

He laughed at her salute.

Love that woman. Love this team. I'd miss them.

Keeping Up is Hard to Do

At the start of 2002, Jiro and Jenny moved to Kuala Lumpur, where she joined the research and development department at MalayGas. Jiro had arranged to be transferred to Tokyo Industrial's new Southeast Asia office, also in 'KL'.

Having her parents nearby was a godsend, Jenny wrote to Simone in March 2003. She had given birth to twins several months earlier. Two tiny, healthy girls.

Simone imagined Jenny's correspondence would become even more sporadic now. Their correspondence. Jiro rarely wrote. *Writing for four*, Simone chuckled.

Single and childless, Simone had no excuse for her weak record, other than crazy job demands. Every six months or so, she would send her own news, share what she knew of Sagan— in case they had not already heard it—and pass along some of her articles and feature reports. Not a terrible record, but she could do better.

Jenny unfailingly thanked Simone for her messages, praised her writing and encouraged her not to give in to detractors. She explained how when she and Jiro read her articles online, they often saw the comments that followed. "So unpleasant!"

"We hope you will continue to cope in a healthy way," Jenny wrote. "It takes courage to confront powerful interests and old thinking. We face our own struggles to keep doing what we believe in when our employers and family would prefer we just go with the flow. That would be much easier, but I think it takes its own mental toll."

Jenny hinted at Jiro's drinking once, when they spoke on the phone, but Simone chose not to press. She and Jenny shared their concerns about Sagan more openly, however. He was subjected to even greater pressures, it seemed. And abuse.

"I told Sagan to make good use of his health plan," Simone wrote. "Massage, counselling, whatever works." She connected with him regularly, as friend and amateur psychologist.

In January 2007, after a long silence, Simone was relieved to get a message from Jenny. It included a family picture taken over Japanese New Year. Yuki and Anna were adorable in their cute little dresses, but Jenny, despite her smile, looked tired. Jiro sat ramrod straight.

How she missed them, she thought, fingering the photo. How she worried about them—young parents, trying to do it all, neither happy in their jobs.

"I hope we can get together some day," Jenny had written. "But travelling with twins is challenging and our limited budget and time is spent on an annual trip to visit Jiro's parents. Namie is quite close to Tokyo, yet it feels delightfully far away. The sea is nearby to the east, and the mountains to the north. The girls love seeing their Jiji and Baba, and it's good for them to breathe the healthy air in Fukushima. KL has become so polluted. Jiro's parents are very generous when we visit. I would not have predicted that. Of course, Katsuo does not visit when we are there, and that is best for all of us. He now works in the office of the national energy minister. Scary!"

Scary indeed, Simone thought. When energy policy and national identity merge, the results can be explosive—as history and current geopolitics showed. She would have to follow that line for a future story.

Being Useful

Gulfport, MI, October 2003

From the day he left home, he had neither been back nor looked back. If anyone from home were to meet him now, they would assume it was a different Elmore Lambert.

Life presents opportunity. You seize it, or you don't. That was the American way. As a guide on chartered fishing excursions, he met a lot of connected men. Influential men. None more than Pete Beauford, owner of Houston-based Pinnacle Asset Management. The 'self-made billionaire,' as business magazines told the story, had taken a small inheritance and moved from one opportunity to the next. Each time, trading up. Cars, houses, country clubs... and wives. Though a writer would do well to leave that part out.

Pete Beauford had taken a shine to Elmore, after several excursions during which his foreign clients had caught the trophy fish they'd dreamed of; been served the food and drink they liked; and enjoyed the flattering attention of some lovely local ladies.

"Elmore," Pete said, as they stepped onto the jetty after another successful outing. "I could use a young fella like you. A guy who solves problems before they become a problem. Ever been to Houston? Ready to take on a new challenge?"

"Why yes sir," he replied, without hesitation, "I *am* ready for a challenge. And no sir, I've never been to Houston. But I'm willing to move anywhere if there's a chance for me to learn new skills and be of service to a respected man like you, Mr. Beauford."

"Well I'm glad to hear that. I'll make arrangements with Claude here to end your employment, if that's alright. I'm sure he'll waive the usual notice period. How long would you need to be ready for the move?"

Elmore was about to say "today," when he thought better of it.

"Well, sir, today is Thursday. If I begin making preparations, packing, and saying my farewells, I could be in Houston by Sunday. Ready to start by Monday, if that is acceptable, sir."

"That would do just fine," said Pete, extending his hand. "I'll have my secretary arrange accommodation. Perhaps an apartment at first. Close to the office. You'll be working some pretty long hours." Pete paused, looking Elmore over. "And I'm thinking you don't own a suit," he added.

"No sir," Elmore said, flushing.

"Easy to fix. Suzy will call someone in for measurements. I get mine tailored. Costs a bit more, but clothes make the man, as someone wise once said." Pete flashed his big grin and added a wink.

"When you get to Houston, check in at the Ambassador Hotel on Main Street. We've got an account. I'll have the contract for you when you arrive at the hotel."

"I'll work you hard," said Pete, his grin gone, "but if you turn out as efficient as I've been seeing here, you'll be suitably rewarded."

"Why thank you sir. I'm sure everything will be fine." Elmore's ears were buzzing.

"Oh, one more thing."

"Sir?" Elmore replied nervously.

"Call me Pete. We're not in the army. Think of me like an uncle."

"Yes sir," Elmore stammered. "Pete! Thank you again Pete. I won't disappoint."

"No, I'm sure you won't. See you Monday. Oh, and take the cooler to my car when you've prepared the fish, will you? They'll be great on the barbecue tomorrow."

Three days to make arrangements! Elmore laughed at that one as he glanced around his rented room near the marina. He would buy two new suitcases. He barely had enough to fill one, but nobody needed to know.

Cassandras

Kuala Lumpur, September 2003

With the afternoon drawing to a close, Jiro shut down his computer. He couldn't wait to check off another day and get home to the twins. He wasn't sure which was more stifling, Malaysia's outdoor climate, or the indoor one at Tokyo Industrial. He was stuck in a grey KL office building, in a cubicle barely big enough to extend his legs, with the air conditioning so high he had a permanent cold. He had no latitude to explore new subjects, or even to share what he was finding.

Just as he was getting up, his phone rang. Long distance, but not head office in Tokyo, the call display told him. When he realized it was a North American code, he snatched the phone from its cradle.

"Tokyo Industrial Investment Bank," he said formally. "Ebitsubo speaking."

"JJ, my tea samurai!" said an enthusiastic voice. "Sorry, I mean *Jiro*.

"Oh, Sagan," he replied softly, looking around to see if any colleagues were in earshot. "So nice to hear from you. Call me JJ if you prefer."

"No, no, you see that's your problem, Jiro. You have to tell people what *you* like."

Jiro chuckled quietly. "As you have often told me. Though it has been awhile."

"The thing is," said Sagan, "I'm calling this time to *get* advice, not *give* it."

"*Honto!*" said Jiro. "You want *my* advice?"

"Well, Simone may be my go-to girl, but one must branch out, right? Diverse opinions must be considered, says the scientist to the lawyer."

"Facts are facts," Jiro said.

"Well there you go, Jiro, exactly what I've always felt. Which is why I end up tying myself up in knots when—"

"Sagan," Jiro interrupted, slightly more loudly, "if you want me to help, you really must be less, how should I say, obscure."

"Right you are, big man. Let me tell it straight and see what you think." Jiro heard him inhale deeply.

"My data leads me over and over to the same conclusion. If all, or even most of the methane trapped in the ground—permafrost, peat bogs, etcetera—and in the oceans—especially in the high Arctic—is released in the mid to latter part of this century, we are right and royally screwed. The problem is, nobody wants to come out and say that. Because they assume nobody wants to hear it. It's a career killer. We'll be accused of being Cassandras—"

"Sorry," said a puzzled Jiro, "what is Cassandras?"

"Ah," Sagan laughed, "Greek mythology. Cassandra was cursed with the need to warn people of what was true, though they wouldn't believe it, or didn't want to. Nowadays, you're a Cassandra if you give unpopular warnings."

"Like about methane, and its impact on the climate?" Jiro offered.

"Precisely. So I find myself pulling my punches. 'Cause that's what everyone else is doing. The data's there, nobody's watering that down, but in our published papers, and certainly when interviewed, we use wishy-washy words. End result: nobody gets the straight goods and we—I at least—feel like shit. A toady, quivering in fear of what others might think."

"Indeed," said Jiro, feeling Sagan's frustration. "I know what you mean."

"I figured you would," said Sagan. "You may not have a solution, but that's probably not what I was looking for. More a friendly ear to bend. And it's been way too long since I bent yours."

"Well," said Jiro, "perhaps all I can tell you is what you always tell me."

"Which is…"

"Be true to yourself. It is never easy, and I am not very good at it, but that does not make it less true."

"Hmm," said Sagan. "And you, Jiro? Is your KL job any more interesting than what you had in London?"

"Ahh," Jiro sighed, "the content has always been interesting. My problem, like yours, is that I cannot tell the full story. The facts lead me to one conclusion about the future of fossil fuel investments and resource extraction—big money can be made doing things unsustainably, but there will be a crash sometime soon, when a lot of people will lose a lot of money—but my company wants me to reproduce the usual advice. Get rich now, and plug your nose." He sighed again, more deeply than the first time.

"Jiro, my man. You have so much to offer. Someday you'll break out and—"

"Easy for you to say!" Jiro felt suddenly irritated. "You have not grown up with this pressure to conform, this expectation—" Realizing who he was telling this to, he stopped abruptly. Then, with Sagan staying silent, he continued.

"Carrying on for the sake of social harmony is more harmful in the end. For all."

"You know it, Jiro. You always have."

"So why am I so weak?"

"For the same reasons I can be. Career advancement, fear, self-doubt."

"Oh, you never seem to doubt yourself. You have shown me what it is to be strong. You, Jenny, and of course Simone."

"You're stronger than you realize, Jiro. When the right moment comes, you'll know. Just don't wait forever. For yourself, and for the people who love you."

"Thanks Sagan, yet again, for the encouragement. I do not think I was much help to you, though."

"You were," Sagan said warmly. "We get by," he began to sing, "when we share with our friends."

Golden Boy

Houston, Texas, November 2006

wo years as Pete Beauford's personal assistant! Executive Assistant was the formal title. *First impressions matter,* Pete told him often.

To say it was everything Elmore expected would be a lie. He'd had no expectations. But if he had, reality would have surpassed them by a mile. He worked long hours when Pete was in town, but had little to do initially when Pete travelled, which he did often. Determined to make the most of such times, he sought permission to take courses in areas that would benefit Pinnacle Asset Management.

Bit by bit, at company expense, he built up his skill set: several courses in office computer skills to supplement his meagre knowledge; some introductory business classes; a spreadsheet management course; a business law course offered online—*The Art of Negotiating the Deal*; even an English course called *Writing for Impact.*

Impact! He liked that word. He wanted to make an impact. In what, he was unsure. But he'd know it when he saw it, and be ready. The American Dream did exist after all, you just had to be prepared to seize your leg up when it dangled in front of you.

His world consisted almost entirely of work, classes and church. Pete had even suggested which church to attend. Forestview—where many of Houston's movers and shakers prayed, and donated.

"I'm not going to get into religion," Pete had said, "but unless you're Jewish or Catholic or something, you might consider being a member at Forestview. Me, I'm one of your Christmas and Easter churchgoers, but Houston is a place where being a church member and benefactor is something a man wants to be known for."

Elmore knew about appearances. He'd come to excel at them. So much so that Pete quickly had him attending some of his bigger meetings, seated right behind him. Even traveling to support Pete during negotiations.

Pete was increasingly calling on him to draft correspondence. His gift with words—a curse for much of his youth, when his clever retorts to others' taunts usually made things worse—had become an asset.

Knowing Your Place

Tokyo Industrial Investment Bank head office,
Tokyo, March 2007

Jiro sat still and straight at the conference table. Wearing his best wool suit, he could feel the sweat forming at the back of his neck and on his brow. He wondered if he should wipe it away. Or if that would just draw more attention to him.

The only sound was of pages being turned—slowly—by Koichi Nakamura, director general of the legal branch. The most senior man in the room.

"Ah yes!" Nakamura said conspicuously, pausing at a marked-up page.

Arrayed around the oval table were three other men. Mid-level managers, two of whom Jiro had met previously. The third, from the company's energy financing division, he had only just met. All sat perfectly still, in deference to Nakamura.

"Mr. Ebitsubo," Nakamura said, looking up. "Remind us please of your responsibilities at the KL office."

Expecting the question, Jiro had prepared a concise version, which he nervously recited now.

"Thank you, Mr. Ebitsubo. Those are indeed the most important tasks." Nakamura glanced down at the final page of Jiro's report. A good deal of handwriting could be seen.

"In any job, there is the formal description," Nakamura continued, "then there are the... expectations." Jiro could see three heads nodding, ever so slightly. "We are interested in your understanding of what the company expects of you, as a loyal employee of... how many years is it?"

He looked to Watanabe, Jiro's immediate supervisor, based in Tokyo.

"Nearly nine years, sir," said Watanabe.

"Nine years!" Nakamura said, feigning surprise. "No longer *junior!* Explain for me please, the kind of advice expected of an employee of nine years. A Cambridge-educated lawyer with a strong technical knowledge of the energy industry."

Jiro was aware of the minefield he would be navigating. The profound deference expected. The self-effacing tone, and coded language: saying so little, while conveying so much. He must play down his technical expertise, his importance to the company; and play up the established policies and well-known preferences of the bank, as determined by its senior management committee, and reinforced in an annual directive.

He could do this. His reports to date had followed this standard format. That is how he had stayed below the radar of head office, while still receiving the annual bonus and a standard promotion after his fifth year. This report, though, was different. He did not expect it to go unnoticed. Indeed, he intended it to be noticed.

"Mr. Nakamura. Gentlemen. I am most grateful for the honor of working for this esteemed company. I understand that my job is to provide an annual report on the legal risks to the company and its shareholders, of our existing investments and ownership positions in energy companies within Southeast Asia and the Indian subcontinent. It is expected that I will identify all relevant risks, whether political, social, technical or security-related. Also, risks stemming from trade and environmental agreements, whether international, regional or bilateral. My job is to support the investment decisions and overall direction taken by the company, its partner companies and the Japanese government. I regret, profoundly if I have missed, or misunderstood anything."

A lengthy pause followed. Jiro's eyes were now fixed on the table in front of him. A bare surface. He had not used notes. All heads save Nakamura's were slightly bowed, yet all eyes were tracking him.

Nakamura took a deep breath. The others quickly followed suit. Jiro too. *Remain calm, at all costs.*

"Mr. Ebitsubo. You know your position well. And yet, would you say this report is indicative of that?"

"With deep respect, sir, yes. It is motivated by my duty to the company."

"How so?" A first hint of, what was it? Not sarcasm... Irony?

The moment had come to walk over the coals. With dignity.

"There is no question that my report breaks with convention. It is not customary for an analyst in my position to make recommendations. Also, it is unusual to flag as risky any of the company's strategic directions, or those agreed to with government ministries."

"And yet, you have done all these things!"

Jiro was surprised to hear the voice of Matsumoto, director of energy financing. A planned intervention? His tone was less polite; *peeved* is how the British might put it.

Jiro did not react. Instead, he turned to Nakamura, seeking permission to continue. Whereas Matsumoto was now flushed, Nakamura remained impassive. Bad cop, good cop. He nodded to Jiro.

"In the lead-up to the Copenhagen Conference, there is discussion of stronger national commitments to greenhouse gas reductions. The EU now has a carbon pricing mechanism, and several American states and Canadian provinces have followed, or are considering it. In light of this, any investment in fossil fuels must be assessed for the exposure it represents to investors and governments locked into a high-carbon economy. This applies of course to Japan, its banks and joint ventures between Japanese companies and ones in countries such as Malaysia and Australia.

Should a stronger target be set in Copenhagen, I felt it prudent to flag which of our investments might be considered risky."

Jiro stopped at this point, testing for any reaction. None came. Again, he looked to Nakamura. A slight nod signalled him to continue.

"As it is one of my specific issues as an analyst, I have been paying particular attention to nuclear safety."

"Indeed." It was Matsumoto again. Jiro paused and turned to the speaker. He was met by an intense stare.

"Mr. Ebitsubo, your commentary on nuclear safety is unexpected," It was Watanabe.

"Possibly even alarming. Or should I say alarmist?" Endo, the company's technical expert on nuclear energy, spoke for the first time. Now in his sixties, Endo had decades ago acquired the nickname "Atomic Guru." His jovial expression and rumpled appearance led most to assume he was a congenial man. Jiro, though, had been warned by a colleague early in his career: "Never challenge the Atomic Guru!"

Jiro had taken great care not to. Until now. This report would be seen as a direct challenge to Endo. To his rigour—if Endo's alleged errors were in fact errors—or his credibility, should they be a carefully crafted whitewash of the safety systems of Japan's reactors. Tokyo Industrial was a member of the consortium that manufactured and operated nuclear power stations.

In raising concerns, however gently, Jiro had inserted a stick into what might be a nest of very excitable wasps. Tokyo Industrial was deeply invested in the sector. Nuclear power was practically a national religion. However improbably, Japan—the only country to ever suffer a nuclear attack—had fully embraced nuclear power under the guise of energy security. The Japanese economy relied on it to power much of its industrial might, light its cities, and even heat homes.

Jiro's report contained a number of assertions regarding the risk of pursuing nuclear energy as a central element of the company's investment strategy. First, the extraordinary cost overruns of recent projects. Second, the heavy reliance of nuclear stations on public subsidy. Third, the wholly inadequate insurance protection available to plant operators and investors in case of a catastrophe, meaning significant exposure to legal action. Fourth, and most damning to Endo and others, Jiro had laid out what he recently learned about weaknesses in the safety systems of a reactor type in common use in Japan, and now marketed to other countries. Several international bodies had recently concluded that there were fundamental flaws in the light water boiling water reactors (BWR). Reports authored by Endo dismissed those findings.

Jiro Ebitsubo, a self-effacing and loyal employee, had decided he could not submit a report which concluded that Tokyo Industrial was adequately protecting investors. Instead, he showed how, by continuing to weight their investment portfolio so strongly toward fossil fuels and nuclear, they were missing out on a growing opportunity—solar, energy storage and the automated systems that optimized their effectiveness.

While writing, Jiro had a flashback to a memorable evening lecture. A fateful night, he recalled fondly.

He found himself channelling some of what he had heard there, but mostly what he later learned from his wife, her colleagues and his own research. The report in front of four senior managers presented the most promising opportunities for a safer and truly sustainable energy future.

Nakamura's invitation to Endo, to "please share your views" unleashed something Jiro had not known since high school. Even then, he had only ever been a witness, not a target.

What he experienced was a merciless exercise of being put in his place. He had presumed to venture into territory that was not his. Beyond his academic training. Beyond even his mandate to identify promising technologies and possible risks to the company portfolio. By questioning the established nuclear orthodoxy, he had questioned the economic and geo-political security of the state itself.

Endo had the role of *really* bad cop. Something the Atomic Guru apparently excelled at—deputy headmaster, given the cane so the headmaster could keep his hands clean. The headmaster, of course, would deliver the lecture.

Nakamura's closing words were both admonition and warning.

"Ebitsubo-san. Perhaps your report is an indication of naiveté. Perhaps you aimed to impress your superiors with a display of intellect. Perhaps spending so many years overseas has eroded your understanding of the interests of your own country. Whatever the reason, this report is not worthy of a man of your position and privilege."

Then came the stinger. "Your family has an enviable reputation in important circles. This report demeans that reputation."

Jiro absorbed all of this in complete silence. His eyes cast down, and head deeply bowed. *So it has come to family honour*, he thought, shame flooding through him, paralyzing him. He had not prepared for this.

"It is best not to mention again any of what has occurred. I will expect to see your actual report submitted by next Friday. The one and only version. It will reflect a better understanding of your place in this company, and a much greater respect for your father and brother, to whom you owe so much."

Jiro somehow found his way out to the street. He wandered onto Aoyama-dori, and then, without memory of consciously doing so, made his way to Aoyama Cemetery. He had discovered this place, an oasis in a humming city, during final exams in his second year of university. He would find himself returning often.

Jiro made his way unerringly to his favourite bench. It had been more than a decade, yet little had changed. Describing the day to Jenny that evening, over the phone from his hotel, he remembered only the cherry blossoms and warm afternoon sun. This, and the decision which came to him. Clear and strong.

He would begin a new chapter in his life. A chapter he would author himself. Co-author, if she was willing to take the leap with him.

Pursuing Truth

2 January, 2009 9:30 AM
To: Prof. Sagan Cleveland
cc. president@pennstate.edu.org; paul.calwell@pennstate.edu.org
Request for complete data

Dear Prof. Cleveland,

The Climate Truth Project was founded to ensure any papers published on topics related to climate change receive rigorous scrutiny. We believe the public interest is best served when taxpayers have full confidence in the accuracy of work done at universities receiving public funding, and/or with project funding from a federal agency or science body.

We found especially interesting your recent paper on rates of methane accumulation and decomposition in the upper atmosphere. In order to subject this paper to appropriate review, we kindly ask that you provide the supporting documentation listed in the attachment.

We consider a prompt and thorough response essential to maintaining the integrity of research in America. We recognize this is a substantial request, so we are granting you 30 days to comply.

Best regards,
Stephen McMullin
Principal researcher, Climate Truth Project

Oh Christ, Sagan cursed as he re-read the email on his office computer. *It's my turn.* He'd heard about these fishing requests. Several senior colleagues had received them last year. *What a waste. I have courses to teach, grad students to supervise, and my chapter in the IPCC report needs rewriting now that comments have come in from the other working group members. Now this!*

He would not succumb to their blackmail. He knew what would come next. More intimidating emails. Threats to go public with accusations of "publicly-funded researcher hides important data." Still, he had no time.

Dear Mr. McMullin, he typed,

I know a fishing expedition when I see one. I also know your goal is not to defend research, but to slow it down. More to the point, to spread doubt about the accuracy of climate research and question the character of academics like me by finding minor and statistically irrelevant data deviations and accounting errors of a dollar or two in a budget of hundreds of thousands.

Below you will find responses to those questions I can answer without bringing to a complete halt my academic commitments and responsibilities to other research teams and international studies.

- Minutes of all project meetings...; **Detailed minutes are not taken at such meetings**
- All email correspondence between the co-authors...; **This is private**
- All raw data recorded from any earth-based and non-earth-based device; **How big a hard drive do you plan to provide?**
- All calculations performed, with a rationale...; **I threw away that napkin.**
- All draft versions of the paper...; **A draft is a draft. It is scientists thinking aloud.**

- The final version submitted to the scientific journal *Nature - Climate*; **Attached**
- Comments from peer reviewers and changes requested; **Attached**
- A complete accounting of the project's finances...; **Ask the university finance office.**
- The amount of any financial benefits that may have accrued to you and your co-authors... **None, beyond my base salary.**

Best regards,
Sagan Cleveland, PhD

To copy the president, or not to copy the president? He opted not to.

Thirty days later, with the email finally out of his mind, Sagan found a registered package waiting for him at the mailroom.

"Who's sending me gifts?" he joked to the grad student next to him. Signing the form, and sliding it into the tray of the departmental secretary, he went to open the package. The Climate Truth Project.

"Not again!" he groaned.

"Problem?" asked the student.

"The fishing trawlers have their hooks in *me* now."

"That's like the third this month," the student remarked. "The new world of academic freedom, where science is politics!"

What's this?" Sagan said, as he tore off the packaging. "A freakin' hard drive! Somebody has a sense of humour. A twisted one."

No humour could be found in the accompanying letter.

Dear Mr. Cleveland,

Here is the hard drive you requested. We ask that you return it by registered courier within no more than 7 days. Should you fail to provide *the requested information, you alone will be responsible for the consequences. Your president has been informed of your reluctance. He will soon be contacted by several highly respected alumni and major donors to the university.*

Respectfully,
Roger Abrahams
President, Climate Truth Project

Well, that ruins my week. He entered his office to find a note slipped under the door. *Dean's letterhead.*

"Sagan, You and I are off to meet with the president. Yes, this sucks!"

The meeting with the president was somewhat reassuring. But only somewhat.

"Intimidation!" he fumed as soon as Sagan and the dean were seated in his office. "This runs against all our efforts to shield scientific research from political pressure. And we *will* defend ourselves. We have engaged a law firm and a lobbyist in Washington, DC to develop a strategy to prevent such tactics being used in the future.

"But...in the meantime, we've been advised to provide the requested information, to the best of our ability and without breaching confidentiality. Sorry gents. I've assigned someone to get the financial stuff, and our IT office will help you pull the emails and any other documents from the university system. That should take some of the load from you, Sagan."

The president looked at Sagan directly. "Your work is important. To the university and the public. I won't allow it to be derailed." His eyes and tone supported his words.

Working well into the night, every night, Sagan was able to pull together most of what had been requested—*demanded!*—without neglecting his other commitments.

"If you don't count eating, sleeping, getting exercise or even daylight, we're still winning!" he said sarcastically to the dean, as they met to draft a cover letter. The table moved each time Sagan's jiggling thigh made contact.

"Keep it short and professional," the dean advised.

"Must—resist—temptation!" Sagan quipped. They shared a laugh, releasing some of the tension they had been living with.

"It has to stop," said the Dean, who had seen a half dozen such demands. "But for now, go home. Get out on your bike this weekend. You're looking kind of grey."

"I'll be fine," said Sagan, rubbing his bloodshot eyes. "Just tired." He gave his head a shake as he stood up, hoping to banish the hum.

Closing the door to his apartment, Sagan made his way into the kitchen to see what might remain in the freezer. *Oh god, the dishes. What a mess.* In addition to the hum, now he was short of breath. He undid several buttons on his shirt.

A light was flashing on his answering machine. *How long since I checked that?*

Beep. "Hey Sagan, give me a call. Free for a bite at my place after your Wednesday night workout?" *Missed that one. I'll have to make it up.*

Beep. "Well, handsome, if I was the jealous type, I'd be thinking there was another man. No calls. Not there when I stopped by after Thursday men's group. Everything OK? I'm pretty sure you aren't travelling."

Beep. "Sagan. It's Isong—again! Are you alright? It's Friday morning and I was checking if we were still on for the theatre tonight. You know my weekend's full, so I was hoping to spend some, ahem, quality time, with you."

Shit, shit, shit. If he called immediately, they might still make it. He could grab a bite on the way. *Nothing since breakfast.* The hum grew louder.

Beep. "Sagan Cleveland!" said a growling voice. Slowly, pronouncing each syllable as if it were poison. "Mr. Showbiz has an unlisted number. Well, we know how to find you if we want to. Not that we want to be anywhere near you and your kind of faggot scum. Drop the TV show. Stay away from kids. We don't want you queers poisoning our children with your gay lifestyle. It's bad enough you brainwashing them with evolutionist propaganda. Got my drift? Consider this a warning, you sodomist!"

Beep. "End of messages. To delete—" Sagan yanked the power chord from the socket as the fog crept in. *Aw no, I don't have time for this.*

He pulled his cellphone from his briefcase. Battery nearly dead. *Four messages from Isong here too. No wonder he's worried. Please pick up, please, please.*

"Sagan? What on earth is going on? We're going to be—"

"Stop Isong! Get over here, now. I need—" He collapsed to the floor with an audible thud.

Punching 911 on his cell, Isong grabbed his keys and rushed out the door.

Ottawa Herald, March 15, 2009

Simone Cohen: Eco Voyager

If a German town and Danish island can generate enough energy from 'renewable' sources to earn an income on the surplus, why can't we do the same in Canada? Or could we? *The Herald's* Simone Cohen — '2008 Media Canada Feature Writer of the Year' — is visiting pioneering "renewable communities' to find out. Over the next six weeks, the Herald will share her stories.

Re-energized: Lessons on power from a small town in Germany

Coal is clean. Nuclear is a climate solution. Oil sands are the engine of prosperity, and any harm from drilling for gas is minimal. Listening to recent remarks by politicians and big energy CEOs, you would think conventional energy risks have magically vanished. You might also think conservation, efficiency and renewable sources have been tried and found wanting, leaving us no option but the status quo.

But if this reincarnation of the grey doesn't sit right with you, I'd recommend a day in a little town in Germany. One entirely powered by renewable energy. Actually, 130 percent. All energy requirements are generated from locally-owned renewable sources, and the 30 percent surplus is sold to the national grid.

Freiamt is a pretty little town of 4,300 people—more a cluster of villages—in the Black Forest north of Freiburg. It's a bucolic region with a rural conservatism and an independent streak.

The local economy is dominated by farming and tourism. For the good burghers, matters of 'the environment' come down to one question: How to protect the soil, water, forest and natural beauty, while harnessing them for local benefit?

This explains why Freiamt is tackling its energy needs in a way that accents self-reliance, resilience and joint problem-solving. For the last five years, it has been pursuing energy self-sufficiency. Though the strategy is still young, it is clearly working; in a way that defies conventional beliefs that energy security resides in big generating stations, big energy companies and big investment.

Frieamt generates so much power from its small-scale renewables that it is turning a "profit". It did so by adding four wind turbines and 800 rooftop photovoltaic (PV) systems to its existing small-scale hydro and biomass installations. It now generates 13 million kilowatt hours of power each year. Since it only consumes 10 locally, the surplus is sold, generating income.

The Freiamt story is as much about 'power' as energy. Although much of the technical expertise and all the equipment comes from elsewhere, the citizens were adamant that they wanted to own their future. The turbines are jointly owned, as are solar projects on buildings such as a soccer clubhouse. Other solar arrays on homes, barns and garages are privately owned.

Biogas digesters have been built on several farm properties in a "co-op" arrangement whereby a group of citizens invest together, spreading the risk and sharing the revenue. In addition to earning a return, these biogas systems offer a solution to farm waste that can pollute water and emit methane.

Several ingredients are critical to success. First is citizen support. The buy-in of individuals came when they were convinced the financial return made it a safe investment, and the presence of wind turbines and solar arrays would not cause significant visual or noise pollution. In the words of a local farmer, "if the wind turbines are yours, they're beautiful, if they are somebody else's from far away, they're ugly!"

Underpinning the financial case is a federal law that guarantees suppliers of renewable energy at any scale get a premium rate for the electricity they feed into the national grid. This provides security and certainty and makes lending interesting for banks. As a result, tens of thousands of Germans and dozens of towns, co-ops and companies have installed such systems.

Is Freiamt's success only possible because of the 'feed-in-tariff', which some view as a subsidy? At this time, yes. That's a political choice supported by the German voter—to 'level the playing field'. Dirtier sources such as coal have received state support for decades, while creating a burden of pollution and waste.

Germany wants to improve energy autonomy and stimulate a new industry, and it is working. So much so that others are following their lead: Spain, France, and even Ontario now.

Freiamt offers a glimpse of what real power looks like.

Letters

Eco Voyaging, without the greenhouse gases

Thanks for the uplifting "Eco Voyager" series. I get depressed by all the sky-is-falling news. Even if much is true, there is so much good out there in the world. I wish the media would focus more on that. I may never get to see the places described in this series, but the stories and photos make me feel like I have. Besides, imagine the emissions if we were all eco voyagers!

Jan Richardson
Perth, Ontario

Reality check

The writer needs a reality check. Her examples are from old cities in Europe. They are dense. The taxes on cars and fuel are crazy high. Of course people use transit and cycle. But Canadian cities are sprawling, and many of us like it this way. It's instructive to see how social engineering works in Europe, but count me out of being forced to live that way.

Xavier Richter
Brandon, Manitoba

Reader Comments

User name: Right_proud
Your bike obsession gives me saddle sores. Hope you've got them too!

Simone Cohen: Eco Voyager
Earth Day Special, April 22, 2009

Marketing green:
Selling a better future with the present

It's Earth Day. Time for the ritual guilt fest. Right? Wrong! Convincing people to sacrifice—to live with less for the sake of the environment—does not generally work, because it runs counter to human nature.

Most of us crave comfort, convenience and choice. What does work—as every advertising exec knows—is showing people that they can have better. They deserve better!

It's an appeal to emotion: getting you to feel; to want.

Everyone wants a healthy planet. The challenge is selling the steps that will get us there. We want clean air and safe food. We want to keep polar bears from drowning. But do we want to lose our jobs to make it possible? Do we want to spend the winter in bulky sweaters, gathered around a single heater? Do we want to live without access to a car?

Of course not. Nor should we, and nor would we. But that's not the impression many have. Whether by poor communication from green proponents, or outright deception from merchants of the status quo, a myth has grown around what a more sustainable lifestyle, a "greener" society, might look like. It equates green with deprivation.

The challenge of marketing sustainable living is to boldly counter that myth, with the offer of a colourful, vibrant, rewarding alternative. With a vision of communities that are safe, healthy, full of human interaction, art and energy. With a picture of an economy that delivers efficient, reliable products and services, and good jobs that don't pollute.

This should not be hard to sell, because it's fundamentally true. But it will be if it's not done with a twinkle in the eye.

This "life-style designed for permanence," in the words of E.F. Schumacher, must also be designed to benefit more than the lucky few of today. Any path that continues to massively favour a fortunate minority (that's us, dear reader) quite simply cannot last. Ask the Romans.

This idea of fairness we must also learn to sell!

Can we do it without exaggerating and manipulating? Can we portray a sustainable future without relying on futuristic images of what the world *might* look like? Yes. To sell the possible, we can use the actual. Everything we need exists somewhere already.

In *The Geography of Hope*, Chris Turner introduces us to people that make the world's most sustainable villages and buildings and farms and companies function. From his and similarly-inspired books, articles, websites and films, it is no great leap to conclude that human society already has the tools we need to build a lifestyle of permanence.

- Green roofs provide the protection of a traditional roof, but the plants they hold help cool the building and surroundings, while retaining and cleaning water and adding biodiversity.
- Energy-plus houses generate more energy than they consume, and are comfortable to live in.
- Urban agriculture is back in style. People are re-learning how to grow a portion of their food on balconies, allotment plots or vacant land.
- The (re)discovery list goes on: the clothesline; the bicycle as a tool for going places and getting fit; the farmers' market as a source of local produce and interaction; shutters, awnings and fans as elementary forms of home cooling.

There is no one-size-fits-all answer. Each idea must be understood and tailored. What does work everywhere, though, is "solution banking," where people share what they have done.

If you were to map the places where you can find the most solutions in practice, it would inevitably lead you to Europe.

- To the German city of Freiburg to see "smart growth" in action, with solar panels galore.
- To the Swedish cities of Stockholm and Malmo—to see communities that tackle energy use, transportation, waste reduction, water use and social challenges holistically.

- To France to watch people flocking back to rail. Domestic flights are often less quick or comfortable than downtown-to-downtown trains. In dozens of cities, 'tramway' systems have been built or upgraded.

It is harmful to think North Americans cannot do as well. We are developing plenty of our own ideas. But the countries of Northern Europe have been leaders on a broader level for some time now. Germany, the Netherlands, Sweden and Denmark have been willing to adopt strong laws and use policy and fiscal tools to shift individual, collective and corporate practices.

But Europe is still full of bad habits—highways are clogged with (diesel!) trucks and cars, the EU subsidizes wasteful fishing and farming practices, and then there's Italy's garbage mess.

The geography of hope is being built on more than just hope. It is also one of inspiration and confirmation. Promoting greener practices and places can lead us to dream of better, knowing it's achievable.

Reader Comments

User name: Right_proud
Crazy Cohen's going to make us all Europeans, riding bikes and living in tiny apartments! How much does she get paid for her fancy vacation, spewing green hoax gases! Do us a favour and stay home.

Working Holiday

Pressing send, Simone sat back in her hotel room chair and rubbed her eyes as the final article and photos winged their way across the Atlantic. *If it's Tuesday, this must be Samso, Denmark.* She had seen six countries, five airports, fifteen train stations, 11 cheap hotels and three B&Bs. She'd even 'couch-surfed'. Over 30 site visits and interviews had gone into producing eight feature articles. She had shot hundreds of photos, then spent hours selecting the 20 best. She had even shot video.

Increasingly, writers were expected to do it all. *Squeezing as much as they can out of us, while questioning every expense.* Simone had seen two waves of staff cuts, and more were rumoured. *Don't complain if you want your job.*

Her mother was always telling her she worked too hard. But now, two weeks of holiday awaited her.

"I am out of the office until May 15, 2009," she wrote, "and will not be checking email or voice mail." She smiled and stretched her arms behind her head. As she went to shut down the computer, she recalled one more task. A critical one.

"Sorry for doing this last minute, guys. Here are the tour specifics. Meet at Amsterdam's Eastern Docklands at 1 p.m. on Saturday. Here's a <u>map</u>. Bikes are taken care of, as well as the guided excursion fee. It's on my credit card. We'll work it out later. Hope your flights go well. If anyone is delayed, you'll have to rent another bike and chase down the barge!" She smiled at the image.

She and Sagan had taken several bike holidays together over the years. This would be different. All four of them, plus children, spending a leisurely week together. It had been way too long. She was keen to see Jenny and Jiro and meet the girls, but she especially needed to see Sagan.

He was doing fine, he had assured her. Recovered, and looking forward to fresh air and exercise. His doctor had cleared him. The medication was doing its job. Side effects were minimal, Isong confirmed. But she needed to see him. And touch him.

She'd been told exercise was one of the best prescriptions for depression. For many mental health issues. Still, she worried this might be too much.

Sometimes, it's Tough

Yuki and Anna laughed as they chanted the Spanish children's song for the third time that day. With her exaggerated gestures and expressive voice, the kindergarten teacher from Madrid was the centre of the girls' world.

Many of the adults on the rear deck of the *Flower of Delft* smiled at the scene as they enjoyed a cold drink at the end of a day of touring. Their fourth, and the longest of the trip, they'd been assured.

"Doesn't that poor woman want to spend her holiday doing something else?" Jenny said, marvelling at Violetta's connection with the twins.

They were 24 on the barge, a refitted canal boat that functioned as hotel and restaurant for tourists who wanted to experience the Netherlands by bicycle. Simone had proposed this 'bike and barge' holiday. "It's a great way to take a group vacation," her parents had raved following their own tour with friends a year earlier.

Choose your route, week, and style of bicycle, then let the operator handle the rest. Each day, the clients—a random party from across the globe—would cycle anywhere from 40-60 kilometres. With plenty of stops for snacks, lunch, and photos.

The day began with a bell announcing breakfast. Hans, their guide, would present the itinerary and confirm if anyone was taking a day off and staying on the boat. He would then move the required bikes onto shore, while everyone prepared a brown bag lunch from the assortment of sliced meats, cheese, bread, fruit—and chocolate bars. The girls had been surprised when Jiro let them choose two each. A little bribe to get another hour of effort from a tired child.

Jiro, no more a cyclist now than at Cambridge, would not be with them. But he wanted to be sure that the girls would enjoy riding, and not be too much trouble. While Jenny, Simone, Sagan and the twins were riding with the group, he could go for a long walk after the barge had docked in the next destination town. On the second day, the barge stayed in its berth, and the cycling itinerary was an out-and-back loop. Jiro seized the opportunity to take a longer trek to a cluster of historic windmills.

On the third day, the whole family stayed on the boat as it motored from Leiden to Delft, where they explored the old centre together. This gave Simone and Sagan a break from pulling the twins on the 'tag-along' bikes.

Jenny had not ridden since settling in Kuala Lumpur, other than spinning at the gym. But after a little warmup, she was able to handle the daily circuits, almost entirely on cycle paths, rural roads and—in the cities—dedicated lanes.

"Sagan and I can take the girls!" Simone had promised when she first floated the holiday idea. That was good enough for Jenny and Jiro, who might not otherwise have agreed, at least not with six-year-olds. The twins were loving it, thanks to Uncle Sagan and Aunt Simone with their songs and games.

Evenings were full of "yackity-yack," as Anna put it.

The adults began by catching up on the mundane parts of their lives. Then came Cambridge reminiscences: "Twelve years ago! Hard to believe." Gradually, they moved toward meatier subjects. It began with Jenny's remark about the limited internet service. She had wanted to send photos to the two sets of grandparents.

"Excellent!" Sagan exclaimed. "A week without trolls."

"Trolls?" Jenny was not familiar with the term.

"People who harass you online," he explained, "and send abusive emails."

"Wow," said Jenny, "I didn't know such a thing existed."

"Lucky you," said Simone, her neck pulsing. "For some—journalists, politicians, even research scientists—it's a hazard of the trade!" She looked toward Sagan.

"Especially when you work in a controversial field," he confirmed, furrowing his brow. "Like stem cell research, or climate. Do you remember that nonsense about the emails from a British researcher?"

Jenny and Jiro looked at him blankly.

"Climate-gate?" he tried.

"Oh yes," said Jiro tentatively. "Scientists manipulating data, right?"

"Not exactly," said Sagan, shaking his head. "That's what one was accused of—falsely!" There was an edge to his voice.

"But you know how it started?" He didn't wait for an answer. "There are people who are paid to pursue researchers."

"Wow!" said Jiro. "What do they want?"

"To sow doubt!" Simone couldn't help interjecting.

"Exactly," said Sagan, nodding. "Create confusion and smear the messenger."

"And they do that," said Simone, "through little tricks. Like finding cracks in the honesty of one or two scientists. Or implying researchers are making big money off the public purse."

"I wish!" laughed Sagan. "It's hard enough to get tenure. But these harassers—"

"Merchants of doubt!" Simone interjected.

"—they're the ones making big money. But they're accountable to nobody. Only their secret funders."

"Some are the exact same people, said Simone, "or PR firms, that have been sowing doubt for decades, on all kinds of science." She felt her face growing hot.

"Who pays for them?" asked Jenny.

Sagan nodded to Simone, knowing she was researching the world of 'dark money'. Looking behind the veil.

"That's complicated," said Simone, taking a deep breath. "Actually, it's simple *and* complicated. It's mostly oil, gas and coal companies, along with some big investors and the foundations of a few mega-wealthy individuals."

Jenny was scowling. "Don't people see through this?"

"Surprisingly, no. Sagan will have his own take, I'm sure. Most people know the climate is changing. It troubles them. And because it's so troubling, and serious action would require dramatic changes to our lives, or governments to force us, they choose not to know. So when the spin doctors hold conferences, put up websites and plant slick 'experts' on CNN and Fox—casting doubt on the science, and now the scientists—can you blame the average schmuck for believing the science isn't settled?"

"For *wanting* to believe it!" Sagan corrected.

"Belief plays a powerful role," agreed Simone. "Religion, too."

A squeal from one of the girls took their attention to the far side of the deck.

"Is everything OK?" Jenny called across.

"Anna's always interrupting," Yuki whined, her tone announcing tears.

"Twins!" Jenny got up. "We can't expect Violetta to entertain our daughters all evening. You guys carry on. Besides, I'm getting depressed."

Simone stood up as well. "Another cold drink?"

"I'll try the Amstel this time," Sagan replied. Simone shot him a worried look.

"Doc says I'm allowed two before my hair falls out. But thanks Mom." He grinned.

"I'll take an Orangina," said Jiro. "And some of those cookies."

Sensing this would be a rare moment alone, Jiro turned to Sagan and spoke directly. "The stress is very difficult. More than you are admitting."

"Ah well," said Sagan airily. "It goes with the territory."

"Still..." Jiro was not going to let him off. "Simone says you get very personal attacks. That is hard, even for a joker. I have had my own issues, and without Jenny I don't know how I would have made it. But you have no such partner—."

"Actually—" Sagan began.

"One Amstel, one Orangina and a heaping plate of *spekulaas*. And some *stroopwaffels*!" Simone announced, attempting the Dutch pronunciation.

"Thanks dahling," Sagan replied softly.

Jiro placed a finger to his lips. Unsure what he meant, Simone sat down quietly.

"You were saying," Jiro prompted, "about support."

"Jiro," Sagan declared loudly, "I've found religion!"

His friends laughed. Jiro out of disbelief and Simone at the choice of words.

"That sounds like something I'd joke about," Sagan admitted. "But I've found a church, a community really, and it's her fault!" His thumb indicated Simone, who nodded confirmation.

"A few years ago, when I was dealing with some things, quite depressed actually, struggling with some family issues, Simone suggested I check out my local Unitarian church. I barely knew anything about the UUs."

Jiro shrugged his shoulders.

"Unitarian Universalism has been around for ages," Sagan said. "It was born out of a Christian tradition, but questioned a number of aspects. I'm no theologian, and frankly, that isn't what interests me. Some say we're the 'un-church.' Others from more dogmatic religions say it as well. But less kindly, if you get my drift."

Jiro nodded. He'd encountered the fundamentalist shift in Islamic Malaysia, and in his brother's branch of Shinto-Buddhism.

"Unitarians support one another in seeking our own spiritual calling. Finding the holy within ourselves. Building a personal relationship with a higher spirit. Nature, even."

"Sagan's telling stories?" Jenny whispered to Simone. She had slipped back into her seat, holding a plate of cookies. Her face fell when she spotted the first, now half-empty.

Sagan paused. "Never too many *spekulaas*," he reassured Jenny. "None will go to waste. Just to *the* waist!" He pointed so nobody would miss his pun.

"OK, Sagan, carry on," said Jiro. "We've only got a few days. Time for everyone to share, or we'll wish we had." Eyebrows raised, Simone glanced toward Sagan.

"Spoken like a man who had an epiphany," said Sagan. With a wink at Jiro, he resumed where he'd left off. "I found a home. For the first time I'm exploring *me*. Why I care so much about science: how the natural world works, and why we humans should care. Were we put here to dominate, or even to manage the natural world? Are we so deeply connected that any harm to it is harming ourselves? I look at the rate of suicide in some places, the depression in professions like mine, and wonder if people can be healthy amid all the abuse? Between humans, and against nature. "

With the others silent, he continued. "Any psychologist—which I'm not—says it takes energy to ignore what's obvious. It takes massive effort to buy into a lie."

He looked at each of them slowly, then smiled. "Sorry for the lecture!"

Jiro shook his head. "No, no, it was well said."

Jenny nodded. "We've had similar conversations, Jiro and I. We wonder if we're alone, or do others feel this way?"

"More than public discourse reflects, I think," said Simone. "I interview so many people who are working to do the right thing in their personal lives, but feel out of sync with the world around them, having to check their feelings at the door when they go to work or out in public; to ignore their inner compass. It makes me think of critical moments in history. When we could have acted to stop something or save someone, but didn't. You know, like slavery, the rise of Hitler, various genocides—"

The dinner bell rang, cutting Simone off. Jiro hopped up to fetch the girls, who Jenny had allowed to watch a video in the cabin of a French family.

* * *

Though they had made a point of mingling with others at meal times, this night they stayed together at a smaller table. Once everyone was served, Sagan called for silence. "I have an announcement," he said, his serious expression prompting uneasy glances around the table. Everyone went silent.

"I'm getting married!" he declared, his eyes widening.

"Sorry," said a puzzled Jiro, putting down his fork.

"Who's the lucky man?" asked Jenny.

"Man?" wondered Anna, looking to her parents.

"We'll explain later," Jiro said quietly.

"Congratulations to you and Isong!" Simone exclaimed.

"Who's Isong?" asked Jenny, Jiro, Yuki and Anna simultaneously.

Sagan recounted how he'd met Isong—an intern minister from Philadelphia—at a regional church retreat several years earlier. When the position of full-time minister came open at Sagan's church, he encouraged Isong to apply. What began as friendship had turned into something richer, he explained, nervously fingering the gold medallion he wore on a chain. A gift from Isong, Simone guessed. She had never seen him like this.

"He supported me through some difficult times," he explained quietly. "We became very close, and then, well... He's the love of my life, and he claims I'm the guy for him. Why would I doubt a minister?" They laughed.

"Marriage seems the obvious next step, now that it's legal. In some states."

"I hope you'll live a long and happy life together," said Jenny, her eyes watering. Grinning, Jiro nodded agreement.

"When is your wedding?" wondered Yuki.

"Can we come?" her sister asked before Sagan could reply.

"We'd love to have you," began Sagan, "but we've decided on something very small. We still have to confirm if we can marry in Pennsylvania. If not, another state. You two can make us a nice *big* card," he said, spreading his arms. The girls immediately began discussing what they would draw.

"Now that's settled," said Jiro, "I have one question. Does Isong like Queen?"

"We had to set some ground rules from the outset," said Sagan. "He tolerates Freddie, and I put up with Sting!"

"Alas, Isong doesn't cycle," Simone lamented. "On the bright side, though, he's fine with the two of us carrying on with our getaways."

"That's true," said Sagan. "Speaking of which, I did invite him to join us this week, but he declined. Getting away would have been tough. Most of all, he knew how important it was for me to have time with you."

"Sounds like quite a guy," Jenny remarked.

"Oh, he is," Simone confirmed. "Sagan's a lucky man."

"Sagan's quite a guy, himself, let's remember. said Jiro.

Sagan bowed his head, acknowledging the compliment. "I'll be calling you two for tips about give-and-take."

Glancing at her husband, Jenny spoke for the couple. "We can't claim to be experts. Any couple who pretends marriage is not constant work is lying. But Jiro and I occasionally refer to some wisdom we once heard." She paused to recall the words.

"If you treat your partner as if they are the best and last you will ever have, then there's a good chance they will be."

"That's good!" Simone exclaimed.

After dinner they took a stroll through the narrow streets of old Delft. Though the twins had claimed they were tired, Simone and Sagan soon had them dashing about playing hide-and-seek among the large trees and deep doorways. Jiro and Jenny strolled hand in hand in silence.

Back from the walk, Simone and Sagan prepared tea in the lounge. Jiro would be up after putting the exhausted girls to bed, but not Jenny. It was her turn to stay with them. Company policy required that young children never be unattended.

"All is good?" Simone asked Jiro as he took a seat beside them.

"All is excellent."

"They're the sweetest kids," Sagan said. Simone detected a note of envy.

"When they're not squabbling," Jiro noted.

"My brother and I fought constantly," said Sagan. "Still do. Though we don't see much of each other.

"Hey," said Jiro suddenly. "There's something you still haven't shared, Sagan."

"Mmm?"

"When you're not fending off trolls, what are you actually researching?"

"Methane release and its impact on the upper atmosphere."

"How does that differ from 10 years ago?"

"Not much. But the speed of change is phenomenal. The last two summers have been mind-blowing. The rate of thaw... and the weather is getting freaky. They're seeing more snow and heavy rain in places that were cold and dry in winter, and mostly mild and dry in summer. Coastlines are receding. It's crazy. It's not a theory anymore. We don't need fancy modelling, other than to predict the speed of acceleration."

"So how do deniers get away with their lies?" Jiro asked.

"I ask myself that often, and I think I know the answer. First, when it comes to Arctic impacts, that's not real to most people. It's far away. Not my problem. But at its heart, public understanding of science is not only poor, it's getting worse. So when somebody throws out red herring explanations, or presents a tiny portion of a bigger graph, and says 'see, it's not really getting warmer,' or use decoy arguments like the climate is always changing' or 'weren't they predicting an ice age in the '70s?' most people lack the basics to skeptically assess this."

"And when people doubt, they opt for inaction," Simone added with resignation.

"Your TV shows—that's your way to improve science literacy?" Jiro suggested.

"And have fun. If I wasn't doing science, I'd be doing stand-up comedy."

Jiro shook his head. "How do you find the time?"

Sagan laughed. "Must be my good clean living."

"No, seriously. You must have some tricks to share."

"Tricks, Jiro? No. I try to do just one thing at a time. Set a time to do a task, then move to the next. It's getting harder to stay focused though. Constantly being texted and emailed." Sagan shook his head. "And don't get me started on Facebook."

"Social media can be a black hole," Simone growled. "Nasty, too. You can't just brush that stuff away." She pinned Sagan with a stare.

He looked away before responding. "Simone's right. I can kid myself everything's fine. Pretend I'm Superman." They waited for him to elaborate.

"I have what some people call manic depression. I'm bipolar. When I'm up, I'm really up. And most of the time, I am. But then when I'm down—boom!" Sagan smacked the table, startling everyone in the lounge.

"I can go quite a few years without crashes," he continued more quietly, his eyes glazing over. "If I'm careful, and lucky. When it comes, though, I need to catch it, or hope somebody catches me. I used to think it was just a mood thing. That I could pull myself out with sheer willpower. I certainly wasn't going to *tell* people."

He turned to face Jiro. "Society says they understand now. But few people do. Mental illness makes them uncomfortable. So, yeah, thanks Simone, for reminding me."

He turned to face her. "Really," he added softly.

"You're welcome," she whispered, reaching across the table to touch his arm.

"Hey, thank goodness for university health care! We can't all be Canadian," Sagan said, to lighten the mood.

"Speaking of the university, what do they think of your shows?" Jiro asked. "Star professor!"

"Sure," Sagan acknowledged, "but stardom has its costs: people thinking I'm not a real scientist, or resenting the attention."

"Like your namesake," said Simone. "Carl Sagan worked hard to promote understanding, but took major flak for selling out!" Sagan nodded.

"I was thinking recently about that," said Simone. "How people seem content to let almost anybody take the holy scriptures and dumb them down to the point where they're outright wrong, or way too literal, then go out on a stage, or national TV and call themselves a preacher. Yet they dump on a popular scientist."

"Speaking of religion," said Jiro, "You were saying something earlier about the role of churches in climate denial. What did you mean, Simone?"

"Right," she began. "You see, there's an odd alliance between a certain kind of Christian, and the deniers we were talking about. They share a desire to do as little as possible, or at least to delay action, but for different reasons. The religious motive, at its extreme, is about bringing on the apocalypse. There are people, sects even—"

"That's crazy!" exclaimed Jiro, sitting up in his chair.

Simone nodded slowly. "To most people. But if you're someone who can't wait for our mixed up, Satan-worshipping world to come to an end, so the Second Coming—"

"Encourage a climate catastrophe?" Jiro's eyes bulged. "So Christ will return?!"

"Like I said, it's complicated. The alliance at least. But for those who want to squeeze 20 more years of profits out of their coal mines, any fanatical opponent of action is a convenient ally."

"Are there a lot of them?"

"It's hard to say. There's the broader evangelical group whose skepticism about climate change—whether it's happening, or whether humans are a cause—is anchored in a belief that it's God's plan. That means everything from ecological collapse to natural disasters should simply be allowed to run their course. It's fatalism. Though you can dress it up as 'faith' if you want."

Jiro had relaxed a little. This made sense on some level.

"You can walk into some American churches and hear the preacher denounce climate science as part of a diabolical conspiracy." Simone's eyes narrowed. "I have. End Timers, some call them. There's a Jewish angle too, but, well, that's too complicated to explain after a long day."

Jiro turned to Sagan, dumbfounded. "Have you encountered these people?"

"Sure," Sagan snorted. "Some troll me. There's the irony, Jiro. People who accuse scientists and tree-huggers of using scare tactics to raise money, are doing just that. Only they're better at it."

Jiro was trying to make sense of what he was hearing. "Well Saga—and Simone—I respect your courage!"

"Thanks JJ," said Sagan. "Jiro!"

"Yes, thanks," echoed Simone. "We're never alone, and that helps."

When she and Jiro rose to head for bed, she noticed Sagan had not moved.

"Coming?" she asked.

"Soon," he said. "I need a moment alone to clear my head."

"You OK?" she said gently.

"I'll be fine. I like to do a meditative walk after an emotional day."

She placed her hands on his shoulders and gave them a squeeze. "G'night."

* * *

"A treat from the cook," Simone announced to Jenny and Sagan, stepping onto the rear deck with four desserts. They were settled at a table watching the long midsummer day draw to a close. It looked to Simone as if nothing could move them. That day's ride—their second last—had been the longest.

"One each!" she scolded Sagan. "You're not the only one burning calories."

"I can't have Jiro's?" he said innocently, loosening his grip on the fourth bowl.

"No," Jenny confirmed. "He'll join us as soon as the girls are settled in bed." Sagan looked perplexed, recalling the rules.

"Relax," said Jenny. "He picked up a child monitor here in Haarlem. We'll hear if anything is wrong. And they can call out to us."

"Spying on your kids!" Sagan needled, wagging a finger. "It's come to that"

"Just don't tell the crew," said Jenny.

"Jiro and Jenny turned Bonnie and Clyde!" he chuckled.

"First they escape their corporate shackles," Simone said, playing along, "and now they're breaking all the rules."

"Mid-career renegades," Jenny declared with a smile.

"*Mid-career renegades!*" echoed Jiro as he appeared carrying four full bowls. "Good company name. I wish we'd thought of that!"

"Oops!" he said, spotting the remains of the first round of desserts.

"Shh!" whispered Sagan, a finger in front of his lips. "Nobody needs to know." Jenny and Jiro looked around furtively.

"Look at them," chided Sagan. "Feeling guilty already."

"Sheepish renegades?" Simone proposed, earning laughter from her targets.

"Quick. Destroy the evidence!" ordered Jiro. Giggles broke out in waves as they raced to empty their bowls.

First to finish and regain composure, Sagan broached the topic that had been skirted all week. "OK, renegades. You guys have done something drastic. Time to confess."

"Please," added Simone.

"Confess, *please*," said Sagan, shaking his head. "Freakin' Canadians!"

Jenny turned to her husband. "Want to go first?"

"No way!" Simone scolded. "You've been way too quiet, Jenny."

"Alright," she consented. "I'll give my version, but it started with him."

"Not really," said Jiro. "I just triggered something we'd both been moving toward."

"Alright," Jenny began a second time. "As you know, I went to work for MalayGas." Simone and Sagan nodded. "I found a way for my research on batteries to be of value to them, like you suggested, powering equipment in remote locations. Though too often I was asked to design standard, diesel off-grid systems."

Simone lowered her dessert bowl quietly.

"I voiced my frustration, but to little effect. When I got pregnant, the company decided I should resign, or shift to another project. While on maternity leave, I decided to write a proposal that would give me a chance to grow, and be of more value."

"Drumroll, please," said Sagan. Jenny smiled patiently, and continued.

"I proposed that MalayGas fund research on turning our abundant natural gas into a power source with reduced emissions."

"Hydrogen!" Sagan blurted. "Reforming natural gas to create hydrogen?"

Jenny gave him an admiring nod.

"There had been a lot of talk about the 'hydrogen economy.' Are you familiar with that?" She glanced at Simone, who tilted her head.

"Quick review," said Jenny. "Hydrogen has been held out as a holy grail of storage. You can create it in many ways. From fossil fuels—natural gas being the cleanest—and from electricity, ideally generated by renewable sources. This has the advantage of mass storage, making 'intermittent' renewables more viable; as part of a system where electricity will be there when you need it."

"And in cars," Simone noted.

"Yes. Hydrogen can be a portable fuel source which, when used to power a fuel cell, would propel a car, a bus—even a boat—with no emissions. It could replace the stinky diesel on a barge like this."

"Amazing, isn't it?" said Jiro.

"If," continued Jenny, "the system can be produced at sufficient scale to be cost-effective. But as long as you're competing with cheap, dirty fuels, nobody has an incentive to switch." Simone noted how Jenny's brow had furrowed. "Governments need to tax pollution from fossil fuels, or stop offering the massive subsidies they do, or support cleaner alternatives like hydrogen with fuel cells."

"How was your proposal received?" asked Sagan.

"It wasn't an easy sell. But luck was on my side. Malaysia got bad publicity around that time regarding air pollution. The government wanted to show leadership."

"And there she was," said Jiro.

Jenny smiled. "Don't call us, we'll call you," became "When can you start, Dr. Fung? Now here we are, about to announce a portable hydrogen fuel cell product that can be used in buildings or large vehicles."

"Whoa!" Simone said, leaning forward. "You skipped a whole step!"

"Did I?"

"Of course. From starting a project at MalayGas to starting your own company!"

"Sorry about that!" Jenny shook her head. "I got caught up in the technology. The project was making progress, but we had to develop a new fuel cell system so as not to infringe on patents. That's not easy. We had a prototype, but the government was growing impatient."

"They were becoming more interested in biofuels," Jiro interjected. "Palm oil."

Jenny nodded confirmation. "Which left MalayGas with a partially developed system, and several patents that had not seen a return. With a skeleton staff and budget, I was given six months to be production-ready, or have the project shut down."

"Brutal!" said Simone.

"It was. But then Jiro made his leap." Jenny gestured to her husband.

"Cue the big guy!" Sagan said with a dramatic sweep of the arm.

"Oh my," Jiro said, looking at his watch, "nearly 11 p.m. I should see if the monitor is working."

"Not so fast," said Sagan, grabbing Jiro's other wrist. "We've been building up to you. 'Jiro escapes from the clutches of corporate mind control'. If we fall in a canal tomorrow, we'll never hear your story. I'm good until midnight. You guys?"

"I'm in," said Simone, sitting up in her chair.

"Another half hour," said Jenny, yawning.

"You guys know about my frustration," Jiro began, placing his hands on the table in front of him, "so let me tell you a story about names."

"Japanese boys are often given names of two types. One is so literal it's hard to believe it has survived in modern times. Basically, it translates as 'number one' and 'number two.' With today's low birth rate, it is rare to get to three. The second is a name with a character trait. Things that imply power, or skill, or honesty. For girls, they are traits such as 'delicate' or 'compassionate', or they are nature-based. My parents followed this tradition, which is how my brother became Katsuo—meaning manly and self-confident—whereas I was named Jiro, which means quite simply, 'number two son.'

"Throughout my childhood, I was 'number two', with 'powerful leader' for a brother. Katsuo owned his name, and I owned mine."

Simone shuddered. Sagan gazed intently at his friend.

"In my family, it was clear where I belonged." Jiro's voice had lowered. Anyone passing would have wondered what deep secrets were being shared.

"So!" he declared, startling everyone, "When I found myself on my bench in Aoyama Cemetery, psyching myself up to tell my family of my reprimand, something snapped."

Jenny, knowing what was coming, sat up with a smile, and waited.

"I was not going to be number two for anybody again. I would do something, anything, where I could make my own plans. Where I could dream, even!"

Jiro paused, looking straight ahead. Proudly. Then, despite himself, he turned to his friends for affirmation. He received none. Not in words. This was a personal decision. Not a group one. Not even a family one. Yet Jenny was there beside him, as she had been from the beginning. She reached out and placed a hand on one of his.

Simone broke the silence. "That must have been a powerful feeling for you, Jiro."

He nodded confirmation, followed by another glance around the table. Sagan, who had been silent, reached across and placed a hand on top of Jenny's, his fingers making contact with Jiro's. Silently, Simone used two hands to complete the pile.

The four were now alone on the deck, apart from the first mate checking the barge's lines.

"You know," Jiro said, "I really do want to tell you about my plans, *our* plans. But it is late. We have our final evening." He stood and reached to help Jenny from her chair.

He was taller than they remembered.

* * *

In Amsterdam harbour, the wi-fi connection was a strong one. After her post-ride shower, Simone took her laptop to the lounge to check for personal emails. A tingle of excitement ran through her when she spotted his name. Ronald Dugas. The girlish feeling surprised her.

Simone had been seeing Ron since January. *Seeing!* She laughed to herself. *Dating. Hooking up.* Five months, but between her schedule and his, it might as well have been one.

As a wilderness expedition guide, Ron was often away. From February through April, he was out West, guiding backcountry ski excursions. In July and August, he guided canoe trips in northern Ontario and Quebec, plus an annual Yukon trip. In October and November, he guided cycling adventures in Cuba and Costa Rica. It was little wonder his marriage hadn't lasted. Or that he did not have custody of his 10-year old daughter, Jacinthe.

Ron loved Jacinthe dearly, Simone knew, and she adored him. He was an attentive father when he was around. All the more reason for Jacinthe to consider Simone a rival. After a couple of tries at joint activities, Simone had suggested they wait. In a rational moment, during one of Ron's longer absences, she had even concluded that the relationship was doomed. Yet here she was, as thrilled as a teenager at seeing his email. And photos.

"Who's the handsome man?!" exclaimed Sagan, who had somehow slipped in beside her at the table.

"A rugged adventurer!" He nudged her with his elbow. "Just what you need, Simone. Don't worry, I won't steal him. I'm engaged!" He flashed his new medallion, then laughed a big, hearty laugh.

"You couldn't steal him," said Simone. "He never stays still."

"Ooh," Sagan ribbed. "I detect hypocrisy, from the woman who can't be pinned down. Have you tried sexting?"

"Sagan!" Simone slapped him on the hand. "You've outdone yourself."

"Excellent. Today was my last chance."

"Why are you fighting?" Now it was the twins who had arrived unnoticed.

"Who's that man with the big beard?" asked Anna.

"Is he your husband?" said Yuki. "Or do you have a wife?"

"Oh dear," offered Sagan without sympathy. "You got 'splainin' to do."

Simone had held off telling her friends about Ron, not sure if it would doom an already complicated affair, or make it more real. When Jiro and Jenny joined them at the table, and with the twins busy drawing, she listed the complications: her unpredictable schedule, his long absences, and his jealous daughter. And yet... having Ron in her life provided a calming influence. Even while travelling, he took time to send emails with poetic and perceptive commentary on where he'd been and the people he'd met. His photography was remarkable. And Simone knew some great photographers.

"Ron has to be the most grounded, unflappable man I've ever met," she said.

Jenny nodded approval. "Good traits in an adventure guide."

"That's who I'd want leading *my* trip," said Jiro.

"Of course, of course. I just wish he wasn't away so much."

"On the other hand," Sagan offered, "you won't get on each other's nerves like most couples. Present company excepted," he added with a smile.

"If you want my advice," said Jenny, "take it slow and savour the good things. Jiro and I had a highly unusual relationship for years. Now look at us."

"Indeed," Simone agreed.

"Speaking of which," said Sagan, "you've left it to the final hours to tell us about your venture. Industrial tycoons in our midst."

Jiro did the talking at first. What had started as a tentative idea was now a registered 'clean tech' company, he explained, with an office, staff and revenue-earning products.

"I had the basic legal knowledge to set up the company and raise start-up capital. My years with Tokyo Industrial were frustrating, but I learned a lot and made useful contacts. Jenny has shown not only the engineering talents we know about, but a sharp mind when it comes to business plans and marketing. I assumed we'd have to get our marketing plans from a consultant, at a high price, but she seems to have a nose for clients, and ways of getting their interest."

Simone could feel the admiration in his voice. It was mutual, she knew, from her private conversations with Jenny.

"What exactly are you making?" asked Simone.

With a glance at Jiro, Jenny spoke in a voice they had never heard. "I will direct this press conference. Two questions per journalist only."

Simone and Sagan exchanged amused looks.

"NiMa Energy makes an innovative hydrogen fuel cell for buildings and large vehicles," Jenny answered. "The technology was developed by engineers now employed by NiMa. We purchased the patent and development rights. Our ultimate goal is to provide design services for renewable energy generation and storage systems. Also, to partner with shipping companies to create systems for moving freight cleanly."

"Any more questions?" said Jenny. "Dr. Cleveland?" She nodded at Sagan.

"Two questions," he said, playing along. "Is natural gas your main feedstock?"

"As I indicated, renewable is our ultimate goal. We are exploring partnerships with some Japanese and Chinese solar panel manufacturers. Not yet with wind or hydroelectric producers, but that is in our plans. Your second question?"

"Storing hydrogen is notoriously tricky. How will you address its volatility?"

"You have some insight Dr. Cleveland," she said, nodding. The best current technology uses titanium-coated tanks. It is very expensive, and supply is limited. We are negotiating with a company that I cannot name which will be a game-changer for storing and transporting hydrogen. Stay tuned for an announcement."

Jenny made a show of looking around the room for other hands, before returning to acknowledge Simone. "Ms. Cohen, one final question." Jiro and Sagan sat back and chuckled at Jenny's act.

"Hearing your ambitious plans, I really need to know when you sleep?"

Jenny took a long time considering her response. "We don't. Why do you think we needed this holiday?" At this point she burst into laughter, joined by the others.

"The face of NiMa Energy in the making," Jiro remarked proudly.

* * *

Nobody was making a move toward bed. It had taken over a decade to get together, and it might be just as long until the next occasion. Conversation wandered from Simone and Sagan's cycling holidays to family—supportive and otherwise. Revelling tourists would occasionally call out in greeting from the boardwalk, mere metres from where they were perched on the barge.

After a prolonged lull in the conversation, Sagan broke the silence.

"Jiro, my favourite nuclear sceptic."

"Mmm?"

"There's a raging nuclear debate among big names in the battle to halt climate change. A few have come out in support.

Not because they like nuclear, but they see it as the only way to replace fossil fuels fast enough. Still against it?"

"Absolutely!" Jiro felt a shot of adrenaline run through him. This was happening often. He was learning to use conscious breathing to calm himself. He liked the *new Jiro*, as Jenny fondly referred to him, but not how quickly he could go from energized to hotheaded.

"Nothing has changed to convince me otherwise."

"Is that ideology, or reason speaking?" Sagan was just poking, but he felt compelled to respond.

"It has never been ideology. Nuclear power is unsound *economically*. Without persistent subsidies, there would be no industry—R&D grants, guaranteed long-term contracts, construction and refurbishment costs typically at double or triple the estimates. Those are just the visible costs. The invisibles are the killer. Even with no accidents, there will be massive decommissioning and waste storage costs—plus 100,000 years of monitoring. Can you picture that? A commitment to contain, protect and respond to an emergency for millennia! Can anybody get their head around that?"

Jiro shook his head. "Governments can't plan even 20 years into the future. And yet, and yet..." *Breathe Jiro*. He took a quick breath and continued. "... everybody plays the game of believing we'll find a solution to waste storage. So we have nuclear power still being sold as affordable and safe, and now as our climate saviour."

"A plug-your-nose kind of saviour," Sagan qualified.

"You can't fit a nose plug tight enough to keep out the stink of foolishness!"

"You know what really sickens me, what drove me to make my 'leap', as you put it, Sagan? It's the unlevel playing field. Governments throwing money at nuclear, and leaving future costs off the ledgers entirely, while claiming poor when it comes to cleaner alternatives. *Oh, it will raise the price of electricity. It will hurt the economy.* That's bullshit! We get the same bullshit in the news." Jiro glanced at Simone, then continued.

"What is the result? The conservation and efficiency measures which might have slashed our energy use have never been fully implemented. Thanks to Germany and Denmark, the cost of wind and solar is plummeting, but this could have been prompted long ago. German households pay a premium for renewable electricity of just a couple of Euros per month. Nobody is bankrupted. Germany is weathering the global recession better than most."

"Though that's not what the media says," Sagan noted.

"The media—Simone and a few others aside—trots out nonsense!"

Simone smiled wryly and nodded.

"Look at 'Germany's foolish energy policy,' as they put it. The *poor* big power companies. Oh, those *poooor* coal and nuclear conglomerates. Crushed by the mean little solar midgets. We *must* offer them more corporate welfare, so they can keep little guys like us down for a few more years. I can't stand it anymore!"

He felt Jenny touch his arm. *Breathe and relax.*

"You never could stand it," Simone said, "but now you've found your voice. Have there been any changes in Japan?"

"Ha!" he huffed. "Nuclear utilities are as sacred as ever. And, sacred is the word. So closely tied to the government, to banks, to industry, that nobody dares to criticize. How can they? We have allowed ourselves to be locked into the fallacy. Everything is fine. Don't question the gods!"

Simone snorted. "Sounds like other countries, where a *fossil fuel* is the god. You know, oil and gas for decades in the US, and now the tar sands in Canada. Oops, they're the *oil* sands now. George Orwell would be impressed. Saudi Arabia and Nigeria, of course. Venezuela, Iran, and especially Russia. Anything to do with the industry is above reproach. And the money being made is so great that those in power have the means to cling to it. There's even a term for this: a *petro-tyranny*."

"There's a history of this going back to coal," she continued. "We have modern versions now, like China, India, Indonesia, the U.S. and Australia. *Carbon-tyrannies.*"

"Exactly," said Jiro, clenching his fists. She was illustrating his argument.

"Australia—if ever there was a country with the perfect mix of sun, wind, and hydro! It could be 100 percent renewable. So susceptible to crippling drought, heat waves and fire, with biblical flooding thrown in, but a hostage to climate denial!"

"Follow the money," said Simone, shaking her head. "Did you know it's high treason now to criticize the Alberta tar sands? Oh, did I say *tar* again? Bad Simone. Nasty, traitorous journalist."

Sagan laughed loudly. Slowly, the others joined him.

"Well," said Jenny, looking around the table, "I love you guys, but that was quite something. A vacation with burning souls."

"The burning souls road trip?" Sagan suggested.

As they headed down the stairs to their rooms, Simone pulled Jiro aside.

"You should meet my cousin someday. François has been grappling with the nuclear issue most of his life. He thought he'd escaped it by moving south, but there it was waiting."

"Southern France," said Jiro, his eyes shining. "The next road trip!"

Windows Open, Windows Close

Just the Guy

Houston, Texas, August 2009

Elmore had Pete Beauford's complete and unwavering trust. An intangible that brought very tangible benefits. A salary increase, naturally; a company car and parking privileges; membership at Pete's country club, and the right to fly business class.

As contriving as Elmore may have appeared to a few Pinnacle employees, his devotion to Pete was total. Which is what Pete was counting on in early 2007, when he called him into his office for "a little chat."

It was a spacious, bright suite on the 30th floor of a modern building. But the furniture was all dark, heavy oak and leather. Old school, like the man who chose it.

Pete began by reviewing some basic facts about Pinnacle. "We're heavily invested in oil and gas. Who isn't, in Houston? But our recent success is the result of some unconventional, riskier plays. Deepwater drilling in the Gulf and off California. Some Alaska projects. A joint venture with the Russians in the Black Sea. And a number of domestic shale oil projects. Fracking is bringing the industry back home, and it's just getting started."

Though Elmore knew the specifics of every project, he listened intently.

"Many of these projects, especially those on public lands and near-shore sites, are restricted by a ton of red tape. Environmental legislation of every kind. It's slowing down approvals, sometimes even blocking projects. And that's costing a load of money for companies where we're major shareholders."

Pete was building up steam. Elmore could tell something interesting was coming.

"So, if it weren't enough to be saddled with more and more domestic rules—air quality, water quality, NOX, SOX, POX, whatever—now we're looking at international agreements to limit emissions of carbon dioxide and what they call greenhouse gases. Now don't get me wrong, Elmore, I'm as much for protecting the health of Americans as anyone. I think Teddy Roosevelt did a great thing, creating our national parks. I even supported Nixon when he created the *Clean Air Act*, when I was young and foolish, like you. But it's out of control!"

Elmore liked to see his boss riled up. It didn't happen often.

"No sooner did we beat back that crazy Kyoto Protocol when along comes the next round of global socialism. President Dubya saved us from Gore, but that hasn't kept the EPA from planning something else, emboldened by Obama."

Where Pete's eyes had wandered at first, now they fixed on Elmore.

"Son, I'm just back from a weekend with some major players in American industry. Congressmen too, federal and state."

"No wait," Pete said with a wave of the finger, "you didn't hear that. These confabs are totally off the record. Imagine that in the New York Times!"

"Hear what?" asked Elmore innocently.

"Good," chuckled Pete.

"Well late at night, some of us got to talking over cigars and bourbon. A fella from one of these big PR firms was there. God knows what they charge! He's reminding us how the tobacco lobby held off the lawmakers. They didn't have to prove tobacco *couldn't* cause cancer, they just had to create doubt about studies proving it *did*." Doubt and confusion. About the science and the motivations of people doing it. 'So use the same tactics against these campaigns targeting fossil fuels,' he tells us."

Here it comes, thought Elmore as his chest tightened.

"Now this is nothing new to us. We've been funding PR firms for decades. You know, to question the so-called consensus that Gore rants about in that propaganda film. Full of errors. Our guys proved it. What this fella was suggesting though, wasn't to fund *competing* science. He thinks the most effective way to go now, especially with the internet, is to question the integrity of the scientists themselves. Shoot the *messenger*!

"Though he didn't really mean shoot," said Pete, lowering his voice. "Not literally. Harass them. Look into their publishing records. Any plagiarism or funny stuff with grant money? Make their life difficult in all kinds of ways."

Elmore's mind began to race ahead. By the time Pete made his request, Elmore had figured out what would be asked of him. It was nasty. It could even be illegal. But these scientists were living high off the hog already. 'Sucking on the taxpayer's teat,' as Pete liked to say of bureaucrats. He could feel the adrenaline rush starting.

"What I'm asking, son, is entirely off the record." Though Pete's voice was just above a whisper, Elmore felt the intensity.

"What we need is some kind of unit to coordinate these little guerrilla actions. No nuclear bombs—just the occasional guided missile. Unmarked of course. Get my drift."

Meeting his boss' gaze, Elmore responded in a measured voice.

"Sure, Pete. A couple of guys maybe. Do some research into who in the science world is having the most influence. Then look for weaknesses. Chinks in the armour. Professional misconduct. Harassment suits, falsifying data, that kind of thing."

"You're getting it. I knew you'd be the right guy. Said so that night. 'I know just the fella,' I told them."

Elmore blinked several times quickly.

"Now don't you worry," said Pete. "No names. Just said I knew the right guy. But I get where you're coming from. Set up some smart-sounding organization. You'll figure something out. It won't come back to any of us. You neither."

"I'm glad to hear that," Elmore said. "I'm pretty anonymous, and I'd like to keep it that way. Just a couple of questions to get started."

"Shoot."

"Budget. I can draw you up an initial one once I've done some thinking, but who's paying for this? And what ballpark are we looking at?"

"Couple of million to start," suggested Pete. "There's gotta be at least 10 people I can get to cough up their share. Anonymous, of course, or as hidden as IRS rules allow. We've got tame accountants, but haven't yet tamed the tax collector."

Elmore smiled. "How much will you want to know, once the campaign starts rolling out?"

"Hear no evil, see no evil." Pete smiled briefly.

"Plausible deniability," Elmore nodded. "And my final question: are we playing softball or hardball?"

"Definitely hardball," said Pete, his eyes narrowing. "Nobody gets hurt though. Not physically. We're protecting investments, not starting a civil war."

"I hear you," said Elmore. "Good to go."

"Oh, Elmore. Hire whoever you need. You'll want some computer experts. Hackers, I guess they call them. Just keep them way outside the building, will you."

"Naturally."

"Outside the country, if you can pull that off. There's bound to be some tech-wizards in India, or Russia or somewhere. Bill them as telemarketers." Pete laughed.

Elmore laughed too. "Telemarketers. Good one!"

He had met a former hacker. The guy taught courses at the business school he'd attended. Advanced classes in corporate computer security. For small companies. Big ones hired their own specialists. *Time to improve my skill set.* At company expense.

Video games never appealed to him. But hacking was real. So was the danger.

* * *

Elmore was meticulous in planning out the steps he felt would lead to the end goal. He began by devising names that resembled existing, official bodies or conservation groups. Start with *The Institute for*, *The Foundation to* or *Friends of*. Add in evocative words like *truth* or *freedom* or *protect*, then include *climate*, *science* or *public interest* and there you had it. A think tank or NGO that only an expert could tell from the real ones. But he was targeting the general public, not experts.

Domain names were registered, websites created, some offices were even leased. How could you suspect a legitimate sounding organization with a slick website, a board of advisors with letters after their names, an address in Washington, D.C., and a live person to answer phone calls? It was amazing how easily you could set up a little Potemkin Village.

Elmore couldn't help marvelling at his handiwork.

At the same time as these fictitious bodies were being spun from nothing, he took to criss-crossing the country, networking with 'like-minded individuals.' They were easy to find. Alternative climate conferences happened regularly. You could count on finding a retired scientist, or somebody who had always wanted to be a spokesperson or 'senior fellow.' A little stipend, travel money and occasional media appearances was all it took.

Building target lists was just as easy—prominent scientists and advocates for action all had publications. They attended conferences— legitimate ones. If you registered, you often got a list of delegates, with full contact details. It was legal, and simple. It just took time, legwork and cash.

Pete arranged the cash. His initial list of likely donors ballooned quickly, when employees, friends and spouses were added. Most were all too willing. They had what Elmore knew was the most precious motivation: a vested interest in sustaining fossil fuel production and consumption.

All this was stimulating. But the dark side of the operation provided the real excitement.

Working from a rented space above a coffee shop, Elmore brought in a 'network security consultant' happy to work both sides of the street. Evening tutorials looked at the basics of cracking passwords, probing for network vulnerabilities and impersonating account holders in ways that could lead to being handed the keys to people's accounts. They took care to do no harm. *Open the door, have a look, then lock up behind.*

"Haste leads to mistakes, Elmore. It's when a hacker gets cocky that they start leaving trails. Trails lead to prison. That's a restaurant I don't recommend!"

It wasn't long before Elmore took delivery of some sophisticated tools. Password generators, phishing scripts, techniques for setting up fake IP addresses, ways to reroute activity through multiple servers in multiple countries. All things he hadn't known existed. Soon he had mastered them. Not long after, he parted ways with his consultant. Without ever divulging whom he would be targeting, or why.

By late 2009, Elmore's handiwork had borne fruit. Very ripe fruit.

The Freedom of Information requests brought some results. Among his like-minded individuals were people with enough science knowledge to find gaps and inconsistencies in a haystack of data. But these were small victories. More effective were the mind games being played with America's top scientists. On top of the time-consuming requests for information.

Elmore enlisted a small army of 'grunts' to do 'trench work.' He enjoyed the military metaphors.

"Keep the target worried," he told his grunts. "Like the Viet Cong did. You want them distracted from their work. Seeing ghosts. Enemies everywhere: 'friends' on Facebook; members of panels they sit on; even their grad students. *Who can I trust?*"

Most of the techniques were classics: Letters to the editor, comments online, calls to talk radio. As for voice messages— disguised or otherwise—that was out of bounds. Too easy to trace.

Then came Twitter.

"Thank the Lord for Twitter!" Elmore remarked more than once. Amazing how much damage you can do with 140 characters.

"People take it so seriously!" he would laugh.

The goldmine, when he found it, was in the most unlikely of places. A small university in England he'd never heard of.

He'd had some modest success with American academics. Many of the big names in the field. Mostly their personal email accounts, blogs and websites. *Such smart people, yet so careless. And we're supposed to believe their science!* But apart from gathering salacious correspondence between a couple of professors and their students (filed for future use), he was mostly disappointed.

As for official email, that was a different world. The major universities, just like national science bodies and federal agencies— NOAA, NASA, NCAR and the EPA—had security walls beyond his skills. Following a hunch one night, he did a probe into the defences of the University of East Anglia, often mentioned in scientific journals.

Suddenly, he was in.

Some would call it an orchestrated attack on science. Others a conspiracy by scientists to withhold evidence and falsify results. "Climate-gate" is how most knew it.

Over 1000 emails and 3000 documents were illegally obtained from the secure server of the Climate Research Institute. They included personal emails, technical discussions and a great deal of conversation about how hard it was to present climate science in a way that was sufficiently convincing to motivate action.

Multiple independent inquiries would conclude that the targeted scientists had done nothing wrong. No data had been falsified. The global climate consensus had not been affected. But the affair—or at least the coverage—left a very different impression on the general public. To the delight of Elmore's backers.

"What Facebookers and Tweeters and even *New York Times* readers now believe is that you can't trust scientists on climate change," he reported to Pete and a small group of backers in a private room at the golf club. "The average Joe thinks something fishy is going on, even if they can't tell you what."

"Son, I knew I could count on you. But holy crap, I never expected this!"

"Why thank you Pete. I aim to please."

Sizing up the rest of the men, Elmore felt he should ask a crucial question. "Would you like me to stand down?" Seeing little reaction, he continued. "Or, if I may suggest, should we just lie low for a bit. There's a lot of intelligence agencies sniffing around. Maybe pause while this blows over. Then re-engage with a new strategy?"

"Now what might that strategy look like?" asked one of the men.

"Well sir," Elmore said, taking care not to seem hasty, "I have done a bit of thinking. I see little to be gained from making scientists our only target. Maybe it's the decision-makers and influencers we should be working on, and in some cases, working with. Elected officials and journalists. Major media companies. Talk radio and certain TV shows. Syndicated columnists, of the correct leanings. That's where I'd put my money."

Seeing nods, he continued. "I can put together something more concrete, if you like the general thrust."

Pete looked to the rest for confirmation.

"Works for me! I'm in! Where do I send the cheque? Excellent work, Elmore!"

"Now Pete, don't you think the boy deserves a bit of a raise? And maybe some time off for good behaviour?"

Time off. Elmore didn't even know the meaning. *Stay busy, stay out of trouble.* Still, it was worth a try.

The Show Must Go On

State College, Pennsylvania, January 2010

Since his breakdown 11 months earlier, Sagan had taken a number of steps to lower his stress. Medication helped, though it left him sluggish and prone to weight gain. Regular exercise was key, producing hormones that offered a natural lift. As for workload, he had stepped down from two international panels and the board of a major journal.

The university had granted him a reduction in teaching load. "For as long as necessary," said the president, who had taken Sagan's breakdown personally.

He had become a major draw: for undergrads choosing a college, and for grad students from around the world. More than that, people liked him.

Dropping the TV shows was an obvious step, but when Isong suggested this, Sagan rejected it outright. Even cutting his visits to schools was unthinkable.

"I know how it must look," Sagan said. "The guy gets course reductions and passes work on to colleagues, but has time to go on TV and play science games with kids. What nobody realizes is that if I had to choose, I'd pick public education over another study on methane burping from the floor of the Arctic Ocean."

Isong gave a weak smile.

"Without an educated public, nobody will care about the rest," Sagan continued earnestly. "Bringing science to people is where we've failed. But it's what drives me. And every time I do one of those shows as Professor Sagan from Penn State, that's better than a dozen recruiting campaigns."

"I get it," said Isong, sounding anguished. "But I don't ever want to have to listen to your head thud on the floor again." The veins in Isong's long neck were pulsing as he stared hard into his partner's eyes. A look Sagan had never seen.

"Finding you there, in a pool of your own spittle is not part of the married life I signed up for."

Sagan reached out, only to have his hand brushed away. "I'm sorry you had to go through that. It must have been scary as hell."

"Damn right!" Isong's eyes were starting to tear up. He looked away, then thought better of it. Turning back, he accepted Sagan's consoling hands.

"If you're going to do the show, then find a way to ease up," he pleaded. "Stars that last are supported by a *team*. Let others do more writing. You have a producer. Stop meddling."

"I don't meddle. I offer suggestions. Frequently." Sagan, as usual, turned to humour. Isong was still learning to read it.

"*Joke*, Isong! Yes, and thank you. I hereby solemnly swear to stop meddling and just be the star."

Isong laughed, in spite of himself. The contradictory emotions of the last few minutes had him thoroughly confused.

"You understand, right? Why I need to keep doing my shows?"

"Yes, I do," said Isong. "Let me know how I can help."

"I will, my love, I will."

Sagan knew he should mention the message. He still hadn't erased the tape. He was going to, several times. Its presence tempted him to throw out the machine.

"You can do all that digitally," Isong had hinted more than once. "Free up some counter space." But Sagan had a sense he might need it some day. The tape, and a machine that could play it.

My Own Column

Journalism was a precarious career. Simone knew that. With the advent of the world wide web came an explosion of online news and commentary, of mixed quality and astonishing quantity. Print journalism was particularly affected. It had taken little time for a sizeable public to abandon paid newspaper subscriptions and seek its daily dose of news online. Efforts to force readers to pay even nominal fees had been largely unsuccessful.

Coinciding with this shift was the rapid growth of Google, Facebook, YouTube and other competitors for attention and, more importantly, advertising dollars. This further upset the business model of news organizations, leaving them producing content with fewer resources. Quality reporting, expert analysis, and the time- and money-intensive work of doing investigative journalism suffered in particular.

When reflecting on this upheaval, Simone had more than once commented how *you get what you pay for*. People were wanting more and more information—for free. Almost overnight, this was the new normal. What few noticed or chose to worry over was the erosion of quality and the growth of 'sponsored content,' whether from corporations, interest groups or governments. The term propaganda had fallen out of fashion just as it was proliferating. But who could tell? Who even cared?

For HeraldMedia, owned and staffed by people devoted to serious journalism, these trends were a challenge on every level. The loss of advertising, the speed of the news cycle, the use of

Twitter and the implosion of paid subscriptions—all pointed in the same direction: more work performed by fewer staff, less devotion of employer to employee; and vice-versa. Simone and her colleagues—half as many as when she was hired—lived each day as if the axe could fall. Still, the survivors took solace in knowing they received a decent wage to do the only thing they ever wanted to do: trying to explain the fascinating world around them to a public who cared enough to read their words, view their photos or, now, watch their videos.

The medium was changing. The media was changing. What remained constant was the need for facts—as free as possible from influence and bias.

Pressure to keep costs down inevitably led to senior reporters and editors being offered buy-out packages. The holes created were only partially filled; mostly with eager graduates from journalism school. At a lower salary, and with fewer benefits than when she had started, Simone noted.

With the latest wave of layoffs came an offer from Anthony Poulson, the *Ottawa Herald*'s new editor. Simone would write a regular column.

Instead of spending days, sometimes weeks, producing feature stories and pitching in on the occasional breaking news story, she would write two columns per week, of a national interest, to be offered to the full HeraldMedia chain. This made for a different pace and—to some degree—audience.

"The columnist is a molder of opinion," Anthony reminded her. Part provocateur, part trusted friend. Someone to stir you up one day, and make sense of a complicated issue the next. Decision makers read the columnists. Particularly ones who have established themselves as influential. They read them and react to them."

"Expect equal parts praise, equal parts outrage," Anthony warned, with a grin.

Her audience would be bigger than before. HeraldMedia had swallowed up several regional chains in a recent merger. They'd closed papers too, Simone noted with some sadness. Less local coverage in small markets. Less diverse voices overall. Neither was healthy.

Her column's focus had been the subject of considerable discussion. An agreement was eventually reached. She would have freedom to choose her topics, for the most part. The editorial board would suggest ones on occasion. The publisher would also want to have some input.

Simone had bristled at this suggestion. "Do you mean 'proposing' a topic, or 'instructing' me what to write about? And more to the point, providing me with the position to be communicated?"

There was a line she would not cross, Anthony knew. He had been coached on how to address it.

"Stephen Northam wants you to know he is committed to a diversity of viewpoints. You were selected because of your dedication to issues and points of view that are too often left out, or pointedly dismissed by the corporate media. You have a talent for poking at old paradigms. The world is changing quickly, and people are being left behind, in addition to the ecological damage you've chronicled. There has to be a new way forward. We want you to write from that perspective."

Simone smiled. *Neither left nor right, but moving forward* was a slogan used by the Green Party. Her initial indignation was dissolving.

"You're going to make some readers crazy," Anthony predicted. "You're going to get some subscriptions cancelled. Though half the people who make those threats are reading us online for free," he scowled.

"But If I know you, you'll win over twice as many readers as you lose, skewering hypocrisy and finding light in the gloom. Does that work for you, Simone?"

"I can work with that," she replied.

"Don't sell Stephen Northam short. Not every media baron's a Rupert Murdoch."

Simone scowled at the name. As she rose, Anthony remembered something.

"Oh, Simone..."

"Uh, huh..." she responded warily.

"I'd like you to do a bit of mentoring. These kids fresh out of J-School, they look up to you. Someone who still has the fire. We old farts tend to pour cold water on it."

Simone chuckled, but only partly agreed. She knew some old farts who were still breathing fire.

Anthony wasn't done. "Also, the climate thing. Mr. Northam's fine with mentioning it occasionally. Just try not to bring it into every column. It can be a turn-off if overdone."

Simone grimaced. *Overdone! If only people knew.*

Trust readers with the truth, she believed, *then they will trust you.*

Poking Bears

Simone and her boss both knew she'd piss some people off. They just hadn't expected it to happen this fast, or prominently. It had only been last week that she took on the gig, Simone reflected as Anthony closed the door and invited her to sit in the chair facing his oak desk. If she was about to get fired, she hoped it would set a new speed record: 'Shortest stint as national columnist.' Did Guinness have a category for that?

"Simone, Simone, Simone," said Anthony with a slow shake of the head. Did I ask you to write a maiden column that would get the Prime Minister's Office making livid calls to our publisher?"

"You did not," she replied hesitantly. "Though you did warn me I'd be attacked from all sides, at one time or another. In fact, you indicated that if I was not, then I wasn't trying hard enough."

"That sounds like something I'd say."

"Has Mr. Northam expressed his displeasure?" asked Simone. "Am I relieved of my duties before I've properly figured them out?"

"No, Simone, relax." He flashed her an enigmatic smile that vanished as quickly as it appeared. "Stephen Northam requested I relate to you his chat with the PM's press secretary, in which he took great pleasure reminding the apoplectic Tory flunky that if he would stick to his job, we would ours. Both being pillars of Canada's democracy."

"Really?"

"Really. Though I added the big words for effect."

Simone laughed. She hated to think her East Coast trip was about to be called off, and her next two columns—already submitted—spiked or shredded.

He picked up a copy of the article and began to read.

A sizeable part of northern Alberta is arguably administered or policed by the energy companies that work there, or at their bidding. Wait, though, isn't this public land? The highways and airspace are still Canada. Nobody declared them private property, or can legally do so. Yet those who venture close enough to view or photograph active sites or tailing ponds can expect a trespass warning or fine. Forcible removal even. A private pilot now needs a special permit for this 'no-fly zone.' A photo of what's happening down there is now a security threat, apparently. Informed discussion might break out.

When other countries act this way, we call it tyranny. 'Petro-tyranny' is used to describe Russia, Nigeria, Venezuela... states where the vast wealth generated from this one resource, this one industry, so dwarfs all others that it is swallowing up nearly everything.

If the Harper government is exclusively promoting oil and gas, then it would be wise to ask just how forward-thinking and sustainable this strategic direction will be in five or ten years, when global commitments to reduce greenhouse gas emissions take hold. And what it is doing to our democracy.

"Reader response has been... robust," Anthony continued, no longer reading.

"So substantial, and from all sides, that we're devoting Saturday's Opinions page to letters you stimulated. I believe we've got the premier of Alberta weighing in angrily. A couple of farmers and ranchers too—but on your side, you'll be happy to know. Apparently they have a new hero. A diminutive cyclist from Ottawa. Mighty Mouse has everyone talking."

Simone smiled at the new nickname. "Talking about my piece, I hope. Not me."

"Well," said Anthony slowly, "both. Debating the content, while sizing up the new columnist. Reaction varies by city, you won't be surprised to hear. Mr. Northam had to sweet talk our Edmonton and Calgary editors into running the column. Advertisers!"

Simone nodded. She was gratified to learn they'd had the courage to print her column. In Saskatchewan also.

Anthony, despite his initial mind games, seemed tickled pink.

"Enough with the tar sands fluff pieces," he huffed, "and the lazy business writers! Way too close to their subjects. *All hail the 'oil' sands and the booming stock markets they bestow upon us!* It was time some meaningful questions were asked, and you had the chutzpah to start it."

He stood up and reached out to shake her hand. She quickly followed suit.

"Go see if you can make them just as mad on the East Coast. Drive up readership there too. Find us a lobster tyranny or something. Make one up if you have to!"

Simone could tell the smile he offered was heartfelt.

Good News for Sharing

Dearest Friends, Simone wrote.

Though email and expanding 'social media' were laying waste to conventions of letter writing, Simone held fast to certain things. Punctuation. Paragraphs. A proper greeting. The messages she received these days made her cringe. "Hey," was typical; "Whazzup" and even "Yo" shockingly common.

I have great news to share. First, I've been promoted to columnist. Not just for my own paper, but the national chain. I won't have to travel as much, since I can write from home most of the time. On the other hand, since I can work anywhere, I may just show up and file from your living room.

The big news is.... drum roll... I got married! Despite our schedules keeping us apart; maybe because of it. Neither of us could deal with a big wedding and we were going crazy trying to find a date. So Ron looked at me and said, "You free tomorrow?" I was. Off to City Hall we went. So we're 0 for 3 in attending each other's weddings!

More news you might find interesting. I'll be heading to the Atlantic coast to write some pieces on the economy nearly 20 years after the Canadian government imposed a moratorium to protect collapsing cod stocks. While doing research, I came across a man at a small university in New Brunswick campaigning to highlight the connection between ocean health and the poor economic health of fishing communities. Somebody with a love of boats—especially cleaner propulsion? Did anyone guess?

I've told the whole story to Ron. He's fine with it. As you know, that comet flamed out. Still, it will be interesting to see Paul. I recall Jenny saying he had a hard time completing his thesis, and then finding work. I'll share what I learn.

NiMa Energy Press Release
Kuala Lumpur, February 28, 2011

Clean energy technology company NiMa Energy announced today that its innovative hydrogen fueling system will go into production in April. NiMa has solved the elusive problem of containing hydrogen for regular refilling using a patented high-density ceramic coating within a standard thin-walled stainless steel tank. The breakthrough takes the form of a nano-particle coating, modeled on the smooth and dense shells of the abalone.

- The Churchill 97 holds 1000 litres of hydrogen at high pressure, enough to provide the electricity needs of a mid-sized building in a business park, combined with a fuel cell system such as NiMa's Rocket.
- The Clare 98 is a compact 60-litre tank, sufficient to operate a fully-loaded 18-wheel truck for an average distance of 800 kilometres. Combined with the Pocket Rocket fuel cell propulsion system, all emissions are eliminated.

"There is no need to even have a chimney in a building equipped with a Churchill 97/Rocket fuel cell system, nor an exhaust stack on a vehicle equipped with the Clare 98/Pocket Rocket system" stated NiMa co-founder and president Dr. Jenny Fung. "The only emission is a trace amount of water. It can be collected to water indoor plants, or—in the case of a thirsty truck driver—to drink." she declared.

NiMa Energy's corporate mission is to produce safe, efficient, affordable electricity with minimal air pollutants and greenhouse gases, so as to help tackle the global problems of polluted air in major cities and the growing threat of climate change.

NiMa currently produces fuel cell generators in addition to the new Churchill 97 and Clare 98 fuel tanks. It holds patents on an innovative lithium-ion battery system which will reduce the size and weight of vehicle battery banks, and avoid overheating. NiMa also designs custom energy systems for corporate and municipal clients.

Reversing Tides

March 12, 2011

Simone was halfway into her rail journey when her phone buzzed. She'd slept better than expected in her compartment, followed by a tasty breakfast. "Relax and take the train," said the ads. *Relax indeed*, she was thinking, just before the interruption.

Probably Ron, she figured, as she watched the phone dance across the table. Checking in after his final day of cycling in Cuba. He planned to join her in Halifax in three days' time.

Simone got up and moved quickly toward the train's 'politeness zone', pressing answer as she did.

"Simone, mon amour," came his slow deep voice. She felt the usual tingle. *I wonder how long this will last, now that we're married?*

"Sorry to call so early, but I saw the news. I figured you'd know more."

"Actually, I was making the most of my mini-break on the train. I haven't gone online yet myself. What did I miss?" Simone heard him take a breath.

"You sitting down?"

"No," she said, reaching for the seat in the alcove. "Another terrorist attack?"

"No. A tsunami. A big one. On the coast north of Tokyo."

Simone felt an instant rush of blood.

"Doesn't Jiro come from there? His father works at a nuclear plant, right?"

"Ye-e-s," said Simone, constructing a mental map of the region. "Yes to both. What the hell happened?" An older passenger gave her an admonishing look.

"That's what I was calling to ask you!" Ron reminded her. "I forgot you'd still be on the train. All I know is what the rolling headlines are saying on BBC World. I'll read it to you. *Major tsunami hits towns and villages. Thousands feared dead. Nuclear plant taking emergency measures to avoid damage.*" He paused.

"There's some mind-blowing footage showing a town being ripped apart."

Simone's mind was halfway around the world now.

"Ron, I love you, but I've gotta go. I need to grab my laptop and go online."

"*Desolée, ma belle.* Sorry to be the messenger. Thought you'd know already."

"Of course. Don't apologize. Very thoughtful, but I gotta go."

"Hold on," he said, "are we still on for Halifax on the 15th?"

"I don't know. This kinda changes everything."

"I figured as much."

Simone hated to back out on her work plans and her romantic getaway with Ron.

"Here's what we'll do," she said. "When are you back? Tomorrow, is it?"

"Yeah, tomorrow afternoon," Ron said.

"I'll send an update by email, and leave a voice message at home, OK? Either we're still on for you to fly to Halifax, or I'll be in Ottawa waiting for you when you get there. Or... who knows. I'm a journalist. Anything could happen!"

"That's what I figured," Ron sighed.

* * *

Children screaming, old men wailing, dogs barking, fishing boats lifted far inland, entire neighbourhoods swept up river valleys then washed back down again, with people clinging to wreckage. Some trapped in their cars.

"Wah!" Jiro cried to his computer screen.

He had been in meetings all morning, unaware of the 9.0 magnitude Tohoku earthquake or the massive tsunami that followed until he arrived back in the office. Many of his colleagues were in tears, Jenny among them.

By then, hours of footage had been uploaded onto the internet, from police helicopters and people's video cameras and cell phones, shooting from atop hills or the balcony of buildings. In a daze, he viewed the waves washing through, washing away Minamisanriku, Kamaishi, Watari…

Namie? It would have been in the tsunami zone. And what if something had gone wrong at the Fukushima Daiichi station? It was accident-proof, the authorities said. His father said. But this was no ordinary accident.

Mechanically, he booked his flight. He did not know what he could do, or whether he would merely be in the way, but he couldn't just stay in KL and worry.

* * *

The arrival hall at Narita Airport was crawling with media. Simone could pick them out. Smell them. Here she was—one of them. Even if she had another motive.

At one time, several Canadian news agencies would have had a reporter stationed in Tokyo. Full-time, covering Japan and the region. Beijing would have had one too. Cutbacks put an end to that. Now Canadian TV networks and newspapers made do with a British or Australian reporter repackaging their commentary.

This story was too big though. On hearing Anthony Poulson's pitch in the emergency teleconference, the publisher didn't hesitate.

"She used to live there? She speaks Japanese? Sheee-it! Get her on the next plane. First class, if you have to. Get her fully equipped. Camera, tripod, recorder. We can sell her stuff to radio *and* TV."

Unlike a lot of publishers, Stephen Northam had worked in the business.

Simone's Japanese was never particularly good, and in the 15 years since she'd left Tokyo her only practice was a little friendly banter with Jiro. She would need a translator. A fixer. A Canadian journalist doesn't just waltz into a disaster zone. Not when entire villages, sizeable towns even, had been wiped out. Not when they were in what looked to be a nuclear crisis.

She had Jiro, of course. But she was coming to support *him*. She wouldn't lean on Jiro for anything; beyond a little commentary from an affected local. She wasn't even sure she would ask him to go on camera.

The rapid departure had left Simone shaken, where it would normally have offered a thrill. She was abandoning commitments, to people who had made time for her in New Brunswick and Nova Scotia. To Paul.

He'd been looking forward to it. She could tell, when she called to cancel. Professional disappointment, she assumed.

She'd been looking forward to hearing about his work. He appeared to have found an outlet for his energy, his conviction. What often came out as arrogance. Knowing you were on to something, and being willing to hold to it, no matter the cost. A trait they shared. She had learned to soften her approach, though. To accept the possibility she may not be right.

Paul seemed destined to do things the hard way. The curse of the genius. Star athlete. Male model. All rolled into one, in his case. She thought he'd have learned about teamwork in sport. Perhaps this explained the ceiling he'd hit in hockey.

And yet, as a lover, she recalled with a blush, he was so generous. He could read her better even than she had learned to. He was always there, where she wanted him, without knowing it. It was so perfect, though it sometimes seemed cold. Like he was playing an instrument, without feeling the music.

How unfaithful, she chastised herself, thinking of Ron. Ah well, it's just a memory. He has plenty of his own, she knew. They'd shared many.

Her farewell to Ron was bittersweet. They arrived back in Ottawa at almost the same time. He was just emerging from the shower when she closed the front door.

"Great timing!" they declared. They made love passionately, aggressively.

The next morning, savouring the moment together, in a bed too often half-empty, everything was slower and softer, as if the beauty and tenderness they were creating might somehow provide solace to broken hearts across an ocean. Simone's mind was already half in Japan, where pain and suffering awaited. Ron could tell.

Death by tsunami. How utterly random. By the time the alarm was sounded, it would have been too late for almost everyone. The wave went higher and deeper than anyone could have predicted.

The nuclear disaster, however, was different. There had been plenty of warnings: about the location of the Fukushima Daiichi Nuclear Plant; about the inadequacy of critical safety features in the design of the reactors; about the vulnerability of the back-up electricity supply, which would be critical for running any emergency shutdown operation.

Jiro had described all this, years earlier. Here, she sensed, was where the story lay. She would report on the human disaster, of course, and the physical destruction. But Simone Cohen would dig deeper, into places she was not wanted.

She hadn't been sent all this way to report from a hotel room, narrating over the same images they'd be showing on CNN or *The National*. *Take risks.* That's how she'd make her reporting stand out. Simone needed to experience the crisis firsthand.

Simone took the first train she could get from Tokyo to Fukushima City, where Jiro said he would meet her. The station, like the train, was packed. She wondered what was taking them all there. Disaster relief, funerals, the desperate search for loved ones, or the search for a hot story? Looking around her, trying to spot Jiro, she felt suddenly sick. Was she just another vulture?

Her doubt melted away as soon as she saw him in the crowd. As they moved slowly towards each other, their eyes stayed locked. A friend in need, she saw. He would be stoic of course. But she knew him too well for that.

"Tell me how I can help you," said Simone as they pulled back from their long embrace. "What was covered up, and how can I help tear the covers off?"

The first thing Jiro did was get Simone fitted with a dosimeter to record her exposure to radiation. The second, was to show her how to use a geiger counter.

"We go in fast. Take pictures, shoot video, then get out," he said. "After, when we're at your hotel, we'll go over the images and I'll explain to you what it all is. OK?"

Jiro had already been in once, three days after the explosion and fires. It was forbidden, he knew, but what did that mean? Protecting the public from harm would be part of it. Allowing first responders to focus on the task of finding tsunami survivors and removing bodies was too. But Jiro knew too much to believe that was all. Safety systems had failed. Communication had broken down. Foolproof designs got fooled. And now a lot of people were looking to save their jobs and reputations.

Now was precisely when outsiders should be taking notes and taking pictures.

"Tomorrow, my father will walk you through what he knows," he told Simone. "Today, he's resting. He's part of the emergency command centre. His knowledge of the plant's design is critical. They're trying to figure out a way to avoid a meltdown."

The 'China Syndrome' Simone recalled, thinking of the Hollywood film named for the theoretical situation where meltdown of a plant's radioactive core would cause the mass of fuel to burn its way deep into the earth—'all the way to China.'

The film was inspired by Three-Mile Island, North America's biggest near-miss in 1978. The accident eight years later at Chernobyl, Ukraine, was far worse. Still, despite the rudimentary equipment in use there, meltdown had been prevented.

The lessons drawn from Three-Mile Island and Chernobyl varied widely. Some saw them as a warning of worse to come, where others concluded such disasters could evidently be managed— smart people had acted, brave responders did their jobs, now back to business.

Often overlooked, or conveniently forgotten, was the harm and loss of life suffered by emergency crews in Chernobyl—plant workers and soldiers sent in with little protection and for too long.

"When the world goes searching for heroes," Simone recalled François once saying, "they should look no further than those poor guys who saved Europe from catastrophe. Not that they were given a choice."

It would be the same here in Fukushima. In the minutes following an accident, nobody really has a choice. First responders, whether professionals or volunteers, do not need to be ordered. They act. Later we call them heroes, dead or alive.

The men who rushed into the coal pits at Springhill, didn't pause to weigh their chances, or imagine the headlines. Nor the firefighters rushing to the Twin Towers. You go because you're needed. It's a strange instinct, she realized, unique to *Homo sapiens*. But maybe not. You could understand mothers and fathers putting themselves at risk to save their children. Why do it for cousins, though? Or neighbours? Or strangers?

Thank heaven for that instinct, Simone and Jiro agreed. He was describing the first hours after the tsunami, when the power went down at most of the reactors and all hell was breaking loose. The command chain was a mess.

How did it come to this? Jiro wanted to know, and Simone would help find out. It could never happen, the public had been told. Yet it did. And could again. Stopping the next one drove Jiro. Even if this one was far from over.

* * *

Simone's post-tsunami footage—with its precise, insightful narration—played on almost every screen in Canada two days later. Within hours, it was running on several American networks, the BBC and Australia's ABC. Dozens of countries were soon broadcasting her report, dubbed into the local language.

She had made a deliberate decision to keep her narration sparse. Understated, and just above a whisper. The images did the shouting.

Jiro arranged for a local company to do the editing and sound mastering. It made all the difference. This was no jittery Skype report. The world had seen those. Simone delivered the first, and ultimately the best uncensored footage of eerie ghost towns that had been thriving, living places just days earlier.

Her second report—longer, at nearly 20 minutes—offered a moment-by-moment breakdown of the nuclear accident. With the help of detailed site plans and design drawings of the four Daiichi reactors, animated sequences pulled together by a production house in Tokyo, and eye-witness reports from people who had been on the inside, Simone's video and written commentary was a sensation. Every HeraldMedia paper and many major dailies across the globe ran the double-page spread. Only in Japan did her work not see the light—officially. It was all over the internet, of course, and alternative news sites had posted Japanese translations 24 hours after it hit streets and screens elsewhere.

What was a sensation outside of Japan was 'sensationalist' inside. The power authority, the national government and all the tame media outlets—which Simone knew to be the majority—mentioned her work only to dismiss it as 'poorly researched', 'full of inaccuracies', and 'scare mongering'. Yet, most Japanese could see through this. They knew well the cozy relationship between government and media. Power companies were very much part of it. Anybody who cared to had developed the habit of looking to foreign media for more fulsome coverage of controversial domestic events.

A few Japanese papers made a pretence of remaining arm's length. But in a situation of national crisis such as this, wagons were circled. This would partially account for the failure to warn the public of the extent and gravity of the accident, and what they should do to protect themselves. It would take an independent report many years later to reveal the extent of collusion—before, during, and after the disaster.

* * *

Poorly researched, my ass! I used firsthand observation and local sources.

In considerable secrecy, Jiro brought together a number of industry insiders: men who worked at the plant and wanted the truth told; journalists who had raised safety concerns over the years—to little effect and at considerable risk to their careers; even a material supplier who knew of abnormalities in contracting. Only a few were prepared to go on record; mostly retired workers.

In Japan, nobody would be arrested for speaking out, but powerful people had ways of shutting mouths. Simone understood Jiro's desire to end this truth chill and the culture it engendered. She was his vehicle and collaborator.

"It's easy for me," she said. "I get to go home. For you, this is home."

Jiro knew a lot of feathers had been ruffled by their work. But it was worth it, if it brought about change. For that though, more than good journalism was needed. It was one thing to shine light on the folly of nuclear energy. It was another to end it. That would take a lot more work, and a viable alternative. He recalled Simone saying how her relative in France had reached this conclusion decades earlier.

Malaysia had been good to Jiro, but his work was in Japan now. His spiritual home. He hoped Jenny would understand. And the twins.

Ottawa Herald, April 22, 2011

The Cohen Column:
Lest We Forget

Do not build your homes below this point!

Passersby could be forgiven for missing the roadside stone marker near the village of Aneyoshi. Like other 'Tsunami stones' along Japan's east coast, it has been there for a long time. Such markers were erected to remind future generations of the high water mark reached by murderous ocean waves.

1611, 1896, 1933, 1960... 2011!

Like many lessons of history, these warnings were eventually forgotten, the markers covered by moss, their message ignored by settlers and town planners.

If the marker had been granted greater authority, perhaps serving as the focus of an annual event, some of the destruction brought by the next great tsunami could have been avoided. Sure, boats in the harbour would have been swept inland, or perhaps out to sea. But town centres, schools, factories and entire neighbourhoods would not have been built in the path of a massive wave. Above all, nobody would have permitted a nuclear plant to be built so close to the shore. Least of all six, with emergency power supplies below the level of that ancient marker. How easily we forget.

As a nation mourns the toll of this latest tsunami, tries to resettle the survivors, and contends with remediating hundreds of square kilometres of radioactive soil, those who 'should have known' must come to terms with their collective failure.

This inevitable period of reflection and recrimination will—for the first time—take place in the shadow of a nuclear crisis. A multi-billion dollar engineering exercise is underway to cool and contain the remaining nuclear fuel at Fukushima Daiichi, and prevent groundwater and rainwater from leaving the site and washing out to sea.

Decades of critical containment work are required. The people of Japan, or whoever rules this land in millennia to come, will be tasked with constantly verifying the condition of the site, responding to future emergencies affecting it—including the next earthquakes and tsunamis—and keeping people away.

There are now over 100 nuclear generation sites around the world, most with multiple reactors. Considerably more sites house military reactors, waste storage facilities and aging nuclear weapons, ships and submarines. All must be managed, sign posted and monitored to keep our distant descendants from wandering in and, who knows, building a town, port or farm; as oblivious to the risk as the people of Japan seem to have been.

Since the Fukushima crisis, a number of European countries have questioned the future of their nuclear programs. Several, including Germany, Switzerland and Italy will phase them out entirely. Public pressure played a strong role. So did the knowledge that every additional year spent generating nuclear energy adds more waste to the management challenge. Every additional ton of radioactive material adds cost and risk. Each additional year of operation carries the risk that the catastrophic event that 'could never happen' just might.

With oceans rising and shorelines moving inland, many of the world's nuclear plants—reliant on ocean water for cooling—will be ever closer to a storm surge or, heaven forbid, a tsunami. It's not as if they can be moved to safety on higher ground. A decommissioning takes decades, and costs billions; money that nobody has set aside.

Not all plants are on the ocean. The rest are on a lake or river. That's a problem too. Many are prone to flooding, though Lake Ontario, the Rhone or the Mississippi will never see the kind of surge that occurs on the ocean's edge. Here, however, the risks are drought and heat. In the devastating heatwave that hit southern Europe in 2003, several of France's largest plants had to greatly reduce operating capacity, as rivers proved too low and too warm to meet cooling requirements.

In a warming world, the glacier-fed rivers of today will almost certainly be drier and warmer. Just at a time when some countries are counting on nuclear energy for essential power; as a low-carbon source. They, we, would do well to think of that stone sentinel on the Fukushima roadside.

An average human lifespan may be 70 or 80 years. An average government lasts considerably less. Nuclear waste requires active management for centuries, then vigilance for millennia. If the people on a tsunami-prone Japanese coastline can forget a stark warning of death in less than 100 years, is it likely that nuclear waste will be anything less than a toxic time capsule with a warning sign nobody can read?

High dwellings ensure the peace and happiness of our descendants, says the stone.

Trouble with Trolls

State College, Pennsylvania, October 2011

"It's an epidemic!" Angela Wainwright declared. Dean of Science at Penn State since 2009, she was reaching the end of a presentation to senior colleagues that included a chart of recorded incidents: threats, hacks, service denials through bot attacks, and demands for documentation and data files.

"You understand of course how hard it is to work." She was trying hard to sound calm in the presence of senior colleagues. "But now it's getting scary."

Systematic harassment was compromising research and teaching through lost time and emotional stress, she underlined. Centres of excellence felt it most, to the point where this emergency meeting had been called.

She advanced to the next slide, a chart of personal threats received in 2010, by type: physical violence - 37; rape - 13; harm to children or spouses - 7; general death threats - 45; detailed death threats - 5; packages triggering hazmat response - 3.

"The police are barely interested. They can't track the senders, and since nobody has been physically hurt, they're writing off all threats as pranks. They suggest we do too." Her hands were visibly shaking as she advanced to the final slide.

"Then there is this, which I was shown this morning."

The pastiche letter of cut-out words from different magazines caused several in the room to laugh initially. One by one, they went silent as they read it.

"Ladies and gentleman," declared Dean Wainwright, "all is fun and games until somebody gets hurt. Well somebody has been!" She paused to let her words sink in.

"What can this university do to make our law enforcement agencies act?"

* * *

The vacation had done Elmore good after all. He'd always wanted to see San Francisco. An epic road trip from Houston, his new car rising to the test.

Three weeks in new places gave him time to reflect on how far he'd come. From bullied weakling in a town with no future, to the BMW-driving go-to guy for the country's wealthiest, and arguably most powerful men.

As interesting as his job with Pinnacle could still be, most days had become routine. It was the special project that gave him something to look forward to. Yet now, even this covert work was starting to drag. It was time to take some risks. The world needed a little more Elmore.

Back in his Bat Cave with its array of monitors and high-speed connections, he began to build his spreadsheet of people to influence, and influencers to get cosy with. There was the pink column on the left, and the blue on the far right. Pink for thought leaders with known vulnerabilities. Blue for clever people with a shared agenda and fondness for working outside conventional circles. They were the future. But first, a little fun with the pink ones.

* * *

The response to Sagan's 'comic book' had been overwhelming.

KlimateKaos was crafted to illustrate what was already happening, what was likely to happen under various emission scenarios, and who would be most affected. The solutions he proposed had neither a free market bias, nor a big government one. Or—the unthinkable—a 'world government' one. He simply showed what each choice—be it policy, fiscal tool, or personal behaviour—could be expected to accomplish. If anything.

With humour, he depicted the relative futility of many *Common Gestures*: cloth bags, recycling... all the little things kids are taught in school. In contrast, he used graphs rather than humour to highlight the importance of *Game Changers*.

Have smaller families. Fly less. Don't eat meat. Don't own a car.

Nobody talked about these in polite company. Certainly, they never made it into a school curriculum.

Less driving, less meat, fewer flights, fewer kids? The car lobby, the beef, pork and chicken lobby, the airline and travel industry lobby, and above all the lobby from any number of religions would be banging down school board doors if anybody tried teaching those to children.

Regardless, Sagan believed facts could speak for themselves, and should be offered unfiltered. With illustrations, to connect both sides of the brain.

Have one child instead of two. Basic math. The chart showed it so clearly.

One couple begets 2 children begets 4 grandchildren, begets 8 great-grandchildren. OR, one couple begets 3, begets 9, begets 27 great-grandchildren. Those 27 great-grandchildren in India, consuming and emitting at a typical level for India will produce 9 tonnes of CO_2 per year. The same 27 Swedish or German great grandchildren will emit 81 tonnes. As for 27 Americans or Canadians, expect 243 tonnes. At only 8 great-grandchildren, though, those numbers plummet to less than 3 tonnes for India, 24 for Europe, and 72 for North America. *72 vs 243! Basic math.*

He'd expected *KlimateKaos* to generate some outrage, but had to shake his head now at his naiveté. Weeks of interviews and talk shows followed the book's publication. These begat book signings and speaking engagements, which begat more vitriol, which in turn begat more media interest. Through all this, he tried to focus on the science.

"Facts are facts," he said. Over and over. "What people do with them, or choose not to, is up to them. I'm a science educator, not a politician. All I'm trying to do is show what's happening now, why it's happening, and what are the paths a person and government might take as a choice."

His publicist—forced upon him by the university—helped craft a memorable line: "In this land of free speech, I, thank God, have the liberty to speak the truth. Americans have the liberty to refute the truth, reject it or embrace it, and act accordingly. Nobody is forcing you to take a train, be vegetarian, ride a bicycle or use a condom. But those must all be options in a free society!"

The *Comic Book Caper*, as he had dubbed it early on, was everything Sagan hoped it would be; and everything Isong feared.

At least people are talking, he chuckled to himself as he approached the front door of his dark townhouse. He'd grabbed a takeout meal, knowing Isong would be home late. *Nobody to share the love letters and hate mail.*

The process of dealing with mail had become a routine for Sagan. At work, where most correspondence came, and again at home, with the smaller amount. The publisher had somebody handling email sent directly to them. Most such messages would neither be passed on to Sagan nor responded to at all. Best to ignore the trolls.

Place mail on table. Sit. Slit open letters, but not anything bulky. Place those in Ziploc bag. Campus security had a process in place.

Remove letter and scan for content. 'Love letters' on left for careful reading and response, as time allowed. Requests to speak in middle, for more rapid response. Most would have to be declined.

"Health comes first," was the mantra for Sagan, Isong and the doctor.

Then the nasties. *Hate mail to right, unread.* In theory. *Never read the comments,* went the meme. But sometimes you couldn't help yourself.

There was something unusual about this one. Thicker than normal, yet not really a package. *What is this? It's like something from a crime novel!* A message—with each word cut out of a newspaper in different fonts. By the time he had scanned it, there was no going back.

This was no death threat. He'd seen plenty, and learned to take them for what they were: empty words, meant to scare. Was anyone really going to murder a climate scientist? In its own twisted way, this was worse. Sagan would not be killed. Everything he had built, though, might. Everyone he loved would be hurt; their trust and devotion tested.

> Sagan Cleveland you pedophile. Keep your hands off the children. A boy says you fondled him after one of your shows. Others say you do it often. You are disgusting. You are going to pay. The media will soon know. You are going down sleezebag sodomist! Down and out. You and your faggot excuse for a husband and minister!!
>
> EL Capitan

* * *

Sagan called Simone the next day, following a sleepless night and an emergency meeting with his lawyer, his dean, a university lawyer and a publicist. There had been nothing in the media at that point. Nor had there been calls.

He read Simone the letter, described the strategy being considered, then asked her for advice. Strictly as someone versed in media practices.

"You know I can't intervene in any way, right? As a journalist."

"That's not what I'm asking, Simone."

"Of course, but I had to make it clear. So here are my initial thoughts. First, I have absolutely no doubt that you're innocent. That will put me in a very small group of friends and family." She paused, realizing what she had said. "Is your family aware? Your parents, brother and sister?"

"Michelle is," Sagan said in a tired voice. "She says she'll try and get my parents to call me. Doesn't want to be the one to break it to them."

"And how is she on this?"

"Rock solid, she says. I have no reason to doubt her."

"They'll come after your family," Simone warned. "That's the first place the media will go. Along with your employer and neighbours. Ditto with Isong."

"His family is all in Nigeria," Sagan said. "If the media can track them down, you can be certain they won't be supportive. They'll have no choice but to condemn him, to disown him. That's how it is for gays and lesbians in most of Africa right now."

"*All* of Africa," Simone clarified. Though it had not always been so.

"OK," she continued. "You have to hope your sister is as solid as you believe, and your parents will give you a fair hearing before they have to decide whether to throw you under the bus, or be tarred by association. They'll be under a lot of pressure."

"Don't I know it." Sagan sounded more sad than she had ever known.

"So, cutting to the chase—this will likely jibe with what your advisers told you, but maybe not—if it goes public, issue a short statement declaring your innocence and intention to clear your name."

"Written, and ready to send. If needed."

"Do not go into hiding!" Simone said forcefully. "Not unless your life becomes untenable. Continue your regular routine if possible. Stiff upper lip, old chap!"

Her upper-class Brit impersonation coaxed a short laugh from Sagan.

"But seriously, my good man," she continued, without the accent, "do not comment on this to anyone outside your innermost circle."

"Naturally."

"And Sagan…"

"Listening."

"Under no circumstance, and I mean *no* circumstance, try to be funny. There is no joke, no smile, no goofy grin that will do anything but hurt you. Child abuse is not funny to anyone, anywhere."

"Of course not, do you think I'm—"

"All your life," Simone cut in, "you've relied on humour. When things get rough, crack a joke. This is one situation where you must resist your programming. OK? It's who you are. It's what everyone—almost everyone—loves about you. You've got to make a herculean effort."

She had been lecturing. Now she adopted a softer, empathetic voice.

"You're hurt. Let yourself feel hurt! You're the victim of an injustice. Make that obvious." It won't require acting, she was thinking.

"One more thing."

"Say it sister."

Simone took a deep breath. "No matter what happens, your life will never be the same. This is a smear. That's all it is, and we know it. But smears stay with you. I really, really hate to say this. Start thinking about the next phase of your life. You and Isong. Nobody can take away your accomplishments, but they can steal your good name. You will eventually earn back some of that, but only some."

"Yeah, I'm getting that. The show's dead. Unless this whole thing never sees the light of day. This time, though, it feels different. Somebody has taken the gloves off."

"Let's hope not, but… hey, I should have asked from the outset, how are you holding up?"

"OK," he said, in a dejected voice. "Considering. Last time I was utterly exhausted, and I'd never seen this kind of thing. This time, well... I've been preparing."

"First they ignore you," quoted Simone. "Then they laugh at you, then they attack you..."

"Then you win." Sagan completed the saying, but did not sound convinced.

"They're attacking, my friend. But whatever it takes, you are going to win."

"*We* are going to win," he said, sounding a little more convinced.

As soon as they hung up, Simone began searching for a phone number. *Leave no email trail. We don't know who they are. But we will find out, and make them pay!*

* * *

"*New York Observer*. To whom may I direct your call?"

Simone provided the name, and her own. The extension was ringing.

"Phil here. Is that really you Simone? *Clare Hall* Simone?"

"Phil? *Wolfson College* Phil? Simone mimicked. "Got a minute?"

"For you girl, all the time in the world." Though she'd been in New York for nearly a decade, Phil's distinctive Iranian-British accent hadn't changed.

"You did great stuff on Fukushima! Have I told you that? We ran all of it."

"Thanks, but listen Phil." Simone was in no mood for small talk. "I'm pressed for time. I've got a story I can't chase myself. A good friend. Some arm's-length research might lead to a scoop, and prove his innocence."

"Journalistic ethics?!" Phil exclaimed. "Haven't stumbled over *those* for a while."

"Yah," Simone chuckled. "Some of us do try."

"It doesn't go unnoticed, girl. By your peers. So, what's troubling your friend?"

"Remember the 'climate-gate' thing? Did you guys have more luck than me, or the British police for that matter? Tracing the hacker?"

"Nothing we could make stick," said Phil. "Just a solid hunch. Lawyers wouldn't let us run it."

"That's what I figured. For the sake of this dear friend whose name you might soon see attached to a very sordid—and I must say false—accusation, could some of your sleuth squad be put back on the job? It's a big ask, but I guarantee there's a story in it. It may lead to high places. Important people, getting very dirty."

"This sounds fun! What have you got?"

Philomena Barkley-Satrapi, 'PB-S' or 'Phil' to just about everyone, had to be the smartest woman Simone ever had the pleasure of working with. Cambridge first boat rowers were like that. Smart and tough.

* * *

The story did break. But three days later, and only on some obscure right-wing websites at first. It seemed the person behind this was having a tough time getting mainstream media pickup. Lawyers would have instructed them to hold off until the key facts could be confirmed: Who was making the accusation? Was the minor in question named, or was there a parent prepared to make a public accusation?

Anonymous tips were always trouble. Unless you were the *National Tattler*, or some of the jock/talk show hosts. They'd grab at anything. Then blame it on an unnamed source and take a chance on a lawsuit.

The major media could not be counted on to be any more ethical. Just smarter. If a small-market paper or special interest website got the ball rolling, the big guys could use the old 'as reported in the *Whachahoochee Journal*' trick. *We were just sharing what was already public. Sue them, not us!*

When one goes public, the pack follows.

But Phil and her cyber-punks were a step ahead of the pack. Three days was all they'd needed, once Phil put them back in the hunt with a fresh scent. With the new information—keywords from the paste-up letter and a little carelessness on the part of EL Capitan—it fell rather quickly into place. Or apart, depending on your perspective.

Had Elmore Lambert been careless? Or was he suffering from a serial criminal syndrome? Did he secretly—unknown to himself even—want to get caught? Whatever led to it, the *New York Observer* was ready.

"Fabricated Accusations Target Science Educators," read its banner headline.

Phil's article, co-authored with two of her top reporters, hit the streets—and went live online—mere hours after the story began trickling out on the evening shows of some 24-hour news channels. Though two major dailies and a number of morning television and radio shows were by then reporting the accusations, along with several dozen political sites and bloggers—"Penn State Climate Scientist Accused of Sexual Touching of Minor"; "TV Host Fiddling with Children, Accuser Says"; "Can't Trust Prof With Science or Students!"—most were promptly withdrawn. Retractions would follow several days later, after the university let loose a storm of lawyers.

The *Observer* article focused not on Sagan, but the larger pattern of harassment of scientists nationwide. As evidence that 'an orchestrated campaign' was underway, and had been for some years, the authors referred to 'a recent accusation against a science professor at Penn State University,' and two other examples. These were qualified as 'unfounded and almost certainly untrue.'

The choice not to elaborate on the nature of the accusation against Sagan had followed extensive discussion among the paper's editors, lawyers and the investigative team. With no evidence that the allegation had substance, printing details of his alleged crimes or misdemeanours would constitute becoming party to the original slander. No accuser could be found and no victim had been named.

The harassment campaign appeared to be both systematic and criminal, the *Observer* concluded, meriting serious investigation by law enforcement agencies.

Phil's story recounted the history of threats to scientists at various universities and agencies, as well as to citizen climate campaigners. All had a record of advocating prompt and serious action to reduce greenhouse gas emissions.

The article chronicled the rise of 'false flag' organizations purporting to stand for public interest and open science, despite a track record of the opposite. Several prominent funders were named, culled from some leaked lists of tax receipts issued to donors who were deducting the expense from their personal or corporate taxes.

Though much of the money raised and spent by these groups could not be fully traced, a distinct pattern emerged. Major funders were often directly or indirectly associated with oil, gas and coal companies. Others were affiliated with the automotive, air travel, chemical and manufacturing industries. All had an interest in the unrestricted use of fossil fuels.

Three other curious linkages emerged. A correlation had been found between funders of climate science denial campaigns and certain evangelical churches or organizations. The majority of donors were from states in which fossil fuel companies were a major player and employer. Finally, significant support was coming from counties and states where the Tea Party movement was strong.

The paper took care not to associate specific funders or supporters with the harassment. They could not prove any one individual or company knew of or endorsed these techniques. But in an accompanying editorial, the paper took a damning position against people who would blindly support an organization without taking an interest in who ran and funded it, or whether it engaged in unethical and even criminal actions.

The editorial gave a strong rebuke to people of religious conviction who would knowingly endorse harassment of scientists and employees of scientific agencies, or choose to look the other way.

"Surely any person of faith, any follower of the teachings of Jesus Christ, should find such acts abhorrent. One must hope these repulsive incidents will open the eyes of Americans to the dirty little war against climate science, and scientists. There is no excuse for such ignorance—either of sound science, or campaigns to suppress it."

* * *

The *Observer* coverage became the subject of substantial comment and curiosity. Media watchers wondered how the paper had been so ready with its sophisticated reporting and editorial broadside. Had they known of the accusations in advance? Who were their sources, and how did they access so much correspondence and bring so many of these denial organizations into one dragnet?

Most people agreed on two things: It was a great piece of investigative work; and there was more to the story.

* * *

Ten months later, Elmore Lambert went on trial for blackmail against Sagan Cleveland and other scientists. He received the best legal defence money could buy.

At the trial, he admitted to hounding scientists by initiating freedom of information searches, but he portrayed these actions as "protecting the public interest, since climate-gate proved these scientists could not be trusted." He denied planting a slanderous story or authoring the original letter to Sagan Cleveland.

The initials in EL Capitan were pure coincidence, his lawyers argued; or an attempt to frame their client.

"Mr. Lambert has no history of using the name EL Capitan, or the term Capitan, in Spanish or any other language."

They speculated that other threatening emails and letters obtained by the *Observer* and the subsequent FBI investigation had been authored by people with the means to impersonate their client and a desire to incriminate him. Elmore Lambert, a mere personal assistant in a large investment company, had neither the means nor the motive.

Much of the material assembled by the *Observer* was subpoenaed as evidence. It had collected a substantial dossier of correspondence from across the country.

"Can you explain how these emails and letters found their way into the hands of your newspaper?" a lawyer for the defence asked Phil on the witness stand. The implication was clear.

"Once it became known we were seeking victims of intimidation similar to that suffered by Professor Cleveland, evidence came flooding in."

"We have four more just as thick as this one," Phil said, as she lifted a bulging binder.

Expert witnesses were able to describe how the complicated trail of data and IP addresses established a link between organizations created by Elmore and many recent targets. They admitted under cross-examination, however, that it was difficult to prove he personally authored or sent any particular message or would have been aware of them all. None of the computers, hard drives or private servers used had been located.

At trial, the prosecution presented financial records and donor lists obtained by the *Observer*. Many major donors were connected to Elmore's employer—Pinnacle Asset Management— and boss. Since it was Elmore Lambert on trial, however, and not his funders, the only issue at stake was whether he had planted a story with the media that defamed Sagan and 'caused or may have caused suffering, loss of personal and professional reputation and loss of future income.'

After a week of trial proceedings, the prosecution had yet to present a smoking gun. It had no witnesses to confirm it was Elmore who planted the story, which had been offered to a small set of media contacts, in an email from a masked account.

There was, however, a final piece of evidence. The case would turn on an old answering machine recording.

"Drop the show. Stay away from kids...We don't want you queers poisoning our children with your faggot lifestyle... Got my drift. Consider this a warning, you sodomist!"

Similar terms. *Sodomist*, rather than *sodomite*. Similar message. Above all, it was the voice of the man now on trial. Despite his amateurish attempt to disguise it.

Nobody in the courtroom needed to wait for the final beep.

In rendering his verdict, the judge made a point of admonishing not just Elmore, but supporters of his false flag organizations for engaging in gross public deception and attempting to "distort and diminish" the important work of scientists and public institutions.

"There are many legal ways of engaging in scientific and political debate in this country. The right to free speech is protected by the Constitution. What we have witnessed in this affair, however, is not an act of free speech. It is a calculated attempt to intimidate and silence. Affected individuals and institutions may launch their own legal action in the future, but I am called to render a verdict today with regards to Elmore Lambert's blackmail of Sagan Cleveland and others."

"I find the accused guilty as charged."

Court reporters noted how Elmore seemed neither surprised nor disappointed.

"It was as if the trial had been part of the plan, part of a bigger strategy from the outset," one wrote. The same reporter noted how Elmore seemed to have built as great a following through the trial as Sagan Cleveland ever had.

As part of his sentencing, Elmore was given six months of community service. He was ordered to pay a fine of $1 million, all legal costs and another $1 million in damages to Sagan. *Chump change to the big boys*. He could barely suppress a smile.

Sagan chose not to pursue further civil action. The formidable resources behind Elmore Lambert ensured any return to court would be long and emotionally draining.

"Besides," Simone counselled, "it won't help your image to be seen pursuing a large award. Wrong as that is, seeking damages will just stand in the way of moving forward. Which you need to do, for your sanity and future with Isong."

Six months later, his community service with a Houston soup kitchen completed, Elmore would leave town. Though Pete made a show of thanking him for his years of excellent service, he scolded Elmore for his ultimate clumsiness.

"Up until that foolish act, you were just executing orders, anonymously, and with imagination. Your game plan for cultivating a network is working like a charm. We have people in positions of influence. Higher by the day. But you crossed the line."

"I don't know what you were thinking," said Pete. "You who plan so carefully. Well, you've made a name for yourself. It's America—you'll cash in handsomely. Just don't show up in any room I'm in. You pissed on my carpet."

Elmore nodded. He could have thanked Pete for his mentorship, and trust. He could have apologized for his lapse, and the damage it did. But he didn't. He was moving on. No point dwelling in the past.

Family Sins

Nobody survives an accusation of pedophilia unscathed. Certainly not family.

Isong weathered the saga despite the grotesque reference to him in the letter. He remained Sagan's rock, but at considerable emotional cost.

Sagan's parents cut themselves off entirely. Curtains closed, they ventured out rarely, and only at night.

His sister Michelle was a different animal.

"Ya, I'll comment," she announced when reporters converged on her house the morning after the initial rumours were being reported, and just as the *Observer* article went live. Standing defiantly on her front step, she let loose.

"A shame on you all, and your vulture owners! My brother is innocent. One hundred percent innocent of touching any child in the wrong kind of way. Ever! So go and write that!" She scanned the assembled group slowly, pausing to make eye contact with each of the dozen or so reporters assembled on her small lawn.

"But while you're here, I have some things to say. Don't any of you come near my children or my husband! Got that? Speak to *me*. And stay away from my parents. They're old, and they're sad. In this community it is still not acceptable to love someone of the same sex. Being gay, being black and gay, is no crime. Yet, it's treated that way in this neighbourhood. In most black communities in this country, and all over the world. And that's nothing to be proud of."

"Ms. Cleveland-Walker—"

"Just hold your horses, 'cause I am not finished. My brother is the kindest, gentlest, most generous man I know. He is also gay. And he is married to another decent, loving black man. So ask yourselves before you report anything on this false accusation, what is the story I am chasing? Is this some uppity nigga who needs to be taught a lesson? Hmm? What's the story here?" She paused, glaring fiercely at the reporters.

"The only thing Sagan Cleveland will be found guilty of is being smart, black and gay. Any combination of which this country just cannot allow. There's your story. Good day and go home. 'Cause if I see anyone near my children, I just might commit a crime!"

"Ma'am?"

"Michelle?"

"Just one question..."

With a firm, unhurried gesture, she had closed the door. A handmade sign swayed gently for a few seconds: DO NOT DISTURB.

"Get that on camera?" a TV reporter asked her cameraman.

"Even got the sign swaying!"

"I got all I need," commented a local writer. "*Smart, black, and gay is no crime.* She just wrote my lead!"

Demar dealt with the news very differently, when he learned of it from a regular supplier on the street. There were plenty of Clevelands, and not many followed the news in his circles. Or watched science shows. But he and Sagan bore a striking facial resemblance, and both had a thing for fashionable shirts and gold chains.

"You related to that guy messing around with kids?" said the man, who had been watching the news in a pizza shop. Demar's look was as good as a bullet between the eyes. He delivered the real one that night.

Retribution took a week to arrive, but arrive it did. Tit for tat on the streets of Detroit.

Sagan and Isong travelled to Detroit together for Demar's funeral, at Michelle's invitation. Her parents were against it, she'd said, but she insisted they be welcomed, and that was that.

They waited until the service was underway before slipping into the building; worried they might be a distraction, and worried there would be reporters. Alone in their pew now, towards the back of the half-empty church, they sat slightly apart. "Out of respect," Sagan had suggested to Isong.

He felt badly about it now. *Respect for who? For what?* After everything Isong had done to support him, here he was distancing himself.

Demar, who had caused no end of trouble since the age of thirteen, gets a proper funeral, while his law-abiding older brother and his loving, decent husband have to sneak in and pretend to be strangers. It made no sense. Sagan slid quietly over until his hip was pressed up against Isong's. He took Isong's hand and gave a gentle squeeze.

It *was* time for a change. Simone had been right. Life must be lived forward. Attending the funeral would be the first step in Sagan's painful return to Detroit.

Four Elements

Fukushima City, September 2013

Sun, wind, water, earth. Jiro's *Four Elements Movement* was born to offer an alternative to nuclear power. He had drawn an image of a four-petalled flower. A four-pronged approach, with the core occupied by economy. *Oikonomia*—the art of running the household. The careful management of resources. Temper your desires and align them with your needs. Efficiency and modesty.

Like the logo, the movement's name was as an elegant symbol. It was also a reference to, and a poke at Japan's 'Four Pillars' policy of the late 1960s, which promoted the 'peaceful use of nuclear energy' domestically, while staunchly opposing global nuclear weapons proliferation.

Lack of a domestic coal and oil resource, and the resulting drive to acquire a reliable supply for an industrializing society, had played a pivotal role in the rise of Japanese militarism in the 1930s. This would lead to imperialist expansion across Southeast Asia and China, culminating in the Pacific War, the destruction of many cities and, ultimately, the detonation of atomic bombs in Nagasaki and Hiroshima.

The scars left by the bombs—Japan was still the only country to have been the target of a nuclear weapon—made it unthinkable to the majority of 1960s Japanese that nuclear technology, even for peaceful purposes, would be developed on their soil.

Nonetheless, opposition to nuclear power waned over the ensuing decades, prompted by aggressive pro-nuclear propaganda, the courting of 'host regions' with generous construction jobs and financial transfers, and the fostering of a close alliance between the ruling party, industry and media barons.

A series of economic setbacks over the ensuing two decades, however, reset the economic and political landscape. Even before a series of 'minor' accidents in the late 90s and early 2000s, support for the nuclear industry was waning. It was no longer the golden goose it had been, and people were less willing to overlook risks to plant workers and host regions. Then came the tsunami.

Four petals, growing from a centre of careful stewardship.

In his initial draft of a manifesto, Jiro made frequent reference to Japan's culture and history. A spiritual approach would be important to 'selling' the Four Elements Movement. Making an emotional connection, not just an intellectual one. He believed he could undermine nuclear power; and fossil fuels for that matter; by showing how foreign they actually were to Japan. How the Japanese had built a sophisticated culture prior to the Industrial Revolution; certainly prior to nuclear energy.

"Nobody remembers this, though," Jiro would say when speaking in public.

"We have been fed a myth—that the nuclear industry is a symbol of Japan's great technological strength, and nuclear power represents independence from imported resources. Sure, the way we built our economy and cities relies heavily on cheap energy. But we can change that. We have just been reminded that nuclear exacts an enormous price when it goes wrong."

Channel Japanese innovation toward a zero-carbon world, declared the published version of the Four Elements Manifesto, which Jiro refined in collaboration with other members of the fledgling organization.

We can achieve a zero-nuclear future through the Four Elements and an emphasis on modesty and self-restraint—such important aspects of Japan's national character, the code of the samurai and Shinto-Buddhism.

It was a veiled dig at the extremism Jiro had often heard from Katsuo. The Fukushima disaster had been a blow to ultra-nationalists, and a source of shame. Even though some refused to accept any responsibility.

In the aftermath of the accident, people demanding a freeze on nuclear expansion and a thorough review of plant safety across Japan had the wind in their sails. What better time to launch an ambitious campaign to promote conservation and renewable energy? The true path to energy security and resilience.

The manifesto laid out the basis for a resurgence of the economy and Japanese pride. It also emphasized two initial regional goals: first, stabilizing the energy grid—through the rapid enactment of conservation measures and extensive local installation of solar panels with storage; second, rebuilding tsunami-damaged housing and community facilities where it was safe to do so, using Four Elements criterion.

New communities would be built, and damaged towns rebuilt, but only in areas unlikely to see another tsunami, and well outside the radioactive exclusion zone. This zone was off limits to all except workers engaged in scraping and bagging contaminated soil and mapping 'hot spots.'

Jiro took a strong interest in those areas recently declared 'safe for habitation'. He had ventured into them illegally on a number of occasions—always with a geiger counter, and wearing his dosimeter.

"So I can tell just how badly over the annual limit I am," he joked darkly to Jenny by FaceTime.

He did not trust government assurances. Low-level radiation remained in most places and random hotspots had been detected outside the cordoned-off perimeter.

Officials like to draw neat circles: *Safe outside, dangerous inside.* But rain and snow do not fall in circles. Wind does not blow uniformly. Radiation had fallen at the whim of the weather in the first days after the accident, something nobody in the Japanese Defense Force or the power authority could control. Hot spots were badly mapped and marked.

* * *

Three years after the tsunami, Jenny had still not visited the region. Not even Fukushima City—40 kilometers from the damaged plant—where Jiro was living in his parents' tiny, 'temporary' apartment. Like most displaced by the disaster, they preferred to remain close to 'home'. Jenny and the girls would see them in Tokyo each summer, meeting up at Katsuo's house, their visits coinciding with his absences.

Jenny would gladly have welcomed her parents-in-law in Kuala Lumpur. They had an extra room. Not large, but there was a generous kitchen, living and dining room, plus an outdoor veranda and a yard. Space was not the constraint in KL that it was in Japanese towns and cities. Though this was changing.

"Urbanization is affecting Malaysia, just like much of the world," Yuki had written in a report for her Grade 5 geography class. Her research led her to a recent UN study. She was reciting some of what she had found to her mother and sister one Sunday evening, in the comfort of their modern, air-conditioned dining room. Anna had her own school assignment to finish, and Jenny was working on her notes for a speech.

"Did you know that 74% of Malaysians now live in cities? The global average is 54%, but that's expected to reach 66% by 2050."

"Wow," said Jenny, pausing to look at Yuki. "Two thirds of the world population!"

"And did you know that KL has grown from 2 million people to 6 million in just 20 years?"

"The air's filthy too," said Anna without looking up. She was writing a report on pollution. "But I'm glad we don't live in Lagos or Dhaka. Or just about any city in China!"

"Tokyo is the world's largest city," recited Yuki. "With 38 million people."

"I don't ever want to live in Tokyo," Anna announced. "It's too crowded."

"There's no chance of that," Jenny said calmly. "Even if it means we don't see Daddy as much as we would like."

"Why doesn't he live with us anymore?" asked Yuki. *Kids get right to the heart of it*, Jenny thought, as she considered her response.

"Daddy has important work he needs to do in Japan. The tsunami was hard for your Jiji and Baba. Also, it was hard for Daddy because it made him sad to see what happened. He needs to do something to help rebuild those towns in a way that makes them more—you'll like this word, Anna—resilient. That means better able to withstand shocks and disasters. Like earthquakes, and floods and being cut off from gas or electricity."

"Why does it have to be Daddy that makes them resilient?" Yuki wrinkled her forehead. "Why doesn't the government do it?"

"You girls ask such good questions," Jenny chuckled. "Ones that aren't easy to answer. You could say that governments tend to do what they've always done. They repeat mistakes over and over, because they don't like to take a risk on something new."

"Also because they are influenced by powerful people who make money doing things the old way," said Anna. "People with a vested interest."

"Wow!" said Jenny, putting a hand on Anna's arm. "Where did that come from?"

"I read things," Anna replied in a matter-of-fact tone. "On the internet, and in journals Mr. Lewis recommends. My *radical* history teacher, you called him."

"Are you and Daddy radical?" asked Yuki.

"I never used to think so. Though I *have* always wanted to change things." Jenny paused and smiled.

"Perhaps that does make us radicals. I guess either we're getting more radical, or everybody else is working harder to defend the 'status quo.' Look that one up, Anna. But tomorrow. You have to get to bed, and I need to prepare for my announcement. NiMa Energy pays the bills for us. And your father and grandparents."

"I miss Daddy," Yuki whispered to Anna, after the lights went out.

"Me too. At least there's FaceTime."

"FaceTime doesn't give hugs."

Welcome; Not Welcome

Le Tilleret, Drome, France, September 2013

"I can't believe something so promising soured so quickly!" Nicole said to François.

Sitting at the rustic dining room table on the second floor of the restored main house, he pictured the body language that went with her exasperated voice at the end of the phone line.

"*Some* countries are flourishing," he argued. "The Arab Spring didn't implode everywhere!"

"*Some* countries! Open your eyes François, we're talking about ONE. Tunisia—but it's on a knife's edge. Egypt—boom! Morocco and Algeria—smaller boom! Libya—mega boom! Syria—oh god! Even Turkey, going backwards under Erdogan."

"Not that Turkey has much choice," he said, "with Daesh at the borders. Kurds agitating again. Syrian refugees flooding in. Putin playing empire builder.

"François! He's a dictator in a business suit."

"OK, OK. I'm not defending him, just noting the circumstances. But if you want to talk dictators, remember that today's imploding states were kept secure by iron fist rulers. People rose up. Nobody could have predicted how badly that would go. Not in Egypt or Libya at least. Syria, sure."

"François—you called me for a different reason—but Libya *was* predictable. No history of democracy, no civil society... how was that going to work? Arm the rebels, take out the regime, and what's left? Rebels with ambition. A recruiting ground for Daesh. Add in the stranded foreign workers, people pouring up from the south..."

"I knew we'd get to the reason for the call!" François chuckled, willing Nicole to laugh. His wife, his separated wife... the mother of his children.

"You're right to laugh, François," she said dryly. "I wish I could. It's a mad world, and this refugee crisis is maddest of all. The generosity of some, the meanness of others. With no end in sight. I need a break!"

Unseen by her, a smile had appeared on his face. "You're welcome here any time. The children too," he added quickly. "Our adult offspring," he clarified, seeking a better descriptor for twenty-something professionals.

"I don't know, François." Nicole's voice was colder now.

"You wouldn't recognize the place. The buildings, the farm, the permaculture garden, the pond. The village! From nearly dead, to hosting music festivals."

"I'm glad to hear your enthusiasm. We should have spoken sooner, but..."

He sighed loudly. "I know, Nicole. It's hard—"

"Well, we're talking now," she stated, "about refugees. Your refugees. Which makes me think I wouldn't be getting a holiday there after all. Migrants here, migrants there..." she chanted facetiously.

"So, I was wondering, Nicole, can you handle more in Strasbourg? Or if not there, can you suggest somewhere else?"

"Our settlement centre's swamped," said Nicole. "The city is helping, but we're maxed out. No money. No housing. No jobs—official or decent ones, that is. I'll check with Mulhouse and Metz. How many are we talking? Age, country, languages?"

"At the moment I have eight," he said, doing some mental math. "In the big barn. There's 12 more being housed by some neighbours. I think we could provide work and housing for, say, two or three each. So we'll need to move about 15 before the next police sweep. The next deportation orders. As if they have anywhere to go back to! They're mostly young men. My friend Yves has a married couple, with a newborn."

"Country and languages?" Nicole repeated.

"A mix, as usual. Sudan, Somalia, Niger, Congo. Even Bangladesh. Poor guy got stranded in Libya when things fell apart. Forced to work for free."

"Trapped, then victimized," said Nicole. "I've heard the stories."

"A trip through hell, just to reach another one!"

"Our nice, civilized Europe, reaching the end of its rope. Or maybe just at the beginning..." she trailed off, meekly.

"The guys from Niger and Congo speak basic French. Quite an accent, and dialect, but they learn fast. The rest? A smattering of English. Which has my neighbours waving their hands and talking louder at them." They both chuckled.

"Education varies wildly," François said. "A guy who couldn't afford to continue medical school. A farmer who had no soil left. Both would be happy to sweep streets in London, given the chance." He sighed loudly.

"Well François, aren't you glad we had this uplifting chat!"

"Sorry for dumping on you like that," he said.

"Both of us still trying to save the world. Me, the casualties, you... the web of life.

"The casualties have found me now too," said François.

"There will be a place in heaven for you."

"*St. François!*" he mimicked caustically. "Don't get started. That nickname has followed me. Only some here prefer *le Petit Diable*. Not everyone admires my work."

"The lot of the change-maker," Nicole said, in a consoling tone.

"I'd better go. Time to show a young man how to drive a tractor. He says he knows, but I'm not just taking his word. So, you'll look into reception centres? Some of the locals are restless, speaking of critics. I'd guess three days at most before the sweep."

"I'll let you know by tomorrow," said Nicole. "Is email OK?"

François laughed. "It's probably watched, but then this phone could be tapped."

"Everyone's being watched now," said Nicole.

"Give my love to the kids, um adults."

It was the first time they had spoken in years. Many more would pass before they did again.

Downtown On the Farm

Detroit, October 2013

This your first visit, ma'am?"

Simone reached out and accepted the steaming cup of coffee with a smile. The border crossing had taken less time than expected. Finding the diner, on the other hand, had been a challenge. Not because the building was badly marked, but because all the others on the block—as scouted beforehand on satellite view—had vanished. Either they'd recently been demolished, or Google wasn't bothering to update this part of town.

This had been a thriving, middle-class community, with decent homes, big yards, schools, parks and... a diner. Simone would never have known about the rest, if not for the television report she'd recently seen.

"Yes, it is my first time," said Simone. "I came to check in on a friend."

The elderly woman smiled weakly.

"And speak of the devil..." said Simone, rising to greet Sagan as he stepped through the door. Instinctively, she did a scan of his eyes and face.

"The food here is great," said Sagan in a flat voice, "but I'd skip the local shops. You'd do well to check out the gardens, though. There's a farmer's market tomorrow which might interest you. And if you're into cycling, I can take you to the most dahling

261

little bike builder." He had slipped effortlessly from a bland tour guide to a camp one.

Simone had all she needed. "Shut up and give me a hug!"

They embraced warmly. He had put on weight, and lost a lot of muscle tone.

"Mmm, that's good. It's been too long girl."

Emails and calls had been rare since Sagan had returned to Detroit nearly two years earlier, and he had declined her offer the summer before to join her on a bike tour.

"I'm really into something right now," he'd explained. "Permaculture. You don't just learn about it, you do it. And I need all the practice I can get." That's how Simone learned about Detroit's urban farms.

When the economy collapsed after the 2008 mortgage fiasco, Detroit's long slow slide hit rock bottom. Some people tried to stay in their homes, even after water and electricity had been cut off. Others moved in and squatted. But it was getting dangerous; more from the condition of the buildings than from crime. So the city moved in with bulldozers and completed the task.

Sagan first visited Center Street Farm on a tour organized by a community developer from church. The same church where Isong was serving as visiting minister. A temporary position. Reflecting the community it served, the congregation was small, its finances non-existent. In winter, they kept their coats on during the service.

They were treating it as an adventure. Sagan had money in the bank from the court award, and they had job prospects in other cities, when they were ready. Returning to Penn State had been an option, until Sagan let the two-year limit expire. By that time, they had settled into a different life.

"Time flies when you're having fun," Sagan said to Simone, gesturing to her to sit down. "Farming for two seasons, reading and writing for the other two. Some days I miss my old life, and others not at all."

"Have Ida's club sandwich," he said, pointing to the menu written on a sign above the counter. "Local ingredients, from the farm. Right next door."

"I couldn't believe there was still a diner here," said Simone. "With everything else gone."

"Yep. It had a stay of execution. The protest made the evening news. A bunch of us in overalls, waving our rakes and hoes, chanting 'Save Ida's Diner!'. 'I thought you were done embarrassing me,' Michelle says to me. 'Just getting started,' I told her. 'But I'll keep my straw hat on.' Only she'd know it was me. And my parents."

"How are they?" asked Simone.

"Not so well. Let's save that for later. We're here to talk *farming*! You say you've got a feature to write. You lose your column or something? Demoted to the gardening beat. Too outrageous for readers? Poking people in the eye about End Times. Ooh, don't get those people mad!" He waved an admonishing finger at Simone.

"Don't I know it," she laughed. "Plenty of riled up folks over that one. Who knew they read the *Ottawa Herald* in rural Mississippi."

"It's called *the internet* Simone. It'll reach Canada eventually."

"Rascal!" Simone gave Sagan a playful swat. "No, I've still got the national column. Though I'm wearing out my welcome. I'll take my severance pay and come farm with you. A gardening column—great tip!"

"If you can get a work visa. We're becoming wary of Canadians."

"So I hear," said Simone. "I had no problem today though, despite being a journalist. This trip is special. I assigned myself, so no travel budget. Show me where I can pitch my tent." She made a show of peering out the window.

"Journalism has fallen on hard times," said Sagan. "Like a lot of people." He gestured towards Ida. "Owner, server and cook."

"Pretty much," said Simone. "Though not quite as hard. I found this Detroit story fascinating. There's plenty already written, but I want to take another angle. The breakdown of social order and the rebirth that follows."

"Reporters!" Sagan said with disdain, only partly feigned. "Gotta fight you off with sticks. Photographers, film students, sociology professors too! We're a working farm, not a zoo."

"Come to think of it," he said, a smile emerging, "a zoo *would* bring in cash."

Simone chuckled, shaking her head. His humour had survived just fine.

"Hey, I got a mountain bike for you." Sagan announced abruptly. "It's a big area we'll be visiting. You can leave the car here."

Simone's eyes narrowed. "Is it safe?" she asked without thinking.

"Safe!" he shrieked. "Ida, tell the woman. Is it safe?"

"Safest it's ever been, honey. Thieves are in the 'burbs now. They don't know what to do with chickens. Certainly not kale."

"I love kale!" Simone said, her eyes lighting up.

"You've come to the right place," said Ida. "Kale central!"

The three-day visit gave Simone everything she came for. Interviews, photos, video and some surprisingly philosophical comments from people of minimal education and work experience. More stereotypes slain.

Most of all, she confirmed that Sagan was healthy. His cheeks were a bit puffy, but that would be the medication. She'd feared the series of blows two years earlier had been too much.

Sagan had taken awhile to find his feet, but here he was—in work boots.

Breakdown and rebirth.

Sometimes a society needs to hit rock bottom before it's willing to admit the old way is no longer working, Simone wrote.

Another bandage on top of previous ones won't help. The first step to rebirth lies not just in charting a different path, but asking 'Where do we need to get to, as a community and a society?' In this, a community resembles an ecosystem. The great ecological leap forward comes after great devastation. Massive forest fires lead not only to a new forest, but a different one. Yellowstone was thought to be lost in the 1990s, and now it is vibrantly renewed. Detroit is showing similar signs, in unexpected places."

The article, with accompanying photos and video, highlighted the human dimension of the urban agriculture movement: black Americans reclaiming the right to till the fields as a choice—a dignified activity, where it was once done by force or out of desperation; former auto workers 'finding rewards in working with living organisms and plants in sunlight and under rain,' where once all they knew was "assembling uniform parts under artificial lighting"; people making connections between the work of rebuilding the soil and rebuilding human bodies and the soul of a community, *deadened after generations of take-it-or-leave-it work, substandard education and highly processed food.*

Simone's reporting won a national award. Her first in many years. Though she'd been nominated twice for her columns.

"There's a book in that," Ron said, after reading her piece.

"Maybe," she said, drifting into thought.

"Ron," she added, after a long pause. "Tell me if I'm crazy. One day I want to co-author a book with Sagan. Or make a documentary."

"Nothing crazy about that," said Ron, putting his arm around her. "Two different but complementary talents. But think of the ego clash!"

She smiled and shook her head. He wasn't wrong.

"When Sagan's ready to be back in the public eye, of course. He's doing great where he is now. Farming, and running discussion groups about science and religion. Facilitating them, really." Simone had sat in on one of these sessions. "He gets the participants to do the talking. Most have no idea who he is."

"We get more from listening than talking," said Ron. "Somebody smart once said that."

"A lot of people," said Simone. "But talking still gets all the attention."

A Big Decision

Jiro's devotion to his Four Elements initiative was putting a strain on NiMa Energy as well as the family. Though many of his work tasks could be performed from afar, using the technology available, it was obvious to Jenny and the management team that he was no longer truly with them in spirit. The passion he had thrown into launching NiMa was now directed to where he felt it was needed most.

"That's great for Japan, and the people you've inspired there," an exasperated Jenny said during one of Jiro's rare trips to KL, "but you've left a gaping hole here! I can't, we can't carry the extra workload any longer, or wait on decisions because you're preoccupied with Four Elements."

Jiro had no answer. Not able to handle her stare, he licked a finger and began to rub a circle left by the marmalade jar on the kitchen table.

"Hello! Jenny to Jiro, are you reading me?"

"Yes!" he replied, more harshly than intended. "I'm listening. But I'm thinking. I'm trying to figure out how I can be in two places at once, without letting everybody down. Especially my family."

His last words served to cut the tension. Jenny knew she could find a new business partner, but not a new husband. Certainly not a new father for her children.

"Oh Jiro. We've been through a lot, and somehow we've always held it together. More than that, we've kept growing. But this time, I feel things slipping. The staff is feeling it, the girls are feeling it—even if at their age they won't let on that they want to be with their parents—and you and I just can't keep this up. Too many balls to juggle. Too much travel. Too little sleep."

Jiro reached out and opened his hands across the table, willing Jenny to place hers into them. She rested her much smaller hands in his, welcoming the connection.

"So, my Malaysian dynamo, what do you suggest I do?"

"WE do!"

"Yes, what do you think *we* should do. I just keep going in circles."

"That's because none of the options are good ones. All of them feel like you're letting somebody down. Right?"

Jiro nodded.

"So let's try a different approach. The very best thing you can do is devote your energy where only you can play the role. Where only Jiro Ebitsubo is *the man*."

He smiled.

"Instead of asking, 'Am I the best person for this job?', ask 'Am I the only person?' Hold onto what only you can do, then give it everything."

"Like being a father. And a husband. Right?"

"That's what I was hoping you'd pick. But we both know that's not enough. So, what next?"

Jiro was silent. Apprehensive. He hoped Jenny would decide for him.

"I can tell you'" she said. "But it needs to be you. Not 'my wife made me do it'. You'll resent me forever. Just say it. You know it."

Jiro breathed in deeply, sat up straight and looked his wife in the eyes.

"I can be replaced at NiMa Energy. The company is humming along beautifully, except when I'm holding things up. Junior people can step up to take on a bigger role. And you can hire somebody else to do the legal and financial jobs. Legal advice does not have to be in-house. As for finance, I've reached the limit of my skills and contacts. You need somebody with networks and deal-making talents I don't have."

"There it is," said Jenny. "The irreplaceable Jiro can be replaced."

"Upgraded even!" he suggested. For the first time that visit, he laughed.

"In the areas you mentioned, sure. As a father, a husband, a *son*, never."

"How about as a brother? You left that out."

"Jiro, as a brother, you're just fine," she said, peering into his eyes. "It's the other guy who needs upgrading."

As Nature Intended

Papineau, Quebec, August 2014

L ying on the deck of Ron's cabin—*our cabin*, she had to remind herself for the first years after the wedding—Simone was at peace. The cabin was where she went for rest. A kind she had never known until her first time there alone. Totally alone. First you empty your mind, then you start to think, really think—for yourself.

Her favourite time was August, when the days were hot, the nights cool and the bugs in decline. May and June were hopeless. Bug-slapping hopeless. September could be nice, but by then the working world had gone from shutdown into high gear.

There was no cell phone or internet at the cabin. Surrounding hills and forest took care of that. They could have installed landlines, but that would have been absurdly expensive and marred the landscape with poles and wires. By choice, they had no power lines either. A solar panel charged two batteries; enough to run lights and charge a laptop and other compact tools.

They had friends with cottages that sported all the comforts and distractions of home. Simone and Ron agreed that there was no point heading into nature just to watch TV or be on Facebook. Ron's daughter, Jacinthe, had a different view. She'd loved the cabin in her youth, but now complained it was 'prehistoric.'

All the better, thought Simone, lying in the sun. People can't reach me, I can't reach them. In an emergency, someone will come find me.

Nothing but gently rustling leaves, occasional chirping, a few croaks from the pond... Simone looked forward to these moments. Uncovered like a solar panel, taking in the energy she'd been starved of since winter and would need come fall.

Come September, she would once more assume the burden of writing about things nobody should have to know about, let alone research and share. Still, it had to be done, and she got paid for it.

It could be worse. She could be the subject, suffering as the people she wrote about did, as the species and ecosystems on whose behalf she wrote did. Really, I have no right to complain. *I do, though, need to recharge.* That thought came to her one afternoon, lying naked on their deck, at the top of the hill, camouflaged from neighbours by the dense forest that stood between the cabin and the lake.

She wondered why more people didn't spend time in the wild. The answer was obvious, though. Few had any experience of the outdoors. The real outdoors. How lucky she was to have been raised—immersed—in a world of water and forest. Playing in the great outdoors, in all four seasons. The lives of the majority involved little or no vacation, and not even a park of consequence. Even in Canada, in relatively green cities like Ottawa, how many people thought of going out into the woods, or to a lake? Or could, if they wished? Not many.

Despite their middle-class upbringing, modest salaries and relatively non-materialist life, she and Ron were—unwittingly, unintentionally—part of the 'One Percent'. Maybe the 'Three Percent'. In the circles they traveled in, certain things were a given: *I'll take my car, you take yours. Let's serve a pinot gris with the salmon. When we were in Florida for March Break... Sorry, the kids are at summer camp that week. We're thinking of getting the kitchen remodelled. I'm popping up to the cottage...*

When her mind went on one of these excursions, it was hard to know where it would land. Increasingly it ended with a reminder to count her blessings. That's how she came to invite Sagan and Isong. What right did she have to keep this place to herself?

Sagan was initially skeptical. "We're not really wilderness people." His Arctic trips were an anomaly, and he had been glad to let grad students take those over.

Isong's family came from a rural Nigerian village, but never looked back after moving into the city, despite the noise and pollution.

"Come in mid-August," she'd urged Sagan. "Bring books and towels. Ron's an ace with the BBQ. He likes to show off his wines too."

"Barbecue! Wine! I'll pack my speedo tonight!"

Simone had trouble erasing that image.

She used to have friends up to the cabin regularly. With and without Ron. Lately, though, it had become her retreat. She even came in the dead of winter, snowshoeing down the lane and up the hill. Seated by the wood stove, with a good book, a pen and paper, sometimes a laptop. But she preferred the notebook, from a slower time.

* * *

"The expression on your faces when you stepped out of the car!" she ribbed them. "Like you'd landed on another planet."

The first night in the guest bunkhouse, thirty paces from the main cabin, Sagan and Isong slept badly. Too many noises, they said. "Bull-frogs, owls, maybe even a bear." They slept all day, though. On the dock and in the hammock. The second night was better, despite heavy rain.

"Hey sleepy head," Simone called to Isong as he stumbled onto the deck of the cabin. She was finishing up her yoga routine. "You seem to have settled in."

"Co-ffee!" Isong responded robotically, his arm extended.

She smiled. "Just let me finish. Nearly done."

Isong went to the deck rail to see the last wisps of mist burning off the lake.

"You know," he said, turning to face her. "The weirdest thing happened last night."

"Whoa, Isong. What happens in the bunkhouse stays in the bunkhouse!"

"Wicked girl!" he laughed, wagging his finger. "No, really. I was sleeping soundly when the storm hit. The rain was pelting on the roof. A real din. I awoke and for a moment was completely lost. I had this flashback to our village in Nigeria. I must have been... maybe ten. I'd lie in bed at night, hearing the rain, thinking 'please let it be enough to bring a good harvest, but not enough to wash us away.' That happened to some shacks, you know. So last night, that's what hit me. Hurray, the rains have come, but not too much please. I snapped out of it when I remembered where we are—lost in the Quebec woods. I slept like a baby after that. Or maybe like a 10-year old back home again. Not that Nigeria will ever be home again. But the rain on the tin roof..."

"Memory is funny," Simone said, sitting up straight. "Smells and sounds—they can transport you back, can't they? You recall exactly where you were."

"Mmhmm. Coffee does that too!" Isong nodded toward the cabin. "Please."

"I get it, I get it. How about you roll up this mat while I put on the coffee. You can help with the pancakes. Guests are put to work here."

* * *

"I think if I become clear in what I believe and why, and how that motivates my work, then I can see if there are any points of intersection with these others—the biblical literalists, the libertarians."

Sagan was explaining to Simone his personal journey since they were last together. The three of them were seated on the screen porch, enjoying tea and shortbread, sheltered from the mid-afternoon sun.

Sagan had come to realize he was dismissing anyone who objected to his worldview. Yet, he had never taken the time to reflect on what his core beliefs actually were. Beyond the superficial.

"Perhaps there's nothing there, no common ground, and we're doomed to talk past each other," he said. "Or shout at each other, each hoping to win the other over. But it's clear to me that stalemate will mean the end of us all."

"Isn't that what they want, a hastened end?" Simone said with mischief.

He nodded. "Some do, or think they do. Though I'm pretty sure a hastened end is going to be ugly, and those who think they'll be spared the ecological unravelling haven't a clue."

"So, you're on this quest… to find points of connection."

"To follow the slow arc of history, tending towards justice. Remembering that no legal systems are perfect. Ditto for governments and religions. That's why all of them should be allowed to evolve: constitutions, legal systems, dogma. At a point in time, they were the best people could come up with. That hardly makes them perfect, or necessarily relevant today."

"So, is that how people should approach religious parables and edicts?" asked Simone. "Wise for their time, but imperfect in today's world? Due for updating or re-interpreting through the lens of new knowledge?"

"Faith updated by scientific discovery," Sagan suggested, shifting forward into the sole ray of afternoon light still hitting the screened porch where they were seated.

"How could you expect rules or stories from hundreds, even thousand of years ago to reflect what we know now?" said Isong. "They can't, of course. They represent the state of thinking at that time. Fine enough way back then, but due for an upgrade."

"That's a tough one to swallow," said Simone. "Not just for Christians. Many people like the certainty of a holy book. Divine, immutable rules to guide them through life."

"People do like certainty," Isong nodded in agreement. "The trouble is, it's not working any better now than it did then."

"Hygiene works better than prayer," Sagan declared with a grin. "Vaccinations too. Birth control works a lot better than the rhythm method. It's fact versus faith."

"Though society is stuck in a place that's halfway between the two," Simone said.

"What almost everyone forgets," said Isong, his voice rising, "is that these holy books are *recollections*. Interpretations and stories. Not the word of a divine being, recorded on reel-to-reel."

Simone and Sagan chuckled.

"Sorry to interrupt!" said a deep voice with a Franco-Ontarian accent from the shadows of the nearly-dark cabin. The three of them jumped.

"I didn't mean to startle you," said Ron, stepping onto the porch, "but I have this rack of pork ribs. Oh geez, I forgot to ask. Anyone vegetarian? Jewish? Muslim?" He extended his hand and a big grin to Isong.

"So, you're the guy who holds it all together!"

* * *

"That was some heavy discussion you guys were into when I arrived." Ron and Sagan were doing the dishes while Simone took Isong for a stroll to the lake to put away the chairs and paddleboard.

"I hovered there for awhile, without anyone noticing. Is that what I'm in for?"

"Afraid so," Sagan said. "You're stuck at the cabin with a preacher, a born-again spiritual seeker and a provocateur."

"That sounds like the start of a joke. Or maybe a slasher movie."

Sagan laughed. "Please join us. If we reach four members, we can register as a cult and get charitable status."

Ron chuckled. "Oh, I don't know much about religion."

"Me neither. I'm just on a quest to find out why I do what I do, and can't let go."

"Maybe we're not so different," Ron said. "Though I find my guidance, and a lot of my fulfilment in nature. And with that little firecracker woman I love."

"*I've* loved her *longer*," Sagan chanted. "Though you needn't worry," he added, in a reassuring voice.

"Worry about what?" asked Simone as she opened the screen door.

"Firecrackers," said Sagan with a grin. "Dangerous!"

"Yeah, Sagan was telling me he's scared of firecrackers. Something about a prank gone wrong." Sagan and Ron's laughter resonated through the log cabin.

Simone nudged Sagan away and hugged Ron from behind, her cheek against his broad back. "He makes me laugh too. When we can be in the same place."

"Well, you are now," said Sagan. "We could leave you alone."

"Stay for now," she said. "Later tonight, though, ignore the howling. There's animals in these here woods."

"Simone!" Ron blushed. He'd never seen her joke like this with another man.

"You think you know your partner until they meet up with old friends," said Sagan with a wink.

"That will make for an interesting couple of days," Ron declared.

Ottawa Herald — September 8, 2014

The Cohen Column:
What's this Bug?

One of the greatest obstacles to getting Canadians to take climate change seriously enough to demand meaningful policy like a carbon tax or make substantial changes to our behaviour, such as reducing flying—is that we're not seeing it. We're the proverbial frog in a kettle, which does not notice the water getting hot until it's boiling.

Sure, we blame the climate after an especially hot or dry spell of weather, but then make dismissive comments each time a cold or wet spell comes around: "Where's global warming when you need it?"

Experts tell us not to confuse weather with climate. One is short term and highly variable, the other is defined by long-term trends.

I was thinking about this during my vacation at the cabin. Whereas in the city I rarely make time to pay attention to the natural world around me, I'm much more observant in the woods. I've been a regular visitor to the forests north of Ottawa for most of my life. What have I observed over these past two decades?

The seasons are changing, though it's not linear. This year was an early spring, last year a late one, but still there are some clear trends: Snow is gone earlier, and buds and blackflies arrive sooner; Thanksgiving is as likely to be spent in a t-shirt as a fleece; the lakes are not always frozen at Christmas.

When it rains, it rains harder, and these intense showers are far more frequent.

The trees are increasingly stressed by heat and drought. I see it in the leaves and die-back of some older trees. Those heavy rains run off before they can soak in.

Then there's poison ivy. It's been around for a long time, but seems to be thriving. The increased level of carbon dioxide is like steroids for poison ivy, and the chemical to which people react—urushiol—is getting more toxic.

Exotic pests are not so exotic: the emerald ash borer may have come from away, but warmer winters have allowed it to thrive, whereas it might have been delayed or wiped out by our winters of old, before it devastated our ash trees.

There is a distinct loss of frogs, and fewer songbirds. The frog loss is a baffling one: chemicals, acidity and water temperature are all possibilities. As for the birds, this may be more about pesticides, habitat loss and other threats to reproduction and migration. Bell your cat, please, or keep it inside. Birds pass through dozens of cities as they travel to and from our region.

As for insects, we find ourselves asking "what is that thing?" I used to know all the bugs in my woods. Now there's this weird greenish fly, and a giant version of the house fly. Neither bite. That's reassuring, but where did they come from?

Speaking of insects, Ottawa Public Health started giving away free tick removal keys last year. That's thoughtful, but how did it come to this? Nightly tick inspections are now on my to-do list. Lyme disease is wicked. I know five people who have been infected. Then there's West Nile Virus. Also on the rise.

Those are my amateur field notes. Experts will surely weigh in, but I know one thing for sure: a lot of things are changing, and it looks and feels more like a trend than a spell of odd weather.

Online Feedback:

She says more drought then more rain. It can't be both!

* * *

You're not alone Simone Cohen. I've noticed a lot of small changes over these past decades in the woods. But it seems they're accelerating. I hope it can be stopped. I liked my cold crisp winters with the blue skies and squeaky snow. These slushy, grey ones are depressing. I'd have stayed in Holland if I wanted that kind of winter.

* * *

I remember plenty of Christmases with the lake not frozen. No news there.

* * *

So summer is longer. Enjoy it and shut up about the climate thing. It's a hoax, and she should know better. Unless she's part of the inside job, getting paid to lie about it.

* * *

DELETED BY MODERATOR

~~Dumb bitches don't deserve to be published. Take her out before somebody else does.~~

Things Come Apart

Prosperity Gospel Academy

St. Petersburg, Florida

Elmore had never had much use for religion. In his youth, the people who made the greatest spectacle of praising the Lord were rarely the most upstanding individuals. He'd seen far too many using religion as a crutch or cover: praying to God instead of doing the hard work; blaming God for their latest bad run of luck, ignoring their own poor decisions.

God works in mysterious ways. It's the will of the Lord.

His father had little time for such thinking. "Lazy minds!" Zachary would often declare. "Hypocrites," he would say of the men and women who proudly drove up to the church of their choice in some shiny new vehicle, after a good week of underpaying their employees or doing a roofing job with cheaper shingles than promised. Maybe pouring their solvents out into the creek, or getting a little slap and tickle with somebody other than that well-turned-out spouse sharing their front seat each Sunday. Then there were the preachers. There were decent ones, of course, especially in the poorer churches. The shiny, new temples of prayer were another matter—sprouting up along the highways, with their 5,000 seats, air conditioning and miles of parking lots; their finely coiffed, slick-talking orators; their business managers.

Elmore shared his father's disdain for hypocrisy and laziness. He was not one to pray for deliverance or accept being part of somebody's larger plan. He had moved from being ready to do what it takes to survive; to ready and capable of being who he needed to be to thrive. He saw a life beyond survival; something his father had never known. Hard work and honesty only take you so far!

Money was never Elmore's main motivation. Though he did like the look and feel of quality objects. Clothes and fishing reels. Later, cars and guns. A finely made hunting rifle was something to behold—and hold.

It was something of a different quality entirely that turned him on.

Elmore rapidly learned that good manners, attentiveness to detail and readiness to serve men of importance would make an indelible impression. Money well spent provided him an image. Knowledge, though, especially about people and how they worked, offered influence. Influence in turn gave access—to all kinds of useful things and people. Access offered power. Power to mold things in the way he wished. The way the people with whom he chose to associate wished.

He had spent his first eighteen years as an outsider. What people rarely understood about outsiders is how they spend a lot of time watching and thinking about how the world works. Not how it is supposed to; how it really works.

Working for Pete Beauford was like a training ground. Pete and his coterie determined the *what* and *why*, but he was given carte blanche with the *how*. This provided latitude to experiment. He did not disappoint. Except the once.

Elmore had targeted Sagan Cleveland for his unique profile. *So poised, yet so vulnerable.* He assumed that would be enough: to have his show cancelled; to get him fired; to smear the climate science community with the same broad brush.

He had been partly right. But he'd never intended the mainstream media to pick up the story so quickly. He'd expected rumour and insinuation offered to 'friendly' alternative outlets to be sufficient. Once out, you can't get it back. Elmore knew all about this, in the microcosm of a small town. But today, the whole world was that microcosm. The internet had power. Sometimes for good. But mostly to do harm.

What am I doing? he asked himself once, maybe twice. He knew what his father would think of all this, of what he was becoming. 'Never act out of hate, Elmore. Not hate, not envy, not anger.' Noble sentiments, but what had they ever done for Zachary Lambert?

What Elmore knew now about Sagan Cleveland was that he too was connected. To people with influence. With an agenda. Anti-oil, left-wing, interventionist, big government friends. All part of the global warming hoax. Enriching themselves while eroding the liberties of hard-working Americans. They'd spin their chicken little tale as long as it brought them readers, advertisers, government grants, trips to Bali for their over-hyped 'Conference of the Parties' where they could eat out on the taxpayers' dime while plotting how to expand the powers of government and the United Nations.

Elmore had names now. Some outed themselves in the fag professor's defence. That was convenient. He noted who had real influence, and who was just along for the ride. The question now wasn't who, or what to do about it. It was how, and when.

Elmore had plenty of contacts, even if the network was no longer being maintained as such. A few wealthy parties were funding their own smaller network of institutes. Some were quite public about it. All the ravings of the *New York Observer* and the trial judge amounted to diddly squat. Denial was mainstream.

What surprised Elmore was how faithful some of his original network had remained to him. Once the rupture with Pete and the Houston clique happened, and he made his move to Florida, it was a mere matter of days before people sought him out.

An odd menagerie, it was. Plenty of regulars from the oil and gas sector, with a new breed of frackers and pipeline builders in the mix. Purveyors of 'clean coal', cutting jobs and blaming it on 'environmentalists.' In Democratic states even. The libertarians, naturally—folks who wanted an America fashioned in their own guise. Plus, all the supremacist and anti-immigrant groups who imagined Elmore to be a champion of their cause, seeing in his story a shared bond of persecution and injustice.

Above all, there was a religious coalition he hardly knew of in the year when he hatched his plot to take down the queer TV host. America was rife with them: not just homophobes or anti-gay marriage proponents; it had spawned a loose, but growing movement of religious leaders and congregations that saw in Sagan Cleveland a symbol of all that was wrong in America. In Elmore Lambert, they saw a martyr, and now a figurehead for what must be done to make the country great again.

In a world so messed up it was producing people like Sagan Cleveland and giving him access to children, the Apocalypse could not come too soon. Then would come such a day of reckoning that only the most pious would be saved. The Lord Jesus Christ would return as prophesied, and all the agents of Satan would be damned—the new Pope and his socialist snake oil sellers would be among the first to go.

But it was taking too long. Anything that could hurry things up was welcome. Nuclear war was looking promising once again. So was a war among religions. But, if scientific predictions were right, it was climate change that would be the trigger. It could be a century before things got so hot as to bring on the end, but with the state of the world—al-Qaeda, drought, flooding, civil wars, Ebola and mass migration—a little more warming was just the thing. So anyone who was committed to hastening this end deserved support. Especially if he had contacts.

Sure, Elmore realized, some of these people were certifiable. Nutbars of the highest order. But that wouldn't be a first. From Pete's circle of high rollers, to the funders and experts he'd pulled together, Elmore was accustomed to a motley crew. Comfortable with one, even.

As for the End Times stuff, it went a few steps too far. Still, there were days when he felt a firm press of the reset button might be the only hope for our sorry little species. Maybe even the future we deserve. As for hastening it, through intentional political decisions, dismissal of climate science, even provocative military actions... he had to wonder what made these people so confident they'd be among the chosen. He had little faith he would be.

But the game was as good as any. And this new team chose him as their captain. *Bringing down America so as to raise it up again?* He had trouble with the logic, but not the offer.

Elmore settled quickly in St. Petersburg. Within a year, he was running a well-oiled machine. *The American Prosperity Gospel Academy.* Impressive headquarters; smart young staff, many straight out of Bible college; a computer network second to none—impenetrable, yet ready and willing to penetrate; and a fundraising branch with astonishing reach. Game on.

Enter Andrew

Kuala Lumpur, June 2014

breath of fresh air. A gift from heaven. Too slick for me. Andrew Ma's arrival at NiMa Energy triggered a range of reactions.

They'd used a professional headhunter. No time for a long, traditional recruitment process. Work was piling up, the annual audit was due and a big product launch was fast approaching.

His CV was impressive. Undergrad from a Hong Kong university, five years with a Swiss pharmaceutical company doing business in China, then, as if icing on a cake, an MBA from the University of Toronto. Languages, international experience and contacts in China—what was not to like?

Andrew Ma had been flown in for an interview, with two other short-listed candidates. A head above the others, he proved, despite his diminutive stature. He was prepared, acquainted with NiMa's products and sales record, and briefed on the latest studies of market potential, notably in China and India; Indonesia and the Philippines too. He had useful insight into NiMa's competitors also, where they existed.

"He's the best, by far!" Jenny declared.

Jiro agreed. "A bit slick, though, didn't you find? The clothes. The hair. The earnest way he looked at you when you asked a question."

"Maybe," said Jenny. "But he was trying to make a good impression. I don't imagine him dressing that way all the time. Not here in the office. You're not jealous, are you?"

Jiro locked on Jenny for a moment, no longer distracted as he was much of the time; by all the things to do while in KL, the girls' growing needs, the work waiting for him in Japan.

"Jealous? Of what? So he dresses better than me—who doesn't?" Jiro chuckled. "His looks? Well, he's got 15 years on me, and I'm a gangly guy at best. Jealous of his skill set? Grateful, really. Especially the China contacts. That's going to be our big market. We'll need joint venture partners to crack it. Plus the cultural knowledge to keep us from getting taken to the cleaners. We'll be counting on Mr. Ma for that, won't we? Then I can focus on what I do best; uniquely, as you say."

"So, we're agreed," said Jenny. "We offer him the position?"

"It's hard not to. Any reservations? Last chance, Jenny"

"His references are excellent. The Interpol search came out clean. I hate to do that, but there's way too much organized crime in Southeast Asia. Chinese syndicates recruit young."

"Still," she said, looking affectionately at her husband, "he's no Jiro Ebitsubo!"

Jiro blushed at the compliment, then deflected. "Oh, that's probably a good thing. I haven't been much use these past couple of years. Time for new blood!"

Jenny nodded, her smile turning serious.

"New blood will be good. And you have held us back sometimes. Never sell yourself short, though. You had the foresight to imagine NiMa. You developed and executed the business plan. You inspired me and most of our leadership team to make the leap. Our people hold you in very high regard. They know you always have their interests at heart when you act. I hope that helps them through this transition. Knowing you have endorsed Andrew Ma will be important. He must be seen as your successor, not your replacement. Can you find a minute to do that, before you fly back?"

"Of course Jenny. Let's call Mr. Ma back in for tomorrow morning. I'll witness the contract, if he's able to agree to it that fast. Then we can meet with staff right afterwards. I can say a proper farewell. I'll still be co-partner, but I don't see myself coming in for anything more than the annual meeting. Even then, I'm likely to video link. Keep my KL visits for family, when I can."

Jiro's intuition was right on all fronts. He never again attended a meeting at NiMa Energy headquarters. His visits were kept to family, and became less frequent. Andrew Ma brought new blood, new energy and very useful contacts. A tighter, more outcome-oriented management process was put in place, with sales getting greater attention, and in-house R&D, less. Revenue surged, to the point where Jiro and Jenny could breathe easily for the first time.

"We earned this!" Jenny would tell Jiro.

Andrew Ma, like Jenny Fung in her first few years, was a whirling dervish. They made a formidable team. The new chief operating officer was smooth, funny and cultured. Within a year they were making initial sales in China, with good prospects for a joint venture and lower cost manufacturing for their hydrogen business—especially the power systems for transport trucks—and the lithium-ion battery factory that Jenny had envisaged.

"Combine our batteries with Chinese electric vehicle technology and we could blow Nissan out of the water," he predicted. "Maybe beat Tesla to market."

"Look out Elon Musk!" Jenny said more than once to Andrew. Her ambition had climbed a notch. Perhaps two.

It would have been easy not to see the signs of trouble.

One of their longest-serving product engineers had intended to share his concerns when he met with Jenny to announce his wish to retire early, but lost his nerve. "I have a different philosophy about internal product development than Mr. Ma," was the best he could muster. "The importance of protecting our patents. I'm sorry."

Jenny was sorry too, but could not talk him out of it.

Andrew, also expressed disappointment, but believed it was for the better. "People reach the limit of their potential, and a company needs fresh ideas to grow."

Jiro, far away in body and spirit, had no idea. About the growing rift among NiMa Energy employees, and the growing closeness of the two at the top.

Ottawa Herald — June 29, 2014

The Cohen Column:
Jiro Loves Sushi, We Love Plastic

I love sushi, and I have a dear friend named Jiro. How else to explain my outing to a quirky documentary about an old man and his sushi counter. *Jiro Loves Sushi* is centered around octogenarian Jiro, his reticence to pass on the business to his son, and the reflections of both men on quality, in a world where so few value it.

I worked in Japan for two years in the mid-90s. It was my first job out of school. Fish stocks were shrinking, and prime species harder to get. My older colleagues bemoaned the tastelessness of "today's sushi" after an evening of eating it.

I didn't get it. Everything I tasted seemed excellent. On my salary I could manage one such evening per month. But the company would bring in platters for office parties. We foreigners would gorge, earning smiles from our colleagues. Never in my dreams could I have eaten at a place like Jiro's. And today, with my (slightly) better salary, and (slightly) refined tastes, would I be prepared to drop $200 for sushi at an unassuming restaurant? Not when there's "all you can eat for $15" here in Ottawa.

It may not be Jiro's, but who can tell the difference? That is the question.

The world's oceans are so over-fished that we think nothing of eating species our ancestors would not have touched. The tastiest fish, like the precious bluefin tuna, are hard to find, and much smaller when they are, leading to surging prices for those determined enough. Or substitution with 'junk' species and farmed fish. We've even come to see 'mock crab' and other composites as normal. As selection and quality heads downhill, we've stopped noticing, or pausing to ask what happened.

In parallel with the oceans being emptied of fish, we've been restocking them with something of our own making. No, not the farmed fish—plastic!

There are now 18,000 pieces of plastic floating in every square kilometre of ocean. Another eight million metric tons is added to the oceans each year—that's a garbage truck per minute.

The plastic we toss may soon occupy more space in the oceans than fish ever did. But unlike fish, our plastics do not biodegrade. Not truly. Some break down into smaller pieces, but that's not a good thing. They can be ingested not just by whales, dolphins and tuna, but even by the smallest denizens of our oceans, lakes and rivers. If our marine mammals, fish and birds do not die from choking, many will from dehydration or starvation, as plastic occupies the place in their stomach that food or water should.

What does Jiro think about this? Devotee of quality, and host to generations of Tokyo sushi connoisseurs, he does not see himself as an environmentalist. He has never campaigned for better ocean management, and certainly not to impose quotas on the Japanese fleet. Or any that supplies his staple fare, while strip-mining oceans and depriving his son (certainly any grandson) of a similar career to his.

Comments on the state and scarcity of fish come late in the film. We see how hard the son must work to be at the Tsukiji Fish Market before dawn, just to have a chance at a few kilos of the most desired species. Some elude him. Some are now extinct.

Overfishing is a subtle, secondary message of the film. Mostly, it offers a window on the art of serving food of exceptional quality. Are Jiro and his faithful customers responsible for the decline of the oceans? In a small way, yes. Just as we all are.

Has Jiro ever asked about his supplier's fishing practices? Has he asked about the abandoned nets or the styrofoam containers, bobbing their way across the Pacific? No. But nor have his customers.

Jiro loves sushi. I love sushi. You may too. But if we want to maintain anything like the variety and quality of fish Jiro goes to such effort to serve, we'd better start asking questions.

Japan Loves Four Elements

Support for the Four Elements Movement came quickly in the months after it launched. Disgust over the mishandling of the Fukushima Daiichi crisis led to passionate support for a safer approach to supplying the country's energy. Membership reached one million within a year of its founding. Donations poured in. Most important of all, people were out in the streets, protesting the government's ties to the nuclear industry. They wanted a new direction.

The Four Elements Movement was ready, willing and able to offer it, with a set of policies and actions it had 'crowd-sourced,' from citizens as well as national and international experts. They took pains to stay clear of Japan's longstanding power brokers.

Local and prefectural governments were encouraged to adopt some or all of what Four Elements was developing, beginning with the 'Two Quick Wins' campaign. Small-scale renewable systems—chiefly solar—would be installed on any viable building or site. At the same time, property owners would perform deep retrofits of their buildings, taking advantage of tax incentives, grants and technical guidance. The impact of any one of these projects would be small, but the cumulative impact large. Four Elements was advocating widespread adoption of these short-term steps, while additional, long-term ones were being explored.

The scale of change needed to replace multiple nuclear plants was enormous. Replacing just one or two was not enough. Four

Elements supporters wanted the entire fleet phased out. Not overnight, but rapidly.

Jiro knew that change was often easiest to initiate locally. Now, as more towns and prefectures adopted the Four Elements Manifesto and implemented at least part of its prescription, the percentage of renewables on the Japanese grid was inching its way up. From under one percent of electricity in 2011, to almost ten by early 2015.

Still, this was not a time for complacency. Renewed effort would be needed to maintain the momentum. Vigilance also.

Entrenched interests were feeling threatened: industry, governments, even trade unions. As every month went by without additional bad news from the accident site, people's memories would fade. Their commitment would slip. Powerful people, quiet for several years, would reactivate. Lobbying, undermining, twisting arms, greasing palms.

The media, briefly vocal after the tsunami, quickly reverted to being a lapdog—whimpering when scolded by its master: owners, advertisers, government ministers. A draconian new 'state secrecy' law enacted in 2013, had created a deep chill. Few dared to criticize government policy or even to publish claims by whistleblowers.

A whistleblower was at particular risk.

Jiro knew that the only chance for sustained change would be if Four Elements and the economic activity it was stimulating were seen as an *economic* force, not just a social movement; as profitable someday as the industries it aimed to replace.

He also hoped that the independent hearings on Fukushima Daiichi, recently-concluded, would issue their report soon. It should be damning. Coverage should be extensive. But this was Japan.

Ottawa Herald — April 6, 2015

The Cohen Column:
Expectations of Comfort

My friend was telling me recently about his teenagers rebelling against the towels he dries on a laundry line. Apparently they feel like cardboard, or something equally awful. He did a decent imitation of the whine. 'Why can't you use a *dryer* like *normal* parents!'

Let's be honest, though. Such expectations of comfort are not limited to teenagers. I hear grown people, friends and family included, gripe about minor discomforts all the time. It seems we have reached the point as a society—we in the lucky 'twenty percent' of the world's population that are able to have such things as a dryer—where we can't imagine doing without all sorts of things. Things that would have been unthinkable luxuries less than a century ago.

In honour of wartime grandmothers, I whipped up a list of things most of us are sure we would die without.

1. Running water. Non-rationed and safe. Hot too, for daily showers.
2. Plentiful food. Enough that some can be wasted.
3. Refrigeration for food. Reach in, grab what you want.
4. Electricity that is reliable and cheap. Yes, Ontarians, I hear you whining.
5. A single-family home or apartment. With a separate room for everyone.
6. A choice of clothes. *What shall I wear?*
7. Car(s), and paved roads to drive them on, with free/ cheap parking.

I can understand if you consider all of this to be essential. It's what everyone else has or assumes they should. What about this next list, though? Have the following moved from luxury to essential? Things we cannot live without?

- Fresh brewed coffee, dark chocolate, craft beer, tropical fruits in winter;
- A family holiday once, maybe twice a year, involving road or air travel;
- A smartphone/tablet/laptop and/or TV for each family member;
- A destination wedding where the entire party flies to an exotic location;
- Class trips overseas for high school students;
- Grad parties involving new dresses, suits and shoes. Plus stretch limo.

Then there's the next list. The little things, which cumulatively have led to people's garages no longer having room for a car, and personal storage rental being one of North America's biggest businesses: capuccino/ice cream/popcorn makers, beer fridges, power washers, exercise machines, barbecues as big as a car. Toys, toys, toys. Shoes, shoes, shoes.

To set the record straight, I've got a few of these and I love them. But would I *die* without them? Which, on any of the above lists, could I truly *not live* without?

Here's an exercise. Make your own list, then ask these questions:

1. If it's essential, shouldn't all 7-plus billion on our planet be entitled to it?
2. Is it possible for this planet to supply everyone with everything on my list?
3. If that seems impossible, which could you share or give up, so it might be?
4. If the answer is nothing or not much, do you believe you have that right?
5. Are you willing to defend that right?
6. Would you kill?

What if natural disaster, war, economic collapse, famine or widespread disease were to severely restrict your access to these things. Would you have the physical and mental ability to carry on without them?

As the global population surges and ecosystems collapse, with millions taking to the roads and seas to assure their survival, isn't it time we tested ourselves?

Like when the towels are a bit stiff.

Elmore Joins Up

A clown. A rich guy with bad hair and poor speaking skills. A mere sideshow. That's what Elmore thought of Donald Trump. If he was going to get behind one of the candidates, it would need to be one with substance. And a chance of winning.

After eight years of a Democratic president, the nation was likely to flip in 2016. That's how it worked. Getting in early on a winning campaign, and helping make it so was the proven way to earn favours. Some of the people in Florida who'd elected 'Dubya', the second Bush, were glad to share their insight with Elmore. They, of course, were backing Jeb. Supposedly the smarter brother. But even in Florida, where he had served two terms as governor, a win was not guaranteed. A smart, younger candidate with close ties to the Hispanic community was waging a serious campaign. So having lunch with the CEO of the American Prosperity Gospel Academy would be time and money well spent for a couple of Bush strategists.

Elmore Lambert would be good for a healthy chunk of a certain kind of vote, they figured. Useful for fundraising too. His track record there was impressive, in such a short time. There was his unfortunate tangle with the law. Still, he wouldn't be the first guy in politics with a record. Besides, he'd be in the back rooms, where his name wasn't likely to come out. If it did, well, it seemed to be playing well with his base regardless. Notoriety wasn't always the death sentence you'd expect. Love that accent too. Louisiana? You don't say!

The lunch went well. Both parties got what they came for. The Bush boys made their pitch to somebody with an important constituency, while Elmore received a primer on the workings of a campaign. Also, he learned enough to confirm his assumption. Early supporters, loyal supporters, get rewarded. These two had under George W. Not top posts, mind you, but lucrative, and influential. Get in early, stay loyal when it gets rough, and your chance is as good as anyone's. To be a player.

As for their candidate, Elmore didn't see Jeb going all the way. Better to check out Rubio. Momentum matters, and he was looking strong. Though Trump was building a head of steam. Best to keep an eye on him after all, however crude he was proving. Like a middle-aged flasher, only older.

It isn't necessary to like the candidate. You just have to be able to work with him. For that, you have to figure out how he works. In Trump's case, it was simple. Ego and insecurity. Elmore could work with that.

Who did he know in the Trump camp?

Our Common Home

"**M**embers of the congregation, please join me in welcoming Doctor Cleveland, a.k.a. DJ Sagan. Doctor or DJ, we are so pleased you could come to Boston to kick off the *Laudato Si* discussion group."

"Thank you Father Donohue," Sagan said as he surveyed the hall. "What a treat it is to be greeted with such open arms to the Cathedral of Saint Paul. Amazing! While some things about America seem headed to dark places, I'm reminded often that this is a great country when we can hold a discussion like this without being arrested."

"Me or you," he added, grinning.

Light, nervous laughter travelled across the large room. Every seat was filled, despite the hosts adding extra tables and chairs that morning. Looking out over the group, Sagan felt a tingle. *Toto, we're not in a Detroit basement any more.*

"We've come a long way in America," he continued, in a serious tone.

"That distinguishes us from other countries when it comes to religious and spiritual exploration. You will know from my advance billing that I am not a Catholic. I am that most misunderstood—or just plain ignored—creature. Though one with a storied history here in Massachusetts: a Unitarian Universalist. But I'm not wearing a religious hat today. Nor that of climate scientist. I come as a mere spiritual seeker. Which makes us all equals in this room, indeed equals on this earth."

He saw people nodding, many with smiles.

"The work I have embraced is to help people of all faiths and backgrounds search for their spiritual calling.

"Some of you may reflexively say, when challenged, 'I'm a devout Catholic. End of discussion.' That would not be honest, though would it? You'd be fooling yourself and holding up a caricature. I'm quite certain that you're looking for more. From yourself, your church, your country and even the Vatican."

"That brings us to the encyclical, doesn't it?" Sagan held up a copy of *Laudato Si.*

"*On Care for Our Common Home*, an eagerly-awaited letter from Pope Francis. More eagerly awaited by some than others, I hasten to say." He had lowered his voice.

This brought chuckles and nods of recognition. The papal encyclical was not without its detractors. Within and without the Catholic faith. Particularly from prosperity gospel adherents. What Sagan referred to as 'Christians for Capitalism.'

"It's been kind of funny. Funny and sad. Suddenly everyone knows more about Christianity than the Pope."

"What!" Sagan exclaimed, in a high mocking tone. "Jesus Christ didn't preach getting rich as a tribute to God? He didn't advocate slave wages or strip mining the earth? No! I can find those passages right here in the Bible. Give me a second."

He could see heads shaking, recognizing the people he was ridiculing.

"OK, before I go on too many tangents, Sagan Cleveland is going to remind himself, that he is a *facilitator*, not guest speaker, or even leader of this exercise."

People smiled, warming to his shtick. The self-effacement.

"So, I'm going to open with a few passages, then turn to you for reaction. Once we've done this a few times as a group, I'll ask the facilitators from your own congregation to each take about ten people so everyone can share.

"You've all read the entire encyclical, am I right? Of course not! I never did my homework either. But by show of hands—you can't fool the Lord—how many gave *Laudato Si* a thorough read, maybe even underlined some favourite parts? OK, that's over half. That should help. How many gave a quick read? Good, that's most of the rest. Everybody else just read about it on Facebook, right? That could be good, or NOT!"

"So, let me read from the opening chapter.

"*I believe that Saint Francis is the example par excellence of care for the vulnerable and of an integral ecology lived out joyfully and authentically...he shows us just how inseparable the bond is between concern for nature, justice for the poor, commitment to society, and interior peace.*"

Sagan was reading slowly, giving people time to absorb each line.

"*Saint Francis, faithful to scripture, invites us to see nature as a magnificent book in which God speaks to us and grants us a glimpse of his infinite beauty and goodness. Through the greatness and beauty of creatures, one comes to know by analogy their maker.*

"And finally, '*The urgent challenge to protect our common home includes a concern to bring the whole human family together to seek a sustainable and integral development... particular appreciation is owed to those who tirelessly seek to resolve the tragic effects of environmental degradation on the lives of the world's poorest.*'"

Sagan looked up from his notes and surveyed the room.

"Who'd like to give us a brief comment on one of those passages?"

The morning went well. The mood was positive and the presence of youth in the room bode well not just for this session, but the future of the congregation. Still, there were more grey hairs than not. Youth were as rare as unicorns in most churches Sagan visited. Not so the big gospel churches, he knew, but he hadn't been invited to them.

Laudato Si offered a trenchant critique of consumption, wealth accumulation and both economic and social injustice. In a liberal place like Boston, he anticipated a warmer reception than in some other cities, where the critique of capitalism, even from the Pope—perhaps especially from the Pope—was being portrayed as a kind of foreign socialism.

Breakout groups were asked to respond to one particular passage.

A true ecological approach always becomes a social approach; it must integrate questions of justice in debates on the environment, so as to hear both the cry of the earth and the cry of the poor.

Agreement was universal that morning, but in sessions outside of a church setting, he occasionally heard the view that people should just let nature be. Nature was not merely a resource to satisfy human needs.

'The world would be better off without us,' was a comment made by some, usually by younger participants. 'Nature survives or humans survive. Not both.'

Sagan would agree it was a point worth debating, but then ask who in the room was prepared to give up their place, or that of their family to make space for nature. It was usually acknowledged that the human race was not about to voluntarily step off the planet; though a catastrophic, early demise was entirely possible. This, however, would likely come at the expense of *all* species. *Most*, at least, and quite randomly. So perhaps it was best not to wish for a quick end to *homo sapiens*.

A young woman did raise her hand during the morning wrap-up. A supporter of Hilary Clinton, the button on her vest indicated. She was bursting to speak.

"Go ahead," said Sagan.

"*Economic interests easily end up trumping the common good and manipulating information so that their own plans will not be affected,*" she read.

"Did you get that?" she asked the group. "*Trumping* the common good and *manipulating information*." She smiled broadly, pleased with herself.

"Good catch," said Sagan gently. "Though I urge everyone to try and be non-partisan today. Even Pope Francis is refraining from intervening in the presidential election. Hard as that must be."

With a chuckle from the audience, they broke for lunch.

"The gospel of creation!" In a booming voice, Sagan opened the afternoon.

"If there was ever a word to set the cat among the pigeons in this country, it is *creation*. With its equally charged cousin, *evolution*. The Pope acknowledges how political any discussion of creation has become, and encourages in this encyclical the involvement of people of all points of view in solving our ecological crisis:

"I would like from the outset to show how faith convictions can offer Christians, and some other believers as well, ample motivation to care for nature and for most of the vulnerable of their brothers and sisters."

"This takes us to one of the thorniest issues. Let's look now at some short but controversial words, and how they have been interpreted and distorted. I speak of course of *have dominion* over the earth, as well as *till and keep*.

"At this point let's recall that the Bible has been translated, transcribed, and in some cases rewritten. Even the language of today's most popular versions use English from centuries ago. So when we use words like *dominion* and *keep*, it is a grave mistake to assume today's meanings.

"If you were to have told your parents 50 years ago that you spent the day at church with a queer man, but that nevertheless, you had a gay time, they would infer something much different than if you said it today."

Older participants chuckled at this, while younger ones appeared mystified.

"So, the encyclical reminds us that we are not God, and that interpreting these passages of Genesis in such a way as to grant Christians the right to do as we will with the earth and with other creatures is both incorrect and disingenuous. *Dominion* is not *domination*, and *till and keep* implies working with the land: *caring, protecting, overseeing and preserving* as opposed to depleting, using up and owning.

"Let's break out again and think about how *dominion* has been interpreted and applied over centuries to endow humans with power and privilege that the scriptures may never have intended. Does this idea still hold sway in your faith community, and in the way you live in the broader community? How might we embrace stewardship instead?"

With the groups engaged, Sagan took a moment to absorb what was enfolding. This work was more rewarding than many of his scientific lectures. And yet, he realized, he would not be where he was without having taken the path he had, even with all its painful detours. A moment like this was one to treasure. This congregation, outside of the most progressive Episcopal, Unitarian and Jewish ones to which he had been invited, was as easy as it would get. But progress was not achieved by doing the easy thing.

Sagan wondered how he might get into some fundamentalist churches. What would it take to be invited through their doors and, more importantly, to have a real conversation? While there was time.

Still, he'd found his way into a major Catholic church, with *Laudato Si* as the door jamb. People were clearly interested in reconnecting their lives with their values, and this remarkable document was an important means.

Sagan could find plenty to fault in the Catholic church, not least its position on birth control and homosexuality. These, and the insistence on a celibate priesthood, were at the heart of much suffering and injustice. The church, like so many institutions, like life itself, was full of contradictions.

He closed the final session by reminding people the encyclical deserved more than a passing read. "Look at ways in which your church and archdiocese could put into practice many of these lessons. Think about your home and work life. How might we transform our workplaces and the companies we purchase from?"

It would be hard, he acknowledged, recalling Viktor Frankl: "What is to give light must endure burning."

Ottawa Herald — January 19, 2016

The Cohen Long Read:
Mental illness and one planet reality

Hardly a day goes by without a report about rising rates of mental illness around the world. Depression being most common. Clinical depression, that is, which is not the same thing as having a bad day. The good news is that depression is better understood than ever and the stigma around it is lifting. People are seeking professional help. Family and friends are more accepting and ready to offer support.

I recently wrote about depression among natural scientists. With the state of the world continuing to deteriorate, they find it particularly hard to deal with the pressure of knowing what they do. Knowing, yet refraining from sharing all they know, as starkly as they should, for fear of being shunned, harassed, gagged or fired. Anxiety and breakdown is common in some fields; suicide is becoming so.

Stress, leading to anxiety and breakdown, is not quite the same as suffering from the medical condition broadly labelled as depression, but it is connected, or can be. Depression can be triggered in someone predisposed to it by fatigue, the use of drugs and alcohol. It can also be brought on by stress in people with no known predisposition.

Readers clearly know this. I received insightful feedback, as well as the usual hate. One thing stood out. You asked me to think about the effect not just on messengers but also on recipients living with the message. "What about all of us who must find ways to deal with the message?" said one reader. "Is there not an impact just as great or greater on the recipient?" Clearly, there is.

I start with tales from readers about their challenges dealing with the 'endless doomsday barrage.' These are the people who know enough about how badly we are collectively trashing our planet to stop listening or reading.

"When I know we are f---ed, why do I need the latest proof?" said one reader. "Somebody do something meaningful, or show me how I can. Otherwise it's just more unusable science." A common response I call 'Enough, already.'

Then there is a reaction to observing the 'cognitive dissonance' in the world we navigate each day. What we see is governments, industry, our neighbours and our family members consistently doing the exact opposite of what evidence and our own gut tells us is fair or healthy. The hypocrisy of people doing the opposite of what they say, the pain of seeing our world heading in the opposite direction to what evidence tells us is sustainable becomes too much to handle. So some stop trying.

Making sense out of the nonsensical won't work. But since we must still find a way to cope, we shut down our analytical brains and suppress emotions connected with what is happening. If we did not, the confusion would be too great, the pain too strong. Nobody wants to see homelessness grow, millions held in refugee camps and species driven to extinction when we have the means to solve them, yet don't. So we stop looking. Stop caring.

Psychiatry tells us it takes a huge physical and emotional effort to suppress what is objectively true. Some people are capable of keeping it up over many years, yet the toll shows in various ways: strained relations, violent outbursts, emotional numbness and unhealthy coping strategies. Which brings me to my own theory. I pose it as a question.

Is it possible that the spike in depression and other forms of mental illness is related to the deterioration of our planet? The psychiatric profession now recognizes this as 'eco-anxiety.' The two are happening simultaneously, after all. Are more people succumbing to the pressure of experiencing a failing planetary home and the inadequacy of the human response—even consciously harmful economic and political behaviour?

I recently participated in a pair of workshops in two American cities. In each city, there was a session for people over 30, and another for a younger group (18-30). A strong theme that arose from facilitated discussion in the older group was the lack of trust most people have that their institutions or even their neighbours and friends would 'do the right thing' in many situations: make ethical purchases, conserve energy, protect local trees or lakes.

Older participants felt that no government would ever muster the courage to make tough decisions on behalf of a healthier planet. This was because politicians are constantly being forced to meet short-term demands of individual voters, who place far too much value on immediate needs or wants; despite people professing to want visionary leadership and long-term thinking. The result is a profound cynicism in the majority of over-30s that leaders will actually show leadership, and therefore they should as well. A Catch-22.

It reminds me of a remark by economist Mark Jaccard. "We put politicians in the impossible position where they must support all of the things we desire, yet dare not tell us about the trade-offs we do not want to see and the costs we do not want to bear."

The younger cohort proved just as interesting. They described how their initial optimism of youth is crushed at an early age. Labelled as lazy, many 'millennials' are in fact working two minimum wage jobs just to pay rent. Meanwhile their grandparents take cruises on their savings and pensions. Millennials are constantly reminded of society's rules, while subjected to highly-placed people in business ignoring rules, and politicians revising rules to benefit the wealthiest.

Is it a surprise that so few people make it out of high school, let alone to age 30, with a sense of wonder and intrinsic innovative drive? They describe 'early onset cynicism' that manifests in bouts of self-harm and excess. A thumb in the eye to society; to people and institutions that never do what they promise and—worse—claim to be doing one thing while, in plain sight, doing the opposite.

Youth today often see right through the cognitively dissonant world around them.

'You used up all the resources in our country, trashed the lakes and rivers, then did it all over again on other continents. You've left us little to work with, but we'll have to fix the problems you've created. You don't want to make the changes or consider the sacrifices that could right this ship, but we're the lazy millennials!'

I heard it over and over. This stinging critique of political, economic and social behaviour, as well as ecological.

How can living with all this not mess with your head? I heard many wondering 'Am I the only one who feels like this?' And when your head is messed with, out comes the harmful behaviour, shared in real time on YouTube.

What will get us out of the feedback loop of denial, crude coping and mental illness? How about calling out what is false, and saying what is true.

Which takes us back to state-of-the-planet science. If we wish to address depression, anxiety and suicide, especially their steady rise among youth, we must become devoted truth tellers about our planet. And truth livers, anchored in reality.

More Bite

nthony Poulson was one year short of his full pension. What was once normal in his profession, working until retirement, had become exceptional. Corporate downsizing and regular mergers were at the heart of it, which in turn led to writers and editors becoming less loyal. Now it was normal to jump across to another media outlet, many of which were entirely web-based. The days of print, radio and television dominating the news landscape were over. Though some were putting up a fight. He'd noticed how the Manchester-based Guardian had become a go-to global source for progressive readers; speaking for the marginalized, against a shrinking but increasingly powerful elite.

Simone Cohen had on more than one occasion praised the Guardian's dedication to covering international development issues. She'd challenged HeraldMedia to raise its game. Then she'd gone a step further. In a memorable column, written prior to the Paris climate conference, she spoke of "the woeful record of Canadian media, both private and public, in covering the climate crisis—its urgency, viable solutions and the extent of ecological deterioration and biodiversity loss as a result of resource extraction, industrial agriculture and accelerating urbanization."

Of the world's major English-language media, the only ones doing what she considered their moral and professional duty were the *Guardian*, the *New York Times,* the *Washington Post* and the *New York Observer.* With its stranglehold on Canada's print journalism, HeraldMedia had a duty to be informing the public and "speaking truth to power." That was Simone: plain-spoken and increasingly difficult.

Moral and professional duty! Easy to say, but with what resources? And, who, after all was HeraldMedia? To be precise, who was HeraldMedia today? Anthony Paulson had hung in, but he was tired of adjusting to the whims of each new owner. Tired of lowering his journalistic standards, pretending to be "sharper and edgier, to meet the needs of our fast-paced world."

Produce more with less, is what the owners meant. *And faster.* Really, though, they were producing worse with less.

Above all, Anthony was sick of drawing up lists of who would stay and who would go. These were people: colleagues, and often friends. Dedicated professionals performing a critical public service.

Serious journalism was one of the few remaining bulwarks of democracy, in the slide towards corporate influence over everything. Not that many seemed to share his opinion. 'The liberal media. The left-leaning media. The corrupt media.' That was Donald Trump's take in his wild and crazy—though certainly doomed—campaign for the Republican nomination. As though a mega-wealthy guy doing business with tyrants and plutocrats would have any moral high ground. Corrupt media, my ass! Who'll have the last laugh there, Herr Trump, poster boy for conflict of interest?

Anthony was also sick of giving instructions to people who didn't need them. Nobody was above a critique. Even a veteran, syndicated columnist should be open to that. But his insides went liquid each time he had to deliver a message to a leading member of his team. As he would today. Just as soon as she had filed her column.

Simone knew it was more bad news. Anthony had a way of wrinkling his brow when "Can we meet?" meant "The boorish louts who own our paper for a brief period of time need me to tell you something." Not that it happened often. And so far, she'd survived each purge, though she'd often wondered how. With each round, she'd tried to imagine a life outside HeraldMedia. There would be one of course. But other than her two years in Japan, the *Ottawa Herald* was her life. Her career.

Career. The term sounded quaint now.

"Hi Anthony. Sorry. That one took me awhile. I was having a little trouble with the closing paragraph. A call to action, but not too 'holier than thou.' Apparently I can come off that way. Or so some readers feel."

Anthony chuckled. He had mentioned it on occasion.

"It's a fine line, isn't it Simone? We read a column because we value the insight of the writer. Sometimes we even consider them a friend, or a wise aunt or uncle. Yet, if we think they're placing themselves above us, telling us what to think or how to act—boom! Don't read the comments, Simone. Don't *ever* read the comments."

She laughed. Someone was reciting it daily. You always regretted it, yet it was so hard to resist.

"Anthony, why do we even keep the Comments section, knowing how they've played out? If anyone's still dreaming they'll evolve into a place of respectful debate, woo-ooh, time to wake up!"

He shook his head slowly. "I know, I know. When the *Globe* shut their Comment section down, we talked about it, you'll recall. But the publisher thought it still has a place. It gives people somewhere to vent. The more intelligent readers send us a letter to the editor, knowing *it* still has value."

"*Somewhere to vent,*" Simone echoed in a sarcastic tone. "As one of the most frequently 'vented at,' forgive me for taking a different view. Might I assume that's why we're having this chat? Something I've written. I can't be getting the axe—there would be somebody in a suit, giving me a box and 30 minutes to pack." She smiled wryly.

He shrugged that one off. "Something you've written? Yes, and no. More like something you're going to write."

Simone shuddered. She was open to suggestions on *how* to write, but *what* was sacred.

"As you know, the paper is shrinking. Short and punchy is the new direction. In print and online, though space should never be a constraint there. But we know most readers start drifting at about 300 words. Scrolling or clicking onto a second or third page seems beyond them. So we're told by the data miners. My dear, it has been decreed that columns should aim for 500 words maximum. No more of your 'special exemptions.'"

She obliged him with a smile, just as he had obliged her on many occasions.

"Standard column length is 500 words. But shorter is encouraged."

"Shorter is encouraged?" She bristled. "As if there's anything worth saying in 300, or even 400!"

"You can do it Simone. I know you can. Here's a little more instruction from the heavens. 'Less context. More bite'."

She snorted. "Is this a pit bull fight? More bite just gets you more enemies! If they want me to tweet for my salary they should say so." Huffing, she stood up and walked to the window.

"Brevity is already killing insight. It's killing complexity, forcing us to oversimplify complex issues. Worst of all, brevity is killing civility. You have to read so much between the lines that everybody just assumes the worst."

"I know, I know, Simone."

She turned to face Anthony, her eyes bulging. "God, you must hate your job!"

"I do," he said, looking away. "Mostly, I do. But I can't imagine you're enjoying yours any better."

"Someday, Anthony. Someday soon... I'll pack it in and take up guiding bike tours. There's more *context*."

"Thanks Simone," said Anthony, chuckling. "Thanks for this brief chat."

He reached out to shake hands. Highly unusual. Placing a second hand over hers, his eyes communicated empathy. It was brief, but enough to re-establish their connection.

Ottawa Herald — July 20, 2016

The Cohen Column:
The Great Failure of Appeasement

Next to the word appeasement in the dictionary is a photo of Neville Chamberlain. That's a cliché of course. Shorthand for his role when Hitler's armies staged 'friendly take-overs' of Czechoslovakia and Austria, in search of a little living room. Hoping to avoid a war that could consume the whole house, Chamberlain chose to sign the Munich Agreement—giving away the entire neighbourhood.

We'll have "peace for our time," Chamberlain declared. *Hitler won't dare go any further,* he must have been thinking.

It didn't work out so well for Chamberlain. Hitler, seeing that those who might have opposed him had neither the resolve nor the means, did what any megalomaniac would. He signed a non-competition deal with Stalin, made friends with Italy and Japan, and kept arming himself. By the time the Allies truly became allies, he'd taken what he wanted, and then some.

If you're thinking you've stumbled on a history column, you are partly right. I studied history and my family 'has history': part Ukrainian and part Jewish via France.

So when I see what Putin is up to in Ukraine, it is personal. It is also straight out of the dictator/bully playbook. Take a little of this and see what happens. Then a little more. It's amazing what you can get away with a bit at a time, when everybody is worrying about ISIS and Syria.

It's also easier when it's 'just Ukraine'—'part Russian' and so very far away.

It's a classic ruse by an expansionist Russia, from a leader using the proven strategy of bolstering domestic support by playing the victim. *They're all against us. Look at me, I'm a tough guy!* Works every time. Especially when you've neutered the media and imprisoned the opposition. Those who haven't died mysteriously.

Is annexing Crimea and waging terrorism in eastern Ukraine a first step towards a new Russian empire? Maybe not. But if you are Ukrainian, Lithuanian, Estonian or Latvian, are you prepared to become Russia's living room? Again.

As the world learned in 1939, you cannot appease a country or leader with territorial ambitions. Least of all, one with a sense of inferiority and wounded pride. If Canada and its NATO and non-NATO allies want to avoid joining Chamberlain in the dictionary, a stiffer resolve is needed. Now. Once they get going, it takes a lot more work.

In a similar case of bullying and appeasement, look at the US presidential race. Donald Trump is going way beyond acceptable behaviour and seeing what happens. Instead of roundly censuring him, many Republicans and the formerly moral majority are simultaneously cringing and celebrating. Hedging their bets, because his tactics are working. He is filling arenas by going public with what was only said in the darkest corners of the internet.

This is a case of appealing to aggrieved outsiders to turn against people who are even more the outsider. Pick on the weak, so you can feel powerful. In 1930s Germany it was Jews, gays and gypsies. Now it's Mexicans, gays and Muslims.

The outsider candidate, as Trump fashions himself through vitriol towards all that is establishment, is a magnet for every type of malcontent. Should his strategy defy all experts and win him the Oval Office, he will find himself surrounded by angry white men. And beholden to them. He will be governing a new country in a new world: where it is okay to grab bitches by the pussy, taunt gimps in wheelchairs, question the patriotism of classmates with dark skin, and march in white sheets.

Whatever the election outcome, this hatred is not going back into its cave. The beast has slipped its chains.

Media Advisory

October 12, 2016

NiMa Energy and Bright Future Industries will make a major announcement that will transform the automobile industry.

Date:	October 15, 2016 at 11:00 a.m.
Location:	Orchid Palace Hotel, Jalan Ampang, Kuala Lumpur
Contact:	Andrew Ma, vice president, NiMa Energy ma@nimaenergy.com

* * *

More than 20 national and international journalists had attended the press conference. Jenny and Andrew were not surprised, given surging interest in electric vehicles, boosted recently by the much-hyped Tesla cars and battery 'giga-factory' in the United States. But the Chinese government's strong support for electrifying the vehicle fleet in its heavily polluted cities was stimulating demand for smaller cars in a lower price bracket than Tesla. Or even Nissan, with its pioneering Leaf.

Market conditions were ripe for an economy model for millions of potential customers throughout Asia. Bright Future Industries had the design and manufacturing capability, Andrew Ma had the contacts to sell in China, Thailand and Malaysia, and NiMa had the breakthrough battery chemistry and high-speed charging software to power the cars.

NiMa's "dynamic duo"—as the *KL Mirror* labelled them in a recent feature—had forged a joint venture that was "sure to have Elon Musk looking over his shoulder."

"You did a fantastic job today Jenny." Andrew was driving, taking them back to company headquarters.

"My speech was OK?" She had felt it, but wanted validation.

"You nailed it. Almost without reading."

"And the questions in Cantonese, from the Chinese media?" She looked at his face as he drove, trying to read his expression. Though raised speaking Cantonese in her early years, most of her education had been at English-language schools. English was also the lingua franca with Jiro and the girls. At NiMa Energy, English was the language of commerce. Malay was only spoken at some government meetings and events.

"No problem with the Chinese press." Andrew's voice was reassuring. "Excellent with the Bloomberg and Asian Wall Street guys too. A media relations dream."

"That's nice to hear." Jenny had come to enjoy the rush of a press conference.

"Not only that, you looked great." He caught her eye for just a second, then looked back at the road.

"Confident you mean? Self-assured?"

"No, I mean you looked great. Look great. That's a power outfit you're wearing."

"You think so?"

"Most definitely, cougar boss."

"What's that?" Jenny asked, not sure she'd heard correctly.

"A cougar? Well, it's a woman of a certain, umm... maturity, who looks good beyond her age. Striking."

"So, it's a compliment?"

"Oh yes," he said nodding. "Most definitely a compliment!"

"Even though it sounds sexist."

"Oh no. Nothing sexist in it at all."

Jenny was not convinced. "Still, young man, it's best you keep those remarks to yourself. I'm a married woman, and a mother, as well as your employer." Jenny was aiming for a serious tone. Not so much scolding, as mentoring.

He nodded, keeping his eyes on the road.

"Of course, my professionally dressed, married boss lady." He smiled and turned, ever so briefly, to check her reaction.

The eyes. The big, charming smile. It reminded Jenny a little of Sagan. Only Andrew lacked his innocence. Andrew loaded on charm when he wanted something. She'd seen him in action. In the boardroom, in staff meetings, with potential clients.

She had to put him in his place, but it was flattering that a younger man should find her attractive. A panther, was it? She'd have to look it up. Her daughters might know. But, no... it wouldn't be right to ask them. Simone would know for sure. But that would just lead to more questions than Jenny was prepared for. Simone was close to Jiro. Equally faithful to both of them.

Faithful. An interesting term. Jiro's visits were infrequent now, as were hers to Japan. When they were together, their interaction had become more and more businesslike. On the phone, FaceTime and in person, even when they were not discussing business. There was always so much to catch up on. The twins would soon enter high school. Important decisions had to be made. Not just about the school, but the country, and language.

Then there were the NiMa decisions. Jenny valued his advice, and usually had a list of things to be covered. Jiro in turn was keen to share details of his own projects. He similarly sought Jenny's input and technical insight. Was it any wonder the physical part of their marriage was wilting?

She missed his touch. She assumed he missed hers as well. Though there had been little sign of it when they were together in August. A family vacation in Hokkaido. But the fresh air, and two weeks away from their work with the girls, had done everyone good. There had been sex, a couple of times. Like an old married couple, she'd realized. Familiar routines and positions. It wasn't bad. Just not particularly good. Comforting, but without spark. Had their lives come to that?

The presence of two mysterious men at the press conference had briefly caught Jenny's attention.

"Who were those guys in the smart suits with the slick hair?" Jenny asked as they came to a stop in the NiMa Energy parking lot. "Bodyguards for the Bright Future men?"

They would soon be breaking ground on a massive battery factory in Guangdong Province. Bright Future Industries would build the factory and develop three car models.

"Oh, them," Andrew answered casually, not taking his eyes off the wheel. "Don't worry about those guys. They come from one of our major investors."

"I've never seen investors like that. More like mafia," Jenny joked.

Andrew's face darkened. Then, as he turned to her, his bright smile returned. "Mafia? Ha! That's a good one, Jenny. Just investors, keeping a low profile. There are many ways of making fortunes in today's China. Don't worry about it."

You handle the technology, I'll handle the money. He didn't say it, but his body language did.

"So..." Andrew said after an awkward pause, "I'll pick you up at 7 a.m.? Big trip. I'm looking forward to checking out the factory. Things move fast in China. Less red tape."

"When you know the right people, it would seem." Jenny remarked.

He flashed her his smile. "That's why you pay me the big money, right?"

Who Saw that Coming?

Ottawa, November 8, 2016

Lying in bed unable to sleep, as stunned as much of the world was, Simone could not imagine a worse result. For everything she cared about. Honesty, respect for the media, equal rights for women, climate protection and the transition to renewables, the importance of democratic institutions, the separation of church and state... the list went on. Instead, we get what? Bigotry, misogyny, serial lying... with unheard of influence from billionaires, the coal lobby and religious zealots. Conflict of interest on steroids. It's as if the Russians had dictated the results, helping to elect someone so erratic, so tied to laundered money that they would be able to get away with anything. There had been rumours. Sure, they were just rumours, but in this strange new world anything was possible.

Ron, though just as appalled by Donald Trump, seemed less *bouleversé*—turned upside down. He explained this to Simone with some ancient words; supposedly a Chinese legend, where on learning of a terrible event, a wise old man would respond: "It might be good, it might be bad. Time will tell." Sometimes in the longer arc of history, it proves to be for the better. Though at first this is hard to imagine.

Fearing the worst, it was this tale and Ron's next words that calmed her a little.

"Maybe he and his ilk will trigger such a visceral rebellion that we'll make more progress on the big issues than all the polite agreements and global conventions ever have. Perhaps the applecart needed upsetting."

"You think?"

"Maybe this is the short, sharp shock we've been waiting for. You know we need one. All our puny efforts aren't getting us anywhere."

"But think how much damage will be done before people march!"

"One way or another, my love, damage will be done. Nothing moves forward without it, sorry to say. Ecosystems flourish after a forest fire."

"Yes. A moderate fire. A scorcher leaves the ground sterile for generations."

Elmore in Power

lmore didn't sleep a wink. He'd watched with disbelief, turning to satisfaction, then pride as the results came in. Winning states like Florida, Ohio and Wisconsin was big. But Michigan and Pennsylvania? Unbelievable! They had seeded the grounds of discontent, added a little water and watched it grow. In fields already shriveled and dry, they had lit the match. Then they'd added fuel until they could stand back and watch it roar.

Working behind the scenes, Elmore had done much of the groundwork in Florida, Georgia, Mississippi, Louisiana and then Texas. Places he knew well from his time with Pinnacle. Places where he'd cultivated contacts. Religion and politics—it was all the same to many in the prosperity gospel world. The end was what mattered.

Doing God's work. Honouring the Lord Jesus Christ with the power of positive thinking and action. Nothing does more to spread the good word and establish the terrain for healing of the sick and salvation of the poor than creating conditions where all can succeed: lower taxes and less government. To many outsiders, it was an incoherent jumble of ideas and ideology. But to the faithful, it was clear. Success in all walks of life was the best way to praise God. They had been a big part of Trump's success, more than any outsiders would know. More even than most insiders.

Elmore could not be sure how much the president-elect himself would know. But he would have plenty of time to remind him, as his closest campaign advisors began the critical task of choosing the new team—placing the right people in the most influential roles. Elmore would be part of the inner circle, if the reaction of people tonight was any indication. Backslaps, high fives and words of praise became more and more effusive as sleep deprivation kicked in and victory drinks took effect.

"Put in a good word for me at Trump Tower!" he'd heard more than once.

Elmore imagined himself in charge of proposing appointments to the new president. In anticipation, he would draw up a list. People who would be the most effective. People who were owed favours. People who could do the most damage, where damage needed to be done. Professionals and lunatics. Everybody had a role.

Blame the Gypsies

here was a reason why so many rural properties in southern France had gates. Walls too, or fences, at least along the edge bordering a road. Theft was frequent enough to justify some basic level of protection. François had been surprised at first. Such barriers were rare in Alsace and much of the north.

The rash of thefts in the region during the summer and fall of 2016 was a shock. These were not just petty crimes. What they were seeing in the Drome, and hearing about in adjacent regions, was more organized, more sinister.

Market day chatter often began with "Did you hear about the theft?" As the numbers grew, a pattern emerged.

Jacques Dutoit lost the grapes from eight rows of vines two nights before he would have harvested them. The hot and dry weather guaranteed an exceptional year. Across the Rhone, three different vineyards reported thefts. Two winemakers had oak barrels stolen, along with some new processing equipment. Just to the south, a neighbour's cousin had his peach trees stripped bare in one night. Just before harvest.

With a little internet research, François learned of the scale of these crimes, under-reported so far in the national press. Across much of France, southern Germany and Italy, orchards and vineyards had been victims of major operations. As planned as they were, they could also be brutal. Vines and fruit trees were left badly damaged and irrigation equipment ripped out.

On more than one occasion, a farmer, vineyard owner or local police officer had been tied up and beaten.

It was rare for an arrest to be made. The German police had, however, interrupted an operation in progress south of Freiburg. The sophisticated sting led to the arrest of two drivers and 40 pickers, and the capture of two refrigerated trucks. The trucks had Austrian plates, but police concluded the operation was being run by Serbian mafia, using mostly Bulgarian and Romany pickers. 'Gypsies.'

In response to the disturbing new type of criminal activity, many rural farmers were working with police to improve security in advance of the next harvest. Hotlines were set up and roving "SWAT" squads with helicopter support would be brought in.

As reassuring as these measures were meant to be, François was troubled by the growing mood of suspicion. Reporting foreign-plated vehicles was encouraged, along with dark-skinned pickers and tourists looking out of place.

"What a strange world," he had mused to friends over dinner one night. They agreed, but with livelihoods at stake, and the risk of bodily harm as well, was it not better to be cautious?

It was all too easy to put refugees and migrants from Northern Africa and the Middle East into the same basket as the fruit and grape thieves. Fear was coming to the region, as it had to Paris, Brussels and Nice. François knew it was going to get harder to retain local support for the humanitarian and resettlement initiatives he and his neighbours had created. Settling two Syrian families in his village had been a monumental accomplishment. He suspected it would be the last.

The winter brought a new and different wave of crime. This time it was the properties of the rich, usually unoccupied in January and February, that were targeted. Stories emerged of a number of estates being emptied of their contents. Entirely!

The initial reaction of most in the area was laughter. The rich were getting their due. But amusement soon turned to concern. The thieves had disabled elaborate security systems and emptied two entire estates, right under everyone's noses.

Do you think they have local informers? I wonder if they use drones to case out the scene in advance. That would be clever.

The teenage son of the school teacher in Le Tilleret, normally painfully shy, spoke up in the middle of such speculation at the Easter village feast.

"Drones are possible. But who needs them? Just go on Facebook. Most people love to boast about their fancy cars. They take pictures to impress 'friends.' Post selfies on vacation. Where they are and when they'll be back. Drones would be good to case things out just before a crime. But satellite and street view tell you all you need to know."

To a silent hall, he went on. "You don't need an informant. The internet is spying all the time. Welcome to 2017!" With a roll of the eyes he ambled to the dessert table.

Ottawa Herald — February 26, 2017

The Cohen Column:
Let Them Drink Coffee Substitute

It started with coffee. Regions that grow many of our favourite beans are under threat from heat and drought. We may soon have to look elsewhere than Ethiopia, Colombia and Java. Places with appropriate soil and climatic conditions. Before the shortages kick in, because a "What, no coffee?!" revolution is going to be nasty. Unless people are too drowsy to revolt. But I can see them mustering the energy if the alternative is 'coffee substitute.'

Next came wine. A calmer, more dignified crisis. What happens when Spain stops producing Rioja, Italy fails on Chianti, California strikes out on Chardonnay and Champagne can't make champagne? French winemakers are onto it, apparently, buying up land in Dorset and Somerset. English grapes? *Mon dieu!*

Then it was chocolate. This may beat out coffee for revolutionary potential. I'll be marching at the front with the other middle-aged women! Husbands, children and colleagues beware! Chocolate is complicated. The trees which produce the cacao bean are finicky. You don't just transplant them in Eastern Ontario. Such a pity.

That brings me to tea, the jolt of the civilized. There's violence this year in the Darjeeling region of India. Drought and heat are factors. There are issues in Sri Lanka too (once called Ceylon), where inconsistent rains and rising heat are putting centuries-old tea estates at risk. Problems are steeping.

As for brewing, hops are under threat in some critical regions for the burgeoning craft beer market. If you want to ensure a reliable supply, better get hopping. Pale ale lovers unite to fight climate change!

Then there's California's almonds, devastated by years of drought and threatened by bee colony collapse. Like every crop that needs to be pollinated, almond trees rely on bees to do the hard work; something that cannot be done by hand, or if some day it can, it will raise surging almond prices even higher. My granola!

I'm making light of the threat to our favourite treats because, frankly, I am tired of being the sourpuss. Yet, I am wired to speak the truth—to the powerful and to consumers, who could in an instant find their power; oblivious one minute, then on the march when a life-altering crisis hits. If people can't be stirred to action through sea level rise, torrential rain, lyme disease or withering heat, then perhaps a coffee collapse will make it personal.

I was only getting started, too. The list of items under threat by various forms of ecological breakdown is long. Olive oil, vanilla, pacific salmon, quinoa, rice.... Some might be reborn through 'assisted migration'—replanting in a suitable place—but not all can. So it's not as simple as harvesting Bordeaux in Upton Noble.

Enjoy your addiction while you can, but if you want your supply to last until, say, 2025, best get behind a carbon tax and renewable energy transition.

Screwing Up

It was on Jenny's second visit to the Bright Future Industries plant that she made her mistake, she explained to Simone over the phone, between bouts of sobbing.

"I was starting to feel powerful. Like I could make a real difference. Not just dinky products and pilot projects. Always there was some reason why big success was a few years away. Then along comes this Chinese deal."

Simone had phoned Jenny immediately, in response to her email. "Big problem! Call any time." Now she was letting Jenny find her way to explain the urgency.

"I was so stupid. So blind." Jenny sniffed, then blew her nose.

"Something smelled from the beginning. The bonus payments. The oily people at the back of the room. But I didn't want to know. I wanted to believe Andrew Ma had our best interests at heart. We had checked him out, you know, as part of the headhunting. No criminal connections, no family connections with Chinese mafia, in Hong Kong or the mainland, we were assured."

"But there was?"

"Apparently. Before, or maybe after he joined us. Who knows."

"So what happened? To you?"

"Oh Simone," Jenny was sobbing again. "I fucked up."

"How so?" She was dancing around the real story. Simone could sense it.

"I just told you. I fucked up."

"OK," said Simone slowly. It wasn't like Jenny to use crude language. "Literally?"

"Yes!" Jenny blurted. Then, after a pause, she laughed. A weepy, nervous laugh.

"Go on," urged Simone.

"I've always been so controlled. Everything in my life, planned. Like a science experiment. So for once, just once, I decided to go on impulse. Opportunity. I had never known it. I knew there would be consequences. Yet I went for it anyway. I let the hormones decide.

"With Andrew Ma?"

"I knew better. But I didn't care. In that moment."

"Whew," Simone exhaled. "Did something happen with Jiro? Things haven't been easy for you guys, but it didn't sound bad enough to trigger this."

"Not by itself, no." Jenny's voice was calmer. "The night before the China trip, we spoke for quite awhile. I called to ask if he had followed the press conference. He had been wary of the deal, but not in a firm way. I had assured him everything checked out. That Andrew had done a thorough vetting, that some top commercial lawyers in Hong Kong and our own counsel in KL were comfortable with the terms. We were giving away some NiMa ownership as part of the deal, but controlling interest would remain in our hands."

"Yours and his?"

"Exactly," said Jenny.

"Then what?"

"I fucked up. Sorry, but it says it all." Again, Jenny laughed. Simone could tell she was exhausted."

"After the visit to the Bright Future plant, we were on a super high. Construction was ahead of schedule. The first prototypes were ready. Really nice. Three models. A little city car that will blow the wheels off the Smart or the Fiat. A utility vehicle for commercial fleets. Then this super slick sedan to rival the Tesla. Only way cheaper.

"Sexy car, big banquet, too much alcohol. It was a heady day for me. For both of us. I was sharing all this with Andrew. *The dynamic duo,*" Jenny added, sarcastically.

"Yes, I'd read that."

"Jiro hated it. For the first time, I heard jealousy in his voice. Jealous, then bitter. Almost mean. That's what led to our big fight. I told him that since he couldn't do the job himself, he would have to trust that Andrew and I would. He had no business reprimanding me when he was hardly able to do his own job, as a business partner, or a husband."

"Ouch! You said that?"

"Yes!" Jenny said defiantly. "I may have gone too far, but that's how I felt. I don't see my husband for months at a time, and when I do it's: 'How's the house, how are your parents, how are the girls?' He took this very badly, of course. He said he's doing everything he can to be a good father, a good husband, a good son, and now the leader of a social revolution. But it's all just too much." Jenny paused before continuing.

"Then I said something really hurtful."

"Even worse?"

"I said he seemed content to collect his salary as vice-president for so little contribution, while working in Japan for no pay. Some of us at NiMa had a right to ask why we're subsidizing his revolution."

Simone winced, then waited.

"That one stung," Jenny said quietly.

"I imagine," said Simone. "Because it's so close to the truth."

"Exactly. First he went silent. Then he said, very calmly, 'since you feel that way, I guess it's time for me to step away entirely, so you can keep that money and pay it to Andrew instead'."

"Yikes!"

"Then Jiro told me of a decision he had made. He was intending to run for governor. Of Fukushima Prefecture. Just as soon as Four Elements registers as a political party. They vote on it next week. He was certain it would go through."

"That's a big step!" said Simone.

"It is. A bold one. I just wish he'd discussed it with me. I told him that. What's the point of being a couple, if we're not sharing big decisions? Ones that affect everyone?"

Simone exhaled loudly. "It's come to that, has it?"

"We still share a lot," Jenny acknowledged in a flat voice, "but it's not the partnership we once had." Simone heard her sigh. "So, the call ended badly. Both of us accusing the other. Then him saying something which gave me an excuse."

"Which was?"

"You seem to have Andrew to meet all your needs now."

"Yikes!" Simone exclaimed, as a shiver ran through her. "*All* your needs! Do you think he meant that?"

"In a moment of jealousy. Or disappointment. But it was enough to... free me."

"To screw up?"

"Exactly," said Jenny. Simone waited. There had to be more.

"Andrew started out on the limousine ride back to our hotel after the banquet, doing what he does: complimenting my clothes, calling me a cougar."

Simone had a sudden intake of breath.

"He says it's a compliment, but I know not to believe everything he says."

"Cougar?" said Simone slowly. "It could be a compliment, but only in a crude—"

"No," Jenny interrupted. "Don't tell me now. What we did next was pretty crude too. I was drunk by then. When he invited me—no, dared me—to come to his room, I just figured what have I got to lose?"

"A lot," Simone said, barely above a whisper.

"Everything," Jenny corrected, sounding like she was fighting tears again.

"Everything?"

She told Simone about the video camera. About Andrew saying how exciting it would be to know they were doing it for the camera. He would erase it right after, of course. She was too drunk to object. And aroused, she admitted.

"And did he erase it?"

"He made a point of it. *Watch—I'm dragging the file to the trash. I've emptied the trash.* Then we slept. The next morning it was over. Everything. My impulsiveness. His interest. All in the trash. Like my life," Jenny sobbed. "Trash. Like me!"

Simone spent a long time consoling her.

Jenny had indeed messed up. Worst of all, she suspected the file had not been destroyed. Andrew hadn't said so, but everything about his behaviour since then did, according to Jenny. He was slowly and meticulously taking over NiMa Energy, daring her to stop him. Knowing she could not, or would not. Not if there was a video. Enough to ruin her, ruin Jiro, and devastate their families.

Simone had helped friends out of plenty of awkward situations, but this one felt like a bridge too far.

Eco Anxiety at Home

When Simone first moved in with Ron, his daughter Jacinthe's visits were limited to occasional weekends and holidays. In those early days, Simone gave father and daughter as much space as possible. Jacinthe was prone to bouts of anger and anxiety. Worse than she'd have expected from a typical 10-year old.

She tried to put herself in Jacinthe's shoes: a father who she only saw occasionally, and whose travels made a regular schedule impossible; a mother who was hell-bent on securing her loyalty by buying her things, and letting her do whatever she liked; and now Simone, 'the rival' who insisted on respect and civility. Gently, but firmly.

It was clear to Simone that Jacinthe needed both discipline and a role model, things her mother Jennifer seemed ill-equipped to provide. She accepted the challenge, and tried not to show whatever resentment she herself felt. The girl needed love and limits. If she only got it on weekends and holidays, it was better than nothing.

Simone found Jacinthe's anger easier to handle than her anxiety. You could sense it building, with enough time to take cover. Then, in a flash, it was over. The anxiety came on slowly, lasted far longer and hit Simone right in the gut. Self-doubt was outside her experience.

Simone was determined not to let Jacinthe's moods define her, though. She was curious, intelligent and she loved the outdoors. The rougher and dirtier the better. She'd be called a tomboy, if that word hadn't fallen out of fashion. Rightly so, thought Simone. A girl should be free to be as scrappy—or dainty—as she wanted. No labels.

Things would improve. Simone was certain. Then Jennifer died in a car crash.

Suddenly, three years into her marriage, Simone was the mother of a deeply traumatized teenager; resentful and incommunicative, even with Ron. The home dynamic changed considerably. Instead of being free to travel at almost any time, Simone and Ron had to constantly negotiate to ensure one of them could be present.

When Simone switched to being a regular columnist, some of the logistical challenges eased and Jacinthe became hers to 'mother', in reality if not in name. To Jacinthe, she was always 'Simone', and a common retort to any request or instruction was a dismissive 'You're not my mother!' Simone was surprised at how much this hurt.

Slowly, things did improve. Jacinthe came to thrive on the structure that Simone provided. She learned to trust Simone's judgement on many things, from course selection to peer pressure. Though she chafed at house rules and curfews—often left to Simone to enforce—she grew to realize her father's wife was actually on her side.

Especially when, at the age of 16, she chose to voice the confusion she had been holding inside. She did so when Ron was away.

"Simone," she began awkwardly as they emptied the dishwasher. "What would you say if you thought I was attracted to girls. To women—*umm*—as opposed to men."

"Well," Simone said, putting down the bowl she was holding and turning to face Jacinthe. "I would say a couple of things. First, that doesn't really surprise me."

Jacinthe flinched, then let out a weak laugh.

"Second, I would say that you have all the time in the world to figure things out. Only you will know what feels right for you. And it doesn't have to be one or the other. Let nature tell you, not other people."

"Wow!" said Jacinthe exhaling fully. "That was easier than expected."

Simone reached out and took Jacinthe's hands into her own. "I'm glad. Not everything will be so easy."

A year later, in Jacinthe's final year of high school, Simone remarked to Ron that it felt as much like a mother-daughter relationship as she would have expected from a biological child. A lot like she remembered having with her mother at that age. Normal, but not always easy.

All the more reason why Jacinthe's outburst in January of Grade 12 surprised and stung her. They had been discussing a March Break student trip while preparing dinner. Jacinthe was sufficiently ambivalent about it that she had yet to even request permission to go.

"They pretend it's about doing volunteer work in a developing country, but really it's an excuse to party," she said dismissively.

Simone had heard this about these commercial trips, and nodded in agreement. "It's a lot of money that could be going toward university," she said. "Besides, just think of the carbon emissions."

Suddenly, Jacinthe turned on her, with an expression she had not seen for years. "Carbon emissions! Shit, Simone, don't you ever get tired of loading that stuff on people? You're the freaking Gestapo!" she spat.

Simone stared at Jacinthe, feeling the heat rising to her face. Finally, in as calm a tone as she could muster, she issued an order.

"Do not ever use that word in my presence, in my house again!"

It was Jacinthe's turn to be taken aback.

"Bad choice of words. But I meant everything else. You lecture us every week in your columns, then off you go on another plane trip to save the world. Now here I want to take one—"

"You weren't even sure you wanted—"

"I don't know if I want to go!" Jacinthe screamed. "But if I do, I'm not going to feel guilty. We're screwed anyway. You say so all the time. As if we didn't know. And what have you really done to stop it?"

Simone took her time responding. "Is that how you really feel? That we're screwed anyway? And I haven't done enough."

"Not you specifically." Jacinthe was still agitated but no longer shouting.

"You do more than most people. Of your generation. You guys got to live high off the hog on the whole world's resources, while my generation has to live with the stinking mess." Jacinthe's eyes bored into Simone's.

"You talk about mental illness. But you have no idea how deep it goes for us. Seeing your planet trashed, your friends getting electronic toys and drugs to entertain their brains, the adults all pretending it's fine, trying to sell us more stuff, and even people like you and Dad, with your big talk and your bicycles and solar panels and hanging the laundry... but look at your fucking air miles! You want to know why my generation is depressed, talking about suicide and trancing out on mystery pills? 'Eco-anxiety?' Try hypocrisy!"

Simone let Jacinthe vent. She didn't do it enough.

"If you're not even going to defend yourself, I'm not going to waste time staying here. I don't even want to go on that stupid trip." Jacinthe was standing, her arms crossed. Daring Simone to speak.

"I'm going for a run. Don't wait for me." Jacinthe headed for the door in long, powerful strides, closing it firmly behind her.

She had the decency not to slam it, thought Simone. And she reads my columns!

Justice in Japan

From: Simone Cohen
March 17, 2017 3:35 PM
Re: Incredible - Japanese Court Delivers Justice!
To: Jiro Ebitsubo

Dear Jiro,

Thinking of you. This just came across my desk. I don't know if you're only reading the Japanese press, which may not have run this. Here's the full article.

All the best to you and the girls. Hope you're finding fulfilment.

Love Simone

- A local court has ruled for the first time that both the government and the operator of the Fukushima No. 1 nuclear plant were responsible for failing to take preventive measures against the March 11, 2011, earthquake-triggered tsunami.
- This shocking ruling was the first to find the state and Tokyo Electric Power Company (TEPCO) negligent. It called the mega tsunami predictable, and said the subsequent nuclear disaster could have been avoided.

- "TEPCO was well aware that a large tsunami could flood its premises and damage safety equipment, such as the backup power generators," said the ruling.
- The state failed to impose stricter measures, despite its own 2002 estimate of potential damage from a major tsunami.

Meeting Day

Washington, DC

Elmore Lambert was running this show. He knew it, and so did a small group of insiders. Few others, though, and that suited him fine. While the White House seemed to be perpetually in a state of chaos, Elmore's agenda was going to plan.

"On schedule, on target, under the radar," he reminded his team when they met to review progress, six months after the presidential inauguration. There were eight of them, housed in an obscure Washington building without any sign to identify them. Officially, the Appointments Task Force did not exist.

"Don't get distracted by the revolving door at the top. Our job is to fill positions few people know about. Some of our choices will be seen as unconventional. No matter. Our goal is not to find people with the best credentials, it's to put in place people who will carry out the president's agenda. People with too many letters after their names can get it into their heads that they're running the show. That they have a duty to protect the agency and all the projects sucking up taxpayer money. *Protecting the public interest*," he sneered.

"Well, who is the public?" he said, smacking the table. "The people who elected Donald Trump, that's who! The president was elected *by* the public, and he made it clear what he intended to do to make America great again."

"*That* is the public interest," Elmore declared, relaxing. His team stayed silent.

"Shrink government. Repeal Obamacare. Eliminate rules that create delays and drive up the costs of mining and drilling. Allow business to get back to making money and creating jobs for Americans. I could go on, but you know it by heart." He chuckled.

"Clear the decks so Americans can make an honest living again. Help the unemployed to pull themselves out of poverty, not wait for another handout. America has gotten lazy, and the liberal agenda encourages it. The media tell them it's okay—they've had a hard life. Boo hoo, who hasn't! But not all of us use it as an excuse."

Elmore looked around the room. Everyone was nodding. Then smiling, as they saw him doing so. It was a small table. His team was small, and he would keep it that way. He needed loyalty, to the agenda and to himself. As much as he trusted this group, he was watching them. None had more than a portion of the work plan or appointments list. Easier to find the source of a leak, if it came to that. And take necessary action.

"We meet to talk about problems," he emphasized. "What posts are we behind in filling. Which appointments are causing grief. Skeletons in the closet too big to cram back in. Anybody trying too hard to be popular with their staff.

"Brittany!" he said, turning to the only woman in the group. "What's with National Parks? Who's failing to crack the whip?" Brittany Coates had been brought in from the FBI. Referred by one of the president's legal advisers. "She's one of us," he'd assured Elmore. "Whip smart, with a quaint little '*Noath Carolahna*' accent. Most important, she's discreet."

As they made their way around the table, Elmore took careful notes. Agencies and people causing problems. Positions nobody wanted.

Filling the top posts had been easy: an EPA head who wanted to strip the agency's mandate; a secretary of energy who knew so little, he was willing to accept the script he was handed; a secretary of state fresh out of the oil patch. But the next level down was harder. The pay and perks weren't good enough for some of the party faithful. The State Department was especially tricky. Everyone wanted to be an ambassador to London or Paris. Nobody wanted Lagos, or Baku.

"Thank you gentlemen!" He winked at Brittany. "Next Monday I want this list to be very short. Understood?"

"Yes, sir!" said eight voices.

"Dismissed. Everyone except Scott and Fred."

Elmore had assigned his two most trusted people—brought in from the Prosperity Gospel Academy—to work on a special list. While much of the team's work was filling positions, an equally important job was eliminating them. The position, or the person occupying it.

Most of the targets were public servants. Meddlesome climate scientists and negotiators had been shown the door quickly. Many resigned or accepted early retirement. Some, though, were proving tenacious. They would have to be hounded out. Embarrassed out. This, he knew, had to be done with delicacy. And no trail.

Which brought him to the journalists. The president had a particular dislike for media, with a few exceptions. Donald Trump relished making life difficult for certain organizations and their reporters. But that sometimes backfired. Elmore was working on several techniques that would be less obvious than, say, not taking questions from a *New York Times* or CNN reporter. Or always favouring Fox. That just looked petty.

Elmore had a special list. Journalists who would find it hard to get media accreditation, or included on important lists, where once it was automatic. He was not above using lawyers to file frivolous lawsuits, or pursue allegations of tax evasion. That's why the Justice and IRS appointments had been so important.

For foreign media, he had a new tool in his kit: impeding entry or re-entry by failing to renew work permits and visas.

Six months after the election—the appointments having taken longer than anticipated—he was just getting started on his media list. Two women were at the top. A Canadian would find it much harder to enter the United States than her previous 47 times. A British woman would have trouble returning from her next family visit to London; awkward for a divorced mother with a mortgage and two daughters in a New York school.

"Fred," he barked. "Where are you at with the immigration lawyers?"

"I've got a novel approach to suggest, sir. Something a Texas governor used once on a Mexican journalist."

Tit for Tat

Jenny's meeting, as expected, was short.

Andrew Ma welcomed her politely into her own boardroom, then asked a lawyer she had never seen to walk through an offer. She had insisted on bringing her own counsel.

Frances Cho had spent the previous day with Jenny, preparing for various scenarios. Jenny had been candid, describing the video, to which Andrew had made several allusions during the preceding weeks: "A file that nobody will want to see on the internet." Whether he had it, or was only pretending was moot. Unless Jenny was prepared to call his bluff.

"We could expect to win a blackmail case in any country with a more robust legal system," Frances commented. "When it comes to influence by powerful people, Malaysia has been sliding. Even in a Sweden, though, you would not reach trial without much of the case being made public. The video might never be viewed by a judge or jury, but the whole world would learn it existed or was said to, which means you and your family would get dragged through the muck. A win would feel like a loss."

Jenny concluded she was better off negotiating a golden parachute than fighting for justice. "If it allows me to take care of the girls and my parents, I'll plug my nose!"

In the tense days leading up to the meeting, she made a point of signalling to Andrew Ma that she was reviewing all options with topnotch legal advice.

Malaysia was a sexually conservative society. China as well.
The video could play two ways. Jenny would surely be shamed
over it, but Andrew and his partners would too. While the 'loose
woman' would come off worse than the 'virile, scheming man',
the Bright Future brand would be tarnished, just as they were
preparing a major launch. Both sides had an interest in making
the takeover mutually beneficial.

When the written offer was placed in front of her, Jenny
requested that everyone leave the room for 10 minutes while
she and Frances reviewed it. Once alone, they sat together and
went over each line. It was short, but also generous. In exchange
for them signing over all ownership, Jenny and Jiro would each
receive a US$8 million buyout.

Notably, there was no mention of a compromising video in
the document. Nor had it been mentioned by Andrew or his
lawyer. Once everyone had filed back into the room, Jenny was
the one who raised it.

"I wish to put on record, witnessed by myself and Frances
Cho, that a video was taken of myself and Andrew Ma
engaged in consensual sex at a hotel in Guangdong." There
was a rustle as everyone turned to look at Andrew. He had
turned beet red.

Jenny continued, in a forceful voice. "Andrew Ma claimed
to me he destroyed this video. Its existence, therefore is *not*
consensual, and should be considered illegal. The video was part
of a scheme to force me and my husband to sell the company.
I require that you, Andrew Ma, confirm that this statement is
true, to be witnessed by my lawyer."

Andrew and his lawyer looked at each other, then turned
to one of the unnamed men also seated at the table. The others
present looked awkwardly at the floor.

"Well…" Andrew began. "I, um, I do not believe—"

Jenny cut him off sharply. "Or I will initiate a very public
lawsuit against Bright Future Industries for conspiring to commit
extortion."

Andrew's lawyer whispered something to him and then the mystery partner, who nodded. "Yes," said Andrew. "What you have said is the truth."

"Good," said Jenny. "Now, I require you to acknowledge in our presence that the video has been or will be destroyed, with no copies retained in any form. Do you commit to that?" The three men again exchanged glances. The silent man nodded and Andrew read aloud from a sheet Jenny presented to him.

"Excellent!" said Jenny. "Now give me a moment to check some notes on my tablet. Hmm," she muttered, swiping and tapping the screen several times. Frances, meanwhile, looked to be glancing at messages on her own phone.

"Ah there it is," said Jenny. "Good. How about you Frances?" Frances nodded.

Jenny sat up straight and scanned the others at the boardroom table, making eye contact with each. Then in a voice that was stronger than her apparent position, she declared: "As despicable and illegal as all of this may be, I accept the offer. Knowing that I am protected by more than a verbal declaration. This entire meeting was recorded on my tablet as well as my lawyer's phone, and the files have been successfully transmitted. They will be stored for as long as necessary."

"You can never be too careful," she remarked to nobody in particular, as she signed the copies of the agreement in front of her. Jiro would be signing an identical set.

Rising from her seat, Jenny spoke in a clear voice.

"I will not be shaking the hand of anyone in this room. Instead I will shake the hands of some faithful and honest staff. Such people do still exist."

Time's Up

Simone's meeting with Anthony Paulson was short.

Seated at the far end of the same conference room table, was a stern woman in a formal jacket and skirt, her bun tied so tight Simone imagined it stretching her forehead. Anthony nervously shuffled his notes and prepared to speak.

"Simone, you know what this means."

"Sure, Anthony," she replied.

"I am to read to you some terms, once we've had a chance for a few personal words. Then Ms. Fitch has a form for you to sign, after which she will escort you to your desk, where you will pack your belongings and exit the building. No long farewells today."

"I know the routine," said Simone, "I'll go quietly."

"Okay, here we go." Anthony sat up straight, mustering his courage.

"Simone, it has been a pleasure working with you. I've challenged you, and you've challenged me. You accepted feedback and criticism as it was intended." He had been speaking from the heart. Preparing now to read from a sheet with HeraldMedia letterhead, he cleared his throat.

"Recently, you were given specific direction as to how your pieces were to be modified to meet the requirements of HeraldMedia. In the view of the publisher, you have not sufficiently complied. Furthermore, on several occasions, you made disparaging remarks about the media in such a way as to impugn this company. In recent months, the feedback of our readers to your work has been overwhelmingly negative, to the point where it is felt your position as a columnist is to the detriment of the interests of this company. It is my duty to inform you that your employment with HeraldMedia is terminated. A standard severance package is offered."

In the silence that ensued, Simone heard a chair slide.

"Just a moment, please," she said firmly, turning to Ms. Fitch. "I'd like to express my gratitude to Mr. Paulson." A barely perceptible nod indicated consent.

"Anthony, I'm not going to dispute anything. There's no point. It has been an honour to work with you. You have a very difficult job, in a very difficult industry. Thanks, and see you on the other side."

The next half hour went according to script. Simone offered a nod and a smile to the few colleagues she passed. Half the desks in the newsroom were unoccupied.

"Good bye, Simone. Good luck girl. Cycle on! Stay in touch."

It could be worse, thought Simone. For more than a decade I could say almost anything I felt needed to be said. I could have had Ms. Fitch's job, holding the door for each departing team member. Confirming they had left.

"Thanks Ann," she said with a nod, as she passed through the door.

"You're welcome, Ms. Cohen. Best of luck."

As Simone reached the waiting taxi, she thought she heard something. It sounded like "I admire your work." She turned to see a dark suit and tight bun disappear into the building.

Birth of a Party

T he past few months had been difficult for Jiro and the people of Fukushima. Tens of thousands remained displaced. Many were jobless. Depression was common and the rate of suicide was high and rising.

The people affected by the tsunami and its fallout deserved better. Japan deserved better. Jiro believed this and so, apparently, did local members of the Four Elements Movement. Enough to fill the community hall for this critical meeting.

Jiro had been preparing for this night for months. For years, if he counted back to the founding of the movement in 2012. For much of his adult life, maybe. Certainly since Cambridge, when Jenny had entered his life. But he couldn't think about that now. He had a political party to launch and a job to win.

Oddly, the collapse of his marriage and loss of NiMa Energy freed him to focus on this one goal. The buyout money would allow him to settle his parents into a proper house and carry on his work, regardless of the outcome. He could easily afford the girls' boarding school fees when they moved to Tokyo in the fall. This wasn't about money.

Jiro began tentatively. He had given plenty of public speeches, but this would be his first 'political' one.

On a number of occasions, people had encouraged him to run for office. He routinely brushed off these overtures. He disliked confrontation. His place was in developing policies and

348

technical solutions for politicians—other people—to implement. But confrontation was inevitable. The systemic changes proposed by Four Elements were a major departure from how things were done. Especially by the power companies. They were accustomed to deciding what was best for people, designing the systems and selling the power.

The Manifesto he had helped write was endorsed three years earlier by a coalition of local manufacturers, trade unions and builders. Some had made a substantial effort to put it into practice. For serious progress to occur, though, governments at all levels had to come on board. Many towns and villages were enthusiastically applying their ideas, but the prefectural and governments were not. And Four Elements couldn't make them. It was a people's movement with no formal power.

Jiro now saw that the most effective way to alter how government worked was to become government. He and the majority of Four Elements directors concluded they must form an official party. Perhaps one day on a national level, but initially, in Fukushima Prefecture. Tonight, the general membership would vote on two questions: whether to form a party, and whether to choose Jiro Ebitsubo as leader and candidate for governor.

Jiro had begun by reading his printed text, reminding members how Four Elements came to be. Several minutes in, he sensed rustling and coughing. He'd wanted to speak without notes, but brought them for support. Now he was losing people. If he wanted to inspire others, to be the leader they needed—the leader he needed to be—he had to do better. Jiro took a deep breath and put aside his speech.

"I dream of a renaissance," he began, looking out at the faces of people he had come to know and trust and love. "I dream of a Fukushima powered by its people and the four elements—sun, wind, water and earth." The rustling had stopped.

"I dream of a society that embraces its traditions and its institutions, but is not tied to them." Jiro's shoulders relaxed as the weight he had been carrying fell away.

"I dream of a Japan that knows and values its story, but will not allow it to hold us down. Preventing us from making the leap to a better future."

Standing tall, his eyes shining, Jiro raised his arms and opened them. He was offering his energy to the audience, and in return they gave him theirs; entrusting him with their collective power.

By the time the board president called for the vote, the outcome was obvious. Fukushima had a new political party and a late entry in the race for governor; Jiro had a renewed mission; and Japan's traditional parties, power companies and nationalists had a new target.

Fault Lines

Le Tilleret, June 2017

François was the one who initiated the community meeting. With growing unease he'd witnessed his neighbours turning against each other during the 2017 presidential election. A local man with strong views about immigrants and a conviction that providing refuge was breeding crime had done shockingly well. He'd concocted a conspiracy involving 'Muslims and gypsies' from the Balkans recruiting North African and Syrian criminals to form a super-network that undermined the social fabric of not just France but 'Christian Europe'. It was crazy, but it worked.

His populist oratory, combined with local insecurity, gave him a slim victory in the advance round of legislative voting. Though moderate voters banded together to block him in the second round and elect Emmanuel Macron's *En Marche!* candidate, seeing neighbours flirt with such extreme nativism put a chill into the start of François' year.

Then in May, two events put people on edge. A teenage boy from one of the Syrian families so warmly welcomed into the village was accused of assaulting a classmate at a party. Two days later, a farmer was shot and wounded in the pasture of his farm in the hills to the east. Several sheep were stolen, along with his pickup. He could not identify the assailants—'it was dark and they wore hoodies'—but he was certain they were 'African'.

Suspicion turned immediately to Chloe and Pascal Martin's farm next door, where three African migrants were living and working. There had been a feud brewing between the wounded man and the couple, who accused him on several occasions of cutting down their trees for firewood.

François knew such things happened—land disputes, theft, assault—and had to be dealt with appropriately. But as individual incidents. Not lumped together as proof the world was falling apart. It was time to act.

With three village elders, he invited local residents to an evening of music and food, to be followed by a community conversation. He had a personal reason for bringing the community together. His farm offered refuge and training to migrants. Mostly they were men. Energetic young men in need of a home, where they would be safe and could earn money—to save, or send home to family.

Though others harboured more migrants than him, François was a leader in developing training modules for youth in areas such as building renovation, PV installation and irrigation. On his farm he provided opportunities to build skills on real projects; implementing ideas he had not found time or money to advance.

His 'Global Village' concept was meant to showcase an integrated approach to construction, energy management and permaculture. François labeled his own property 'Global Village Assisi', or just GV Assisi. When such Global Villages became widespread, he believed, they would be a way to build community bonds. To calm fears even. You mistrust what you don't know.

He hoped this meeting would help people get to know each other again. And allow some of his team to tell their stories.

The night got off to a rocky start. Three members of a skinhead group calling for 'direct action against illegals'—rushed the stage to protest the presence of migrants. They miscalculated badly. Knowing the event was to have begun with a musical performance by a popular local singer, the crowd was in no mood to be bullied. Barely into a denunciation of François and his treason, Mario, the leader, was drowned out by calls to get off the stage. Cursing loudly, the three stormed out of the hall.

This ugly display served to enhance interest in what followed. Nobody wanted to be associated with such extremism.

Two men who had recently completed training programs at GV Assisi and now worked as on-site caretakers were due to speak. Spooked by what they had just witnessed, they appeared reticent to go on stage. Sensing this, François took the microphone and addressed the assembled community.

"Who would like to hear what these brave men have prepared to share with us—in a language that is not even their mother tongue?" He paused.

"I would," shouted a woman at the back of the hall.

"Us too," echoed a father. His adolescent daughter began to clap. Her younger brother quickly joined her. Soon the entire hall was clapping and chanting: "Speak, speak, speak!"

Taking courage from the reception, the two young men approached the microphone, smiling nervously. The stories they would share were not easy to hear. Nor, of course, were they easy to tell. In turn, they described the desperate conditions they had fled and their harrowing journeys. Then, with poise and pride they spoke of the skills they were now learning and their desire to contribute and be accepted.

By the end of the evening, after a wide-ranging discussion period, more people wore smiles than François had seen for a while. Not everyone was won over, and not everyone would host a Global Village, but people were now talking about ways to make use of the migrants' strong arms rather than to how to rid the country of them.

"An evening well spent," he said to his crew as they helped sweep and put away chairs. He would lock up the hall when they were done.

When they emerged, Mario and his followers were still in the parking lot. They sounded angry, and they were not alone.

"Hey, François!" a male voice called from the shadows. Startled, he turned as the man approached. It was his neighbour Pascal Martin. Next to him were three other men. Even in the dark, he knew Robert Giroux and his equally large teenage sons.

"We thought you might want company on your walk home," Pascal said, pointing to the noisy group. "They've been drinking, and it hasn't made them any smarter."

Chautauqua Heads South

*The majority of people living on our planet profess to be
believers. This should spur religions to dialogue among
themselves for the sake of protecting nature, defending the
poor and building networks of respect and fraternity.*

Laudato Si

Sagan was headed to New Orleans. For months, he had been
reaching out to religious leaders in the South, in search
of a congregation open to his chautauqua—"A facilitated
conversation to find common ground in this divided country and
divided world, for the sake of our community, our descendants
and God's great Earth."

It was the pastor of a pentecostal church in one of the
parishes most devastated by Hurricane Katrina that responded
to his overture.

Dear DJ Sagan,

I spend a lot of time thinking about these issues.
Since Hurricane Katrina, and the insufficient
response from our leaders, I have questioned
many positions previously held by this church.
What was God's plan in sending us the winds and
floods? Were we not living a sufficiently righteous

life and was this his lesson? Many of us sin in word and deed in our daily lives, yet profess to be God-fearing folk. We have idolized money and power, and turned to acquisition rather than inner development and the message of Jesus to help and to love our neighbours. I have come to see we have erred by failing to embrace the call to stewardship over all of God's creation. I know that many in this country do not see this as a duty. I believe they are misled. There is money and power in exploiting God's earth, and we have found it convenient to bend the teachings of the Bible to align with self-serving choices. This may yet be judged our greatest sin.

But here I am writing a sermon, not an invitation. I and my fellow church leaders will be pleased to host you. We cannot pay for your travel, but we can offer a bed and some fine New Orleans cooking.

Sincerely,
Evander Washington

* * *

Sagan prepared a short study guide for all who registered. While there was a strong Catholic presence in Louisiana, this was not a Catholic church. Basing the discussion around the Pope's words would be unwise. Though he did include mention of the *Laudato Si*, and some direct quotations, mostly he used original biblical references. Also, he drew on some of the lines from the encyclical, without specifically naming it. This was a discussion, after all, not an academic exercise. The guide also included passages related to stewardship of nature and the Earth from holy books of other world religions.

Then, he took a chance on passages from the works of Michael Dowd. Sagan had not yet met the man, but had followed with admiration his writings, videos of his talks and his bestselling book, *Thank God for Evolution*. The subtitle, "How the marriage of science and religion will transform your life and our world" could serve as a mission statement for Sagan's own journey since leaving academia.

In Sagan's mind, there was nothing controversial about Dowd's message. But people cling tight to beliefs. Dowd was asking people to let go of confining, literal interpretations of passages from the Bible and recognize that by failing to integrate science with religion, and by failing to accept and embrace 'reality' and fact, they were in effect worshipping a kind of virtual or alternate reality.

By failing to understand and respond to how the world actually works—based on our ever-improving scientific understanding of it—and by failing to recognize how human behaviour was so dramatically altering our world, God's world, the true believer would not be capable of saving her own species. Blind to reality, blinded by doctrine and ideology, even by idolatry—placing man above the rest of creation—fundamentalists of many religions were hastening the end of civilization.

This was heady stuff: theology, philosophy, anthropology and more. It had taken Sagan, a highly educated scientist, several years of reading and thinking to get his mind around the work of Michael Dowd. Now he was trying to introduce it as just one part of a discussion that would span a single evening, and then a follow-up morning session.

He'd be lucky to get people to stay for both. That's why he packed as much as possible into the evening session. This would be more of a lecture than he liked. Time was always too tight. Which was why he sent the study guide in advance, with links to readings and websites for those with the time and inclination.

Like Dowd, Sagan was convinced it was possible and necessary to develop a story of our place in the world that reconciles science with religion. It would have to appeal broadly to people who clung to a biblical creation story and rejected human activity as a primary cause of the breakdown of Earth's atmosphere and biosphere.

"We, as God's prodigal species, can come home to God, by coming home to reality, to scientific truth," Sagan declared.

After a full night of lecture and discussion, Sagan was building toward his conclusion. It was not the packed hall he had been hoping for, nor the level of engagement of Boston, but decent, considering parish demographics and the time slot. Some had drifted away early, not willing to have their established gospel called into question. Others left during the break, as it was approaching 10 p.m.—the scheduled end. But an attentive group of 50 still with him so late on a Monday night in New Orleans had to be considered a success.

There had been a man at the back throughout the evening. Sagan noticed him on and off, taking notes, but not participating. More than just a skeptic, he assumed.

"If I may again draw on Dowd's language to close," said Sagan, "our new gospel, our revised gospel must be *a 'pro future, pro-science, nature-honoring'* one. I thank you for staying and being open to other ways of viewing the world and the gospel."

The applause that followed was genuine. Not particularly enthusiastic, but many were still processing what they had heard. Some appeared shell-shocked, or just exhausted. Sagan observed the man with the notepad heading quickly for the exit. He paused briefly in front of the pastor, seeming to rebuke him. Sagan would have to ask what that was about.

You Can Be Anything

"If you have to get fired, let it be in time for summer."

Simone knew from the very first evening, when she broke the news to Ron, that she would take the summer off. For riding, reading, canoeing—maybe one of Ron's expeditions—and for thinking. Most of all for thinking. She'd been running since the starter pistol went after her bachelor's degree. Go, go, go... Japan, Cambridge, the *Herald*... write, write, write. Always curious, always provocative. She knew what she wanted to do, and she did it. What she had never done was pause to reflect.

"What do I want to be now? More importantly, who do I want to be?"

She posed this to Ron, as they sat on their back deck, late into a long June evening; drinking craft beer, eating organic, free-range chicken with a locally-sourced salad to match. To any observer, they had it all. Jobs that offered excitement and freedom. The mortgage paid, and a daughter in university; on scholarship no less.

"I've been paid to give advice to the nation—to tell people how they should live, and governments and corporations how they should do their business—on the assumption that I know it all. Or by doing enough research and talking to the smartest people, I will sound like I do."

"It seems to me you do," Ron said, with no hint of sarcasm.

"But am I living out the values I profess? Am I the model eco-citizen, the compassionate supporter of immigrants, the mentally ill and the drug addicts that I pretend to be; and cajole my readers to be?"

"You're being pretty hard on yourself!" Ron said. "You ride your bike almost everywhere, then take the bus most of the time when you're not. We eat local, organic and mostly vegetarian. The house has been retrofitted from top to bottom. Every appliance is ultra-efficient. You wear a thick sweater and those dorky insulated slippers in winter. We still don't have air conditioning, because you think fans and insulated blinds will do. You even shut off the modem at night. Who does that!"

Simone began to chuckle.

"Wait!" Ron held up his hand. "I'm not done. You joined the Ottawa Renewable Energy Co-op and made me become a member too. Even though we already had solar panels on the house. You switched to a credit union—and made me do it too!"

"Suggested. I don't make you do anything, Ron."

"Yah, OK. 'Suggested'. Let's see, what did I miss? You buy carbon off-sets for every flight you take. Geez, Simone, is there anything more you could be doing?"

She was chuckling now.

"Oh, yeah, you want us to get an electric car. The damn things aren't available, but you're on two waiting lists."

"OK, OK. So why do I feel I'm not doing enough, not meeting expectations?"

"Whose expectations?" Ron shrugged. "Mine? Nope. Our neighbours'? Nope. They already think you're a fanatic. The only expectations you can't meet are your own. Am I right?"

Simone was no longer laughing. After a long pause, she answered.

"Yes, I set a high standard for myself. Because I don't see others doing enough, I feel I have to overcompensate. Then there's feedback from readers. Some think I'm overbearing, others take shots at me for being a hypocrite. 'I bet she still has a car. Look at all the flying she does.' That one really gets me. I'm telling everybody else to stop flying, yet I do it all the time. Buying offsets won't suck the CO_2 back out."

"So, there it is," Ron announced. "The great Simone Cohen, hero to many, eco-feminist bitch to a few, has a flaw. She flies. And it makes her a self-loathing wreck."

"I am *not* a self-loathing wreck!"

"I exaggerate. But that's what it comes down to. You've failed to persuade the entire world to live up to your standards, *and* you're a hypocrite for flying. What are you going to do about it?"

Simone took a long time thinking. Ron had cut to the heart.

"I can see two options," she said, finally. "Stop flying, or lower my standards. I don't know how to do either. And I refuse to do the second one."

"So," Ron said, "let's start with flying shall we. And I say *we*, because I rack up as many miles as you do, and I'm not as rigorous about buying off-sets. Sorry to break it to you."

Simone wagged her finger, but said nothing.

"I've been thinking about that too, you know. I'm tired of flying. Sure, if I wasn't, somebody else would be stepping in. They might not even buy *any* off-sets. But, mostly, I'm just tired of flying all over to guide tourists. It was great for awhile, but it's worn thin. I'm 56. I don't tolerate airport security and lost luggage anymore. I want to stay closer to home, or run my own company where the plane is a choice, not a must."

"There you go, Ron." Simone leaned forward and looked him straight in the eyes. "How do we do what we do, where flying is occasional, not automatic? How do we have more time for one another? Holidays together. Stay-cations, or local trips. By bike, by train—"

"Electric car, once you find one," he added. Simone laughed.

"So, when we've got the EV, and we're only flying once or twice a year, and maxing out our carbon credits paying for energy retrofits of low-income housing for disabled, refugee women with dyslexia... we'll be perfect!"

"Ron!" Simone tried to sound indignant, while suppressing laughter.

"You see! We have to be able to sit back and say, 'I'm doing my share, and I feel good about it.' Or else you'll never feel good. And nobody likes a bitter, old eco-bitch!"

Simone laughed. A deep, long laugh. Ron joined her. In the silence that followed, he poured them both another glass of local, craft-brewed, organic ale.

"I'm not really an eco-bitch, am I?"

"When you are, you have good reason," Ron said, his tone supportive. "Too many people are just plain eco-sloths, and make all kinds of excuses for it. Then they attack people like you, because it somehow makes them feel righteous."

"Or because I've been too self-righteous?"

"I think you're honest in your writing. You're upfront about your imperfections, Simone. That's important."

She took a sip and looked up at the sky, which was finally dark.

"Are you doing any canoe trips this year to a really remote place? Where we won't see other people, but plenty of wildlife?"

"Sure. My Arctic trip. Alsek River. It will involve planes, though." He grinned.

"I'll buy more solar shares, and flog myself before breakfast."

"Don't do that. I can put you on polar bear duty at night, instead. How are you with a rifle?"

"Haven't touched one since my biathlon days," said Simone. "But I used to be a crack shot! When's the trip, again?"

"First week in August."

"Perfect. I'll do my long bike trip now. Go visit Sagan in Detroit. Or entice him over to beautiful Windsor, so I won't have to cross into Trump-... *He Who Must Not be Named*-land. Then we can spend most of July at the cabin. Me at least. You when you're free. Jacinthe, when she's back from tree-planting in BC."

"Not sure she'll want to," Ron said wistfully. "She used to love it."

"Until it became uncool to be with parents. That and the lack of cell coverage."

"Oh, about that," said Ron. "I was at the outhouse, in April, and suddenly my cell phone beeped. I usually shut it off, since there's no reception. But I forgot. I received a batch of text messages. Must be the new tower."

"There goes the neighbourhood," said Simone ruefully. "Now everybody's going to be glued to their phones, like in town."

"It could change things, that's for sure. It also means we can be tracked, if somebody wanted to."

"We'll have to remind friends not to geo-tag photos," Simone said. "Remember when Jacinthe did that?"

"The way you ripped into her, I doubt she will again," Ron said, standing and gathering up their plates and glasses.

"Yeah. Not one of my finer parenting moments. I was angry. Me in my very public work. It just set me off."

"You never asked to be *the stepmother*," Ron said placing his hands on her shoulders. "And with me away... If I haven't said thank you enough, I'll say it again now." He kissed the top of Simone's head.

She sighed deeply, consciously absorbing this gratitude.

"I do love her," Simone said. "I sometimes even like her. Wow, she's turning 20!"

"Home from university and appreciative of all we do for her," Ron said in a sing-song voice.

"Yeah, right," Simone laughed. "But there's time."

"Ron," she said affectionately. "Thanks for supporting me in my mid-life crisis. I'll get going in a few days."

"Ships crossing in the night!" He moaned. "Speaking of which..." His voice sounded hopeful.

"If I were a ship," Simone said, putting him off, "what kind would I be?"

"Hmm, a tug boat? Not a canoe, you're not stable enough." Ron laughed. "I know! A zero-emission racing boat, with solar sails and a tank full of hydrogen."

"That sounds cool. I'll get Jenny to whip one up for me."

"Ah, yes, Jenny," Ron sighed. "Poor Jenny. And Jiro!"

Simone nodded. "Come to bed. Let's make positive energy for struggling couples."

"Duty calls!" said Ron, giving her a salute.

Digging Deep

June 29, 2017, North of Kamloops, BC

Grab seedling from bag, jab shovel in ground, pry, wedge seedling firmly, punch hole closed and repeat. Jacinthe's back ached. Her eyes stung from the sweat. Her boots were water-logged and her socks stunk. All of her stunk. And she was happy as hell. She grinned, though there was nobody to see it. The nearest member of her crew was 300 metres away. Not Isabelle. Not today. Today it was Weird Wendell from Victoria.

Jacinthe stood up and arched her back. *Ooh, that felt good.* She was over the hump. Out of the fog.

The last weeks had been tough. This was her second season of planting in British Columbia; she knew what she was getting into—the isolation, the food, the strange customs and the aching muscles—but this year was different.

It was the fire. The *fires*. This year, fires were everywhere. If the smoke didn't get you—and it did—the growing sense of futility would.

You think you're making a difference. Trees need to be cut, people need wood, locals need jobs. If it's done carefully and responsibly—that being relative—the ancient forest can be replanted. Never replaced, or even replicated, but at least replanted. That's why you came. The noble reason, at least. A lot came for the pay, but deep down even they were motivated by a desire to do good. You could make just as much doing harm somewhere, so why not do good. The pay was way better in *the patch*—the tar sands, as she insisted on calling it.

Tree planting attracted more than its share of idealists. Like her. Isabelle too. Another of Izzy's qualities. Which is why the camp felt so different this year. Just over the range, just down the valley, or up, the forest was burning. Torching last year's growth. Or if it wasn't last years, it was the year before's. And the one before that.

What was the freakin' point? Cut, plant, burn and repeat. It hit them hard. Night after night, talking it through, smoking joints and drinking. A few quit. Too hard on the lungs, too many planting days lost, too depressing.

She'd thought about leaving, but Isabelle talked her back. "Despair is natural. Feel it, own it, breathe it." Then breathe again, some of the pure morning air when the wind wasn't blowing smoke through camp, and remember that you have a choice.

"Give up, or stand up and be counted," was how Izzy put it. She had chosen to stand. To stay, and to plant. So Jacinthe did too.

Simone would be proud. Her Uncle Sagan would be even more so. He knew more about what she was going through than any. Somehow, he always found a way to get back up.

Living in integrity. "Deep ecological integrity," he put it. You define it, you embrace it. What else is there?

She was sore and she was filthy and she was fit as hell. There was smoke, but there was also the scent of resin and humus. And the powerful musk of sweat. *Isabelle*, Jacinthe smiled. By day, and at night.

TPoT Blog — *The Power of Truth*
A Blog is Born

September 10, 2017

Welcome to this inaugural blog: *The Power of Truth (or TPoT)*. A blend of original comment and pointers to the best reporting on earth science, social justice and climate breakdown. As I am no longer employed by a corporate entity, my blog will be constrained by three things only.

1. **Is it true?** I will never knowingly publish anything untrue. Should I learn of an error, I will correct it.
2. **Does it add value?** I aim to share unpublished or under-published information.
3. **Does it need to be said?** Sometimes it is positive information that needs to be more widely known; other times depressing reports that we would rather not hear, but must.

Over my summer of reflection, I thought hard about what and who I want to be in this next phase of my career—and life. I am quite proud of what I've done to date, and who I've been. But more of the same is not enough. So, while I redouble my efforts as a truth teller, I aim for greater alignment with a philosophy I've long aspired to: *living lightly*.

That means reducing my resource footprint to the smallest I can manage in a world where you can't just be a hermit. That's one way of living lightly. The other is to carry yourself in a way that is less weighty, to yourself and those you are trying to influence. Nobody likes a bore or a nag, a scowler or frowner. We can do important work with levity and humility, and we must. I must.

In practical terms, I will be doing very little flying, I will be eating very little meat, and I will have no more children. A recent study indicated that despite these being the most significant things anybody in an advanced industrial country can do to protect the health of our only home Earth (less flying, less meat, fewer children), these are also the most socially and politically sensitive. For this reason, they are rarely acted upon or even mentioned.

The first two will be as hard for me as many readers. The latter a bit easier. I am 44, and beyond my best childbearing years. My 'somewhat older' husband supports me in this pledge. We have a beautiful daughter; mine by marriage. I have never given birth. I may yet regret not doing so.

As for income prospects, not flying presents challenges. I will have to forego some useful research, networking, first-person witnessing and the in-person meetings we use to establish bonds and build trust. I will, of course, make the most of 'virtual' connections.

My life journey has been amazing. I have learned what matters to me and where I now wish to devote my energy. So today, I launch what is not just a blog but a community. The *TPoT* community. A tempest, anyone?

In a time of fake news and echo chambers, we need trusted sources to help us weed through an overwhelming and often toxic information environment. I rely on certain news outlets, journalists and personal contacts for just that. I will share what I gather from them as I will share with them what I gather. You, as a visitor and **subscriber** (hint!) will receive the best we can give. You will also be welcome to share.

Which brings me to a couple of key points.

I need to earn money. I will rely entirely on members and contributors to this TPoT community. Give what you can. Give more if you can. On that note too, I wish to be transparent. Any contributor over $5,000 per annum will be listed as such. Climate deniers and false think tank supporters may be happy to stay anonymous, but I won't emulate them. If you were thinking of giving more than 5 grand, don't be discouraged. You will be standing up publicly for what you believe.

Second, I wish to encourage feedback, but I will not tolerate abuse. Journalists are subject to a staggering level of online abuse and harassment. When you are a woman, it is worse. When your name is Jewish, take it up a further notch. No more! I am using a custom filtering program (NastyBlockerTM). Somebody truly creative and malicious will find a way to get around it. But at least they'll have to use their brains, which should exclude many. If you find your feedback blocked, take a close look at what you wrote, then try again.

What can you expect for your subscription? I aim to post three times a week. Sometimes there will be bursts of activity, sometimes silence, when I'm involved in other projects.

As for content, I aim to do the following:

- Manifest positive energy, even when signs point towards darkness. There are millions of points of light: in the form of people, groups, innovative products and ideas.
- Focus on small wins. Big wins usually start this way.
- Never shy away from hard truths.

And one last thing: language. I am committed to language that is accurate, evocative and necessary. No more euphemisms. I will use the term *climate breakdown*. I will refer to planet Earth as *our only planet*. Thanks for the nudge, George Monbiot. And for this thought:

"We are blessed with a wealth of nature and a wealth of language. Let us bring them together and use one to defend the other."

* * *

There it is, thought Simone, as she logged out of WordPress. The inaugural post.

It had been a summer like no other. The wettest ever in Ontario and Quebec. Still, she had logged more kilometres than she had since her early twenties. There had been the glorious, intimate canoe expedition in August with a small group of Ron's regular clients. Canada's North and West had experienced exceptional heat and drought. Then came the cabin: reading, hosting friends and her parents. She'd even spent a pleasant weekend with Jacinthe.

As for her working future, there had been two very productive stops. In Toronto, she accepted an offer from the Canadian Spotlight—an upstart, online journal devoted to 'countering the erosion of democracy and the growing power of global corporations and elites.' The editor jumped at the chance to bring Simone into its fold as an occasional contributor. She might also be asked to join a crack team of reporters on stories of large international importance.

The second stop was meant to be purely social, but Simone's three days in Detroit resulted in an exciting new project. Sagan had been approached to write a book about his experiences in educating the public about science and spirituality, and his thoughts on the country's future. He had a working title, notes and some scattered ideas, he explained, but he needed a skilled co-writer.

"You've been with me on the entire journey. You've been on a similar one yourself. I hope you'll partner with me." She said yes.

"Good," he'd said. "Now I can confess—it was me that got you fired. How else would you make time for a book?" Seeing his straight face morph into the grin of old, she began to chuckle. Soon they were splitting their sides with laughter.

Simone was thrilled to see Sagan in such fine form and excited about the idea of writing together. A remarkable outcome from a meeting that almost didn't happen.

"Reason for wishing to enter the United States?" the young female officer had asked Simone as she stood at the heavily fortified border control booth, supporting her bike.

"I'll be visiting a friend in Detroit," she replied, handing over her passport. The officer took it and ran it through a scanner. Simone glanced casually around as she waited. She counted a dozen or more microphones and cameras.

The officer tapped a couple of keys. There would be an extensive file, Simone knew. This must be the hundredth time she'd entered the United States. Rarely did it take more than a couple of minutes. Sometimes they wanted details of her work, or even a letter from her employer. Occasionally, an overzealous officer would ask whom she planned to interview or what story she was reporting on. For a journalist, this was sensitive territory. Simone had memorized the agreements to which both countries subscribed, and could even cite previous legal decisions, though she rarely had to. Not at the U.S. border. Entering some other countries as a journalist was a different story.

Today, however, she was crossing as a friend, not a reporter. The hyper-partisan new America, with all its border anxieties, wasn't her problem. Until she caught the frown crossing the woman's face as she gazed at her screen.

"Ma'am," the officer said, her voice cold as steel. "Take your passport and your bicycle and go to the interview building. Or you can turn around and head straight back to Canada. But if you wish to be considered for entry, you will have to report to the counter just inside."

Inside the building, she was instructed to fill out a form providing the address of places where she would be staying and, where applicable, the names and contact details of her hosts. Filling out the form took under 5 minutes, but she would wait 55 more until her name was called. By then, her sweaty cycling gear had turned cold and clammy. *Grin and bear it*, she told herself. *And bite your tongue.*

A large male officer came into the glass-walled interview room to which she had been directed. Placing her passport on the table in front of her, he sized her up and down with his eyes. Then he made a snorting noise, and shook his head. Finally he cleared his throat and began to read from an official form. 'Conditions of Entry' she made out, upside down.

"You will be granted entry for 72 hours," he stated in an officious voice. "You will be expected to stay with your 'friend' Sagan Cleveland. At no time will you be permitted to conduct interviews, file stories or post remarks critical of the president or administration. You may expect at any time to receive an unannounced visit at Mr. Cleveland's address to confirm you are in compliance. Is that clear Mizzz Cohen?" he said, his eyes toggling between hers and her breasts.

"Yes sir," she said.

"Enjoy your stay." He smiled as he slid her passport towards her, making no effort to look into her eyes.

Simone pedaled some distance toward downtown Detroit before letting loose.

"Holy shit! Making America paranoid again."

Writing sessions with Sagan would have to take place north of the border. Online discussion would be kept to a minimum. But who were they kidding—phone calls could be tapped, email messages intercepted and letters opened. The 'right to privacy' was just a fiction now.

Surprise Win

"Everybody, please welcome to the podium our first Four Elements governor!"

The age of the volunteers and supporters assembled on election night told much of the story. Other than Jiro's parents and some veteran community activists, this was a crowd of young people. Many were high school and university students, young professionals, even the young unemployed or underemployed. They saw in Four Elements and its earnest leader something no Japanese political party had shown in decades. A commitment to take the country in a fundamentally different direction; and the absence of ties to interest groups or old boys' clubs.

Naturally, this ruffled feathers; the implied and often overt criticism of so many traditional practices. Jiro's opponents had been quick to make him out as a radical, ready to turn Japanese culture on its head. He was subjected to a sustained campaign of innuendo throughout the campaign. A 'visitor' who knows little of Japan. The founder of a company now in bed with the Chinese. Married to a *Chinese* Malaysian.

His daughters had even been brought into it. A poster appeared in some towns late in the campaign. It showed a photo of Jiro and the twins with a very simple text: "Mudblood!"

This slur went far beyond what the people of Fukushima would tolerate. Most posters were torn down promptly by passersby or irate supporters, but the internet made sure it was seen. A flood of donations and volunteers followed.

Stepping up to the microphone, Jiro acknowledged with a wave the resounding ovation. Before speaking, he gestured for Yuki and Anna to join him. Excused from school, they had been working seven day weeks for the last month of the campaign, showing dedication and sophistication few would have imagined from 14-year-olds. His parents had been equally supportive, though health and age prevented them from playing any active role. When he beckoned for them to come onstage, they waved him off, preferring to stay seated in the front row, their pride evident.

Katsuo sent a note of congratulations. "Brother. You ran an excellent campaign. Be careful of changing too many things. Change is a double-edged sword."

A warning, Jiro wondered, or a threat?

The note from Jenny was far less ambiguous. "Well done Jiro! You deserve this victory. I hope it offers you the means to make the difference you so wish to. Keep the girls safe."

Where There's Smoke

TPoT Blog — *Major divestment from fossil fuels by Catholic church*

October 3, 2017

On the anniversary of the death of Saint Francis of Assisi, more than 40 Catholic institutions from around the world will announce the largest ever divestment from fossil fuels by faith organizations, the *Guardian* reports.

The German Church bank and the Catholic relief organization Caritas said that they will divest more than $7 billion from coal, tar sands and shale oil.

Stefania Proietti, mayor of the Italian town of Assisi, announced it is also slated to sell its fossil fuel holdings to mark Saint Francis' feast day in an important symbolic move. Proietti–a former professor of climate mitigation–told the Guardian that investing in fossil fuels "strays very far from social justice," since the poor are affected most by the impacts of climate breakdown. "But when we disinvest and invest in renewable and energy efficiency instead, we can mitigate climate change, create a sustainable new economic deal and, most importantly, help the poor."

This international climate action project was advanced by the Global Catholic Climate Movement, but its origins lie in Pope Francis' *Laudato Si* climate encyclical.

Clean Break

"Jenny, I'm so glad you called! Where are you? HOW are you?" It had been four months since Simone had spoken with her.

"I'm at home, in KL. My parents haven't disowned me. They're just disappointed." Simone's shoulders relaxed. Jenny sounded much calmer than the last time they'd spoken.

"Besides," Jenny laughed, "they're in *my* home!"

"The girls are in Japan," she continued, with a note of sadness. "Jiro has his own house now, so they're with him and their grandparents. Though they're at boarding school in Tokyo during the week."

"That's the *where*," said Simone. "And the *how*?"

"Oh, slightly better. I go back and forth between feeling like a sucker and wanting to blame everyone else. I can't say I've sorted much out, other than making sure my blood money is out of reach of the wrong people, and the girls are in good hands."

"That's a start," said Simone in an upbeat voice. "But don't confuse housekeeping with having your head on straight. Make sure you have people to talk to. Professionals, I mean. Friends are useful—you can call me any time—but get a good counsellor."

"Mmm," said Jenny, without enthusiasm. "It's not something we do much in my culture. But you're probably right. I never established a network of friends here in KL. Too busy with work, the twins, holding a marriage together..."

"And… the marriage?"

"Thanks Simone. Straight to the point!"

"You're both my friends, remember. I need to know how to navigate this thing myself. Are you trying to work it out, or have the lawyers been called in?"

Jenny coughed. "No, we haven't gone that far. To be honest, we haven't gone anywhere. Jiro only wants to talk about the girls—by email. He's been consumed by the campaign, and then taking office. We've let the marriage dangle."

"But it can't stay that way…"

"Of course not," said Jenny.

"It seems to me," Simone offered hesitantly, "you'll need to go all in to save it, or make a clean break. As amicable as you can manage." After a pause, she dove right in.

"What do YOU want, Jenny?"

Jenny sighed. "I don't know. I really don't. I could take all the blame and ask for forgiveness. Leave KL, move to Japan—if Jiro agreed. Be the good daughter-in-law and governor's wife, with only a few Japanese phrases to get by. Or I could stay here, take care of my parents and start a new business—something quite different."

"Or try a *third* option."

"What third option?"

Simone did not immediately respond.

"Are you still there? I said what third option?"

"Still here Jenny. Just thinking. Hear me out. I'm making this up as I talk."

"Sure."

"Maybe it doesn't have to be rushed," Simone suggested. "Jiro feels betrayed. Grovelling won't help. Sure, you messed up, but he had a role in that. He's going to be so busy in politics, and making time for the girls on weekends and holidays, that you guys wouldn't stand a chance working through this. It would take intense marriage counselling and a deep commitment from you both. I'm not seeing that right now. Am I right?

"As usual," said Jenny.

"OK." Simone's voice was growing more intense. "I'm going to take you back to our bus ride in Rio. And then Cambridge. You never wanted to be a corporate dragon lady. You wanted to improve living conditions in villages that had nothing. Your dream was never about building electric cars and mega-factories. Was it?"

"No," Jenny agreed. "That's just where life took me. We wanted to make a difference, and that's where we ended up."

"And it was fun. Right? It WAS fun."

"Sure," said Jenny. "For a while. The big rush that goes with success."

"But looking back, was that you? The real Jenny Fung? I asked myself those same questions. Perhaps that's where you should start."

"And then what?"

"It's too early for that. Get away somewhere. Your parents— would they be alright without you for a few weeks?"

"Dad's due for a hip replacement, but otherwise they're fine."

"Go somewhere that represents a clean break," said Simone. "Somewhere in the hills. A beach house, whatever. Take some books. A note pad. Your favourite music. Walk, swim, write, whatever. Ask yourself, what do I want as my legacy in 40 years? What do I want people to say about me?"

"What do I want to think about myself!" corrected Jenny.

"Even better. Do that, then call me. I'm sure it will help. If the marriage is meant to be repaired, maybe resurrected..."

Jenny laughed at the image. "Back-from-the-dead," she said in a zombie voice.

"Good girl," Simone laughed. "Have some fun. Oh, and one more thing."

"Ye-e-e-s?" Jenny said, warily.

"Get some exercise. It'll clear your head. Everything else will follow. Trust me."

"I do," said Jenny. "I still don't know why, but I do!"

TPoT Blog — *Bad news that didn't (yet) make the papers*

November 28, 2017

Most bad ecological news never makes it onto TV or survives the algorithms that decide what you read. After all, who wants more bad news? Terrorism, opioids and the White House are enough. But what you don't know could and most likely will hurt you. So here is my (least) favourite ignored news from the past six months.

- The rate of sea level rise is... on the rise. As many as 26 million people have already been displaced from coastal settlements globally. Sea levels along America's southern Atlantic shoreline from North Carolina to Miami "rose dramatically between 2011 and 2015," according to this recent published study. Expect the pace to pick up.
- Experts describe as unprecedented the two wildfires that burned this summer in Greenland. Rapidly shrinking glaciers are exposing land to sunlight, leading to drying in summer months. A feedback loop is expected, as soot from these fires lands on remaining snow and glaciers, which will in turn accelerate their melting.
- Large groups of subsistence farmers are on the move across Central Africa as drought, combined with degraded land, leads to crop failure for people who have no other means of eating or making an income. A fierce famine threatens to cause mass starvation in Somalia, Somaliland, South Sudan, Yemen and Nigeria. Famines that traditionally occurred every six to eight years are now happening every second year.
- The remaining wild portion of the Amazon straddling Bolivia, Peru and Colombia, but mostly in Brazil is under intense threat once more from logging, mining, agriculture and, above all, political corruption that allows

for these supposedly restricted activities to take place in areas where they are ostensibly forbidden.

- Tailings ponds constructed in northern Alberta to prevent the toxic byproduct of bitumen extraction from entering lakes and rivers will cost billions of dollars to remediate. As insufficient funds have been set aside to do this, the Alberta taxpayer will foot much of the bill. A recent report estimates costs at $44.5 billion as of 2016, with $6.8 billion more likely to be needed for reclaiming land, treating water and future monitoring and maintenance.
- Flooding in South Asia from monsoon rains has affected 16 million people in Bangladesh, India and Nepal, with over 600 reported killed. While the monsoon is a normal occurrence, this year's rains are unprecedented.

TPoT Blog — *Good News that Deserves More Attention*

November 30, 2017

If you look for it, there is good news about the transition from an extractive, carbon-intensive economy to a regenerative, low-carbon one. Whether the tide is turning rapidly enough, and whether these trends will become a large-scale movement, remains to be seen.

- The California legislature has extended its innovative cap-and-trade carbon pricing program. In a show of bipartisan leadership, close to a third of Republicans supported the extension. No wonder, given the economic boon to the state that such climate-friendly policies have proven to be. The state has attracted billions of dollars in clean energy investment and created a half million jobs.
- Rafts of black solar panels floating over the flooded site of a former coal mine in China symbolize "a mindset change" taking hold in Asia faster than in North America, a senior HSBC banker writes in the <u>Financial Times</u> of London.
- On a Friday in April, Britain went through a full working day without coal power, for the first time since the Industrial Revolution. As natural gas and renewables have come to play an increasing role, less coal has been burned over recent years. Coal accounted for a mere 9% of electricity generation in 2016, down from 23% in 2015.
- The country of Portugal generated all of its electricity demand over the course of three days in August from renewable sources—mostly solar and wind.
- Enough construction jobs to hire everyone unemployed in Canada today could be created by 2050 through a planned, aggressive transition to a low-carbon economy, says a Columbia Institute <u>report</u>. A low-carbon economy could create almost four million direct jobs in the building trades.

Power for the Global Village

Dear François,

You do not know me, but I am a good friend of Simone Cohen. I am intrigued by what I know of your work on electricity and pumping systems for rural villages, and your low-tech approach to green building. If I may be so bold, would I be welcome to visit in the coming month and learn all about your Global Village concept?

I will gladly pay someone in the area for a home stay. And you can put me to work. I want to get my hands dirty. Make my muscles hurt. I am quite skilled with electrical equipment, renewable systems and energy storage.

Please let me know soon if this is viable. I am in rather a hurry. I wish to get a break from my current situation and leisure time makes me bored.

With best wishes,
Jenny Fung

* * *

Chère Jenny,

My English, he is not so good. Please come to stay at Global Village Assisi. If you say when you arrive, I ask a friend to find you at the aeroport.

À bientôt!
François

* * *

A clean break. On the flight, Jenny crammed as much elementary French as she could. *Je m'appelle Jenny. Je suis une ingénieure.*

The villagers Jenny met and the people she taught during her month at GV Assisi marvelled at her technical knowledge and interest in them. They, in turn, helped her.

What do you want to do? *Design power systems for self-sustaining villages that don't rely on finicky technology. For villages, boats and farm equipment. Not one technology, but interlinked, resilient systems using whatever the local climate and geography has to offer. Elegance, not brute force.*

Who do you want to be? *Jenny Fung took her money from years of hard work but which came with so much pain, and invested it where it was needed most. She did no harm.*

TPoT Blog — *Global Witness Toll Mounts*

January 15, 2018

Once more, courtesy of the *Guardian*, I offer this update on the campaign by Global Witness to document the deaths of 'Defenders'—people protecting their community's land or natural resources; dying to prevent an even greater death: ecological, cultural and human. In 2017, 188 Defenders were killed. These are real people, though, not numbers. Here are some of them.

> *Killed on 16 August 2017 in Tanzania*
> **Wayne Lotter**, a leading elephant conservationist and head of an anti-poaching NGO shot dead in Tanzania.
> *Killed on 1 September 2017 in Peru*
> **Elías Gamonal Mozombite**, one of six Peruvian farmers shot dead in a land rights battle reportedly linked to the palm oil trade.
> *Killed on 14 September 2017 in the Philippines*
> **Ruben Arzaga**, a village leader and environmental officer shot while arresting suspected illegal loggers.
> *Killed on 24 September 2017 in Pakistan*
> **Inspector Manzoor**, one of two rangers shot after intercepting bird poachers in Punjab.

Every story is unique, but they have one thing in common. They went up against powerful interests. People who stood to make money or acquire power—usually both. Oil companies, timber barons, ivory poaching queens, governments (elected or otherwise), organized crime, warlords...

Who would want to stand up to such people? You're liable to get yourself imprisoned, run out of town or killed! Yet they did it. For themselves, for animals, for ecosystems and for marginalized people. For our only planet. For us.

Since 2015, more than 150 defenders of land and ecosystems are known to have been killed in Brazil; the most of any country. Most were people trying to stop illegal logging in the Amazon. The Philippines is second on the list, with about 80 such deaths. Per capita, however, Honduras is the most dangerous place to be a Defender.

View the breakdown per country, and the full list of murdered Defenders on the *Guardian* website. While you are there, please subscribe. Real journalism costs money.

Making Earth Great Again

It took Sagan and Simone less than six months to have their book ready. Two intensive working sessions, one at the cabin and another at the house in Ottawa, was all they needed to pull together what they'd sketched out using a secure video conference and document exchange service. What came off the press was a beautiful book, to hold and to read.

The original concept was for a semi-autobiographical first part telling the story of Sagan's life and career, and a second that would present his personal insight in the form of essays, speeches and reflections—on the search for common ground, renewed civility and living in ecological integrity. What emerged was quite different.

As soon as they began working together, Sagan insisted it be "our book." First he argued with Simone, and then with the commissioning editor. "She's been with me for two decades. Present in my life and career as if we were a team."

Simone was flattered, but wanted none of it. "I took my path, you took yours. We supported one another. We checked in frequently. We bounced around ideas, and made fun of each other. But your life and career are yours! Geez, take your moment of glory."

"I don't need glory," Sagan bristled, "and I don't want it."

Simone suggested a compromise. They would weave together their two life stories, and present his best speeches, her best writing and some original essays co-written over the past months.

Making Earth Great Again was released in North America by Paradigm House, and one month later in the U.K. Its critical and commercial success assured it of a wider international audience, initially in France and Australia. Paradigm House was fielding interest from other countries too.

A successful launch typically demanded a tour, but after Simone's last border experience, she didn't want to chance another crossing. She suggested doing as much as possible by video conference. One of them could travel to the writers festivals and launch events in their home country, and the other join in on a large screen. "We could use the autopen devised by Margaret Atwood to sign remotely. Or something like it."

For local events, they would travel by bus, train or the cleanest car they could get. For events across the continent that required flights, they would insist on video-conferencing. Paradigm House balked, certain this would harm sales.

It was Sagan who suggested making it a PR campaign. The 'Low Carbon Book Tour' became a story in its own right, pulling in larger-than-normal audiences, propelling sales and generating interview requests and talk show invitations.

Still, Paradigm House insisted Simone join Sagan at some of the biggest events in Boston, New York and Chicago. She could take the train, or drive her new Bolt. That was when she mentioned her border issue.

Paradigm House put its best lawyers onto Simone's case. They learned that she was "on a list," but the reasons for it were confidential. All they could get from Homeland Security was that she was "denied entry for suspicion of involvement in activity inimical to American interests." She would have to go to court to learn more.

Paradigm House threatened to launch a high-profile action. Simone Cohen may be Canadian, they argued, but her co-author was American, and this was an *American* book. In response, she received a temporary exemption, allowing her a three-stop tour. It came with absurd caveats. She was to receive no appearance fees, and she was not to engage in other book-related visits, even informal ones, such as visiting book stores.

"Book stores?" Sagan quipped. "Are we visiting the Amazon warehouse?"

In place of fees, her share from book sales could be given to charity. "The petty bastards!" said an incensed Simone. "I'll split it between Puerto Rico hurricane victims and California forest fire crews!" She agreed to the deal, however. She owed it to Paradigm House and to Sagan.

More than 5,000 people attended each of the three events. Larger venues had to be booked at the last minute. The book rapidly became a bestseller.

The Hard Part

I n the heady early days, Jiro was greeted with smiles and deep bows. Within months, though, people were asking when they would see progress. Notably with housing and jobs. But a prefectural governor's powers were limited. On many issues, he needed support from the national government. He decided to temper his criticism of the prime minister in speeches and interviews.

In her congratulatory email, Simone had reminded Jiro of the need for speed. He had momentum and would be afforded a brief grace period by the media and public.

Rookie mistakes are forgiven in the first few months, but never again. Set your agenda, keep it simple, focus on the 'must dos,' let go of the 'nice to dos.'

You can't please all of the people. The media may be friendly, but are never your friends. He received a lot of advice, but that did not make the job easier. Not when you were on a collision course with landowners over expropriation, the building industry over net-zero energy goals, the banks and power companies over promoting co-operative alternatives to their services, and the discredited but ever-present nuclear lobby over restarting plants closed since 2011.

"We don't need the electricity, and we don't want it either," Jiro declared, whenever the suggestion arose. But the public was susceptible to whispers. 'Manufacturing is stalled because there isn't enough power'. 'Solar energy is unreliable'. 'Imagine a blackout in the dead of winter, or when your mother is in surgery!'

His brother was playing a strange game. One day he was an ally—"I just thought you should know what so-and-so is saying," and the next an opponent—"Don't overstep your mandate in this area, or I will make life difficult."

The ultra-nationalist groups Katsuo had belonged to for much of his adult life had friends in all the right places, even if they stayed mostly below the radar. Jiro's victory under the Four Elements banner made him a prime political target. Maybe worse. Security was tight around his house, and he was often accompanied by plain-clothes officers. "We have credible information, Ebitsubo-san," his police chief warned.

When weekly protests began outside the prefectural offices, security was stepped up another notch. "A waste of money," Jiro told his team. "Our police have enough to do without adding this to their load!"

One Four Elements promise that he quietly put on the back-burner related to the settlement of immigrants. Members felt they had a duty to take migrants from neighbouring Asian countries where rising ocean levels and increased storms had left many destitute. Some small island nations were on the verge of being submerged. They had proposed petitioning the national government to accept 1000 such migrants per year. A drop in the bucket compared to countries like Germany or Sweden, or even—especially—Kenya and Uganda, but too much for the Japanese, he was advised.

Jettisoning this promise was painful. It would have been a small but meaningful gesture, at a time when compassion for the world's hardest hit was shrinking.

High Road

"How did you handle the harassment Sagan, and the threats?"

"You too now?" Sagan said. He looked fondly at his friend on the tablet screen. So stressed. So earnest.

"Oh," Jiro said, "it has been going on for a long time. But it has become more intense. More organized." Sagan nodded.

"What is especially hard is when I know my brother is behind it." He paused and tilted his head. "Not *all* of it. But he does nothing to stop it."

"Hmm," said Sagan. "Still stuck in his little world of honour and certainty."

"More than ever," said Jiro.

"Boxed in by pride, with no escape route," Sagan suggested.

"He doesn't want an escape route. What he wants is to push me out a trap door."

Sagan laughed. "Keep up the humour, big man. Some days it's all you'll have."

"I can't believe you are still laughing Sagan, after all you've been put through?"

"Put through? Put myself through mostly. We're still our own agents Jiro—of destruction or salvation. Most of the time. But…" Sagan added, "we're also agents of compassion, for ourselves and, on a good day, others." He wrinkled his forehead. "Yes, on a good day at least."

Jiro was silent. Sagan could see him nodding ever so slightly.

"Advice, Jiro? You want advice? What I know for sure is we can't control others, much as we might wish to. Only our own actions, and thoughts. So be gentle with yourself. Try to see the hurt that drives people like Katsuo. But don't let it do the same to you."

"So, keep to the high road?" Jiro suggested.

Sagan smiled. "That's all I've ever known from you, my friend."

"How we act defines us," said Jiro.

Dear Maman

U sing a knife from the kitchen drawer, Simone slit open the letter from Jacinthe and sat down at the table. The house was silent. Ron was playing his Monday night hockey game. Jacinthe had enrolled in a graduate programme in environmental design at the University of Calgary in September. She had barely managed a monthly email or video call since. Not even to Ron. Why suddenly this letter, Simone wondered, addressed specifically to her?

Dear Maman,

Simone paused and blinked, confirming she'd read correctly.

I hope you won't mind, but I've decided to call you Maman. I spent many years resenting you for sharing Papa's affection, and punishing you for being the devoted mother my own never could be. I was petty, and I'm not proud of it. So when I heard you and Sagan interviewed on As it Happens last night, I knew I had to fix this. I was so damn proud. Honoured to have

395

you as my mother, but ashamed of my 'bitchy step-daughter' act.

Simone couldn't continue. Fetching a tissue from the counter, she dabbed her eyes and blew her nose before returning to her seat.

I hope you will accept my apology. And agree to be called Maman. Mother is too formal, and Mom just isn't you.

Simone let out a choking laugh.

It honours the French side of our families too.

People were talking about your book in one of my study groups. Nobody knew Simone Cohen was my mother. That's the upside to a different last name: I don't have to answer for you. The downside is I don't get any of the glory.

I love this programme. My classmates are great, and the profs too. One reminds me of you—in a good way!

I understand better what you mean about living in integrity. I felt this when I was planting trees two summers ago. Then when I interned with the energy co-op last summer. And every time I ride my bike, or put on a sweater instead of turning up the heat, or make the effort to cook a veggie stir-fry instead of grabbing a burger. It's not for other people, it's for me. I'm not doing it to save the planet (or only a little), or to save money (well, a little) but because it feels right. Even if this whole homo sapiens experiment goes down the toilet and takes so much beauty with it, I'll do what I can.

Now I'm rambling, like my mother! So without getting too teary-eyed, I just wanted to say THANK YOU! For being supportive, and firm. It's actions that matter, isn't it?

I love you Maman! Papa too, of course. And don't you dare show him this letter!

Reading the letter over again, Simone cried some more, and laughed at the digs a second time. She smiled as she got up, placing it where Ron would see it when he got home.

The Ultimate Challenge

On the coat-tails of their successful book, Sagan suggested to Simone an ambitious plan for producing a 'state of the planet documentary series'. It would focus equally on regions where things were going badly and places where a positive transition was happening.

Are You a Leader?
Join Us and Show It!

Sagan Cleveland and I will be taking an 8-week 'virtual trip' to places ravaged by climate breakdown, and others where meaningful steps have been taken to tackle it. We are issuing a challenge to decision makers and influencers of the world to 'join' us. All it takes is two hours of your time every Sunday night for the 8 weeks of the SmartView show. They're waiving the monthly subscription for these 8 weeks.

But there is more to joining us than watching. We are committed to solving the very real crisis of climate breakdown and ecological collapse. Will you join us?

You can do so in several ways:

1. *Declare that we are living in an ecological and climate crisis, and that you will make this a top priority for*

your time in public office or a position of influence. If that's you already, fantastic. Don't feel obliged to come on the trip. You have big work to do.

2. *Admit you are unconvinced and would benefit from seeing 'proof' first hand. Agree that if you find our evidence compelling, you will communicate publicly how you reached this conclusion. You will then make a declaration, as per 1.*

3. *Acknowledge that you never will 'believe in' climate science or that ecosystems are collapsing, and declare that the plight of those living with or fleeing from their effects are of no concern to you. How is this 'joining us'? We can stop wasting valuable energy engaging with you.*

4. *There is no fourth option. You are with us, open to evidence, or immune to evidence.*

The *Are You a Leader?* appeal was sent out through social media, where it spread rapidly. Full page ads were purchased in major English-language dailies across the world, and on news sites of all political persuasions. SmartView had deep pockets.

"You can't take it with you," one of the channel's billionaire founders declared when he launched SmartView a year earlier. He had made his money off a popular social media platform, and wanted to atone for it.

The show's format was straightforward. Local teams were hired to film scenes illustrating the chosen themes. Nobody knew the real story like a local, Simone learned early in her career. She and Sagan would be together in a studio in Windsor, Ontario. A short drive for Sagan in his Leaf. A local host, live on location in the places they were 'visiting' that episode, would comment on what was being screened, and answer questions from Simone and Sagan.

On launch night, *The Now or Never Show* took viewers to places ravaged by heat and drought, where safe water no longer existed, aquifers were exhausted and the land was toxic. Bangladesh served as the main site visit, but Spain and Saskatchewan made effective 'First World' counterpoints.

By the time it aired, almost every elected official in the English-speaking world had been enticed or guilted into 'joining'. Many had already declared support, or agreed to watch the first episode and see what it was all about. Canadian Prime Minister Justin Trudeau 'doubled down' by hosting a viewing party on Parliament Hill to which he invited every elected member. The British and Australian prime ministers also declared support, but their body language spoke for itself. No response had come from the White House.

Around the world, members of congress, parliamentarians, governors, premiers, mayors and city councillors were showing their colours. Category 1 'supporters' hailed in first, to no one's surprise. Some Category 3 'non-believers' seized the opportunity to declare the whole thing a scam—the science, the show and especially the hosts.

"Lunatic lefties," a Senator from Nebraska muttered when scrummed. The head of the U.S. EPA went on record declaring that Sunday was for prayer, not television.

The second episode featured locations where ecological destruction and dwindling resources—notably water and fish— were bringing neighbours to the brink of violence. Use of the Tigris and Euphrates rivers being a historic source of conflict, the opening report noted how drought had been a contributing factor to the war in Syria and recent fighting in Turkey.

Hosts in Canada and the U.S. looked at how the Columbia River and the Great Lakes were generally well-managed, but why conflict sometimes arose. Scenes of a dried-up Tagus River introduced a report on Spain and Portugal's historic dependence on the river for agriculture, urban drinking water, electricity production and, more recently, cooling nuclear plants.

The third episode looked at the appalling living conditions in the world's growing megacities, with visits to Jakarta, Mexico City and Rio de Janeiro. Archival footage had to be used for

Shanghai. The Chinese host and her team were detained two days prior to broadcast.

The fourth episode looked at mass migration out of Africa as a result of drought, famine, disease and violence. Hosts at refugee camps in Uganda and Kenya described the scale of migration, while images illustrated the desperate conditions of people who must walk hundreds of kilometres without food or water. Hosts in Libya and Italy described the challenges of protecting and settling large numbers of migrants.

By the time the fifth, sixth and seventh shows aired—with their emphasis on solutions—audiences were dwindling. Online feedback was clear: "This is overwhelming!"

They should have known better. Indeed they did, and had debated whether to alternate scary and inspiring shows. That would dilute the message of urgency, however, leaving an impression that half the time everything is fine. Simone, Sagan and the show's backers wanted to show as starkly as possible that things were really bad already for billions. Viewers shouldn't wait to act until they—the U.S., Canada, the U.K. and Australia in particular—were in a similar state.

They had lined up some fascinating material for shows 5 through 7. An update on Fukushima featured the work of Four Elements. Jiro hosted that section, contrasting long-term damage from the nuclear accident with progress in shifting to a society of ultra-efficiency, and decentralized renewable energy. An emphasis was placed on community building and the role of co-operatives. François' limited English prevented him from hosting the segment on France's revolutionary Global Village model, but his neighbour, Chloe Martin performed admirably in his place. Other featured models included Transition Towns, born in England and now thriving in many countries.

The seventh episode was devoted to education of girls and the role of women in politics, economics and technology. It opened with a look at the prominent role of women in developing renewable energy co-ops in Ontario, then leapt to the poorest parts of South Asia. In Nepal, Empower Generation was enabling women to create clean energy businesses and manage a sales network. Overcoming cultural resistance, they were taking communities out of energy poverty while developing leadership skills and setting up businesses employing both women and men as agents. In India, Frontier Markets was running an organization called Solar Sahelis that supplied clean, reliable light and energy to nearly a million people, replacing kerosene.

As the series progressed, Sagan was finding it progressively difficult to get fired up. Where he had entered the project bursting with enthusiasm, he now struggled just to make the drive into the studio. His demeanour jarred with the content: upbeat for the early depressing shows; flat for the uplifting ones.

Simone, feeling immense pressure to execute a risky finale, was at a loss for how to help him beyond urging him to see his doctor.

Despite all of this, the series was making an impact—much of it initiated by others. Students at Oxford University launched an online scorecard, calling on other students, faculty and universities to 'join'. Cambridge students rose immediately to the challenge, as did the administration, and soon a university rivalry spread worldwide.

Though the show's target had been decision makers—mostly political—anyone was welcome to declare support. After seven weeks, the Oxford scorecard indicated 68% of respondents had 'joined', 10% remained unsure, and 22% never would. Though the scorecard had little statistical validity, it showed *The Now or Never Show* was engaging a global audience.

The heavily-publicized finale opened with Simone providing a recap, speaking over images from earlier episodes. She then shared video footage and photos submitted by viewers in response to the show. At this point, Sagan was to have risen to provide a spiritual commentary—delivered standing and without notes. Instead he remained seated, reading from a script. Few would remember this, though. Simone's closing eclipsed everything.

"I would like to thank the dedicated people who helped produce and host the eight episodes," she began. "And of course you—the viewers—who came, stayed and brought friends on this important journey. As for decision makers—the 'leaders' in politics, business, civil society and faith communities—you were our intended audience. Our goal was to get you to acknowledge the extent of this crisis.

"I congratulate those who declared themselves supporters. I want to equally praise those who were unsure, for whatever reason, but who had the courage to take the journey and then declare where they stand. Finally, I want to acknowledge those who had the honesty—however misguided—to declare themselves unreachable. History will condemn you. I do not have to. Your names are public. When we sign off, a current list will go live.

"Our lines are not closed though. If we got anything wrong, let us know. Did we miss you? Are you just tuning in, and want to declare your stand? Go ahead. But before I read a final special list, let me reiterate that this is a dynamic process, just as the physical and natural systems of the Earth are dynamic, ever changing. If you change your mind, one way or another, let us know. That was, after all, the point—to change minds through reality.

"To quote from the French, 'Il y a que des imbéciles qui ne change pas d'avis.' It is only imbeciles who never change their mind. Or, from Neil de Grasse Tyson: 'When facts are what people want to be true, in spite of contrary evidence, witness the beginning of the end of an informed democracy.'

"So, let's talk about democracy. In many countries of the world, it is under attack. But for all its failings, democracy is still the best system of governance. Many of us believe it worth pursuing, protecting and improving. Many powerful people, however, have no interest in democracy other than to use the word as cover while they work to undermine it—with money and with privilege, which amount to the same thing.

"The focus of this show has been on halting and reversing ecological deterioration and climate breakdown. That is very closely linked to democracy and the will of people at a local level. We see that when people organize at the grassroots, they rarely choose to act in ways that undermine the natural systems that keep them alive.

"But the further away you get from the grassroots, the easier it becomes to take a political or business decision that does harm. Then there is one step further. When your life is organized around making profit, acquiring and holding power, and influencing people to adopt your views so as to maintain a hold over them— as it can be in a world where the only thing that counts is the number of people in your pews and on your donor lists, or the quarterly returns on your investments—then you have moved as far from the grassroots as you can get."

Simone paused, and made a point of showing a sheet of paper to the camera.

"Which brings me to the names." She lowered the list and began reading, slowly and carefully, looking to the camera after each name. The list had been compiled over many months. Carefully researched, then vetted by SmartView's lawyers. It would stand up in court, they assured the company's executives and funders, and the show's producers and hosts. *It is not libel if it is true.*

"The following are known to fund organizations and campaigns that actively work to discredit ecological and climate science." There were 17 people on the list. A who's who of American, Canadian, British and Australian 'dark money.'

"The following are known to be engaged in activities which impugn the character of public servants, scientists, activists and journalists engaged in science, and working to protect the public commons." It was a list of 53 people, mostly media owners and populist hosts in the United States, though 11 were Canadians.

"And finally..." Simone looked at the camera and took a steadying breath. "This person is known to lead a campaign on behalf of the U.S. president to remove people from public office, or prevent them from carrying out their work in the media, academia and the private sector by highly unethical and often illegal methods. You will not find his name or office in any official listings. You can, however, find something of his past online. His name is Elmore Lambert."

Simone stared at the camera, steely-eyed and unblinking until she received the signal that they were off the air. Then she began to shake. She had stayed composed throughout the entire show, despite the added pressure of covering for Sagan. She had carried through with the lightning strike, and nobody had leaked it.

With considerable mental effort, Sagan stood and approached a slumped Simone. Reaching out his hand, he prompted her to stand and melt into his full, gentle embrace. "Supersonic woman," he whispered.

After a long silence, and with producers and crew gathering to congratulate them both, she whispered back: "You hung in. Now we'll get you help."

Sagan would normally return home—a mere 30-minute drive, depending on border delays. Tonight, he had planned to stay for the party, with Isong joining them. At the party, he sat glassy-eyed, his beer untouched. Occasionally people came to congratulate him; mostly SmartView executives and funders who had not been aware of his deteriorating state. Crew members kept their distance.

Glancing regularly over at Sagan, Simone did her best to chat with the show's backers. Several conversations began with a "My, oh my!" or raised eyebrows, or both.

"Gutsy!" the legal counsel declared.

"You assured me it was airtight." Simone's voice betrayed her sudden nervousness. "Now you tell me it was gutsy?"

"Nothing is certain with the law, my dear. Especially with powerful people. They might not have a case, but they can eat up a lot of your money and time. Word to the wise, stay on this side of the border for a while."

Simone let out an odd, high-pitched cackle, attracting puzzled looks. "Sure! I'll just stay right here on my side of the wall. I hear Mexico's paying for it."

In the middle of the night, sleeping uneasily in her hotel room, Simone heard her phone buzz. A text from Jacinthe. Midnight in Alberta.

Two thumbs up, Maman! You're a hero. Get some rest. Love J!

Isong's text came shortly after. Her reason for leaving the phone on.

Sagan's OK. Went to emergency. Moving to private clinic in the morning.

Wide awake now, she decided to check her emails. One from Ron.

Nerves of steel! Je t'aime ma belle. Rest.

Then another text from Isong.

As we drove, he kept singing one line: "You're my best friend."

Simone responded immediately. *Friendship takes two. Sometimes three.*

Elmore Explodes

Elmore texted his staff immediately after the show. *My office, 9 a.m.!* Nobody would get much sleep.

Elmore hadn't been sleeping well for several years, since early in the presidential campaign. First it was the drama of the race, then something harder to define. The pressure. To make a good impression. To complete the job he'd taken on. To show he was a dependable member of the team. Above all though, was the growing pressure of his conscience. He could shut it out by day, but never at night.

Sleeping pills could help him get to sleep, but they couldn't protect him from the night people. Their numbers grew by the week, as his list got shorter. Another one gone and another one gone, but they all return at night. Accompanied by his father.

Zachary Lambert, shrivelled, often doubled over in pain, insisted by night, as he had in real life, right to the painful end, that when Elmore went out into the bigger world, he must not abandon the values of his people, brought at such sacrifice to the deltas and the bayous. *Do unto others… Honest living, honest speaking, do no harm.*

Elmore had tried. He could honestly say he had tried. But when you know what it is to sleep in a house riddled with mold, with a roof that leaks in a hundred places, and you haven't eaten a proper meal in months, can the rules you live by always be golden?

Zachary, who could do no wrong in the eyes of his neighbours, was not without faults. So what business did he have coming into Elmore's head, night after night, siding with the night people against his son? The son who took care of him until the day he was laid to rest.

When Elmore's sleeping pills were no longer up to the job, he switched to stronger products. Easy to find when you knew the right people.

The team assembled early. They were only three now. At this point, their job was to replace people—those not up to the job, and those enjoying it too much. They eyed each other nervously, sipping coffees quietly. All had seen the show.

When the door burst open, the three cringed. When Elmore slammed it shut, they jumped. Then braced. Their boss had been changing; turning on his staff.

"What in holy fuck was that!" he screamed. "Who fucking told her about this unit? And why in flaming fuck was I named? Stop whatever you're doing and get me an answer! What we do is secret. Somebody is going to pay with their balls, and I'd better not find out it was one of you." He stared down each of them, one at a time, his red eyes boring into theirs.

"Get out! I have thinking to do."

The three skulked out in silence. "One of us has nothing to lose," smirked Fred, glancing toward Brittany's crotch.

"Only my job," she responded.

"Not sure I still want mine," remarked Scott. "But if any of us quits now, it'll look like an admission." The others nodded. Keep your head down, and make a show of looking for a traitor.

Alone at his desk, Elmore ran through the people who knew of the unit and its secretive work. Current staff were an obvious possibility. How devoted were they, really? Scott and Fred, who'd been with him forever. But can you ever know for sure? Or Brittany, with her intelligence background. Too obvious, he concluded. It would be *former* staff. They'd signed an oath of secrecy, but what did that count for in this administration? Time to put feelers out. Find the loose lips.

It was also time to finish his personal list. Down to three. Everyone else had been taken out—no longer a threat to the administration, the president, or him.

Just three. One, he would learn shortly, had been hospitalized. Possibly for a long time. Convenient, but maybe not sufficient.

Another was reaching renewal time for her green card. He'd been waiting for this, patiently. No point being obvious. British, with an Iranian parent, she had been harassed returning to New York each year from her summer vacation in England. But she'd been careful not to leave the country too frequently, and never took both children with her. One was always left in the U.S. with the ex-husband. Breaking up a family was bad optics. The president learned that the hard way. But this coming summer, they were all due to visit Iran for a wedding. The trap would be ready.

The *New York Observer* had it coming, and "Phil" Barkley-Satrapi in particular. PB-S they called her. How appropriate. Taking down PBS! He smiled at his cleverness. Nobody knew what he was capable of. One more thing to keep to himself. He opened his desk drawer and found the pill bottle, downing two.

Finally there was the Canadian. The bitch that outed him. Tagging her file with Border Services had hobbled her, but she was clever. Possibly the smartest of the three. Certainly the quickest. Best friend of Sagan Cleveland, he now knew. If he'd known earlier, he might have gone for her sooner. But it wasn't until he found himself in this building, with access to digital intel—every email, text and phone call, if he wanted it—that he acquired the means. For how much longer though, now that he'd been denounced?

By that afternoon, he had his answer. *Fake news*, tweeted the president.

The White House spokesperson spent several hours dodging questions arising from the show. "Yes, he is employed by the administration. No, he is not engaged in illegal activity. Yes, we know he made mistakes earlier in his life." Then she attacked.

"Who here never did anything illegal in their youth? Had a drink while underage? Smoked marijuana! Anyone here never done that?" *Don't get high and mighty about Elmore Lambert,* was the message to the press corps. *We know stuff about you.*

Elmore got a reprieve but was now on borrowed time. Better hustle.

Fruitful Collaboration

"Incredible!" François could be heard exclaiming off screen as the camera panned across a group of villagers gathered to watch the raised concrete cylinder descend into a water-tight tube of the same diameter. A jet of water shot out the hose at the bottom and into the turbines of the micro-hydro engine.

On sunny days, electricity for GV Assisi was generated by an array of solar panels and a small wind turbine, providing power as needed via a battery bank and inverter. Any excess, though, could now be used to lift the cylinder. When the batteries were approaching depletion, this water displacement device could be set in motion. Reliability through diversity was the idea. Science and technology transcend borders and language, Jenny found, with the help of diagrams on paper.

A prototype was built and tested during her visit, but she could not stay to see the full-scale version in action. François promised to send a video of her system in action.

Jenny was tingling with excitement as she watched it on her tablet several days later. The applause and wondrous expressions told her everything. How exciting it would be to share it with her daughters. She would forward it to them at school.

She had been confident it would work, and was already preparing a refined set of schematics, using different materials. She wanted it to be so simple that it could be easily replicated in any region. But certain materials had to be of a quality to last for a long time between repairs and replacement.

Jenny had linked up with a non-profit based in India that specialized in bringing intermediate technology to remote parts of Asia. The more that could be built *in situ*, the cheaper and more sustainable it would be. Teach people to fish, don't give them fish. Some parts would have to be brought in—the engine, the inverters and the gaskets. Most of the electronics, though, were or could be assembled in any country under a rights-free patent.

Patents. That was how Jenny reconnected with Jiro. Could he suggest a patent agent? One who could protect her inventions in a way that kept them available to anybody? People before her had taken the 'open source' route. She wanted to join the club.

Jiro wrote back promptly, but cagily. *Why do you want to know?*

When she described the project, he seemed to warm up. After suggesting several agents, and offering his own ideas, he opened the door a centimetre wider. *We should talk. The girls miss you. Are you in KL?* Polite, but nothing deeper. Nobody was ready to venture down the raw path of emotions. Neither had ever been good at that, and both were out of practice.

Jiro had a political motivation to re-engage. He was keen to bring clean energy jobs to Fukushima Prefecture. Jenny would need parts suppliers. Notably, for the micro-hydro engines. She had been working on another idea as well: a compressed air system. Any electricity source could be used to inject pressurized air into a robust expandable pouch.

She had someone ready to test it on a light, recreational boat. The results could help her raise money to scale it up for larger craft. Ferries, barges and fishing boats in developing countries burned dirty bunker fuel. They were an obvious target. She had wondered if it could go larger still. Ocean-going vessels emitted huge volumes of CO_2 and spilled fuel. One step at a time though. Big dreams are realized in small steps, her father had taught her.

Jiro was impressed by her concepts. He wasted little time connecting her with a possible partner in Fukushima. Someone with an idled manufacturing facility that once supplied parts to the nuclear industry. He also arranged for lodging. She could stay with a Four Elements member named Kimiko; a woman in her sixties who had lost her family in the tsunami.

Kimiko posed no questions about Jenny's relationship to the governor. Her English, like Jenny's Japanese, was limited. Enough to share an apartment and some meals, but little else.

Jenny would split her time between KL and Fukushima City, which allowed her to see the girls regularly. She would take them out for a meal as she passed regularly through Tokyo on her way back and forth to Malaysia and India.

Jenny's frequent flying had become a source of personal discomfort. The girls had commented on it. Both were taking a strong interest in personal choices and their ecological impact. It was time to do her part—but with aging parents in Malaysia, and projects in villages across Southeast Asia, that would not be easy.

The Professor

S agan spent three weeks at a private clinic, and then two months at home under regular surveillance. Isong shared status updates with Simone. Once cleared to do so, he arranged for video 'visits'. The first was seven weeks after Sagan's *Now or Never Show* breakdown. This incident—Isong had shared—was far more severe than the first, a decade earlier.

Sagan brushed it off in typical fashion. "It's just my nineteenth little one," he joked to Simone by video.

"Oh dear," she said. "You're channeling Mick Jagger now."

"Must be the drugs." He attempted a grin. "Feels like there's cotton in my head."

Sagan's stay at the clinic and ongoing medication costs were enough to bankrupt him. Over the past several years his income had been limited to fees from workshops, modest book royalties and the SmartView contract—far short of a regular salary. Salvation arrived by way of a peculiar email from Scotland. A message that was almost deleted.

Isong had been doing a daily scan through Sagan's inbox, checking for genuine messages. '*Important inheritance information*', read the subject line of one. Another scam, Isong figured. But there was something different about this one.

It started the typical way—*solicitor for a distinguished professor seeks to make contact with rightful heir*—but there was just enough personal detail to make him think twice.

With Sagan back home, Isong was reading aloud from the backlog. Most were notes from friends and supporters. "Here's an odd one," he said to Sagan, who was lying on the living room sofa.

Dear Mr. Cleveland, I am writing on behalf of the estate of the recently deceased, professor emeritus at the University of Edinburgh, Robert McIlraith."

"I know him!" cried Sagan, sitting upright. "Or *knew* him—it sounds like."

In a shaky voice, Isong continued.

Having no surviving family, the professor left his entire estate to two individuals, to be divided evenly. Ms. Simone Cohen of Ottawa, Canada, and Mr. Sagan Cleveland, formerly of Pennsylvania State University.

Sagan was perched on the edge of the sofa now.

In his final months, suffering from terminal lung cancer, Robert McIlraith, being of sound mind, dictated to me his instructions. His wish to bequeath his estate to 'a virtual stranger' was out of deep respect for your dedication to both the pursuit of truth and to reconciling scientifically-observed reality with faith and spirituality. He spent his life attempting such a reconciliation. It was upon seeing your recent show that Robert McIlraith made this decision. He watched avidly until he succumbed to illness prior to the final episode.

In addition to bequeathing the sum of US$724,212.00, he wished to convey the following message: 'We had a fine night at the pub. You acquitted yourself as well as any American. You exhibited a keen intellect and sense of humour. Above all, you went forward into the world to make your mark. Use this money as you see fit. I have only one demand. Raise a pint of Scottish ale in my memory."

Please have your bank contact me to arrange the transfer of funds.

"Professorrr McIlrrraith!," Sagan exclaimed, shaking his head. Then he leapt up, pulled Isong from his chair, and led him in the closest thing to a Scottish jig he could muster.

"Easy boy," cautioned Isong when they collapsed on the sofa, breathless.

Raising a pint together would have to wait until he was cleared to drink and to travel, Simone had to remind Sagan when they spoke later that day.

"We could clink by FaceTime," he proposed. "Just a wee dram!"

"Let's do that," said Simone. "We'll raise a glass by video when the money comes in, then do it properly at some pub in Windsor when you're mobile."

She raised her hand, as if holding a tankard. "To the Prrrofessorrr!"

"To Robbberrrt McIlrrrraith!" he mimicked.

* * *

By July, Sagan was up and about. Keen to get outside, he volunteered to help out with weeding and some lighter tasks at Center Street Farm.

Word of his improving condition reached his old colleagues at Penn State. Angela Wainwright, his former dean, recently retired, was the one who thought of nominating him for the American Science Academy's Science Communicator Award. She brought together two of his former colleagues to seek their views, and see if they would co-sponsor the application.

"The competition is bound to be stiff," noted the current dean, Pavel Smit. "But I can't think of anyone more deserving, and who has reached such varied audiences."

"Against all odds too," said Denise Benzema, one of Sagan's former graduate students, and now an associate professor. "If you know what I mean."

Angela and Pavel nodded. A lengthy silence followed, interrupted finally by Angela, bringing them back to their task.

"My only misgiving would be his fitness. The recipient is expected to deliver a substantial speech. Between 60 and 90 minutes. Do we know if he's up to it?"

Pavel and Denise shook their heads.

"I'd hate to set him up for a relapse," said Angela.

"Or put a target on his back," suggested Pavel. "Again!"

"Naturally," Denise said, with a grimace. "But he could always decline, if he thinks it's too much. Assuming he's chosen."

In early September, Sagan was surprised to receive a letter from the American Science Academy. He was even more surprised to learn that he would be honoured at the Academy's gala in Washington, DC in late November. And that he was expected to give the keynote address.

Though immensely flattering, the offer presented a dilemma. He was supposed to avoid stress. Furthermore, he didn't feel up to drafting the calibre of speech they would no doubt expect. Sensing he may never again have such an opportunity, he turned to Simone.

"You give me the basic outline and key messages," she proposed after hearing him out. "I'll create a structure to keep you focused, with some quotes and facts to draw on. Then you run with it. But only if you're sure you *want* to."

"It's *Now or Never*," he chuckled. I'll get you my outline in a week. And I'll ask Lady Doc about easing up on the cotton wool that night."

"Sagan!" admonished Simone.

"Only if she thinks it's safe! *Mom*."

"Don't play around," she growled. "The twentieth breakdown won't be so little!"

Sagan's doctor prescribed a modest tapering off for the week leading up to the speech, followed by gradual ramping up the day after. The two colleagues she conferred with felt it was safe.

Bearing More Truth

"When it comes to the climate, facts are what matter. But why believe me, and not, say, the dozens of organizations making alternate claims? Apart from my PhD in a field actually related to climate science; apart from my dozens of reviewed papers; apart from every one of my lectures, TV shows and even comic book treatments being available for scrutiny, well... just look at this face."

Sagan's exaggerated grin brought light laughter. *Not bad, but I can do better.*

"No, really. I have absolutely nothing to gain from lying. I could have made more money arguing climate change is a hoax. A lot more. I wouldn't have had my emails hacked, my sexuality made a national story, my friends harassed and my life threatened so many times the police don't bother returning my calls."

He sighed, and shook his head. Looking up, he locked eyes with a young woman in a headscarf.

"I could have led a quieter life. But could I have lived with myself if I'd told anything other than the truth? I do not *wish* what I know to be true. *Au contraire.* I wish it were not. But nature doesn't care what I wish. The climate will do what it does no matter what the politicians, the paid skeptics and the rich men pulling their strings would have you believe. No matter what anyone believes.

"You see, when data, collected in enough places by enough people comes together to tell a coherent story, you have the start of fact. When enough people offer a hypothesis to explain that data, you have a theory. Over enough rounds of critique, modification and efforts to disprove, you have a theory that is as close to scientific truth as will ever be possible."

He could see people nodding.

"Climate change, substantially attributable to human actions is a *fact*. It is accelerating, in lockstep with emissions of carbon dioxide. It is surging in response to releases of methane from oil and gas extraction, from cattle, frozen arctic soils and wetlands and even from the sea floor. Escaping refrigerants are a big factor too. We have proven all this to be true. Other explanations do not coincide with observed temperature increases. The *only* factor which can account for our increasingly hot and chaotic planet is emissions from human activity, which are at a historic high in the upper atmosphere. The highest in *800,000 years*."

He paused to emphasize the point. "Any of you around back then?"

Sagan was loosening up. His tongue more or less under control. Dry though. He took a sip of water. No need for notes here. He owned this stuff.

"Climate change, climate chaos... I prefer climate *breakdown*. For its accuracy, without hyperbole. Call it what you want, but deny it and you are deliberately misleading people. If in doing this, you enable inaction, then you are accountable. For lives, and livelihoods and the future of our species on this planet. But if that's not enough to make you worry about the day you meet your maker, I suggest it's time for *climate deception* to be treated for what it is: a crime against humanity. Against all species. But I'll settle for crime against humanity, with all the legal implications."

Now they're paying attention. Sagan's eyes flashed and his breath grew short as he built towards his crescendo. "If the fear of God is not enough, then handcuffs and a long spell in jail surely ought to be."

Pausing to regain composure and let things quiet, he offered a rueful shrug.

"Alas, we are not there. My very strong views may get me an audience with you fine people, but not the president or UN secretary general. Even if it did, the former hasn't the will, nor the latter the means to treat climate action as an obligation, enforceable by law. So I content myself with science and the occasional burst of politics.

"When the Paris Agreement was adopted, scientific consensus set '2 degrees Celsius above pre-industrial levels' as the temperature never to be surpassed. Lamely, it also named a 1.5 degree rise as a target that all countries should *aim* to achieve. Lamely, because the atmosphere was already on its way to hitting that level in 2015, and is now, in 2018, locked in to blow past it.

"So remember 2. Two's the magic number, because if we surpass it, only magic will save our sorry little civilization. The conditions which allowed for relative peace and stability since 1945 will be gone."

Sensing a growing murmur, Sagan paused to stare down one of the offenders.

"I'm all for debate, but this is *my* speech. And I'm half done."

He smiled, as several people applauded.

"A 2 degree warmer planet is not one that has ever supported our species. Sure, the planet's been warmer. Much warmer. But neither humans, nor most of the critters, trees or crops that are a part of our era existed then. Nor I believe, could they survive it. The atmospheric conditions and ocean acidity and hydrologic cycles would very likely set off a death spiral for all of today's ecosystems.

"Stability and civility will no longer be possible. You watch the news. Mass migration out of Africa; caravans of desperation out of Central America; social breakdown and extreme economic uncertainty. What we're not yet seeing is collapse on a scale where people give up entirely on government, the police, courts, hospitals and schools. Where we enter a world that is basically survival of the meanest. Heavily armed, with nuclear weapons and unmanaged chemical and biological waste.

"Will the human condition be any better than short and nasty and brutish, Mr. Hobbes? *No arts, no letters, no society...* I find it hard to imagine a non-Hobbesian outcome above the 2 degree tipping point.

"Conjecture, Dr. Sagan, I hear some say. You promised us facts."

He could see several people nodding vigorously, defiantly.

"I did. So, where are we now, and what would be required to stay under 2 degrees? I'll examine the numbers. Then I'll venture into the ugly world of policy and law—where the real battle lies. It was never about the science.

"Avoiding 2 is almost impossible. Fact! Global emissions would have to peak in the next 2 years, then go into steep decline. Fact! But too many economic choices, investments, vehicle purchases and building decisions have been made and locked in. Look at the entrenched lifestyles in countries like ours, and the dreams of people in poorer ones. Multiply *us* by 4 or 5 billion *them*. Fact!

"Short of an overnight replacement of all fossil fuel with renewable energy; a total revolution in how we travel—and the belief that we *should* travel; a total shift in investments into an ultra-low-carbon economy; a radical change in what we eat and how much; and—the kicker—a major collapse in global population, it's just not possible to stay below 2 degrees."

"Ffff..." he began, his arm raised. "Fact!" shouted most of the audience as he dropped his arm. "Fact indeed!" he chuckled and shook his head.

"But it could have been possible, and so much easier. In 1992—when agreements were signed and noble statements made. Even 1997, under the Kyoto Protocol. It was already a stretch in 2009, when countries like ours sabotaged the Copenhagen Accord. But by 2015, when there seemed to be real global will, it was out of reach. Commitments by Paris signatories in early 2016 set the planet on track for no better than *3.6* degrees warming. Little has improved.

"For the United States, responsible for the largest single share of historic emissions and morally obligated to play a leadership role, I feel profound shame. We knew what needed to be done, and yet—as a government, a free market economy and a highly educated society—we failed. Worse, many elected leaders chose to *ignore the science*. Major companies whose own studies rang an alarm bell failed to change business models. Think tanks with the means to develop intelligent, market-based policies and fiscal tools for guiding the transition away from fossil fuels did the opposite. In so many cases, these institutions and individuals engaged in *predatory delay*. They misled or outright lied. Many are still doing it. They have blood on their hands."

"Aw, c'mon!" A booming voice rang out. Sagan heard others grumbling too.

"Too strong?" he challenged. Trembling, he waited for the murmurs to subside.

"I say not enough." He could feel his anger. Time to let it show. "The delayer and falsifier is a traitor. To family, country and species. A traitor to God!"

He let the sharp intake of breath from around the room wash over him.

"So," he challenged, "what are you going to do about it? For the sake of your children and grandchildren and descendants that may never be born." He paused for one short beat. "Before you face your maker—sooner than you expected.

"If America were to have any chance of doing its part, the Trump administration would have needed to adopt Obama's best policies and carry out even stronger ones at a speed not seen since Pearl Harbour. But did it?"

A number of people shook their heads. "No indeed."

"Imagine we had taken seriously the fine words coming out of Rio. Imagine we kept the window open, wide enough to allow Earth's systems to stabilize and recover. Where might we be?"

Sagan scanned his audience, giving them time to think.

"We'd be living and working in buildings built to net zero energy standard. Schools too. Shops, pools, hotels, consuming 90% less than today. Many generating more than they consume. We have the knowledge and technology. We've had it for years. Think of it: electricity bills of $20 a month instead of $200. Or maybe a cheque.

"Yes!" He pumped his fist for effect.

"Food production would have been reformed on a similar scale. Less chemical inputs and pesticide use and energy, working with natural systems. More local production. No more '2000-mile salad.' Above all, though, an end to food waste. That's not a technology problem, it's a system failure.

"Would we all be vegetarian? Not necessarily. But very close to it." He smiled at the moaning, then offered an exaggerated frown in commiseration.

"Travel? Way less of it. Dashing across the world for a vacation twice a year might be twice in your life. *Oh no, I'd die without my cruise!*" He held the back of his hand campily to his forehead, earning scattered laughs.

"Really? Our ancestors took one long boat ride, and that was the last. Globe-trotting is a learned behaviour. Trips for work, conferences, weddings, or simply to get away? If we can learn it, we can unlearn it. Think spitting in public, or smoking. Think slavery.

"Oh, and the economy. Some countries have 'decoupled' their consumption of resources from their GDP. Look at Sweden. Each year its GDP grows, while energy use stays stable or declines. But even that's not enough. What's needed is an economy of renewal. Of remediation. Of renovation. If that sounds like sacrifice—it shouldn't. That's the *old* story that put us in this mess, not the one that will get us out. *Renaissance* means *re-birth*. A new way of seeing, living, and being with each other.

"But we didn't do those things did we, when the window was wide open? And it's too late now. The spiral is speeding up. The unravelling in full flight."

Sagan shook his head slowly.

"So what *can* we still accomplish, to survive as a civilized species?"

He paused and took a sip of water. Time to pump it up.

"It's called *deep decarbonization*. As an entire society, we must leave almost all known coal, oil and gas *in the ground*. That's not a political statement, it's physics.

"*But that is most inconvenient*," Sagan mimicked a Texan drawl. "*My savings are invested in companies whose value depends on selling those resources. In companies that make cars, fly airplanes and build highways. They rely on free-flowing travel, and conspicuous consumption and BUILD BABY BUILD!*"

He had been speaking faster and louder, almost screaming the final phrase. Many in the crowd, he sensed, were shell-shocked. Sweating, he persisted.

"*The only way to ensure a future is to leave everything in the ground?*" he said in a mocking voice—his eyes bugging out. "*The economy will implode! You want me to undermine my interests, to protect my interests? That's... that's nuts!*"

Much of the audience was nodding. Sagan wiped his brow on his tuxedo sleeve and resumed his normal voice.

"It *is* nuts. To do all of this now, at breakneck speed would be insane. Because it defies all rules of accepted behaviour and economics. Still, nothing less will do. So when I prescribe something this disruptive, all I can say to support my case is: *the automobile*, *World War II*, and *the internet*. Something on the transformative scale needed now *has* been done before. We have more than once thrown ourselves into action, not knowing how it would end."

Sagan took a long pause, scanning through his notes. Just use what you need, Simone had said.

"Deep decarbonization!" he exclaimed. "Living a meaningful life, maintaining a civilized society with far less fossil fuel and drastically lower emissions. To avoid climate breakdown, we'll need to embrace the concept of a per capita carbon budget. Each person allocated a measurable quota per year.

"Since measuring an odourless, invisible gas is a hard concept to grasp, some clever people decided to measure energy consumption instead. Their idea is to respect a per-person carbon budget of 2000 *watts* per day by 2050. That number is not grabbed from thin air—pardon the pun. It's derived from the remaining 'carbon space' in the atmosphere, divided by the number of people on the planet. Daunting, right? Especially when I tell you the typical European is at 6000 and North Americans are over 10,000!

"I find two aspects of this approach intriguing. First, it's not some arbitrary target. Second, it goes in both directions. People who are way *below* 2000—the poorest on the planet—must be allowed to *increase* their energy use, where the rest of us have to scale down, drastically. We could, of course, set up a system where those not using their full quota could sell some. We buy from the poor, and get a softer landing. Most potential sellers are in the rural global South, or slums, or massive refugee camps." Sagan shook his head and sighed audibly.

"As awful as such transactions sound, they could help with the transition, when we're learning how to scale down, and taking overdue steps in, say, insulating our walls, or sub-dividing overly-large houses, or learning to carpool.

But this is unthinkable, isn't it? Raise your hand if you'd vote for someone who limited you to 2000 watts per day." Sagan made a show of scanning the room, nodding slowly. "Oh look, one. And a second. Two votes for the 2000-Watt Party!" He caught the gentle laughter. "Politically unthinkable. And yet… it's the only moral thing to do."

He spread his arms wide and looked at the ceiling. "I'm travelling through a cold, merciless universe with 8 billion people, and my spaceship has ecological resources and carbon room for 1.5 billion only. Is it defensible for me to use the share of 20 Ethiopians, or 10 Indians, or 4 Chinese or 2 Europeans? Is my current lifestyle more important than the future of *homo sapiens*? That's not a question anybody has wanted to ask. Nor one any politician or religious leader has asked of you, with very few exceptions. But it's precisely what deep decarbonization will demand. Are you up to it? Can you cut your consumption and waste by 90 percent?"

He paused to wipe his brow. His sleeve had become wet.

"You don't think so, do you? But I think you can. I admit it's a whole new worldview, and it must be phased in—there's much to lose from imposing it overnight, and few will self-impose it. It will take two years at a minimum for the new economy and the jobs it generates to begin to flourish, and to wind down industries that block the way. But it has to start now, and it starts with a carbon budget and a plan. It will also require measurement, and enforcement—yes, *enforcement.*"

He paused, nodded and smiled. "I see your faces. I wish we could do it out of a sense of morality or patriotism. Alas, we've proven ourselves a bit more selfish than that. There's a story from wartime England, where fuel was strictly rationed. It went like this: it only takes one aristocrat in an idling car to undermine the resolve of an entire community. People *despise* a cheater!

"A carbon budget is just one approach though. The transition can be achieved through a range of instruments. Above all, a price on carbon. Make it a tax, cap-and-trade, or fee-and-dividend, but pick one. Otherwise our finite atmosphere will remain a free dump. Emitting carbon already costs us, so charge for it. Then increase it in stages to reflect its harm. If you're a capitalist, note that this is a market-based tool: true-cost pricing. The alternative is regulation. Who prefers intrusive regulation?"

He again scanned the room for effect. No hands were raised.

"*But I don't want regulation or a tax!*" he mimicked, in a nasal whine. "*Climate change isn't bothering ME.*"

"*Really,*" he said, in a deeper, louder voice. "When will it be enough to 'bother' you? More hurricanes and mega-fires? More of the country declared uninsurable?"

"Oh, and I nearly forgot…" He hunched forward and stage whispered. "There's a messy little thing called *mass migration*!"

Resuming his normal posture and voice, Sagan scanned Simone's notes.

"Those tens of millions fleeing their homes? Who are they and why are there so many? Are they 'climate refugees'? That's too simplistic. There's war and corruption and persecution and more. But the chaotic climate is a very important player. Then there's a growing set of ecological problems: no water, no harvest, no fish, no forests... no future! If ecological breakdown doesn't cause hundreds of millions to flee, social collapse will."

So why me, and why now? Are you ready to feed, shelter and integrate another 200 million in the next decade or two? That's how many could choose the U.S. of A. as their preferred destination. Don't want them? How big a wall do you think we'll have to build? How many naval vessels and drones will we need to turn them around, or torpedo them? Is that where you want your tax money going? Is that a job you'd wish on your granddaughter? Pulling that trigger?"

Sagan paused to allow the crowd to consider his words. He took another sip of water and wiped his brow. In a gentle voice, he resumed. "Or, we could go with a carbon budget. Starting Monday. But no cheating. Right?"

A quick glance told Sagan he was moving into the final section, drawing on his Chautauqua material. He was physically drained, and his mouth as dry as parchment, but his head surprisingly clear. No more notes.

"What should we make of our dilemma from a Christian perspective?" he began. "Many here follow another faith," he noted, looking around the hall, "or have no formal religion. But you may still recognize yourself in what I'll say. Some believe humans are at will to use all the natural world can offer. We are not only the dominant species, but it is our right and privilege to use and *use up*." His emphasis triggered grimaces.

"I won't accept that this is what anyone's god had in mind. Most religious scholars agree. It is a perversion, excusable when the planet was scientifically unknown and its bounty limitless, but no longer.

"From this twisted understanding of our place in the world, comes a fanatical and influential group of people who downplay or deny the threat to our only planet and discourage collective action claiming that this is somehow the Lord's will. That to consume conspicuously is to honour God. How nice for them— and their allies of convenience: the dirty fuel flogger and the ultra-conservative, who attack any agenda of collaboration and ecological protection. That there is such a twisted movement here in our country, I find disgraceful. My faith, my god, has been hijacked.

"Picture for a moment the scene in 2030. Coastlines of every continent are flooded. Tens of millions are on the move. Desperate, they are prey to all manner of criminal. Continental regions that were once fertile are barren and abandoned. Oceans have been emptied and can sustain little. Forests are decimated by infestation, and burning out of control. Safe water is a scarce, privatized commodity.

Sagan paused and held up his near-empty glass, taking a slow sip, for effect. People stared, entranced.

"Cities seethe with malnourished, unemployed, diseased and angry refugees from a countryside where there is no living to be had. Violence is rampant. Countries are at war over remaining water and food. Nuclear plants have long ago been hastily shut down, or worse, with nobody watching over them.

"The true believers, of course, are patiently waiting to receive the return of the Lord. The few, that is, who haven't starved, perished from disease, been irradiated or shot. Lo and behold, Jesus Christ steps out onto the mountain or the roof of a Trump Tower and surveys all of God's Creation. There could only be one possible reaction.

"*WHAT IN HELL WERE YOU THINKING?!*" Sagan screamed.

The room deathly quiet, he continued in a quieter, anguished voice. "*Did you think God created Earth so you could do THIS? He gave you everything you needed to prosper, to share, to ensure nobody went hungry. He gave you dominion over Earth so you could be Stewards of Creation. And you did THIS! What did you think I*

*would do when I returned? Pat you on the back?! I have only one
thing to say: The horror! The horror!*

"Then Jesus would fall on his knees and weep. For the plants
and animals and insects. The running rivers, the snow-covered
mountains, the spring awakening and the autumn harvest. Music
and dance and literature. All lost. The failed human experiment.

"Then, as he came, he would leave. Shoulders slumped,
sobbing."

Sagan himself slumped over the lectern. If he had looked
up, if he could have looked up, he might have seen the effect
of his tale on the audience. But eliciting tears from others had
brought on his own. For several breaths, he remained immobile,
summoning the strength to finish. This was not how he wished
to be remembered. With both arms, he pushed himself upright
once more and looked out over the room.

"So…" he began tentatively, "what you want to know, what
I want to know is whether there is still a useful role for me? Is
the demise of our promising but flawed species part of God's
plan? The natural evolution of the cosmos, perhaps? If the end
of a liveable Earth is approaching, what is my place? Do I work
harder, pray harder, scream louder?

"Beats me," he shrugged, smiling weakly. "All I know is
there must be a way to live my values in as full and honest a
way as I can. Staring down the obstacles and opponents and
deteriorating conditions. Working to make hell on Earth just a
little bit better than if I had never been here, instead of shirking
that responsibility and praying for a better afterlife. Though I
don't know how long I'll be playing a role on this Earth, I *have*
found my meaning.

"Michael Dowd has done some extraordinary work in
conceptualizing the dilemma we face: reconciling science with
religion, and evolution with creation; placing evidence at the
highest rung; showing how observable reality can and should be
compatible with many fundamentalist beliefs. He sees the great
reckoning as a 'great homecoming'; and promotes a gospel that

is resolutely 'pro-future and pro-science' while clearly honouring nature."

Sagan spoke slowly, catching the eye of the academy president who had introduced him. Ages ago, it seemed. She smiled, willing him forward. Sipping the last drops from his glass, he looked up and squared his shoulders.

"Allow me one last meander. A point about character, which both Dowd and Pope Francis discuss in their own way. "*Sacrificing for the common good and standing for the future must be honoured as sacred.*" That's Dowd. Pope Francis, for his part, reminds us there is no shame in living with less, in being humble and gentle—it takes more effort than to rage and bully. Anybody who has raised a child knows this. We have proof from the White House too. Gentleness and empathy take work. Protecting is harder than trashing. This is what makes the gentle path sacred."

Sagan put his glass again to his lips. It was empty. A young man at a table near the stage leapt forward with a pitcher of water. Sagan smiled and nodded.

"I ask myself often what we can do to redeem ourselves. As individuals. As a society. For we can no longer undo the devastation. Fortunately, redemption does not hinge on this. It does, though, require us to choose a new path. How we act will define our legacy… or ensure we have none."

Sagan stepped to the front of the stage and placed his palms together.

"I applaud those who are with me on this journey to find and act in ecological integrity. I invite everyone else to join. It is really the only trip worth taking in our one precious human life. *Namaste.*"

As he bowed people began to clap. Politely at first, building to a roar. For nearly three minutes he stood, bowing repeatedly, allowing his tears to flow freely.

Scattered around the room, barely visible, a dozen or so were not clapping.

Into the Twitterverse

Simone spent the entire morning fighting the temptation to call. On the chance Sagan might be sleeping in late at his Washington hotel, she waited until noon. By then, she had read through the dozens of tweets at #ASAgala. She knew better, but this time it was temptation that won.

"He's back, and telling it as straight as always," said @ProfHashimoto.

"What a thrill to have the highly-respected Dr. Sagan Cleveland give his first public address in many years to American Science Academy members and guests. Well worth the wait!"

Nice, thought Simone. But it was from the Academy's communications office. What else could they say?

There was more. Lots more. Mostly praise, she was pleased to see, but not everyone was being nice.

"Delivery as garbled as his so-called facts," @realsciencetruth had written.

"Climate deception? Crime against humanity? There was only one traitor at the #ASAgala and he was on stage. Lock him up!" said @FriendsofPOTUS.

And then, the piling on began, from people who had clearly not even heard the speech. But why let that get in the way of an opinion? "Lock him up?" @FullRightNow had tweeted. "More like string him up. Or take him out. Know what I mean?!"

Simone knew she had to get out and leave the twitterverse to what it did best—or worst. The only thing that mattered to her was how Sagan was doing—whether he had made it through the ordeal on his lowered dosage and come through unscathed.

"So?" asked Simone, when Sagan answered his phone. "How did it go?"

"Most people stayed," he answered flatly. "Some applauded. And I think my sentences all had a noun and a verb."

She laughed. "What about the speech outline? Was it helpful?"

"Dahling," said Sagan. "It was perfect. I even used some of it."

The deep chuckle that followed told Simone what she needed to know. He would be OK. Best not to mention her little trip among the trolls, though.

Strange Find

Detroit, April 2019

What a stench! Diego Ramirez strode deliberately between two long rows of dead corn stalks. He liked the smell of soil, recently thawed. Rich, musty, but slightly sweet. "Earthy," he chuckled. Makes sense.

But this was different. Out of place.

Diego had surprised himself. When the judge proposed field work and an urban farming course as restorative justice for stealing tools and vandalizing a storeroom at Center Street Farms, he'd pictured his grandparents back in Honduras. Peasant work. He hadn't come to America for this! Then again, it beat another stint inside. He wasn't a minor now. This time it could be as much as 12 months, his lawyer warned. Locked up with some mean dudes.

The class work had been easy enough. He hadn't cracked a book since finishing high school two years earlier, but he had once been a good student. Still was, it seemed. It was the feeling of using his hands, though, that proved a revelation. Planting, digging, watering and watching his plot grow that first summer.

Free to move on after the harvest, Diego instead registered for a class in permaculture during the winter months, and worked at the community market on weekends. Now, with spring approaching, he'd volunteered to help prepare the fields. Corn stalks—left standing through the winter to stabilize the soil and act as a wind break—needed cutting. They would be ground up and used as mulch during planting.

It was eerie, walking through the stalks at this early hour, out of sight of the others. Diego set out for the far end of the row. He'd work his way back, cutting the stalks one by one. There were machines for this kind of work, he knew, but he liked the feel of hand tools, especially the machete. So beautifully balanced, able to slice through a stalk as thick as his wrist with one well-aimed swing. He admired the newly-sharpened blade as he advanced up the row, skating slightly in some viscous mud.

There it was again. The smell. Acrid, like a burger left unattended on the backyard grill. A whiff of gas too. Had kids been holding bush parties out here, cooking hotdogs? Threw some in to see what would happen. It looked like a bonfire site. He could see the circle up ahead, and smell the charred meat. Some stalks had been blackened.

Whoever they were, they'd left a mess. Partially burned rags, it looked like, at the outer edges of the circle. *Pigs, littering up a good field! And the reek.* Gasoline and something bitter.

Disgusted, Diego switched the machete to his left hand so he could gather up some of the singed pieces of cloth. As he bent down, he was drawn to what appeared to be a gold medallion in the fire pit. *Nice. Careless as well as stupid,* Diego thought as he reached out.

Grabbing hold of the medallion, he realized the chain was hooked on something. A sharp tug failed to free it, but was enough to uncover what it was attached to. *What the hell?* He was looking at a scorched human head. And the eyes, badly burned, were looking at him.

"Aie! Madre de Dios!" he screamed.

Dropping the piece of jewelry as if red hot, he tossed the machete aside, looked frantically left and right, then turned and ran back down the row as quickly as his shaking, sliding legs would carry him.

* * *

Keeping gawkers away from a crime scene could be difficult, the Detroit Police officer had learned, but now they had drones to contend with too. Zipping about like hummingbirds, diving in for a close up, then darting away before you could take a swing. *Freaks!*

On the positive side, she mused, at least we can't be accused of tampering. Everything's on video, posted in no time.

* * *

Michelle was first to learn of Sagan's death. She was on recess duty that morning. Facing across the asphalt playground toward the side door of her elementary school, she'd been watching a game of tag when the door opened and her principal emerged with a female police officer at her side. The principal looked her way and pointed. The officer's gaze followed until they made eye contact. Michelle's neck stiffened, as if ice water had been poured on it from behind.

"No!" she had howled, seated in the principal's office, just her and the officer. "How can I have both brothers murdered?!" Tears streamed down her face.

"I am so sorry Ms. Cleveland," the officer said. "So you understand, though, it has not been ruled a murder. Not yet, at least."

"Tell me you'll do your best to catch the killer," Michelle said, staring directly into the eyes of the officer. "You'll promise me that at least, won't you, Inspector Williams?"

"That I will," Shaun Williams replied. "My very best."

* * *

Working from home that morning, Simone had been expecting a call from the editor of the *Canadian Spotlight.* They were working on an investigation of Canada's National Energy Board and Simone had agreed to contribute.

"Hey, Vicky!" Simone answered, in an upbeat voice. The silence took her aback.

"Umm, Simone, is it possible you haven't heard?"

"I guess the answer is yes."

"Oh my," Vicky gasped. "Gosh, this request was going to be hard enough to make, but I hadn't planned on being the messenger too."

Simone had no idea what she was on about. "Whatever it is Vicky, giving it straight will be easiest."

"No, Simone. There's no easiest way to tell you this. It just came across the news feed out of Detroit." Simone shuddered at the word.

"Your friend—"

"Not Sagan!" Simone braced herself on the desk with her right hand. "Not another breakdown."

"Not exactly," said Vicky, clearing her throat. "They're calling it suicide. At least the police statement used the euphemisms for suicide. 'Death by misadventure. Foul play is not suspected.'"

Vicky had expected an emotional reaction from Simone, but not the one she got.

"No fucking way!" Simone shouted into the phone. "Suicide! Absolutely no fucking way. Send me what you've got Vicky. I'm getting onto this right now."

Vicky took a moment to respond. "Uh, Simone. I don't think it's appropriate to ask you this. Certainly not now. Probably never was. But I wanted you to have first right of refusal, given your close ties." She paused, then finished her thought. "Would you like to write the obituary, or should I assign someone else?"

The veins in her head and neck pulsing, Simone needed a moment to answer.

"I wish I could, Vicky, I really do. You could run it by me for fact-checking, but I'm too close. This is too soon. You understand, don't you?"

"Of course, Simone. And Simone… please accept my heartfelt condolences."

The call over, Simone placed her arms on the desk and lay her head down. Breathing in, she felt her chest and back quiver. Breathing out, she made up her mind.

I'm sorry Sagan. I will do this, and do it right, but everything in its time. First there are calls to make.

* * *

It was midnight when Jiro received Simone's email. He called her immediately.

"Simone. I like to hear from you, but so late as this? I fear it is bad news."

"Jiro, *tomodachi*, Sagan is dead."

"*Honto?*" he gasped. "Dead! How?"

"The police suspect suicide. Isong doesn't believe it. I don't believe it. And there's something fishy about the way the police are acting. I'm putting out feelers."

"Suicide!" Jiro said softly, thinking. "It is possible. But no, I do not think so."

"Jiro..." Simone said awkwardly, "do you know where I might find Jenny?"

He paused before answering in a matter-of-fact voice. "I believe she is travelling. I can ask the girls in the morning."

"I've emailed," Simone said, "but sometimes she isn't able to receive messages."

A long pause followed. Finally Jiro spoke. "Will you let me do this? Let me give the news."

Simone was puzzled. "I guess, if you really want to."

"She can get the details from you, Simone, I know that. This isn't about details."

"Of course not, Jiro. Of course not."

Let something good come of this, thought Simone.

* * *

Jiro knew exactly where Jenny was. He reached her at the guest inn near the girls' school. It was after midnight, but this call was already overdue.

"Jiro!" said Jenny, "what a surprise."

"Are you free to meet first thing tomorrow? A walk in Aoyama Cemetery?"

"Yes, Jiro, yes I am. What's this about?"

"Everything," he replied.

The cherry blossoms were in full bloom, petals blanketing the ground. Jiro and Jenny walked together in silence toward his favourite bench. He had just delivered the grim news.

Brushing petals gently from the bench, he gestured for her to sit. Eyes on him, she lowered herself. Clutching the cotton bag he had been carrying, he sat beside her, looking forward. Finally, he turned and cleared his throat.

"I cannot deny I have been hurt. I still am. But I am also tired of hurt."

Blushing, Jenny nodded.

Jiro then opened the bag and took out a thermos, two cups and a smaller paper bag. He poured tea for each of them, then, with a crinkle, placed two scones on a napkin. With both hands, he offered one to Jenny. Watching her intently as she accepted it, he spoke again.

"Can we start over?"

Her answer came out in choked bursts. "I think... that's what... Sagan... would suggest."

Searching for Meaning

Pointed Fingers

I song had never felt so angry. Was it not enough to have my husband, my partner for life ripped away? No, they have to tear us apart in the media and online too. Now, when we should be grieving, we must deal with the rumours, the pointing fingers, the grotesque remarks. His head hurt, he couldn't eat and, above all, his heart ached for Sagan. Sweet gentle Sagan, doused and burned to death. Let him have been dead already, Lord, let him not have felt the pain.

The circumstances of Sagan's death demanded a full investigation, he had shouted at the Detroit Police press conference. It was so obvious.

Everyone heard him. There, and all over the world. "Sagan Cleveland suffered from depression," he yelled, "but he was not suicidal. This was murder!"

Be careful what you wish for, somebody might have whispered to him. First to be investigated will be those closest to him. Especially ones who stand to gain financially. Underpaid preachers, and hard-working sisters with children to raise on a pathetic kindergarten teacher's wages.

Indeed, the first to be questioned were members of the family. Standard procedure, they were told. Isong was subjected to a thorough and aggressive interview. A husband under stress from caring for a partner with depression, who had recently inherited a substantial sum. Sister Michelle came next. Sagan had recently

BURNING SOULS

taken out life insurance; with Isong and Michelle as benefactors. The only two in his will. Had she known?

Both had solid alibis. Isong was giving a guest sermon in Pittsburgh. Michelle went to bed at her normal time and stayed there, her husband Clause swore. Their car was in the shop for servicing. No taxi or Uber drivers had come forward.

* * *

Much of Detroit took a morbid interest in the case. The *Detroit Free Press* assigned a reporter to it. Young, soft-spoken and diligent, Antoine Stillwell had impressed the city editor in his first year at the paper, assigned to the crime beat. This would be a new challenge. Something was odd about the way local police were acting.

Antoine had read the statements. He'd been at the press conference. He'd spoken with family and a number of friends. He'd read the social media chatter—the supporters and the trolls; the science community and the Alt-Right.

The harassment finally got to him. Wasn't it just last year, his breakdown? Lots of people had it in for him. Black, gay, climate scientist, critical of the government... Some supremacist nutcase, I'll bet. They're homophobes as well as racists! And wasn't his brother involved in a gang? Got himself killed.

He'd even waded into some FullRight sites. *The freak had it coming. Couldn't keep his mouth shut. Or hands to himself. Or kids' mouths off of him!*

Forget the chatter, ugly as it may be. Follow the money, Antoine knew. Who stood to gain? Bank records for Isong and Michelle showed no unusual transactions, the police divulged. Same for Claude. A contract killing costs money. A down payment, then the balance on delivery.

The case for suicide appeared weak. Though Sagan's history was well known, he'd been in good spirits, even resuming his farm work. There was no note either. He would surely have wanted to explain himself, or bid farewell. His husband and sister insisted he'd shown no suicidal tendencies. His close friend and collaborator, Simone Cohen could corroborate this.

Then there was the method. Could his body have been that badly burned if he'd set the fire himself?

* * *

Few knew about the gas container. Shaun Williams had taken photos of it as soon as she'd arrived, and then carefully covered it with a blanket to protect it from rain; and drones. She'd found the blanket sitting off to the side, near the container; dry and neatly folded. She wore gloves, of course. But before touching a thing, she'd meticulously photographed the entire area.

The autopsy found no evidence of foul play. No wounds. No evidence of poison. No drugs, other than what Sagan Cleveland had been prescribed. The fire had done substantial damage to the body, she knew. She'd seen it up close. Taken the gruesome pictures. No skin remained, and his stomach was too badly burned to support a reliable analysis of its contents.

* * *

It was the *Free Press* that first raised 'the list.' What about the people outed by the SmartView show? Any one of them might have wanted to harm him. And what about Elmore Lambert? He had a history, a criminal history with Sagan. Was nobody investigating him? Shouldn't the FBI be onto that? Had they even been called in?

They had, a senior FBI official stated at a press conference the next day.

"We are partnering on the investigation. Everyone on the list is a potential suspect, but we have no reason to suspect that any were involved in the death of Sagan Cleveland. Should we have more information germane to the case, we will make it public at the appropriate time. Thank you, and good afternoon!"

Sagan had enemies, the *Free Press* had written, but most were critics or detractors, not actual enemies. He was not known to have harmed, cheated or threatened anyone. He did not owe money, and none was owed to him. His political convictions, scientific stands and sexual orientation might suggest a motive. People had been killed for less, and Sagan *was* threatened on multiple occasions. But threats were one thing. Did anyone actually want him dead?

The newspaper's lawyers advised against naming Elmore Lambert a second time. Friends in high places. That advice—or was it a warning?—made Antoine more determined than ever. This kind of complacency, corruption even, was what drove him to pursue journalism in the first place. His editor supported him continuing to sniff around. But he would be 'freelancing,' should anyone ask.

PB-S was Antoine's first call. She was preoccupied by immigration problems, he learned; barred from returning to New York, her green card rescinded. She was fighting it, but without much success. Simone was his second call. Unknown to him, she was already deep into her own investigation.

Simone warned him to avoid all electronic communication, including phone calls. Could he meet her in Toronto? Did he cycle? He might like Toronto's ravines.

Then There Were Three

Isong and Michelle agreed on a small, private funeral. Anything else would become a media spectacle. The autopsy and investigation had delayed it, but allowed time to reflect on what Sagan would have wanted. The cremation versus burial discussion was a ghoulish one, his remains being partly incinerated already. But Michelle was not one for sentiment.

"I want to grieve and then celebrate my brother's spirit. What happens to his body is of little importance to me, as long as it's done with respect."

This opened the door for a suggestion Isong had been reluctant to make. A 'natural cemetery' had been created adjacent to some of the urban farms, not far from where Sagan had grown up. It was affiliated with a funeral co-operative as well. They could keep things simple: a light, biodegradable casket, not some massive one made of rare hardwood. Principle, not money was the issue, he said. Isong was sure Sagan would have liked the idea.

Michelle responded with a roll of the eyes and shake of her head.

"Living by principles, dying for principles, getting buried with principles! Go ahead, whatever. I doubt he'd have wanted a second cremation. Too many emissions!"

Like brother like sister, Isong remarked. Nothing was too sacred.

"Besides," she added, "if the investigation requires us to dig him up later for another look, better that he's all together, not blowing around the farm!"

For the memorial, Isong sought Simone's advice. He wanted to host it at their church in central Detroit. Simone had to remind him she would not be able to attend, and it might prove difficult for Jenny and Jiro, given visa requirements. They agreed on two events. Isong would hold a memorial in Detroit for American family, friends and colleagues, while she would plan "something special" for Canadian and international friends.

* * *

The celebration of life would be at her own church in Ottawa. Tears were guaranteed, but she wanted food and music and a sharing of stories. Isong would come, perhaps Michelle, Claude and their boys. Ron of course, and Jacinthe, who was fond of him. Her own parents would come, though they'd only met him once, when he'd stayed with them in Montreal. A number of Canadian academics who had worked with him were sure to attend. The big unknown would be Jenny and Jiro.

* * *

Bohemian Rhapsody, the Freddie Mercury biopic had been released the autumn before. It garnered a lot of awards, she knew. And criticism for taking liberties with facts, among other things. She hadn't seen it. She was far too busy during its initial cinema run, and again when it returned after the awards. But here it was now, playing at the Mayfair, their local arthouse cinema. Ron, never much of a Queen fan, offered to accompany her.

She cried through much of it. This was Freddie's story, she had to tell herself, not Sagan's, but they kept crossing over in her brain. In her heart. A jumbled mess of memories and regrets.

"I could have stopped it! I could have saved him!" she declared to Ron, turning to face him on their slow walk home.

"Oh sweetheart, don't do that. I've never seen anyone do so much for a friend."

"It wasn't enough!" she barked, her face turned ugly. "I'll bring those bastards down, if it's the last thing I do!"

Ron knew his wife to be determined. Fixated, sometimes. But never like this. Finally he spoke, carefully.

"I know better than to try and stop you, the Mighty Mouse, and why should I even want to. But don't do anything rash—not yet. There's something else you can do for Sagan first. Something you are uniquely suited for."

* * *

Simone and Ron were waiting for Jenny and Jiro at the airport. They'd taken the same flight from Vancouver.

"Looks promising," Simone said to Ron, when she sighted them together on the escalator. As they approached it became clear they were both smiling.

"Even better," she said, half whispering.

"Best of all," Ron exclaimed, when Jiro and Jenny joined hands.

* * *

Simone had put her heart and soul into the celebration of life—from tracking down invitees, to picking food and ale, to choosing readings. Above all, was the music. She didn't know how many would get it, but this was for Sagan.

And for her.

Bicycle Race, I Want it All, Fat Bottomed Girls, Don't Stop Me Now, Play the Game, Under Pressure, It's a Hard Life, I Want to Break Free, Lazing on a Sunday Afternoon, Good Old Fashioned Loverboy!

"My lord!" Michelle declared, when the two of them finally had a moment together. "Those stories. Such warmth. And so much laughter." She stepped forward and gave Simone a warm, lingering hug.

"Thank you sister. That was truly unique."

"It had to be!"

TPoT Blog — *The Defenders: Sagan Cleveland, 1973-2019*

February 17, 2019

> Scientist, comedian, spiritual seeker,
> shooting star, planetary defender.
>
> Murdered for speaking truth to power.

> *It did not really matter what we expected from*
> *life, but rather what life expected from us.*
>
> Viktor E. Frankl

Unconvincing Suicide

S elf-immolation. The act of a despondent man, suffering from mental illness. The Detroit Police and FBI had followed every lead and considered all motives. Gas was stored in a shed 300 yards away. He knew that, and had a key. He would have walked to the middle of the field, a place he knew well. Case closed.

Seeking attention in death as he had in life. Death by fire as a symbol.

Sagan's close family and friends refused to accept it. Former colleagues were less sure, not knowing his state of mind in recent years. The public seemed split, breaking down heavily along racial lines—another black life not mattering. Even a prominent, internationally accomplished black. Protests in Detroit brought out mostly black objectors, but on the campuses of Penn State and Cambridge, a full rainbow of students, staff and professors had marched.

The internet was rife with conspiracy theories.

The three least willing to accept the verdict but with greatest means to do something about it had to tread carefully. People in high places wanted the case closed. Antoine and Simone were following a trail into ever deeper and darker places. Then there was Inspector Williams.

Shaun Williams had been alone at the scene for fifteen minutes, with nothing but a notepad and phone. Something seemed odd from the outset. Meticulously, she photographed everything: gas container, blanket, unburned boots, medallion. Both sides of the medallion. In the highest resolution her phone was capable of. When she heard the first drone, she quickly and carefully draped the blanket over the red gas container.

In the following days and weeks she witnessed many troubling things, but didn't know anyone she could trust with her suspicions. Her job, perhaps even her life, could be on the line. She would carry on with her duties and keep her mouth shut. Copies of the photos were in a safe place.

Open and Objective

Tokyo, December 2019

"So we are clear," Katsuo said, "no minutes are taken. This meeting never happened." He looked around the table at the four others in the room. The president of Japan's nuclear safety authority, the chief executive officer of TEPCO, the energy minister and the prime minister's chief of staff nodded, faces grave, eyes shifting back and forth from one to the other.

"We need to get more reactors online. It is nothing short of a miracle that the grid has not yet crashed. But we can't expect the people of Japan to sacrifice forever. At some point—quite soon, if our polling is correct—they will rebel, and it will be this government, this party that pays the price. And everyone who benefits from a stable government." Katsuo looked up to emphasize his points. All nodded once more.

"Tomorrow, we will announce the creation of a new Electrical Security Commission. I will be one of the members. The four others will include two reputable academics, a trade union representative and an invited American nuclear expert, so as to demonstrate our openness and objectivity." Again, the four nodded.

"The mandate is simple. To ensure electrical grid reliability, and that any restarts put public safety and taxpayer protection ahead of other interests."

"With the support of the press and our intelligence agencies we can steer public opinion towards the..." he paused, but only briefly, "the *obvious* conclusion."

Katsuo looked directly at the prime minister's chief of staff, the corners of his mouth curling ever so slightly upwards. "Four Elements policies are little better than fantasy, as the rigorous and unbiased report of the Electrical Security Commission will demonstrate."

"Quite so!" declared the TEPCO officer. The others nodded.

Cohen's Comment
How to Erode a Liberal Democracy

Canadian Spotlight, December 18, 2019

There are many ways to undermine a liberal democracy—defined by a free and universal vote, an elected government and opposition, independent judiciary and media, freedom of speech and assembly and an assumed desire for equality of opportunity for all citizens.

The first is through the political process. Once elected, those in office will move to acquire greater powers, and limit those of the citizen and independent institutions of the state. This would be done transparently, through party policy and even changes to the constitution, brought to the public for approval at election time, or through a referendum.

The second is for a government to gradually allow people of influence—be it corporations, the church, or a particular insider elite—to gain influence over affairs of the state. Look at the track record of governments working in close partnership with the fossil fuel and nuclear industries, at the expense of cleaner alternatives. Subsidies, tax breaks, weak environmental protection and low royalty fees are common.

Another example is reduced testing and oversight of the pharmaceutical and agri-food industries. Not only are products finding their way onto shelves without third-party testing, in some cases/ countries, it is actually illegal to label a product as "organic" or "non-GMO" or "Wild Fish" because that would be "unfair competition." When we aren't even allowed to make a conscious consumer decision, what can this be but a transfer of power to the corporation/investor?

The third way to undermine liberal democracy is by tightening control—through state surveillance, influence over the judiciary, media harassment and imprisonment, and curtailing the right to oppose, protest and speak. In its extreme, it is by intimidation, incarceration, loss of employment, eviction from housing and ultimately elimination (murder) of voices of opposition. We are or have been watching this play out in countries where it once looked as if a liberal democracy was taking hold. Kenya, Nigeria, Pakistan, Hungary, Venezuela, Brazil, Poland... I could go on.

The most egregious cases in recent years would of course be Russia, Turkey and the Philippines. Assassination of journalists, lawyers and defecting whistleblowers is a common practice to silence not just the individual, but all who might consider speaking truth to power. In Turkey, sweeping 'security' measures have done much to silence opposition, imprison or impoverish an entire intellectual and professional class, and turn the clock back on women's rights. Turkey appears to be the biggest jailer of journalists in the world. Though how does one confirm that?

If you think your country is above what I'm describing, look again. You may have recognized yourself in the first two categories: the election of governments who promise to fix our problems by taking more power into their own hands and out of yours; or who make no such promise, yet do so anyway through the transfer of power from the public's hands into private and corporate ones. But if you think you are safe from the third, it's time to wake up. My American friends know best of what I speak. *Kakistocracy:* government by the worst. Can you count on rights you assume you have?

In Britain, entitlement is back, before it truly left. But the entitled is now an odd amalgam of lineage and wealth, with a strong corporate presence. Everything is owned or sponsored by some corporate entity; often with Russian kleptocracy, Gulf oil or Asian "dark money" connections. Been to a soccer game lately? Who built the stadium, and who finances the billion dollar payrolls?

As for Canada, the nice liberal democracy, don't get sanctimonious. Corruption in this country is not overt, and that is the problem. Dark money is creeping into how this country is run. Fossil fuel, agriculture, the media, school curricula...

Wake up, then put your savings in a local credit union. Look at where you get information. If it's from one of the few independent sources left, take some money and subscribe or donate. Sources don't stay independent when they can't pay their staff, or lawyers to defend against libel chill. Wake up and do more than vote. Politics matters. It's happening in front of you. Do more than sit online complaining and liking.

Liberal democracy needs us to engage, constantly. It is a fragile thing, with many enemies.

The Heat Is On

The summer of 2020 had been exceptionally hot and dry across Europe. Worse than 2017, the year they gave weather a name—*Lucifer!* Worse even than 2018, when an airport runway in northern Germany was too soft to land on. By July it was clear records would be broken. *Hades*, they were calling it.

For farmers across the continent, this meant acute water shortages. For fire fighters, it meant a constant battle. As lake levels dropped, it was harder and harder to use water bombers.

The Drome received good rains in May, but June winds were stronger than ever, drying fields before they had full crop coverage, and whipping up grassfires. A total fire ban was in place. Mechanical equipment, even axes and spades had to be used carefully. One spark was all it took.

François' permaculture approach, broadly adopted in much of the region, helped with water retention. Good tree cover, healthier soils and no-till farming were essential. Most farms had constructed reservoirs underground now, knowing their surface ponds would dry up by August.

What concerned François most was the plummeting Rhône, which supplied cooling water for two nearby nuclear plants. During the 2003 drought, a number of stations tailed back or stopped generating entirely in order to protect against critical overheating. He had less confidence in these operators now, or in government oversight. They would generate for as long as possible, trying to extract every last drop from their stranded asset.

You could do all the right things in your little enclave, but it would never protect you from larger forces around you. No Global Village is an island. He would stick with what he could control—more or less, considering the drought—and pray for the best; for nuclear workers, firefighters and farmers, the elderly in their overheating apartments, and the migrants in their rickety boats.

Family Secrets

"It is the birthday of your nieces, and your mother and I want the family together. Now get over your inflated importance, and be here on Sunday, at 2 p.m. Bring flowers for your mother!"

Jenny had never heard Jiro's father speak so forcefully to anyone. Least of all Katsuo. She, Jiro and his mother had overheard the phone call, one side of it at least. They were finishing an early dinner together before Jiro went out for yet another evening meeting. Jenny only understood part of what was said, but she could tell it involved Katsuo, and that Ebitsubo-san was uncharacteristically angry.

"Pompous prick!" he muttered as he returned to the table. "He's had his way for too long. '*So sorry, I have important engagements*'," he mimicked. "On a Sunday afternoon! Try canceling your golf game with the prime minister, or your secret handshake meeting with your little racist friends!"

Jiro's mother coughed, while he and Jenny made eye contact and struggled to stifle a laugh.

"So he's coming?" his mother said innocently.

"Damn right. And I'm sitting at the head of the table. Got that?" He fixed a stern gaze at his wife.

"Yes, husband and head of the family!"

This time Jiro could not contain himself, letting out an audible chortle.

"Sorry father. You have always been head of the family to me."

"Yes, yes, run along honourable governor. Don't you have to be somewhere?"

"Indeed I must," said Jiro, rising and thanking his mother for the meal. As he passed behind Jenny, he leaned over and kissed the top of her head. She reached out and brushed his back as he made for the door.

Her return to the household had been smoother than she could have hoped. It began with a separate room, for a trial period following their return together from Canada. When the girls arrived for summer vacation, they would be one room short, however. It was Jiro who suggested a return to the shared bed. Not that they'd been avoiding physical contact. They had begun gently. Hand holding. Affectionate kisses. The rest followed in one rush, neither wishing or able to stop it.

Forgiveness had come quite easily. Trust, she knew, would take longer to rebuild.

Jiro's parents said little. Only "Welcome back! We have missed you."

As little as possible of their marital situation had been shared with Katsuo. As far as he knew, they'd been busy pursuing their own lives and had a similar loveless marriage to his. Only with children. Another sore point, Jenny knew. That they had children, and that they resembled her.

The party for Yuki and Anna started off well. The birthday songs and opening of presents helped to cover the tension.

"Seventeen!" their grandfather exclaimed. "You must be done growing now."

The twins were already taller than him, but would never come close to Jiro in stature. They had Jiro's chin, but Jenny's small nose, cheek bones and slim physique.

"Streamlined," declared Anna, a promising distance runner.

Both were set on becoming engineers. Jiro was happy to support them in whatever they chose.

The meal went well enough, with conversation directed mostly to the girls. How was the science fair? How did the track meet go? Sensing the tension, Anna and Yuki gave more elaborate answers than usual. Katsuo said little beyond asking a few questions about school. Though often with an edge. *International school!*

His wife stayed silent. As did Jiro's mother. His father, though, rose to the role of patriarch in a way that seemed caricatural. "Now I would like... Now I think..."

A great deal of alcohol was consumed. By the time the men went out into the garden for air and to await their coffee, they were visibly unsteady. Once seated at the garden table, Katsuo was quick to turn to politics. Namely the failure of Jiro's policies to deliver results. Jiro had been anticipating this, and was determined not to play second son.

"That is true. Many of our ideas have been slow to develop. It's a shame that we are undermined constantly by old and failed ideologies."

"*Ah,*" remarked Katsuo, raising an eyebrow. "And those would be which?"

The jousting that ensued came to a crescendo with Jiro railing against the national policies which placed all of Japan's energy bets on nuclear.

"There is blatant collusion between government, regulators and industry and the failure to implement sufficient safety measures is criminal." Jiro was flushed and sweating.

"Criminal!" shouted Katsuo. "Is it a crime to keep your country free of dependence on *Malaysian* oil and gas? Hmm, is that criminal? And does this make our father a criminal? He was as much a part of it as anyone."

"Enough!!"

Jiro and Katsuo were startled by their father's shout, and fist hitting the table.

"Enough from both of you. There is something you both need to know, and I have been silent too long. It is killing me!"

In silence, they listened as their father, his face blank, told the story of the Fukushima Daiichi safety systems.

"I was 30 years old. A good engineer. Top of my class. I was hand-picked to lead the team that would design the backup power systems. It would have been perfect, if constructed as intended. If the plant had been built on higher ground, as recommended."

"None of this had to happen," Ebitsubo-san spat. "Yes, the structure may have been damaged. Yes, there would have been flooding, but we could have kept the cooling system operating. We could have avoided major damage to the reactor, sitting like a time bomb now."

He shook his head ruefully.

"But others had different ideas. It was simpler to build lower down. Easier to access by boat. What were the chances of a tsunami like this hitting Japan in the lifetime of these plants? That's what they said. People senior to me. People who had to keep the project within budget. People who wanted to prove Japan could be a leader in building affordable reactors.

"I did what any company man does. I made my case, then I went about my business keeping the systems running the way I designed them. Only with inferior materials and in the wrong location."

"As the years went by, I got over it. Maybe they were right, and we didn't need to be so cautious. I made a good living, became a senior manager, and then retired in 2010. But now I know I was just a coward. A flunky, following orders."

He was grimacing now. His face contorted, in a way Jiro had never seen.

"That's what Japanese officers said after the war. *Following orders. Everyone else was doing it.* Those who ran the horrific camps, in Hong Kong, Burma, Indonesia... *Just doing my job.* Those who set up 'comfort women' stations. Sometimes 15 or 20 soldiers per day per woman. Until the women died of bleeding, or infection."

"That never happened!" shouted Katsuo, jumping up and glaring at his father. "It's a propaganda lie, to discredit our honourable soldiers."

"Sit down and shut up," Ebitsubo-san said firmly. "You embarrass me. You know so little, you question so little. Like your fanatical friends. It's all about injured pride. Some perverted idea of honour. Do you know what honour is?"

"Of course. But you will tell me differently, and expect me to take your word."

"I don't expect anything from you," Ebitsubo-san said, his eyes growing moist. I had to stop years ago. You've always been attracted to myth. Did you ever do your own research? Did you talk to people who lived under Japanese occupation? To the courageous women who came forward with their stories, and shame."

"I don't talk to sluts. Or liars!" Katsuo mumbled, staring forward, his arms crossed defiantly. Jiro could do nothing but shake his head in disgust.

"Katsuo," his father said with regret. "There is something I have spared you. I should not have. It might have taken you on a different life path. One which included humility, empathy and the search for a higher truth. Real Japanese values. Honourable ones. Unlike this nationalist nonsense. You're no better than those supremacist marchers in America."

"We're more Japanese than you," snarled Katsuo. "Or this weakling," he said, glancing briefly at Jiro, "with his half-breed kids."

If Jiro had been a different man, he would have knocked his brother to the floor. Instead, he took a deep breath and turned to his father.

"I believe you were about to tell us something important."

"Thank you Jiro. Yes, you know this story. I shared it just before your wedding. Your brother needs to hear it now too, whether he wants to or not."

"Katsuo, I will make this short. I am tired of your presence. Your grandmother, the one you never met... she was a Korean woman, forced to provide 'comfort' to Japanese soldiers home on leave. A victim of acts so atrocious most to this day deny it is part of our history."

Katsuo stared at his father in stunned silence, the blood draining from his face.

"Your grandfather was one of a thousand possible soldiers, looking for comfort from the body of a slave. This of course means your mother is half-Korean. That makes you..."

"No! This is not true," said Katsuo shaking his head. "How could you have done such a thing? Marry the daughter of a Korean prostitute?" Katsuo was glancing back toward the house where he knew his mother was. Spittle had formed on his lips.

"Katsuo, I have a great shame to atone for—my weakness in not standing up for the safety of my community—but marrying your mother is the one time I did the right thing. I hope you can find peace in knowing you were born out of love. Now go. Never show yourself again, unless it is to apologize to your mother and your brother."

"That will never happen," Katsuo spat.

"You," he said to Jiro, his lip curled in disgust, "have seen the last of me. I'm not protecting you any longer!"

Katsuo jerked open the paper sliding doors and stormed through the living room where the women had been seated. Grabbing his wife violently by the arm, he pulled her outside to the car. In the silence that followed, Jiro's mother turned to her grand daughters.

"Happy birthday my dears. Now you know everything!" She walked slowly out to the garden where she kissed her husband affectionately on the head as tears streamed down her face.

Jenny only understood a fraction of what had been said, though she heard everything. It had been impossible not to. But she knew the story already, and could read body language.

The girls exchanged wide-eyed glances throughout. Now, alone with their mother, Yuki looked at her and Anna before speaking.

"Half-Chinese-Malaysian, three-eighths Japanese, one-eighth Korean. No wonder we like so many foods." The three broke into laughter, breaking the tension.

Shortly after midnight, Jiro's father swallowed a bottle of pills. Anti-depressants he had been taking since 2011.

Katsuo did not attend the funeral.

Shining Light

Toronto, September 15, 2020

Simone's story—the *Canadian Spotlight's* story—was incendiary. Slowly, meticulously, obsessively even, Simone and two young researchers had assembled the pieces. With outside help. Some arrived anonymously, most did not. Most were from credible people, brave people, ashamed people who needed to share what they knew. Off the record, of course. The risk of being named was too high. This—her inability to use names—was the story's big weakness. Yet even without attribution, it would be a cruise missile in the middle of the 2020 American election, and the dogfight for the presidency.

Simone knew all of this. As did her two co-authors, editor-in-chief and the *Spotlight's* legal counsel. Five in total, sworn to secrecy. They knew what was at risk, and who. They shared her passion for the truth, her devotion to getting the facts right and her commitment to justice and fairness. But none of them were tied to the story like Simone. For them, it was a big story, a really big story. For Simone it was personal.

She had failed to prevent his murder. She should have. She could have. If she'd looked harder, tried harder. Stopped the bastards earlier. Stopped Elmore Lambert. She knew it was him. It had to be. But she couldn't tie it to him. Not him specifically. Or anyone else. Hard as she had tried.

Simone couldn't bring Sagan back, but there were things she could do. She could bring down the people, the kinds of people at least, who tormented him. She could shift the balance of power in the White House, the country, and other countries as well. And this was her chance.

'Dirty Money, Dirty Deeds'. They had been sitting on the story for six months. It had been fact-checked, and double fact-checked. It fingered a lot of powerful people. *It isn't libel if it's true.* But a lawsuit, however frivolous, would ruin them. Rich people, rich aggrieved people could bankrupt you long before you proved your innocence. They could also hurt you.

The only ones who knew about the story were gathered in a locked Toronto boardroom. They had been here before, four weeks earlier. But this time, Simone knew, the outcome would be different.

Running the story would put their sources at huge risk, they'd agreed at the initial meeting. Most sources were American. All had spoken on condition of anonymity, something a writer went to great lengths to protect. A recent U.S. Supreme Court decision had, however, eliminated the media's right to protect sources, while also gutting whistleblower protection. "State security is paramount," it ruled.

The *Spotlight* was Canadian, as were the five of them in the room, but the Canada-U.S. Border Agreement, renegotiated in 2020, obliged their government to arrest any national accused of a crime against an American. With sufficient evidence.

With the presidential election eight weeks out, a strategic decision had to be made about running the story. If it helped defeat the Republicans—prominent members and friends of the government were named—an extradition request was unlikely. But if the Republicans saw electoral advantage in pressing for immediate extradition to show they would not allow foreign interference in an election—the five had a good laugh at that one—it might become a *cause célèbre*; a useful distraction from bigger issues dogging them.

It was complicated, and so unpredictable. The Canadian government could always refuse to extradite. The border agreement was not intended to cover libel, and the *Spotlight* had a reputation for accuracy. But would this new government, this untested True North Party, wish to take such a stand? Especially as some of its own supporters, Americans *and* Canadians, were named. No matter how you cut it, they would be rolling the dice against bankruptcy and imprisonment.

It went further though. The unsolved deaths of four journalists in the United States and two others in England—each of whom had recently written about the American government and its supporters—had caused a deep chill. Canada's long, porous border offered little protection.

Plenty had been written on the growing role of dark money, extreme religion and ultra-nationalism; the connections between them, and the increasingly violent tactics employed to further their interests and silence critics. Did the world need another exposé, the five had asked themselves? Not more of the same, they agreed. But this story wasn't. It described specific incidents tied to specific individuals in meticulous detail, corroborated by witnesses to the crime or its planning—corruption of justice, violent intimidation and murder.

But if witnesses couldn't be named because they could no longer be protected, their statements were of minimal value. A 'confidential source' or a 'witness who does not wish to be identified' was easily dismissed as more fake news.

They'd opted to wait. "Two more months," Simone had agreed reluctantly. The thought of an election being fought without these facts appalled her. Details of illegal, abhorrent acts not reaching voters and the remaining independent media.

"What would Sagan do?" she'd asked herself. Over and over, for four long weeks, until she knew. Back in Toronto now, she announced her decision.

"I'm prepared to take the risk. We'll publish under my name, on my blog. The *Canadian Spotlight* can link to it if you wish. But nobody else needs to be involved."

The others protested immediately. When the uproar subsided, she spoke again.

"You have young families. Assets. This publication means a lot, to a lot of people. It's a livelihood for dozens now. Most of my assets are tied up in non-redeemable 20-year solar co-op shares. The first won't come due for 12 years!" She laughed. Alone.

"The house is Ron's. The cabin is Ron's. So much for the liberated woman, eh! They can take my bikes, but I'll use the good one for my escape." This got a few smiles.

"I saw that!" she said, getting a chuckle from everyone.

"I have to do this. If there's the smallest chance it will stop this slide into fascism, oligarchy—*The Handmaid's Tale*—I'm throwing my chips in. Hero, or martyr."

A long silence followed. Each was thinking. *Do I join her? How do we stop her?* It was the lawyer who spoke first.

"I get it," Emma Kazmersky said. "I could never do it. But I'm glad as hell you will. So I want to help. *Pro bono!*" She smiled.

She advised Simone to wait four more days. "I'll shake down some people on how to delay extradition. *Extraordinary rendition*, more like. Be ready to vanish on short notice, Simone, and keep moving!"

"Alright Emma. I know how to keep moving. I love you guys. This is your story as much as mine, but I'll wear it."

A Kinder, Gentler America?

I n the summer of the election year, a Democratic victory seemed
certain. The administration was deeply unpopular; its list of
unethical and illegal acts long; its list of blunders longer. Its
dance with extremists had pushed some lifetime Republicans to
leave the party entirely.

The Democrats took away from their surprise defeat in 2016
that simply being a moderate, progressive party was not enough.
Not without a serious plan to address the deep grievances and
fears of the many who found themselves marginalized, abandoned
by the global economy and suspicious of 'elites'.

Trust us, we're the good guys wouldn't fly any better now than
it had then.

The 2020 Democratic platform was deep, detailed, positive,
and built from the bottom up. Not just to appeal to voters
lost in 2016, but actually designed by them. This was a plan
to rebuild manufacturing, revive agriculture, clean up America's
multiple toxic sites, and create employment in clean energy, land
restoration and efficient transportation infrastructure. Above all,
it was unabashedly pro-climate action. Because that's what people
were finally demanding.

Four years of alternating droughts, flash floods, forest fires
and coastline incursion was taking a massive psychological toll,
and had become an undeniable economic burden. If there was
one moment that had brought many reluctant Americans around

to understanding climate breakdown, it was Hurricane Frieda, the monster which hit Houston in early October.

When the category five-plus storm made landfall, watchers knew it would be far worse than Harvey, in 2017. The city of 7 million people was situated on flat land; heavily paved, apart from its creeks, rivers and suburban lawns. Its flood defences remained inadequate, despite Harvey's warning.

The impact of the 25 foot storm surge on the Houston Ship Channel—home to multiple ports, and mile upon mile of oil, gas and chemical refinement facilities—matched the worst predictions. Ships were ripped from their moorings, and most of the storage tanks and pipelines became untethered, first tumbling inland into residential neighbourhoods, then back out into the channel and on to Galveston Bay, along with an estimated 100 million gallons of chemicals and oil.

The resulting shutdown of all affected industries, pipelines, roads and railways had a massive impact on the economy of the region and the country. Gas prices surged, and shortages led to lineups at pumps across the nation, with waits of up to two days. Strict rationing had to be introduced. Airlines were forced to ground most of their planes, as jet fuel prices quadrupled, and a refuelling quota system was introduced.

In greater Houston, freeways and roads were undermined, forcing indefinite closure for structural inspections. Over one million people were left homeless. It was America's worst natural disaster in history, and surpassed Japan's 2011 tsunami and nuclear explosion as the world's most expensive.

Overnight, the Republican platform was modified to declare climate change a significant threat to the American economy, and a hastily assembled plan was released. Coal was notably absent. Instead, it touted nuclear energy and ethanol as 'made in America' solutions.

Just hours before Hurricane Frieda, with 15 days to the election, Simone posted her article. To her dismay, it received far less attention than she expected, despite the allegations of Oval

Office-sanctioned murder. A *Guardian* reporter was one of the few who pursued it—once all Frieda questions had been exhausted.

More lying foreign media, was the response.

"Nasty woman," tweeted the president.

Any reporter who pursued Simone's allegations received a deluge of death threats. Attending a Republican rally, even venturing into 'red' districts, became dangerous.

One week before the election, a devastated Simone received a registered letter at her home, on the letterhead of a prominent Toronto law firm. It instructed her to remove the libellous article from her blog site and informed her that a lawsuit had been launched jointly by six people identified in her article, through an Atlanta firm. She had 48 hours to issue an unqualified retraction and apology. Failure to do so would trigger a $50 million suit against her in an Atlanta court.

Time to execute Emma's strategy. Within 24 hours of signing for the letter, Simone would leave home in one of three cars departing simultaneously. Only the drivers should be visible. All cell phones, GPS or other tracking systems must be off. The car in which she was hidden would travel to a friend's farm by an indirect route with no stops. All cars would be old ones, with no onboard navigation or communication.

She would stay at the farm for a week at most, before moving on to the next in a series of 'safe houses': cottages and fishing camps across Quebec's near north. Ron's knowledge of remote, off-grid locations was vast, and his friendships with their owners strong. Each location was given a code name and each had a contact who could get there to relay information to and from Simone. But the order in which they would be visited would be chosen at random, Simone drawing the next one out of a bag as needed, then relaying it to Ron, who was in constant contact with Emma.

Keep moving. Throughout the late fall and early winter, she did.

They had ruled out using their own cabin from the outset. Too obvious, they felt, even though its location was known to few, and finding it was complicated. But these would be resourceful people, possibly aided by Canadian intelligence or law enforcement.

On January 12th, Ron's birthday, he and Emma agreed that the post-election chaos south of the border presented a window of opportunity. No extradition request had been made, and it was not likely to happen until the political and security crisis settled. Ron could take Simone to the cabin, where she would stay until further notice.

Access was limited to a single rural lane, with a gate. Followed by another narrow lane, which was now booby-trapped—a deep trench with thin plywood and earth spread across it. Old fashioned, but enough to disable a vehicle and make a racket. An infra-red alarm system had also been installed.

Simone would be ready to slip out the back into the woods. From there, she could travel for hours along ski trails invisible from the air, and known to few.

Should someone make a stealth approach on one of those trails, by ATV or snowmobile, they risked being garrotted by the wires Ron had strung between trees on the two paths to the cabin.

"Anyone who tries to play rough with my wife will get what's coming!" he announced to Emma, who cringed, then smiled.

Knowing Simone's biathlon history, however brief and long ago, Ron had suggested bringing her a rifle. "Once a good shot, always—"

"No!" Simone said firmly. "A gun is like a hammer. When you have one, everything looks like a nail. Including friends and family." He took her point.

Simone had shared what she could with her nearest neighbours. They knew what was at stake. They also provided a way for Emma, Ron, Jacinthe or her parents in Montreal to alert her if she was being sought—officially.

Her phone would remain off, as it had since late October. No exceptions. Though there was still no reliable service at the cabin, all it would take was a few seconds of roaming, or one short text message, for a tower to register her location.

Switching to Glide

Tokyo, November 1, 2020

The Foreign Correspondent's Club was packed. Any mention of the Titanic—even halfway around the world and more than a century later—attracts the press.

It was a publicity stunt, to showcase the latest energy generation and storage technology being built in Fukushima, and highlight potential applications, ranging from small villages and boats to—one day—large ocean vessels. It was also a chance to help an old friend.

"I am excited to announce today our sponsorship of a world record attempt." Jenny had not stood in front of the media for years. Though she hadn't missed it, her experience showed.

"The Clean Atlantic Crossing will take place in July, seven months from now. A Canadian vessel, designed and piloted by a former classmate of mine, will retrace the route of the Titanic. The vessel will be crewed by just one person, and powered entirely by pollution-free, renewable propulsion systems. They include a solar sail and a unique mast that harnesses wind—which you will hear about in a minute—along with a pressurized air chamber, in combination with an innovative pump and micro-turbine. These last three are manufactured in Fukushima Prefecture."

"Now…" announced Jenny, pausing for effect, "through video hook-up to Saint John, New Brunswick… here is the smartest engineer I know… Mr. Paul Racine."

"You'll do a better job avoiding icebergs than the Titanic did, right Paul?" she joked as his face appeared on a large screen. The English-speakers laughed politely.

"Of course, Jenny, er, Ms. Fung," a smiling Paul replied after a brief time delay. "*Switching to Glide*, my boat, is equipped with modern iceberg detection. And I will not order 'full steam ahead', unlike the captain of the Titanic!" Paul laughed. "Besides, I have nobody to give orders *to*. It's a solo crossing. I plan to not only stay afloat but set a speed record for a zero-carbon boat!"

"Now, if you're ready with the video there in Tokyo, allow me to describe the SolarSail, the unique PowerPole, and how they are networked in a system I designed in collaboration with that brilliant woman in front of you."

At Loose Ends

Washington, DC, November 15, 2020

T he few personal effects Elmore had in his office fit into a single leather carryall, his spare shirts and suit in a matching garment bag—all he'd needed for a term of service.

Four years. He was amazed he'd kept his job that long, what with the revolving door and the media howling for his head. Now, suddenly it was over. In the midst of the mayhem, here he was out of a job and under suspicion.

Big deal! He'd lived his whole life under suspicion. Or feeling like he was. Like everything he did wasn't enough.

But this was different. This was murder. "Conducting a covert campaign to silence persistent opponents and protect the president."

Not quite right, you little Canadian bitch. This wasn't about the president. Maybe it had been at first, but it hadn't been for ages. His days were always numbered. Presidents can be swapped out. His allegiance, their allegiance, was to a bigger goal: a country of small government and the freedom to succeed. Where Americans ran their own lives. Rise to the top, if you have what it takes. Choose to sink or swim. Not rely on handouts that keep half the country in poverty or addiction. Talent and hard work—that's what mattered!

Under suspicion? A good legal team would take care of that. No job? A new one was easy to find. The murder allegation would raise his standing in some places. He didn't need a job right now anyway. He had one waiting.

She was a smart cookie, he conceded her that. Arrogant though, from day one. Didn't have time for him. And if she had, would it have mattered? It's not like *she* had anything to offer. She came and went, like all reporters. Still, though, why had he left her to last? Bleeding heart journalist. Holier than everyone. Where were you raised? How was junior high for you? What choices did you have to make to survive?

Simone Cohen. Why *had* he held off for so long?

Sagan Cleveland, though—he hated that one. So comfortable in his skin. Couldn't faze him. Everywhere you looked, the showboat kept popping up. Didn't he know who he was up against? Tried scaring him off. Several times, but he just kept at it. If he'd stopped then, they could have left him alone. Bad enough attacking big oil. But no, he found religion, didn't he? Those folks are ours! Those votes are ours! Start losing their support, and then what? He'd heard the recording. He'd read Fred's notes, from New Orleans. Sagan Cleveland sealed his fate then and there. But Elmore kept his hands clean. No trail, no trace.

Opening his locked desk drawer, he removed the only three things it had ever contained. From the bottle he took a pill and popped it in his mouth. Taking a sip of water, he grimaced and swallowed. Then he picked up the memory stick and held it for a moment in his right hand. Smiling, he slipped it into his breast pocket. Finally, he flattened the much-fingered sheet of paper on his desk for a last look at his handiwork. His special list. Every name crossed off but one.

Mighty Mouse.

More Than Hanging Chads

It was 2000 all over again. Both parties had brought in a phalanx of lawyers, to prove they were the rightful victors. Unlike 2000, however—a time of relative calm—this was a nation divided. The previous twelve years had polarized Americans in a way not seen since the Civil War. Some saw another coming. Riots broke out in more than a dozen large cities, where crowds felt the election was being stolen in front of them.

Simone knew every detail, courtesy of the radio. She'd always loved the radio: *Ottawa Morning, The Current, All in a Day, The News at Six* and *As it Happens* on CBC; *All Things Considered* on National Public Radio, the one non-corporate American source; and of course Radio-Canada, the French-language CBC, which often pursued stories the English media wouldn't touch. With no cell phone or internet, and only occasionally some television or a newspaper brought to her by Ron and the small group of trusted friends who sheltered her and kept her moving, her radio was her lifeline. Long live the radio.

In Atlanta, a pitched battle was raging. The National Guard had been called in to protect stores and homes in wealthier areas. The courthouse was under siege. For Americans, it was a mess. For Simone, a reprieve.

Using a secure satellite telephone Ron carried, she and Emma reviewed the options. "Stay put," Emma advised, "even though extradition doesn't seem imminent."

"One more thing," Emma suddenly remembered. "Someone's trying to reach you. He said it was highly sensitive. I told him I'd try to pass on his message, but by no means would I let him contact you directly. The name was... here it is, Antoine—"

"Stillwell?" Simone blurted. "Tell him to come to Ottawa. Ron will get him over to Gatineau with a map. Tell him to bring warm clothes."

"Warm clothes? What is this..."

"Big. Very big. It's related to the *Dirty Deeds* story. He's been investigating Sagan's death since the start. Freelance. Antoine believes the suicide verdict was a cover-up. Tell Ron Thursday at noon at Healey."

"Alright," Emma said skeptically. "Noon, Thursday, at Healey. Wherever that is."

"Perfect. And Emma... I'm out of dark chocolate. It's an emergency."

"Now *that* I understand." she laughed.

China Syndrome

Things started to go wrong at Reactor Number 4 in late February, ten years after the tsunami. The molten core—which had been kept stable and cool by surrounding the tangled mess with the world's most expensive ice wall—had begun to heat up. Images appeared to indicate a shift. But it was anybody's guess whether the engineered floor was intact enough to keep the core from melting its way out. None of the cameras or robots lasted long enough to maintain observation. Safety crews had to make do with occasional, short bursts of footage. Consistent images for comparative purposes did not exist.

Jiro had been alerted immediately as part of a new protocol he insisted on. In 2011, it took far too long to get messages directly to key decision makers, and what was passed on did not adequately stress the severity and urgency. He was up, dressed and into the emergency room in under 15 minutes.

"Governor. If this is not controlled quickly, the core is headed to China."

"More like Brazil," Jiro replied. The chief engineer looked puzzled.

"Sorry," he added quickly. "I have a tendency to make jokes at difficult moments. A trait learned from a friend."

"Of course sir. Brazil. Heh, heh!"

"Now walk me through the isolation measures."

Three days of intense procedures were required to get enough coolant around and underneath the fuel lump. Three days of high stakes maneuvers, and a massive mobilization of people and equipment. The world's media pressed to get as close as possible, their unauthorized drones battling for air space.

"That's 10 billion yen we'll never see again," Jiro was heard to mutter. "Let's send the bill to the power company and see if they pay this time."

Crisis averted, but Jiro knew it was only a matter of time.

Cabin Fever

Simone stayed as informed as ever. What else was there to do? Load the stove, melt snow for water, read, go for a snowshoe and listen to the radio. In two languages.

Street violence had subsided, but no fewer than 12 states were holding plebiscites on secession from the Union. Houston's oil refineries were beyond repair. Abandoned. Oil companies were exploring other cities as replacement locations. Canadian producers, after 18 months of low prices, were working to get bitumen production out of mothballs, now that a barrel was hovering around $200. The lack of adequate pipelines—long debated and protested, but never built—meant more shipping by train. People all along the rail lines were planning blockades.

Climate activists and opposition parties in Canada were arguing that this was the moment for a massive investment in renewable generation. If there had to be any movement of energy, they declared, it should be through an upgraded electrical grid—a high voltage grid with smart switching technology—not high carbon fuels. Electric vehicle producers had ramped up production, but they were as hobbled as anyone by the cost of fuel for making and shipping cars.

Overseas, the French had restarted five nuclear plants along the Rhône. Over half the national grid was now supplied by renewables, but the rapid shift to electrification for heating and transport in Europe had created pressure to bring some nuclear back online. The plan was to run them in winter and spring only, when demand for heating was high, and reactors could be safely cooled. Plants would need to be monitored extremely carefully in light of low water levels. The near-meltdown at Tricastin in August 2020 had left everybody spooked.

Food rioting raged in many African and Middle Eastern countries; shades of 2008. The Arab Spring, Simone recalled wistfully. Numerous states were teetering on the brink. Force was being used to quell dissent and protect important infrastructure.

Men with tough talk and easy answers float to the top, history told her.

There was good news out of Quebec City, though. Les Démocrates Vertes ("Les DV")—a coming together of young Parti Québécois members with disaffected Liberals and a resurgent Green Party—won power in the snap February election. Their rise was explained by many factors, above all a desire to counter the reactionary new federal government. One of the DV's first acts was to assert Quebec's unique control over certain international affairs, notably immigration and trade.

Disgusted by how easily Canada's parliament had acceded to a series of White House demands when the True North government took power in October 2019, millions of Québécois took to the streets. The DV government rapidly passed a law rejecting the new Canada-US Security Agreement which granted Washington access to Canadians' private information. Also included in the DV law was a rejection of the even newer Extradition Protocol.

It was finally safe to come out of hiding, Emma felt, as long as Simone stayed in Quebec. "With the crisis in Washington, even if it's resolved soon, you're as safe in Montreal as at your cabin," she advised. "Besides, I think you're going stir crazy!"

Simone agreed. "Better to be dragged off by Marines than in a straitjacket. At least I'll get a show trial."

"Good!" said Emma. "You'll need your humour for a while yet. The lawyers in Atlanta and Toronto are working to get you arrested by the RCMP. That'll cause a ruckus, I can assure you. We're ready to take it public."

"If we have to," Simone clarified.

Emma hesitated, before responding. "Yes, only if."

"Though you should know," she paused, "four others have joined the libel suit. And another thing: the *Spotlight* has assembled a dossier to substantiate the article. *Your* article. They added Antoine's material. It's massive, so we have it uploaded and ready to go live the second you and I authorize it. We felt comfortable writing a piece that comments on the evidence. Dozens of American outlets created links to your allegations without consequences last time. Apart from being forced to remove them, which they took their sweet time doing.

"Oh, if you missed it on the radio, Miami police made an arrest in that 2019 Jacksonville murder, the CNN reporter. They were shamed into it, despite the governor's interference. They've fingered the killer, but not the people who paid him."

"Good to know," Simone said bitterly. "Though the damage is done. You can't revive a dead journalist or restore a family. Or un-chill the climate for reporting."

"What do you think of Quebec City?" Simone said, after a long silence.

"I love the Winter Carnival!"

"Smart ass. You know what I mean. I was hoping to visit my daughter."

"Springtime in Quebec City!" Emma chanted. "Just keep a very low profile. No cellphone. If you're going to post anything, use a public computer. And never the same place twice. Also... get a pair of those big glasses with the false moustache."

Simone laughed. "Thanks Emma. I owe you."

"Nope, I owe *you*. We *all* owe you!"

Lightning Rod

B y 2021, the Four Elements Party was in power in five prefectures and had elected 63 deputies to the National Diet. Fukushima was the proving ground.

Construction of new housing was progressing. Over 100,000 new units in apartments and townhouses had been built to Energy-Positive standards. A Cool Roof policy ensured that any new building or renovation incorporated reflective material, solar panels or natural 'green' roofs. More subsidized housing had been built: close to 20,000 units. People displaced by the twin catastrophe continued to receive special treatment, particularly seniors and single parents.

Improved public transportation was now available in rural areas, and greater frequency had been achieved in towns and cities. Electric vehicle adoption had reached 45 percent of private cars in the prefecture, and 90 percent for municipal and institutional fleets.

There had been a modest return of manufacturing to the region, though larger economic factors continued to act as a brake. Namely the exchange rate and high wages relative to neighbouring countries. Makers of specialty materials for Energy-Positive buildings were doing especially well, along with niche producers of ultra-efficient heating and cooling units and components for renewable power systems.

Jenny's efforts continued to bear fruit: over 150 people were employed making micro turbines and 100 more building compressed air systems.

Jobs had been created in retrofitting older buildings and constructing dedicated cycling infrastructure. To the amazement of many, a local bicycle manufacturer had opened: an industry lost decades earlier to Taiwan and mainland China. They specialized in electric bikes for transporting children and cargo, and a unique model for taking seniors on outings.

Efforts to label Four Elements a failure rang hollow in most people's ears, but opposition parties had not stopped trying. Oddly, a growing wedge was the inability of government, any government, to stabilize the Daiichi reactors. That Jiro had been saddled with this failure was one of the ironies of politics.

"When you're in power long enough, you wear everything," Simone had warned.

Unknown to most, Jiro had been visiting the exclusion zone regularly. He felt compelled to see and measure how effective the clean-up efforts had been. He wore a radiation dosimeter and was careful to respect recommended annual limits. One day he hoped to witness the safe return of citizens to their ancestral villages. It would be a meaningful legacy.

On the morning after presiding over New Year's Day 2021 celebrations, Jiro visited his doctor to discuss chest pains he was feeling when climbing stairs. After several tests he received the diagnosis: lung cancer, likely incurable. It would progress slowly until the pain became unbearable. Jiro told nobody, but curtailed his exclusion zone visits.

"Avoid unnecessary stress," the doctor had said. Seeing him laugh, she joined in as she recalled who he was.

Like anyone in public office he faced endless demands and expectations. He had always believed he dealt with that kind of pressure well. It was mostly a matter of setting priorities, and knowing when to turn things off and go home. What he found hardest was the criticism. Some of it was shockingly personal. Simone had warned him, and offered good advice.

"People will blame you, insult you and occasionally praise you, but remember it is rarely actually about you. It stems from their own fears and prejudices. People believe they have no power over their lives, so they go after those who do, or appear to."

Looking for You

Quebec City, July 5, 2021

Simone had been in Quebec City for six weeks. Forty-two days, at the suburban home of Jacinthe's partner Isabelle, and she hadn't worn out her welcome. Jacinthe and Izzy —a champion mountain bike racer, now owner of a popular bike shop—made it clear she could stay as long as she wished. Or had to. Simone felt loved and she felt safe from extradition here, and yet, she felt like a fugitive. A fugitive until the threat of arrest vanished for good, or she faced charges head on and proved herself innocent—by demonstrating every allegation she'd written was factual.

Recently, Simone had been denounced as a terrorist by several FullRight news sites. Terrorist was a loaded term, its definition greatly expanded in the U.S. and Canada. Punishment for aiding and abetting a terrorist had been similarly enhanced, while the right to a public trial on terrorism-related charges had been curtailed.

Simone's personal story was now widely known, meaning she was too. In Quebec, where she had been granted sanctuary, the government and media treated her as a hero, lauding her stance against powerful people in Ottawa and Washington.

Though she felt comfortable circulating freely here in Quebec City, she preferred to stay anonymous. You could do wonders with summer hats and glasses, she found. A bike helmet with wraparound shades worked particularly well, as she experienced again today.

Several days a week, Simone rode into Old Quebec on the hybrid bicycle Izzy had fitted up for her. She would eat lunch with Jacinthe at one of the several cafes near her workplace, then take a longer route home. Today's trip into the city had been particularly hot, yet she'd done it faster than ever. She was getting her legs back!

She chose an indoor table out of the sun, sitting with her back to the entrance. Switching her helmet and shades for a Nordiques ball cap, she tugged the peak low over her face. Then, knowing she had plenty of time, she dove into that day's *Guardian* on the tablet Izzy had lent her.

"See-moan Cohen?"

Startled by the voice beside her, Simone had the presence of mind to pretend not to have heard. Not to be who this woman assumed she was.

"See-moan?" The woman repeated. *Southern accent.*

Scalp tingling, she turned slowly, lifting her head just enough to examine the speaker. *Fifties, short, fit, plain.*

Directly in front of her now, the woman showed her palms, then slowly opened her purse. *Unarmed. Perhaps.*

"Do I know you?" Simone said as casually as she could, glancing sideways toward the door.

"No," the woman replied calmly, "but you know my former boss."

A jolt shot through Simone.

"I'm not on his side," the woman quickly added. Simone nodded warily.

"Brittany Coates." The woman extended her hand formally. "I spent four years working with Elmore Lambert." Registering Simone's reaction, she continued. "Figured the name would be a shock. Four years pretending to be on his team."

"May I?" she asked, pointing to an empty chair. Simone nodded.

"Let's just say a lot of people in government felt it our duty to keep an eye on that administration. Sometimes, you have to disobey to be patriotic."

Simone nodded again, trying to parse where this Brittany Coates was going.

"Look, I'm not going to beat around the bush. I'm way outside my jurisdiction. I tried more conventional means. You don't check your email, it seems. Nor voice mail. You're no longer at home. Nor your parents' place. I even tried commenting on your blog. Seems you have a blocking device. The word 'kill' gets blocked, is that the trick?"

Simone could feel sweat rolling down her sides. "A filter," she said quietly, her voice cracking. "To screen out abuse." Her eyes darted around the room.

"I finally figured that out. You see… " It was Brittany's turn to glance around. "I need to warn you about an imminent risk. I'll be blunt—Elmore Lambert intends to kill you. We lost track of him two days ago. We think he's searching for a cabin you own. We don't know if he's tracked you to your daughter's home here. That took us awhile, what with her partner owning it. And we have more resources than him, now that he's lost his access. But there are still people who'll help him."

After a pause, Simone spoke slowly and deliberately.

"It seems I have little choice but to take you at your word, Brittany. I can't think of any other explanation for you tracking me. Unarmed. Unless you're the advance party for my extradition." She watched Brittany's eyes as she said this. They had stayed locked on hers.

"Ma'am. I can assure you that if extradition was my goal, I would be male, six foot five, with three colleagues of similar stature waiting in a big black SUV with tinted windows around the corner from your daughter's home. We would haul you out of bed at 3 a.m. and drive straight to the border. A special lane would open and nobody would hear from you again. Unless we wanted them to."

Simone's ears were ringing.

"I came to warn you, not arrest you. I've done what I can to prevent the new people from acting on an order issued some months ago. But that won't hold. More importantly, we have a deranged man who has killed before."

"Sagan?"

Brittany flinched at the name, but said nothing.

"Did he kill Sagan Cleveland?" Simone had dropped her voice, but it couldn't mask her anger.

"We were not able to prevent that one," Brittany replied, looking briefly at the ground. "I am sorry. It was that act which showed us he had moved from intimidation to... a higher degree of violence."

"But can you confirm he killed Sagan?"

"I can confirm he did *not*." Simone wasn't expecting this response.

"However," Brittany continued, "I *can* confirm he made the contractual arrangements. Proving he was more dangerous than initial assessments indicated."

Simone was growing lightheaded. "What now, then? Where's the safest place to be?" Then a more frightening question came to her.

"My family!" Her voice had grown louder. "Are they at risk?"

"He has never targeted family. His gripe is with those who cross him."

"That's a relief." Simone said, without sarcasm.

"I wouldn't spend more than tonight at your daughter's though. The extradition order could go through any time, though we can't be sure when your own police will act on it."

Brittany surveyed the near-empty cafe. "I shouldn't even be here."

An energetic shift was occurring, her professional demeanour melting.

Simone's mind was racing. She needed to get out and working.

"Ms. Cohen," Brittany said tentatively, "I have seen and done things I'm not proud of. You have to prove your loyalty when you go under cover. You do things you never thought you were capable of, to prevent worse ones. I didn't expect Elmore Lambert's 'special list' meant murder. He kept that list to himself, and his intentions. He only referred to it. People he would 'take care of personally.'

"It was when your friend Mr. Cleveland died, in that gruesome way, that I, we, understood how far he might go. In those last days, when it was clear our unit would be wound up, he was muttering things. By the end, it was just me and him. That's how I got your name. Though he never actually said it. Just gave enough hints. He's a vain man. I believe he was telling me how powerful he was."

"*That's* how you concluded he intends to kill me?" Simone said, her voice rising. "Hints!"

"Yes," Brittany nodded. "But you'd have to be stupid not to reach that conclusion."

She reached into her purse. "It's all on here." She offered a memory stick to Simone.

"Listen for yourself. There are two sound files. One referring to Mr. Cleveland's murder. One, to his plans for you. There's other useful material on there too. Do what you will with it."

Simone looked carefully at the stick, then accepted it as one might poison. She placed it quickly in her courier pack. Then she looked Brittany straight in the eyes as she spoke. Her voice firm, words carefully chosen.

"Thank you. That's not easy to say, knowing what you might have done. Odious acts for odious people. Knowing you might have prevented a dear friend's death."

Brittany held her gaze, nodding only slightly.

"But I admire your courage. I've often wondered how people can go under cover. It has to mess with your head. Your soul, even. So I'm thanking you for any good you were able to do. And could still."

"You're welcome," replied Brittany, in the quietest of whispers.

"Just tell me, though, these files: will releasing them put your life, or anyone else's at risk? I won't put a life at risk to save mine."

Before Brittany could answer, Simone's eyes swivelled toward the door, where Jacinthe stood, looking puzzled. Brittany turned to examine Jacinthe, then back to face Simone.

"I'll be fine," Brittany said, her eyes empty. "We'll be fine. We take risks."

Abruptly, she pushed back her chair and stood to shake Simone's hand. Then, waving to Jacinthe to come closer, she addressed her directly.

"Young lady," she said with surprising gentleness. "You have an amazing mother. Get her far away."

Mother and daughter watched as Brittany strode briskly into the street.

"Who was *that*?!" asked Jacinthe, confused by what had just transpired.

"It's a long story," Simone said, gathering her things. "But not here. I have to get to my laptop. I'll fill you in tonight." With a peck on the cheek she handed Jacinthe a ten-dollar bill and slipped out.

"Like the wind," said a baffled Jacinthe.

Brother, Where Were You?

Fukushima City, July 2021

J iro sensed trouble when he learned 18 months earlier of Katsuo's appointment to the Electrical Security Commission. Its agenda seemed clear—to assess whether any of the 24 reactors shut down in 2011 could be safely restarted—but only on the surface. Other interests would be at work.

"The grid is teetering," Katsuo had just declared at a live, televised release of its report. "More capacity is needed, and quickly."

What would take years to build out through renewables could be switched on in a matter of months by restarting just five nuclear plants, its study determined, with a national investment of no more than 400 billion yen. Some of which could be found by cancelling new off-shore wind projects. Refurbishment and safety checks would be performed on the five plants judged most ready and safe. Two were close to Tokyo—one of these in Fukushima.

The government of Fukushima was opposed, Katsuo noted, but the governor should consider the interest of all Japanese. He must show leadership with the security of the country at stake.

"Leadership?!" Jiro shouted at the television in his office. He had not been invited to the press conference where the commission released its report. Provocatively, they had chosen to hold it right under his nose, at a local hotel.

"Supporting a reckless, politically motivated, rapid restart is leadership?" he fumed. "Spending billions of taxpayers' money, and suspending renewable initiatives is leadership? And I am supposed to accept this madness?"

His staff had never seen him this way. When he announced he was heading to the venue to get his views on the record, his press advisor and security guard tried to dissuade him. Failing, they chose to accompany him. They arrived as Katsuo was being scrummed in the hotel lobby. Jiro strode straight for him, in time to hear his broadside.

"I am ashamed to say my brother's cowardice betrays the people he represents. One accident must not condemn 50 years of safe operation. It is time now for a phased restart. This of course, takes courage."

"You!" Jiro shouted as he barged blindly into the scrum, pushing aside anyone blocking the path to his brother. "How dare you speak of cowardice and courage! A man whose life has been spent hiding behind nationalist myths."

"Ah, and here he is now, the brave governor," Katsuo said.

Standing less than an arm's length away, straining against the security staff, Jiro levelled his arm at the smirking Katsuo.

"Where were you when the tsunami hit? I do not remember seeing you helping displaced citizens; those you now pretend to speak for. I do not recall you arranging housing or raising money for widows and seniors. Quite the contrary, brave Katsuo. What I remember most are your efforts to protect your party and the power company officials with whom you play golf, and who visit the same temple."

Katsuo used his right hand to mimic an orchestra leader conducting Jiro's tirade.

"I remember your brave stand to return people to the exclusion zone before it was safe," Jiro shouted. "Your threats to cancel support for those not willing. But you, I do not recall seeing at your family's village, with a geiger counter and a camera."

Jiro paused to catch his breath. "No," he continued, as Katsuo appeared about to respond. "Not on any of the visits I took into the hot zone to map ongoing contamination did I see you, brave brother. You must have been busy, writing your report, to support the conclusion made in Tokyo before the study had even begun!"

"That is nonsense," Katsuo began, looking to his left at the other members of the commission who had been watching in stunned silence. "Our report is independently—"

When he turned back to the journalists, he realized nobody was listening. There was a murmur, followed by someone shouting for an ambulance.

"The governor needs air. Give him room!"

Jiro, clutching his chest had dropped to his knees. A TV reporter was propping him up, waving away the other cameras. "Give him space to lie down!"

Katsuo took a step towards his brother, then stepped back and adjusted his tie.

Jenny received a call while inspecting a shipment headed for Laos. She was at the hospital in under 20 minutes. Anna and Yuki received the news that evening from the school headmistress.

Jenny's email to Simone was rejected. Inbox full.

In for a Penny

S imone had prepared her blog months earlier. The evidence long pointed to this. Also the testimonials. From people who had been in rooms where things were said. Trusted people. Loyal to the party, their bosses, the police, the intelligence agencies that employed them. People who one day reached a point where loyalty was no longer enough to excuse what they had seen, heard, done or been ordered to do. At what point does an oath, a confidentiality agreement, an expectation of loyalty lose its value? Where is that breaking point, when every mirror is looking at you, and you don't dare face it?

Simone had witnesses and statements, photos and coroner's reports. Police reports too—the near-final versions, just before they were changed. What she did not have was a single person willing to go on record. A moral stand is one thing, the courage to put your name to it is another. Jobs, memberships, marriages, families, lives—any or all are at risk when the whistleblower goes public. It had prevented her from publishing many stories. Truth is not the same as proof.

"We need something stronger, Simone!" The refrain of the lawyers.

Now it was different. There were no lawyers. Just herself, knowing that all she'd written was true, and that the public interest must be served. The only tests that mattered. Brittany's sound files were the missing piece. Her photos of hit lists, dates

493

of meetings... those were useful, but how can anyone deny the voice of Elmore Lambert giving directions to cover up Sagan's murder, and boasting of his plans to carry out hers?

Simone would add these to the dossier compiled by her *Spotlight* colleagues; drawing heavily on Antoine Stillwell's meticulous work.

There was the Detroit Police's 'draft' report, with tracked, time-stamped corrections 'suggested' by the FBI. Important things had been removed. Inspector Williams' original notes and photos made this clear. The blanket had not been taken to the site by a suicidal Sagan. It was purchased a week earlier at a Walmart. CCTV footage gave a clear image of the purchaser. Footage lost, and now found. The gas can in the photo was different from the one shown as evidence. And the medallion? Sagan's in every way but the miniature swastika and stylized FR—for FullRight—scratched on the back beside the dedication from Isong. It would have been added just before the match was struck. With Sagan unconscious from the sedative he'd been given when he answered the door. Trusting to the end.

Finally, there was the drone footage made by the FullRight lieutenant contracted to kill Sagan. He had a thing about recording his work, it seemed. Later, when he realized his days were numbered, he had provided the file to the Detroit police as part of his appeal for amnesty. Everything was in high resolution.

Simone did not need to change much of her pre-written blog. Just a few words. 'Allegations of committing acts of physical violence' became 'proof of violent intimidation and murder.' She named Elmore for what he was. Then went one step further.

To her list of more than two dozen people described in her original *Spotlight* article as the architects, financiers, accessories and facilitators to a series of illegal and violent acts stretching back over nearly four years, she would add the word *murder*. One obvious murderer, and many who had made it possible. Some were still in office, part of the power-sharing administration still being negotiated. They would dismiss Elmore as a rogue operator and spare no effort to defend their good names and destroy hers.

By destroying her.

Simone's thumb hovered above the trackpad, the cursor arrow on the "publish" button. Her post would appear in the morning, unleashing events she could only guess at. Once published, that was it. *Breathe in, breathe out.* When you commit, you commit.

America's most expensive lawyers would be on the case within hours of the blog going live. Canada's too. Three on the list were True North government ministers. She would have no protection from a deranged man already in the country, or RCMP officers under orders from people you could not refuse. At 7 a.m. tomorrow, the hunt for "terrorist Simone Cohen" would begin.

When she pressed on the trackpad with her thumb, the sound was barely audible. The days of making herself heard were over Simone understood. Now her freedom, her life even, demanded the utmost discretion.

Suiting Up

Jiro's stitches had ripped. He could tell. The sharp pain, and now the oozing blood. But it was the only way to get into the suit—the awkward contortions. Nothing could be done now, anyhow. And it was too late to matter.

"Breathe in, sir. It's going to be tight. Closing up the torso section."

He complied with a deep, painful breath, holding it until they said to exhale. Working quickly and quietly, his three young collaborators took the final steps to seal him in. It had been harder and slower than expected.

"The aging knight, donning his armour for battle," Jiro joked, his smile rapidly replaced by a grimace. So much pain, despite the anesthetic.

"More like Iron Man," one assistant replied, the others nodding.

Ten minutes left. If he wasn't ready, all was lost.

This will atone for my failures. My many shortcomings.

Rapidly, systematically, they guided him through the suit's features. He knew them by heart, of course, but only from the outside. This would be his one chance on the inside.

Flexing his right hand, he watched as the massive armoured glove opened and closed with a high-pitched whir of motors. Grasping a brick, he squeezed and felt it crumble.

The perimeter gate was open now, but not for long. Security would be working frantically to neutralize the hack.

"Get into the van, please. We have only a minute or two."

"Helmet now. Last step." Four capable hands placed it carefully and locked it in place. He heard the hiss and click. With the respirator on, he took a first breath of cool air. Enough for 20 minutes, he knew. Other systems would likely shut down by then anyway. Fried.

Seated in the cargo area, facing towards the back doors, he bowed his head to the three men who had built this special suit for him in secrecy and at great personal risk. He could no longer communicate with them. The suit did not include an audio system. There was no point. It was a one-way mission.

They would get the video stream, though. Confirming if he had pulled it off.

"*Gambatte kudasai!*" all three shouted together.

Through the radiation-resistant glass, he noted their deep, simultaneous bow.

Spy Novels

Seated at the kitchen table, Simone's laptop open in front of her, Jacinthe read carefully through the dossier her mother had uploaded a few hours earlier. The entire contents would go live in nine hours on Simone's blog site, courtesy of a programmed time delay. Seven o'clock—as people began to feed their morning news habit.

While Jacinthe read, Simone quietly ate her cold supper. The silence was broken sporadically by Jacinthe's gasps and curses. "May he rest in peace," she whispered, when she came to the video of Sagan's murder. She chose not to view it.

Simone would never have posted the video, if there had been a choice. But it had to go public, and this was the only way now, without involving others. She trusted Sagan would understand. This was her cross to bear.

"Vile, evil creature!" Jacinthe spat after hearing Elmore boast about Sagan's murder, and his plans for Simone.

"Maman," she said, pushing away the computer and fixing Simone with a stare. "You have to disappear. Deep cover," she added. "Somewhere nobody will guess. You can't tell anyone, or even send us messages. These people, with their connections and search engines, will scour the internet. They'll have drones looking anywhere you're connected to. Facial recognition from security cameras."

Simone nodded slowly. *Deep cover.* She was at a loss for where that might be, or how to reach it. "Where would you suggest?" she asked Jacinthe.

"You're not listening, Maman! If I know, or even think I do, it won't stay hidden."

"You think someone's going to pry it out of you?" Simone said without thinking. She knew the answer, and clearly her daughter did also.

"You've lived all over the world. You have friends everywhere. So think who—"

"I'm not putting a friend at risk just for me!" Simone protested.

"*Just* for me?" Jacinthe mocked. "Simone Cohen, admired by millions for her courage. Many would gladly return the favour. But you just need one."

"I can't!"

"Yes, you can. For Papa, me, your parents... everyone who has ever backed you. Give the rebellion a chance to make a difference."

Simone laughed. "You're mixing spy novels with Star Wars!"

"So I am," Jacinthe said frowning.

"Who do you think I should—"

"There you go again," said Jacinthe, her hands raised in frustration. "If I even thought I'd given you a clue, that's what I'd reveal when they tighten the thumb screws."

"Noooobody expects the Spanish Inquisition!" Simone chanted.

"Good," said Jacinthe, chuckling now. "Absurd humour for absurd times. Now go to bed, and while you're lying there unable to sleep, instead of thinking up radical plans for saving the world, think up one to save yourself. You've done your part for the world. Besides, the world will need you alive to clean up the mess in a few years."

"Years? I'm supposed to vanish for years?"

"Yep," said Jacinthe. "Hatred has a long half-life. And a lot of people have a hate on for you. Not just the one scumbag!" Simone could not argue with that.

They prepared for bed in silence, each wondering if this would be the last time they'd stand side by side at a bathroom mirror.

"Bonne nuit, maman. I love you." Jacinthe embraced her mother in a long, crushing hug. "You'll come up with a doozy. You always do."

Simone watched as her daughter walked into her bedroom and closed the door. Izzy had long ago gone to sleep. She rode each morning, before opening the shop.

As she lay in bed, her mind swirling, an envelope slid under her door. Something meant for later, Simone understood.

* * *

Undetected. Simone began the process of sifting, analyzing, calculating. *A friend who would put their life on the line. Deep cover. Hatred has a long half-life. Give someone the chance to step up. Nobody can know.* Be unpredictable. Avoid all obvious choices.

By morning Simone had a partial plan. A series of scenarios. Not perfect, but good enough. *Now for something completely different.*

Since Sagan's death, she had been obsessed with finding the truth. With seeking justice. Possibly even revenge. But that was then, and this was now. No saving the world this time; just her sorry little ass. She chuckled at that, preparing a pot of tea in the dark. Little was not how people described it. Muscular, sure. Fat—*oh Sagan!*

One mug for her. A cozy to keep the pot warm. Jacinthe would be up with the sun in an hour.

Simone opened the door to the basement, took several steps down, then closed it quietly behind her. Moving quickly now she made her way to the work bench where Izzy kept a complete set of tools. Most for repairing things, but some for destroying them. She placed her laptop on the workbench and lay a small screwdriver beside it. Then with a deep breath, she prepared to send her final message.

"Dearest Ron, you are my partner, my rock, my lover. Our time together has always been too little. Absence may make the heart grow fonder, but if there is a limit, I am about to test it. My darling, this is *adieu*, until we meet again." SEND

No time for tears, she told herself when she felt her eyes misting. There would be plenty later, but if there was to be a later she could not allow tears to derail it. Simone sniffed, wiped her eyes quickly with the bandana around her neck, and picked up the screwdriver. Methodically she extracted the hard drive, placed it on the basement floor and lifted a crowbar from its hook. One, two, three strong blows with the heavy tool and the details of her private and personal life were locked away from prying eyes. Only two blows were needed to pulverize her phone. How oddly satisfying.

Five minutes later, Simone slipped out the basement door, a small backpack on her right shoulder, hiking boots on her feet, retractable poles in her left hand. *Telegraphing*. She could walk all the way into the Laurentians from here, and that's what she wanted people to think.

"A hike at this hour? In this heat wave?" That's what 'the neighbourhood watch-lady' across the street would tell the man 'from the government' when he came.

"Her family is worried about her," he'd explain, a genuine note of concern in his voice. "She's been under a lot of stress. Do let me know if you hear or see anything."

One more stop. *A dépanneur.* Hurray for corner stores. Closed, but with an ATM in the vestibule. Out came Simone's cards. Debit—maximum withdrawal. Ditto for the VISA. The one that earned Air Miles, she chuckled. She maxed that one out too. Mission accomplished: $1000 cash. That would be important. As was this visible transaction. Last seen withdrawing large sums before disappearing into the woods.

Imagine if we'd been stupid enough to fall for that 'cashless society' crap, she thought as she slid the bills into a zip-up pocket. Every transaction tracked and saved.

* * *

Every move had to be right. She had written it out and memorized it. Then ripped it up and flushed it.

Be seen by a neighbour. *Check.* They'll be searching as far north as Parc Jacques Cartier. *That buys 2-3 days, easily.*

Use a bank machine. *Check.*

Upon entering the trail system, rather than heading north she took the cycling path which led to a commercial street a kilometre to the east. She broke into a fast walk. Running in boots would draw attention, and hurt.

Avoid injury. *Check.*

Simone approached Cycles Izzy cautiously. In under two hours, store managers would be arriving all along the street. She circled around to the door in the back lane. No cameras and no alarm. Jacinthe had mentioned how Izzy kept forgetting to set it. "One day, she'll get robbed and the insurers won't cover her. Stupid jock!" *Hurray for stupid jocks. Generous, stupid jocks!*

Using a spare set of keys she'd taken from the house, Simone unlocked the door. Izzy would open the front door at 9:45. Her usual routine. She would find nothing amiss. Perhaps not for an hour or two.

One modest touring bike. *Check.* Comfort was more important than speed. She'd have many long rides ahead of her, if all went well.

Panniers, clothing, touring shoes, bandana, tools, spare tire and tubes, helmet, two bottles, energy bars and gels. *Check.*

Smog mask and sunscreen, of course. And a powerful LED light. *Check.*

Sum total: $1800. Maybe $1100 before mark-up. She'd done some daring things, bent a lot of rules, but never, ever committed theft.

One more job. Using shop tools, she removed the tracking chip attached under the bottom bracket. A common device to help track stolen bikes.

When she slipped out the alley door she was as ready as she could be: seat and handlebars adjusted, tires pumped to full pressure, bottles filled and other items stashed in one pannier, day pack jammed in the other, with the hiking boots.

Locking the door carefully, Simone opened the envelope she'd prepared in advance, added the keys and the chip from the bike, and sealed it. She'd drop it in a mailbox. It would arrive several days later. As well as the key and chip, Isabelle would find an apology and a promise to repay her.

Somehow.

Was she making it more complicated than necessary, she wondered as she rolled downhill towards the heavily-used road along the St. Lawrence River. *I could drive. Or take a bus. I could have taken Jacinthe's bike and left her the money. No, you made this plan for a reason. Start doubting now and you won't get past city limits!*

Who would expect a terrorist to be escaping on a bicycle? She smiled. If it was a scene from a Le Carré book, it wasn't one she'd read. *Cool plot idea. Spy novels, under an assumed name. I'll have time on my hands.* She'd always wanted to try fiction.

Think like Le Carré! In the middle of the night, she had recalled being impressed by the little tricks Justin Quayle used to avoid detection when he made a run for it in *The Constant Gardener.* Withdraw a load of cash, then ditch the credit cards and phone.

As she approached the river, Simone turned east in the direction of Montmorency Falls. To anyone that might take notice over the next quarter hour, she was a middle-aged woman on a touring bike, dressed in a red t-shirt and yoga tights, her blonde pony tail flapping from side to side in the wind. When she passed by again, heading west, she was a Cycles Izzy squad member on a morning training ride, with requisite jersey, shorts, sunglasses and aero helmet—hair squashed inside. There would be little reason to notice the bike was the same, other than the panniers—odd for a training ride. Then again this could be a team rider heading to work with a laptop and a change of clothes. She'd done it often enough.

It was a modest feint. The hiker act was the better one.

Riding at a steady clip alongside the Plains of Abraham, she would soon be in sight of the high bridge over the river. Though it was legal to cycle on the bridge, few did. For the 10-minute duration of the crossing, she would be in full view of commuting drivers. Would any have reason to take notice?

Simone felt a wave of relief when she rolled down onto the quieter streets of Lévis. Spotting a cafe-bakery with an adjacent alley, she dipped out of view to make a final change. Off came both shirts, leaving her in a sleeveless blue sports top. She'd run through her full wardrobe. The bike tucked out of sight, she stepped into the busy place and ordered a large breakfast and two sandwiches for the road. The frenetic first three hours had been fuelled on tea and a banana.

She could drop the spy games now. Today and the next would be plain hard riding. Challenging, physically and mentally. Cycling alone on a straight highway offered lots of time to worry.

Going In

"Stop where you are!" cried the frantic security guard over the loudspeaker. "You are in a highly radioactive zone!"

He has no idea who I am, thought Jiro. *What I am. Or what I intend to do.*

The cargo van had dropped him at the approach to the mangled building. Only a human had the mobility to penetrate the dark, obstacle-strewn recesses. A human, in a very non-human suit; engineered to lift or crush objects well beyond the capacity of even the strongest man; rigged with night-vision enhancement to allow its operator and some future image analyst to see what the human eye could not; armoured and coated to withstand as much as five minutes of exposure at 400 sieverts an hour. No previous probe, unmanned probe, had lasted more than a minute. Still—even with full-body cooling and robotic enhancements—the suit, the entire Hail Mary campaign, was only as good as the humans behind it. The dying human inside it.

"I'm not dead yet," he uttered aloud, and chuckled.

Though nobody would hear him, he knew of several who would have laughed. They would be cheering for him. One dead, one missing, and one he had not found the courage to warn.

Raising his eyes, he saw droplets form and begin to trickle down his visor. A light rain. Surfaces would be slippery. He must take extra care not to fall. The suit gave him superhuman strength, but limited his movements. And he was never particularly nimble.

Sixteen minutes of oxygen, the display on his visor read. Power for 20 minutes, give or take—depending on the amount of heavy lifting the motors would perform and the temperature of the battery reserve.

Batteries. He felt a sharp pain. This time it was not his diseased lungs or torn stitches. This was a dagger in the heart.

What kind of divine justice this would be if he could protect her, and so many others, using batteries she conceived of as they discovered love together.

With a shout of "I will do my best!" he forged ahead into the rubble and the dark.

What Does not Kill

pproaching Rivière-du-Loup in the late afternoon, Simone had been pedalling steadily for almost eight hours with just a brief lunch, several bottle fill-ups and a couple of roadside stops. Water in, water out.

"Squat, and don't hit your shoes," she heard her mother say. *Outdoorsy parents! You curse them when you're young, but thank them later—often in absentia.* She hoped she'd thanked them enough. Jacinthe would fill them in as best she could in a few days' time. Or if her disappearance hit the national news.

For now, let ignorance be bliss. A farewell message could be passed on later. Assuming she didn't get forcibly extradited. She recalled Brittany's chilling description. Bastards, the Americans. Spineless bastards, the Canadians.

On the outskirts of town, she pulled out a map from Jacinthe's old road atlas, found on a bookshelf with various travel guides. Simone had torn out the pages she would need. The inset map for Rivière-du-Loup lacked detail, but had all she needed. A smart phone would have been so much more convenient.

There was a public park, down by the river, in sight of the ferry to the north shore.

Taking the north shore route would have knocked 30 kilometres from her day. She'd already covered almost 200. *But the hills. Oh Jesus, the hills!* "Toughest part of my entire cross-Canada ride," a friend once told her. There would also have been the ferry crossing. Cameras everywhere. And the north shore was one of her false trails, she suddenly remembered. There *was* a method to her madness.

Time for a nap. The air was cooler by the river.

Awakened by the deep horn of a departing ferry, she reflexively reached for her bike. Still there. Nearly 10 p.m., her watch told her. Watches, maps, and now a pay phone. Old school. There might be one at the truck stop.

A courtesy USB plug in the park had provided her new light with the charge it needed. Simone mounted it on her handle bars and switched it on.

WOW! She'd purchased a self-defense weapon. Choosing the lowest setting, she returned to the main road. She'd need 20 minutes to reach the crossroads with the Trans Canada. *Ow, ow ow.* Her muscles had seized as she slept. All the more reason to find the right truck. *Luck be with the lady tonight!*

Rolling slowly through the parking area for big rigs, she spotted a couple with Nova Scotia plates. Two drivers were seated at a picnic bench, chatting loudly over a late supper. Friendly voices. A clear Maritime accent. Simone limped toward them, pushing her bike, the light off.

"Good evening, gentlemen."

"Oh, I wouldn't go that far ma'am," chuckled the older of the two. "Donny here, he's lots of things, but never a gentleman."

"Look who's talking now, Stephen Lahey. I'm guessing you've got a lady in every city. Prob'ly a brood of kids too!" Jovial. Simone's instinct was confirmed.

"Oh, sorry ma'am. Are we sharing too much?" said Donny.

"Keep going," she replied. "It's just getting interesting,"

"Well, not without an introduction." said the smiling Stephen. Large. Fit. Sixty-something.

"That's fair," said Simone. "Catherine's my name. Cathy, actually."

"That's better. How can we be helping ya, Cathy? Fall off yer bike?"

"Fortunately not. Just aching muscles. Thought I was fitter than this. I set out from Sherbrooke three days ago. Planning to get to Halifax by the end of the week. Meeting my husband there. But it's slower going than I planned."

"Sherbrooke!" Donny said with a whistle. "Further than I've cycled in my life."

"That's as much as you'll want to know about Donny's life, I can assure you," Stephen said, getting his own back. Simone smiled.

"And you'll be wantin' a lift?" Donny ventured, ignoring the jibe.

"You read my mind."

"Not too many reasons why a nice girl would be hangin' around truck stops," said Donny. "Got room in that cab, Stephen? I'd offer, but I'm headin' the other way."

"I'd be honoured," said Stephen. "Leavin' shortly."

"I'd best be headin' out too," said Donny. "Boss tracks every minute. Prob'ly listenin' now. 'Just in time' delivery. Modern slavery it is!"

"Slavery, my backside," Stephen countered. "Freedom of the open road!"

"True, true, and we still have jobs. Can't be said for some of the boys workin' the oil sands. Banks repossessin' their pickups. Well, if I want to keep mine, I'd best be movin.' Nice to meet you Cathy. Yer in safe hands with Stephen. Never mind my jabs."

"See ya soon Donny. Keep yer eyes open."

"Good to meet you, Donny," Simone called after him.

Walking toward Simone, Stephen reached for her bike. "Brand new! I'll be careful."

"Thanks," said Simone. "Just let me grab the panniers. And bottle."

Once he had his rig up to cruising speed, Stephen glanced over at Simone, who was struggling to hold her head up.

"Decent bed back there," he gestured with his thumb. "No point hurtin' yer neck."

"Umm, oh of course," she said groggily. "Wish I was better company, but it's been a long day."

"Never you mind. I got my beauty rest already. Woke up just before you arrived. Pull the sheets off and help yerself to the spare set in the cupboard," he instructed. "I'd change them, but—"

"Don't be ridiculous. You've been generous enough. So, I just lift this handle—"

"Yep. It swings in and you step through."

Sitting on the mattress, Simone abruptly swivelled and stuck her head back out.

"Stephen, do you mind if I call my husband. Assuming you've got a phone? I left mine back at a diner. At least that's where I think it was. I'll try and trace it when I get home."

"Here you go," he said, reaching back. "Glad to help you keep in touch. I'm away a lot, but we call every day. Darlene often joins me... Oh dear, how am I going to explain the pretty woman in my bed?"

Simone shook her head. "Just say, 'We took turns!'"

"Good one." They both smiled.

Sitting up on the surprisingly comfortable bed, Simone wondered how sound-proof the divider was. She fished her wallet out of the pack and removed a card on which several numbers were neatly written. No names, just hints for each number.

Habs was her code for the man she was calling. It was ringing. One. *Would he answer?* Voice mail was too risky. Two. *Shit, it's past midnight.* Three. *Was this number still valid?*

"*Allo. C'est qui, Stephen Lahey?* Do I know you?" He sounded wide awake.

"Paul Racine?" she said quietly.

"Who wants to know?" he answered loudly, his tone testy.

Simone looked nervously around her, though Stephen couldn't possibly overhear them, not with the noise of the engine.

"I won't say my name, and please, please don't say it either Paul—"

"*Tabernac!*" She heard him exclaim. "It can't be."

"Don't say it!" she urged, her voice rising. "Don't say anything, or you'll get us both in trouble."

"If you insist." He was speaking more softly now.

"I'm going to ask several yes or no questions. Please just say yes or no."

"O-K," Paul replied slowly.

"Is your big adventure going ahead as announced?"

"Ye-e-s," he said, clearly working to decipher her cryptic question.

"If you'll be alone, and there is room for *cargo*," she said calmly and clearly, "can you be found at your usual hangout in about 26 hours?"

"Wait a sec, 26..." he was calculating. "Yes."

"Thank you. I'm hanging up now. Please don't call back."

"Thanks Stephen," Simone said in a jovial voice as she returned the phone. "My husband's an insomniac. Everything's fine. I'll get some sleep now."

"What the hell?!" Paul exclaimed, alone in his home office. *Thought she'd be arrested by now. They're more likely to whack her, though. Like the Russians, only they use poison.* He had not spoken to her in ages. Not since she arranged to visit and interview him, he recalled. *Cancelled at the last second. Some sort of crisis. Right,* he recalled, shaking his head. *Fukushima!*

He'd followed her, though. For two decades.

Paul leaned back in his chair, hands behind his head. *Hard to know where she wants me to take her, but that can wait. It wouldn't change much anyway. Couldn't.* He pulled out a pen and added several items to his final shopping list, imagining all scenarios, as an engineer and mariner would.

- Life jacket. (W - small)
- Wet suit, flippers, snorkel, goggles
- Wool sweater/hat/socks. Polypro shirt/tights. Rain shell/pants. Boots (W4/5?)
- High energy food (light, sealed)

That should cover it. Wait...

— Cash: Pounds/Euros?

Not that he could afford either. He'd nearly maxed out his cards. *Expense it to Jenny. She'll understand.*

How to get her on board? He smiled, warming up to the game. *What would Jason Bourne do?*

Simone woke up when she felt the truck slowing. By the time it came to a halt, she was sitting upright. Stephen was already stepping down as she stuck her head into the cab.

"Where are we?" she croaked.

"Mornin' sleepin' beauty!" he called up.

"You flatter me."

"It's what I say to my wife. Habit. Time to use the facilities. I was going to wake you. Figured you'd be wanting a bathroom break too. Rules say I have to rest now. We might as well grab breakfast together."

"That's kind Stephen, but—" She searched for a plausible reason to decline.

"Food's pretty good here. I only stop at the best. If cash is a problem..."

"I'm OK, really. What I need most is a good stretch. If you wouldn't mind, though, could you bring me tea and some kind of breakfast sandwich? I'll be over on the grassy area," she pointed. "It's a little weird going into a truck stop in lycra, you know."

"As if we're gonna judge. Then again, a fit lady in lycra..." He chuckled as he walked away.

Simone hobbled to the far side of a bush and relieved herself. Then she limped to where she had indicated, sheltered from the building by Stephen's rig. In this summer of drought, the grass was brown and thin. Despite the roughness, it felt good to kneel and stretch. She was settled into a child's pose when she heard approaching footsteps. Wary, she turned her head as the voice reached her.

"Carry on, Cathy— Jeez, the soil is parched!" He paused to kick at the turf.

"Sure is. Thanks for grabbing me a breakfast. That's so sweet."

"Bein' a gentleman, like my ma taught. Good advice, when I remember it."

"I'm sure you do often." Simone moved into a seated position, crossing one leg over the other.

"I try, but I admit to feelin' old-fashioned. 'Ordinary decency', feels more and more like I'm some kinda fool. Barely 60 and I feel like the world has raced by me into a new era. One I don't much like."

"Can't say I like it much either," Simone replied.

"There's a meanness that's crept in. I listen to a lot of radio as I run my routes."

Simone stood up and gestured to some picnic tables. "Shall we?"

"It's been festerin' fer a couple of decades," Stephen continued as they walked together. "Tea Party take-over of the Republicans brought it to a head. Everyone competin' to be most outrageous. People think it started with Trump, but nah, he just raised it a level. Or lowered it, I guess."

"I've been watching it for awhile too," Simone said. "There, and in Canada,"

Stephen nodded. "We had our Rebel Media and its stunts, and that Sun TV."

"The late and little-lamented," Simone offered.

"Oh, don't kid yerself. They had their fans. Those folks didn't go away. They just moved onto the internet, where they could find what they wanna hear. And worse."

"Too true," Simone said, suppressing the urge to expand. *Stay in character.*

"Don't you think that's where civility died first—the internet?"

"I do believe you're right, Stephen."

"Those Breitbart and Alt Right people," he added, glowering, "ugly as it was, now it seems like just a rehearsal for this new gang of FullRight fanatics."

"I have to say, Stephen, you're exceptionally well informed."

"For a trucker?" he suggested. There was an edge to his voice.

Simone shook her head vigorously. "Well informed, period. I despair—"

She was cut off by a musical ringtone. *Farewell to Nova Scotia.* She'd learned it in school. Stephen reached for his phone.

"Hi honey!"

Simone decided to stroll back to the truck and give him some privacy.

Ex-Military

Seeing her in the passenger's seat, Stephen climbed behind the wheel and closed the door. Instead of doing up his seatbelt, he went silent. He stared forward for several breaths, then turned to address Simone.

"Cathy. Or should I say Simone?"

"Umm," she began, feeling her spiders awaken, "I don't know what you mean."

"I think you do," Stephen said gently. She held his gaze for as long as she could. When she felt her face blushing, she had to look away.

"There's an arrest warrant out for Simone Cohen. My wife Darlene says the public's asked to report any suspected sightin's."

"Oh my," Simone responded feebly, processing this news. She stared directly at Stephen now, trying to make out his intention. He saved her the trouble.

"I want to make one thing clear. Whatever's behind this extradition thing, if I'm ever asked to side with those crazies in Washington or their stooges in Ottawa, least of all against Simone Cohen, who I consider one of the few clear-thinkin' voices still left... I'm with her!" He stopped to let her absorb his words.

"Stephen," she began carefully, "everything you've said and done leads me to believe you're a good man." He nodded. "If I'm going to avoid arrest, I'll have to trust *some* people. But each time, I take a risk. And everyone who assists me is—"

Stephen held up his hand, halting her mid-sentence. "Do the words Medak Pocket mean anything to you?"

"Croatia? Shit! I mean, wow! You were there?"

"I was," he nodded. "I know about risk. And trust. And teamwork. A team you can trust will get you further than on yer own. They'll also cover for you."

"Alright Stephen." She offered her hand. "Simone. It's an honour to know you."

"The honour's mine. Besides," he laughed, "you were never a Cathy!"

Simone reacted with a nervous giggle. "How long have you suspected?"

"The midnight hitchhiker act was clever enough. But yer voice seemed familiar. Then this business of avoidin' the diner, skippin' bathroom breaks…"

She nodded slowly.

"My wife's call though. Darlene wanted to tell me, in case I wasn't listenin' to the radio. I normally would have, but not with you sleepin'. We're fans. And subscribers."

"Well, I'm flattered!"

"So, now we've got that straight, *Simone*, where am I takin' you?"

Paul had been fielding media well into the evening. Live interviews on the dock used up critical preparation time. He'd barely found the hour he needed for his list. Now came the final check.

Connections to the solar array on the roof and deck and the photovoltaic Flexy-Mainsail mast were in order, as was the critical mast turbine. Just installed, this revolving PowerPole was his pride and joy—lightweight, salt-resistant and ultra-efficient. The idea was not his, but he'd refined it substantially. It made for a complete, all-conditions package. Barring multiple days of heavy cloud with no wind, a boat departing fully-charged could make a high-speed transatlantic crossing without slowing.

All systems go!

With the journalists finally gone—off to sample Saint John's pubs and get some sleep before the scheduled 7 a.m. departure—Paul was enjoying the calm when his phone rang. The display said Stephen Lahey, so he was expecting Simone.

"I have delivered your cargo safely," declared a deep voice.

"O-K," Paul said slowly, somewhat puzzled.

"When the dock is clear, take a stroll to the south. There's a camera above Warehouse 10. Disable it. Double check you're alone. Knock on the side door. Remove the lock. It's broken, but looks intact. Put it back when you're done. Say nothin'. Move fast. With cargo and bicycle."

"Bicycle?!"

"Am I clear?" barked the voice. It was a command.

"Clear."

"Godspeed Paul."

"Thank you Stephen." *Ex-military*. Like Paul's father, and grandfather before him.

Sail Away Sweet Sister

As the first rays touched the spires of Saint John's uptown steeples, *Switching to Glide* hummed out of its berth to the cheers of onlookers. Cameras were trained on the vessel from every angle. Television, webcasts, amateur photographers and a dozen drones.

Paul steered confidently into the deep harbour. He'd sailed these waters since childhood. Depth would once have been a problem, though never at high tide. Rising sea levels over the past several decades, though, had added a further margin of safety. For anyone piloting a boat, that is. On shore those sea level changes made life less safe.

Paul pictured the ice sheets of Antarctica and Greenland giving themselves up so he could skim over the shoals. One benefit from melting ice caps and glaciers, set against all the harm. *A rising tide floats all boats,* he'd often heard. But how true was it? For him, at this moment, sure. For the yachts of Miami, of course. But for the owners of those yachts, in a growing number of coastal cities, swelling tides were to be feared.

From the window of a lofty oceanfront condo, Miami's wealthy could still savour the sight of boats bobbing happily between hurricanes. Best not to think about their Porsches, though—the massive pumps working to keep garages dry were in a losing battle. Or the streets—keeping saltwater away was a major expense. Front lawns were a relic of bygone days. Most residents, though, were still hanging in. Not so in Dhaka, and dozens of sea-level mega-cities in poorer countries.

Boats float, people don't. Nor crops, or homes…

Flight from flooding was behind a renewed wave of global migration. Even less accessible countries like Japan and New Zealand were seeing hundreds of boats reaching their shores. Could Europe's refugee crisis of 2020 soon reach Canada?

Here he was sailing into the heart of it for kicks, or so it might appear. Mostly, it was to attract investors to his Clean Freighter concept, so he could scale up to where it might replace some of the most polluting ships on the oceans. They still numbered in the thousands. He could help change that, if anyone cared to listen. *That's* what this was trip was about: making people listen.

Paul was in love with the ocean. The sick, tormented ocean which would quietly suffer the many forms of abuse people gave it, and then suddenly, in a fit of rage, strike back. He'd launched one campaign after another to end the use of the ocean as a chemical dump, a nuclear disposal site, a place to drill for gas, a recipient of every type of plastic, the object of all manner of abusive fishing practices and now a 'sink' for so much CO_2 it was turning the ocean to acid.

Most of what he loved about the ocean was dying. He'd known it was in trouble back in 2001 when he'd defended his thesis. 'The potential for hybrid solar/wind/sail-powered boat propulsion to replace liquid fuel engines, reducing greenhouse gas emissions and petrochemical releases to the world's oceans.' *Yah, right.*

Technically yes. Commercially, maybe. But never politically. How do you sell an idea that has opponents in high places? *The fishery is fine. Toxic effluent? No big deal. Radioactive waste? The ocean is vast. What plastic gyre? Have you seen it? I haven't. The coral reefs? That bleaching is temporary.*

He'd lost those battles, but never entirely given up. For the longest time, he'd struggled to bring his ideas to market—out of the university lab and into production. He'd had little success until he received a surprise email one day from an old class-mate.

Jenny Fung had read about his PowerPole and Flexy MainSail prototypes. She wanted to know more. She had money to invest and a manufacturing facility at her disposal. The rest happened quickly.

Paul smiled. Here he was, suddenly with two amazing women from his past. One who would help make people pay attention. The other whom he would help disappear. That headstrong, mischievous woman he'd loved all his life, but couldn't keep. He'd have her for just a few days, then set her free. Alive, and with a chance.

A buzz off starboard brought Paul out of his revery.

First, get out into the shipping lane. Next, set course as per plan. Then, with the sun truly down, the drones called home and the ocean as dark as it gets, open the hatch and let Simone taste her first breath of fresh air in almost 18 hours. Him? He'd taste the thrill of resistance.

Stowed away below deck, Simone's mind continued whirring long after activity had ceased. Eventually the rocking of the boat lulled her to sleep.

Footsteps overhead startled her awake. She sat up abruptly, alert. Excited voices could be heard, then the cheer of a crowd and the unmistakable buzz of drones, which prompted her to lay carefully back down again.

The rules were clear: 'a mono-hulled boat, electric engines, no fossil fuels, solo, unsupported.' If ever a second person was detected on board, it would undermine the whole enterprise. And who knows what they'd make of Simone Cohen being spotted on board. There was no category for 'supported by a terrorist stowaway.'

Nothing to do but wait. Simone used the time to write several notes on a pad she had found in the galley space. She would ask Paul to post them when back in Canada. This would accomplish two things: reassure family of her continued liberty, and create another false trail. Assuming...

Simone looked carefully at the items Paul had evidently bought for her. When she caught herself neatly setting aside the sales tags as she removed them, she stifled a laugh. *It's a tad large, Paul! Could you exchange it for a small?*

Still, it was useful to confirm the fit. Too large would be okay, but too small would waste valuable pannier space. He had erred on the roomy side, she saw. What was with the wetsuit and snorkelling gear though? Was he expecting her to swim? With a bike? Then again, he hadn't known about the bike.

Paul had thoughtfully supplied a set of all-season gear, for whatever came next. Even a wool toque. No Montreal Canadiens cap, she chuckled. *Ooh, catty!*

Killing time, she set to stowing her gear as efficiently as possible, beginning by emptying out her panniers. At the bottom of one, among the energy bar wrappers, was the envelope Jacinthe had slid under the door. "Open when you think the time is right," it said. Now was as right as any.

Fighting a rising wave of emotion, she slit the envelope open with her folding Opinel knife. Inside she found cash, a note and a piece of jewellery. She counted about $300 in several currencies. *Dear girl offered every bill she could find.* Picking up the necklace, Simone felt her chest tighten. On a silver chain was a ring she'd only recently given to Jacinthe. She'd worn a slimmer one when she married Ron. What had belonged to Simone's grandmother, and then her, and only briefly Jacinthe, was back in her hands. Perplexed, she read the note.

> *Maman, neither of us knows how this will end. The chain will remind you of our friendship. I have around my ankle the one you gave me when I was younger. The ring is for you to do as you see fit. If it's of more value traded for cash, or freedom, then that's what it was meant for. If I marry someday, that bond will be worth more than a ring. Bonds of love are toughest to make and break."*

Through watering eyes, Simone examined the ring in her palm. *Far have I travelled, with further to go still. To safety, if there was such a thing.*

Paul and Simone had barely spoken the night before. "Oh merde, you and your bikes!" was how he had greeted her. No hugs. Not even a handshake. Just an order to stay still and silent. Now, with the sun down and the boat on auto-pilot, they began their awkward reunion.

Sensing Paul's hesitation, Simone opened her arms for what proved a very brief embrace. To her surprise, he was the one who terminated it. He was trying hard not to cross any boundaries, she sensed. She did not wish to either. Least of all, the fundamental rules of the voyage.

"You must never be seen," he explained curtly. "It's a solo crossing. That's the basis for this trip. It's also how I got permission to enter ports and territorial waters. Fear of human smuggling is high. Particularly entering back into American waters on the return. Though I suspect that's not your intention."

He might have smiled, but did not. Or could not.

Paul looked older and considerably heavier than Simone expected, though he was still powerfully built. He was also visibly nervous. Seeing him here, as he was now, her heart went out to him. Her life had been a blessed one. Until the past few years, at least. Paul, though, seemed to have spent his life perpetually looking. Giving his all from the start, but when that was not enough, quitting and moving on.

He was doing it again, she thought. His purchases were the first sign. He must have understood her predicament even before the surprising phone call. When it came, he had responded in full. For this she was grateful, but was he hoping for more?

So far so good. They were 32 hours into the voyage, and the *Switching to Glide* was performing flawlessly. By day, the panels, sails and mast provided power to propel the boat, while also replenishing the innovative sodium-ion batteries. *Full marks to*

Jenny and her Japanese partners for those! This ensured the hyper-efficient motor could operate at full power, apart from periods when favourable winds allowed for the massive spinnaker to take over entirely. Power saved by day came in handy at night and, if needed, in poor weather.

As they approached mid-point in the crossing, with the afternoon sun due west, Paul invited Simone to join him on deck. "I'll be performing a special ritual," he explained. "I thought you might want to take part. Given your... predicament."

Simone appeared puzzled. The invitation contravened his explicit instructions, he knew, and he had been vague about his intentions. What he was about to do, though, was bigger than any rules, and a clearer description was bound to scare her off.

"The sun will do you good," he said, trying hard to entice her. "And the energy we invoke will serve you well."

At the precise spot Paul had calculated to be the middle of the route, with the ocean remarkably calm, he stripped naked, faced the sun and silently raised his arms to the sky. Revolving towards the direction of what was now just a light breeze, he knelt and prostrated himself. Rising, he picked up a rod with a small cup attached. Extending what proved to be a telescoping pole, he dipped the cup into the ocean, retracted the pole and splashed the water on his face. Finally, he took a short knife from its sheath and pricked the index finger of his left hand. Using the cup, he caught a drop of blood as it fell. Then, extending the pole again, he immersed the cup briefly in the water, just long enough to rinse off the blood. Placing the rod down, he bowed once to each of the four points of the compass.

Still naked, he turned to Simone and asked if she wished to perform the same ritual. She nodded consent, but asked him to explain its meaning.

"I will," said Paul, "as you are performing each rite."

As soon as she was ready, similarly naked, he began his narrative.

"We honour the sun, which provides all energy to our bodies and our Earth; we honour the wind, which creates motion and constant change; we honour the ocean, from which we are born and without which we die; we offer our blood, as symbol of our commitment and contribution to the healing of the great oceans. To the four directions and all the elements of Mother Earth, we thank you and dedicate ourselves to your protection and renewal, and ask in return for your protection."

Simone, he guessed, was not used to pagan ceremonies, but she appeared intrigued—moved even. At least she hadn't laughed—at his self-made ritual, or him. For a brief moment they locked eyes, then he turned away, suddenly self-conscious.

Dressed, he stood at the bow looking east toward Europe. Simone, also dressed, joined him in silence. The feeling of her small hands wrapping around one of his much larger ones took him by surprise. As did her gentle voice.

"I am honoured, Paul. You have a profound connection with the ocean. I respect that enormously." He hesitated before answering.

"You can't know how good it is to hear that," he said, turning to face her. "I've followed you all these years with admiration." He could feel himself redden. Taking a breath, he continued. "You have a certainty of purpose I wish I had. Whatever I set out to do always falls short of the impact I want to achieve. I cry for the oceans and what we've done to them, but I've done little to stop it."

Simone shook her head. "You've done a lot, Paul. Impact is not about prizes."

"Says the lady with a roomful!" he mumbled in response.

"No," said Simone, fixing her gaze on him. "Only a couple. Some of us are in the public eye. But the ones in the trenches, on the boats, freeing right wales trapped in nets… what you do is as important as anything those of us with our names in print do."

"Hardly. What have I done that will be remembered?"

"Who designed this boat?" Simone said with a sweep of her arms. "Who earned Jenny's backing? You've built a winner, Paul. Me, I'm going into hiding. You, you're our great hope. My great hope. For getting me to safety, and then taking up the torch."

He looked her in the eyes, as she issued a challenge. "Sagan passed it to me, and I'm passing it to you. Will you take it?"

"I guess," he said softly. Her eyes told him he could do better.

"Yes," he stated more loudly. "I'll do what I can."

"You'll do amazing things, Paul! Maybe someday we'll do them together."

"I hope so," he said, feeling a tug at his heart. "We weren't meant to be, as a couple. But I'd be honoured to work with you. I hope we'll have the chance."

"Which brings me to a very important request," Simone said gravely.

He nodded for her to elaborate.

"I can count on you to say nothing, right? You never saw me, OK? Not even if probed by Jenny, or my family. Definitely not the police."

"I would never—"

"I know, Paul. Not on purpose. But things slip out when we're trying to be helpful. They might ask. You'll want to reassure them. Wink, wink. Right?"

"I guess," he nodded. "Yes, it would be hard not to. The police I can handle. *The bitch! She broke up with me. Why would I help her?*" He said it like he meant it.

She laughed. "That could work. But not with Jenny. I'll find a way to get a message to her, while you focus on making these boats a going concern. Tell her that's how you're going to honour Simone, *wherever she is now—the bitch.*"

"Deal!" said Paul, clasping her hands and smiling. "Now get back under cover and load up on carbohydrates. You'll need it, wherever you plan to ride that bike."

At the end of the third day, with darkness and the coast of France approaching, Paul was forced to press for details. "Just stay on your planned route," she had said when he first asked. "We'll figure out how to get me ashore later."

By the rules of the challenge, *Switching to Glide* would be timed on the return voyage from the moment it passed between two specific buoys just off Portsmouth, until it crossed a similar finish line near the Statue of Liberty. Paul had chosen to go after the less-heralded Saint John to Cherbourg record as a warm up of sorts. On arrival, he would dock in France for two nights to take on supplies, perform a mechanical inspection and get the sleep he would not be getting during the closely-watched return leg.

He had a more personal reason for taking this particular out-bound route, though.

On August 19, 1942, Alphonse Racine was among the 4,963 Canadians who took part in an ill-fated Allied raid on Dieppe. He would be one of 912 Canadians killed by the heavily-entrenched Germans. On June 6, 1944—D-day—close to 14,000 Canadian troops landed at Juno Beach. Alphonse's younger brother Jean-Paul Racine was among them. He would return home to marry and have three children. His youngest son, Jean-Pierre, would in turn have three children. The oldest, Paul, had never been to Juno Beach, but it had been his lifelong wish. Now, he intended to offer a special salute to Alphonse and the other Atlantic Canadians who died at Dieppe. When he first planned this detour he could not have known how fortuitous it might prove for another Canadian.

"That's perfect!" Simone exclaimed when he described it.

Now, with under four hours to go until they reached Juno Beach, at Courseulles on the Normandy coast, they made a plan to get her ashore with as short a stop as possible. *Switching to Glide* could get to within 200 metres of the beach at the estimated arrival time of 3 a.m., according to the computer navigation system. The inflatable life raft would be prepared in advance, along with the bicycle and loaded panniers. For speed, she would enter the water wearing only flippers, and propel the raft until she could stand and walk it in. With bike and panniers offloaded, she would towel dry and quickly dress, then place towel and flippers in the raft. Pulling on a thin attached line, he would retrieve the raft, deflate it and stow it. The entire operation should take under ten minutes.

Paul had filed his plans with the French government and received approval to approach—but not land—at the beach. But there was always a chance the captain of a particular vessel would be unaware of this, or Paul might stumble into an anti-smuggling operation. That summer's surge in human smuggling along the coasts of France, Ireland and England had prompted an escalation in preventive measures in all three.

At 2 a.m., with the sea dead calm, the clouds parted to reveal a three-quarter moon. While this made navigating easier, it increased the chances of being seen.

In total silence, they prepared the inflated boat, roping Simone's bike firmly to the gunwales. When Paul gave the thumbs up, they lowered it slowly. Once in the water, the two panniers and a dry bag with Simone's riding gear and filled bottles was lowered in. In response to a beep from the computer, Paul cut the engines. At that precise moment, and as Simone was stripping on the deck, a voice barked over the radio.

"This is the French Navy, identify yourself." Handing Simone the line he would be holding during her swim, Paul raced to answer.

"This is *Switching to Glide*. Captain Paul Racine here."

"Acknowledged. What brings you into French waters?"

"I have permission from your government to approach the beach. I wish to perform a brief ceremony to honour Canadian soldiers who came ashore here in 1944. I have the form on file and can send it to you, if the water is too shallow for you to approach." Paul desperately hoped it was.

"*Merci, Capitaine Racine.*" came the response from the navy ship. "We have your authorization. You will understand, it was necessary to confirm your identity. Most boats approaching our coast do not have French interests at heart."

"Yes, of course," Paul empathized. "You have a difficult job. I commend you!"

"That is generous, *Capitaine Racine*. Oh, and one more thing…"

Simone held her breath as she crouched exposed on the deck.

"On behalf of the people who lived under Nazi occupation, I and my shipmates extend our gratitude to the Canadians who came ashore. Break that record, *Capitaine!* "

"A Canadian is almost as good as a Frenchman," he added.

Paul laughed with relief. "I'll break it for us both."

Over the calm water, the conversation would have been audible on the beach. Paul hoped the windows of nearby homes were closed against the ocean breeze.

Through his binoculars, Paul watched Simone with admiration. When she emerged from the water, he had a clear view of her in the moonlight. He continued to watch as she towelled off, dressed and meticulously performed each act they had rehearsed. At last, she turned toward him and passed her hand slowly in front of the light. Once. Twice. Three times. Her signal that the raft was ready to be retrieved.

It also meant farewell, he realized.

Another One Gone

From: Jenny Fung
7 August, 2021 11:40 PM
Re: Jiro my hero
To: Simone Cohen

Dear Simone,

It is with great sadness that I write. Our beloved Jiro is dead. Before I explain, I must say how worried I am about you. I just learned of your escape. I hope you will receive this message.

So to Jiro. You perhaps did not receive my short message after his collapse. It seems he had been suffering for many months from lung cancer, without telling anyone. A result of exposure to radiation. This now explains many things.

Jiro was in hospital for several days, and then returned home to rest. He had no more than a few months to live and was in great pain, but wanted to set his affairs in order. He was determined to make sure that his mother and the girls are taken care of. I am financially independent, but my status here in Japan is uncertain. His death would make it more so.

Now the circumstances. As you know, the most damaged of the nuclear reactors was never fully stabilized. One obstacle to containing the fuel mass is the debris from the original accident, which is in the way of capturing good images, and ultimately getting underneath it—wherever that 'underneath' is. Japan's best robots get destroyed before they can perform the required work. The radiation is that intense.

Here it gets crazy. Jiro arranged to be suited up in a kind of 'Iron Man' outfit that would temporarily protect him from the radiation, and whose motorized parts would provide super-human strength. Apparently he was working secretly over the past year with people who develop suits for mine rescues and prototypes for space missions. They say he has been obsessed with this idea for even longer, but only when he knew his time was short, did he decide it must be him to take on the fatal mission. Some use the word 'suicide', others 'insane', but most prefer 'heroic'. I think it was all of these.

Jiro did the impossible. He removed the troublesome debris, leaving an unobstructed path for the essential work of cooling the radioactive mass, and getting underneath it. He also sent back clear images. If there is such a thing as a noble suicide—*Hara Kiri*—this must surely be it. I am overcome equally with admiration for what he did and tears for what he would have felt. Fukushima Daiichi is his tomb.

There is another silver lining to Jiro's efforts. The national government has declared that Fukushima prefecture will be a nuclear-free zone in perpetuity. The campaign to bring this about was led by Jiro's brother Katsuo. What he could not find the moral courage to do while Jiro was with us, he has found now that Jiro is gone. To our enormous surprise.

Jiro has been suitably recognized. Honourable in life, honoured in death.

Life with him was not always easy. Of course, I was not easy to live with either. But I could not have hoped for a more devoted partner, nor a better example to our daughters. In recent years, with helpful counselling—mostly about communication—Jiro and I reinvented ourselves as a couple. I think this led to our both being more confident and at peace with ourselves as we followed our own paths.

I will miss him enormously. As of course will the girls and his mother. Though I think she will not be in this world much longer. Soon it may be just the three of us. My parents died last year, as you know. We will need to make a decision about where in this troubled world we wish to be, if we have that luxury.

Simone, when you can, send me a message. But only if it will not put you at risk.

Jiro has joined Sagan. I know they are looking out for you.

Your Sister Jenny

Deep Cover

Eerie Ride

This was not the France Simone cycled in the fall of 1998. Where it had once been lush and welcoming, it was now desiccated and suspicious—verging on locked down. The public fountains and faucets, so much a part of any town square, were mostly dry, contaminated or had warnings against filling containers for resale.

'Pay what you can' food boxes once common on rural roadsides were rare, and often empty. Simone had to make the most of whatever safe water posts she could find, outdoor food vendors on market days, food boxes in more remote areas and—when desperate—raiding fruit trees. Paul's energy bars were not going to last 6 days and 900 kilometres.

She might have taken a more direct route. She might have walked into one of the hundreds of stores she passed. She might have bought an occasional cooked meal. If it weren't for facial recognition. One good image could be processed and an alert sent around the world in less time than it took to pull up her bandana. Nobody must know she was in France. Nobody but Paul did, and even he didn't know if she would stay.

Interpol would have an alert on file. Simone Cohen—wanted terrorist. It would include personal details, fingerprints, iris data and a set of facial images from all angles. The French had been early adopters of security cameras in public spaces, and who could blame them? She would be passing hundreds, if not thousands. All it takes is one.

535

Simone rode with a smog mask and dark glasses by day. If dust had not been as pervasive as it was, this would have been highly suspicious. Most people on bikes were wearing such masks, or a scarf over the mouth and nose.

For safety, she preferred night riding. It was cooler, required less water, and she rarely had to resort to a face covering. Her powerful light, which Paul had helped fit to her helmet, would blind any camera. While night riding lowered some risks, it increased the danger of collision and attack. A cyclist on the road in the middle of the night was also a red flag to state security.

The closer Simone got to her destination, the more impatient she became. Energy bars gave her calories, but her stomach was empty. Aching, gnawing. In a race there were feed stations. On a tour there were stores and bakeries. Here, there were no such luxuries. Bakeries were closed at night, and convenience stores had cameras. For her final two days, Simone switched to daytime riding. The nights were too short, and the dangers too great. She was passing through some remote areas where homeless migrant numbers were high, and local vigilante patrols equally so.

For 48 hours she kept a punishing rhythm: sleep from 10 p.m. until dawn, crank from 5 a.m. until noon, nap wherever there was shade, then do another stage from 3 p.m. until dark. Mostly she ate berries, nuts from her jersey pocket, and the last of the energy bars.

Thirst had proved the greatest challenge. A never-ending thirst.

At 3 p.m., six days after Paul delivered her to Juno Beach, she set off on what should be her final leg. It would be 70 kilometres into a head wind with nothing but unripe plums and barely half a bottle of water.

* * *

Twenty-three years had passed since her first visit. Fifteen since she had stopped in on a working trip. Only three direct communications between them, yet somehow he knew. As dusk turned to dark and Simone dug deeper than ever before to climb the final short hill that she knew continued beyond the farm gate and into Le Tilleret, there he was. Swinging open the gate, with a nod and a sweep of the arm.

"Simone," he said—with warmth, but no hint of surprise.

"A much better stop!" he added with a broad smile, as she brought the bike to a halt. François' face had weathered and thinned. His body seemed thinner too, but all sinewy muscle, belying his 65 years. Wrapping one arm around her and pulling the bicycle with the other, he propelled her up the lane.

"Let's get a roof and some walls between you and your demons!"

"How did you know?" Simone gasped.

"The animals," he explained, with a wink. "Your disappearance was in the news, but it was the animals that told me you would come here. And when."

'Saint Francis or not, Simone couldn't believe his connection with animals went this far. Her expression said as much.

"*Non, ma petite Canadienne*," he laughed. "I am not speaking with foxes and snakes. It is simpler than that. When anybody reaches the corner at the start of the long climb to Le Tilleret, Pauline's dogs start barking. I used to find it a nuisance. Now it's a crucial early warning. It happens so rarely that I notice it each time. Then I raise the alarm for neighbours down the road, and in our own little village, GV Assisi."

He pulled an old walkie-talkie out of his pocket. "It's linked to a relay system in the hayloft of the big barn. A warning goes out to others. Sad that it has come to this."

François' answer was convincing as far as it went. But why did he seem so unsurprised by her arrival? They had reached the top of the gravel drive and stepped into the small barn, one of many new buildings since her first visit. He leaned her bike against a wall, then offered his arm as she limped towards the entrance to the main house. There in the shade, lying on a blanket just outside the door, legs not willing to haul her up for a proper greeting, was a very old dog. Her tail flapped madly.

"See," said François, as he gave the border collie a scratch behind the ears. "The animals!" Belle knew you were coming. She was prepared to wait. Just like me."

He described how Radio France had done a long feature on Simone's struggle to achieve justice for Sagan. "Belle listened carefully and yipped each time a clip of your voice was played. Then whimpered when it was reported you had gone missing."

"Clearly your visits left a good impression," he added sincerely.

* * *

Two weeks after Simone's departure, Jacinthe uploaded her mother's final post. The memory stick had been well hidden. Like every family member, and most of Simone's friends and collaborators, Jacinthe had been visited by a trio of well-dressed men, arriving in a large SUV with tinted windows. They learned little. Brought in by the RCMP for further questioning on the afternoon the blog appeared, Jacinthe freely admitted to posting it. She denied, however, having knowledge of her mother's destination, or word from her since. The iris scan to which she willingly submitted bore this out.

"No waterboarding," she later quipped to Ron. "Yet!"

TPoT Blog — *To You I Pass the Torch of Truth to Power*

I write this final post with a heavy heart. Readers will know that my work to share the truth is not always appreciated. I am comfortable with criticism. I am even accustomed to abuse, though I shouldn't have to be. I have learned to live with death threats, knowing these are empty acts by people with no intelligent alternative. But now I am in real danger.

For some months, I have fended off an attempt by prominent people to get me extradited on charges of libel. Recently, charges of terrorism have been filed by the American government, and a separate extradition request formally made. I have resisted these attempts to silence me with the help of a dedicated legal team, sanctuary from the Quebec government, and the support of family and friends. But in the past several days, I have learned that someone is seeking to kill me. Elmore Lambert, and those who back him, have a history of intimidation, violence and murder, as documented in my fully corroborated recent <u>post</u>. In normal times, we could count on government and law enforcement agencies on both sides of the border to defend the freedom of speech of a journalist and protect her from a murderer. These are not normal times.

I must go into hiding and disconnect myself completely from my former life. Two weeks will have passed since I wrote this message. Nobody has been told where I am going. Please respect the privacy of my family, who do not know and may never know my whereabouts. Though I will look for a way to signal that I am safe.

My case highlights the erosion of our once-proud liberal democracies, including the corruption of our justice system and the role of the media.

I must take a break from speaking truth to power so as to take care of myself. I wish to live to fight another day. Or just to live. The fact that I have a reasonable chance of staying alive and finding another calling somewhere makes me fortunate. Thousands, even millions of truth tellers before me have paid with their lives.

Some may criticize me for running. I get that. Where I am headed—fortune be my friend—I hope to continue doing important work, even if you never hear of it. I will be fighting as always. I urge you to step up and fill my shoes, tiny as they may be. This is not a time to be silent.

May peace and truth be with you.

Simone Cohen

I Want to Break Free

August 2022

Simone plunged her hands into the recently-turned soil. It felt deliciously cool on this hot afternoon. The line of trees bordering the western edge of the vegetable garden provided partial shade now against the late-August sun. Low enough to begin planting fall lettuce. This exposed plot had lain empty for most of the summer.

François' efforts to encourage shade trees was paying off. It had taken several decades to bring them to this point, tortured as they were by the Drome's strong winds and growing drought. *L'homme qui plantait des arbres.* Simone smiled as she recalled the Jean Giono story her parents used to play in the car. Long ago. Outside the fence.

Visible between the trees was the three-metre fence François installed in 2019. Motion detector lights were attached every 30 metres. He told her how he'd hated doing it, but the level of insecurity left him no choice—the streams of desperate migrants seeking food, shelter and work, and the gangs that preyed on them; the paramilitary forces doing regular sweeps to round them up, and the vigilantes who did as they liked with them. His buildings and equipment needed protection, but above all this fence was for residents in refuge.

A week earlier they'd added cameras: ten in all, two on each edge of the property plus two at the gate, transmitting to a pair of monitors in the main house. Now they could watch and record activity in the adjacent fields on three sides, and along the road on the fourth. A two-metre high stone wall separated them from the road, interrupted midway along its length by the gated entrance. Or exit. Simone had not passed through in thirteen months.

These defences were mostly for show. It would take little to penetrate them: a large vehicle or a small explosive charge, perhaps. Any determined individual could scale the walls or, easier still, cut through the fences. This was no medieval fortress. Just a farm, where residents were doing their best to stay alive. Their only weapon was a hunting rifle that François had acquired years earlier for scaring wolves, kept under lock and key. In case. Of what, he did not know.

Inside, looking out! Simone sat back and wiped away the trickle of sweat before it could sting her eyes. Through the fence and across the fields to the east she could see the farmhouse in the distance. On a clear day, she could just make out the steeple in the village to the south. Almost close enough to touch.

Confined to GV Assisi, with no end in sight. But plenty to keep her occupied.

For the first few months, that was enough. Now there were twelve acres of land, 10 buildings and up to 60 residents at a time. François had taken over the adjacent farm in January, when his neighbours had abandoned it. This was a hive of activity and productivity. A green oasis, compared to the land she had ridden through.

For several more months, it was almost enough. Staying busy and physically active had always been her way to calm buzzing thoughts. It still worked, most of the time. There was water, food, shelter, security, and energy to provide. There was medical care and counselling to offer. Even the occasional baby to deliver.

GV Assisi was bigger than a lot of villages, but it had come to feel claustrophobic. As months stretched to a year, and now into a second, she struggled with moments of panic by day, and nightmares by night. Would she be here forever, waiting to be found, or found out, without a say in her own future? What of Ron, Jacinthe, her parents? Jiro, Jenny and Isong? Were they thinking of her? Or would her long silence have them fearing the worst?

At GV Assisi, Simone was in deep cover. Only François knew her real name or much about her beyond their agreed-on cover story. Village rules forbade taking photos, making phone calls or connecting by video. This, like the other rules posted inside the gate and in all three living quarters, was strictly enforced. A code of conduct to ensure social cohesion and the physical and psychological safety of residents.

You handed in your phone on arrival. Anyone unwilling to do something this basic could not be counted on—to respect their outside neighbours, pull their weight or take responsibility for the safety of GV Assisi. François did what he could to provide as secure and welcoming a haven as possible, for as many as possible.

Simone had taken on roles that François was struggling to perform. The departure of so many friends and longtime partners left large holes. She couldn't fill them all, but was determined to contribute in every way possible. As long as it did not require outside interaction.

François invited Simone into his own living space from the outset. She was family, and she had to be kept hidden until it was clear if she was being pursued. New arrivals assumed they were married, such was their intimacy. She had even adopted the name Nicole on her third day. It was the safest thing they could think of.

"This is my wife, Nicole, just arrived from the city. In need of fresh air." He had never mentioned a wife to the residents, but then he had shared few personal details. It was his property, and he sheltered and fed them. Who were they to question?

Masquerading as Nicole was odd. Creepy even, Simone sometimes felt. But for François it was simply what had to be done. She needed an inside identity. As for visitors, she must avoid being seen at all. They might wonder. Or take pictures!

Inside GV Assisi, she was now Nicole. Outside, she didn't exist. Not to neighbours, security forces, cameras—which started at the nearest store and community centre—and, of course, drones.

The confinement could drive her crazy, or force her to evolve. Where Simone's playground and office had once been the entire planet, now it was what she could see and touch. Every person she would visit, every act she would perform, every challenge she would face was less than a five-minute walk from where she slept. Much of humanity lived a similarly confined life, finding contentment and fulfilment, but she had little experience of this. A week at the cabin, or housebound with the flu was the extent of it. But even when bedridden she *could* have made a call or gone out. Or online.

From the age of 20, most of her life, she'd had the internet. Email, chat rooms, webinars, Facebook, YouTube, Skype... other than a chosen period of isolation in the wilderness or on a trip to the remotest of places, she had always been connected. Bored, curious or lovesick, she'd just had to text, log in or update her status and somebody was there for her. It ended the moment she'd handed back Stephen Lahey's phone.

Nobody could know where she was, or even how she was. Far worse, she could not reach out for news of the people who mattered to her. There it was, though, every day, tempting her on François' laptop. At one point, when she had almost succumbed, she asked him to install a blocking password.

He had already dealt with the lure of the confiscated phones. They were in an old steel safe in the kitchen, their batteries removed. "Plenty of people beyond your family wish to follow you," he explained to new arrivals. "None are friendly. But I'll return your phone if you choose to leave."

Then he would ask about implants. Most migrants were forced to accept them as a condition of entry into Europe. Easier to track, easier to control. Easier to hunt down. Fortunately, the extraction operation was quick and simple. Nobody objected.

They understood the risk. To themselves, and the village that welcomed them.

Tracking people did not require an implant, though. Simone knew this. She'd written stories on the topic. Going online and doing a few searches was enough to expose you. She'd discussed it with François—how to search for news of loved ones without leaving tracks. How she might send a message, or leave one somewhere; coded, or using nicknames. But even François, far from an expert, knew that all could be tracked, sifted and collated to reveal what you thought was concealed.

"Your words can and will be used against you," he reminded her. "My computer, my accounts and my IP address have established behavioural patterns. If you went online pretending to be me, you wouldn't get past your first five Googles, or Facebook visits. From the language of the sites you visit, to your choice of news outlets, to the search terms you use, to the topics that interest you, each are gifts to a sophisticated watcher. Your enemies, Simone—short of having died or lost interest—will have set up systems to trap you."

That's why the internet—beyond looking over his shoulder as he did his own news searches, with camera and microphone off and taped over—was forbidden.

Even François was careful not to do anything unusual. No deep dive into news from Canada. No following up on family, like Simone's parents, or mutual friends such as Jenny—even though Jenny had visited him and they had exchanged emails previously. They had been out of touch for more than a year when Simone arrived, so why the sudden interest, highlighting the connection between the three of them?

* * *

News of Jiro reached Simone entirely by accident. François was reading the newsletter of a nuclear watchdog to which he subscribed. Plants in more than a dozen countries were powering down as water temperatures climbed and levels dropped. He had been reading a global summary of plans to phase out reactors. It referred to decommissioning in Japan and the role 'Jiro's Law' was playing. Not familiar with the term, he clicked on the link for more detail. Up popped an article in English.

"Simone?" he called out, his tone indicating he needed her help. "Could you translate this for me?" Chewing the last bite of a late supper, she made her way casually from the kitchen to the dining table where François sat at his laptop.

"Jiro!" she blurted, as she read over his shoulder. "What the hell?"

François waited patiently as she scanned the article, dated a year earlier. For a moment she stood perfectly still, apart from her blinking eyes. Then, without warning, her legs buckled. François lunged sideways, too late to keep her knees from slamming on the floor, but in time to prevent her keeling over. His lap served as a resting place for her head as she sobbed, warm tears soaking his worn jeans. One hand on a shoulder, the other on her head, he cradled her in silence. When at last she stopped shaking, he helped her stand and guided her toward the couch. Once settled, her head on his shoulder, but shell-shocked eyes staring forward, he spoke to her gently.

"This is Jiro, your friend? Jenny's husband, *n'est-ce pas*? Tell me what made him so special."

Blinking several times, Simone gradually emerged from her shock.

"Gentleness," she said softly. "Honesty. Devotion. And the quirkiest sense of humour." She smiled, a small rueful smile, thinking of his resemblance to John Cleese. *He's just resting.* Like the parrot, though, 50,000 volts would not bring Jiro back.

Now we are two. I need a sign, Jenny. Then I will find a way to give one back.

The strange dreams and recurring nightmares came more often after she learned of Jiro's death. The four of them were together again. In Cambridge. On bicycles, fleeing black SUVs. In a truck, driven by Stephen Lahey. Jenny and Jacinthe, trying to talk Jiro out of going into the reactor. Sagan calling to get out: "Move it JJ. She's going to blow!"

She could go many nights without them, too tired from a 16-hour day for anything but the deepest of sleep. But in the early hours, especially on Sundays—a day off at François' insistence—the dreams came, in all their garbled glory. Always the women pleading with the guys to save themselves.

"The world doesn't need another fucking martyr!" she would scream, waking up with those words ringing in her head and smoke in her nostrils.

Saving Italy

June 2020, Off the coast of Sicily

T*hud.*

Angelo lifted his head abruptly. He must have nodded off. It had been a calm night on the Mediterranean.

His friend Roberto had promised action.

"We turn away some boats before they get close. The Italian Coast Guard doesn't have the balls!"

They'd force a few to do U-turns; tow them back into Libyan or Tunisian waters if needed. Have a little fun. Run interference between the big Operation Samaritan ship and the filthy illegals in their rotting boats. Sure, it was a drop in the ocean, but one less boatload of brownies diluting Europe meant fewer thieves, rapists, welfare bums and their dirty little spawn.

Most nights, they stopped at least a couple of boats, Roberto had said. From 20 to 200 in a boat. Or they impeded the work of the Samaritans for long enough to make a difference.

"Samaritans! What makes helping rejects and disease carriers an act of goodness? We know whose side they're on, don't we?"

Angelo had nodded, and shaken his head. He hadn't always thought this way. But now they were crawling all over the public squares and city parks. Something really did have to be done.

"Come out with us tomorrow night," Roberto had said. "For Italy. Less black boys making brown babies. Right Angelo? For your mother and sister."

Yes, he'd said. He would take a stand. For Italy, for a Christian Europe.

Thud. Thud.

Hitting hard objects in the dark could damage the boat. Why wasn't the captain slowing? And why was each impact accompanied by a cheer?

Wide awake now, Angelo pushed his way into the cluster of Save Our Italy volunteers gathered at the bow. Proudly wearing their windbreakers and caps.

Thud. "Goal!" came the cheer. Like soccer fans.

A smiling face greeted him, and an arm pushed him forward to where he could see better.

"Goal!" went the group once more.

Blinking as his eyes adjusted to the bright spotlights illuminating the dark, calm waters, Angelo could make out floating wreckage. Wood, plastic seats, lifejackets and...

Thud. "Goal!"

No! Were those heads? Barely above the water line, barely kept afloat by flimsy lifejackets.

Thud. "Goal!" The prow had struck another head.

Struggling to comprehend what he was hearing, and now seeing, Angelo caught a different sound. A high-pitched cry. Faint. Off to his left.

"There!" he shouted. Pointing to port side, he called for someone to swing a light in that direction.

There it was. Clear to all. A tiny child, whimpering, clinging to the neck of a lifeless adult.

"Quick," shouted Angelo. Somebody get a rope, a stick or something.

Nobody moved.

Incredulous, Angelo scanned the many pairs of blank eyes facing him.

This was not what he had come for, Angelo cursed as he stripped to his underwear. "We're supposed to be sending them back, not murdering them!" he cried, fighting with the laces of his boots. As he plunged into the cold water he heard the first mocking calls.

He had come to teach the migrants a lesson, Angelo thought as he swam powerfully through the water. Instead, he was learning one.

Taking the small crying child onto his left shoulder, he corkscrewed his legs to turn himself back towards the receding boat.

"Hey!" he cried, treading water furiously. "Show what you're made of!"

Struggling to keep a grip on the weakening child, he watched the boat carve a wide circle and head back for him. Forced to squint under the intensity of the spotlights Angelo had a hard time judging its speed.

Thud.

"Goooooo-al!"

News of the World, 2022

Every night at dusk the front gate was secured, the motion detectors activated, and a pair of veteran residents assumed watch. In addition to occasional walking inspections, the video system now allowed for full-time monitoring of the perimeter.

Most nights, Simone and François settled in to read, listen to music or simply talk. Simone often found herself working the dials of an old radio. It was an ancient Sharp boom-box—a 'ghetto blaster', before the term fell out of favour. This one had four radio bands in addition to the broken cassette deck. FM pulled in several dozen stations. Most were French, but a few were English. Commercial ones brought music into the house, but were useless for credible information. The news and talk shows they offered reflected their conglomerate owners: as reactionary as much of their audience, often more so.

There were pirate stations too, many of which fanned the level of anger and blame beyond what the French government would tolerate from a licensed broadcaster. These were neither governed nor governable.

In Rwanda, three decades earlier, radio had been used to foment genocide, but not even the most provocative French stations were promoting such violence. Populism was their standard fare—tirades against 'weak' President Macron and other centrist politicians. Their sights were also trained on the dozen European leaders who had banded together to support orderly settlement of migrants and greater cooperation in a shrinking European Union and cash-starved United Nations.

This 'Coalition of the Still Willing' was a rump of previous EU and UN membership. Financial contributions to the UN had plummeted since American withdrawal in late-2021 triggered a similar move by Russia, the United Kingdom, and most OPEC countries. The Coalition was struggling to hold together the critical work of international and domestic health agencies.

Call-in shows of 2022 France had descended to the depths Simone knew from the rise of the Tea Party, Trump's 2016 campaign and the unexpected election of Canada's True North Party: echo chambers of xenophobia, isolationism and libertarianism. Several stations added an evangelical message. Prayer and tithing, said on-air preachers, was the answer to economic and social problems, and would protect the righteous from storms, drought and fire.

Not everyone was peddling populism. Simone found several stations offering both tolerance and responsible reporting. A global network of independent stations was generating and sharing news and commentary, doing what public radio had done in many countries until recently.

Of the remaining public broadcasters Simone could find via shortwave bands, only a few continued to offer what she considered objective news and informed commentary. Most were now overtly influenced by the governments that funded them.

With a set of old headphones and a deft touch on the dials, she could still follow much of what went on 'out there.' Most evenings she listened alone, seated in the kitchen. Occasionally she would call out to François with a particularly striking piece of news. Generally, he preferred not to know. The mind is healthiest and sharpest when not polluted by a daily fix of random and remote news, he maintained.

"I like to focus on what touches me and what I can influence, in my own small way," he explained.

There were times, though, when he could not help responding to a passionate "François, you've got to hear this!" Late summer of 2022 offered plenty.

The disasters of 2017 through 2019—record drought, fire, flooding and winds, with a price tag to match—were a mild prelude, in hindsight. Events of 2021, though, sent markets into extended free-fall, brought on by the bankruptcy of municipalities, indebted countries and most of the world's insurance and reinsurance firms.

By 2022, with markets at last stabilized at under half their previous values—shored up by massive state intervention in support of the world's largest corporations and their 'stranded assets'—10 trillion dollars' worth of properties, industrial facilities and power plants along vulnerable coastlines were no longer insured or insurable. In rare instances where insurance could be obtained, premiums were prohibitive. This made many activities in disaster-prone areas too risky, destroying thousands of small businesses, suppliers and the families they supported.

Tourism suffered first and worst. Hotels, resorts, ports, highways and associated facilities lay abandoned in areas until recently considered holiday paradises. There was neither money nor will to dismantle structures or rehabilitate coastal zones destroyed by wind and storm surges. Scavenging had occurred on a large scale, with valuable metals taken for recycling and resale. It was carried out in the most rudimentary fashion, leaving areas at water's edge scattered with pulverized concrete, shattered glass and a soup of fuels and chemicals. Simone was glad to be spared the visuals.

By August 2022, simultaneous fires, floods, drought and storm damage had not only displaced hundreds of millions, it had wiped out productive agricultural land, coastal fisheries and aquaculture zones. Most of the world's coastlines were beyond remediation. Aquifers and surface water were polluted to a point where drinking, cooking and bathing would be dangerous for centuries.

Then there was radiation. Flood water—whether from coastal surge or continental deluge—collects and redistributes everything it touches. Bad enough when this was animal or human, including medical and pharmaceutical waste. Worse still for pesticides, landfill leachate, industrial waste, tailings ponds from mining, or various oil, gas and coal byproducts. But the worst was nuclear waste. Now that so many sites had been flooded, radioactive contamination of soil and water sources was widespread.

François took no satisfaction from having told them so. "*We all live downstream*, our bumper stickers said."

With some governments incapable of providing even basic oversight of the civilian nuclear industry, the problem would get worse. François kept a close watch on news related to France's plants—along the Rhône in particular, and especially the nearby Cruas-Meysse plant. A group of concerned citizens—mostly retired scientists and workers—had formed an international response team to act where governments wouldn't, or couldn't. They had dubbed themselves 'Atomic Angels'.

This unravelling of ecosystems and democratic institutions was painful to hear about. The warnings and predictions Simone had spent years sharing were being proven right—and wrong. It was happening as predicted, but not in any linear way. More like a cascade. Rippling out wider and faster than expected.

When Belle passed away peacefully one hot July night, Simone couldn't help feeling that she was the lucky one. Blissfully unaware of how crazy the world could be, and spared from worrying about how chaotic it was becoming.

Everywhere, people were mired in a daily struggle, trying to stay ahead of the next local crisis. Ron, Jacinthe, Maman and Papa—she assumed—but her place was here now, doing what she could for people she could touch.

Sometimes she wondered what all her years of reporting amounted to.

TPoT Blog — *2018 So Far*

June 18, 2018

For those who like information in bite sizes, I've assembled a "best/ worst" roundup for the year to date.

Climate breakdown to create 'world's biggest refugee crisis'
Over the next decade, climate breakdown will force tens of millions of people from their homes, creating the largest refugee crisis the world has ever experienced, according to a recent report. American defense and security experts believe Europe will experience massive challenges.

Shipping Executive Chides Industry 'Prostitutes' for Inaction
A British marine shipping executive has accused his industry of infiltrating its international oversight body in order to mislead the public about its paltry attempts to reduce its emissions.

Global atmospheric CO2 levels hit record high
The amount of carbon dioxide in the earth's atmosphere grew at record speed in 2017, hitting a level not seen for three million years. Sea levels at that time were thought to have been 20 metres higher than today. Will we see a similar rise? Yes, but there is a time delay between CO_2 reaching the upper atmosphere, and its full impact on polar and glacier ice, as reported.

Madagascar plague has infected 800
Health officials in Madagascar are struggling to contain a pneumonic strain that has infected 800 people. Many cases are the most virulent form of the pneumonic plague — the Black Death, as it was known in the Middle Ages. Pneumonic plague can be deadly, and spreads easily. More

Doctors sounding the alarm over global 'Antibiotic disaster'
Bacteria that contains a gene that confers resistance to the antibiotic colistin has been spreading across the globe at an alarming rate since it

was discovered 18 months earlier. In one area of China, 25% of hospital patients now carry the gene. Colistin is the 'antibiotic of last resort', so resistance to it has scientists fearing a bacterial apocalypse. More

No wild Atlantic salmon found in a major New Brunswick river

A New Brunswick river once teaming with Atlantic salmon no longer contains a single fish in the species, alarming those who blame this on the spread of aquaculture sites in the area. More

Warning of 'ecological Armageddon' after insect disappearance

Three-quarters of flying insects in nature reserves across Germany have vanished in 25 years, with serious implications for all life on Earth, scientists say. Insects play a critical role as both pollinators and prey for other wildlife. Destruction of wild areas and widespread use of pesticides are likely factors. Higher temperatures as well.

Pollution kills millions, costs trillions per year

Pollution kills at least nine million people and costs trillions of dollars every year, according to the most comprehensive global analysis to date -- the *Commission on Pollution and Health*. It warns the crisis "threatens the continuing survival of human societies." Pollution deaths are triple those from Aids, malaria and tuberculosis.

'Regreening' Planet' Could Cut 11.3B Tonnes of Carbon by 2030

Of the greenhouse gas reductions humanity must achieve by 2030, 37% could be provided through tree planting, peatland protection, and better land use, according to a new study. "Better stewardship of the land could have a bigger role in fighting climate change than previously thought," concluded an international research team led by The Nature Conservancy.

Renewables Will Lead American Job Growth for a Decade

Renewable energy will generate jobs in the United States "twice as fast as other occupations," predicts the U.S. Bureau of Labor Statistics. More

Local Rumblings

July 2023

News from outside their walls was grim. Cooperation and community were gone, friends and neighbours reduced to squabbling over what few resources they still had. A spirit of abundance through collaboration replaced by one of scarcity.

On a larger scale, some of the biggest migrant camps—in Spain, Italy, and Greece—were regularly rocked by food rioting. Though French camps were better managed, and those locked inside better fed, the cost was enormous. President Macron's support for open borders, for a humane, orderly process of resettling the masses of refugees—two million in the past year alone—had stretched public support to breaking. Re-elected in 2022 by the slimmest margin, the deciding factor had been his position on migration: was it not better to help the world's desperate settle in France and a small number of likeminded countries, than join the ranks of nations forcing back boats and barricading highways and rail lines?

"It's a question of humanity," he restated in a New Year's Day 2023 broadcast. "Are we people who put up walls, who believe others must die so we can live, who will kill to protect our patch of soil?"

To this, François added, as he and Simone listened, "Do we wish our souls to live, or do we kill what's left, beyond our physical body? A hot, dry, crowded France; or a hot, dry, walled-in France, its people morally dead."

"Yet here we are at GV Assisi, stuck inside a fence of our own making," Simone noted, wryly. François took a moment before responding.

"I would like nothing more than to take it all down. If our family was not at risk from native vigilantes and traffickers."

"Fences within fences." Simone shook her head. "Everyone's a prisoner."

Leaders of other countries had challenged their electorate to share their good fortune, and lost. Australia, Malaysia, South Africa, Austria, Greece and Denmark. The Spanish government was teetering on the edge, but the country had fractured in 2021 into three separate regions. Spain proper was half its original size.

Even in France, the central government was having a hard time maintaining authority. A number of *départements* close to Spain and Italy barely recognized the president. Those with a Mediterranean coastline were threatening to secede unless strict controls were enacted and policing increased.

The dilemma every desirable region faced was both moral and practical. Bans or quotas on refugees involved repelling people at the border; sending boats back out to sea. Dilapidated, overcrowded boats, without water, food or fuel. A death sentence. But accepting them meant more would keep coming. More mouths to feed, shelter to provide and fences to erect. There were limits to how many a country could properly resettle. Limits long surpassed, Simone knew. Hence, the holding pens.

Outside these pens, life was little better for migrants. Without jobs or housing, they resorted to begging, stealing or trading what little they had. For men, there was dangerous and illegal physical work, arranged by people thriving in this new economy. For women it was worse, if that was possible. A very few might be offered farm or domestic labour for meagre wages. That market was saturated. So was the one for sex workers. Which left sex slavery—service in exchange for a place to sleep and something to eat. Until you were used up. And replaced.

Fences within fences. GV Assisi struggled to protect its 60 residents from outside danger. Beyond 60, conditions would not be sustainable. More bodies could be packed in, but there was a limit to food, water and sanitation capacity. Land had to be reserved for growing, and water for irrigation. Overcrowding would breed disease.

Disease presented a major dilemma: to treat people who arrived with disease, or to bar them? A dilemma facing much of the world: how many, and what to do with the rest?

By the summer of 2023, external forces resolved the dilemma for François and Simone. Not a single migrant had made it to their gates since March. The few who were risking the open road were being scooped up long before reaching them. Paramilitary groups had grown in size and influence, funded by 'takings'. Small businesses and farms were forced to pay 'protection' in food or cash. At one time, protection might have been welcomed in the area: from the gangs that targeted harvests and property, and from petty thievery by passing migrants. Now, the greater threat was these self-appointed protectors.

Failure to pay was punished. Sometimes by seizure of food or equipment; sometimes by torching of fields or buildings. In the case of a refuge like GV Assisi, it might be through seizure of residents with market value.

In July, two young men from GV Assisi had been accused of stealing supplies from a bakery in a neighbouring village. Once owned by friends of François, it was now run by a family that had long opposed his vision, the local consensus vision, of welcoming migrants. He had won that battle, but made enemies. Like the Lepines.

Mario Lepine, the youngest son, had moved away for several years, taking his nativist message to Marseilles, where he was said to have linked up with a supremacist paramilitary. Now he was back, sporting a White Wolves uniform; extending the group's reach and revenue by confiscating viable businesses.

The Wolves focused on basics which everyone still needed: Groceries, building materials, gasoline and generators, solar panels and small wind turbines. Recently they had targeted drinking water, trucking it to areas where wells had gone dry. Where they acquired it, and how, one could only guess. They were said to be logging public forests and confiscating good agricultural land to the east—things the organized crime syndicates had been doing for several years.

Saving Humanity

June 2020, Off the coast of Sicily

Adriana Cologna was exhausted. Night after night, patrolling the Mediterranean. Triage, triage and more triage. Always needing to stay sharp. Making split-second decisions with life-changing consequences. Quarantine or no quarantine? Separating friends from friends, parents from children. One mistake, and even more lives would be lost. One mistake, and more volunteers would be infected. One error with her gloves, or mask, or suit, or end-of-shift shower, and she would be infected too. Then what? Then who?

Night after night. With no end to the stream. The floating bodies. The misery.

Operation Samaritan had 12 boats in the water at its peak in 2017, but only three now. Not because the need had dwindled. It had grown 10 times. A tsunami of need, rising with the oceans.

Turmoil in so many of its European donor countries translated to less state support or private contributions for frontline intervention. Meaning fewer volunteers, reduced levels of service, deferred maintenance of equipment and the gradual collapse of the network.

Adriana had served 53 tours of duty over nearly five years. She'd gone from rookie, to veteran, to old grey mare. Only one of the ship captains had served longer than her. But he didn't have to look at the faces. Or touch them. The living, the dead, the nearly dead. He didn't make life or death judgements dozens of times a night. Thumbs up, thumbs down, for 20 nights in a row.

When she'd started, it was six nights on, then a mandatory four off. Never 10 in a row; 20 was unthinkable. People can't function.

But they had to. The only other option was to call off the operation. Declare it over, a failure. Plenty of critics would have loved that. The first year, they were heroes. Soon, as the need and response grew, they became targets. *Facilitators of misery. If the bleeding hearts weren't encouraging people to keep taking to the sea, the crisis would end. They'd stay home.*

Home. What home was that? Which of them had a home? Now, or when they started the long march of misery and predation.

Still, tired as she was, Adriana could have had a worse job. She might have been a snatcher, if she were bigger and stronger. Reaching out from the swing arm to spot and snatch living bodies from among the dead. Bobbing for bodies in rough seas. They were the real heroes. Tonight, Luca had pulled off another miracle, snatching a little African girl from the hands of a badly injured man.

"Strangest thing," Luca said. "A big, strong Italian boy. Built like a competitive swimmer, wearing just his underwear. Died just after we pulled him out. Severe head wound."

"Tell my mother I did like she taught me", the boy said.

"I hope his mother will know. We couldn't find any ID."

Wolves at the Door

"Wolves!" François shouted to Simone from the living room.
"What did you say?" she responded, removing her headphones.

"A pickup truck at the gate. Five or six men!"

"White Wolves?" Simone blurted as she ran into the room. She stopped in front of the monitor where François sat, her brow furrowed and heart racing.

The Wolves had not seized any farms in the Drome as far as they knew, but productive ones were bound to be targeted. The best any farmer could do at this point was provide advance warning to others of intimidation in the area. Giving time to flee or hide. Resistance would be difficult.

"Watch the screen for trouble along the perimeter," François instructed Simone. "I've already alerted Robert."

"I'll gather a few of our men and find out what they want," he shouted from the door as he yanked on his boots. "If they breech the gate, stay out of sight."

Though itching for action, Simone agreed. She'd be of little use in a physical confrontation. Yet knowing what these people were capable of—said to be engaged in—she wished there was a way to knock them down a peg. But with what? She noticed François had not taken his rifle. Probably wise. He'd be badly out-gunned.

She knew where the key was, and the ammunition. She'd have a great sight line from the open bathroom window. How could she just sit and watch?

The confrontation lasted 10 minutes. Mostly Mario Lepine shouting through the gate at François from the bed of the pickup.

"Traitor! *Kaffer*-lover!" Simone heard over the monitor. "Bring them out and let them pay. Or do you train them to rob locals of their hard-earned goods!" It would be laughable, this random tirade, thought Simone, if it weren't for the imbalance of arms.

Distracted by this noisy activity at the front gate, she failed to notice that the camera facing the southern fields had gone black. Now, as she ran to the kitchen window to get a direct view in that direction, she heard frightened shouts coming from the dormitory for single men. Then shots. One, two, three, four.

From the kitchen, she saw two hooded men running from the scene, towards the main gate. Each brandished a pistol. François and the others would be turning to face them, unarmed.

Sprinting to the bathroom window, Simone raised the rifle she had loaded in anticipation. They were less than 20 metres away and walking slowly now, anticipating a gunfight. Breathe, hold, sight, squeeze. One went down. The other came to an abrupt halt, baffled, searching for where the shot had come from. Breathe, hold, sight, squeeze. Two down. Both men had dropped their pistols now, and were making a gesture of surrender. From the road, she could hear hollering and banging.

"Open immediately, or we torch the place!" screamed Mario.

Over the din, she made out a deep roaring sound, growing as lights flooded the road. Back at the monitor she saw Mario and his accomplices leap down, seconds before their pickup was knocked onto its side by a giant purple truck. Robert Giroux emerged from it with his two sons, brandishing rifles as the White Wolves disappeared into the dark of the field on the far side of the road.

Simone's heart was pounding. A natural shot, the biathlon coach had called her. Muscle memory, she recognized, as her jittery hands put the box of ammunition and rifle back where François kept them. *How are we going to explain this?*

They wouldn't have to. Outside events took care of it, though not in time to spare residents this latest trauma; certainly not in time for Khalid and Samir. Friends who had escaped the Russo-Syrian invasion of Lebanon, making it all the way to France, only to be shot in cold blood. For a fabricated theft of bread. Mere boys.

Local outrage was swift. Members of the Lepine family escaped by car mere minutes before the bakery was set afire. It would mean the loss of jobs and a valuable resource, but to people forced to suffer the insult of bowing to thugs, it was worth it.

The Lepine clan, supported by a ragtag unit of the White Wolves, had been doing more than running a profiteering and protection racket. They had begun to traffic in slave labour for the farms and workhouses of Drome and Vaucluse. They were also peddling opioids, creating new clients by lacing some of the alcohol and cigarettes sold in their shops with chemicals produced in the labs of affiliates in Spain. The use of guns that night was not typical. They preferred to punish by quieter means. Dusting personal items of an intended victim with fentanyl, or even deadlier opiates, was so much easier, and hard to trace. Hats, work gloves, steering wheels… the handlebars of a bicycle.

In a different time, police would have been called. Arrests would have been made, trials held and sentences served. Today, a rougher justice was used.

Samir and Khalid were buried quickly, as was their custom. One of the older residents led the funeral. Tears were shed by a few. Most were incapable.

The injured assassins were treated for their bullet wounds. One had been hit in the buttocks, the other in the shoulder. "I'd have preferred a clean shot through the heart," Simone muttered darkly to François, the evening of the funeral. "I just couldn't find one." She had never killed, but now felt that she could.

Wounds cleaned and dressed, the pair were driven out to the highway, where they were left to fend for themselves without food, water, money or weapons. While some clamoured for physical punishment, a few calling for their death, François insisted this would only bloody everyone's hands.

Any expectation that their White Wolves comrades would take care of them had evaporated when they learned the fate of five of the six who fled into the dark. A villager stumbled across their bodies in a ditch less than two kilometres away, stripped of their uniform shirts and caps. The cause of death would never be confirmed, but seemed obvious. A half empty bottle of vodka lay beside one of them. Furnished by the man who provided their telltale uniforms, then took them back. He did not want witnesses to his failure.

Like the rest of his family, he had vanished. But for how long? A fresh squad of eager Wolves was easily recruited. All it took was a shirt, a cap, food, cigarettes and alcohol—with a little extra to keep them loyal. For as long as they were needed.

Hearts in Other Lands

On the following Sunday, five days after the night of violence, François led a special service at the local Catholic church. It was open to anyone, GV residents included. It began with a symbolic freedom march along the road to Le Tilleret. Friends and parishioners had scouted the surrounding area in advance and called around to confirm the region was quiet. On each approaching road, a hidden sentinel kept watch.

Simone did not attend. Instead, she led a ritual for three residents who, like her, chose not to venture out. As the rest were led out the gate by François, two of the women in niqab, she imagined herself in their place. Her face fully covered, but feet free to step over the line. The idea left her trembling.

François' service was a hybrid. Catholic, Muslim, Jewish, Buddhist, pagan; he brought together common stories and shared values of world religions. Mostly around care for the downtrodden. Crosses and overtly Christian symbols were supplemented by embroidered sashes and painted banners that represented important symbols of other faiths. Rather than covering over this obviously Christian place of worship, he and its parishioners had chosen to add to it.

Sitting at an open window with the others in quiet contemplation, Simone recognized the music. Sibelius's *Finlandia*, carried by the breeze. She hummed along at first, then sang as some of the English words she learned at church came to her.

... other hearts in other lands are beating,
With hopes and dreams as true and high as mine...

* * *

"Why do you think the *Laudato Si* encyclical had so little impact?" Simone asked François later that night, after he recounted how moved he was by the neighbours' show of solidarity. They were sitting in the living room, lit by a single candle.

"Didn't you think it would have more of a galvanizing effect," she said, "uniting Catholics around the world?"

"I thought it would," he answered. "But when I began leading discussion groups, something became clear. You see, this was not just an 'environmental encyclical,' as some had heard. It went so much deeper. Pope Francis speaks of humility, compassion, gentleness and caring—for less fortunate humans and for animals who require our protection. He reminds us that those who are genuinely strong, like Joseph as presented in the Gospel, must be capable of great tenderness. Such tenderness is not a sign of weakness, but strength."

"People had trouble with that?"

"By itself, this appeal for a kinder way of living wasn't a problem. We hear it all the time. Yet we live in a world that is the opposite—full of bombast and self-promotion. Our internet world is all about 'look at me, look at me.' Few people remember how to do good things for the simple personal satisfaction. So, when you hear the Pope reminding you that the road to fulfillment is not about wealth and power and the latest gadgets, this is an attack not just on our society, but our identity."

"And nobody wants to face *that*," said Simone. "To hear they've got it backwards."

François nodded. "Living a bad life, a wrong life, when they believe they are good. Because they give to charity, and purchase free range chicken."

Simone laughed. "Though that's not exactly what he's saying."

"It isn't, and yet it is. Here..." He picked up the candle and walked to the bookshelf where he found his worn copy of the booklet.

"I haven't opened it for years," he admitted, standing in front of Simone. "It carries bad memories, but good ones too."

"How so?"

"The feeling that I failed to inspire people; to adopt a healthier way of living."

Simone shook her head. "You and me both!"

"Yes, I guess so." François eyes met hers. He looked tired. The recent events had taken a toll. "There are some particular lines I felt sure would resonate, and yet often had the opposite effect." He placed the candle on a side table and flicked on a reading light.

"*Why are we here?*" François read from a dog-eared page. "*What is the goal of our work and all our efforts? What need does the earth have of us?*"

He skipped forward a line. "*We need to see that what is at stake is our own dignity. Leaving an inhabitable planet to future generations is first and foremost up to us. The issue is one which dramatically affects us, for it has to do with the ultimate meaning of our earthly sojourn.*"

He skipped forward several pages. "*Reducing greenhouse gases requires honesty, courage and responsibility, above all on the part of those countries which are more powerful and pollute the most...*"

"I can hear a finger being pointed," said Simone. "Do you think that's what irritated people? Getting called out by the Pope."

"Partly. Mostly, I think it was the prescription. What they were being challenged to do, and be, was just too far from what they imagined themselves capable of."

"When embedded in a society that is almost the polar opposite," Simone added wistfully. "You know: 'What will the neighbours think?' Or maybe: 'The work I do conflicts with my values, but I need the job'."

"Yes, yes." François said. "I recall one passage being hardest of all to swallow. Some of those Capitalist Christians went berserk. In America, but even Australia and Africa."

He flipped through the booklet until he found the page. "*When profits alone count, there can be no thinking about the rhythms of nature, its phases of decay and regeneration, or the complexity of ecosystems... biodiversity is considered at most a deposit of economic resources, available for exploitation, with no serious thought for the real value of things, their significance for persons and cultures, or the concerns and needs of the poor.*"

"The Pope, questioning the free market!" Simone mocked. "Heaven forbid."

"Oh, but he gets worse. Radical. Socialist even."

"You mean, like Jesus Christ?"

"Yes," said François slowly breaking into a smile. "Like Jesus. Who some now think was on the side of the money lenders and slave traders."

"Weird, eh? How far people can get from their own gospel."

"Here," he continued. "*It is not enough to balance, in the medium term, the protection of nature with financial gain, or the preservation of the environment with progress. Halfway measures simply delay the inevitable disaster...*"

"Sounds like the debate over pipelines in Canada," said Simone. "Pump more oil to fund the transition from oil. The Trudeau government, trying to have it both ways. I'm sure I wrote something like that."

"Trudeau, and pretty much every government—throughout history."

"True," Simone acknowledged. "I don't know if there was any other way to get elected, and stay in power long enough to change things."

"So here we find the real prescription. Pope Francis talks about the need for all of us to develop self-awareness, to understand that real satisfaction comes from within."

François ran his finger under the line as he read. "*Obsession with a consumerist lifestyle, above all when few people are capable of maintaining it, can only lead to violence and mutual destruction.*"

"Though consumerism is all most have ever known," said Simone.

"*A person who could afford to spend and consume more, but regularly uses less heating and wears warmer clothes, shows the kind of convictions and attitudes which help to protect the environment. There is a nobility in the duty to care for creation with little actions.*"

"Good line!" Simone chuckled, nodding. "I often felt that way. I got a thrill from 'little actions': turning off lights, shutting down everything at night, and when I went out. Riding my bike... but you can't go around preaching. People hate that."

"They do. I know it well."

"St. François?" she poked. He glowered briefly, then read some more.

"*We need to take up an ancient lesson, found in different religious traditions and also in the Bible. It is the conviction that 'less is more.'*"

"Simplicity and sobriety when lived voluntarily is liberating," he added, in his own words.

"Living lightly!" Simone said, quoting with her fingers. "That's what I called it."

"He comes not from above but from within."

"There's so much there," she said.

"So demanding," François countered.

"So easy to dismiss," she concluded, sadness creeping into her voice.

Stay or Go

October 2023, Hokkaido, Japan

"So," Jenny asked, "do we stay or do we go?" One glance between Anna and Yuki was all it took.

"Do we stay or do we go now?" they chanted, leaping up and doing a pogo dance to the eighties The Clash hit.

"No," Jenny laughed as the floor underneath her armchair began to bounce. "I'm being serious!"

"Right," said Anna, promptly halting. "Yuki, we're being serious!" she declared with an exaggerated frown.

"Beep, beep. Switching to serious mode," said Yuki, plopping back into the sofa she and Anna had been occupying in the sparse living room of their Hakodate apartment—home since they had moved to the island of Hokkaido, 18 months earlier.

"Ahh, you two kill me," said Jenny, rolling her eyes.

"Better us, than someone else," said Anna. It had been meant as a joke, but once it was out, all three went silent.

"Well, that brings me back to my question, doesn't it?" Jenny eyed her daughters in turn. "Go now, while we have a chance, or stay and prepare for the worst?"

"Mmm," said Yuki. "The problem is, we don't actually know which will be worse. Staying or going."

"We do know one thing," said Anna. "It's bad and getting worse in China, and now they're exporting it. Those boats trying to land in Ishikari Bay are going to overrun Sapporo soon. Just down the road." She glanced toward the small open window which looked onto the street.

Jenny agreed. "If not by armed force, then infection."

"Pneumonic plague," said Yuki, hacking and gagging. "Evil!"

"Exactly," said Jenny. "We're lucky it hasn't hit Hakodate yet. Just the few isolated cases. But you know it's going to. So…"

"Do we stay or do we go?" Anna finished the sentence, without humour this time.

"Then there's your military service," Jenny reminded Yuki. "Anna's done her basic naval training. You're next. Twelve days until you report. Only this time, I don't think they'll be permitting draftees to return home once the 3-month training is over."

"You can't *not* report!" Anna said, aghast. "That's a prison term."

"Precisely," said Jenny. "At risk of repeating myself—again!"

"It's now or never," said Yuki. "To leave, that is."

"But where?" said Anna. "And how? Our navy isn't just keeping *out* the Harbin Chinese. They're keeping *in* deserters."

"*Traitors to the Emperor!*" Yuki mimicked.

"Did you say *our* navy, Anna?" Jenny was incensed. "Since when is it *our* navy. As if Japan ever accorded us the benefits of citizenship. Me, at least."

"Sorry, Mama." Anna leaned over and stroked her hand. "Half Japanese, you know. Half Malaysian."

"Three-eighths Japanese," Yuki corrected.

"Be that as it may," said Jenny. "We were lucky to get a place here, courtesy of the governor and his interest in the Clean Freighter business, but our days are numbered. JSS Enterprises will be one of the first targets of any Harbin drones; to figure out where our parts are being tooled. The sooner we get the last two freighters loaded with our assembly equipment and on their way to Vancouver, the better. At least there's a chance of Paul keeping the business going there. And your navigation systems out of prying hands," she said to Yuki.

"*Our* navigation systems," Anna corrected.

"OK Anna," said Jenny. "*Your* navigation systems." Yuki rolled her eyes.

"You know they won't just let you cruise out of Japanese waters," said Anna. "With all our intellectual property. You do know that, right Mama?"

Jenny nodded. "Why do you think we haven't left already."

"We need AN ESCAPE PLAN," Yuki declared to Anna, opening her eyes wide and flashing a demonic grin.

"A DIVERSION," proposed Anna. "BANG, BOOM, POW!"

"And soon," said Jenny, without a trace of a smile.

Radio GaGa, 2023

This is the BBC World Service. In the news tonight:

- *Hurricane Yuri pummels Haiti before soaking Cuba a second time;*
- *Government troops battle to suppress militias in Texas and Oklahoma;*
- *Wheat crop failure in Australia foreshadows end of domestic agriculture;*
- *Bee colony collapse in South America reduces fruit and crop yields by over half;*
- *And, the World Health Organization calls for air travel ban to curb Ebola outbreak.*

The radio brought a relentless storm of bad news. Still, Simone had to listen. "Better to know what's coming than to be caught off guard," she would say.

"Better to find strength and grace in small moments of beauty than to be sapped by events beyond your control," François would counter.

Simone listened and mulled. François read, and meditated. Sometimes they shared. In tandem, they struggled to support their shrinking family.

Illness had taken several. Tuberculosis, the highly-resistant strain. Madness took several more, borne out of the sense of imprisonment Simone knew so well. Three suicides in a week. She remembered such epidemics in northern Canada. Eventually, it runs its course, and there is stability. Then it starts again.

Four residents had left. Young men, determined to make it to a city where they felt sure a friend or relative would take them in. It beat staying cooped up. Like fish in a bowl, with cats prowling all around. Off they had gone, carrying supplies and warnings of what to expect on the road.

Simone had taken a similar chance two years earlier. Now would be far worse, she reminded herself. Every time she was tempted.

In Canada, the situation was not as bad, said the radio. Distance and three oceans had kept migrant numbers below five million. Most arrived via the United States. A long and violent trek by foot, bicycle, horseback or whatever vehicle you could commandeer and find a way to run. While some states were friendlier than others, all routes traversed several where refugees were officially and blatantly unwelcome. Nobody bothered to detain or arrest now. *Just patrol the highways and keep 'em moving.* Samaritan groups offered food and water, but rarely refuge.

The border wall with Mexico was being torn down as fast as it could be rebuilt. *Let 'em through*, many argued, *then keep 'em moving north.* Hunger and disease culled the numbers who made it to Canada. Also kidnapping, for farm labour or the slave trade.

Like the four chancing the roads of France, the millions fleeing South and Central America knew what to expect. But they kept coming. The alternative was worse.

Brazil, Uruguay, Paraguay, Colombia, Venezuela, Peru, Bolivia, Central America, and Mexico... Each had followed its own course, but there was a pattern. To start, some combination of drought, flooding, deforestation, and overfishing. Leading to the next stage: hunger, thirst and infectious disease. Then profiteering, and the growth of criminal gangs in place of, or competing with elected government.

Much of South America was experiencing some level of state dissolution. Brazil had fractured into five separate states. Amazonia was run by a warlord, clearcutting nature reserves and state parks. Tens of millions had flooded north and west from the main cities, hoping to claim a patch of land. Biofuel and soya cartels supported by their own private armies were seizing property.

The big cities had exploded, with the exception of Curitiba and Porto Allegre. Rio de Janeiro was abandoned. The incessant rains of 2022, followed by a hurricane and storm surge, did massive damage to wealthy enclaves along the southern beaches and took out coastal roads, the airport and the industrial area along heavily-polluted Guanabara Bay. When several hillside favelas began to slide, residents poured into the damaged hotels along the waterfront. Until they burned.

Nobody knew who lit the initial fires, but copycat arsonists soon torched Leblon and Ipanema. From there it spread across the city. With key infrastructure destroyed, and water badly polluted, cholera ran rampant.

Sao Paolo was spared the worst of the rain, but events in Rio unleashed a pent-up rage. All that was wrong with Brazil simply erupted—the racial divide, the corruption, the decades of failure to share its abundant resources. The first targets were banks, luxury goods stores and gated compounds of the elites. Followed by government offices, courts and, inexplicably, power plants.

As bad as things were in Brazil, the *Highway from Hell* countries sounded worse. Panama, Costa Rica, Honduras, Nicaragua, Guatemala—food and anything portable stripped, forests and wildlife raped. In Mexico, the federal government crumbled in 2022 under the weight of civil strife. A simultaneous drought and collapse of bee populations set off the famine. Crops failed, as they would across North America, but the riots in cities were over water.

With so many people malnourished and poorly housed, and so many more in sprawling internment camps—exposed, drinking foul water and using tainted drugs—Mexico's large cities were a breeding ground for disease and violence on a scale nobody was equipped to contain.

Criminal gangs had been quick to step in to the vacuum. By 2023, Mexico consisted of multiple fiefdoms. If pledging allegiance to the local boss was the way to gain protection and food; if joining the battle with a rival was demanded, so be it. Desperate times.

Simone marvelled that anyone was still reporting. She wasn't sure whether to be thankful, or wish she could be spared. Still, she listened.

Not all regions were in chaos. In North America's Pacific Northwest and Atlantic Northeast, as in Scandinavia and Western Australia, people had rallied around their elected governments and institutions. Order was holding, and economic activity was sufficient to meet people's needs. Surely, it must be in some other places too.

Not in New Zealand, where a class war was raging. Ultra-rich from all over the world had flown in to use the bunkers they had been building in anticipation of this chaos. They were prepared to spend whatever it took for basic supplies, which left poorer locals and migrants unable to afford what remained. Force was the only way.

Secession in many countries grew out of disagreement over admitting migrants and redistributing land. Germany and the Netherlands had recently fractured into anti- and pro-resettlement regions.

Enough is enough! But where will they go?

* * *

By mid-2023, the open exchange of ideas, information and even private messages had mostly disappeared. To think people had once spoken of the internet as a tool for democracy. If not for the Global Freenet—the bold idea of some students in Ireland, supported by a pair of Silicon Valley retirees—it would no longer be possible to send electronic messages, free of corporate or political interference.

The Global Freenet was, as its name implied, 'free to access, free to use, and free from censorship or advertising'. Its administrators—*Seekers*, they called themselves—could not guarantee freedom from surveillance, but they were working on an encoding service that would make this possible. Soon.

Simone followed these developments with growing frustration. By radio.

Soon, they said. But would it be soon enough?

A Curious Death

onsoir! You are listening to Radio Canada's weekly world news digest. In this edition, we focus on international cooperation, as 15 more countries withdraw from United Nations membership, citing inability to pay. The UN secretary general warns that its partner agencies will no longer be able to deliver basic human health programs, or engage in oversight of atmospheric or marine health. In a report by Chloe Duhamel, we look at what this could mean for struggling efforts to fight recent outbreaks of infectious diseases.

Later, we look at how some democratic leaders are forging pragmatic ties with authoritarian breakaway states in a bid to limit regional violence, protect water supplies and prevent desertification of crop lands.

In her report titled, 'What to do when you can't stomach your federal government', Vancouver correspondent Yvette Deschamps describes the new cooperation agreement signed by British Columbia, Washington and Oregon, and compares it with the deal made last month to bring Quebec and the Atlantic Provinces into a tighter alliance with some northeast American states.

Our agriculture specialist, Paul-Luc Tardif gets his hands dirty, as he investigates what crop disease in much of Europe means for the hungry continent.

And we'll close with Koichi Yamashita in Tokyo, who sheds light on the curious death of energy innovator Jenny Fung.

"François!" Simone cried. "Something happened to Jenny!"

He rushed into the room to find a trembling Simone, her arms wrapped tightly around her knees, rocking back and forth in the kitchen chair. As the opening reports wore on, he was able to coax her onto the sofa, where they sat in silence, waiting.

Things were going badly in Japan. They knew this from reports of clashes between its fledgling navy and Chinese ships sent out to ensure safe passage for 'boat people' fleeing crop failure and an avian flu pandemic. The departure in 2020 of the US Navy from its bases in Japan had prompted a full-scale Japanese military buildup.

François had been careful not to track Jenny's progress, worried this would be cross-referenced. Her friendship with Simone was well known.

"Here it comes," Simone said anxiously. He held her hand as the reporter, a Japanese man speaking in French, began the tale.

In her 50 years, Jenny Fung lived more than most could in two or three lives.

As successful as she was in many things, her life was afflicted by a series of blows: the murder of a dear friend in the United States; the loss of her parents during ethnic riots in Malaysia; the loss of her husband in his act of heroism at Fukushima Daiichi and almost immediately after, the disappearance of Canadian journalist Simone Cohen—a close friend—now presumed dead.

François felt Simone flinch, but she remained riveted to the radio.

Recently, in partnership with daughters Anna and Yuki—engineering prodigies in their own right—and the enigmatic Four Elements governor of Hokkaido, she created JSS Enterprises, with boat yards and design services in Hakodate and Vancouver. She and her daughters were seen by many as beacons of hope. If anyone could help the world find a way out of the darkness, it would be her. Them.

Why then did their car burst into flames and plunge into the ocean? The only eyewitnesses—an elderly couple coming the other way along the curving coastal highway—saw a massive explosion in the distance, then a fiery object plummeting into the water. Drone footage from several craft in the air at the time—too far to provide clear images—confirms the sequence of events. Divers later tried to locate the vehicle in the deep water. Two pieces of the car were salvaged, but no bodies.

A hydrogen vehicle explodes. Sad, but simple. Then again, why?

Recently, Ms. Fung would have witnessed battles off the coast of Hokkaido and raids by the Harbin secessionist regime. Refugees had been landing in large numbers, many carrying pneumonic plague. The three women had many good reasons to leave, but indicated no signs of doing so. Which feeds the rumours.

Was it a contract murder? Enemies of her husband, perhaps? Vengeful nuclear investors? Maybe the American, Elmore Lambert, architect of one friend's murder and now an active player in organized crime.

Or the simplest explanation: a suicide pact between three women who endured too much. Perhaps a distraught mother's murder-suicide. One guess is as good as another.

For Radio Canada International, I'm Koichi Yamashita in Tokyo.

That's world digest for this week. Tune in again soon. We might be on the air.

After a long silence, Simone blurted "They're alive! You know that, don't you?"

"No," said François candidly. "But you seem to."

Simone went to bed with a smile. She would give Jenny a month, then reach out through the Global Freenet.

News of Family

September 2024

The next morning at breakfast Simone confronted François about his family, a subject he had resolutely avoided. Where were his children? Why were they not in touch? What was the status of his relationship with Nicole? Her questions verged on aggression.

'Missing, presumed dead.' She was desperate to contact her family, and had an idea for how.

For three years he had brushed her off, politely. But now, taking a deep breath, he began his story.

"It was never my intention to hurt anyone. I needed a break. I had to get away and clear my head. I couldn't see a way to... press the reset button. Not in Strasbourg. The things I was drawn to do were so different from our life there. I came here to see if there was another life. I knew there would be consequences, but I was no longer the husband or father I wanted to be."

She examined François' face carefully. His eyes betrayed a deep sadness.

"I was harming those I loved, and to stop this I had to find internal peace."

"Did you think your separation would be permanent?" Simone asked.

"I didn't really know. I was hoping if I established a comfortable life here, a place that appealed to Nicole and the children, they would come to share my dream."

Simone eyed him intently, then shook her head.

"That was arrogant, I know now. I suppose I wanted both— my family to be a happy unit again, but here in this place I was creating."

"Though you misjudged them," Simone said, her brow furrowed.

"Yes," he said softly. "We each have our own dreams." He paused, chewing his lip, then looked away towards the window, where the sun was now streaming in, promising another hot day.

"They never even gave it a chance!" François' tone was higher. "I understood Nicole not visiting. She knew the place already, and she was the one I had split from. I thought the children would want to see it and establish some kind of relationship with their father. But no. They must have felt rejected. Like I had walked out on *them*."

"Which you had."

"Yes," he said, "but I hoped they'd see it wasn't about them."

Simone had never seen him this vulnerable. "Did you ever hear from them?"

"At first. A polite card at Christmas, and on my birthday. I assume Nicole put them up to it. A few times a year I'd write to share what I was doing. Invite them to visit."

"And?"

"Sylvie came once. With a boyfriend." He shook his head. "I'd forgotten about that. He was intrigued. Helped out a lot. But she spent the whole time angry. Making remarks about my 'hermit' lifestyle. They left early."

"And Marc. Any word from him?

"Not once. I wouldn't even know about his marriage, or the birth of his son two years ago, if it weren't for Nicole's sister. She thought I should know."

"Any recent news?"

François again looked out the window. He sighed, then turned and gave her an embarrassed smile, his shoulders hunching up. Simone thought she saw tears forming.

"I admit I Googled them a few times. As recently as... 2021, shortly before you came. I found some basic information. Career stuff. Both were in Paris for awhile. Then Sylvie was in Bordeaux, where she was in public relations or something. But it felt terrible prowling that way. I decided that if they didn't wish to share their lives with me, it wasn't right for me to stalk them. Besides, it only made me sad."

Simone nodded. "I can imagine. A severed connection. Whatever lies underneath—pride, bitterness maybe—it's hard for people to move beyond those feelings."

François' thoughts were drifting, his expression stoic.

"And Nicole?" Simone continued. "You were in contact for a while, right?"

"At first. Decisions about Marc and Sylvie. I let her make them. The easy route. It was guilt I suppose, lessening my pain, but increasing theirs. A father who doesn't care enough to have an opinion; that must be how it looked."

"Yes, I suppose it did." Simone paused, choosing her next words carefully. "You were in touch regarding refugees... you told me once."

"That's right. She was involved in settling refugees. Working for the city, in social services. She advised me on helping some young men. When this was just a farm. We worked together to arrange safe passage. But then..."

Simone waited. "Then?" François looked at her, momentarily lost.

"We let it drop. The numbers were too great. Strasbourg couldn't take more. Nor could others in her network. Full up. She was burning out. I invited her to visit, the last time we spoke. But she declined."

"Do you think she sensed you wanted more?" Simone probed. He nodded.

"And did you?"

François' face turned red. "It wasn't planned," he said defensively. "There was a bond. Still. Deep down, there was respect."

"Hidden under the pain, and resentment."

François looked at his hands, cracked and rough, as he considered her words. She chose not to wait. "Did she ever remarry?"

"No," he replied cautiously. "I expect there were other men, but…"

"You see," he resumed, "we never divorced." Noting Simone's surprise, he gave a half-hearted explanation. "There was no reason to, once the children were adults."

She offered him a warm smile. Then made her move. "I've been thinking…"

"Mmm, about what?"

"Family. Connections. Regrets." She paused.

"I'll get to the point," she resumed, speaking quickly and loudly. "I need to contact my husband, my family. They have to be struggling with the thought that I may have died. You heard that report. It's not fair to leave them like that. Nor me. *I* need to know how *they* are. Sure, I could find a way to Google them, or whatever we do on this sad excuse for an internet. Find a few crumbs. Some indication they're alive and well."

"For the first two years, I could comfort myself by trusting they were fine." Simone was speaking more calmly now, but her heart felt like a clamp had been attached. "It was me that was the worry. But now, with the violence and disease, I can't assume anything. I need to know. I need them to know."

"I understand," François said softly. "That news about Jenny changes everything." Simone nodded, fighting tears.

"I'll understand if she needs time before hailing in, but I want her and my family to know about me. They deserve it."

"So you need my help. And Nicole's?"

Simone's mouth dropped. Had she been that transparent?

"If you don't mind," she said. "If you can, and think she would. I have a plan that could work, without putting any of us in jeopardy. Least of all her, or you. Besides, the inconsequential Simone Cohen must be the last thought on anyone's mind now, however much I pissed them off. Secession, gangs, pneumonic plague... What kind of a grudge would have you chase me across an ocean when the world's falling apart?"

"Still," warned François, "there's no point being foolish. Tell me your plan."

When she was done, he took a moment to test her on possible pitfalls. They agreed that the first part posed no security risk. The second, however, would be trickier.

The first hurdle did involve emotional risk, though. The phone call. Simone left François alone for that. She had work to do and residents to check on. A pregnant young woman was overdue. *By decades*, thought Simone. This mad, ugly world. So much for perpetual progress. Or the arc of history tending toward justice.

Violence and general insecurity in their region had abated, as disease ran rampant across southern and central Europe. Internment camps along the Mediterranean served as breeding grounds. For tuberculosis—the virulent new strain; for a highly contagious influenza; for several strains of bacteria that resisted all antibiotics; and now for Ebola. The ban on commercial air travel agreed to by most states a year earlier came too late, and far too many private planes were still flying.

A disease prevention strategy enacted by the French government six months earlier achieved minimal success. Despite strict protocols, almost all quarantine efforts failed. Too few trained staff and volunteers and too little medication and effective vaccine. Disease was creeping northward, carried by medical workers passing through quarantine zones and escapees who felt their chances of survival were better outside.

Europe's highways were strewn with corpses and abandoned vehicles. Drivers and passengers succumbing to disease, starvation or dehydration on the road to somewhere better. You couldn't escape a threat that was already in your car or bus. Not all had died from disease. Even the healthy could run out of fuel, then food and water.

Most were choosing to stay put though, hoping quarantine measures in their towns, gated communities or apartment blocks would be sufficient; everyone praying that food and water would last until the outbreaks ran their course.

Water would be the prime disease vector, followed by insects, birds and feral animals. The communities faring best were ones like GV Assisi, where water, food and power could be locally sourced and gates kept closed. GV Assisi could last a while yet, but not if 2024 brought more extreme heat and drought. Water supplies would fail. Crops and fruit trees too. As for medicine, they had none to speak of. Only herbal remedies, to complement prevention through nutrition and hygiene.

A reliable energy supply meant they had hot water for hand and dishwashing, and the means to sterilize drinking water. A special meeting had been held to walk the remaining residents through the protocol. Hand washing with soap and hot water after every visit to the toilet or composting outhouse. The same before every meal. Sharing of drinking glasses was forbidden. Cooks and wash-up teams were given special instructions, and posters with images were pinned up in all food preparation areas.

Little stood in the way of insects and birds, though. Spraying was out of the question. Without pollinators, all was lost.

Leaving François to his task, Simone began her daily inspection of the green perimeter, looking for dry patches. What rural residents feared most was fire. Even where there was no tree canopy, a fire could spread rapidly through planted fields or fallow land. GV Assisi and its remaining neighbours had instituted fire prevention practices on their own properties. Each had a reservoir and the ability to pump. In peak season, a daily wetting routine was followed. As long as the water held out, a green perimeter would be maintained. All non-metal roofs were wetted at dawn and dusk.

She had done three quarters of the tour when she noticed the humming sound. *Drone!* Instinctively, she turned her back while pulling up her bandana and lowering the peak on her cap. It had been months since they'd heard or seen one. When she turned to look, it was practically upon her. Close enough to capture a clear image, if not for her protective gear and glasses. She gave it the finger.

Now she had to warn the others. As she strode toward the living quarters of the twelve remaining residents, she saw the drone peel off and disappear toward the west. *Flying range about 10 kilometres. Better keep a rifle handy.* They had two lightweight, modern ones dropped by fleeing White Wolves.

Coming quickly around a corner, she nearly collided with François. He was beaming. News of the drone could wait.

"Go on!" she urged him. He beckoned to a bench.

His call had taken Nicole by surprise, he recounted. She was headed to the market for opening time. Pickings would be slim by mid-morning.

He told her how news about an old friend made him anxious for his family. Nicole seemed touched by his concern, but wary. Marc and Sylvie had long ago insisted she not serve as go-between. She assured François they were both alright, but in financial difficulty, like most, with so little work available. Both were in quarantined sections of their cities. Everyone was healthy: Marc, his wife and young son, as well as Sylvie.

As for herself, she'd left her job. Pay had been cut in half and the strain was too much. Nicole was volunteering at the hospital, but worried about pneumonia. Also, security in the streets. Especially after dark, with power cuts so common.

Simone listened patiently, interested in François tale, but anxious to get to their plan. He described how he'd looked for a natural segue. The call might be monitored, after all. Everything needed to sound spontaneous.

He'd asked about Nicole's parents, and family in France and Germany. Elderly relatives had succumbed to illness: Nicole's widowed father and several others. A second cousin in Germany had committed suicide.

'What about family in Canada?' he'd asked, as naturally as possible. Nicole said she had last spoken to Nadine and Edward several months back. They'd been healthy and in reasonable spirits, considering. They'd seemed resigned to the likelihood that their daughter was dead. Better that, though, than some of the uglier alternatives, Nadine had said darkly.

Simone cringed. How painful it must be for her family.

Ron and Jacinthe had stayed hopeful for longer, François learned. Convinced Simone was resourceful enough to find a safe harbour, and wise enough to lie low. But with no reason to stay in hiding now, her failure to contact them did not bode well.

They were all in Quebec City, François said. Living with Jacinthe and Isabelle. The economy being as it was, plus disease, they felt safer together. The home was big enough, with a garden. Street crime was less than in Montreal.

François hesitated now. Like a boy, Simone thought, looking for the right words.

"She accepted!" he blurted suddenly.

Nicole had been thinking of leaving, he said. She'd thought of the Drome, but hadn't found the courage to ask. The train journey would be tricky, they'd agreed. There would be security checks, health inspections, unreliable connections and the risk of infection in a closed compartment. But she could try for Lyon, if he came to fetch her.

François smiled sheepishly. "We'll speak in two weeks."

"Well now," Simone chuckled, "things are getting interesting. Good for you. And thanks. You can't imagine how much it means, that little bit of family news."

"Yes," said Francois, reaching out to take her hands. "I can."

News from Canada had travelled to Europe. But how to send it back?

Wanting Contact

October 2024

The Global Freenet somehow managed to keep a basic message service running, despite the breakdown of government and loss of infrastructure in many regions. *Resilience through diversity*, was its motto. With enough servers, high-speed conduits and sources of electricity, the thousands of volunteers dedicated to preserving open communication seemed able to get service back online almost as fast as it went down, or was taken down.

The Freenet had a simple goal: allowing people to stay in touch, no matter where they were. Hundreds of millions had come to depend on it. There were limits, of course. Personal security and disease had taken out service in parts of South America and much of Africa. State censorship and sabotage continued to limit service in Russia, Turkey, northern China and several regions of the United States. For the most part, though, anyone with a terminal and a regional Freenet provider could create an account and send a secure message.

The Freenet Bulletin Board was the basic venue for people to post messages letting their loved ones know they were alive, and how to reach them. Anyone could post, and there was no way to be certain of their identity. A search for a particular person might yield many results by that name. A short 'bio-data descriptor' was linked to each account holder. To view a post, the searcher had to perform a 'handshake', by answering a series of security questions. It was rudimentary, and there would be impostors and code breakers, but since the goal was to reunite people, anything more strict would defeat that purpose.

Once this handshake was established, future messages could be sent using the Freenet's separate, secure messaging service. But if one party was not who they claimed to be, despite correctly answering the questions, security was compromised. It was a chance you took. A chance millions of people, continents apart from loved ones or separated in transit, regularly took. How else to find someone when you don't know where to start? When phone service is dead, and postal service abandoned?

François set off for Montelimar after lunch in his pickup. The batteries were full, but they had degraded with age and infrequent use. There had been few reasons to drive, and plenty not to. It was a risky mission, but he anticipated few people on the road. His biggest worries were sharp debris and checkpoints where he might be delayed in quarantine. Rapid tests were apparently being performed on locals, using some new kind of nasal probe and iris scan; results available in under 30 minutes. Even that might be too long. He didn't want to be driving in the dark.

Best case scenario, he could reach the city, get through the checkpoint, and be at the library in an hour. He'd budgeted 30 minutes online there, to create an account for Simone using bio-data she'd provided, and to post an initial message. He would also search for the six names she had given him. He would not be able to perform a 'handshake' between them and Simone. Instead, he would note the security questions for each account. Later, she could write out the answers for him to enter on the next visit. All of this could be done on his home computer, but at a far higher risk, and only if the service was up, which was rare now.

In theory, only a small number of Freenet administrators could see the identity of an account holder and trace their location. In theory.

Creating the account went smoothly. Simone had provided 10 security questions and the answers to them. Access would be granted to anyone who could answer five correctly in 90 seconds or less. But there was a hitch, he had just discovered. It could take up to 20 minutes for the new account to become live. Rather than waiting, he began his search for the accounts on her list.

When he failed to find a match using Ron Dugas, he tried again with Ronald. Toulouse, Rimouski, Philadelphia, Ottawa— *voila!* He wrote Ron's questions carefully in his notebook. Time was ticking. There was something else he needed to do.

Jacinthe Dugas. Instant match. Hurray for unusual names. Writing faster, he realized he was sweating. His handwriting would be hell. Edward Cohen was another long one. He did not try Nadine. Simone said one should do, since all four family members were in the same house. But you couldn't count on it.

Not a single hit for Jenny Fung. On a hunch, he tried the daughter's names. Yuki Fung, then Anna Fung. Nothing. What was their father's last name again? Endo... Edo... Best leave it and move on.

Last was Paul Racine. Way too common. Yet there it was, first try. But in Vancouver?! 'Engineer, ocean protector, inventor,' said his bio-data. Had to be him.

Nearly 30 minutes at the terminal. There was a line-up now. One last task. Complete Simone's account. He hadn't a clue what any of it meant. But she assured him others would.

> *Username: FBGirl.*
> *Password: Ride!2021*
> *Message: Alive, well, living in Oz. Two out of three ain't bad. Bruce.*

The Cruas-Meysse station had four water cooled reactors, but two had been shut down in 2022 as part of France's energy transition. Much of the spent fuel was stored in barrels outside the station. To be monitored forever. Containment vessels exchanged over and over.

Same problem all over the world. You have no clear idea what you're going to do after a mere 50 years in service, but you build it anyway! Typical blind faith in technology. Willful blindness.

The haze was terrible, but from his vantage overlooking the Rhone, with good binoculars, he could make everything out. There was activity on the site. People in white suits, with pink epaulettes. *Les Anges Nucléaires!* The Atomic Angels. Self-appointed guardians of abandoned plants and storage sites. A risky job, when everyone else had run for the hills. Investors, managers, lobbyists and politicians just walk away, leaving the people to clean up. Because they live there. The Atomic Angels were former plant workers, retired or recently unemployed. They had made it their mission, even if it killed them.

A third reactor had been idled for repairs, but never brought back online. The fuel, according to François' sources, had yet to be removed. A time bomb. Then there was the fourth, still operational. The company that last owned and operated it was no longer in business. Which meant no paid staff. Again, the Angels. He wondered if he'd have that kind of courage. Like Jiro. *Ebitsubo! That was the name. Merde!*

Just one more thing to check. It wouldn't change anything, but he had to know. Like Simone, listening to her news.

Water levels were so low now that intake pipes had been extended, despite the impact this would have on navigation. But there was little barge traffic on the river now. He estimated from the vapour plume that the reactor was operating at half capacity, a quarter even, its intake pipes partly exposed. This confirmed what he suspected—another month without heavy rain, another winter without heavy snow in the Alps, and it would have to be shut down completely. A good thing, but only if somebody was around to do it properly. There were a dozen more such places in France alone. Hundreds across the globe, if military sites were included. As for submarines and other atomic reactors...

Time to go. François floored the pedal as soon as he had the door closed. The sun had dropped below the mountains. Behind the wind turbines, just visible through the haze. Opening the gate would put everyone at risk.

Risk, everywhere you looked. But you had to take some.

News of the World, 2024

M any of Simone's regular stations were compromised by funding cuts or a change of mission. A few went silent entirely. Some became mouthpieces for regimes determined to spin the news. Voice of America went early, but the new Radio Free Cascadia—based in Seattle—provided informative coverage from western North America. Australia's ABC, Canada's RCI and France's RFI seemed to be operating on a shoestring, making constant appeals for donations. Radio Japan, covering Asian news in English, went silent when Tokyo fell to the militarist government now struggling to hold off invasion from China.

She was down to four. More choice wouldn't change the facts, though. Elected governments were few, and under siege. Famine and mass migration had made teetering countries ungovernable. Increasingly, it was a smooth-talking strongman running the show. A common formula saw authoritarian leaders leaving control of trade and economic activity to a network of criminal gangs.

Then, there were the religious extremists of all colours. When the world was going to hell, enter the preacher with a simple message: *Return to the right path, and ye shall be rewarded. Join today*, Simone understood, *and take part in the meting out of punishment.*

Adventurism by Russia, Iran, China, Pakistan and Turkey had changed the political map of Asia and eastern Europe. Securing a water supply offered both incentive and excuse for cross-border incursions, where the quest for oil or access to ports or pipeline routes had once done so. Simone was amazed that nobody had used a nuclear weapon yet. Or biological, though who could confirm that?

In countries with a history of tension, the deteriorating social and political environment triggered internal fracturing, often along religious lines or older ethnic identities. Indonesia, Spain, the United Kingdom, Nigeria and the Philippines were among the earliest. China's dissolution was only partial. Russia, while losing some states, had reclaimed others from its heyday as the USSR.

The Coalition of the Still Willing had crumbled entirely. Efforts to work collectively on a narrow set of urgent issues—climate, overfishing and monitoring nuclear and chemical waste—succumbed to the pandemic, and the panic. In which order it was hard to tell, and no longer relevant.

Bad as it was, Simone could not resist playing with the dial.

"I'm hoping to find a new country, unspoiled by modern idiocy," she joked to François one night, as he challenged her again on why she kept at it.

"Try Radio Mars!" he called out in response. She could hear his chuckle from the other room. Nicole would arrive in two days.

Riding Today

"François, you won't believe what I learned from my Aunt Nadine! Simone is alive!"

During their final call before Nicole boarded a quarantined overnight train, she was bursting to share her news. "She sent a message on the Freenet."

He said nothing, unsure if he could fake the right tone.

"François, did you get that? Isn't that incredible?"

"Sorry Nicole," he said cautiously. "I was stunned. Did she say where she was?"

"No. Well, yes. Oz. Clearly a joke. She made some reference that her father says is from Monty Python. You know, those silly British guys from way back. Uncle Edward says she did it to prove it was her."

"So nobody actually knows where she is?" François tried to sound innocent.

"Not yet. They're hoping that by establishing a handshake, a secure link, she'll be able to share more. Everybody has completed their part. Now she has to do the final step. You still have the internet, right? A Freenet account?"

"I do have internet access, yes," he said carefully. "Though it's very unreliable. I've never used the Freenet." He felt the sweat on his brow.

"That's not a big problem. We can find somewhere with a better link. There are public libraries nearby, right? Like in—"

"Sorry to cut you off, but I have to do something urgent here. Everything's still in order, right? Lyon Central at 10 a.m.?"

"Yes, if it's on time."

"Look for me at the charging station."

"Fingers crossed. See you soon."

"Ciao," he said, hanging up. *"Ciao, my love,"* he had almost said.

François set out for Lyon just after dawn. It was a two-hour drive in normal times, but these were anything but. He had no idea what the road would look like, nor what kind of inspections he'd encounter as he entered the city. Most worrisome though, he could not do a round trip without charging. He needed at least an hour of charger time, at or very near the station. *If* they were working. *If* it was safe to leave the vehicle unsupervised. *If* it was safe to supervise it.

Seeing his hand shaking as he poured tea into his travel mug before setting out, François realized he was nervous. Not since his early days in politics had he felt such anxiety. He'd faced a lot of adversity these past five years, but nothing had reduced him to this. He laughed.

"Like a teenager preparing for a date," Simone had ribbed the night before.

"Not at all," he'd replied seriously. But she was right. That's exactly how he felt. The arrival of Nicole was full of unknowns. Would it be like welcoming an old friend, sharing a home, and nothing more? Or would there be more? It could get complicated.

Her arrival would certainly require adjustments. To habits, sleeping arrangements and names. Now they would be three in the upstairs apartment. The patterns he and Simone had settled into were going to change. Who would sleep where? The women in the same room? He and Nicole together? Not at first, that seemed certain. Simone offered to move downstairs. There was plenty of room. They were now only 10, counting long-time residents and the baby.

"One thing at a time," he had said.

The issue of names would be the first to tackle, they'd agreed.

François approached the centre of Lyon just after 9 a.m. The drive had been uneventful, but informative. There were few debris on the highways, indicating some kind of organized cleanup was happening. To his surprise, there was no health checkpoint. Less surprising, there was minimal traffic.

The biggest surprise came at the charging station. One stall was occupied by an old Renault ZOE. The other was out of order, its cord missing.

There were other stations in the area, he recalled, but with no way to check if they were working either, he opted to wait. Surely the Renault owner would return soon.

An hour later, with the train due shortly, he was still waiting, and getting increasingly agitated. He had a right to charge as well. He could unplug the other car briefly; 30 minutes might be enough to get them home. Besides, this ZOE had to be charged by now, or nearly. Public chargers were for sharing!

It was the arrival of the train that prompted him to act. He could feel the rumbling, hear the brakes screeching. Nicole would be there shortly.

His palms sweating, François grabbed the plug, pressed the disconnect button and halted the charge.

Click. As he made to remove the plug, he heard another click, this one closer. At almost the same moment, something hard and sharp pressed against his throat.

"That's my car!" said a man's voice behind him in English. His own English was poor, but he understood the meaning of a knife.

"Put it back" ordered the cold voice. "Then give me your money and drugs."

"I put back," said François, fumbling to insert the plug with his right hand, while holding the left aloft. "I geev money," he said, to indicate his intentions. He showed his right hand now, then slowly lowered it to remove the small amount of cash from his pocket.

"Stop," ordered the voice. "Turn so I can see." The knife was lifted just enough to allow him to turn.

François slowly slid his hand into his pocket, not wanting to give the man any reason to use the switchblade. Fishing for his coins, he lifted his head to make eye contact. Just as he did, he caught a flash of movement, heard a metallic clank and saw the man's eyes roll back as he crumpled to the ground. The knife clattered across the pavement and disappeared under the truck.

"François!" Nicole cried, dropping her day pack on the ground. The steel thermos strapped to it was severely dented. She stepped forward and opened her arms.

"Nicole," he muttered in disbelief, as they stood entwined and shaking.

The return drive began in silence, both of them still in shock.

While the truck charged, they had lifted the knife-wielding man into the shade. He was unconscious, but breathing. From here on, they'd agreed, he was not their problem. With neither an ambulance to summon nor police to be found, there was nothing more to be done. Rules were different now, when there were rules at all.

It was Nicole who broke the ice. Reaching across to the steering wheel, she stroked François right hand and loosened its grip. Then, taking it in hers, she spoke tenderly but firmly.

"There's a lot of water under the bridge. Let's just take it slowly."

He nodded, turning to look at her as he spoke. "Yes, Nicole. Nice and slow."

"So, let's start with news of family and friends," she said, launching into a thorough and often painful update. He listened attentively, asking the occasional question, and biding his time. When she seemed done, he thanked her and cleared his throat.

"Nicole, I have some rather surprising news."

That Simone had been living with François for the past three years was indeed a surprise to Nicole. And an enormous relief. When he told her how Simone had adopted her name, indeed her identity for safety reasons—limited as it was to within GV Assisi's fences—she went silent. He feared a strained reunion.

Stepping back from a long and warm embrace, Nicole stared at Simone, then laughed awkwardly. "You've been Nicole Grod all this time, and this never reached me? That's weird!"

Simone was quick to agree. "Creepy, I think I called it. But you get used to a new name, when you have to. I didn't really use your last name. The only people who ever met me were our Assisi family. They just knew me as Nicole, François' wife"

"What if you had to go to a hospital? Would you have done so as me?"

François intervened. "If it was a matter of life and death. You'd have wanted that, right?"

"Fortunately it never came to that," Simone said. "But I see how strange this is. I needed an identity, so residents had a name and a story. I'm truly sorry."

Nicole thought for a moment before speaking.

"It's okay. I'll get over this... creepy feeling. Like there's two of me." Suddenly she snorted. "That could have been useful at times. You know, sending one of me to a meeting I didn't want to attend!"

She smiled at Simone. "The question is, who are you now? Or who am I?"

François and Simone nodded. They'd discussed it, but found no clear solution.

"What makes more sense?" Nicole wondered. "Switch back to Simone, and explain this to the residents? Or both go by Nicole in public? We could say I was a friend with the same name."

"Though we look so much alike," she noted, after a moment's reflection.

Simone had a suggestion. "Let's say our mothers were sisters with a strange sense of humour? It's not that far off." They all smiled.

"Or the third option would be for Simone to remain Nicole, and I get a new identity. I've always liked Esmeralda. Or one of those great African names, like Precious." Nicole's joking helped clear the air.

"Seriously though," said Simone, "either there's a credible explanation for why we're both Nicole, or I revert to Simone, and own up to the name games."

"Why not just come clean," François said. "Do you still have enemies, with the world as it is? I know we're being careful on the internet, but that may now be making your life more complicated than it needs to be."

Nicole glanced between the two of them. After a long pause, Simone spoke.

"I hate this 'deep cover'. It must be miserable for my family—"

"It is!" Nicole confirmed. Simone sighed, her heart aching.

"But…" she continued, "I've always trusted my hunches. You've seen the drones François. Someone wants to identify me. So let's both go by Nicole. Cousins. No explanation required. Though we must never go outside at the same time, uncovered."

She looked at Nicole, her eyes flashing warning. "You should also make sure not to be photographed."

The most pressing issue settled, temporarily at least, others proved easier. *Les Nicoles* would occupy the master bedroom, while François moved into an empty room on the ground floor.

"Closer to the gate," he added, in a serious tone. "One rifle with me, one with Simone—I mean Nicole—and one with Cedric in the resident's house across the courtyard."

Simone and Cedric would take the White Wolves' high-powered rifles. There was not much ammunition, but it was good for morale, François thought: being something other than sitting ducks while on watch duty. Cedric was familiar with the rifle. He had served as a sniper in the Tunisian army. Until they were overrun by a Libyan warlord in 2021. He and six others had escaped to Corsica, while it was still part of France.

Cedric instructed François and Simone in the care and use of the weapon. On two occasions they had taken target practice together, Simone learning the critical skill of zeroing the scope. She now took it with her, slung over a shoulder, when out in the open.

Twice she would use it to take shots at a drone. Missing, but sending it fleeing.

Always to the west.

Nicole et Nicole

T wo months after Nicole's arrival, the three of them had developed a comfortable evening routine. Simone rarely listened to the radio, preferring Nicole's news from the outside. Nicole in turn wanted to know how things had been going in the region, and at GV Assisi in particular. She marvelled at the elegant working farm François had built. Also, at how they had kept the area so green.

"It isn't hard," François responded. "Not the concept. Creating mutually-supporting systems. One's waste is another's input, basically. But it requires good planning and questioning many habits; anything that only works with continual outside inputs will eventually fail. We tried to do that with our local Tournesol Co-op as well until..." He stopped, his expression wistful.

After a lengthy pause, Simone switched topics.

"I've been thinking. The time has come for me to see the outside world. You don't want me going crazy, do you?" They nodded in empathy.

"I have a bike. I have a rifle. And there's nobody out there who I won't see or hear for kilometres. I won't be on roads much anyhow. What I really want is to get into the Saou Forest, then up into the mountains. I'll have a great view of what's going on."

"I think that's an excellent idea," François said.

Nicole agreed. "I don't know how you've stayed sane all this time."

"You're making assumptions!" Simone laughed. "But I'll be cautious. It'll take a while to build up my strength anyway. These legs haven't been on a bike, or up an incline for a very long time. I'll let you know where I'm going. Though I'm not sure you should come after me if..." her voice trailed off. "I'll be fine!" she added quickly.

Simone spent the next day tuning up the bicycle. The tires were cracking, but would hold up. All the cables needed tightening, the shifters adjusting, and the chain and derailleur lubricating. Not bad though, considering.

That night, she prepared all she would need. Bandana, water bottles, food, walking shoes, binoculars, François' old trail guide and a general topographical map. The rifle would be strapped along the cross bar, unloaded. She had ammunition handy in a pouch worn on her hip. Speed might be important.

The next morning, face beaming, she wheeled her bike out the door. Hearing a hum, she turned instinctively to seek the source and found herself facing directly into a camera. It would have been one second at most—enough for a clear image.

Quickly she spun away, covering her face with one arm while lowering her sunglasses and pulling up her bandana. Already, the drone was flying away to the west. Spooked, she sprinted down the gravel drive pushing her bike. Slamming the gate behind her, she mounted the bike and accelerated down the road toward the south. Once around the corner she might be able to catch sight of it again. The fields were large and open.

It did not take long for her screaming legs and lungs to put an end to her mad dash, but she had what she needed. The drone was headed straight to the nearest town. Many of the buildings had been burned out, but the church was still standing, its steeple intact. That's where he'd be. She was certain. He'd have no idea she was coming. Out of shape, but well-armed.

By the time she reached the church, 20 minutes had passed. There had been a climb, and a strong headwind. She could see tire tracks and smell exhaust—it was burning poorly refined fuel—but there was no vehicle. *Missed by minutes.*

It was always in the morning, the drone, around 9 o'clock. Creature of habit. *Next time, you'll be the one with the stunned expression!*

She could catch him. Shoot him, if she wanted. But was it too late?

Simone's first hike was a short one. Her legs were jelly, and her mind preoccupied. She didn't made it high enough for a view, but she would. It would take a couple of weeks until she was fit enough to make the nearest summit, with a view over the entire valley—the A7 highway, the Rhone, and of course Cruas-Meysse.

Recounting the story that evening, but leaving out her pursuit of the drone and plans for springing a trap, she shared her worry that she'd been filmed. Full facial view. Nicole listened intently, then offered a solution.

"For the next few days, assuming it's back, I go out and intentionally let myself be filmed doing your usual tasks, and tuning up the bike. I'll react slowly, letting myself be captured prior to covering up. That way there will be multiple shots of me—Nicole *Grod*—and just the one from today of you, my identical twin. Somebody, or some machine will be confused. It's clearly me, except for one that is almost me. They're likely to discount that image as an anomaly, since there can't be two of us. Can there?" She looked at Simone and François, hopefully.

"That's brilliant!" François declared.

"Very clever," Simone said slowly.

Three mornings in a row, Nicole allowed herself to be filmed. Harvesting carrots, cleaning the bike chain and walking the perimeter. Each time she play-acted covering up.

On the third morning, Simone was already in place across from the church. She had ridden the seven kilometres as the sun was rising, in cool, late-November air. Dusty and smoky, but cool. From her vantage point, the bike hidden, she watched as Mario Lepine opened the door of his Range Rover and entered the church carrying a bulky case. At 8:54, she heard the hum, then saw the drone exit the steeple and head east. Twenty minutes later, it returned. When Mario stepped out of the church door, she was ready.

He had put on a lot of weight, and was moving slowly with the case in his arms. As he opened the vehicle door, she opened fire. One to the left leg. Two through the case. As he scrambled into his vehicle, dragging his leg, blood visibly soaking his pants, she calmly took aim again. One through the front tyre. One through the rear.

It would take him a long time to get home. Longer still before he would think of returning.

She could have killed him. Should have killed him. But she didn't have it in her. Collecting her bike, she strapped on the rifle, and quietly continued her ride toward the forest. She would make it half way up the mountain before the adrenalin caught up and she vomited her entire breakfast.

François and Nicole rushed out to greet her as she pushed her bike up the drive in fading light.

"We heard shots this morning. We've been so worried!" said Nicole.

Simone paused and leaned her bike by the front door. As she removed her shoes, she acknowledged Nicole. "I can't say Mario will never bother us again, but it won't be for a long while." She unstrapped the rifle, handing it to François to hold while she removed the panniers.

"I think I'll have a drink," she said as she entered the house. "It's been quite a day."

I'm Back

When he saw the images, Elmore's perpetual scowl transformed into a smile. Four years of hunting, using every search tool, every contact, every clue from her past. France was an obvious hiding place, but she wasn't with her cousin in Strasbourg. Her name showed up on no registry, no bank account, no health care record, no hospital visits. Not even a financial transaction. *You can't live without creating a digital trail! It wasn't the 18th century, or even the 20th.* He had hacked her cousin's emails early on, along with her Facebook account and even the closed-circuit camera records from her apartment building; all came up empty. The resemblance between them was uncanny though.

There had been the one public Freenet post, from somebody named François Dirringer in a region he'd never heard of. But the guy couldn't be traced to a location precise enough to be of use. A public library terminal in Montelimar! *A library! The French still have those?*

Then came the video, and some stills. Not great quality, but sharp enough. Two women. Identical, yet not. He ran a program to clean up the best two images, then uploaded the files to the facial recognition database maintained by the CIA. Still had access. Getting lax, those guys.

Image one: Nicole Grod. We know her. Image two: Simone Cohen. Finally! Elusive little cunt. Probably there all this time. Putting out for the François guy in exchange for food and shelter, no doubt. He chuckled at the idea. Sex for survival. Like the women he'd been trafficking.

Thank you, Mario of the White Wolves! Affiliate of the White Eagles. Probably just as creepy too. But we can't always choose our associates. Like family—you make the most with what you're dealt. Elmore's circles were not nearly as refined as they once were. Or as highly placed. But he got by. A network was a network. Once again, he was a man of influence. People did him favours, knowing he could reciprocate.

These were not nice people. Then again, when had they been? Pete and the Houston good ole boys? The oil and coal men? Sleaze bags and profiteers. Just like the Florida holy rollers, and the slick operators in D.C. It was all about the money for them. Getting respect. Calling the shots. Making others do your bidding. And sometimes, making people pay the price for getting in your way. Different suits, same goals!

Elmore the insider was again Elmore the survivor. Fingered for his role in silencing people that certain associates found troublesome. Accused of murder; accessory to murder. By the Canadian whore. Then some leftie journalists. Fucking *New York Observer* never gave up. Until they fell apart. But that had taken awhile. Then there was Michelle Brown. Sister of the queer scientist. Didn't back off until she received the photos of her children, with the nasty artwork.

One by one, they'd all backed off. The police, the FBI… he just waited them out. With the help of a good lawyer. *Good* was a flexible word.

The supremacists gave him a new home, though. 'A man like you could do us a world of good.' They'd been moving up in the world, while he was moving down. From a ragtag bunch of conspiracists, to a sophisticated global operation. Ku Klux Klan meets Hell's Angels meets Russian mafia. With some Japanese yakuza and Chinese triad thrown in. What they'd needed was serious organizational skills. A strategist. A nose for weakness in security systems.

He'd focused on North America, England and Australia. Wasn't much for languages or cultures. They all spoke English though, the people he dealt with. Even Russians. Especially Russians. Loved their accents. And their hacking skills! Hoowee, what they'd done to Ukraine, the Brexit vote and Hillary. Some street cred.

Elmore's Washington years left him with the best Rolodex going. He liked that term. So 'inside the beltway.' Boasting about the size of your Rolodex. Everything was digital now, of course. What were they supposed to say? 'I got the biggest stick in Washington.' Rolodex or stick, Elmore had a big one, and he wasn't afraid to wield it.

A year in the wilderness, then back he came. Applying his skills in new ways. Year by year, things grew. Loose alliances became signed agreements. Regional gangs came together as an international syndicate. He'd been at the big meeting in Singapore, when the deal was inked. Blood was spilled, but they'd worked things out. What was the point of killing each other when there was plenty to go around?

Negotiating turf had been the tricky part. By geography and line of business. As long as everyone got a guarantee of spoils, they liked the idea of not having to sleep with a gun under the pillow, or worry about ingredients you hadn't ordered in your drink.

The supremacist stuff mostly took a backseat to business. Racism had always been about fear, anyway. Fear of losing jobs. Hunger. Somebody taking your women, or your land. It's what made it easy to recruit from the lowest rungs. Rural America and the rust belt. Who wanted to be 'white trash'? Not when you could muster a little army of the likeminded to go taunt some Blacks, or Latinos, or Natives. Muslims especially.

It worked pretty much the same in any country. Then there was Eastern Europe. They made a mean kind of grudge there: race, religion, ethnicity.

They all came together as the World White Web. Elmore's idea. White Eagles of America, Polar Bears of Canada, White

Wolves across much of Europe. White Bears in Russia. White Foxes across Scandinavia. Delivering goods and services people needed.

With so little supervision, it couldn't have been easier. No food or drug inspectors meant an open market. Buyer beware. *Very* aware. Even for legal products. Though what was the difference now? Legal drugs, illegal drugs? All for the taking. At a price you can't refuse. You pays your money and you takes your chances. Heart medicine, anti-depressants, anti-anxiety meds. Crack, crystal meth. Most of all, it was opioids. They even sold naloxone kits. Mustn't kill off a customer too quickly.

Ready to do or sell anything, the World White Web was. Weapons. Vehicles. Solar panels. Wherever there was a market, or they could corner or create one. Wood from illegal cutting, sushi from protected whales or marine sanctuaries. The Japanese loved getting whale meat again! Water, diverted from somebody's river, or taken from somebody's spring. Plus, the services. Disposal of toxic and radioactive waste. Approved sites were such an unnecessary expense, when you knew somebody, who knew somewhere. And fossil fuels. No government can tax your carbon, or sell you an emissions permit when they don't know who you are or what you've been burning.

Free trade at its finest!

Sure, there was the ugly side. The misery. But this was a business, not a social agency. If they weren't going to do it, somebody else was. Besides, the people they traded were one step short of the grave. Nowhere to sleep, nothing to eat. The days of anxious moral debate were long past. With billions of jobless and homeless, humans were just another commodity.

Elmore didn't get too close to that side. Plenty of 'white collar crime' to keep you in whisky and caviar. Not that there was caviar left; real caviar. Mostly the luxuries were real chocolate, coffee, wine and whisky that wasn't tainted with something. Folks paid big money to get the real stuff. Or so they thought.

Simone, Simone, See-moan! All this time, hanging out at some organic farm in Provence. Just how did you stay below the radar and fool the best searches money can buy? Laying really low. But stealing your cousin's identity? Evil! Pretty good with a rifle too. So un-Canadian. But how good are you, when you're not expecting it?

He'd thought of contracting this Mario dude and his White Wolves. But after all these years, he couldn't leave it to just anyone. They'd offered to film the hit and post it. Tempting. It *was* a long way to travel. But nah. Somehow, he'd find the time and means to get there. To take care of her personally.

Cross-border travel was a problem. Even with connections and influence. Travel by boat was risky, getting to the French coast particularly so. He could source a fast boat and a good crew. The Web had plenty. He could arrange trouble-free docking. It was pirates that made things sticky, especially in the busy waters of the Channel. Pirates, and the French Navy. Both known to shoot on sight. They'd lost boats and cargo to pirates. Zealous navies too, where they existed.

He would need something fast and stealthy. What was that Canadian boat again? The crazy Acadian who sold out to the lady who died in the crash. That boat was fast! Almost no heat to be picked up by infrared, and no need to refuel. He'd get one of them, as soon as he closed this deal. A breakaway gang out of Vladivostok and some Native crew operating in Alaska, running goods and gals down the West Coast.

So much to look forward to!

Until the pandemic reached New Orleans.

A Night at the Opera

Christmas 2024 was a modest gathering. The three of them, and their family of six. Ibrahim, the veteran. Pushpa, and her husband Vikram. Cedric, amazingly, after a bout with the virus that took so many. Last of all, Yvette, the Senegalese stowaway, and her young daughter Bijoux. Pierre, husband and father, had not survived his illness.

Were they happy to be alive? Only if they could forget. Forget what was happening outside. Forget their families, their friends, their memories of home, and what their future was likely to bring.

It was Christmas at Global Village Assisi, where history, race and religion might be ignored for the time it took to prepare and share a meal. What must not be ignored were the fundamentals of hygiene. Hot water, soap and face masks were all part of the decor, along with a small, scraggly evergreen.

The meal was pleasant. None of the excess Simone, Nicole and François knew from Christmases past. Just some light and warmth, and seasonal music playing on a pirate station. A break from the smoky cold winds blowing across the fields.

In place of gifts, Nicole suggested an exchange of story and song. Everyone contributed, the giver often brought to tears, which in turn triggered others. All but Ibrahim, who was incapable of tears, and little Bijoux, who had yet to learn sadness.

After everyone had gone to bed, Simone put on headphones and tuned in to Radio Canada International to see if they had resumed broadcasting. They'd been putting out a nightly news show at 6 p.m. in Quebec City—midnight in France. Until two weeks ago, when all she'd found was a hiss. She'd try again, but midnight was an hour away. First to Radio Cascadia, the only 'real' station she could find last time.

Good evening listeners around the world, welcome to our Christmas broadcast. Whatever your faith or means, wherever you are, no matter how troubling these times, we hope you'll find something in our show. We have assembled stories from the past year, reflecting the spirit of Christmas. We go to the heart of what it means to be Christian, and the similar spirit found not only in all religions, but in the UN Declaration of Human Rights and espoused by some of history's inspirational figures. Today, we celebrate the best of what it is to be human.

Simone was tempted to wake up Nicole. Until she remembered Nicole was downstairs. Asleep in the same room as François, their single beds pulled together.

The program was all it billed itself to be. Stories of places where the rule of law still held, where tolerance and respect outshone division. Stories of people and communities rallying to help one another. Tales of adversity overcome, and people who tried but failed. Stories assembled by journalists who gave everything to let people make up their own minds about the world around them. Stories of journalists who died.

Simone cried the entire hour. From joy and marvel and deep sadness. When the hour was up, it was time to try Radio Canada. What she found was a recorded message.

"From all who worked here for nearly a century, we wish you a Merry Christmas. There may not seem much to be merry about, but if we look within ourselves we can all find something to celebrate. Let us remember this is a season of giving. Though this station is no longer operating, we have found a way to share the best of Christmas music from across Canada. *Joyeux Noël!*

Simone's tears returned as she listened to song after song from her childhood and much of her life. Artists she had loved, and some she never really did. All brought back memories. Where she'd been and who she'd been with.

She awoke to the pain of headphones digging into her cheek, and the sound of static.

Limitation of Species

January 2025

The winter wind was howling. There had been rain. Enough to replenish the reservoirs and get the stream flowing, but not nearly enough to end the multi-year drought. Inside there was warmth, food and the remains of François' wine.

"Better to drink it than lose it!" he had said darkly.

In the evenings, they often found themselves in conversation. Nicole and François would occupy the living room sofa, a wool blanket over their legs. Simone took the worn leather armchair, her knees pulled up to her chest, enrobed in an over-sized sweater. This night, each was nursing a mug of mulled wine. It might have been a scene from any farmhouse over the past few centuries, Simone thought.

Simone recounted how moved she had been by the Radio Cascadia show—how humans do so many things well, yet constantly undermine themselves with poor governance, poor choices and a misguided understanding of the common good.

"Do you think we suffer from some fundamental flaw?" she asked. "A limitation we have yet to evolve past? Or something so deeply embedded our species will never escape it?" Getting no response from the ageing lovebirds, she continued her musing.

"We had this gorgeous opportunity post-1945, where most of humanity could look beyond survival and consciously choose a path that was ecologically sustainable." Feeling the wine, she carried on unprompted.

"I think of the word 'elegance'—the simplest and most effective way of doing something, but also the most ethical."

"You speak of the late 20th century," said François, sitting up straighter. "As the closest we ever got to living sustainably."

"Not so much achieving it as knowing what had to be done," Simone clarified, "and having sufficient resources to make it happen."

"But what about all the energy consumed to reach that stage?" François asked. "This lifestyle of comfort, that allowed people to move beyond scraping together an existence. And we are only talking about the One Percent here, aren't we?"

Simone looked away as she pondered the question. "I think we could have done better than that," she said. "We could easily have organized ourselves, as late as the turn of the millennium, so that 30 or even 50 percent of the global population could have had the luxury—if you want to call it that—of conscious choice. Actually having choices, beyond mere survival."

"That would have required a more egalitarian society," François said, his eyes narrowing. "An economy that distributed resources fairly, with the political support to do so. Not communism," he clarified quickly. "Communism misunderstood the importance of human initiative, and failed to link material reward to level of effort. But certainly a far more enlightened social democracy. Where markets can do what they do well, but are limited to that. Not the neoliberal mantra so many Western countries worshipped."

"China and India prayed at that altar too," Nicole added lazily. "And the Tiger economies of Southeast Asia—"

"Let's not forget Brazil," said Simone. "How we went from 'Save the Amazon' to 'Oops, what happened to the Amazon?' Massive, corrupt, ungoverned deforestation with eucalyptus and palm oil replacing complex ecosystems. For what? A few years of growth and then FOOM, total collapse. Soil that even chemical fertilizer couldn't revive."

Feeling hot, she struggled to remove her sweater.

"Fertilizers don't revive anything!" François said firmly. "Only healthy soil ecology does that. Fertilizers and pesticides together destroy everything."

"Except the market for fertilizers and pesticides," Simone added mischievously, now free of the sweater.

"Even they stop working after a while," François continued seriously. "Then you start the long, patient process of building soil back up again."

"Where were we?" Nicole chimed in, looking from François to Simone. "Oh yes, the moment in time when anything was possible."

Simone laughed. "Maybe there never was one. We went from scarcity to abundance to excess to deprivation in three generations. At what point might we have been at a kind of equilibrium, I wonder?"

"The fifties or sixties?" Nicole offered. "Certainly not beyond the seventies!"

"It's more complex than just resources, and population," François said.

Simone agreed. "Hygiene, medicine, education, gender equality, farming and fishing practices. You could pick a date like 1967, when my parents met. Everybody had electricity and the telephone, and television and a car. Almost everyone. We had good public schools and hospitals—universal health care had just been established nationally. But look at the other side of the ledger. Houses leaked like sieves. Fridges used CFCs. Cars drank up gas and oil. Rivers and lakes were used as sewers. Same with the sky. Oh yeah, and people smoked everywhere."

All three shook their heads, remembering.

"Right after Rio, 1992, what about then?" François was rising to the question.

"We had reasonably strong legislation in most countries," Simone noted. "Everyone was talking about the Three Rs. But could we have locked in 1990s practices, spread evenly across the globe, and built a sustainable world?"

François shook his head. "Too many people! Forests being clearcut, fisheries in steep decline... and climate change already under way. The first big conference acknowledging it was... when... 1990?"

"1988," Simone corrected. "Toronto. *The Changing Atmosphere: Implications for Global Security.*" She saw François and Nicole exchange a smile, but carried on.

"Maybe we never had all the winning conditions," she conceded. "Every era did some things well and others badly."

François sat forward and looked her in the eye. "That's why I took exception when people said, 'you eco-freaks want us to go back and live in a cave'." Simone heard bitterness in his voice. "Nobody was suggesting that. I felt the winning formula would be to merge the wisdom of natural systems, the best of traditional practices and the best of modern science and technology. With an openness to constant refinement."

"Appropriate Technology!" Nicole exclaimed, nodding. "The most sensible approach, using local resources."

"Elegance!" Simone declared. They had come full circle. Sitting in silence, each lost in thought, she felt the warm glow fading.

Nicole was the first to speak. "If we survive this unravelling, what will be left? As a civilization. Emphasis on civil!"

"People will come through," François said confidently. "There will be clusters of small groups, hunkered down, with elaborate purification systems and renewable power; or even secret caches of gas."

"And lots of canned food," Simone added.

"Yes," chuckled François with the hint of a smile. "Lots of canned food. Nobody can last in a bunker forever, but some just might be remote enough to hold out until the marauders die off, or settle into something more civilized."

"How about on an island?" asked Nicole. "Some remote temperate island like New Zealand? Or Fiji? A kind of Noah's Ark."

"Ready to start the cycle of human history all over again," Simone said cynically. She shook her head at the thought.

"Quite probably," agreed François. "But there will be a new story. A set of teachings will be developed, and passed on—about how to live sustainably, elegantly as you say, based on what was learned. But even this would be tenuous," he admitted. "Could the people who survive have a sufficient grasp of earlier mistakes to pass on any lessons? A list of the things their predecessors did wrong. That's *us*."

"Yes, us," said Nicole. "Our era. We'll need a catchy name for it."

"People were starting to use 'the Anthropocene', Simone recalled. "I prefer something more evocative. Like 'the Great Delusion'."

"This new society," François said, ignoring the women's meander, "or societies— since there could easily be dozens—would have to write all this down or pass it on orally at first. They would create new myths, new lessons, a new 'bible' to live by, with lessons very different from the holy books we know, I suspect."

"New commandments," Nicole suggested.

"This reminds me of the Natural Step," Simone said, in an upbeat voice. "Do you recall the Natural Step?"

"Vaguely," said François. He looked to Nicole, who shook her head.

"No matter," said Simone. "There was a Swedish scientist who was tired of the politicization of environmental issues. He wanted to see if the best thinkers, and not just scientists, could reach consensus on a set of principles to guide society toward sustainability. Sort of like commandments, though they called them 'system conditions'. If everyone could buy into these basic science-based 'conditions' then it would be easier to agree on plans of action."

"So how did that go?" asked Nicole. "Getting consensus?"

François crossed the room to add wood to the stove, which had burned down to embers.

"Surprisingly well," Simone recalled. "He got buy-in from some major players. They agreed on four system conditions based on science; the inarguable. Actually, the first three were. The fourth was social, so it was trickier. It was about social relations and structures, and allocating resources. It took as a given that no society can be stable and peaceful over any extended period if power and resources are unfairly distributed. Too big a disparity will create resentment, subversion, the need for expensive and repressive policing and, sooner or later, overthrow of the regime."

"Was this Natural Step actually implemented?" asked François, refilling their mugs. "Beyond Sweden?"

Simone nodded enthusiastically. "By quite a few large companies. But it was only as good as the willingness of CEOs, and politicians, to use it. It never reached a critical mass globally. I knew a trainer, somebody who went into companies to introduce managers to the Natural Step. She told me how she could quickly get buy-in to the three 'scientific' conditions. Engineers got it. Even lawyers and accountants. But you always ran into objections about the fourth, which was about treating people fairly."

"That doesn't surprise me," Nicole said, her eyebrows raised. "The objections."

"Right!" said Simone. "So she used a clever technique." Simone smiled at the recollection.

"She'd ask these doubters, some of whom were livid at the idea of codifying fairness, to break up into a group of say 10. She'd tell them they were on a spaceship heading to another planet to colonize. But resources had been rationed to ensure they got there. So far, so good. Then she'd assign each a 'share'. *You, sir, are a renowned entrepreneur. You have earned 50%. You two are from powerful countries. You each deserve 20%. You three ladies have college degrees. You merit 3% each. And you four... see if you can find any crumbs.*"

François shook his head, chuckling.

"You can guess what happened," Simone said, looking from him to Nicole. "Everyone was outraged. Even the guy getting the lion's share. So the session leader would give them ten minutes to come up with their own approach. And..." Simone said, trailing off.

"They would agree to allocate everyone an equal share," Nicole suggested.

"Exactly," confirmed Simone. "So the moral is...?"

"If we understand we're on a limited planet, and if we have to interact daily with the people with whom we share it, we would agree to equitable shares."

Simone beamed at Nicole. "Nicely put! We, the fortunate, have failed all this time to agree to fair allocation because we believed in the endless abundance of the planet. We could not perceive its limits. Plus, those *other* people, those starving Africans, or the homeless... well, we weren't in the same room with *them*, so... oh well, life is unfair. Pull up your own bootstraps!"

"But do you think anchoring fairness in a *commandment* could work?" wondered Nicole. "On our island of survivors, that is, with its new story? Would that work any better than all the other commandments, since the time of Moses?"

"Not for everyone," said Simone, nodding slowly. "But wouldn't it be better than not having it?"

"If you're going to have commandments at all!" noted François, who had been listening quietly. "Wouldn't our little society eventually turn all this into a religion of a kind? To suffer the same fate as other religions? Its followers moving gradually from faithful application, that is, to support in word only, then ultimately just ignoring it, or interpreting it to meet their own ends?"

"Probably, yes." Simone acknowledged. "It's what happens to most rules, isn't it? We forget why we created them. If the human condition is to desire sex without restraint, and to amass goods for pleasure or future comfort, and power for security and the thrill of feeling important... If all these are givens of our species—of our 'reptilian brain'—won't that cute little island society just end up where we are now? Is a better end possible for *homo sapiens*?"

"I hope so," said François, his expression darkening. "But we are what we are. Unless human evolution can outpace our capacity to destroy. Otherwise, we'll keep inventing more powerful ways to alter nature, faster than our brain can evolve to curtail the temptation."

"*Hubris*," Nicole declared with a sigh. "Humans, pretending to be gods."

Elmore Gets his Boat

It wasn't the fastest boat, but Elmore knew you were lucky to get anything now. Especially fuel.

His efforts to get the craft he wanted had come up empty. Production in Saint John was shut down when the yard was overrun by death ships from Africa. People stumbling out of the holds; fleeing disease, while bringing it with them.

New Orleans had been protected, until the navy itself dissolved. Not enough fuel, not enough money, mostly, not enough sailors. Who could blame them? Knowing they were as likely to catch something from a shipmate as on shore. It was everyone for themselves. And their families, if they still had them.

He'd put the word out through his networks: self-powered boat, crew, provisions, weapons. He'd even reached the inventor. "What do you need the ship for?" the guy asked. Not "how much can you pay?" like any sane person. "I need a clearer idea of the voyage," the guy said, "to try and supply one from the Vancouver yard." Things were still functioning there. Cascadia! Just a matter of time before they'd go down too. You can fend off invaders and quarantine refugees, but the plague will get you in the end.

The World White Web was toast. Back to local fiefdoms, in pockets, where they'd got hold of the experimental vaccine. Just when he was set to call in favours!

"Where are you headed?" Who did this Paul Racine think he was?

"Crossing the Atlantic!" he'd blurted, when it was clear who held the aces. "You'll be well paid."

"There's more to life than money," the guy replied, from his high horse.

Didn't need him in the end, though. Found a beauty in Fort Lauderdale. *The Libertarian.* Some dead rich dude's Caribbean cruiser. The town practically empty. Eerie. But there it was, fuelled and ready. Two crew, canned food, water filtration, cannons. The racing bike had been procured on the side. Electric. Fast and quiet.

Mario had asked to take her down himself, along with the others. But he'd been crystal clear: "You have your grudge, I have mine. Don't scare my target off if you want the other half of the reward. I'll be there in about three weeks."

News of the World, 2025

Radio Cascadia was Simone's window on the world. Cascadia was Oregon, Washington and part of British Columbia. Portland, Seattle and Vancouver were its urban hubs. Maybe there were other pockets like it. Perhaps Iceland, the Falklands or Maui. But Cascadia was all she'd found. The only evidence of sanity and civility.

Broadcasting steadily and reliably, Radio Cascadia told a story so different from the rest. Yes, there was disease. Yes, there were refugees. They'd had to repel armed attacks. First a Russian fleet, then a self-styled Rambo out of Denver. But if Simone could trust what she was hearing, the attacks had pretty much died away. Like the crime syndicates who'd tried taking over from the inside. Their power had vanished with the second round of pandemic.

Was Cascadia their only hope?

How lucky some were to be there. How desperate the people who heard the broadcasts must be to reach it. Could Cascadia possibly hold off such a torrent? Or would something else kill those wretched folks first? Pity anyone on the open road.

Simone had been on the road frequently. She made it her mission to scout the area and report back. Quiet, she told them, but for the wind. You could hear anyone coming long in advance, in a vehicle at least. Which made it safer than it had been in years. Though there was always a risk of someone lying in wait. And the feral dogs. Lots of them, now.

She could have used the truck. François had maintained it well, with help from Ibrahim, who was trained in EV maintenance in Morocco, before he'd fled the gay purge in 2020. But she preferred the bicycle—the only vehicle you could pull off the road and stash, or use on certain forest trails.

Simone had identified six properties as still occupied. There were likely more, but nobody flew a welcome flag: 'Come on in. We have food.'

How sad that was. After years of constant fear, survivors were hunkered down; when collaboration made greater sense. Perhaps it would return when the fear of disease subsided.

Simone made her first summit in May. May 3, 2025, she wrote in her log. She noted everything: vehicle movement, houses occupied, recent fires, water sources, wild animals—in the mountains or foraging in fields alongside abandoned domestic ones.

By late May, she was doing scouting trips twice a week. She'd have gone out more often, but her help was needed in the fields, and fire-proofing the perimeter. They had decided to cut back any brush and not plant the first 20 metres outside the perimeter fence. A fire buffer. Wetting was using too much of their dwindling reserve.

On her outings, two things in particular interested her. Finding a way to access the Freenet, if it still existed; and watching for signs of Mario.

She wondered if the library in Montelimar was still active. The town was silent, though she'd noticed smoke over the city on a particularly cold morning in late April. A domestic stove perhaps. A biofuel system, emitting steam. To know for sure, she'd have to get closer, running the risk of attack or infection. Best to avoid cities.

At GV Assisi, they had endured several rounds of illness, but not the influenza sweeping the continent. Perhaps she was one of the lucky few with resistance. Best not to put it to the test.

She may have to try Montelimar in the end, but not yet. Let the pandemic run a little longer and pray the Freenet survives. Best try the smaller towns close by.

* * *

Paul had been at the Vancouver assembly dock when the call came through. Not many people knew his satellite phone number, and few these days had access to phone service of any description. He didn't recognize the number or the gravelly voice, and the caller refused to identify himself. "I need a fast boat and now," was all he said. "Money is no object." Paul had felt the hairs on his neck stiffening.

Only when pressed to describe what the boat had to be capable of doing, did the caller offer more. "Crossing the Atlantic!" he said belligerently.

Three words only, but every part of Paul screamed danger. It was Elmore Lambert, and he knew where to find Simone.

Paul could refuse to sell the psychopath one of his new boats—the fastest, most efficient ones on the water—but there were other boats out there. Fast ones too, though most ran on fuel. And fuel had become difficult, and dangerous, to purchase.

He wanted desperately to warn Simone, but she hadn't completed her handshake.

* * *

There was enough food for the three of them for a one-way trip. Fuel to reach Ireland, maybe Gibraltar. The boat was fancy, but a hog. He had wanted something autonomous. Now he'd have to refuel. That's what the guns were for. Protection. Barter. He wouldn't need these assault rifles for her. Just a pistol. Maybe he'd use the knife. Quieter. Slower. Real slow. *Like this goddamn boat trip!*

Eight days to get around Florida and up the Atlantic coast! He could have tried refuelling in Bermuda, but didn't imagine finding any. Hurricane Zelda had ripped it to shreds. Good name. Using a Z for finality. Nobody was naming hurricanes now. Nobody was even tracking them. *You're on our own.*

Elmore laughed. *What's new?*

* * *

Simone tried more than a dozen small towns before striking gold at Sauzet. Outside the town hall, she picked up a strong signal. Odd, as there were no people. But a signal was a signal. Public WiFi, no password. Good start. She found a rear entrance with a staircase, where she could sit out of sight, her bike an arm's length away. Leaning back, Nicole's 5-year old tablet on her knees, she launched the browser.

In her logbook, she'd written answers to the security questions François had noted months earlier. Speed mattered. Vigilance also, and an escape route.

She'd start by contacting Marc and Sylvie from Nicole's account, as promised.

It was her first interaction with the Global Freenet. Username, password, open messages, and in. Nice job Freenet!

A message to Nicole from Sylvie.

> Maman, I don't know why you aren't answering. I'm in Denmark with Alexandre, on a small island called Samso. He had friends here, and we're welcome to stay. There is food, a power system, and so far, no violence. We spent two weeks in quarantine, but were treated well. I think we may be here for a long spell. It's turning to shit to the south of us. Radiation poisoning. What could possibly have convinced people nuclear would be safe? That's a whole other conversation, and I dearly hope we'll have the chance.
>
> Where are you? How are you? Marc and his little Antoine were not well, when we last connected. I don't want to be first to give the news, but Gisele died. Influenza. It ravaged Paris. Too many people, too little clean water. I cry when I think of it.
>
> If you can, please get a message to Papa. Tell him I love him. He did what he had to. I hope you can forgive him too. Bisous, bisous, bisous! Sylvie.

Simone was trying not to cry. She needed her eyes clear, her head clear.

REPLY

Chere Sylvie, you won't believe this, but this is Simone. I am messaging on behalf of your parents. Both of them! They are together at your father's farm. Reunited, and in love, if I may make that announcement. Things are not great here, but we have what we need: tools and determination. Things will not get better, though, with the drought and fires. They, maybe we, will wait for an opportunity to try to get to you. I have some ideas, but that's for another day. Know that they love you, and will want to be with you soon. Love Simone.

SEND

Now for Marc. Damn! Nothing from Marc. Messages from others, though.

SELECT and SAVE

My turn! Here goes. Speed and accuracy.

Edward Cohen. Five questions. Five correct answers. Handshake and... in! One message, dated a month earlier.

Dear Simone. It's Maman, writing for Papa as well. Thank God you're alive. I can only guess where. No, I can't even. But you'll let us know in good time. We're together in Quebec City. Things are getting worse—the violence and plague. We may have to move, if there's somewhere safer to go, and a way to travel. But don't worry. Just get in touch when you can do it safely. We'll find a way to reunite. Love from all. Maman.

REPLY

Dearest Maman!, she tapped on the touchscreen. Her heart was pounding. She could hear it in her ears. But no tears. Please, no tears! *No more hide-and-seek. I have been living with François Dirringer in the Drome. Pretty good hideout, eh? Amazingly, Nicole has recently joined us. She and François have reconciled. There is beauty in all this ugliness. We can hold out for a while yet, but the climate and disease are real worries. Yes, we will find a way. If you move, give me a clue. I'll do the same. Love Simone.*

SEND

Ron now. Questions, answers, in. Simone stared at the empty message folder. Nothing. She tried to scroll down. Nothing. Maybe her mother's message spoke for all of them. She shook her head, breathed to ground herself, then looked at her list for a prompt. Of course! Jacinthe would be writing for both of them.

Jacinthe Dugas-Marinoni. Married! Simone beamed. Until she read further.

Maman! We were so thrilled to get your short message. Alive and well, the Python reference, it had to be you! We were on pins and needles waiting for you to complete the handshake. But here we are, a month later with nothing from you and nothing to share but our grief. If/when you get this message, I am so sorry to have to tell you that death came to call, and we were at home.

Simone held her breath, scanning now.

You must know about the horrible sickness. Our dearest Ron, my Papa, your husband, became ill just a week after you made contact. Within two days, your mother and father also. Amazingly your father has pulled through, but he was the only one.

Simone swallowed hard. When the tears came, they would pour.

> *We were all preparing to leave for Vancouver Island with Izzy's brother, who has one of those ships made by your friend Paul Racine. The departure was delayed. Nobody was sure what to do. But the illness was mercifully short. We were able to bury our beloved Grandmaman Nadine and Papa Ron in the garden of the house. Then we resumed our trip, though Grandpa Edward was reluctant and still weak. We are partway there now, connecting by satellite—the one thing that's immune to the chaos down here. At least I hope so. It's the only way you'll know what has happened, and how to find us. When you get this, wherever you are in your 'deep cover', pray for us as we do for you. Just as Papa and Grandmaman did for those happy days between hearing from you, and passing on. They are watching over us, I know, as we cruise through the Northwest Passage. Come help us make a new home. Love Jacinthe*

Simone could hold back no longer. For several minutes she sobbed in a way she could not remember ever having done. Gasping for air, her chest heaving. Ron and her mother, in one fell swoop! Never to hug or hold again. But her father came through! Oldest of the three. Incredible! And Ron, so fit and healthy. *Focus Simone*, she had to tell herself. There was more.

Two more. What was this one? A request to connect. Yuki Ebitsubo. Alive!

Just at that moment, Simone felt vibrations. She'd have to log off and take cover. *I'll get to you, Yuki.* She slipped the tablet into its pouch, then the pannier, which she cinched shut in one quick movement. There was a narrow path running behind the building and around to the other side. She deftly mounted the bike and slipped out of site. Seconds later, a battered Range Rover belching smoke crunched its way into the gravel lot beside the steps where she had been seated. Simone did not dare look. Her rifle was still strapped onto the cross bar.

From where she waited in silence, she heard the car door slam and the door to the building open and close. Had her signal been detected? Was he able to track her? Or was he also there for the WiFi, perhaps seated at a terminal?

Simone didn't wait to find out. She wasn't yet ready to kill.

The ride back demanded all Simone's concentration. There would be time later to share and process the news.

She had saved the messages. All except the one from Yuki. She'd had to run before attempting the handshake. That was how she missed her plea and warning; and the identical one from Paul.

Infested Waters

They were just off the Spanish coast when the attack came. They'd needed fuel, and would take a chance with Cadiz. One of his crew, the Italian, was familiar with the harbour. He'd run drugs and weapons into Spain, until the pirate problem got too crazy. It was dark, and they were motoring without lights. The first they knew was the sudden roar, then floodlights and a loudspeaker demanding all appear on deck, hands in the air.

Elmore ordered his two crew to flatten themselves and take a position on the lower deck with the big machine gun. He would sprint to the cannon on the upper deck. Standard equipment for luxury yachts. Ocean cruising had changed.

Before he could ready the weapon, machine gun fire raked across the lower deck. Ducking behind the heavy shield on which the cannon was mounted, he couldn't see if his men had been able to return fire. When the noise subsided, he made out screaming. One man. Nothing from the other. No cries, no return fire.

He'd only have one chance. Blinded by the approaching boat's lights, all he could do was squint and aim just below them. Checking first that the gun was ready, the belt of huge shells neatly stretched, he stood and fired in one movement. *Boom, boom, boom, boom...* ten large rounds fired at close quarters. Instantly, a flame appeared on the other boat. Smelling fuel, he raced back to the cabin. Ramming the throttle forward, he steered sharply to starboard. Seconds later the attacker's boat erupted in flames. He was barely out of range when it exploded.

Shaking from the deadly encounter, he motored on slowly through the night, making directly for the Strait of Gibraltar. He'd find fuel somewhere else. Calls to his men went unanswered. He'd roll them overboard at first light.

Elmore had known his own chances of returning were slim. Now they were slimmer. He'd need time to assess the damage before he could carry on towards Mallorca, Marseille, and then up the Rhône. He'd want everything in working order. And fuel. The Mediterranean coast could be crawling with pirates and militias, unless the plague had killed them off. That night's attack was his answer: proceed cautiously.

Better Late

July 10, 2025

She was alive! In Europe, likely still France. But where exactly? It was a big country, and it would take three weeks to get there. That's why he had to leave Vancouver as soon as possible. The others could relay her exact location when she provided it. If they didn't reach her first. It could be too late. That bastard was resourceful and obsessed. A dangerous mix.

The Panama Canal would have been shorter by far, but that was suicide. North was their only option. Around Alaska and over the top, as ships had been doing for half a decade, since the seasonal passage had opened up reliably in summer. It was mid-July, the pack ice would be gone.

The route had its own risks: unmapped shoals and breakaway ice chunks— *bergy bits* and *growlers*, as deadly as pirates, but more of them. They'd be relying heavily on the ice detection system the twins had devised. Without it, they'd be reduced to half speed, which would mean eight weeks. It had to be kept under four. Paul realized he'd need another crew member.

They flipped a coin and Anna won. Excellent! He liked her sense of humour.

As they prepared to depart from their base on Moresby Island, Jenny took him aside and pointed to a heavy case. "Take this, you'll need it."

"Two months of whisky?" he joked.

"A little more deadly," she answered, straight-faced. "You've got a speed advantage, but speed isn't everything. You may need some offence. It could be too late for defence." Jenny had traded some of their best navigation equipment for these guns. She wanted everyone back safely.

"Aw, Jenny," said Paul with an earnest expression. "I'm a lover, not a fighter!"

"That may be. But you'll have precious cargo. Learn to use these. You'll have plenty of spare time."

As they prepared to cast off, the *Rocket Richard* loaded with supplies and an electric-assisted cargo bicycle, Jenny fixed him with a gaze that was equal parts boss and trusted friend.

"Sometimes you have to fight Paul!"

Burning Through the Night

razy woman, thought Mario as he watched her through binoculars from the attic of a farmhouse two kilometres west of Le Tilleret. *Twice a week she goes off on one of her rides. Good, stay predictable. Mario needs you out of the way. I'd much rather kill you, but I made a deal. Besides, it's the old guy I want. Self-righteous holy man.*

* * *

That morning, the wind was from the south as Simone headed out. Tailwind. A headwind for the return—what every cyclist hates!

François had asked her to check out the water levels and report on any activity around Cruas-Meysse. Was it operating? Were the Angels still active? He had given her his geiger counter. A curious thing to own, she thought. One of the few items he'd brought with him from Strasbourg. They used street theatre to get across their message, he explained.

First stop, though, was Sauzet. Simone had stayed away for two days. She'd check in on her family. *The survivors*, she thought, with a heavy heart. Then Yuki. It had been eating at her day and night.

Approaching the town centre, she paused. Silence. *No birds sang*, she noticed, recalling the book by that title. Farley Mowat's account of the brutal Sicily campaign in 1943, and the slow and bloody march towards Rome. A frank depiction of the horrors of war. Shell shock and PTSD, before it had that name, or the respect it would later get. The inability to see that war could never be anything but proof of failure. Not even birds survive full-scale war. An odd recollection at this time, but she was prone to those. Looking back, when forward seemed impossible.

No vehicle. No sound. But a faint odour of smoke, from the fields. Must be far to the south; not much left to burn around Sauzet.

In just a few pedal strokes, she was back in her previous spot. She went straight to new messages. Yuki Ebitsubo. And Paul Racine! On closer inspection, she saw there were actually two from Paul. One was five weeks old.

Seeing nothing from family, she felt her heart fall. Still, she'd send a quick message to both active addresses: Edward and Jacinthe. You never knew.

> *Dearest Papa and Jacinthe, I've been struggling with the news about Maman and Ron. It was such a blow that I couldn't respond. I don't know what I would have said. I still don't. I remain in the Drome, living with François and Nicole, and our adopted family of migrants. Eight of us, all told. We're considering a move. Perhaps to Denmark, to join their daughter, Sylvie. How we'll all get there, I don't know. Please tell me where you are, as soon as you can. So much love, Simone.* SEND

Now Yuki. Five questions.

Jiro's Cambridge nickname. *You're kidding?* "*JJ*"

First name of Godmother. *Oh my, that's me!* "*Simone*"

Boat on which she escaped. *How would Yuki know that?* Simone blanked for a moment. "*Switching to Glide*", she typed. *The questions were made for her!*

Jenny's college. "*Churchill*"

Sagan's hero. *Oh dear. Hero or idol? "Freddy Mercury"*
INCORRECT
What? Got it! "Freddie Mercury"

> *Dear Simone. You're alive and so are we! Jenny, Anna and me. Also your father and daughter. We hope this is not the first you hear of it, but sadly your mother and husband were taken from this world by sickness. May they rest in peace. Edward, Jacinthe and Isabelle are on their way to join us. We have established a base on South Moresby Island—Haida Gwaii, off the BC mainland, as you know. We transferred some of our equipment from Hakodate and Vancouver. That story can wait. You must tell us where you are. Precisely. You are in grave danger. Elmore Lambert is headed for you.*

Simone felt a jolt on reading the name. Not of fear, but adrenaline. High alert.

> *He seems to know where you are, but we don't. Paul Racine and Anna are racing towards France. Send a precise GPS coordinate, if you have one. Satellites are still working. Also, is the Rhône deep enough to navigate? Is Montelimar the best place to dock? ETA is August 25. Do not delay. And be very careful. Yuki*

Simone was stunned. Everyone coming together like that. And a rescue. For her! Stop! Why take that risk? But they'd be most of the way to Europe now, with the trickiest part to come. Gibraltar. Spanish coast. Dangerous as hell. The Rhône? Who knows! She would shortly, but would she have a chance to relay what she learned?

François had told her it was low when he checked in May. But the nuclear station's intake had still been immersed. That was before the summer. There had been little snow in the Alps this year, and only a light spring rainy season. *Better get moving.*

Been here too long. She looked up, checking for any movement, or sound. Nothing. But the smoke seemed heavier. Definitely, there were fires nearby. To the south, southeast, judging by the wind.

> REPLY *Yuki and everyone. Still doing okay. Global Village Assisi is just south of Le Tilleret. Southwest of Sauzet, which is about 35km east of Montelimar. Best port is Montelimar. Take National Road number...*

She banged out the details from memory. It wasn't as if they could stop and ask the friendly locals for directions, she thought grimly.

> *From Le Tilleret we're second farm south from roundabout in village centre. That's Le Tilleret in the Drome. France has dozens. No point rescuing damsel in distress at the wrong Tilleret! She smiled. Humour is rarely wasted.*
>
> *Water levels very low, I fear. Proceed with caution. If too low, use dock south of Montelimar, perhaps Pierrelatte. Watch out for water intake and outfall pipes just below surface at nuclear stations. Gambatte! Simone.* SEND.

The smoke was definitely worse. She had to get out. But not before checking the messages from Paul. His latest one was more recent than Yuki's. A public message. No handshake required. No security offered. That was taking a risk, but she'd left him no choice. She never completed his handshake request.

Hey Fit Bottomed Girl. She smiled. Nice attempt at code.

> *We know where you are. J hailed in. Exchange of messages with S in Denmark. Gave precise GPS and sent map with pin. We're good to go. Not sure how many folks we can carry, but we live by Law of Abundance: love and resources expand to meet need. Stay alert. Keep arms handy. Courage! Paul*

That was ominous. How did this work, the Bulletin Board? There it was.

POST PUBLIC REPLY *You brave fools. Message received. Identify yourselves at gate. Code word is real name for Habs. We have guns and know how to use them! JJ's college mate.*

Roll, girl roll. Simone was pedalling hard towards the Rhône. This would be fun, if it weren't so dangerous. She pulled up her bandana for the first time in weeks and picked up her pace, looking to skirt the worst of the smoke. Where was it coming from? NO! The fire would be south of GV Assisi and headed toward it, or north of the farm and moving away from it. Or from it, she realized with horror. She screeched to a stop.

If the fire was north of the farm, fanned by the strong, hot wind from the south, they would be fine. If south of it, they were in big trouble. If coming from it... she couldn't bear the thought. But what could she do? It was an hour of hard cycling. Faced with this reality, Simone froze.

Complete your task and get back as soon as possible; or turn around, get back to find all is well, but have nothing to show for it; or get back empty handed, and find... She cringed at the image. And the smell. Or was that her imagination running wild?

Simone stood still and closed her eyes, trying desperately to ground herself. Then it came to her. Get to the nearest point with a view, use the binoculars and take a geiger reading. Hell, turn the machine on now. A reading from a couple of kilometres away could be extrapolated, if that was the right word. François would know how.

Pumping furiously, she chewed some dried fruit and gulped down water. She coughed up most of it. Still coughing, she turned and headed up towards a highway lookout area. The A7, once one of Europe's north-south expressways, was empty except for shells of cars and trucks, and picked-over bones. She winced at the sight. A decade earlier, she'd have been riding in the middle of streams of transport trucks and holiday caravans, all honking at her. Now, the endless pavement was hers alone. She'd dreamed on occasion of a world without cars, but never like this.

At La Coucourde, she took an offramp. There would be a clear view from the N7. There they were, the cooling towers. They'd been painted years earlier by a mural artist, to help rebrand the industry. *Your friendly nuclear station. Like us on Facebook!* There was also a highway lay-by, for taking photos: *Look kids, the Rhône with nuclear plant as backdrop!*

The geiger counter, clicking consistently and slowly since she turned it on, had been getting louder since about 5 kilometres out. Now it was shrieking. She shut it off.

Pulling up close to the rail, she yanked out the binoculars and worked the focus ring. Water low. Lots of rocks. *Shee-it!* Was that the intake or the outfall? Only half immersed. Better be the outfall. But if it was, wouldn't the intake be just as bad? Yep. Scanning right to left, she confirmed that every pipe was mostly or entirely out of the water. The river would be tough to navigate. And what about the power stations? They had better be shut down. Properly.

Can't do anything now, she thought morosely. But there was movement. One, two, three men in protective suits and masks running from a van towards the fourth reactor. Last to be shut down, she assumed. There was no sign of vapour in the air. No hum from pumps or any other mechanical noise. Had it been safely put to sleep?

Suddenly, Simone remembered the camera. An old digital contraption. She'd once had one like it. Powering it up, she took a series of shots amounting to a panorama, then zoomed in on where the men were, in their white and pink angel suits. *A few brave men.* Ever has it been so. She dropped all three devices in the pannier and pointed her front wheel for home.

Exhausted and barely moving, she bore down into the wind. She'd been urging herself on for more than an hour. The closer she got to GV Assisi, the less smoke there was. But there was a different smell. A barbecue unattended. She shuddered.

First the body goes, then the emotions, then the mind.

Nearly there, she was hallucinating now. Imagining a dust cloud heading along the wall of GV Assisi, approaching the corner where she would soon be. No, it was real, and moving fast. Simone veered into the ditch, tumbling from her bike. Her right hip and shoulder took most of the impact.

Crouching, she pawed at the straps holding her rifle. Come on, come on.

She could see the nose now. A black SUV, slowly accelerating out of the sharp corner. Reaching into her fanny pack, she loaded the rifle. It was picking up speed. He wouldn't know she was there. Or would he? One of her wheels was protruding into the road. As the vehicle approached to within about 50 metres, it slowed. Then, in a sudden change of mind, it surged with a roar. This time he left her no choice.

Mario was right in the scope now. *One, two!* Her shoulder screamed. The car veered away, toward the hedge on the far side of the road. It was passing right in front of her now, the driver slumped over the wheel. *Three, four!* It hit the hedge, started to yaw, and then crossed to her side, tumbling over and over.

Simone didn't bother to watch. She had thrown the rifle aside and was limping toward the farm. Her bicycle lay mangled in the road.

* * *

Nothing in Simone's life prepared her for what awaited. Not even the forensic photos from Sagan's murder.

Incredibly, the main house was standing, apparently intact. The barn had collapsed, still smouldering. Nearly everything else was levelled. The guest house was burned to the ground. Charred bodies lay outside, and just inside the doorway.

Crumpled on the ground, 10 metres back from the building, two bodies were sprawled over a hose, still trickling. François and Nicole lay together, arms wrapped around each other, their clothing scorched and hair burned away. Most repugnant of all, in a scene so shocking, they were riddled with bullet wounds. François in particular.

Simone kneeled beside them, placing a hand on each of their heads. Then she began to shake uncontrollably.

She didn't hear the footsteps. Nor the whimpering sound. She didn't even notice the hand on her shoulder, at first. Gradually she became aware of the sensation and tensed. Instinctively she looked up, expecting the worst.

A thin, dark haired man, was staring at her. Something in his eyes caused her body to relax: tenderness, pity and a deep sadness; for her and for all he had seen in his thirty long years.

"Madame Nicole?" he said tentatively.

"Oh, Ibrahim. Is it just you and me now?" He nodded.

"Then at least we have each other." Again, he nodded.

"Madame. When you are ready. We have a very unpleasant job to do. But I think it best to begin soon. It will not get easier. I have seen this."

Simone nodded, and accepted his hand. Leaning heavily on him, they walked back toward the one intact building. At the doorway, she stopped and turned to face him.

"Ibrahim," she said softly. "My real name is Simone. Like you, I have been hiding all these years. Enough hiding, *n'est-ce pas?*"

"Oui, Madame Simone."

"Just Simone, please."

I'm a Rocket Ship

Getting fuel was easier than expected. Repairing the critical damage was harder. But someone could usually be found, when you had the means to pay. He'd brought plenty of his universal currency. Drug dealers survive even the worst crises; like rats and cockroaches. They always knew people, who knew other people, who fixed things.

Elmore spent five days in Barcelona's Port Masnou, well outside the city centre, at what had once been a thriving yacht club. Five days with little sleep, always on edge, guns and pills by his side.

The big yacht was once again seaworthy. Just. The biggest holes were patched over with sheet metal and a riveting gun. Good enough, as long as seas remained calm. It wouldn't get him home, but he'd never counted on that.

Now came the big unknown—water levels in the Rhône? They'd be high for the first while. Rising sea levels made sure of that. But at the point where salt water reached fresh water, it could be tricky going.

He'd wanted a fast craft with low draft, not this tank! Fucking Paul Racine!

* * *

Though they had been forced to travel on high alert for six days—throttling back whenever the ice detection system told them to—going over the Pole had saved them several weeks. Whether that was enough to make up for their later start and a journey more than twice that of the boat they were racing, they had no way of knowing.

Anna had little sailing experience, but picked up the basics quickly. Paul was not surprised. She had refined several of the power systems for his boats. Unlike him, she was also nimble, and seemed to operate perfectly on insufficient sleep. *Youth*, he had mused, watching her leap about, adjusting rigging, folding sails like a pro. *And no hockey injuries!*

A day out from Gibraltar, she suggested they take a 24-hour break. Initially shocked, Paul was won over by her logic.

"The batteries are barely half-charged. We'll need maximum speed when we pass close to Spain and Morocco, and then that section after the Strait. We'll be outgunned by any boat still on the water. Speed is our only advantage."

Where had she learned this stuff?

They'd pause, well back from the coast. If they got their calculations right, they could take advantage of ocean current overnight, while catching up on sleep. One could catnap in the pilot's chair, next to the warning system and screens, a gun at the ready. The other could get a proper rest.

They shut the engine down at 10 a.m., 100 kilometres off Cadiz. Anna took the first duty shift from 2 p.m. to 10 p.m.

He was startled by her wake-up call. "I can't believe I slept right through!"

"You needed it," said Anna. "I made you supper. Or is it breakfast?"

Paul smiled, pulling himself up. "Anything to report?"

"Just one boat. Something small, way to the east, and heading north. Fingers crossed for a quiet night."

With no discernible movement or heat source, there was nothing to indicate the *Rocket Richard* was more than a chunk of ocean debris. One more boat ripped from its anchor by a storm, floating loose until it washed up somewhere else, like so many after the 2011 tsunami. And again, following each major hurricane and typhoon. More than 50 in the past few years.

Anna's sleeping shift was nearly over when Paul shouted from above, followed immediately by a summons through the intercom.

"All hands on deck, lassie! We may have visitors." It was 5:45, the sun just starting to light up the sky.

"Good morning Sleeping Beauty," he joked, without looking in her direction as she stepped into the cabin. He was watching the screen and pointing.

"It's coming from Tangier. Won't be Coast Guard. Morocco's too far gone to have one. Nefarious intentions, I think. Here, eat!"

"What do you propose?" Anna asked, accepting the breakfast sandwich and coffee substitute.

"Element of surprise," Paul replied. "If we take off now, headed for the Strait, they can easily plot a line to intercept us. I'll wait until they're within about 20 clicks, then take a false course due east. Classic deke. When I see how they're responding, we can get the sails out and unfurl them if the wind holds. Norwesterly, it looks like. If it picks up as the sun rises, we've got prime spinnaker conditions. A breakaway for the Rocket!"

He looked up and met her eyes. "Ready for action?" She nodded.

"We knew it might come to this. Your mother did. Get the other gun out and loaded please. We should each take some practice shots. Plenty of bobbing plastic."

The approaching boat didn't seem particularly fast, even when it accelerated as it closed in. This would be child's play, unless they were holding something back.

The sun was high, and energy reserve now at 78 percent. When Paul turned to set their true course, the attackers made no attempt to close ground. Or couldn't, he concluded, smiling. Once he'd put 15 kilometres between them, he eased back and plotted out a precise course through the Strait.

"Shooting fish in a barrel," he muttered as it dawned on him just how narrow the passage was. "We're the fish!"

"What was that?" asked Anna, removing her headphones, which she had been using to listen for voice traffic.

"We'll shoot right through, I was saying."

Approaching at three-quarter speed, he kept his eyes on the water in front of him, glancing frequently at the shorelines to both left and right. Anna watched the screen, and kept the headphones on. With a sigh of relief, they cleared the point off Almeria late in the afternoon, and watched the Spanish coast receding. The direct route would now take them between Barcelona and Mallorca, through the Balearic Sea. Instead, they chose to swing east, staying between Menorca and Sardinia.

"Critical hours lost," Paul explained, "but you can't play saviour if you're dead, or left on a beach without your boat."

They'd reach the mouth of the Rhône just before dawn. They'd be watching for rocks and sandbars now. Also ambushes, all the way upriver. They kept the guns out.

* * *

Ibrahim had seen this kind of shock in others: friends he'd escaped with; survivors of the boat ride, after they'd capsized off the coast east of Cannes and spent months in a camp in squalid conditions, with sickness and despair all around them. There would be housing and work in France, they were told. Official refugee status, they were promised. Some day, citizenship. Only there wasn't. Just sub-standard housing in an internment camp, and hard work for little pay.

Convinced they could do better, he'd escaped with three others, walking in the night. Two were caught. One drowned, crossing a river. He kept going, determined to find haven somewhere. And he did. The kindness and fairness and humanity of *St. François*.

But Ibrahim was dead inside by then. Unable to feel. Not willing to let himself. It was how he survived. He could work. He could help. He knew to say thank you, for generosity and kindness received. He knew how to help others, even. But all without feeling. Shock, or whatever you wanted to call it, can last a very long time.

Suddenly now, after witnessing the very worst, Ibrahim felt something lift. This woman—Madame Nicole, now just Simone— she needed him. It was pitiful how she had crumbled. Physically she appeared fine, but in other ways like a baby.

Wake up Simone, it's time for breakfast. Let's go Simone, we need to do our farm work. That's great Simone. Remember Simone, how the security cameras work. We must move a few to replace the two that burned. Today we will repair the fence. Coucou Simone! You must be daydreaming. You were going to collect eggs for dinner. Remember? No, of course not. I'll get them? It will be dark soon. Tonight, Simone, I think we should take a small bath. You can go first. I'll re-use the water for mine, then put it on the garden.

Someone needed him. Completely. That made all the difference.

Simone was aware of each day's activity. Getting up, working, eating, working, listening to music on Ibrahim's little device. He had patched together enough of GV Assisi's surviving panels and batteries to provide some electricity. This abundant haven reduced to so little. Two survivors, barely making it. With autumn coming.

Simone's day dreams had no particular focus. Snatches of memories. Recollections of family. Glimpses of the cabin where life was similarly basic, but without the despair. Then there was the night. Dreams involving trucks with bright lights. Nuclear plants on fire. Charred bodies. Sitting at a computer terminal, trying to figure out how to log on, how to send, but never getting past the subject lines:

Where are you?
Terrible news!
How do we get you?

Then there was the one where a boat came up the Rhône, but couldn't find a place to dock. It was beached on a sandbar. The hull pierced. The crew unable to get ashore. Night after night.

Sometimes though, they were flashbacks. Semi-lucid memories of her childhood, high school, living in Japan. And Cambridge. A strange version of Cambridge, though the landmarks were clear enough. But where were Sagan and JJ? Only Jenny, calling out to her from across a crowded cafe, which she was unable to cross. Too crowded, and her legs wouldn't work!

* * *

"Goddamn, stupid fucking son-of-a-bitch shit heap!"

He'd grounded out completely now. It had happened before, but each time he'd powered his way out, backwards and downstream. Not this time.

"Mother fucking tank is going nowhere!"

What the hell to do. He was getting close to Montelimar, but he was further away than he wanted. The motorbike was charged, but he didn't know the range it would get. Sure, it was big and fast, but he didn't need speed. He needed distance. Not having any other options, he kept the ship's engine running while he topped up the batteries, just to be sure. All the while, assembling what he would need.

There would be the trip itself. What, 100 miles? How many kilometres—150 or something? He couldn't remember the formula, and it would matter. All the signs would be in metric. Stupid metric. The conversion that never happened. Good ole US of A.

It wasn't a suicide mission. He planned to stay alive. Which meant more than a quick dash with a sandwich, a thermos and his pills.

The pills. He'd take the whole lot. For barter, and for himself. More and more for himself. He'd always been above that. Except for his time in Washington. But he'd weaned himself. Mostly. He could quit anytime, he told himself. For the past year, though, there it was—the creeping need.

Some food. Freeze-dried stuff. Maybe a few tins. Couple of containers of water. A blanket. Good boots. A sweater. A raincoat.

It was adding up, and he hadn't thought to bring any kind of saddle bags. This was a racing machine, not a touring bike. He would fill a plastic storage box and tie it down on the rear seat. Which would cut his range.

Getting the bike to shore would be tricky. He'd have to use the life raft, then find a way to get it up the steep bank. Best to float downstream again, looking for a better landing. All this time lost. Weeks longer than he'd intended.

Elmore felt a surge of panic at the thought of his target, his precious target, having flown the coop. Mario better have held up his deal, or no payoff.

Just payback.

* * *

As her mental state improved, Simone took on some of the night watch shifts.

"I might as well, since I don't sleep much anyway," she insisted.

Ibrahim, who was sleeping well for the first time in years, did not argue. They were sharing the upper floor of the main house now. Whoever was on duty would stay in the downstairs quarters, from which they could do a regular perimeter walk and gate check without waking the other. The monitoring equipment had been fried.

Simone had explained her situation to Ibrahim. The danger. His now too.

They could have moved somewhere else. To one of many abandoned farmhouses in the area. The truck had sustained only superficial damage. But how would Paul and Anna find them? This left them exactly where Elmore expected, of course, but with everything they needed. It was a gamble, but what wasn't?

They were starting to harvest the crops and fruit that had survived the inferno. The fire, lit much further south, had gathered so much speed that it leapt right over their fire break and the vegetable garden just inside the fence, which had still been green and reasonably moist. They had lost most of their farm animals and food stores, but they would not go hungry.

What they lacked was water. The depleted reservoir was pumped dry in the urgent effort to fight the fire. Normally it would have been replenished by their protected stream, fed from the hills to the northwest. Not this year.

Hunger plays tricks on the mind. Dehydration also, she knew. Which made sleep even harder. Harder to find, and stranger when it came. Mostly, it did not. Not real sleep. Just a few short hours, snatched from the middle of her nightmares and strange recurring dreams.

Night after night, Simone would dream of filing a story. She would present her written copy to a procession of editors, always printed on a sheet of paper. He would look at it—it was always a man—then tell her in the friendliest of tones why he couldn't publish it.

"Sorry, we don't write about that. You know how it goes." And she would nod.

"You know we can't touch that one. We'll get sued. You understand, of course. You're a pro!" Lame and helpless and silent Simone was, in her dreams.

Then there were the ones where she was at a computer. Posting a blog, or sending in a big investigative piece. She would press send. Nothing. No matter how often and how hard she punched the key, or clicked the mouse, nothing!

Sometimes Simone was not dreaming at all. Rather, she would lie for hours in a state of half-sleep, exhausted, yet unable to drop over the edge. Her mind whirring, reliving chapters of her life. Rarely the good ones. Strange, she thought, for a life well lived. Why all the regrets? Is this what old age is like? Was she getting an early taste? Regrets for a planet, for a species?

Once, in her midnight semi-sleep, she dreamt of a conversation she'd had with François. A year earlier perhaps, before Nicole had come. The weaknesses of *homo sapiens* was the subject. Had humans progressed as far as they would, or could? Was there a fundamental design flaw, or character traits that no education, or cross-selecting or praying or meditation or yoga retreats would ever be able to surmount? If *sapiens* had limits, better to acknowledge them and work with, or around them.

François had pulled out a book. A big one. *Sapiens*, by Yuval Noah Hariri, published in 2014. Originally in Hebrew, but then in English and—apparently—French. She'd seen it. Heard about it. But not read it.

"We have most evenings free," he noted raising an eyebrow. She said she would, but asked him for a summary. What was the 'take away?'

"Oh, many," he'd said, "But I'll try to list the main ones." Which he did, while flipping through the book. As he had with Pope Francis' *Laudato Si*, some months earlier.

"Sounds fascinating," Simone said. "You saved me 500 pages!"

François responded testily. "It's 443 to be exact. I think you're getting lazy!"

"So much to read and so little time!" They both went quiet. It was Simone who broke the silence.

"*Homo Sapiens*, the ecological wrecking machine! Maybe it's a good thing if we drive ourselves into extinction. So other species have a chance. Ones with less blood on their hands. Or at least Earth might benefit from *Sapiens* being culled to some manageable number, and learning important lessons from the crash."

"In one of your moods," François remarked. "I guess that's what's happening now, the culling, only more randomly than any of us would have wanted. The good wiped out indiscriminately with the bad. I think any of the people who, in their dark moments, hoped for such a crash expected greater fairness. Social activists would be saved, and profiteers wiped out. Or the righteous saved and sinners smitten."

"Indeed!" said Simone. "If there has to be an apocalypse, the good guys should be spared. It's not looking like the happy homecoming the evangelists counted on."

"Simone," François said, looking and sounding irritated. "You have often spoken this way of certain believers. You feel disdain, am I right?"

Taken aback by his tone, Simone took a moment to respond.

"I don't know. Sure, I guess so. I can't bear the thought that anyone, any group or sect would actively be hoping for others to be damned, and more than anything, hoping for conditions to get really bad in order for their big moment to arrive. As for the people who encouraged this unravelling, how dare they assume they wouldn't be the ones sent to their imagined hell?"

François nodded. He'd had similar thoughts. Instead of saying so, he prodded her further.

"I've listened to you, and many in the green movement, speak this way about fundamentalist people of faith. But I've also heard you, though not you personally, wish for some disaster to purge the planet of its bad actors. So we can start fresh."

Simone nodded. François took a breath and continued in a softer tone.

"I had periods where I felt this way. But listening to you, it struck me that maybe you, we, they, have more in common than we think."

Simone cocked her head. "How is that?"

"Each of us is dissatisfied with some aspects of human society. We are disappointed with the direction the world has taken. We wish other people to behave differently—more like us. At least more like the ideal we have of ourselves. When they don't, we imagine a higher power doing the hard work for us. Whether through threat of divine wrath or the promise of a place in heaven. But how to earn admission? One way would be to work on improving the behaviour of *other* humans. The other is to work on *ourselves*. This is all very slow and tedious, of course. How frustrating that is for people who are certain how the world ought to be. And maybe just as frustrating for those like you and I, who have a strong sense of how humanity *needs* to act to ensure ecological survival."

"Precisely," Simone declared.

"So all of us, at some time, wish a higher power could just sweep in and fix it. Or wipe away those we consider at fault. You've had such thoughts, and so have I."

"I still do," she admitted. "Look at the evil out there. I can't fix it, but I wish someone could and would. Or something."

"Even if our loved ones and heroes get struck down along with the supremacists and predators? Deep down, although our motives and our expectations for how this global purification will happen certainly differ, we have more in common than we realize."

"Yes, maybe," Simone said. "Or want to acknowledge."

"As your 'maybe' just proved."

Simone smiled. "So how many self-righteous columns must I atone for?"

"Probably not a lot. I'll bet you were targeting the extremes, the worst group behaviour, not each individual."

"With some notable exceptions," said Simone. "Individuals who acted in a manner I consider evil. People who found ways to justify abuse and violence by wrapping it into some cause, when really it was just about ego, or wealth, or power."

"Or fear," François suggested. "Or hurt!"

"Hurt?" said Simone. "I suppose."

A Trail to Follow

All the way up the Rhône they had glided, without seeing anybody. "Are they hiding when they spot our boat, or is there really nobody left?" Anna wondered aloud. Paul was thinking the same.

Since their cautious approach to the mouth of the Rhône, they had made excellent time. Nothing was moving at Port-St-Louis. Nor at Arles.

"Nobody dancing on the Pont," Paul joked darkly as they slipped by Avignon in near silence. No concrete was being moved at Ardoise, no signs of life even at the big Tricastin nuclear station before Mondragon. Just a lot of vehicles, some with their doors open wide.

"There's a story there," Anna remarked as they cruised past. The geiger counter made excited noises. Both felt relief when it calmed as they continued north.

Their first real scare since entering the Rhône came just after Mondragon. Beached on what appeared to be a gravel bar, was a luxury yacht. *Fort Lauderdale,* they read. The boat's name had been covered by a rudimentary patch.

It was listing heavily. So much so, that Paul felt it unlikely anybody was aboard. Still, he reached for a pistol, and urged Anna to take cover. Instead, she snatched up a rifle and tucked herself behind the base of the PowerPole. All was quiet though, as they slipped past.

He said nothing, but inside, Paul feared they were too late. He nudged the throttle up, weighing unknowns below the surface with knowns above.

It was now a straight run into Montelimar—maximum 90 minutes. All that could be was stowed, wind resistance minimized. In near-silence, they raced upstream. Just the hiss of water, wind in their ears and the whine of racing electrical motors.

The bike was ready—charged and pared down to essentials: two bottles of water, energy bars, a first aid kit, a flare gun and a pistol neither of them had tried.

Paul had assumed it would be him doing the cycling. On the other hand, he was now thinking, Anna was clearly the fitter of the two, even if neither had used their legs much in weeks. He wasn't any better at shooting, either. Then again, if it came down to brute force, *mano a mano*, he would have a significant advantage. It was a toss-up. In the end, it was decided on language. She spoke no French. It seemed silly, but what if success came down to language? She agreed.

He would bring the boat into the first decent dock that presented itself on the northern side of Montelimar, or—if the river seemed high enough—he would enter the mouth of the Roubion, and see how far east they could get before it dried up or became too narrow. It would be safer than the banks of the Rhône, he guessed. Less exposed.

Anna would stay on the boat, or better still, secure it well, and find a place to lay low for the day or two he expected to be gone. They had their radios; reliable, but only within about 10 kilometres. Paul would also carry the satellite radio. At noon on the following day, he would use it confirm if all was well and they would soon be leaving.

No news would mean the opposite. Anna would be on her own, to attempt a very long trip home.

"Nobody said there wouldn't be risks," she remarked calmly.

"You're amazing," said Paul. "Smart, resourceful—"

"For a woman?"

"I didn't say that. I most definitely did not say that. Or even think it!"

She smiled. "I'll be fine Paul. It's you I'm worried about. Keep a steady pace. No middle-aged heart attack, OK?"

Approaching the Roubion, the geiger counter began to chatter.

"Whatever is upriver, it must be bad," said Anna.

"Another nuclear station," said Paul. "One more reason to head up the Roubion. Help me get the mast down. There are bound to be bridges."

* * *

She had been dreaming again. Half dreaming, half sleeping. A long and complicated dream. Trump. *Screw you, Trump. Get out of my dreams!*

High school, philosophy, poetry, something about existentialism. Frankl and *Man's Search for Meaning*. Nietzsche. Yeats too. Yeats especially.

Mere anarchy is loosed upon the world...

Her brain was back in high school. 'A little quote factory' one teacher had labelled her. It worked. Top marks in English, vaulted into university, great in sports, lots of friends, straight into her chosen career in journalism. A real job, when everyone else was looking for a summer internship. Driven. She'd always been driven. For the longest time, she was not sure why; or to do what. That would come.

So the dreams would go. Always pointing to the three of them. Over and over, her dreams and reminiscences came back to three people. Of course, there were others. Her parents, her playful and devoted husband, her daughter who had been hell, and then a dear friend. Nicole, then François, and then Nicole again. But in the beginning, they were three. Three plus Simone made four. It started over tea, on a blustery afternoon in Cambridge. Who could have known? How much love. And pain.

...the worst are full of passionate intensity.

Sure, the worst are full of intensity. But so are the best. The best have two things the worst never will. Things the worst may never have been shown. Integrity and, more than anything, love. To offer their friends and the world. Papa, Jacinthe, Jenny, where are you now?

Dogs barked in the distance. Searching for food, fighting over it. Another reason for mending the gap in the fence alongside the field. Simone took a deep breath, trembling as she exhaled. Then, to her surprise, she felt tears, cool as they rolled down her cheeks. Salty, as they reached her tongue. The first in a long time. Sleep came at last. Blessed, overdue sleep.

With a jolt, she awoke. Her whole body had tensed. That cracking sound—had she dreamt it? For a full minute she lay perfectly still, listening.

Nothing. Just another of her strange dreams.

Breathing deeply, she tried to settle again. Voices! She was sure of it. Lowering her bare feet gently to the floor, she felt her way to the bathroom. At the open window, she pulled back the curtain and peered cautiously out. Pitch black. Nothing to see. Or hear, beyond the pounding of her heart.

Then she felt the tingle in her scalp. Could it be? A surge of adrenaline hit her. *Avenge Sagan!* But with what?

Crunching gravel. She was sure of it. Barely distinguishable, but getting louder. What happened to Ibrahim? Asleep? Fled? Or worse? She shuddered.

Now there was a light. A single one; faint, advancing in pace with the sound. Simone went rigid. Then relaxed, as it came to her—there was just enough time to grab the hatchet from outside the door.

Visitors

wo sets of footsteps, and something else. Wheels, but not from a car or truck. Simone stood motionless in the front entrance, just out of sight of the driveway. She'd left the door open. Both hands were needed to grip the hatchet. The head was heavy, designed for splitting. The element of surprise would be hers.

Crunch, crunch, crunch, one more second and they'd be in sight. She rotated her feet to get the best angle for swinging, raised the hatchet just above shoulder height, and tried to relax.

"That's odd," said a voice in French as the footsteps stopped abruptly. "The door is wide open." *Ibrahim!*

"Do you think she might have run for it? The noise could have spooked her."

Simone knew that voice.

"Simone!" Ibrahim called out loudly, "You have a visitor!"

She flinched. Was he being used to lure her out?

"Simone!" shouted the second man, a mere two arms' lengths away. In French.

With a New Brunswick accent!

Flinging the hatchet aside, she staggered out the door and into the arms of Paul Racine.

At the table in the downstairs apartment, Simone examined Paul while Ibrahim boiled water. He was sweaty, dirty and clearly

659

tired, but his eyes communicated something else. Worry, and possibly relief.

"I can't believe you came all this way," she said, shaking her head, "for me!"

"Not just you," said Paul, his eyes on hers. "For everyone who's been worried sick."

Simone nodded. "I know what you mean."

"But Anna and I weren't the only ones coming for you. Did you know that?"

She looked over his shoulder toward the entrance. "Do you know where he is?"

Paul exhaled and looked at Ibrahim, who was placing a pot of tea and some flatbread with honey in front of him. "We certainly do."

"Lying by the gate," offered Ibrahim, as he took a seat at the table. "Unconscious, but securely bound."

Simone turned to him, her eyes wide. "Here?!"

"He was trying to scale the wall," said Ibrahim. "He got snagged on the wire."

Paul chuckled and reached into his rear pocket. "Someday I may have to use one of these, but not yet." He placed a pistol on the table.

"Is that his?" Simone said, her mouth agape.

"It is," said Paul. "Mine's strapped on here." He patted his chest.

"So, what happened?" asked Simone, glancing between Paul and Ibrahim.

"I can tell you what I saw," Paul said, taking a bite of bread, "but your loyal friend saw more than me."

"I heard this high-pitched motor," Ibrahim said calmly, "followed by a loud bang. I got the gun ready and moved to where I could see the road. Ten minutes later, maybe, I saw somebody staggering up the road, clearly injured. As he approached the gate, I stepped back and out of sight, keeping my gun trained on him."

Ibrahim looked at Simone, then at the pistol on the table.

"He seemed to be considering shooting the lock, but decided it would be unwise. Too loud. So he tried to scale the wall, not counting on the barbed wire." Ibrahim stopped and looked at Paul, who raised his mug of tea and emptied it in one gulp.

Simone leaned forward in anticipation.

"I was almost here, on the stretch of road just before the corner. My light was off—to save power and not attract attention. It was pitch black, but when I spotted something, I switched it back on. There was this hulk of an SUV straddling part of the road. And what would you know, there was a motorbike pretty much indented in the side of it, and a bunch of stuff littering the road. Clear bags full of pills, some split open. I didn't see a body, so I guessed the driver had been thrown. I couldn't imagine anyone surviving that, but a wave of panic hit me. Imagine making it all the way here, but coming up short!"

Simone reached out and placed a hand on his arm.

"So I just stood up and cranked like crazy. As I approached the gate, I saw this guy on top of the wall, cursing and pulling. Next thing I know, he tumbles off and lands with a thud on the asphalt."

Paul and Ibrahim shook their heads in unison.

"Delivered to me, just like that," said Paul, gesturing at the table, "this pistol lying next to him."

"I was preparing to shoot," Ibrahim volunteered. "If he made it over the wire—"

"Too bad you didn't!" Simone spat.

For a moment, the three sat in silence, her words still ringing. This time it was Paul who reached out, placing a hand on Simone's shoulder.

"No," Simone said to Ibrahim. "I didn't really mean it. It's what that evil man deserves, but there's no reason why you should be the one to deliver justice."

"If shooting him will bring justice," Ibrahim said calmly after another silence.

Paul poured himself more tea, then cleared his throat. "So… we have this injured man… this very evil injured man," he added, looking at Simone.

"What now?" she said, completing his thought.

"Indeed. To start, we have to contact Anna to let her know we're coming." He looked around the kitchen. "We should bring all the food we can. And, of course, we must decide what to do with Elmore Lambert."

Simone's eyes narrowed at the mention of his name.

Paul looked towards Ibrahim. "What do you think his chances are?"

Ibrahim shrugged. "I'm not a doctor, but it looks as if he has broken one arm. He was limping badly, and he likely has a concussion. Maybe broken ribs."

Simone was listening in silence. Paul turned to her now and spoke directly.

"I know what this man has done to you. You, your friends, your family. It's natural you want him punished—"

"I see three options," Simone interrupted. "Execute him; leave him here to fend for himself; or take him with us." She looked at Paul and Ibrahim for confirmation.

Paul was shaking his head violently. "Ignoring for one moment whether he deserves to be spared, we have very limited means. How do we get him to the boat? How do we get ourselves there, for that matter? How do we feed the five of us? And do we hold him captive the whole way back? For what? It's not like there's a justice system to put him in front of."

Simone nodded. "My rage says shoot him. Or let him die of his injuries—maybe leave him for the dogs, or the next fire. That last one is just plain cruel, though. It drags us down to his level. Somebody who thrives on cruelty. I'm ruling that out."

Paul and Ibrahim looked relieved.

"As for execution… When you kill, it stays with you. I know."

Paul looked mystified.

"That SUV lying in the road…" she explained. "I shot the driver. I could have let him drive past, but I knew what he'd done. It was the only thing to do, I'm sure of it, but it was still murder. I don't know if I can do it again."

"And I couldn't ask either of you." She looked at Ibrahim and Paul in turn.

"Ask Elmore!" said Ibrahim. "He could be made to pick his own punishment."

"If he regains consciousness," said Paul, sounding doubtful, "in time for us to make our departure. We can't leave Anna for long."

Simone looked at Ibrahim. "The truck still works. Is it charged enough to get to Montelimar, with four passengers and as much food as we can muster?"

Ibrahim nodded. "It's been trickle-charging on surplus solar."

"Well then," said Simone, preparing to stand, "we know we can reach the boat. Let's see if Sagan's murderer has anything to say for himself…since we can't ask Sagan for an opinion," she added bitterly.

As Paul and Simone moved to the door, Ibrahim handed them headlamps. He had already put on his own. Just outside, Simone halted and spoke.

"I'm not saying we'll do what Elmore says. But let's give him a chance to do the right thing, if there is one. I believe that's what Sagan would want."

Lying on the gravel by the gate, Elmore's body appeared lifeless. *That would solve things*, Simone thought. Ibrahim knelt down and put a finger to his neck while at the same time listening for breathing.

Suddenly, Elmore stirred. Simone saw his eyes open a crack, then shut in response to the headlamps.

"Aiee!" he exclaimed, followed by a loud moan. He appeared racked with pain.

"Where am I," he croaked, "and who are you?"

Ibrahim turned to Simone, his headlamp blinding her. She closed her eyes and took a long deep breath.

"The last on your list," she said. Then, without thinking, she spat in his face. Nothing came out.

Reflexively, Elmore had winced, but now he was leering. "You've got me all tied up and that's the best you can do?"

When she made her lunge, she was surprised to feel Paul's arms wrapped around her. Slumping to her knees, she started to shake. She could slit the bastard's throat, or kick him over and over until he was reduced to a pulp. But it wouldn't undo a single crime, least of all bring back Sagan.

Gradually she became aware of Paul kneeling behind her. Holding her as she sobbed. Now she was aware again of Elmore, just out of reach. His eyes closed against her headlamp.

"Ibrahim, Paul," she said softly, switching off her light and patting the gravel beside her. They turned off their own lights now and sat next to her, facing Elmore. If he was still leering, she wouldn't have to see it.

"The man who has caused so much damage," she said. "I meet you at last."

Elmore snorted. "Typical!" he said. "We've met before. But you don't remember."

"What?!" exclaimed Simone. "When?"

"A boat trip to see a nasty oil rig. Twenty years ago. Gulfport."

She remembered the trip but not the face, or the name.

"The deckhand. Does it ring a bell? No, why should it?" he sneered. "I asked about becoming a journalist. But you had no time for me."

Suddenly it clicked. "I was under deadline. I gave you my card. I offered to answer your questions, but you never contacted me."

"Huh," said Elmore. "I didn't like your attitude. Too important for the deckhands. Besides," he added in a taunting voice, "I got a better offer. Better pay than you. More power too!"

She shook her head slowly, exhaling. "*Elmore Lambert*," she said, pronouncing his name as a Cajun might. "From first mate to corporate mercenary. You had power alright. And chose to use it in the worst possible ways."

"Chose!" he scoffed. "What do you know about choices. With your silver spoon up your— *Ow!*"

"Paul!" Simone scolded, grabbing for his arm as he pulled it back.

"Everyone makes choices," she said, returning to Elmore. "However bad your childhood, or whatever, there's people who have it worse and make choices that aren't about hurting others." She stared at him, trying to see into his eyes.

"Yes, I had privilege," she continued. "I had choices. Like a lot of people with privilege, I could have gone for power, and done a lot of harm. But I chose respect."

"Respect!" said Elmore, wincing. "Like you have a monopoly on respect. I went out and earned mine." He was not so much taunting as boasting. "I *chose* to be my own man, on *my* terms. Nobody made fun of me again. I chose influence."

"And used it to kill my best friend!" Simone growled.

"Friend!" Elmore sneered. "Couldn't you *choose* better than that?"

Before she could move, Paul reached over to restrain her. "No," she said, pushing his arm away and getting to her feet. "I'm going to take a stroll."

Choosing your friends, thought Simone, crunching her way up the drive into the darkness. What did he know about that? The trust and the love and the work that went into making and keeping a friend. Had he ever known it; been shown it? Or had he just dismissed it?

When she returned to the gate, she could hear Elmore whining.

"My pills," he was saying. "Come on, give me my painkillers. My arm's broken. My kneecap, too. They're in my bottom right pocket. Then you can shoot me."

Paul unzipped the pocket of Elmore's leather jacket and took out two plastic bottles.

"Any one in particular?" he asked gruffly.

"Choices, huh? Now I have choices. I wonder if I'll make a good one this time." He stared at Simone who was now standing over him.

"Why not choose *for* me?"

She observed him for a long time. What was it she was feeling? Disdain, still? Pity? We are all victims of our upbringing. No, not victims, that's a state of mind. We are influenced, but we still have the choice to do good rather than harm. We make our choices, as best we can. But then we start to justify them, to rationalize them. Sometimes to blame them on others.

"So, which pill do *you* want?" said Simone, taking the bottles from Paul. Standing in silence, holding them out in front of her, she waited. She had turned on her headlamp again, clicked down to the lowest setting, so the light would shine through.

Elmore looked first at the larger bottle, full of white pills. Then at the smaller bottle of blue ones. "Blue," he whispered, nodding toward her right hand. Simone handed the larger bottle back to Paul, and opened the smaller one. As she went to tip a blue pill into her hand, Ibrahim knocked the bottle away.

"*Touche pas!*" he yelled. "Let him take them for himself."

"Choices," said Elmore flatly, as Simone untied his hands. "I don't suppose you could give me some water. Please."

"Yes," she replied, "I can get you water."

By dawn, the truck was loaded and ready at the gate. Paul had reached Anna on the radio and was giving her the news.

"We'll be there in an hour with plenty of fresh food," Simone heard him say as she placed a final shovel of soil on Elmore's grave. "Headed for home!"

Home, thought Simone. What, and where exactly was home?

Author's Notes

I am indebted to Ginger Pharand for her guidance, patience and ability to see the story inside the massive first draft, and to Marie Bilodeau for her story-telling craft, and assistance at so many levels. Also to Jessica Torrance for her meticulous copy editing.

Thank you to Tanis Browning-Shelp for believing and encouraging and connecting me to Marie; and to Jonathan Solomon for helping me understand legal language and procedure.

Additional debts are owed to Steven Heighton, Theresa Wallace, Rena Upitis, Larry McCloskey, Mark Fried, Jennifer Tiller and Joanne Sulzenko for lending an ear and offering insight into the publishing industry, and to Jon Connor, Michael Reid and Angela Plant for feedback as early readers.

Special thanks to Raissa, Victor and Luanna for their unwavering support.

Finally, the largest thanks go to Anna for her endless joy, and for bringing me back to reading aloud; to Eric and Gaia for their many acts of love, insight and practical assistance and of course to Marie-Odile for standing by me while at the same time pushing me to reach for my best.

About the Author

David Chernushenko is an educator, author, speaker, film producer and explorer of 'living lightly' in our personal and professional lives. He was twice elected to Ottawa City Council, where he chaired the Environment and Climate Protection Committee and played a major role in promoting active transportation, complete streets, public health and supportive housing. He served as a member of Canada's National Roundtable on the Environment and the Economy, the International Olympic Committee's Sport and Environment Commission and as deputy leader of the Green Party of Canada. He has written three books on sustainable management practices, and produced three films: *Be the Change*; *Powerful: Energy for Everyone*; and *Bike City, Great City*.